SUN
GOING DOWN

JACK TODD

A TOUCHSTONE BOOK
Published by Simon & Schuster
New York London Toronto Sydney

Touchstone
A Division of Simon & Schuster, Inc.
1230 Avenue of the Americas
New York, NY 10020

First Touchstone trade paperback edition May 2009

TOUCHSTONE and colophon are registered trademarks of Simon & Schuster, Inc.

For information about special discounts for bulk purchases,
please contact Simon & Schuster Special Sales at
1-866-506-1949 or business@simonandschuster.com.

The Simon & Schuster Speakers Bureau can bring authors
to your live event. For more information or to book an event
contact the Simon & Schuster Speakers Bureau at
1-866-248-3049 or visit our website at www.simonspeakers.com.

Designed by Jan Pisciotta

Manufactured in the United States of America

10 9 8 7 6 5 4 3 2 1

The Library of Congress has cataloged the hardcover edition as follows:
Todd, Jack.
  Sun going down / Jack Todd.
    p. cm.
  "A Touchstone Book."
  1. Social change—Fiction. 2. West (U.S.)—Fiction. 1. Title.
  PS3620.O318 S86 2008
  813'.6—dc22   2008004619

ISBN 978-1-4165-5048-8
ISBN 978-1-4165-5049-5 (pbk)
ISBN 978-1-4391-6507-2 (ebook)

For Theo and Irene

*In memory of Marguerite, Garnet, Kate, and my grandmother Velma
—the hardriding Jones girls of Brown County, Nebraska*

Her princes within her are roaring lions;
her judges are evening wolves,
they gnaw not the bones till the morrow.

—ZEPHANIAH 3:3

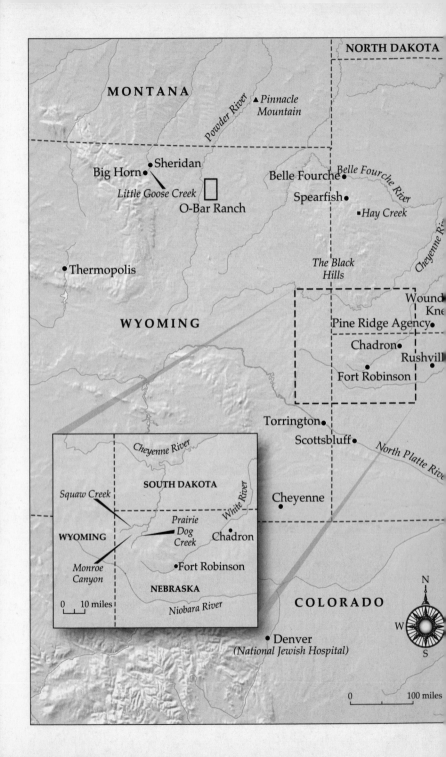

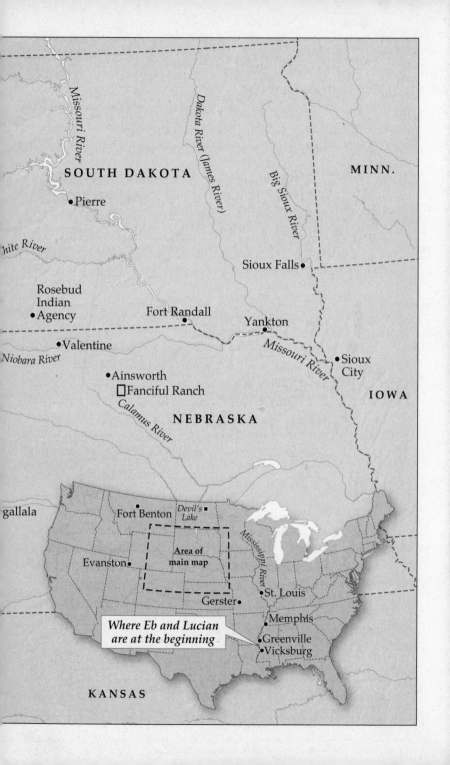

Missouri River

Dakota River (James River)

Big Sioux River

SOUTH DAKOTA

MINN.

•Pierre

hite River

Sioux Falls•

Rosebud
Indian
•Agency

Fort Randall

Yankton

Missouri River

•Sioux
City

•Valentine

Niobara River

•Ainsworth
☐Fanciful Ranch

IOWA

Calamus River

NEBRASKA

gallala

•Fort Benton

Devil's
■Lake

Mississippi River

Area of
main map

Evanston•

•St. Louis

Gerster•

Memphis

*Where Eb and Lucian
are at the beginning*

•Greenville
•Vicksburg

KANSAS

BOOK 1

Leaving
the Mississippi

 The Mississippi River, 1863–1864

⚜ CHAPTER 1 ⚜

Eb Paint woke at dawn to a caressing fog, eyelids fluttering where damp sycamore leaves drizzled mist. He tried to cuss but the word stuck in his whiskey-parched throat; he was too dry to speak or spit. The fire was dead and the stink of wet smoke hung where blackened cottonwood boughs leaked steam. He tried to recall why he hated that smell so, gave up the effort and parsed the river without opening his eyes. There was a good deal a man who knew the Mississippi River could tell by listening. He could hear the rush of water over a bluff reef, the *slap slap slap* of ripples on wet sand around the finger of land where they had anchored the *Marielita*, the whinge of mosquitoes, curlews somewhere, a catfish breaching the surface for a toothful of dragonfly. He strained to listen. Somewhere out there, the big river flexed her tawny muscles. Seldom had the Mississippi been so quiet since the twelfth day of April, 1861, the day Brigadier General Pierre Gustave Toutant Beauregard of the Confederate States of America opened fire on Fort Sumter. Before the war, half-acre rafts and scows and broadheads floating downriver would chance this peasoup darkness, the crews banging pots and pans with tin spoons to warn off the eight-hundred-ton steamboats pounding upriver through the main channel. Only a double-plated fool would chance the river now, not knowing whether the next bend would bring hungry rebels, jittery bluecoats, or some daft and murderous outlaw like Quantrill. Most of the boats on the river were bringing supplies to Grant's besieging troops as the vise tightened on the Confederate fortress at Vicksburg, but in this fog even the Union supply boats were shut down waiting for the sun to burn through.

The *Marielita* was beached on a long finger of sand out there in the mist, creaking as she shifted her weight in the lee of the towhead like an old woman squatting to pee. Eb tried to see the old tub where she was tied fast with two bowropes thick as a man's ankle, knotted to deep-rooted cottonwoods. The effort made his whiskey headache pound like a brass band. He closed his eyes again, went back to listening. There it was again, something out of place in the fog. The thick air muffled the sound but it carried plain enough.

Thwuck. Thwuck. Thwuck.

He rose to shake the sand from his britches and strolled to the water's edge. A shoal of minnows darted left and right away from the manshadow—and by what mysterious semaphore did each tiniest minnow know to zig and zag, rise and dive and flee in a single body and never mistake the direction? You could drill a squadron of crack troops until their heels bled and they would never perform in such singleminded unison. It was a thing to ponder and Ebenezer Paint of Jones County, Mississippi, was by nature a pondering man, but on this day his noggin was thick with whiskey and he had more urgent matters to ponder. At the edge of the towhead, where sand met river, there coiled a rolling shoulder of fog; beyond that it was like trying to look up the devil's arse.

Thwuck. Thwuck. Thwuck.

It came from the starboard side of the *Marielita*, a sound like a rotten watermelon tossed on a wharf.

—Lucian?

Lucian was still wrapped in his bedroll, a scrap of wet blanket hiding the nap of his head. Eb prodded his kidneys with a bare toe.

—Goddammit, Lucian.

He yanked the blanket back and peered into the bloodshot eyes of Lucian Quigley, who regarded him as one regards a man who has taken leave of his senses.

—What?

—What is that goddamned noise.

—What goddamned noise.

—That goddamned noise.

Thwuck. Thwuck. Thwuck.

—Sound like somebody tryin to beat through the hull with a wet hammer.

—Off to stabberd, like.

—Thassit.

—Trouble with fog like this. Can't see a goddamned thing. Could be a ghost.

—Could be a old tree too. You get the damnedest ideas for a white man, like a old slave woman.

—I aint the one tacked that cross o' nails in my left bootheel to keep off the evil spirits, am I? I aint the one afraid to look over my left shoulder at the new moon.

—Man got to be sensible, take precautions in this life.

—Precautions, hell. Superstitions, what it is. Now I'm goin out there to see what it is bangin on my boat. You comin or aint you?

—Aw hell.

Lucian rolled onto his knees. The rye came up with chunks of catfish, all of it hurled over the exposed roots of a dwarf oak. Eb wrinkled his nose and turned away.

—You have to do that? You and your goddamned rye. Stuff tastes worse'n arsenic.

—If it aint to your taste leave it be. More for me that way.

—I swear you make it in a outhouse.

—Didn't hear you complain once last night. Not once. All I heard was *Lucian, pass me that there rye one more time.* You kep at it till my whiskey was most gone. Smack your lips like you was tastin honey from the bee. Yessir, honey from the bee.

—That was last night and this here is this mornin. If you're done evacuatin your innards, can we go have a look, find what's messin with my boat?

They crawled into the skiff. Eb climbed to the bow and left Lucian to row while he navigated by the sound of water lapping against the hull of the old steamboat and the other sound, the metronome beating time to the river.

Mist rolled down their shirtsleeves and trailed off their fingertips. Eb tied the boat fast to the *Marielita* with a bowline knot. Lucian shinnied aboard and led the way with his bowie knife held blade up. Eb followed the sound of Lucian's bare feet going *slapslapslap* across the main deck, three feet above the waterline. The mist was so thick they couldn't see the starboard rail from the larboard, and the deck was slick with damp where Lucian had whitewashed it fresh not a month before. Eb leaned over the rail and peered down into water the color of tar.

—Aw Jesus.

—Hell is it?

—See for yourself. Aint no pretty Natchez lady out for a stroll.

—Lordy. It surely aint.

The corpse, its feet tangled in a drift of willow limbs, had lodged on the upriver side of the *Marielita*. A Confederate officer, by the look of his butternut coat. A wisp of fuzz on his cheeks and upper lip, a man not yet old enough to grow a proper beard, long blond hair now riverdark. A thick black tongue lolled like an eel from his mouth. One blue eye stared off somewhere the other side of beyond but the near eyesocket was pulped with black gore. With every roll of the Mississippi, the dead man's head beat against the hull.

Thwuck. Thwuck. Thwuck.

—Reach me a oar, Lucian.

—Aint we goin to pull him in?

—No, we aint goin to pull him in, unless you want to get caught tryin to dig a hole for a dead Confederate and you a black man. They'd string you from the nearest oak and then hang me from your toes to make sure we was both dead. Reach me a oar, now. This poor sonofabitch is in the only grave he's ever goin to know. May the Lord have mercy on his mama.

Eb took the oar from Lucian and poked the rebel's feet free from the willow drift, then turned the oar paddle down and heaved on the dead man's chest. The corpse spun away from the oar back to belly, like a sternwheeler churning downstream. As he rolled they could see where the ball that took out his eye had splattered the back of his head. Eb turned and retched, caught his breath, tried a second time and managed to tuck the tip of the oar in under the man's suspenders, where he got enough purchase to guide the corpse the length of the boat. With one last heave he shoved the body clear of the sternwheel and watched the current take it. The butternut coat fanned out over the surface and the dead rebel rotated like the hands of a courthouse clock, head to boots, head to boots down the gullet of the fog. Two rotations, three, four, and he vanished, bound for Milliken's Bend, the Gulf of Mexico, the land of perdition. Eb handed the oar back to Lucian and knelt on the deck, leaned out low over the water and vomited rye and catfish into the stream.

—You and your goddamned tangle-foot whiskey.

They slipped back into the skiff and rowed to the sandbar. Lucian pried hot embers from the sand, got the fire going again. Eb roasted green coffee beans in a skillet, filled a buckskin bag with the beans still hot, pounded the bag between two rocks until the beans were crushed fine. They didn't risk another word until the coffee was boiled and they could squat in the sand with battered tin mugs, nibbling hardtack and drinking coffee thick as molasses.

—That was some awful sight.

—Deed it was.

—I seen some things on this river, Lucian.

—Ain't we all.

Lucian fried bacon in a charred pan thick with grease. The fog held, persistent as a bulldog locked on a hambone.

—Y'know, I seen the wreck of the *Pennsylvania*.

—Oh, she was a hard one, that. Hard. I was down with Judge Quigley when she blew and we heard her go two counties south. Folks was talkin about it for months.

—I pulled a burned boy from that wreck was hangin on to a stick of wood no bigger than your arm.

—Helluva thing. The judge said when she went up they found pieces of that boat a mile off and they was a thousand dead on the river they never did find.

—Was more than a mile. They was things from the *Pennsylvania* traveled three mile in the air and was still goin hard enough to kill a pelican on the wing. Brass fittins and boiler plate and hunks of fellas like you and me that was smokin a pipe and jawin about the price of calico in Shreveport not a minute before she went. Seen it myself, but I seen worst things. Last spring I seen a poor goddamned devil Union corporal, tried to take a bath in the river all by hisself. Wild boar, must of been the guns made him crazy, come bustin out of the scrub. Big bastard the color of a rusty nail, longleggedy vicious razorback sonofabitch barrelin along with green foam drippin off his tusks, fast as a racehorse. Run right over that naked corporal, knocked him down and went to eatin him from the pecker up. Soldier beat on the beast with both fists and screamed like Judgment Day but that hog paid him no more attention than you would a gnat, just went right on chewin with the man's innards danglin from his jaws. I dragged out that big ole muzzle-loadin Whitworth rifle figgerin to shoot the beast but there was so much chop on the water I couldn't get no bead on that critter, big as he was. Pulled the trigger and fired a bolt to scare him but that hog was past scarin. Then the boat was on by and around a bend and there wasn't ary thing I could do cept to pray for that corporal's mortal soul. Never forget it as long as I live. You lead a dishonest life, you will find a critter like that razorback boar waitin to greet you personal at the gates of Hell.

—Amen, my brother.

—Don't know that I can take much more of this river.

—Aint goin to hear no aggument from me.

—Tired of listenin to rebels tell me Bobby Lee is a genius and the South aint got no quit.

—Yessuh.

—Tired of wakin to find a dead man's head bangin on my boat.

—Yessuh.

—Tired of thinkin about the misery folks is in down to Vicksburg, ball and shot droppin on their heads day and night. They say women and children is eatin rats and mules cause they got nothin else. We been awful lucky to steer clear of the worst of it.

—Maybe that dead Confederate is a sign it's time to get shed of this place for good. Find a spot where a fellow can eat his dinner without crackin a tooth on a minié ball stuck in the peas.

—They say Dakota.

—Dakota! Dakota? I aint goin anywheres near any Dakota. Full a nothin but wild Indians, Dakota. They scalp you, stake you to a anthill and spread you with molasses, then they slice off your tallywhacker and stuff it in your mouth.

—Lord, Lucian. Where you hear these things?

—Folks.

—Folks that aint been no nearer Dakota than yourself. I was through all that country on the way to California back in 'forty-nine. The Indians didn't give us a peck of trouble and there's plenty of free land up there.

—Free land for a white man, maybe. Aint never been nothin free for a black fella on this white man's earth and never will be.

—That's here in Dixie. Aint the same everywhere you go.

—Aint no nevermind to me. I aint taggin along to no Dakota and that's all she wrote.

—I aint asked you to. Just passin time, is all. Like as not I aint goin to no Dakota neither. If I want to light out, I got to find me some fool wants to buy hisself that leaky little pissant forty-ton store boat we got. World full a fools, they say, but I aint yet met the man fool enough to buy that boat.

—Except yourself.

—Except myself. But I was young and foolish then. Now I got to find another such goddamned fool.

Lucian took his bowie knife, stabbed at a sliver of bacon left in the pan.

—That's it right there. You said a mouthful. World full a fools. Trick to life is to find the right goddamned fool.

✦ CHAPTER 2 ✦

Back in the spring of 1856, old Bonaventure Archambault saw his fool coming a mile off when Ebenezer Paint purchased the *Marielita* for the sum of three thousand two hundred dollars. Archambault saw a young man with money in his pockets from the goldfields of California, a fellow who wanted a piece of anything this side of a hollow log that would give a man a toehold on the Mississippi. Archambault knew the way the river could get a hook in a man's gills, the irresistible pull of it. A fellow could stand on the riverbank and watch the *Eclipse* and the *A. L. Shotwell* race each other upstream from New Orleans to St. Louis, with their sixty-foot smokestacks pouring sparks and black smoke, and find the river had him in her grip and would not let go, the power and mystery of it as seductive as a Memphis harlot. A man who was intoxicated by the Mississippi could spread out a map and run his thumb upriver through Morganza, Waterproof, Tomato, Tipton-ville, New Madrid, Cairo, Thebes, Kaskaskia, Oquawka, Musca-tine, Moline, Genoa, Winona, and Wabasha all the way to St. Paul and imagine that he could feel the planks of the pilothouse vibrate under his feet with the power of the big engines, see the rush of white water past the bow with himself as captain of all that wood and brass and steam. Eventually, he would come to believe that any other life was a pale substitute. Archambault knew how it was because he had once given his soul to the river. Now he was old and crippled up with the rheumatiz and all he wanted was enough money to get out in one piece and spend the rest of his days fishing on the banks of Lake Pontchartrain.

Archambault's boat was Eb's ticket onto the Mississippi. For two years he had cast up and down the river for a steamboat pilot willing to take on a cub with a crippled foot at a time when half the young men along the river from New Orleans to St. Paul aspired to pilothood. The pilots watched him limp along the dock and shook their heads. They wanted healthy teenage boys to act as indentured servants, not a full-grown man who had been to the goldfields of California and back and was lame to boot. What Archambault had to sell was a smallish sternwheeler called the *Lac Pontchartrain,* after his home, the boat, and the business that came with her, a floating mercantile that supplied plantations and one-mule towns between Natchez and Memphis with every need but salvation. He knew the boat was a leaky tub, so what he sold was the river, not the boat. He let Eb stand at the helm on a sparkling May morning when the Mississippi was at her sweetest, let him stoke the boilers, call out the depths as the leadsman working off the bow, watch the pitman rods crank the flywheels, take the helm and feel the tug of current against the rudder. It took every nickel of specie and every ounce of gold dust Eb had left from the goldfields, but when it was done he owned the *Lac Pontchartrain* and everything aboard her. Lock, stock, pilot, and whores, because Archambault threw in a drunken and surly pilot named Tobias Salverson and two broad-beamed, ample-bottomed New Orleans prostitutes who advertised on the hurricane deck and plied their noisy trade in the living quarters of the texas, directly across from his own narrow and monastic chamber. He resisted their charms but he could not resist a remark or two as he watched them sashay to and fro on deck, dresses stretched taut over what they called their "derrears."

—Like two pigs fightin in a gunnysack.

—*Comment?*

—Nothin, darlin. I was just admirin your accoutrements.

—*Comment?*

—That part what you call your derrears. Wide as a steam boiler.

His remark drew a curtsy.

—*Merci, monsieur.*

—Mercy is about right. Lawd amercy.

He rechristened the boat the *Marielita* after a Mexican girl he had fallen in love with when he saw her panning for gold one sparkling June morning on the Feather River in California, her skirts up and her bare brown legs gleaming with droplets of water. The girl nearly cost Eb his manhood when her father held a gleaming silver knife to his private parts, threatening to turn him into a gelding on the spot if he didn't agree to leave her alone. The next day, Marielita and her family had vanished from the Feather River, never to return. In Eb's mind eight years later, her legs still sparkled in the California sunshine, so he named his floating castle the *Marielita*. Three weeks later, Salverson the pilot failed to appear after a drunken night in Natchez Under-the-Hill and Eb decided he could get along without him. The man was sour as persimmons anyway. After a single season on the Mississippi he sent the whores back to New Orleans aboard the *Princess*, their fares on the grand ship paid in full by Ebenezer Paint. He was no whoremaster and their clientele, snaggletoothed and vicious men with rank odors and long knives tucked into knee-high boots, scared off the regular trade. Business was brisk enough, with customers seeking to buy or trade for watermelon, plug tobacco, playing cards, axes, pitchforks, pistols, ammunition, sorghum, molasses, bolts of calico, gingham or muslin, buckwheat flour, cornmeal, chicken mash, hand-tooled canes, the Good Book, and rye whiskey sold by the dram, the pint, or the jug, depending on the victim's thirst and the size of his purse.

A month after the whores left, Lucian Quigley came aboard. The first time Eb laid eyes on him in the blazing heat of a Mississippi August, Lucian wore a long overcoat buttoned down to his toes. The boat was aground in the mud upstream from a three-mule hamlet on the Arkansas bank and there were a half dozen white men aboard her to purchase black powder and ball, the bunch of them far enough into Eb's Tennessee whiskey to make them dangerous. Lucian steered clear of the whites, pulled a tattered rag out of his coat, and went to polishing along the rail as if that was the job he'd done every day of his life. When the white men were gone, Eb looked him over and saw a giant of a man with blue-black skin and shoulders about two ax handles across. Eb tried to make out the face under a battered slouch hat, saw only indigo shadows, and waited for the man to state his business.

Lucian opened the coat. From his wide leather belt a dozen live chickens dangled upside down, secured by their feet with strips of rawhide.

—Name's Lucian Quigley, sah.

—Ebenezer Paint.

—Fella upriver said you was lookin for a supply of chickens.

—I might be. These your chickens?

—They's my chickens now. And I'll sell you ever last one for a dollar a chicken.

—A dollar? For a damned chicken? I'll give you a nickel apiece for them molty birds.

—A nickel? For a prize chicken? No, *sah*! These here is fitty-cent chickens, fat as the behinds of them Loosiana harlots you had on this boat last time you come this way. That's fitty cents in New Orleans, where they got plenty chickens. Way out here, these are one-dollar chickens.

—Two bits. That's my last offer. You aint goin to haggle me no higher so don't even try.

—Then I expect I'll be eatin all these chickens my own self.

Lucian turned to go ashore. Eb let him get one boot into the mud.

—Forty cents.

—Six bits.

—Four bits. Fifty cents a chicken, just like you said in the first place.

—You just bought yourself these here chickens, Mr. Paint. Thank you kindly. It has been a pleasure to do business with you.

—Now hold on. I got to do my cipherin here. You got one dozen chickens, fifty cents a chicken, that makes three dollars.

—No, sah! Fitty cents a chicken makes *six* dollars for twelve chickens. You may be dealin with a colored man, Mr. Paint, but you aint dealin with no fool.

Lucian wrung the neck of one of the chickens and plucked it and they fried it up over Eb's stove to seal the deal, washed it down with Lucian's whiskey. They were picking their teeth with the bones when Eb edged up to the topic that was worrying him.

—You aint no runaway slave, are ye?

—No, sah. I'm as free as you, sah. Got my own patch of Mississippi land. Got my dockaments right cheer.

He tapped the buckskin bag strung over his shoulder.

—You never been a slave?

—Oh, I been. I been slave to three masters. First one whupped me. Second one whupped me and sold my wife and two babies down the river. Third was old Judge Quigley. Taught me to read and do ciphers. Said the day he died I'd be a free man and he was good as his word.

Within a few weeks, Eb couldn't imagine how he had ever run the *Marielita* without the man. Lucian kept the *Marielita* supplied with sweet corn, beans, collard greens, watermelon, turnips, and potatoes from his plot or maybe from other people's plots, Eb never knew for sure. He chopped firewood for the boilers. He built a chicken coop on the hurricane deck and filled it with a dozen Plymouth Rock hens and a one-eyed rooster of uncertain provenance. He learned to read the river so well that Eb trusted Lucian's judgment better than his own. Beyond a common need for self-preservation, Eb and Lucian shared a passion for the game of checkers and a love for what Lucian called "aggument," a free-flowing, long-running dispute over everything from the best way to run the shoals to the religion most likely to usher a man through the pearly gates. To while away a warm night on the river, Lucian would lead them into a thicket where they would debate the exact quantum of blame accrued to God Almighty for permitting this conflict and the degree to which any one man caught up in the great spokes of the wheel of war might still act of his own free will, make his own choices, and live with the consequences. They would chew it back and forth, stake out preliminary positions, tickle it a little, as Lucian put it, see if it squealed. Then Lucian would vanish; Eb would wake up one morning and find him gone. Three weeks later the *Marielita* would steam into a makeshift dock at a village that was nothing but sticks and mud fastened with binding twine to the Arkansas bank and there Lucian would be waiting, squatting on his haunches, holding a spotted barrow on a rawhide leash as if he knew all along where Eb intended to travel before Eb knew himself. He would hoist the little pig on his shoulder and come aboard and resume the argument in midsentence, as though the pause in their conversation had lasted no longer than it would take him to pee into the river.

—. . . and if you choose to blame the Good Lord for all the tomfoolishness men get theyselves up to, you as good as givin every last fella a invitation to rob, murder, plunder, and covet his neighbor's womanfolk. All a man got to say is, "Oh, the Devil made me do it!" and he done assigned all his sins to a higher power.

—You take my meanin and get it all twisted up, Lucian. All I meant to say was that if He let loose this murderous plague of war upon the land, then He has somethin to answer for, same as any general who marches a thousand men to their deaths with no more thought than you'd give to killin a chicken.

—No, sah. Only ones to blame for this is folks like you and me. We the ones shootin and killin and murdering and the Lord Almighty, all he done is shake His head and wished He could start over again. Maybe He put Eve in charge next time, do things right.

Gradually, Lucian took over one task after another on the boat. He left off chopping wood and foraging for chickens and rabbits and became an adept engineer and mechanic, capable of repairing anything from the paddles to the pitman rods. Once he began to absorb the river, he learned so much so quickly that Eb began to rely on Lucian's prodigious memory to recollect every snag, shoal, and bluff reef upriver as far as Memphis and beyond. Lucian could read the river as well as any pilot, could navigate through a starless pitchpine night with no more to guide him than a glimmer from a farmhouse candle or a shadowy bluff that to Eb appeared to have been plunked down in exactly the wrong place. On the protean Mississippi where the landmarks were never the same two trips in a row, where new channels were carved every day and the river would take a notion to run a new cutoff fifteen miles to the west of the old one overnight, nothing seemed to surprise Lucian. Even down in sugarcane country south of Natchez where the slaves piled the shredded cane stalks into great piles of bagasse and set them alight, Lucian could thread the boat through a hundred miles of billowing black smoke and set her down in New Orleans neat as china on a planter's table. For Lucian, there was no malevolence in that roiling brown water, though men often enough claimed otherwise. If a fellow stayed humble, he rolled with the river. It was when he got arrogant, when his pride told him he could tame her like a horse, that was when the Mississippi would rise up to slap him down.

⚜ CHAPTER 3 ⚜

High noon came and went and the fog held so thick you could chew it up and spit out the seeds. Eb fidgeted. Stare into a peasoup fog long enough and you were apt to conjure up most anything: Bright yellow panthers. Pink alligators. Green pelicans. A whole marching band of phantom soldiers or a dead Secesh officer. Why of all places did that Johnny Reb corpse have to light here, smack up against the *Marielita?* Dead men enough on the Mississippi but the river was a big place, big enough you could drown both these warring armies between New Orleans and Cairo and pilot a dozen steamships through the main channel the day after and run into nothing but snags and driftwood. So here came this lone one-eyed rebel bobbing through the fog like he was searching for Eb Paint's boat and no other.

Thwuck. Thwuck. Thwuck.

The sun would have scattered the ghosts. Instead every phantom a mind could conjure danced now behind this curtain of fog: entire bloated battalions of river-sodden, one-eyed soldiers waving rusty sabers, trailing seaweed and swamp grass and belching minnows as they charged, the rebel yell bubbling in their throats. It gave a man the heebie-jeebies. Eb jumped every time a twig snapped, whirled and clutched his knife when an owl fluttered from branch to branch. Lucian saw the ripple before Eb did, a spasm in the water where the towhead met the river.

—I'm goin to get that sonofabitch before he get me.

—What sonofabitch?

—That sonofabitch water moccasin.

Lucian was already on the move, half-handled spade in hand, sidling to his left as the snake poured itself over the ground, its body almost black in the shadow of a gnarled oak. It was a big one, four feet long and thick as a man's wrist. Eb reached for his hickory stick but Lucian was already on it, crouched with one bare foot on either side of its tail as he drove the spade clean through the only narrow part of the snake, an inch behind the trowel-shaped head. The body whipped back and wrapped itself around Lucian's ankle. Lucian slipped the tip of the spade between his foot and the pale, rippling scales of the snake's belly, and as he lifted the spade the snake came with it, headless, the body still writhing. He tossed it to Eb, who jumped back and let it fall, still writhing, at his feet.

—Dang, Lucian. Don't do that. You know I hate snakes.

—He's bait, that's all. A snake that big catch you a dozen catfish.

—Keep him the hell away from me, is all.

Lucian rummaged in the skiff, came away with a bucket they used to bail water, chopped the snake into chunks two inches long, filled the bucket with snake morsels fit to snag a catfish. Eb backed away, keeping the fire between himself and the chopped snake.

—I hate snakes.

—I know you do. Don't know why you want to go to Dakota. I hear they got snakes in Dakota. Big damned rattlers make this thing look like a tadpole.

—You aint tellin me nothin I aint seen up close. I killed a dozen a them bastards between Chimney Rock and the Carson Desert.

—Well then.

—Sonofabitch rattlers can't swim.

Late afternoon the sun broke through. Down Vicksburg way the Union guns opened up as soon as the fog lifted, a distant rumble like summer thunder. The mist tore into rags, the bald sunshine heated the mist to steam. Just sitting on the towhead running bare toes in the mud, they were sweating like stevedores. Eb pulled his hat lower over his eyes, squinted downriver, spat his chaw.

—I expect we should have had the boilers up. Didn't think that fog would lift before sundown.

—You want to head out?

—Time we get someplace else it'll be too late to trade with anybody but the owls. Maybe we just sit tight, drink some more of that arsenic rye. See if you can't snag us a catfish or two.

—I knew you'd be pleased we come across that snake. Folks always say, "Why we got snakes? They aint no use at all and they scare a feller most to death." But they's a use for everthin if you know what to make of it. Water moccasins and razorback hogs and persimmon trees. Everythin in this world got a use.

—Skeeters? You got a use for skeeters?

Eb went to slap one, got three on his forearm in a single whack. Lucian chuckled.

—Aint found a use for skeeters yet, cept they seem to like white meat better'n black. Fella used to whup me afore Judge Quigley set me free, they drove him plumb crazy. Could never figger why they lit on his hide and left me alone. I expect that was just the good Lord foolin with him, lettin him know what he got comin for his sins. Devil aint waitin for him with a pitchfork. He's waitin with sixteen boatloads of skeeters, goin to torment that mean old man for a million years.

Lucian was still chuckling as he rowed out in the skiff, baited the trotlines with hunks of snake, hung them off the stern, and went to cajoling the catfish.

—Fresh water moccasin, honeys. Come to Papa. I killed this snake a-purpose for you and now you goldarned fish is hidin out. Lazy critters bellywallerin in Mississippi mud all the livelong day when you ought to be the makins for a catfish pie. Come to Lucian, now. C'mon. You got a taste for fresh kilt snake, I know you do.

Eb stayed in the texas, out of the sun, fiddling with his charts, poring over ledgers that showed the war was not altogether a bad thing, not for a man with a nose for a dollar. He had pondered some of the right and wrong of it, taking profit off the misery of war, and had not absolved himself entirely, although he knew the greater guilt to be with the men who made powder and shot and the engines of destruction and sold them without favor to the side that could afford to pay the highest price. If not for the war profiteers, the armies that clashed by night would be armed with stones and cudgels, able to kill only at close quarters. If it was wrong to sell a man a watermelon or a pig within the sound of the cannon, surely it was worse to sell the cannon and shot, although he was not certain he would care to argue the point come Judgment Day.

Within an hour Lucian had three big catfish gutted, two of them smoking on forked sticks over the fire while he sliced the third into fillets, daubed the fillets in lard and cornmeal and a sprinkling of salt and tossed them into the frying pan. Eb poured generous dollops of rye into bent tin cups. Lucian tore open a gunnysack of sweetcorn, slipped a dozen ears still wrapped in the husks among the embers of the fire, added four sweet potatoes. By the time they were done licking the grease from their fingers, they were deep into a third cup of rye. They leaned back against the thick trunks of oak trees and watched the sun cast long ropes of fire over black water, a tawdry display lurid with the promise of undiscovered sin. A heron flapped over the river bound for Louisiana, towing its long legs into the sunset. Far out in the swift current of the main channel, a Union supply boat churned past without a hail, hurrying off to war. They sat in silence for a time, watching the river. Lucian pointed to a long sycamore floating past, black limbs and a tangle of roots tumbling out of the water.

—I expect that if a man was to sit on this towhead long enough, sooner or later he'd see most everythin float by, headin for New Orleans.

—Long as he was here to see it. Every little thing passes by is one less thing you're goin to see before Judgment Day and a man never knows how close that day may be. I expect that dead rebel could a told us a thing or two bout Judgment Day.

—Aint it the truth? You ever think about that? How it's all like this big river, goin on and on until they aint no more goin on to go? You see that big sycamore snag and Carter's woodlot yonder, and Cat Island

and the dogleg after Marse Hunter's plantation and the shoalest water at the north end of the Barnaby Slough, and every foot of it is one more foot of river that has passed you by. That river creepin on tomorrow and tomorrow and the day after next Sunday, until they aint nobody round to see it no more and all our hurryin and doin is goin to be washed away with the rest of it, like a caved-in point in the December highwater. It's a damned fool yarn, a whole lot a noise that don't signify no more'n a gutted catfish. It's enough to scare folks right through the door to the first church they lays eyes on. That's what keeps your preachers in business, you ask me. Folks see they don't amount to much more than a stick in the river they got to believe in somethin, even if it's all a lot of mumbletyjumble.

They talked through the night, until the first apricot tinge washed the eastern shore of the river. Lucian declared it was time to get some shut-eye. Eb stayed awake to watch the sunrise, puffing his pipe and listening to the sounds of the river. He was a southerner by birth but an abolitionist in sympathy, the opposite of the northern Copperheads who were pouring into the South, venomous with their hatred of the Negro and spoiling for a fight. Back home, his brothers sided with the majority of the citizenry in seceding from the secessionists, setting up the independent republic of Jones County, Mississippi; it was called the Free State of Jones, a bastion of dissenters in a land of slaves. After the government of Jefferson Davis passed the Twenty Negro Law stating that any man owning as many as twenty slaves was excused from the fight to stay home and keep an eye on his plantation, the two youngest Paint brothers determined that the southern cause was a rich man's war but a poor man's fight and they left to join one of the Jones County regiments fighting with the Federals. If he had two sound feet for marching, Eb would have joined them. Had he done so, he would likely be as dead as they were this very day.

Beyond his abolitionist sympathies, Eb considered himself a patriot. He believed the United States of America was the greatest nation on earth, the one true bastion of liberty, the last, best hope for mankind. But once a wrong as great as slavery had been committed on this soil, could that wrong ever be cleansed? Could a nation as divided as this one ever heal? Would all the blood now being poured into the land act as a baptismal tide, saving a misguided people from the morass of their own sins, or were they doomed by the misdeeds of whole generations of white men? Would it ever be possible to make things right with a fellow who had been whipped until the blood poured from his back? Was there any sound reason why Lucian should not take an ax one night and hack to death every white man and woman he could find?

Eb grabbed his bedroll, stretched out next to what was left of the fire, watched a lopsided moon lollygag across a pale sky, trying to outrun the rising sun and making a poor job of it. He had no answers for the questions he put to the river. The future of the Republic was as murky as the Mississippi and every bit as strewn with boiling whirlpools, unseen snags, flood tides, forgotten wrecks lying in wait. It was like one of those sloughs where the river divides a thousand times and then a thousand more. Only one path will lead you through and only the best river pilots can find the path. The hard part was to find the channel in these perilous times, a task for great-souled men who could see much farther down this old river than he could. Now if Marse Lincoln should happen along one night and sit down cross-legged by the fire, they could worry at it over Lucian's fried catfish and whiskey and by daybreak, the Lord willing, they might arrive at a place where the channel was marked plain as a turnpike, where the river flowed clear and straight and sensible all the way to the sea. He drifted off to sleep at last, into a dream of Marse Lincoln rowing a skiff upriver, his long back and sinewy arms bent to the oars. As the president rowed, Eb poured the man a cupful of Lucian's rye whiskey. In times like these, the man at the helm needed something to warm his innards.

An hour later, Lucian was pounding coffee beans.

—Goddammit, Lucian. Sun aint but half up.

—I thought you was in a hurry to get off this here towhead.

—Goddammit anyway.

—C'mon, Eb. Times a-wastin.

They rode the current south along the main channel of the river, just enough steam in the boilers to keep the paddle turning. They glided past three tumbledown abandoned villages, an overgrown cotton plantation and a long Union raft holding to the main channel, where the current was strongest, Federal troops escorting bales of supplies south to Vicksburg, bayonets glinting in the sun. The Stars and Stripes, waving from the jackstaff of the *Marielita*, granted them free passage and a hail from the troops.

—What we need for this here raft is a little a that steam. Reckon we could borry some from you fellas?

—None to loan, but we'll sell y'all a dozen bolts a fresh steam at three cents a yard.

That brought a guffaw from the raft.

—You goddamned traders would charge a man for a bucket a warm spit and then make him pay double for somethin to warsh out the taste a spit. You fellas got whiskey aboard?

—Three dollars a pint.

—Hell you say. That whiskey you sellin or diamonds?

—Open your throat, it's like swallowin diamonds, it's that good.

—You'll have to save it for a rich man, then. Aint naught here but poor soldiers bound for the slaughter.

The *Marielita* glided on by. If the men called a halt at the next loading dock, they would be thirsty enough to pay three dollars a pint. If not, there would be others. A boat hauling boot leather, plug tobacco, and hundred-proof liquor on the fringes of a war zone would never lack for customers. Within the shadow of conflict, specie became unmoored and floated free and men grew careless of the value of greasy bits of paper, happy to swap piles of dollars for plug tobacco, sugar, rye, paper, boot leather, beeswax, anything a boat could carry.

Lucian pointed to a long, slanting streak across the water a half mile ahead.

—That bluff reef's gettin bigger, boss. Best tuck in close to the labberd bank till you get past it.

Eb obeyed without question. Lucian swept the river ahead with the spyglass.

—Ever occur to you that come this time next year, half of them boys'll be dead or so busted up they's no use to nobody?

—It has.

—I've thought about it considerable. Seein that raft, it's like ridin by a graveyard, only the dead don't know they's dead, so they's a-wavin and a-hollerin and a-lookin to buy whiskey.

—If they knew they was dead, I don't expect you'd get much fight out of them.

—I expect not. Nor sell 'em much whiskey neither.

It was not a topic they cared to explore further. They settled into an uneasy silence. From midriver, both shores were identical dark smudges of vegetation, trees and weeds and brush all tangled together—sycamore, black pine, joe-pye weed, swamp oak, shagbark hickory, possum haw, wolf willow, dwarf cypress, sumac, hackmatack, cottonwood, honeysuckle. A bloom of egrets rose from the Mississippi shore a mile downriver, at that distance like cotton bolls flung into the breeze. Lucian saw them first.

—Watch them birds, Eb. Somethin flushed 'em.

—Might be a alligator.

—Yep. Might be a elephant too, but it aint no alligator and it aint no elephant neither.

—How do you know that?

—If it was a alligator, them birds would fly a ways, then they'd light back on the water. Men around, they keep movin.

—Give me a peek through that thing.

Eb took the glass from Lucian and fixed it on the shore. He could make out two dozen ragged Confederates on a rare sandy stretch where the bush didn't grow right down to the river. They waved madly, like escapees from an asylum, beckoning him to shore. Eb knew what they wanted: they would rifle through his stock, plunge their hands into barrels of buckwheat flour and cornmeal, crack eggs straight down their gullets, lick sorghum and molasses off fingers black with dirt, claw at the chickens as though they intended to eat them alive, feathers and beaks and all. When they had emptied the *Marielita* of everything she carried, they would make a great show of figuring exactly what they owed and pay with a greasy stack of worthless Confederate dollars. Then out of sheer orneriness they would ask if Lucian had his "dockaments" proving that he was a freed slave and pore over his papers a long while even though not one of them could read a lick. Like as not they would take a notion to lead Lucian off and sell him to the first slave trader they came across, documents or no documents.

—Haul that flag, Lucian.

Lucian was already at it, pulling the Stars and Stripes down from the jackstaff and tucking it under the chicken coop.

—What you aim to do?

—Run past 'em. Make like we don't see 'em, see if we can't drift to the Louisiana bank and snug in with some bluecoats.

—I thought they wasn't no rebels this side of the river before Vicksburg.

—I expect they slipped out of Vicksburg in the fog and got past the Federals before it lifted. They're like chiggers that way, get up inside your pants and bite your ass.

Eb eased the helm to starboard. Lucian took the glass, twisted it until he could make out a rebel's battered hat. He scanned uphill, found a rebel battery seated on a makeshift terreplein behind a parapet of fresh-cut logs with three cannon unlimbered and ready, pivoting on their trunnions to bring gaping muzzles to bear on the *Marielita*.

—What you see?

—They got a battery up in them woods.

—They wouldn't fire at us. We aint no warship.

—Hell they wouldn't. Looks like they fixin to do just that.

As he said it, Lucian saw a puff of black smoke from the hill. A screaming came across the water, followed by the report of the cannon. A geyser of white water rose three hundred yards to larboard. Lucian didn't flinch.

—Eight-inch shell, sounds like. Fuzes cut for thirty seconds, maybe forty. Caint find the range yet. You give 'em time to get the range, they can drop that eight-pound shot down a chicken's gullet.

There was another puff of smoke and a long scream that wailed low over the twin smokestacks of the *Marielita* and exploded in a sheet of water fifty yards to larboard. This time even Lucian ducked.

—Looks like they figgerin it out.

—Swing that glass to starboard. There ought to be a Union landing just past that little towhead.

Lucian swiveled the glass beyond the little sandbar and found a line of white water where a rotting jetty thrust a perpendicular jab into the river. Beyond that the Union pier was busy with bluecoats hauling bales of equipment off a long raft. One or two had spotted the *Marielita* and were waving her in.

—They's just past the towhead. Looks like they want us to put in that side. We're awful popular this mornin.

A third shot splashed well off the bow. Now Lucian could see Union troops waving and pointing at the rebels, more bluecoats back in the woods unlimbering their own artillery.

—Damn. We goin to find ourselves in the middle of a shootin match.

—No, we aint. Now you wave at them rebels; let 'em know we're comin in.

—How's that?

—Just do it, Lucian. I aint got time for one of your dang agguments. Do it quick, then get down to the boiler deck, grab every loose stick of lumber you can get your hands on, stoke it into them boilers and get your pitchpine ready. When I ring the bell, you start chuckin pitchpine into the boilers and nothin else.

—I do that, she's goin to gum up and blow a cylinder head.

—Not if one of them shells hits us first.

Two balls screamed over the river in unison, the second near enough to the stern to send a geyser of water onto the hurricane deck back of the texas. Lucian was already up on the bow, waving to the Confederates, letting them think he was putting to shore.

As Eb swung the helm hard to larboard and sighted along the jack-staff to get his bearings, Lucian tore down the steps to the boiler deck and stuffed cottonwood logs into the boilers. He had to brace himself as the Marielita heeled over and came about, reluctant as a fat boy on his way to school. With the boat running toward the Mississippi shore, a rebel shot fell a hundred yards off the stern and the Secesh battery fell silent, waiting for them to come in. Lucian threw another armload of wood into the boiler. Black smoke belched from the stacks and the Marielita hiccuped and stuttered as she gathered speed. Eb tried to watch everything at once: the pressure gauges, the approaching shoreline, the power of the river running crosscurrent to the boat, the sternwheel churning foam as it bit deep into the water. He fancied he could see those Johnny Rebs salivating at the prospect of a supper that might consist of something other than mule meat, roast rat, and peameal bread.

The boiler rattled and hissed steam. It was time.

—You might want to take aholt of somethin, Lucian. She's goin to come about right smart.

Eb watched Lucian brace himself against a rail, waited until the man appeared set, then spun the helm to starboard so hard one of the spokes whacked his wrist. Old oak groaned, metal screeched and the Marielita hunched down low in the water on the starboard side, heeling over so far that for two dozen strokes the sternwheel caught nothing but air. Then the flat keel slapped down on the river, the paddles caught water and the current helped shove the boat into a sweeping turn as she swung downriver, caught her breath, shivered about and at last found her bearings again, bound away from the rebels toward the Louisiana shore. Eb sighted along the point of the jackstaff and aimed her directly at the Union landing. Lucian brought the glass to bear on the baffled Confederates standing helplessly on the shore as their dinner headed west.

Once the rebels saw what Eb was up to, their artillery opened fire in earnest. Geysers of river water spouted on either side of the boat. Lucian's spotted barrow squealed in terror, his Plymouth Rock hens squawked as they tore back and forth looking for a way to escape from the makeshift chickencoop on deck. Lucian ignored the water that splashed down his back, stooped for more wood. Eb spun the wheel back and forth, carving slow zigzags over the water, eyes fixed on the far shore, willing speed from a boat whose quickest tempo was a maddening saunter. He tugged the bellcord so hard he thought the rope would break, signaling Lucian to start tossing pitchpine into the boilers. He pulled the rope again and again until he saw black soot pouring from the smokestacks and the *Marielita* chugged on, her trail vanishing in billowing clouds of black smoke that obscured her passage. The wind was right, blowing straight out from shore to hide the boat behind a widening smokescreen.

The last Confederate ball exploded a dozen feet off the larboard rail and doused the main deck in three inches of water. The Federal dock was now so close that Eb, peering through the glass, could see the faces and beards of the men waving him in. The rebels shifted their attention to the Union battery up in the trees, which was now taking fire and returning it threefold. Eb and Lucian could hear the balls screaming back and forth overhead, see the shells bursting among the bluecoats as the Confederates began to find the range. The din all around them seemed to blend into something almost like silence and they were adrift on a river smooth as glass, in a realm beyond sight and sound where the best a man could do was to pray that he not find himself burned in all his parts clinging to a spar in midriver, a piece of blackened flotsam as unlike to a man as a crawfish or a porcupine.

Lucian spotted the Federal gunboat as it rounded the bend downriver, bristling with armor and weaponry and gleaming in the sunlight like redemption itself. Squat, low in the water, ugly and effective as a bulldog. She was the *John Quincy Adams*, on her way north at the head of a flotilla sent by Ulysses S. Grant to clear the river for supply boats bound to Vicksburg. Eb and Lucian watched as she swung to and unleashed a rolling broadside from her starboard and bow guns that turned the water black with smoke. The rebels forgot the *Marielita* and the Union battery and turned their attention to the *John Quincy Adams* as she fought her way against the current, a target making less than three knots and considerably larger than the *Marielita*. The gunboat was hit first with plunging fire from the heights that collapsed her bridge, then a one-in-a-million shot struck the engine room. The *John Quincy Adams* lost power and began drifting backward with the current, helpless. Before she bowed out of the fight, a last salvo from her guns found the range and knocked out the Confederate battery just as the bow of the *Marielita* nudged into the lowest point of the riverbank, her paddle wheels slowly grinding her bow into the mud. The Federals ashore sent up a cheer. A tug from the trailing flotilla grappled the *John Quincy Adams* and towed her to shore at the makeshift dock, a hundred feet downriver from the spot where Eb had beached the *Marielita*. Litter bearers hauling the dead and wounded off the gunboat slipped in blood and cursed their loads, men drenched in gore screamed as they were dropped and hoisted and dropped again, a longhaired sailor flopped like a gutted fish and died as soon as he was ashore. Eb and Lucian tried to find a way to help, realized they were only getting in the way and stood by, watching the litterbearers stumble ashore with their screaming, shattered burdens. Lucian took a long pull of rye.

—What I heard about them hospitals, it might be more merciful to shoot a wounded man in the head and be done with it.

—Could be, but a man's got to hope. Sometimes that's all he's got.

Shadows of tall pine lengthened over the water, all traces of the recent skirmish vanished with the pitchpine smoke from the *Marielita*'s boilers that scattered downriver with the breeze. A half mile upriver a man in a rowboat was far out into the main current with two or three trotlines out for catfish. Lucian pointed to the boat.

—He aint got the word they's a war on.

—War or no war, a man has to keep on keepin on.

CHAPTER 4

The dock was still bloodslick when the healthy Federals came swarming aboard the *Marielita*, greenbacks in hand. The rye whiskey went first, then the plug tobacco, stacks of coarse gray writing paper, Lucian's chickens, cornmeal, buckwheat flour, hardtack, molasses. Before dark they had sold off everything aboard the ship except their personal belongings and Lucian's spotted barrow. Ashore, a mushroom growth of tents had already sprung up in the shadows, a kettle boiled over a fire at the center of each circle of tents, cooks sliced onions into a rough-and-ready stew of chicken parts, the gravy thickened with possum meat. The wounded who were past help moaned on litters where they had been left to their pain and prayers, their ragged bandages already filthy. The dead were arrayed in a clearing, each with a tattered blanket spread to hide his face and wounds, their sprawled bodies like heaps of old clothing cast aside. The soldiers had torn apart an old fisherman's shack to save the trouble of cutting trees for firewood; they broke up some of the boards, scrawled the names of the dead with chalk on slabs of wood and laid a slab neatly on the breast of each corpse for burial. The burial parties were already at work digging shallow graves in the rocky ground. They worked by torchlight, tacking nameboards to sticks of pine to form rough crosses at the heads of the graves, where the names would endure only until the first shower washed away the chalk. It hardly mattered; most of the time the survivors were hardly sure which body was in which grave anyway. It was all haste and hurry, dead men dropped into peeled ground with a dollop of sorrow and no glory at all.

It was past sundown and they had a fire going on the fringes of the Federal bivouac when Eb noticed his hands were still shaking.

—You hold back any of that arsenic rye of your'n? We sold all that good Tennessee whiskey.

Lucian reached into his bedding, hauled out a three-pint Union canteen full of rye. Eb chugged the fiery stuff like a man quaffing cold springwater, drank until his throat stung and his eyes watered. A dark-bearded sergeant strolled over, said they had taken thirteen dead and thirty wounded off the *John Quincy Adams*. The Union battery ashore had suffered another dozen killed and as many wounded who weren't likely to survive.

—You fellas was lucky. I aint never known the Rebs to miss like that. But you got sand. Aint many like you folks care to operate along this stretch of river.

—If I had my druthers, I ain't sure I care to operate down here no more neither.

—Caint say I blame you. You oughten to sell this boat and get off the river.

—I might do. First I got to thank them fellas on the gunboat that saved our lives.

—They was just lookin for Rebels to kill, same as us.

Eb offered the sergeant a pull of Lucian's rye. He could see where a Confederate minié ball had plowed a furrow in the man's cheek from the corner of his eye to the jawline, the scar showing an angry red in the firelight. The sergeant squatted on his heels for a time, as though he was working himself up to some pronouncement, then took another belt of whiskey and ambled off without saying a word. Lucian stretched out on his back and was snoring within a minute. Eb tried to do the same but it was a long while before something like sleep caught up to him. In a waking dream he saw the *Marielita* take a direct hit and dissolve into splinters of oak and pine that pierced his body as she went down, leaving his corpse to wash up against a boat on some downriver towhead where his skull would beat a hollow tattoo on the hull with every ripple of the Mississippi.

When Eb woke the next morning, the Federals had taken their wounded and vanished to the last man, leaving no one behind where the ancient trees spread their dark secret boughs over pine-needle beds soaked with blood and strewn with bandages caked black in the night. When the breeze stirred the overhanging limbs, the sun flashed lightdark darklight in semaphore on his face until he picked up a rock to hurl at a chittering squirrel.

—Lucian?

—Yassuh.

—Where'd them Federals get to?

—They done lit out. Ever last one. Afore first light.

—How could that be?

—They moved quick and quiet. Warn't no bugles and no reva-lay, they just up and went. Three, four more died last night. Buried 'em quick before they left.

Eb nodded as though burying the dead was as normal a way for a man to start a morning as slopping the hogs. He hauled himself to his feet, crunched over pine needles looking for a likely spot to urinate away from the campground, his eyes still half-closed. His foot slipped on something warm and blue and swarming with flies. He felt his gorge rise: a man's innards on the ground. Farther on he spotted a foot in a torn gray scrap of stocking lying on a sumac root. He stepped a few feet away. This war could wobble a man. No sense to it. He sprayed hot piss on dark ferns like a dog marking his territory, taking a shivery pleasure in this simplest act of being alive. When he was through, he tugged his suspenders back over his shoulders and padded in bright sunshine back to the fire, where Lucian poked at the coals with a stick.

—You hang on to any of them coffee beans?

—Yassuh.

—Could you rassle up a little coffee then?

—Got the water to boilin already.

—It's somethin how all them soldiers up and went and I never heard a thing.

—They was quiet. I expect you was plumb wore out, slept right through.

—I was tuckered. Still, it gives a fellow a fright to know a whole danged batch of soldiers can move off like that and him not hear a thing. Remember how you was sayin most of them is ghosts already, only they don't know it? Maybe they move so quiet cause they're somewhere between human and spirit, vanishin right in front of our eyes.

—Nope, they warn't no ghosts. They was just men in a hurry to get where they got to go.

Eb burned his lips on the tin coffee mug. It was not necessarily true, he thought, that a man was transformed from body to spirit the instant a charged shot tore out his bowels. There was a species of doom that could settle over a fellow weeks before his death, so that near the end that man could pass between you and the sun on a bright day and you would not be in his shadow.

They spent the next three weeks beating their way back north against the flow of the big steamboats and long rafts hauling troops and supplies south, a stream as unending as the river itself. Here and there they put in at rickety mud-and-stick Arkansas towns that in a flood year would tumble into the river and leave no trace, so that the next trip a man would round a bend and see only gumbo and rock and wonder if his mind had not failed him in some significant fashion, restructured a thing as immutable as geography and scrawled in its place an imaginary and now vanished shoreline populated with draymen, storekeepers, gamblers, preachers, rivermen, whores, and their boatloads of filthy urchins. Scavenging troops had long since stripped these towns of anything of value; the few citizens in view hastened about their business, eager to get back inside some shelter, however shabby and impermanent. Eb and Lucian wondered what lure would keep a person bound to a place that offered little more than mud and rock and the imminent possibility of some riverborne catastrophe; they could detect no reason for such curious behavior other than sheer force of habit. A man walked the same path to an outhouse for a span of days, and in time that path came to define his existence as surely as hidden gold or progeny unborn, so that if you were to tell him to pick up his possessions and move to a mansion he would feel the reluctance in his bowels and the soles of his bare feet, which had taken root in that path and that ground. They watched the tattered habitations from the river, untroubled by any desire to put ashore, their own habits linked to movement and current and flow. Empty, the *Marielita* rode high in the water. On any other occasion Eb would have put in to shore every few miles to do a little trading. On this trip he kept to the easy water, venturing ashore only when the ship needed to take on wood, wanting to put as much distance as he could between himself and the carnage around Vicksburg.

Just north of Greenville on the Mississippi side, they called a halt for a week to refit paddles, adjust the hog chains, polish the boilers, whitewash the deck, for all the world as though they were planning another trip. Lucian went along, knowing what was coming before Eb knew it himself.

—We could buy us another load, make another run, maybe two, leave this river feelin like a rich man feels. Man turns a good profit down there.

—He do at that. Long as he don't make too much fuss bout stayin alive.

—That's the nub of it, right there. Which way you thinkin, Lucian?

—I got no stake in it. Your boat, your choice. You want to run down that river again, I'll tend the boilers and the hog chains, scare up chickens to sell and keep a eye out for the Secesh, same as usual. You want to sell up, I would tell the world you're a sensible man.

—Well, I'm thinkin one of these days I might have to sell and get on to Dakota.

—I was you, I'd do the same. Cept not the Dakota part.

—Where would you go?

—Galveston.

—Galveston? You mean Galveston down in Texas?

—Yup. Galveston. My wife and babies was there, last I knew.

—They might be long gone by now. Could be any place south of the Mason-Dixon Line.

—They might. But Galveston is where I got to start.

—Well, let's say I'm sellin up then. We got to put the word about that this boat is for sale. Don't know how many folks is willin to part with Federal dollars for a old tub that has seen her best days come and go.

—Oh, they's folks will buy all right. They see a dollar to be made in death and destruction, you won't be able to scrape 'em off with a spade.

—Don't know that I'm ready to sell just yet. Me and this old boat been together so long, it don't seem right. Anyhow, I'd be sorry to see you go. You're a contrary cuss, but a fellow gets used to the company after a while.

—Nothin goes on forever, not even this old river. I'll stick till you find your buyer, then I'm off to Galveston.

The buyer was Alfonso Posey, a squat, pig-eyed Yankee carpetbagger with a goiter the size of a snapping turtle and a single tuft of coarse black hair over his left ear. The man had in his money belt enough greenbacks to close the deal in fifteen minutes. At the last minute, Eb hesitated, reluctant to see the *Marielita* sold to anyone, much less this venal creature from the alien North.

—You know anything about boats or this river?

—Not a damned thing. Nor care to.

—What you fixin to do with her?

—That aint your worry neither. You got your money and I got your boat.

—Well, she's been a good boat. Kept us alive. A man can't ask a lot more than that.

—That's where you're wrong. Your Mexican and your nigger is content just to stay alive and dip his pecker at night. Your white man, he's civilized. He wants a deal more.

Eb glanced at Lucian, saw the huge fists clench once and relax. The fool wasn't worth busting up.

Lucian Quigley left with five hundred dollars from the sale of the boat. More money than he had ever seen in his life, half what Eb offered, a fraction of what he was worth. Bound for Galveston, determined to scour every square inch of Texas for his wife and babies. Eb embarrassed himself at their parting, weeping like a child until Lucian wrapped a powerful arm around his shoulders.

—We seen some things, done some things.

—That we done.

—I'd feel a sight better if the two of us was bound the same direction.

—I don't have no aggument with that. Only we aint.

—If I had my druthers, you'd be comin to Dakota with me.

—We done talked all through that. First I got to find my woman and them little ones.

—They's Comanche in Texas. And Mexicans. And bandit rebels more dangerous than any Indian you'll ever meet. Crazy Texans would as soon shoot a black man as look at him. Be a whole lot easier if you could leave off chasin a needle in a haystack, especially when that haystack is plumb full a dangerous folk.

—A man can't set still and let a thing like this be, y'understand? If I got to chase my woman and my babies to t'other end of the world where the grass grows out the sky and the fishes climb trees, that's what has to be done. This war aint goin to go on forever and the Federals are goin to win it. You can see it plain as day, all them boats flowin down this river. When it's over they got to set my people free. When they do, I aim to be there so's my family got a place to go and a roof over their heads. But I aim to step careful.

—You do that.

Eb watched Lucian fasten a packsaddle to a gray mule, talking to the mule the same way he talked to his precious catfish. When the mule was loaded to his satisfaction, Lucian mounted a spavined brown horse bareback and rode off south, leading the spotted barrow with a rawhide leash. Eb kept watching until he couldn't see the barrow at all and Lucian was no more than a speck and still he could not convince himself to move on.

CHAPTER 5

Alfonso Posey owned the *Marielita* for three days, sold her to the Federals for a five-hundred-dollar profit. She was re-christened the *Moline* in honor of the hometown of Captain Edwards Pike, a Bible-pounding old buzzard who believed in the liberal use of the lash for such offenses as spitting tobacco on the deck, taking the name of the Lord in vain, and questioning the judgment of the infallible Edwards Pike. Pike died three months later along with four of his crew when the *Moline* threw a cylinder head just as Lucian had always predicted she would and went to the bottom of the Mississippi two hundred miles south of the spot where Pike took command.

A week after bidding his good-byes to Lucian and the *Marielita*, Ebenezer Paint managed to squeeze onto a Federal packet boat bound for Memphis, two hundred miles to the north. He spent the Fourth of July ashore in a city sullen and cowed under oppressive heat and Union guns. Memphis had been occupied for less than a month after General Beauregard ordered Confederate troops to leave the city on June fourth and a Confederate attempt to rescue the city with the fleet ended in a disastrous naval battle; the natives were disinclined to accept the defeat or the Union troops that came with it. The city was now occupied by the Indiana brigade under Colonel G. N. Fitch; southern women and children kept out of sight, not wanting to show themselves to the Federals; old men shook quavery fists at soldiers who laughed and spat tobacco where they pleased. The streets were crowded with soldiers, muleskinners, war profiteers, supply wagons. Turncoat merchants eager to please the victors strung red-white-and-blue bunting on storefronts and prepared to join the celebration. On that Fourth of July the extent of the Confederate catastrophe became obvious from the Atlantic to the Mississippi: Robert E. Lee had been repulsed at Cemetery Hill, Joseph E. Johnston had failed to cross the Big Black River, Zachary Taylor's son Dick Taylor was unable to retake New Orleans despite the panic in the city, and Theophilus Holmes could not capture Helena. The ultimate humiliation, however, came after the long and brutal siege of Vicksburg, when Major General John Pemberton surrendered the starving garrison to Ulysses S. Grant on Independence Day, cutting the Confederate States in two and leaving the great highway of the Mississippi in Union hands.

The news reached Memphis by telegraph on Independence Day and drunken torch parades of gloating Federals staggered through the streets until dawn the next morning. Unable to sleep with all the commotion, Eb wandered and watched until the first red streaks of a bloody dawn sent him back to the packet boat. It was not his celebration; he remembered too clearly a pulped Secesh head pounding the hull of the *Marielita*, Federal innards blue and fly-mottled, a row of graves hastily dug and hastily forgotten. The irony was duly noted: Now that he had decided that the Mississippi was an impossibly dangerous place to operate a store boat and sold the *Marielita*, the fall of the citadel at Vicksburg meant the river would be relatively safe for commercial traffic from Cairo to New Orleans. Given the extent of the Confederate reversals, the war might be over in six months or less and he and Lucian would have been able to run their boat in peace, but there was no going back now. Lucian was on his way to Galveston, Eb was bound for Dakota. He had never been one to worry over things lost or turns not taken. As the celebrations died down outside and he drifted off to sleep, he imagined himself at an upstairs window in a big white house overlooking a river somewhere in Dakota, a passel of children playing on an expanse of lawn below, fine horses in a pasture behind neat white fences, and from the parlor the sound of his wife at the piano, playing one of those Stephen Foster tunes he loved. If a man could latch onto a dream of sufficient power, there wasn't much he couldn't do.

Two weeks later, Eb caught a second packet boat as far as St. Louis, where he found himself stranded without passage up the Missouri. The war had so reduced passenger and freight traffic on the rivers that it was difficult to find steamboat passage at any price. He was preparing to winter in St. Louis when in a dim and derelict waterfront doggery one gin-soaked late summer afternoon he encountered Captain Horatio Leverton, master of the *Western Dawn*, a sleek shallowdraft sidewheeler and one of the first steamboats to make the run from St. Louis all the way up the Missouri to Fort Benton in Montana.

In his cups, Leverton took Eb for his boon companion and fellow river rat and promised free passage as far upriver as Eb cared to go. As they talked and the liquor flowed, the *Marielita* grew until she was a full-fledged steamboat nearly on a par with the *Western Dawn*, with a crew of twelve, a quartet of boilers and handsome quarters for fine ladies willing to book passage on a ship where the wood was always whitewashed and the brass always polished. After innumerable toasts to the river and to the great steamboat pilots who had tamed her, to Marse Lincoln and the Union triumphant, they climbed into the captain's hired phaeton behind a matched chestnut pacing team and pounded through a warren of streets past soot-blackened houses without end, bound for a rambling three-story manse where Leverton promised they would find delights unimaginable, pleasures to put the bordellos of New Orleans itself to shame.

After a night in the arms of a tender harlot, Eb woke to the furious bellow of Horatio Leverton pounding at the door.

—Ebenezer Paint! Ebenezer Paint! Time to take ship! Up and at 'em! Leave the girl be!

The phaeton with its matched team was ready and waiting outside. The chestnut pacers clattered again through dark cobblestone streets, where huddled figures slept, drank, urinated, and fornicated in shadowed doorways or staggered aimlessly to and fro, dodging clear of the flashing hooves as though hauled to safety by some unseen hand. Leverton shouted at them to clear the path and cracked his whip. It was a cloudy, moonless night, the streets running dark as rivers of ink. Eb could not understand how Leverton knew where he was going; perhaps the horses knew the way. The phaeton lurched left and right, clattered over cobblestones and tore through deep mud puddles. Eb had to lean out to vomit over the side.

In a cone of light blown from the open door of a doggery, a man vast as the night itself seemed to rise in the path of the onrushing phaeton, a mudcreature birthed from the mud. The creature stood weaving, drunken, bearlike, blocking their path as though daring Leverton to pass. Eb shouted a warning and braced himself for the impact but the creature leapt aside with the agility of a bobcat, avoiding the flashing hooves as he swiveled his weight to swing a giant's cudgel at Leverton's head. The phaeton was moving too fast. The blow glanced off the rear wheel as they passed. Eb felt the carriage sway and shudder with the force of it. Somehow the wheel held. Leverton drove on, thundering into the night, curses howling in his wake.

They returned to the wharf in the first feeble gray of a watery dawn to find waiting among the draymen, the heaving, sweating stevedores and the confusion of the harbor a phalanx of Holiness Charismatics, the only paying passengers aboard the *Western Dawn*. In his cups, Horatio Leverton had entirely forgotten the Charismatics, who were taking ship as far as Sioux City, where they planned to purchase wagons and mules before carrying on to Dakota Territory. The leader of the flock was the Reverend Augustus Connell, a tall, emaciated preacher with the aspect of a hungry vulture. Until that spring, Reverend Connell had been minister of the Church of the Living Redeemer in Oberlin, Ohio, where at dawn on Easter Sunday he claimed to have received the Sign of the Spirit telling him to pull up stakes and bring his flock to the Wild West to convert the savage heathen. Among the forty pilgrims who had agreed to accompany him to Dakota Territory were two dozen widows of the War of the Rebellion, including several women still in the prime of life. They were accompanied by a handful of males, pale and sorry specimens who were all too old, too ill, or like Eb Paint himself, too crippled to fight. Spread out along the wharf in their dark, dismal plumage, they offered to the carousing revelers a grim reminder that there is a price to be paid for sin, a price some begin to pay sooner than others.

Leverton stumbled from the phaeton and lurched in their direction. In the captain's wake wafted the trail of liquor fumes oozing from his pores. The reverend sniffed with his long nose, shuffled his gaitered ankles back a pace or two and crossed his arms like a schoolmaster. When Leverton extended his paw, Connell took it with the air of a man plucking fish guts.

—You've been drinking.

—A wee dram only, sir. I don't hold with liquor aboard ship, y'see, so I make it a habit to bid the stuff good-bye in St. Louee, but only after a sip or two to fight off the chill. It don't appear so in this heat, but the Missouri can be a mighty chilly place.

The sun was barely up but already the heat brought the choking stench of rotting garbage and dead fish from the cocoa-colored, oil-slicked water at the river's edge. There would be no chill in this day unless a man caught his death of the swamp fever. Leverton knew as much and so did the Reverend Connell. They were not yet aboard ship and already the riverboat captain and the preacher were circling each other like fighting cocks. To head off a confrontation, Eb slipped between them and shook the reverend's hand.

—Ebenezer Paint, sir. The captain has to be taking this phaeton back to the stable, so maybe you folks could begin stowing your gear aboard ship.

Leverton allowed himself to be dragged away to see to the return of the phaeton and the chestnut team while the first mate ordered the stevedores to load the heaps of chests the pilgrims had piled on the dock. Eb stayed on the wharf to watch the furious activity preceding the steamboat's departure. He had seen it a thousand times downriver but he never tired of the spectacle. The sun rose like a rotten tangerine over the molten river, wagons and draymen's carts came and went, the sweating stevedores bent their backs to their loads and the curses of the first mate spurred them on. By the time Leverton returned, the *Western Dawn* needed only wood, water, and pilgrims before casting off at precisely three in the afternoon.

At five minutes before three, the order was given to burn pitchpine and resin and the columns of black smoke pouring from the smoke-stacks offered the first sign that the *Western Dawn* was about to cast off. Old Glory was unfurled from the jackstaff, the last bells sounded, the paddles began to turn, and the boat slipped back into the stream. Eb raced aboard an instant before the stage planks were hauled in, took his place on the bow just back of the leadsman, and watched until they were well out in the channel and the pilot had set his course almost directly into the setting sun, bound due west for Kansas City, St. Joe's, and Indian country. Once they were well under way, he felt a sudden weariness as the previous night's exertions caught up to him. He withdrew to his bunk directly across from the cabin where Lever-ton's snores nearly matched the roar of the engines. The unearthly racket was unlike the sound of the *Marielita* only in volume; Eb found it soothing as a lullaby and fell into a deep, dreamless sleep.

Early in the evening, he tottered out onto the deck to have a look about, found exhausted pilgrims and their belongings every-where. There were no passenger cabins on the *Western Dawn*. The boiler deck and the main deck below it were loaded so heavily with freight that the main deck was barely six inches above the water-line and the only passenger space was out in the open on the rough planks of the hurricane deck, where the pilgrims made themselves as comfortable as possible with tattered canvas awnings stretched to provide shelter from sun, rain, and the black soot pouring from the smokestacks night and day. Some of the Charismatics tried to sleep, others gathered in weary little groups, a few bent over their devotional readings. Reverend Connell himself was stretched out on a makeshift bed under a strip of canvas, one arm flung across his face, snoring in rhythm to the thrum of the engines and the splash and slap of the paddlewheels churning inside their housing. Eb strolled to the stern, lit a cheroot, stood watching the river roll away, mulling what a deal of living a fellow could do in the span of thirty-three years. He had first come this way by oxcart with Horace and Virgil Saleen on the second leg of their passage to the goldfields of California in 'forty-nine, their entire company full of piss and vinegar and sure they were on their way to a land where a man could pluck gold nuggets from the streams like a girl gathering eggs. At the time they were too preoccupied with the journey to take much note of the country through which they passed on that long, dusty journey; now he had time to admire the long V of the ship's wake widening over dark, muddy water until it vanished along a shoreline of low, rolling hills shimmering brown in the late summer heat under a deep blue sky streaked with thin white clouds, as though a painter had emptied his brush on the firmament.

—It's a beautiful sight, isn't it, sir? A reminder of God's bounty upon us.

She was a young woman of no more than twenty, dressed in widow's weeds. Her hair, despite the severe black bonnet she wore, fell in wild, dark curls down the back of her neck. She was of more than common height for a woman, with coppery skin, high cheekbones, a narrow waist, wide-set dark eyes, a frank, open expression. She extended a black-gloved hand.

—Good evening, sir. I am Mrs. Hobart Landry.

—Ebenezer Paint, ma'am. A pleasure.

—I wish to thank you, Mr. Paint.

—Maybe you got the wrong fella.

—No, it's you I was looking for. I wanted to thank you for interceding this morning. I feared that awful captain and our Reverend Connell were about to come to blows.

—Oh, I doubt that. Horatio is a little salty but he wouldn't bust a preacher in the nose.

—Perhaps not, but a man of the cloth would have little chance against such a rough type as the captain. Your diplomacy was noticed and appreciated.

—Well, thank'ee kindly, ma'am.

Eb stood awkwardly, slouch hat in hand, racking his brain for something to say to the woman. She appeared to be waiting for him to speak but faced with that innocent, upturned face, he could think of no topic for discussion except steamboats.

—I believe they've used cast-iron pitman rods on this boat.

—Excuse me?

—Pitman rods. What connects the engine to the paddlewheels. I always thought it was smarter to make your pitman rods out of wood. They don't make such a clatter, and if one of 'em busts on you, you can always hew a new one out of a tree on the spot. Your cast-iron rod goes, you're stuck until the foundry can supply a new one, and they aint always a foundry handy.

They fell silent, watching the turning wheels, the muddy water slipping aft, the tableau of river and sky. Finally, curiosity got the better of him.

—Is your husband amongst this lot?

—I lost my husband at the first Battle of Bull Run.

—I'm sorry to hear that.

—You needn't be. I hardly knew him. We were married but six weeks when he was called off to war, but that was long enough for me to learn that Hobart Landry was overly fond of his drink.

—They's many a fellow like that.

—I might have thought the same of you at first, the condition you two were in this morning.

—Horatio don't mean no harm. He's a riverboat captain. They're a breed not given to fine manners. I'm not a drinkin man, as a steady habit.

—Well, that's a consolation. Perhaps I can persuade you to find the way to redemption.

—If you're talkin religion, I wouldn't want to offer you much encouragement, ma'am. I was brought up Christian as the next fellow, but it's been a long while since I set foot in a church. Seen too much death and destruction to give much credence to all that hocus-pocus.

—Then there is all the more reason to bring you to the Lord. I am not in the habit of accosting strange men, Mr. Paint, but we are to be some time upon this boat and I have detected something in your countenance that tells me you may be receptive to the word of God. I can be a very determined woman when it comes to bringing lost sheep to the fold.

—I'm sure you can be persistent, ma'am. But you'll find this old rock aint that easy to wear down. What come over your bunch to make for Dakota anyhow?

—I'm afraid I am guilty of persuading the reverend of the importance of bringing the word of the Lord to the Sioux. In a way they're my people.

—I thought you looked like you had a bit of Indian in you.

—I do, and I am proud to say so, sir. My father was a trapper who came out here from Ohio and my mother was a Minneconjou Sioux. She died of the smallpox when I was ten and my father sent me back to live with his sisters in Ohio. That's where I met Mr. Landry. After he was killed, I went to a meeting and heard the reverend speak. I was so moved I decided to cast my lot with him.

—You're sure the Sioux are going to make your preacher fellow feel welcome?

—I'm certain they will, once they understand we have come to save their mortal souls. What greater gift could one human bring to another, Mr. Paint?

—We passed south of here in 'forty-nine, and most of the Indians we met were Pawnee and Arapaho, but I don't remember them bein much concerned about their mortal souls.

—That's only because they have not been exposed to the word of the Lord, Mr. Paint. I will assist the reverend to explain it to them in their own language. They will understand.

One of the older women called to her and Mrs. Landry took her leave before Eb could remark that, in his limited experience, Indians were not in any goshawful hurry to flock to anything resembling the Church of the Living Redeemer.

The trip west along the Missouri was a slow one. Compared with travel on the Mississippi, it was almost like an overland journey, an endless battle with sandbars and reefs and snags, the *Western Dawn* beating her way over one impediment after another like a monstrous crawling insect. The trip might have been made in ten days except that the boat seemed to halt every dozen miles, sometimes more often. Off-loading one cargo, taking on something else, unloading three crates of watermelon here, loading four barrels of molasses there. Even when she was beating her way upstream against the current, the *Western Dawn* couldn't move much faster than a man's brisk walk. Eb had time to register each landmark, island, and village as they passed, cataloging them with a riverman's thoroughness and noting every point in the little journal he had kept on the Mississippi. They put in at Augusta, Washington, Marthasville, Holstein, Hermann, Morrison, Chamois, Mokane, Osage City, then Jefferson City for three days while waiting for a load of supplies destined for General Cooke's command on the Platte. They stopped at Hartsburg, McBaine, Boonville, Arrow Rock, Miami, Grand Pass, and spent four days at Kansas City. By the time they reached St. Joe's, Eb and Mrs. Landry had fallen into the habit of chatting every evening on the stern, sometimes talking until the glow of his cheroot was the only light on deck, the smoke keeping the mosquitoes away, Eb always attuned to the boat and her peculiar habits.

—Feels to me like the hogchains is too tight. She aint supple like she ought to be for a shallow-bottom river like this.

—I don't know how you can feel such a thing.

—Spend enough time on boats and you can't help but feel it. Course my river is the Mississippi. I aint been along this way since eighteen hundred and forty-nine. World looked like a different place then.

—I imagine it did. You must have been very young.

—We was. I wasn't but nineteen, a couple of us was younger'n that. We formed a little company down in Jones County, Mississippi. Started out with me and the Saleen brothers. Horace and Virgil. We brought in four more, figured to manage better that way, all pitch in together. Two of 'em was lawyers had just hung up their shingles, so they drawed it all up proper, shares in the California & Mississippi Gold Company to be divided eight ways. We wasn't thirty miles out of St. Joe's when one of them lawyers died of the cholera. Then we lost the other one to drowning in quicksand in the Platte River. Another fellow died of thirst in the Carson Desert along with most of the livestock, then one got hisself shot in a card game in the Sierra Nevada. Time we got to the goldfields, it was just me and the Saleen brothers left.

—I have heard it said there are graves all the way to California.

—Every step. The Carson Desert was the worst. You'd walk a mile, see the bones of a hundred dead oxen and the graves of three dead children, same thing the next mile. That desert was hell on animals and children.

—All for gold. It's hard to imagine. If only men would endure such privations on behalf of the Lord our Savior.

—Gold is a thing that has a power on ye. Most of the folks who went out there was well-fixed in the first place or they wouldn't have had money for the passage. But you get to thinkin about that gold, and how it's just layin there in every stream waitin to be picked up, and all the things it can buy, and next thing you know you're headed for California. Can't help yourself.

—Only the gold wasn't just lying there.

—No, ma'am, it sure wasn't. Well, it was at one time. That's what started the whole thing. That was around Sutter's Mill, the first strike. Time we got word of it in Mississippi and decided to light out for the goldfields, the easy pickins was all picked. You could break your back tryin to shift a whole stream to a different course or strainin rock through a Long Tom from dawn to dusk, work like a slave all day and if you was lucky you could buy your dinner that night, when eggs was a dollar apiece. We was workin for one of the big mining outfits took over when the small miner couldn't make a go of it. They had us hydraulickin, blastin a hill apart with a stream of water to see what's inside her, when half that hill come down on us. Killed Horace and Virgil and twenty other men, hurt about a hundred more. I expect you could say I was one of the lucky ones, but I got my foot caught between a rock and a redwood tree, that's how I come to have this limp. After that I wasn't much use with a pick and shovel, so I took what money I had left and bought two

pack mules. Started buyin denim trousers off a fella name of Levi
Strauss in San Francisco and sellin 'em to the miners along the
Feather River and made a little money. Your smart fella in California, he's the one never panned for gold nor run a Long Tom. The
ones got rich, they let the other man do the dirty work and made
their pile sellin your miner the tools to work himself to death.

—Isn't that always the way?

—Everywhere you go. It's the lawyers and the land schemers and
the merchants get rich while the rest breaks their backs to get poor.

—It doesn't have to be that way. You could put aside worldly
things and embrace the Church of the Living Redeemer. I must
offer you some reading material. Do you know Phoebe Palmer, sir?
Or William Arthur? Have you not read Mr. Arthur's book *The
Tongue of Fire?*

—Afraid not, ma'am.

—Well, I shall be happy to make you a loan of it, provided you
give it back before we disembark. I also have some back numbers
of Phoebe Palmer's *Guide to Holiness* magazine, which you ought
to read.

—Truth is, I'm not much of a reader.

—Can you read?

—Oh, I can all right. I just don't.

—Well, you should, so long as you have the proper material.
She went to rummaging under one of the canvas awnings
stretched out on the hurricane deck and returned with the book
and several well-thumbed copies of *Guide to Holiness.*

—Herein lies the greatest gift you can receive.

—Well, thankee kindly, ma'am.
Her face shone up at him and her fingertips brushed his wrist.

—Your heart must be open, Mr. Paint.

—Oh, it's open, ma'am. Open as a heart can be.
He felt himself teetering forward onto his toes as though his
body was being tugged out of balance. Another degree off plumb
and he would twine his fingers in those curls and kiss her full on
that wide mouth.

By candlelight in his bunk that night, Eb attempted to grapple with Phoebe Palmer's magazine but the effect on him was like a dose of laudanum. He had just enough presence of mind left to douse the candle and then he was fast asleep. After three or four more failed attempts, he had a go at William Arthur's book but the effect was even worse. At most he could read a paragraph before his mind wandered, usually to the widow Landry's neck, or her lips, or those square, capable shoulders, or the way she moved when she walked away from him, her black skirt blown taut against her legs.

She waited a week to bring it up.

—So have you been reading Phoebe Palmer?

—I been workin at it.

—What does that mean?

—It's deep.

—What you are saying is that you cannot penetrate her thoughts.

—Well, it aint like I didn't try. Trouble is, I can't stop thinkin about you.

—It isn't me you should be thinking of, Mr. Paint. It's Phoebe Palmer. I am sure that if you would read it, you would not be subject to the distractions of a mere female such as myself. It is the spirit that matters, Mr. Paint. Not the flesh.

Eb drew a deep breath.

—I expect it's been a good long time since you had a man around, ma'am.

—Mr. Landry has been in his grave a good while, sir. Now Christ is my altar.

—I'm sure He is, but even a religious woman gets to needin things.

—Needing things like what, Mr. Paint?

—Needin a man around now and again, is all.

—What are you driving at? Are you trying to court a poor widow?

—That I am. I am going west with a stake and I aim to make something of myself.

She looked away, drew a deep breath, fixed him with that steady gaze.

—I have no doubt that you will make something of yourself. You are a man of pleasing appearance and a pleasant manner. You are plainly intelligent and I have enjoyed our little chats. But you must understand that I would find it awkward to join my life to a man who did not believe in our faith. Do I understand you plain? That you are asking me to marry you?

—That's about the size of it.

—Well, I promise you I will think on it. Meantime, I will ask you to read Mrs. Palmer and to see if you can find it in your heart to embrace our church. Then we will talk again.

There it was, plain as day. Phoebe Palmer looming between them. Back in his bunk, he picked up a number of the *Guide to Holiness*, thumbed through it for the hundredth time. The letters swam in front of his eyes until they gave way to a vision of the rise and fall of the Landry woman's bosom. It was hopeless. He was a man of the flesh, she was a woman of the spirit. She was the first woman he had truly wanted since Marielita, the Mexican girl on the Feather River. Phoebe Palmer was like Marielita's father, her prose like the knife pressed to Eb's privates, driving a wedge between him and the woman he desired. There were a lot of things he would do for a woman like the widow Landry, but marching in step with the holy widows of the Church of the Living Redeemer was not one of them.

Deep in the night he felt a jar and shudder as the *Western Dawn* ran aground on a sandbar in midstream. The river was low and there was no rain in sight. They were apt to sit for a spell, stuck in Missouri mud. Eb rolled over and went back to sleep.

CHAPTER 6

Eb woke at dawn. It was the twenty-second day of August and Horatio Leverton was shaking him awake with some urgency.

—Ebenezer! I need ye to come quick and quiet.

Fragments of a sweet dream of the widow Landry drifted away. Eb shook himself, tried to focus.

—Hell's goin on?

—Get ye topside and stick this here little gun in your pocket.

Leverton pressed a Manhattan three-shot pepperbox pistol into Eb's hand. Eb tried to give it back.

—Don't trust a toy like that. Thing's apt to blow my hand off. I'll load the Whitworth.

—No, ye won't. Bring out a cannon like that and we'll start trouble. Keep this handy in case we need her, that's all. I want ye at my back and armed.

By now Eb was fully awake and scrambling to his feet. He rummaged in his trunk and came up with his Australian kangaroo-hide bullwhip, a souvenir of the goldfields of California. Leverton nodded his approval: The whip was just the thing to cow a man without starting a gunfight.

Eb tugged on his trousers and boots, tucked the pepperbox pistol in his pocket, and grabbed his hat and whip. By the time he reached the pilothouse, he found Leverton standing next to the pilot at the helm, holding a scattergun in the crook of his arm.

Even the pilot wore a Colt Navy strapped to his hip and his cub held a bowie knife in a shaky hand.

—What the devil is goin on?

—The devil is about, that's just the thing. That murderin weasel Quantrill and his raiders hit Lawrence over in Kansas last night. Rider came by this mornin, said they burnt the town to a crisp and killed every man and boy. Slaughtered some in their beds and then lit their houses afire. We got to be ready in case Quantrill comes this way. We're aground on this sandbar, and we can't run, so we got to be ready to fight.

—This damned pepperbox pistol aint goin to do much good against Quantrill.

—Taint just Quantrill I'm worried about. If we see hide nor hair of Quantrill, ye can break out that Whitworth and see if ye can't put a bolt in his eye. It's the crew worries me. They're Secesh to a man and Quantrill has 'em stirred up. They might take a notion to do to them Yankee pilgrims as Quantrill done to Lawrence.

—Mutiny?

—Don't say that word aboard my ship. Your riverman is a hard sort, but when he looks up and sees this scattergun, he'll think twice about partin with his face.

—Well, I'm touched, Horatio. It's mighty kindly of you to look after Yankee pilgrims. I didn't take you for a abolitionist.

—I aint no such thing, but I got to look out for the payin customers. That crazy preacher and his bunch paid their way as far as Sioux City, and I aim to get 'em there in one piece. If they get scalped a hundred yards from the river, that's on the preacher's head. They aint goin to get stabbed on my boat.

—Seems a slim chance we'll run into Quantrill. If he burned Lawrence, he'll run south, won't he?

—He may do and he may not. Point is to be ready whatever he does and to keep an eye on the crew. We'll stand armed watches twenty-four hours a day until we get off this sandbar and get up the river.

For two days they watched and waited. Eb never moved out of

the texas without the bullwhip coiled at his hip. He could hear the mutterings among the crew, but they were rivermen, not raiders. They scanned the banks for any sign of Quantrill but none came. During the second night a sudden thunderstorm washed the *Western Dawn* off the sandbar and they resumed the journey upriver. The next day, Eb returned the pepperbox pistol to Leverton and stowed the whip in his trunk. All was well aboard ship; for the poor souls of Lawrence, Kansas, there was aught a man could do.

Three days upriver, the widow Landry found Eb in his usual spot at the stern on a muggy morning sullen with the threat of rain.

—Do you know what day it is, Mr. Paint?

—The twenty-fifth of August, I believe. Maybe the twenty-sixth?

—Not that. I mean the day of the week. It's Sunday and Reverend Connell is going to preach.

—Now that's good to hear. I aint been to Sunday meetin in a long while.

—Oh, this isn't Sunday meeting. This is of a different order altogether. When Reverend Connell preaches, it is so taxing that sometimes he does not attempt it again for weeks. Taxing for his flock as well, if the Lord chooses us to make a Sign of the Spirit.

—How's that?

—Oh, you'll see. Promise you'll come? I should very much care to have you there.

The Reverend Connell timed his shipboard camp meeting for six o'clock in the evening, the hour when Eb and the widow were usually perched at the stern having one of their talks. Connell had aboard a heavy oak pulpit, which had been dragged out in the open, where the entire expanse of the hurricane deck would be his church. Even the deckhands had all gathered to hear what the preacher had to say. Only Horatio Leverton and the pilot remained apart; the pilot because he had to stay at the helm, Leverton because he would have no truck with preachers of any stripe, let alone the priggish Augustus Connell. Eb stood at the rear of the gathering, keeping an eye on the western horizon, where a dark smudge that was still barely visible warned of approaching thunderheads.

Connell waited until his congregation was in place, pilgrims and rough shipboard characters alike restless, waiting to hear what he had to say. Once they were gathered, he raised one arm aloft, lowered his white head and remained in that pose as the wind whipped through his hair.

—My children! We are gathered here on the Lord's Day, our day of rest from the mighty toil of saving souls, so that we may ask that Power so infinitely greater than ourselves for a sign, a manifestation, a divine light to guide us on our way.

A murmur went through the pilgrims.

—Amen! Praise Jesus! Blessed be His name!

At first Eb thought the man wasn't much of a preacher as camp-meeting preachers went. Such preachers, half of them escaped convicts or worse, would start off shouting and hollering and work a crowd up real quick and next thing you knew they were passing the collection plate, eager to get on to the next town a step ahead of the law. Connell took his time, beginning so softly that at first his listeners had to lean forward to hear him over the thrum of the engines. He let the volume build bit by bit until his rich baritone boomed over the waters.

—Now, my children, we turn our thoughts to the holy scripture, to the second chapter of the Book of Acts, the sacred words which lie at the core of all we believe, the very sinew, bone, and marrow of our faith. "*And when the day of Pentecost was fully come, they were all with one accord in one place. And suddenly there came a sound from heaven as of a rushing mighty wind, and it filled all the house where they were sitting.*"

Far out over the water a zigzag of lightning flashed, and a rolling boom of thunder washed over the ship. Eb had to hand it to the preacher. He knew when to call a camp meeting. A ripple of excitement went through the crowd.

—A sign, Sisters. A holy sign. The Lord God is among us.

—*And there appeared unto them cloven tongues like as of fire . . .*

—Amen! Praise the Lord!

—*And they were all filled with the Holy Ghost, and began to speak with other tongues, as the Spirit gave them utterance.*

A battlement of thunderheads rose on the west bank of the river, tinged a deep rose at the edges by the setting sun. Lightning signaled cloud to cloud. Captain Leverton shouted down from the pilothouse, where he had taken his place at the pilot's shoulder.

—That storm's comin fast. Cut her short and get your people down to the boiler deck.

The preacher went on as though Leverton hadn't spoken.

—*Now when this was noised abroad, the multitude came together, and were confounded, because that every man heard them speak in his own language. And they were all amazed and marveled, saying to one another, Behold, are not all these which speak Galileans?*

A pale and perspiring young man, his face so red it was almost purple, collapsed onto the deck, surrounded by a half dozen of the older women gathered like black crows in their widow's weeds, urging him on as he shrieked and thrashed and babbled, his bootheels drumming the wood.

—*Eruth-won banaka alaga rowena shnndeth brrala kazurzu kanaba ozenda kanaba* . . .

Eb had heard Spanish, French, German, Chinese, and some of the Indian tongues but he had never heard anything like it for pure gibberish. The young man's eyes bulged, his tongue lolled, he rolled to and fro in a pool of his own perspiration on the deck. A plump woman collapsed to her knees and pulled his face into her bosom, her sobs mingling with the strange words that croaked from somewhere deep in his throat. One of the older widows began to babble in a voice suddenly gone deep as a man's. Another woman joined in and then another. They shrieked, whispered, wailed, and chanted, rolling on the deck or joining hands to face the approaching storm, their voices rising to meet the thunder rolling over the river. The Reverend Connell spread his arms wide and beckoned with his long bony fingers as though summoning the storm to do its worst.

Eb held to the rail, fighting to steady himself against the force of the wind. The widow Landry was the last woman in the line of Charismatics now rocking to and fro with their hands clasped, close enough for Eb to reach out and touch her. Her head was thrown back, her mouth open. Her long black hair had shaken loose and fallen over her shoulders. Her face was radiant, ecstatic. Her body trembled, her arms spread wide as though pulling an unseen lover to her breast. Eb caught her gaze but her eyes looked right through him, fixed on a more distant, less corporeal vision. A moan came from her throat, her body quivered from head to toe in a prolonged spasm. Then her voice joined the rest, and she stamped her feet hard on the deck as she chanted:

—*Abababa kiyi kiyi ababa kiyi kiyi okahe okahe kiyi okahe onha onha akali kiyi kiyi . . .*

Eb recoiled as though he had singed his fingers on a hot stove. He turned away from her to face the storm. The wind was strong enough to bring up whitecaps and a three-foot chop on the water. A solid line of rain advanced across the river toward the boat. A single lightning bolt forked and forked again before it struck the water within a hundred yards of the *Western Dawn*, close enough to send the deckhands scurrying below. Leverton leaned down from the pilothouse and pointed a blunt finger at the preacher.

—Reverend! That storm's comin fast! Get your pilgrims below-decks! Now, by God!

—*And it shall come to pass in the last days, saith God, I will pour out of my Spirit upon all flesh: and your sons and your daughters shall prophesy, and your young men shall see visions, and your old men shall dream dreams . . .*

Leverton tore out of the pilothouse and roared down the steps to the hurricane deck.

—Connell, you sonofabitch. You will get your people below or by God I will move you!

—*And I will shew wonders in heaven above, and signs in the earth beneath; blood and fire, and vapor smoke . . .*

Leverton grabbed the preacher's arm and spun him around. The reverend went on, chin to chin with the captain.

—The sun shall be turned into darkness, and the moon into blood . . .

Leverton flung the man stumbling toward the steps to the lower decks.

—You're done preachin on my boat now, Reverend. The rest of you, get your sorry carcasses down them steps before you get fried by that lightnin.

—We are worshipping our God. The Lord will protect us.

—Goddamn your Lord to hell. This is my ship, and I am lord of this ship. It is my charge to deliver you safely to your destination, and I will get you there if I have to kill every last one of you to do it. Now get below!

—Hellfire and blasphemy! We shall stand our ground, sir, though Beelzebub himself take the helm of this devil's ship.

Leverton backhanded the preacher across the face, a mighty blow that smashed the man's prominent nose and sent him sprawling just as the rain lashed over the hurricane deck from larboard to starboard, drenching the pilgrims. Blood poured down the reverend's lily-white shirtfront. The women, Mrs. Landry among them, crowded round their fallen hero. Eb saw her turn on the captain and watched them argue in mime show, her words drowned out by the storm. The others hoisted Connell from the deck and began helping him to the stairs. The widow looked from the captain to Eb. She didn't say a word, but he understood her quite plainly.

—Well? Are you just going to stand there? Either you are with us or you are with him.

Eb stood motionless, impaled by the laws of the river and his own indecision. The rain plastered the widow Landry's hair to her long neck. She looked up at him, imploring, her beauty a beacon lighting the way down a path where he could not follow. Eb made no move to help. She looked away from him in disgust, marched up to Leverton and hit him an openhanded slap in the face just as a double clap of thunder sounded so near that one of the women screamed. With that, the women poured belowdecks in their soaked widow's weeds like wet coal flowing down a chute. The preacher, still bleeding, was borne aloft by a dozen hands. Leverton grabbed Mrs. Landry's arms and pushed her after the others. Eb watched her disappear, her hands cradling Reverend Connell's white head. She did not look back.

Eb waited with Leverton until the last of the pilgrims was belowdecks, then slipped into the texas for shelter from the storm. The captain went straight to his chest, hauled out a bottle of his best gin, took a long, thirsty belt and passed the bottle to Eb, who drank liquid fire until his eyes watered and he felt the heat rising in his belly.

The fond picture he held in his mind of the widow Landry with her cool dark eyes and composed features had given way to the image of an exalted madwoman. Head thrown back, legs wide apart, unearthly sounds coming from her throat.

—*Ababababababa kiyi kiyi ababa kiyi kiyi akali akali kiyi akali kiyi kiyi kiyi . . .*

When he woke the next morning, it was an hour before dawn. The sky was clear, the air new-washed and fresh as dew. The pilgrims slept under their tattered awnings. He saw the dark figure of the widow standing alone at the stern rail. He left her alone, lit a cheroot, and watched the river flow by.

CHAPTER 7

Leverton would have preferred to throw the pilgrims overboard, but drowned passengers were bad for business. They had paid their passage as far as Sioux City in advance, so he would take them to Sioux City, but he would not put up with any more nonsense. In any case, the Charismatics were no longer inclined to challenge him. Sullen and defeated, they clung to their places on the hurricane deck, parting to make way for a leadsman heading to the stern, then closing behind him like a field of black flowers in a sunless world. Eb stuck to the pilothouse or the bow, keeping the texas between himself and the widow Landry. Leverton drank more than ever and was often soused in his cabin while the pilots ran the boat with quiet efficiency, tallying the leadsman's measurements with their own notes on the river as they were called out:

—Half twain!

—Quarter twain!

The pilots accepted Eb's presence in the pilothouse. He was a quiet man who knew rivers, he did not interfere, he had his own storehouse of knowledge. The younger of the two, Thaddeus Jackson, was happy to impart his knowledge of the Missouri for Eb's benefit.

—Along here you got to wait for your crossing and not rush her. Get your jackstaff on yon bluff, square your stern on the woodlot to stabberd. She's drawin three fathoms forward and three and a half aft this minute, but the Missouri is peculiar as a cross-eyed mule. You'll run a deep channel to either side but when you try to cross her you'll find a sandbar five feet down and right smack-dab in the middle of the river. You got to make your crossing where she deepens again or you'll ground sure.

As they steamed upriver between the Nebraska and Iowa banks, Eb watched the muddy river like a man poring over scripture, studying its whorls and eddies, snags and sandbars. On the Mississippi at neap tide he could read in the sand and mud the river's tale, its moods and disasters, its December high water and the mysterious yearning for the Gulf that prompted the occasional breakthrough to a new channel down a course which a day previous had been cotton fields and haymows. The Missouri might flow into the Mississippi, but it spoke a foreign language, strange as the babble of Connell's pilgrims when they were speaking in tongues. It would take another lifetime of study to riddle her out and he didn't plan to stay on this particular river long enough to get past the first lesson. Still, he listened to the boat, his ear attuned by habit to the strokes of cylinder, valve, and flywheel, the quartet of flue boilers on the boiler deck that delivered reliable power to heave the *Western Dawn* around the twists and turns of the river, almost always through water that was no deeper than it had to be. North of Bellevue he scanned the shoals warily, mentioned to the pilot that it looked like shallow water ahead. Jackson grinned.

—They don't call this boat shallowdraft for nothin. She'll scrape through. I knew a engineer shipped out of Louisville, always kept a dozen kegs of beer aboard. Said if he hit a patch where the river run dry, he could tap the kegs on a hot day and run three miles on the foam.

The Charismatics disembarked in hazy dusk on a September evening in Sioux City. Leverton tried to persuade him to come along for the ride all the way to Fort Benton, but Eb, his plans as vague as his sentiments, said Sioux City would be the end of the line for him.

—I figure to go on as far as Yankton before winter, but I expect I'll stick here for a bit, have a look-see.

—Do as you please, but remember what I said about that pilgrim woman. She's a beauty, I'll give ye that. But if it's her you're after, she'll never have ye, less ye get down on your knees and start babblin and screechin like a mad baboon. Never understood why a man would marry anyhow when he can always find a harlot to care for his parts and a Chinaman to starch his shirts.

—Aint nothin to do with the woman. Seems a likely spot, is all.

—Suit yourself. I aint fool enough to try and turn a man when he's picked up the scent. Just remember, if you don't take to this neck of the woods, you can join us for the downriver passage in a month or so. I mean to have this boat pointed south ahead of the first snowflake.

—Thank'ee kindly, Captain. But I come all this way meanin to settle in Dakota.

Eb spotted her on the dock at twilight. She had lost weight during the passage, and her tall, elegant figure was easy to spot among the broad-beamed women of Connell's flock clucking through the jumble of their baggage. He was tempted to stroll over and offer assistance but thought better of it. Instead he hired a man with a brokendown mule and a spring wagon to carry his trunk to the Grand Hotel, a rickety, two-story firetrap where the rooms were set off one from another by buffalo robes or muslin curtains dangling from nails in the ceiling. Surveyors, river-men, farmers, traders, itinerant millwrights, land speculators, trappers, and a one-armed ex-soldier from the Army of the Potomac coughed and wheezed, snored and farted behind their curtains. Every man slept with his war bag tucked under one ear or fastened around his waist and a pistol or a knife at hand for the sneak thief creeping under the robes at night. A traveling drummer who said his name was Askey recruited Eb to help haul his load of patent medicines up to the second floor, offered white whiskey as payment when the job was done. They sat on their trunks with the buffalo robe curtain pulled back, passing Askey's canteen back and forth. The man had a face like a squint-eyed ferret but he was honest enough.

—Truth is, this here whiskey's the main ingredient in what I got to sell. All ye got to do is take most any herb or root you find along the way and grind it, pinch a little into a bottle, and fill the bottle to the brim with this here white lightnin. Make the right pitch, and ladies will buy it. They can take a dozen sips a day and make like they's only doctorin the rheumatiz, the scrofula, or the lumbago. I've left many a happy settler's wife along the trail on account of this stuff, and took advantage of one or three that sampled a little too much of the product.

Askey claimed that he knew most of Dakota and traveled regularly through Indian country. He even professed a degree of sympathy for the Sioux, which drew hoots of derision from the other travelers at the Grand Hotel. Askey waited for silence.

—I says put yourself in their place. Imagine what a fella in Pennsylvania or Georgia would do if he looked out the kitchen window one morning and seen thousands of painted savages pourin into his territory without so much as a by-your-leave, grabbin up all the land and killin all the game and tellin white folks we can't go here and can't go there. We'd fight, that's what we'd do. Same as we're fightin for the Republic right this very minute. Anyway, the Sioux aint half as dangerous as people says. They's unpredictable, is all. What you don't want to do is to get caught by your lonesome or in a little bunch. They'll light on you so quick they'll be off with that hair of your'n afore you can think "Injuns!" You got a dozen men with rifles who know how to use 'em, the Sioux will most likely leave you be. Anyhow, I aint worried about this scalp.

Askey lifted his floppy hat to reveal a pate bald as a turkey egg.

—What would this look like stitched to the leggins of a respectable brave? Haint worth the trouble, not half. If I had a blond head of hair like your'n, Ebenezer Paint, I wouldn't go near the Indians without a troop of United States Cavalry at my back.

—I aint worried about my scalp. I was clean through Indian country on the way to California in 'forty-nine. Never had a peck of trouble.

—That was then and this is now. Too many settlers pourin in, and the army stirrin 'em up like a man pokin a hornet's nest with a sharp stick. They's been trouble and they's goin to be more trouble.

A broad-backed millwright spat his chaw a foot too close to Askey's boot.

—There ought to be trouble. Goddamned savages don't do a thing with the land. Don't grow no crops, don't make no improvements.

Bunch of no-good layabouts want to shoot buffalo every other week and sleep in the sun the rest a the time, when they aint scalpin women and children. Country aint goin to be safe until we shoot every last one.

Askey had his hand on the pepperbox pistol tucked into his pants. He did not back down.

—You ever meet up with a bunch of real Sioux?

The millwright shook his head.

—You will. Might change your mind. Aint no lazy man in the world can ride like that.

The Charismatics stayed a week in Sioux City, buying mules and wagons and outfitting themselves for the trip west. Eb saw the widow Landry only once, on the board sidewalk outside a mercantile emporium. He tipped his hat.

—Afternoon, Mizz Landry.

—Afternoon, Mr. Paint.

—I hope you been keepin well, ma'am.

—I have, thank you. It seems we've procured the mules and we'll head west tomorrow.

—That's what I hear. I'll be right sorry to see you go.

—Thank you. You were excellent company on that long voyage, sir, even if you did disappoint me at a critical moment. I've been thinking about it, however, and I feel that perhaps our Reverend Connell was in the wrong this time. Captain Leverton was responsible for our safety and as an unbeliever he could not be expected to put the same trust in the Lord as we do.

—You are goin to need every bit of trust in the Lord you got, where you folks are headed. It's rough country out there, and I aint sure the men you got with you are up to the task. It don't pay to be genteel when you're faced with road agents or a herd a buffalo.

—We are not fools, Mr. Paint. You forget that I was born here.

—It aint you I have my doubts about. It's some of those fellas with you, startin with that reverend. How far are you headed?

—We have no definite destination. Toward the Black Hills, I know that much. Reverend Connell says he will know the place when we come upon it. His wish is that we put ourselves among the Sioux, where it will be up to me to explain our purpose.

—I hope they give you a chance to talk. If they don't understand you're part Lakota yourself, they're apt to lift that pretty hair before you get a chance to preach.

She gazed at him, her dark eyes intent beneath the sunbonnet, as though seeking some clue to the inner workings of Ebenezer Paint.

—You are demonstrating a lack of faith. I believe that the Lord will keep us safe. I will pray for your soul, Mr. Paint.

He tipped his hat and walked on, sure that his soul was in need of whatever praying Mrs. Landry cared to do. Early the next morning, he paid a dollar to board a ferry to the west side of the river, where the Charismatics were preparing to depart. It had rained on and off for three days and the heavily laden wagons bogged in the mud every few feet. At best the pilgrims were indifferent muleskinners. Trace chains rattled on the whiffletrees as the contrary animals skipped and balked, laid their ears back, bared their teeth, kicked anyone unfortunate enough to get within hoof distance. Men who had rassled mules all their lives came out for the morning's entertainment, chewing tobacco and proffering contradictory advice.

—Give him his head now or he's goin to balk on ye.

—Take a two-by-four and whack her upside the noggin. Only way to get the attention of a mule.

—Turpentine, Preacher. That's how you get a balky mule to move. Ye lay a dollop a turpentine on their arseholes and they'll step off right smart ever time.

—Watch yer off jenny there, Rev, she's about to kick her traces.

—You got twenty foot of blacksnake whip in yer hand, Preacher. Don't be shy. Use it on the sonafabitch or you aint goin to leave here before sundown.

E. L. Biggs, owner of the biggest mercantile in town and the freight outfit which had procured the mules for the missionaries, was the loudest.

—Aint cussin 'em near enough, Preacher. Mule don't understand a goddamned thing if you won't cuss him.

The Reverend Connell glared at Biggs.

—Now you know we can't do that, Mr. Biggs. And I'll thank ye kindly not to curse in the presence of the women.

—Well, hell.

It took most of the morning for the pilgrims to get their wagons strung out on the trail. The sun was beginning to dry the mud and most of the crowd that had gathered decided the fun was over and headed back to the ferry. E. L. Biggs heeled around. He boasted a belly like the front end of a barge and it was pointed Eb's way.

—They say you run a boat and done some business on the Mississippi.

—Did for a time. Till they started shootin at storeboats.

—Uh-huh. If you can handle the Mississippi, I expect you can run the itty-bitty Big Sioux River. I might have a little proposition for ye. I got a interest in a steamboat down to Omaha, want to start runnin her up the Big Sioux. Around here, men who knows boats and rivers is as scarce as alligators.

—Any damned fool can steer a boat. You don't need me.

—Lemme be the judge of that. I got a whole goddamned general store strung along the bottom of the Big Sioux because of fools who tell me they can run a boat when they don't know labberd from stabberd. War on, or maybe you aint noticed. Nothin left but half-wits aint got sense enough to come in out of the rain.

—I thought maybe I'd head on to Yankton.

—Yankton! Hell's bells. Place is full a big damn dumb Scandahoovian farmers. Scandahoovians and Indians and I don't know which is worst. They aint neither of 'em American, anyways, I don't care if they been here since the *Mayflower*. A Scandahoovian aint happy 'less he's starin at a mule's arsehole all the livelong day, wouldn't know a opportunity if it hit him in the head with a shovel. Nope, Yankton aint no place for a white man. I aim to winter in Yankton myself, but that's only temporary, till it's safe to go back to Sioux Falls. That's the place you want to be. Prime bottomland just settin there since the place emptied out after the Indian scare. We can't settle there just yet on account of the heathen savages, but as soon as we get more troops around here and things in Sioux Falls quiet down, I aim to go back. A man can make a good livin off the Big Sioux, long as he thinks American and not like some damned ignorant Scandahoovian.

Biggs offered a chaw of Mickey Twist. Eb shook his head, not wanting to be beholden to the man for so much as half a nickel's worth of tobacco. Biggs bit off a plug for himself, worked it awhile, ejected a long, thin stream of tobacco juice between his teeth.

—Well, if you won't take my chaw you can still run my boat.

—Depends can you pay me to run your boat.

Biggs guffawed. He laid a paw on Eb's shoulder.

—You and me's goin to hit it off just fine, Mr. Paint. Just fine. Ferry's about to push off. Whyn't ye come on over and we'll talk?

Biggs struck off through the mud, realized Eb wasn't with him.

—Well? Are ye comin or aint ye?

—You go on over. I'll be by.

Eb watched the white canvas of the line of Conestogas flow like hooped clouds where they puffed over the brown hills. The pilgrims sang an old hymn as the wagons lurched westward, their voices carrying across the prairie:

> Rock of Ages, cleft for me,
> Let me hide myself in Thee;
> Let the water and the blood,
> From Thy wounded side which flowed,
> Be of sin the double cure,
> Save from wrath and make me pure.

Eb thought he saw Mrs. Landry peering out of the back of the rear wagon. He raised a hand and waved, saw a hand wave back. Reverend Augustus Connell himself, mounted on a piebald nag, followed the wagon train up the hill. Eb watched until the last wagon vanished behind a copse of cottonwoods. It occurred to him that he ought to pray for Mrs. Landry, not the other way round.

⚜ CHAPTER 8 ⚜

The first week of October, Eb Paint rode out with a mule train bound for Yankton. Nineteen wagons rolling north along the east bank of the Missouri and then northwest as the river bent into Dakota, a dozen braying mules each, muleskinners and men riding shotgun. He rode with the scouts up front out of the dust, topping each rise expecting to see the pride of the Sioux Nation arrayed in all its finery, encountering instead only a few Omaha attired in top hats and leggings. The air was crisp and clear, the sky a deep cobalt blue such as he had never seen on the Mississippi, the sparse stands of cottonwood and ash along the way already turning color. After too long a time spent swapping lies and picking lice out of his hide at the Grand Hotel in Sioux City, he was happy to be on the move and out in the open again, bound for Dakota Territory and a future as free of boundary as the great nation at his back.

In Yankton, Eb found a winter's employment sorting out the books for E. L. Biggs. He moved his kit into a cabin a mile north of the squalid little town, a stone-walled shack abandoned by a real-estate speculator from St. Paul named Lyall or Lytle who had vanished during the Sioux uprising the year before. Lyall or Lytle had bolted before the first hostile warrior had been sighted, lit out alone in the middle of the night and was never seen again. Some said the man had returned to a farm near St. Paul, others claimed he had been scalped and eviscerated and left to die a slow death alongside some forgotten creek. Eb preferred to think that he was back with his family in Minnesota, milking cows, putting up hay, and bouncing his children on his knee. He would sleep better in the man's cabin if there was no cause to fear that his scalpless and bloody ghost would come howling down the stovepipe, breathing tales of wild painted men creeping soundless through the tall grass, of the hiss of arrows in flight and barbs lodged in bone.

The first week of November, it rained for three days without stopping and the roads in all directions were left axle-deep in mud. Muleskinners hauling freight to Fort Randall worked their whips until the backs of the animals bled but the tall thin wheels of the wagons refused to budge unless they were heaved forward a few feet at a time by a dozen men prying with poles behind each wheel. When the rain stopped, the temperature plummeted and the mud froze to axle-snapping ruts a foot deep. Biggs squinted at the sky and declared it was time to shut down the freight business until spring.

With time on his hands, Eb worked to ready the shack for his first winter in Dakota. He put up a little smokehouse and bought and slaughtered a hog, smoked hams and bacon and made sausages, cut shakes for the roof, dug a root cellar to store a hundred pounds of potatoes, propped up the privy, worked at patching the chinks in the stone walls of the cabin with a mixture of straw and mud and tacked old copies of the Dakota *Democrat* over the patches for insulation. A newspaper didn't do much to keep out the cold but as long as a man had tallow for candles he could read the walls on long winter nights. When it snowed, he liked to lean back and look up at the hole where Lyall or Lytle had shoved the stovepipe through the roof and watch the snowflakes drift down to melt on the surface of the clawfoot stove. Over his straw tick he spread four of the old Union Army blankets, blue with the distinctive black stripes at either end; when he was dressed in his woolens with all four blankets wrapped tight around him it felt still as though he were sleeping buck-naked. To keep warm he wore his old Union greatcoat day and night, burned quantities of wood and buffalo chips to little purpose and chalked off the winter days one by one on the frame above the door.

One Saturday morning each month, Eb dragged buckets of clean snow to fill the copper boiler atop the stove, stoked wood in the fire till the water was near boiling. Then he slopped the hot water from the boiler into the galvanized tin washtub on the dirt floor and stepped in, yelping with the heat on his shanks and testicles. Then he bathed with head and arms and feet thrust out in the frigid air of the cabin, torso and buttocks and groin in the scalding water. The baths were the only time that winter he felt warm all the way through.

During the short winter days, Eb watched as the snow drifted against the ramshackle buildings across the road from the freight office. He fished through the ice for pickerel and pike, acquired a smelly old buffalo robe from a Metis trapper, slept under its warmth on nights when it was so cold his breath froze to a film of ice on the wall next to the bed. He dreamed of Mississippi heat thick as syrup, the scent of magnolia blossoms drifting through an open window where a lace curtain billowed in the breeze, the widow Landry tucking her bare backside into his groin to warm his bones. When he woke, the bed was empty and cold, the fire almost out, snow drifting under the door, another howler tearing in from the northwest.

In the spring, Louis Cobb, a bullwhacker out of Fort Randall, came in looking to buy buckskin gloves. Cobb and Biggs were both talkers, so they gabbed the better part of the morning. Eb stuck to his checker game until Cobb hit on a topic that caught his attention.

—They got the damnedest fella up at the fort, preacher name of Connolly, mad as a hatter. He's got a whole bunch with him, call themselves the Christmatics or some sech. This Connolly starts to preachin and they all get to throwin themselves on the ground and rollin around, hootin and hollerin and screechin in languages you never heard tell. Such a racket they put up, sounds like a boatload of heathen Chinee with their balls on fire. Anyhow, this crazy preacher was all for headin to the Black Hills to get the whole bunch scalped but Captain Jack Stanton caught up to 'em about ten miles short of hostile country, rounded them up and brought 'em into the fort. Army helped them build cabins north of Fort Randall, set them pilgrims up pretty as you please. Now I don't usually pay no more attention to a preacher than I would to a buffalo gnat but this old goat has a wife and she has to be about the prettiest thing in the territory. Shapely as a racehorse even if she is a half-breed.

Biggs laughed.

—Sounds like your widow woman has gone and found herself a real studhorse, Eb.

Eb turned to Cobb.

—You say the preacher's name is Connolly? You sure it aint Connell?

—Connolly, Connell. Somethin like that. Ought to call hisself Crazy As A Bedbug, 'cause that's what he is.

—And she has dark curly hair, you say? Tall, pretty as a picture?

The bullwhacker nodded.

—That's her. They say she's a war widow, though she don't hardly look old enough to been married and widowed already. You know her from someplace?

—Came up from St. Louee with that bunch aboard of the *Western Dawn* last summer. That preacher tried to keep 'em all out on deck during a lightnin storm. Captain name of Leverton broke his nose.

—That's him. Nose healed kind of funny, off to one side. Can't see why she married the crazy old coot. Aint nothin wrong with her nose, nor nothin else about her far as I can tell.

—Only betwixt the ears. She must be as crazy as he is. Religion aint safe. Addles a mind, same as locoweed.

Eb went back to his checker game. A woman like the widow Landry hitched to a man who was about as crazy as you were allowed to be and still walk around loose. It was enough to drive a man to drink.

The first week of June, E. L. Biggs persuaded Eb to come along with a company of armed and nervous adventurers from the Dakota Land Company, bound for the abandoned settlement at Sioux Falls. They rode highbooted for protection from the tall slough-grass that would slice a man's legs worse than a freshstropped razor. Redwing blackbirds perched on cattails along every poorest brook or sluice or puddle or stream, redtailed hawks drifted on high eddies against a blue sky, the horses danced lightfooted and eager. Eb rode a palomino gelding purchased from E .L. Biggs. Biggs himself was astride an immense irongray Percheron draft horse, a porkpie hat jammed down over his ears.

When they camped overnight at the juncture of the Split Rock and Big Sioux Rivers, Biggs let Eb in on a secret.

—This yere's the town of Emanija. Bound to be capital of the state of Dakota some day.

—How's that? Enemija?

—Emanija. Indian word. Means "where the water splits the rocks" or some sech.

—You don't say.

Eb looked around. There was not a road, a shanty, a barn, a chickencoop, a pitchfork, a hitching post to be seen in the wondrous town of Emanija. As far as he could tell there was not even a surveyor's stake to mark the site of this future capital of Dakota and metropolis of the West. Biggs read his thoughts, winked and pointed at his noggin.

—She don't look like much now but once we get her rollin, ye'll want to be in on it from the ground up. If I was you and I had a dollar to invest, I'd put her down right yere and just sit back and wait for the money to roll in. Thirty years from now folks will speak of Emanija like they was talkin about Chicago or Paree. If you're one of the first men in on the deal, ye'll be wipin your arse with silk drawers.

Eb took another look.

—If it's all the same to you, Biggs, I believe I'll hang on to my dollars until you got a survey stake or two in the ground.

—Suit yourself. But one of these days when you come to visit the E. L. Biggs mansion right here in Emanija, be sure you tell the

English butler you're the same Ebenezer Paint who wouldn't risk a plug nickel on a bet that is safer'n sundown.

That night as they posted guards and prepared to crawl into their bedrolls, Biggs told the kind of Dakota yarn designed to convince visitors they would be better off elsewhere.

—We're right near the spot where two fellas from the Western Land Company came to grief back in eighteen and fifty-eight. Company sent the poor devils down here tryin to grab some land out from under our noses, right after the treaty was signed with the Yankton Sioux. 'Twas Smith Kinsey, and Wilmot Brookings with him. Kinsey and Brookings, they got caught in a blizzard on the way back to Sioux Falls. Tried to wade the horses acrost the Split Rock but the river was only half-froze and Brookings, he fell through the ice. Time they got to Sioux Falls his feet was froze solid, but Brookings is a lucky fellow, always was. Had a doctor friend name of Phillips there. Doc Phillips sawed Wilmot's feet clean off, saved his life. Wilmot, he's still with us and as busy as any man in Dakota, feet or no feet.

Eb got his first look at Sioux Falls early the next morning. He heard the falls before he saw them, reined in the palomino and listened to the rumble and boom of downrushing cataracts over ancient rock where the river tumbled through a nexus of rock strewn along the riverbed like the aftermath of a tantrum taken by a giant's spoiled child. A spiderweb of chasms ran off in every direction, the falls caught at their vortex like a fly in a stone net. The country on all sides was treeless but for a copse of brush at the head of the falls and a handful of maple and ash trees on an island in the stream, the leaves already a deep summer green under a sky the blue of plucked cornflowers. The spray from the falls bent the light into rainbows and split-tail swallows exploded in caprioles above the torrents.

Biggs gestured expansively, as though he himself had flung this wonder onto the landscape with a mighty hand.

—These yere's the Sioux Falls. Blessed nuisance. Wasn't for

the falls we could load a boat upstream, run her all the way down to N'Orleans.

—If ye didn't sink her on the first snag.

—A sad but potent truth, Mr. Paint. A sad but potent truth.

The odor of wet smoke and old fire clung to the abandoned settlement still, tenacious on the blackened fields now greening with fireweed and the remnants of log cabins where the angry Sioux had torched everything that would burn. Fences had been torn apart and scattered along with the tools the panicked settlers left to rust: adze and pitchfork, hammer and scythe, sewing machine and spinning wheel. The cast iron of the sawmill itself still stood, its rusted skeleton exposed to the elements, the building that housed it gone up in flames along with the rest. In the crook of an old maple tree perched a crudely carved wooden doll in a tattered rag dress, keeping mute and eyeless vigil. At the foot of the tree was an open leather trunk stuffed with old books now so pulped and weatherbeaten there was no way to tell whether they had been Bibles or histories or medical books. The stone building that housed the old Smith printing press would not burn, so the furious Sioux had dragged the press out and hurled it into the river where it lay rusting, a warning to the jittery Land Company men who expected an ambush at every turn. E. L. Biggs held forth on the tragedy of Sioux Falls.

—This yere used to be a cornfield. August the twenty-fifth, it were. Murderin heathen White Lodge and his braves caught Judge Joe Amidon here with his boy. Shot the judge dead right off. Boy was a hunchback, so they put a dozen arrows in his hump. I expect they thought that hump was bad medicine. The boy pulled most of them arrows out a himself afore he died. Helluva thing.

—They kill everybody?

—Hell no. Only them two.

—I thought you said it was a massacre.

—It were. Them two was massacred and everybody else run, most of 'em to Sioux City, some to Yankton. Rounded up what livestock they could find, piled everythin they could get on the wagons and skedaddled. Saddest parade you ever seen, women cryin and kids scared half to death, thinkin they was all goin to be turned into pincushions and scalped afore nightfall. Wasn't nothin but a stampede once it got goin. Hell, I wanted to stay and fight but I weren't about to tangle with no thousand Sioux by my lonesome.

Tom Jackson heard what Biggs was saying.

—Biggs, you're a lyin peckerwood. First off, it was more like forty Sioux and you was the first white fella wanted to run. You wanted to run even before they killed the Amidons. When you saw that boy with the arrows in his hump, we had to hold you back or you'd of run off with the horses and wagons and left the rest of us to walk.

—Well, that's your recollection, Tom. You aint always been the most accurate of men.

—Mebbe not. But when I shoot a arrow, it tends to land in the same county. You tell a yarn, it starts out a mile from the truth and ends up four states south.

They spent the night in a thick-walled sod house owned by the Dakota Land Company, called Fort Sod by the original settlers. They had to share the meager space with a reconnaissance party representing the Western Land Company encamped behind the same walls. The two companies were rivals in commerce forced to band together for mutual protection. The next day Biggs introduced Ebenezer Paint to the handful of the hardy or demented who still believed that white men could make their fortunes here, the footless Wilmot Brookings of the Western Land Company among them. Biggs, anxious to ingratiate himself with Brookings, boasted of the fortune Eb could make for them.

—This yere is our riverman, Wilmot. Run a steamboat on the Mississippi, nigh the most famous captain betwixt Natchez 'n' Cairo. What he don't know about paddlewheelers aint worth knowin. He's goin to figure how to run steamboats up the Big Sioux as far as the Falls. When he does, there will be a handsome dollar in it for many a man.

Eb scuffed a booted toe in the dirt.

—You got to take E. L. here with about a pound a salt, Wilmot. The truth is I run a pissant storeboat on the Mississippi, peddlin everythin from spinnin wheels to yams. When them big steamboats come through, the most I done was to get the hell outa the way. I do know my way around rivers some, so I'll take a peek and see what you might be able to do with a shallowdraft boat on the Big Sioux. What I seen so far, water in that river is thin as a poor man's crop.

Eb stayed a week at Fort Sod before he left to pole a skiff down as far as Sioux City. He tested the depth of the water every quarter mile, drawing up the beginnings of a chart that would be of little use come late summer and low water. Already some of his measurements were in inches, not feet. No matter how shallow its draft, no steamboat could run up the Big Sioux. The first night out he camped on a sandbar where the river widened briefly, thinking it might afford some protection from Indian attack. He missed the Mississippi River with a longing that was like a man's longing for a woman. Like a woman, that river. Like the widow Landry, covered nightly by the spindly shanks of the preacher man.

He slept little, jumped at every sound. He lay on his back watching the stars, the Milky Way a long, vaporous puff from the breath of the Creator Himself. When at last he slept, he dozed fitfully, his dreams a parade of footless wraiths with pulped eyesockets, in relentless pursuit as he sailed the *Marielita* over an endless grassy sea, her paddlewheel churning up dust. Lucian perched atop the pilothouse playing checkers against himself while Eb forked twists of dry prairie grass into the boilers in a hell of heat and noise, the widow Landry whispering in his ear all the while:

—*Abababababa kiyi kiyi ababa kiyi kiyi okahe okahe kiyi okahe onha onha akali kiyi kiyi . . .*

BOOK 2

Big Sioux

Dakota Territory, 1869–1886

⚜ CHAPTER 9 ⚜

The weapon was a fowling piece of some antiquity. It had a sighted, two-stage barrel supported by a full wooden stock, the barrel decorated at the breech with a chiseled ornament and the inscription BUNNEY, LONDON. The side plate, escutcheon, ramrod pipes, and retaining ramrod had all been worked from whalebone by a master craftsman. The flat lock had beveled edges, and the figured walnut stock was carved behind the breech and inlaid with silver-wire scrolls that burst into a delicate filigree of engraved silver flowers. The cast and engraved silver mounts of the butt plate and trigger guard bore the mark of Charles Freeth and the dates 1780–81. The piece had survived a difficult crossing of the Atlantic to Philadelphia in 1797 during which its original owner, Ewan Whitworth, was washed overboard and drowned. It was claimed by his friend and fellow voyager Theophilus Landry, who used the antique piece to put food on the table for his brood, shooting such a quantity of wild fowl in the woods of western Pennsylvania and eastern Ohio that there were mornings when he peered out the window at dawn and wondered that there were birds of the air yet living, such destruction he had wreaked upon their kind. Upon the death of Theophilus Landry, the weapon became the prized property of his beloved grandson Hobart, whose widow inherited it following Hobart's death at the first Battle of Bull Run in the War of the Rebellion. In the summer of 1863, it was carefully packed in a steamer trunk for another journey to this spot on the south bank of the Missouri River outside the walls of Fort Randall, Dakota Territory, where its muzzle was now pressed tight to the back of the unwashed neck of the trooper Archer Swaples, caught with both hands rummaging in a steamer trunk loaded in the back of a canvas-covered spring wagon. It was a hot spring day, and Swaples was bathed in sweat and pungent as a badger's den.

—Soldier, this is a loaded weapon in my hands and that is a muzzle at the back of your neck, so you're going to want to hold real steady.

—Yes, ma'am.

—Do we understand each other?

—Yes, ma'am.

—Then perhaps you would care to tell me why you're pawing through my corsets.

—I was lookin for a pair a wire cutters, ma'am.

—Wire cutters.

—Yep.

—And you thought that a trunk filled with a lady's private things was a likely place to find wire cutters?

—Not exactly.

—Well, what was it exactly?

—I was lookin for wire cutters and I opened this trunk and I seen right off there wasn't any.

—Careful now. It's hot and I'm feeling awfully impatient. My finger might slip if I think you aren't telling the truth.

—Yes, ma'am.

—Now maybe you'd like to start over and be a little more truthful this time.

—That's the God's truth, ma'am. I was lookin for wire cutters.

—And you just happened to come up with two handfuls of petticoats instead, is that it?

The set-to had drawn a little crowd: a troop of returning cavalry filthy after a week on the trail, a half dozen muleskinners camped south of the fort, thirty or forty Hangs-Around-the-Fort Indians, the fort blacksmith, and a government land agent. The Indians watched in dignified silence but the troopers and muleskinners had plenty of suggestions for the unfortunate Archer Swaples.

—Looks like she's got ye, Archie! I'd say a prayer to my Maker, I was you.

—Was ye fixin to wear them bloomers, Arch, or did ye think ye'd hide 'em in your kit and just haul 'em out for a sniff now and again?

—Make a grab for her, Arch! You're quick enough when you're cheatin' at cards. You aint goin to let yourself get bested by no woman, are you?

—I wouldn't move a muscle, Arch. That old thing she's got pointed at your head is apt to go off and scatter what brains you got all over her unmentionables.

The cavalry captain strolled over to see what the fuss was about.

—Mind tellin me what the trouble is here, ma'am?

—I found him in my wagon, where he has no call to be, rummaging through my things.

—Is that so, Trooper?

—I was lookin for wire cutters.

—That's what he claims. He can't explain why he'd expect to find wire cutters in a woman's trunk.

—I didn't know this here was your wagon. I thought it was a fella with them teamsters yonder and he was sure to have wire cutters.

—And which fella might that be?

—I can't recollect his name.

—Do you see him around here now?

—Can't say as I do.

—Did he tell you he had a trunkful of women's things in his wagon?

—Well, no. But I knowed the teamsters comes to the occasional fence, and they got to cut through it. That's why I come here for the wire cutters.

The captain stepped up to take charge.

—Ma'am, if you'll just withdraw that weapon from his neck, we'll take it from here.

—Is he going to be disciplined?

—That's up to the colonel, but I'm sure that he will be.

—And what form will his punishment take, may I ask?

—I have no idea, ma'am. He might be hung by his thumbs. Or bucked and gagged. Or spread-eagled. You can be sure he will be well-punished, in any case.

—For shame. I wouldn't subject a weasel to what you do to these men.

—I'd think you of all people would want to see him punished.

—Perhaps I would, if your punishments were not something from the Middle Ages. I saw what one of your colonels did to a trooper here last summer, Captain. The man was spread-eagled in hot summer because he wouldn't tell where another soldier had his whiskey hid. They staked him out right in the middle of the parade ground and left him there for an entire day while the buffalo gnats crawled in his nose and mouth and ears and the horseflies bit him and the sun blistered his skin. He screamed for water until he could barely croak. By the time they let him loose, he was completely out of his mind and of no use to anyone. That is not justice, Captain, that is sadistic foolishness.

—What sort of discipline would you prefer, ma'am?

—I don't know, but there must be some way to punish a man without half-killing him.

The captain waved a buckskin-gloved hand in the general direction of his troop.

—Them savages? They're almost worse than Indians. You got to half-kill them just to get their attention. You coddle him, the next time he'll be after more than your unmentionables.

—I will not be a party to any bucking and gagging or hanging by the thumbs.

—I aint asked you to be a party to a thing. There are plenty of witnesses right here.

Her arms ached from holding the weapon. She could see the sweat pouring down the back of the soldier's neck, smell his fear. Reluctantly she stepped away from the man and leaned the fowling piece against the wagon. Archer Swaples stood and rubbed his back, his face glowing red with embarrassment through a three-days' growth of stubble.

Before she could say another word, the captain directed two corporals to quick-march the culprit into the fort. The troopers and Indians and muleskinners who had gathered to watch the show shuffled away, disappointed at the lack of bloodshed.

She wiped her brow under her sunbonnet, ducked into the suffocating heat inside the wagon to see exactly what the man had been up to. She had to fight back a sudden wave of nausea. Her undergarments were scattered all over the wagon. The trooper had been pawing through her things for some purpose dark and deviant. She had a sudden uncharitable thought of Archer Swaples bucked and gagged, his arms and legs trussed together and a stick tied in his mouth. Immediately she castigated herself for a lack of mercy. It was this country that did it; a woman saw so much and heard so much that the most casual cruelty to man and beast became commonplace. Those who did not become hardened to it did not endure. It was just as well that she was about to leave and never return.

—Are you in need of some assistance there, ma'am?

A tall muleskinner from the civilian wagon train camped near the river was standing politely next to her wagon, hat in hand, his face obscured by the glare of the noon sun behind him, so that all she saw as she peered up from the darkness of the wagon was a shadow bordered by a halo of light.

—I should think you fellows would have had your fill of the spectacle by now, sir.

—Pardon me, but I just wanted to be sure you was all right. I believe I made your acquaintance before.

—Excuse me?

—Ebenezer Paint, ma'am. We met aboard of the *Western Dawn* coming upriver from St. Louis about five, six years ago.

She stepped out of the shadow and as he turned to the sunlight she saw him clearly.

—Mr. Paint. Of course I remember you. I am so sorry. I couldn't see your face. The name is Mrs. Connell. It's a pleasure to see you again.

She pulled back the sunbonnet so he could see her face. She

looked a little gaunt and worn but it was unmistakably her. She was no older than twenty-six but she was so thin that her cheekbones stood out and there were a few white hairs visible among the dark, unruly curls poking out from under her bonnet.

—Pleasure is mine, ma'am. I didn't figure to see you again, though I knowed you was about. Run into a captain, Jack Stanton. He's the one took you folks up to Fort Randall when you was headed west.

—Oh, yes. I didn't believe so at the time but he might have saved our lives. It was an arduous journey coming here from Sioux City and the men were new to the West. They had trouble with the mules and when they tried to hunt, they didn't have much luck.

She fell silent, staring across the Missouri as though she might find the answer to some profound question out there on the river. Eb hoisted the fowling piece.

—This is quite the weapon

—That belonged to Mr. Hobart Landry, sir. It's the only thing of Mr. Landry's I still possess. I took it this morning to show the base commander because I heard he was interested in old weapons and I thought he might purchase it from me. He offered me only fifty dollars. It isn't loaded. I wouldn't even known how to load it.

—Good thing that trooper didn't know. Them fellas have no manners at all.

—Theirs is a hard life. He is probably dangling by his thumbs right now, or he will be soon enough. I feel I should have done more to persuade them to spare him.

—Pardon me for sayin so, but he's lucky you didn't shoot him. The reverend ought not to leave a woman such as yourself to fend for yourself around the fort. There are rough men here.

She bit her lower lip.

—Unfortunately, the Reverend Connell is no longer with us. The Lord took him last fall. That is why I was trying to sell this old fowling piece, to secure my passage back to Ohio.

—This is ever a harsh country. What happened to the reverend, if you don't mind my askin?

—Died of snakebite.

—They Lord. I do hate snakes. You got to be careful where you step out here.

Eb tapped his own knee-high boots with his walking stick as though invoking a sacred charm against snake venom.

—It was his own fault. He was handling a big diamondback rattler in a church service after we fell in with a band of Charismatics from Appalachia who handle snakes as part of their worship. He was bitten in the throat.

—Awful way to die.

—I'm sure it was, although he couldn't speak to tell us one way or another. My husband thought he had the unique protection of the Lord. I have often wondered what he thought as he was dying. If he felt betrayed by God Himself.

—I don't mean to speak ill of the dead, but he was ever a prideful man.

—He was. I can't deny it. I'm sure you recall his altercation with Captain Leverton aboard ship. I was angry with you then for not defending us from the captain, but I see now that it was the reverend himself who was at fault for putting us all in danger from a lightning strike. It was pride that led to his fall then and pride that led to his death. It would be untruthful to say otherwise. He caused me to lose my faith in his religion.

—So I expect you will be leavin Dakota soon?

—As soon as I am able. I would have left as soon as the reverend was dead and buried but I could not get a steamboat until the ice broke. My aunt found me a place teaching school back in Ohio.

—Well, I'll be right sorry to see you go.

—I take it you have found a suitable existence for yourself here in Dakota?

—I run a little freight business. Bought it off a fella name of E. L. Biggs. He had a office in Yankton but I moved to Sioux Falls once the cavalry took charge. We're all loaded down for a run to the White River but a muleskinner name of Tom Ogle took sick with the appendicitis, so we brought him to the post surgeon. Soon as Tom is able to travel, we'll be headed west.

—Seems we always meet in transit.

Eb twisted his hat in his hands.

—Seems to be the case, ma'am. It's a shame, because I do enjoy your company.

She touched his arm. There was a noise behind them, a grouse flushed at the approach of one of the dogs that hung around the fort. When she turned to look, her corseted breast happened to brush the back of his hand. Eb swallowed hard.

—There's a question I haven't asked ye.

—And what might that be?

—All this time and I never knowed your Christian name.

—Why, it's Cora.

—That's very nice. Cora.

The muleskinner Tom Ogle died that night in a feverish delirium after his appendix burst. The mule train moved out before first light the next morning, escorted by an entire company of cavalry for the trip to the Spotted Tail Agency. Eb saw Cora's wagon was still there when he left, considered rousing her to say good-bye, thought better of it. It was the way of things; sometimes people were lucky enough to land in the same spot, sometimes they weren't.

When the wagons returned to Fort Randall three weeks later, he was surprised to find she was still there, camped in the same spot. Eb found her near dusk, baking biscuits in a Dutch oven in the back of her wagon. She was expecting him.

—A captain from the fort told me you were coming in today, so I made these biscuits. I was about to fry up some ham if you're hungry.

—After drivin mules and eatin dust all day, I could eat a boar hog, bristles and all.

—Then you'd best wash up and I'll put a feed on for you.

Eb did as he was told and they ate sitting side by side on one of her trunks in the shade of the wagon. He helped her with the washing up and they were sitting with steaming bowls of coffee when he got to the question that was on his mind.

—Nary a steamboat through here yet?

—There was one down from Fort Benton. I didn't go.

—Trouble securing your passage? I could help.

—I don't need money for passage, Mr. Paint. I decided to wait for you. You paid court to me at one time aboard the *Western Dawn*, sir. I thought to see if you might care to do the same again, knowing that you were more liable to succeed.

He looked at her, long and steady. Those frank, dark eyes meeting his pale gaze, just as they had when she first approached him on behalf of the Church of the Living Redeemer. It was bold of a woman to say a thing like that but he could see she was firm about it. She would wait for him to ask the question but she had already given her answer.

They leaned back in the grass and watched the sun set over the Missouri, the truth between them heavy and unspoken. He considered asking her about Phoebe Palmer and the necessities of her faith, thought better of it. Spoke of what he knew instead.

—I have never learned to cotton to this river, the Big Muddy. Springtime in Yankton, the streets look pretty much like the Missouri, except maybe less muddy. The Mississippi, she's all a mystery, changeable as a woman, beg pardon. The Big Sioux runs clear and clean over rock. The White River is pretty enough, once you're past the quicksand. The river down in Nebraska some call the Running Water and some call the Niobrara, that's the prettiest river you'll ever see. But the Missouri aint built for fish nor boats. It's made for snakes and centipedes and such. A long muddy crawl all the way from St. Louis to Fort Benton, near as I can make out. Taint a place I care to stay longer than is strictly necessary.

Eb helped himself to two more of her biscuits and drained the coffee and they went for a stroll along the banks of the river. The night air was fragrant; the reflection of a yellow moon danced on the choppy waters. When she shivered, he put an arm around her shoulders. She did not push his arm away but leaned into him instead. He felt himself rigid as a pump handle, his longing for her like a terrible thirst. He pulled her to him and kissed her hard on the mouth and when he started to pull away for air, she hooked a strong arm around the back of his neck and would not let go, her open mouth on his, her probing tongue between his lips. He heard the crickets singing in the dark trees and felt himself go dizzy as though he might topple over and drag her down with him. She would not turn him loose and he felt the length of her pressed tight to his body and lowered his hands to pull her buttocks into him, heard no protest and breathed into her warm mouth something that was like a prayer for the both of them. When finally she let loose, he belonged to her as surely as his hand belonged to his arm. She tangled her long fingers in his hair and whispered in his ear:

—I have to warn you, Eb Paint. I have been a hazardous woman to husbands. Barely twenty-six and I have buried two already. You would be taking an awful chance.

—I aint afraid a that.

—No, I don't suppose you are. Perhaps that's why I haven't stopped thinking of you since that time on the Missouri.

—Nor I. Many a cold night. Wonderin where you was at, what you was up to.

—It has not been a year since the death of Reverend Connell. Some might not think it proper.

—I almost never come across nothin that is writ in stone except the Ten Commandments. Life can be short and precarious out here, and I aint no spring chicken myself. I'm nigh onto forty years old, so if we're goin to do this thing, I'd as soon we got it over with.

—Since you put it that way.

—I aint meanin it's something to be got over, only that if it's going to happen, I'd like it to happen soon.

She pulled her skirts tighter around her ankles, listened to the murmur of the river.

—First you must ask me in the proper way.

Eb knelt with some gallantry, took her hand.

—Miss Cora, I'd be pleased if you cared to be my wife.

—Mister Paint, I accept your proposal.

She helped him to his feet and they kissed again, Eb thinking how a man's life could turn on a dime and give him a nickel change. Here he'd stopped for biscuits and ended up with a wife.

They were married by the post chaplain at Fort Randall early on the morning of Independence Day, 1869, the muleskinners and two women from the original group of pilgrims from the *Western Dawn* standing in a semicircle around them as the chaplain pronounced them man and wife. After the ceremony they watched the U.S. Army on parade, all spit and polish, gleaming spurs and gold braid, glistening matched companies of gray-horse cavalry, bay-horse cavalry, black-horse cavalry, white-horse cavalry. They listened to lengthy speeches on the glories of the Republic, celebrating its ninety-third anniversary after surviving the trial by fire that was the War Between the States. They joined the revelers inside the fort eating plates of roast beef and pork and sweetcorn and potatoes as though all of Fort Randall had turned out to celebrate their wedding. As soon as it was near enough to dark, they slipped away to spend the night in Eb's tent, ignoring the bawdy comments of the muleskinners camped not thirty feet away. With the flap of the tent open, they watched the fireworks, gaudy in the northern sky. When he closed the flap, Eb found her unexpectedly wanton, certain of what she wanted and even demanding, not at all like the demure and churchly young lady he had known aboard the *Western Dawn*. First she peeled every stitch of clothing off him and undressed herself without shyness. Then she straddled him and with adept fingers helped him to the place he wanted most to be. He could not know that it was the first time she had been with a man in this way since her short, unhappy marriage to Hobart Landry but in her passion, he sensed a woman long untouched and eager. As he spent inside her the first time, Eb was sure he could smell magnolias in the air, a thousand miles from Mississippi.

❧ CHAPTER 10 ❧

At dawn on the first day of April 1870, Cora Paint stood near one of her spindly and failing apple trees a hundred feet from the river, watching the rednecked helldivers above the falls soar and plummet into the Big Sioux after carp or perch. After six months in the new cabin in Sioux Falls, she still could not get enough of the spectacle. Eb had ridden out to the woodcutters' camp long before first light, leaving Cora to finish her tea and porridge alone. She added an extra dollop of molasses to the porridge and then another, finished it all with more appetite than usual, rose heavily and waddled to the privy out back. She took her time even with a full day's work ahead: She needed to take the hoe and shovel and turn the earth for her truck garden and she had to boil water to wash Eb's butchering clothes. When she went to feed the chickens, she saw the helldivers and decided to check on her apple trees, knowing the errand was nothing more than an excuse to put off her chores and to linger instead watching the birds and wondering how in that roiling river they could see a fish, much less catch one.

She was so entranced by the spectacle that she ignored the first ripples of pain until one came strong enough to take her breath away. At first she thought it a mere stomach upset, something to do with the weight of the porridge and the extra molasses. Then something inside her belly seemed to shift and she knew that her time had come. She spotted a boy about ten years old downriver, fishing off a cutbank with three poles cut from willow branches. When he saw her waving, he came willingly enough and she asked him to go fetch Mabel Stratton. He left his poles unattended and went pelting off before she could offer more instructions. Between spasms she returned to the cabin, loaded wood into the stove, and put a basin of water to boil, not knowing for certain whether the boy had the foggiest notion who the Stratton woman was or where to find her.

An hour later the sky turned gray. The temperature dropped, blustery winds shook the cabin and the first cold rain mixed with the spray from the falls. Above the sounds of the cataract and the gathering storm, she heard a springwagon pull up outside and Mabel Stratton came in without knocking, brusque as the wind itself, and ordered her to bed. With her head propped on two feather pillows, she watched the woman move from the stove to the bed, the bed to the stove, where she kept the big kettle of water at a boil all day long. Cora was grateful for the warmth, the sounds of crackling wood and boiling water to counter the wind, the gusts of rain that rattled like sand against the windowpanes, the distant roar of the falls. With each gust the muslin curtains she had nailed to the walls billowed like shivering ghosts, the tallow candles guttered, the draft cooled the sweat on her forehead. She tried to ride the wind and the rain to a place where the pain could not touch her but the Stratton woman talked without pause.

—This is a date you're not likely to forget, child. A day only a fool would be out and about. Your man ought to be here.

—They've wood to cut.

—Men. Always got some excuse when they're needed.

—It's not an excuse. The fort needs lumber. Eb has a contract to fill. He'd no reason to think my time would come so soon.

—By my count it's been nine months since you got hitched. He ought to have expected somethin, with you big as a house.

Cora's smile vanished as the breath hissed through her teeth. Her fingers gripped the quilt, the hiss turned into a long, shuddering scream as another thunderbolt of pain ripped through her abdomen. The spasms were closer together now, giving her less time to gather her strength. She was stunned at the power of it, how it could feel like some great metal thing twisting and ripping inside. Then it would pass and she would gasp for air, fight to prepare herself before it was on her again, the pain insistent and demanding and beyond anything she had imagined. How did women do this without pleading for deliverance? How could some women bear a dozen children and more and not perish of the pain? Surely death itself was better than this, the grave a refuge of peace at the end of a river of anguish. The spasm passed and Mrs. Stratton bent to wipe her face with a towel.

—He's in a hurry to be of the world, this child.

—Why do you say "he"? It might as leave be a girl.

—Not this one. This one is a boychild. All set to come out yippin and screamin.

—Eb will be pleased.

—Course he will. That's as far as they think. Get a boy to help with the work. Until they get down to the last child or two, then they always want girls to help 'em totter about when they can barely gum their oatmeal of a morning.

Another spasm came, fierce as the storm, a surge that went on and on and seemed not to stop. Cora heard the midwife telling her to push, so she pushed and the pain subsided for a bit and then it was back again worse than ever until she felt she would split like a tree cleaved by lightning. Again Mabel said "push" and she pushed, harder. "Push!" and she pushed again. "Push!" From somewhere on the far side of the river, she heard herself scream and wondered why her throat didn't shatter. The storm shook the cabin, the pain gripped her and would not let go and she felt herself plummet over the falls into black water a thousand feet below, certain that she would die. Then the Stratton woman was holding up a bloody, slippery, squalling thing still attached to a purplish twist of umbilical cord. Cora looked on as from a great height while Mabel cut the cord and doctored the baby's navel with ointment, wrapped the child in cotton and tucked it into Cora's breast just as another spasm of pain tore through her abdomen.

—That's it, girl. You have to push it all out. One more time. Try.

Cora pushed as she was told. The child tucked into her breast stirred and a hand the size and color of a walnut brushed her skin, brought her back to the sound of boiling water, the rain beating against the cabin.

—Mabel, I forgot to look.

—Look at what?

—Is it a boy or a girl?

—Sweet weeping Lord. A boy. Just a-hollerin and a-kickin to get into this cruel world.

The child stirred and whimpered and Cora held it more tightly, gazed into Eb's pale gray-blue eyes staring back at her as though charging her with some enormous weight of responsibility, infinite care, love without limit. She arched her back, felt the baby roll away from her, clutched him again before he could plunge headfirst to the hard pine floor. Here the child was not three minutes old and already she had nearly lost it. The Stratton woman clucked her tongue, lifted the baby away from her and placed it in the rough cradle Eb had cobbled together against the day when his firstborn would arrive. Another spasm shook Cora to the core. She looked at Mabel in desperation, wondering why the pain that was supposed to end with this birth had not ended.

—They Lord. They's another one comin.

—Another what?

—Another child. You had two babies in that belly, girl.

—You mean twins?

—Two babies is twins, or at least they was back in Tennessee. Out here everything is a bit odd, I'll admit you that. But I do believe twins is still twins.

There was no more time for talk. It was as though she had slipped back in time, into another awful river of pain. Then Mrs. Stratton was again holding that slippery bloody thing as it opened its mouth to squall.

—You poor child. Twin boys.

—Boys. Two boys?

—What I said. Twin boys. Two of 'em. They Lord, you poor girl. Such a burden.

Cora let her head sink back into the pillow, all her strength gone, soaked in sweat and fighting for breath.

—Eb will be so pleased.

—Just like a woman. Ever thinking to some man.

It was past nine o'clock when Eb came in, drenched through from cutting wood in the rain all day. He reeked of damp and sweat, woodsmoke and wet horse and saddle leather. Mabel Stratton sat on a highbacked wooden chair at the table holding one of the babies and Cora, pale and drained and with the dark ringlets of her hair plastered to her forehead, was propped up in bed with the other child. Eb heaved the door shut against the force of the wind and looked from one woman to the other, blinking like a drunk who has stumbled into the wrong house. He removed his hat, leaned over Cora and brushed the hair from her eyes.

—Where did these two come from? These aint our'n?

—They are.

—The both of 'em.

—Both. Twin boys.

—Twins, you say? They wasn't one, they was two all along?

—That's right.

—Well, I'll be damned. And they come just today, did they?

Mrs. Stratton could hold her tongue no longer.

—They weren't here when you left, were they?

—No, they weren't at that. They look as alike as two peas in a pod.

—That's because they's twins. I thought we had that settled. Now you might think to ask after your wife. She has had a time of it.

—I'm sorry, Cora. Are you all right?

—A little weak. It was awful for a while but we have two big, strong boy babies now.

—Sorry I was out so long. We run into some Ponca. I thought there was goin to be trouble, but they left us be.

Cora squeezed his hand.

—You should get out of those wet things. You'll catch your death. I'm sorry there's no supper on.

—I'll rustle up somethin for myself.

Mrs. Stratton stood and handed him the baby.

—This here's the second one born. You hold him and I'll get you somethin to eat. Better than you messin with the stove. Apt to light yourself afire and the rest of us with you.

Eb handed the baby to Cora, pulled the muslin curtain to divide the room and shed most of the wet clothes, then changed his wet long johns for the one extra pair he possessed. When he was dressed again and more or less dry, he took the plate handed him by Mrs. Stratton and ate without thinking, staring at the infants cradled on either side of his wife. He had barely finished eating when the woman snatched the plate from his hands. With the storm outside there was no question of her going home before morning. She eased her bulk onto the narrow tick next to Cora, leaving Eb to sleep on his bedroll on the pine floor. It was not until he had almost drifted off to sleep that it hit him: He was now the father of twin boys. The notion had a good feel to it, like the weight of a bag of gold dust in a man's pocket. Once during the night he heard a baby cry and then Cora's voice and the sound of the child suckling at her breast. For some reason he couldn't fathom, the cry in the night brought a sudden and awful emptiness, as though he were the only being in a deserted landscape. He fell asleep again and when he woke at dawn, the dark-of-night panic had vanished and he was so overwhelmed with gratitude for the bounty of two fine sons that he mumbled a rough prayer as he got the fire started in the clawfoot stove and put water to boil for coffee.

They were named for Eb's younger brothers Eli and Ezra, Mississippi boys from Jones County killed fighting with the Federals in the War Between the States. They had Eb's pale gray-blue eyes and Cora's dark hair, their father's height and their mother's wide shoulders. In appearance they repeated each other in every facet, so that Cora marveled at the precise match of knee and elbow, foot and neck, ear and nose. The only physical feature that made it possible to distinguish one from the other was a birthmark the size and shape of a small cottonwood leaf on Eli's chest, over his heart; at times even Cora had to haul up a shirt to see which brother was which. From the cradle, they were as different in mind as they were alike in body. Ezra would holler over almost any little thing and would sometimes keep them up half the night; Eli rarely whimpered and then only if he was sick. Since both boys slipped through childhood almost without illness, he rarely made a sound. Ezra began to talk nearly a year before his brother; for a long while Eli's silence worried Cora, until she decided that in their own mysterious way the twins had so apportioned things that Ezra would do the talking and Eli would do the thinking and make the decisions for both of them, although how they communicated all this to each other was a mystery she could not penetrate. Ezra's gabbing sometimes drove her to distraction; from the age of two he would discourse on anything and everything while Eli watched and listened. When she wearied of his chatter, Eb would shake his head and grin.

—Ezra has to talk twice as much because his brother don't say a word. Half of that is comin from Eli, only he don't let on.

They were tall, broad-shouldered, rambunctious, quarrelsome, energetic, and bold to a fault, so fearless that Cora worried day and night that they would suffer some unimaginable injury. They would climb anything that offered purchase, jump from any height, attempt to ride anything with four legs, dive into any body of water without checking for depth or current. They threw rocks at every living thing, rode horseback from the age of three, fished and hunted, made their own bows and arrows and learned to fire them with some accuracy and fought grim, silent battles, wrestling in the dust, so well-matched physically that in the end the only thing to separate them was Eli's implacable will. Because Eb was away so often freighting or making deals or looking for new ventures, most of their instruction fell to Cora. She taught them how to ride, how to shoot, how to skin a deer, how to kill a rattlesnake without getting bit. She often spoke to them in Lakota so that they would learn the language, which sounded to them like wind in the pines.

When in successive winters Cora gave birth to girl babies who failed to survive a single night, she swallowed her grief, tended the little graves on a hillside overlooking the Big Sioux and told herself that she had no energy left for daughters because the boys drained her so. By the time they were five years old, she could find barely a trace in the mirror of the young woman who had come up the Missouri on the *Western Dawn* with such Christian optimism twelve years before. Her body had thickened, and her hands were red and rough from the labor of washing clothes, plucking chickens, scrubbing pans, sewing clothing for two boys and a man, gardening in the summer and canning in the fall. She often felt a weariness made worse by Eb's tendency to pull up stakes, moving on and then on again in pursuit of something he could never quite define. As he established and abandoned one enterprise after another, they moved back to the Missouri River near Yankton, then twenty miles upriver from Fort Randall, east to the Dakota River, east again to the Big Sioux, back to the Missouri, west to Pierre for six weeks, back to Fort Randall. No matter where they lit, Eb grew restless again within a month or two, looking to try life somewhere else almost before they had time to unpack the wagons. She protested as often as they moved, but it was like trying to hold back the river with her thumb; Eb always had some compelling reason for the next journey.

In the spring of 1875, Eb stopped in at the post office in Sioux Falls to see if there were any stray letters about that hadn't followed him on his various moves. Louis Dickelmayer dug around in his cubbyholes and found a yellowed envelope addressed to Eb Paint, c/o General Delivery, Dakota Territory. The letter bore the postmark of Gerster, Missouri. It had bounced around some and arrived at the post office six months before. Dickelmayer had no forwarding address for Eb, so he hung on to the letter on the off chance that Eb made it back to Sioux Falls one day. The address had been written in pencil in big block letters and a thick wad of paper had been stuffed inside. Eb took it out into the sunshine and sat on a bench to read it:

Ebenezer,

It has taken many a year for me to get to this and I wouldn't blame you none if you thought I was dead and gone. This here is by way of letting you know that aint the case altho it was close enough many's the time. I went on the trail of my wife and babies back in 1863 and damned if it didn't take four years to catch up to them. I made it down to Galveston but they had moved on with the master that bought them a long while before. They was released when some Union troops come through Texas after the war to be sure nobody was holdin slaves. My wife Betty, she cooked for the Federals some and tagged along with their outfit as far as Oklahoma, but when the troops was moved to Montana she was left to fend for herself. She got as far as Arkansas and she was working for a crazy white lady there when I found her. Betty like to died of shock. My boy Lucian Jr was twelve years old and my girl Lucy was ten and pretty as a picture. They had some hard times but they was still alive—still are, far as that goes.

We looked around some and found a few acres here outside of Gerster, where I have a mule to do truck farmin and such. It aint the life on the Mississippi but with my young ones all growed I'm reaching the point where they can look after me and none too soon. I told them stories about the boat and the river so many times that I don't think they believe a word of it, but you and I know it's all true. We done some things and we been some places and if ary of us was a man of letters we ought to set it all down so folks could read about it a hundred years from now, only we aint.

*There aint much else to tell but I'd be grateful if you could set
down and write a spell, let me know how you made out in the Dakota
if the rattlesnakes or the Indians didn't get you. It's been near a dozen
years since we laid eyes on each other and it could be you're no more
of this earth, heaven knows there is many who aint.*

Your old friend,
Lucian Quigley

Eb felt dizzy when he finished Lucian's letter, as though time
had opened up and taken him back to a towhead on the Mississippi River, a peasoup fog and a rebel's head out there somewhere beating a tattoo on the hull of the *Marielita*. Back home he
sat down to write to Lucian. No matter how he tried, the words
wouldn't come. He couldn't imagine what to say, how to tell Lucian any part of what had happened since they left the big river.
Or rather he could imagine it but it was a story that would go on
and on and would take him most of a year to write. He put the
letter aside and vowed to get back to it once he could figure out
what to say, thinking that once a man had done a certain amount
of living, when it came to talking about it there was no knowing
where to start. He never heard from Lucian again.

⊰ CHAPTER 11 ⊱

The horse trader Samson Dawe came pounding up the road on a frigid March morning. Eb was doing the chores at their latest homestead on the Missouri River north of Fort Randall when he spotted Dawe driving his buggy so hard that the horse was lathered despite the weather, shouting "Cold! Cold!"

On this particular morning, Eb was less inclined than usual to roll out the welcome mat for Sam Dawe. The twins had the chickenpox and were itching so badly that even Eli fussed a little, the sow had crushed two of her newborn piglets, every last one of the new calves had a bad case of scours, Cora was feeling peculiar and a coyote had broken into the chickencoop and murdered half the hens. Now here was Sam Dawe yelling about the weather.

—Cold! Cold!

—Hell yes it's cold. Taint no reason to drive a team that way.

—Not *cold* for the love of God, man. *Gold.* General Custer found it, up in the Black Hills. Nuggets the size of a bull's balls just a-lyin in every crick waitin to be picked up.

—The Black Hills what belongs to the Indians?

—Only on some piece of paper. Word of this gets out, prospectors aint goin to be denied by a sorry bunch of savages.

—That aint no sorry bunch of savages own them hills. Them's the Sioux Nation and that's sacred country, far as they're concerned. You go pokin around for gold up there, your scalp will be decoratin some warrior's pony.

—Aint the Indian alive can get the jump on Sam Dawe. There's a whole bunch of prospectors in Yankton right now, fixin to head west soon as they can get supplied. The army is going to have to protect this, like it or not. Didn't I hear you was a prospector once?

—Went to California in 'forty-nine. By the time we got there, most of the good pickin was already picked. Made a little money sellin pants to miners, but most I got out of it was this lame foot.

—You ought to know your way around a gold vein, anyhow. That's why I come, to give you a chance to throw in with us. You're the kind a fella we're lookin for, somebody knows how to find gold.

Dawe fetched a tattered newspaper clipping out of his pocket and handed it to Eb.

—My sister back east cut this out of a paper called *The New York Times*. Says it wasn't just Custer. Prospectors been in there under this fella Gordon and they found the same thing—gold.

Eb turned the cutting to the light and read that the Gordon party had successfully prospected in the Black Hills before being ushered to Fort Laramie by Captain John Mix of the U.S. Army, who had orders to keep miners out of the Black Hills. Before Gordon was taken into custody, he had found gold aplenty. Eb read aloud:

—They sank twenty-five prospect holes and struck gold in every instance. From the grassroots to the bed of the rock they found numerous gold and silver-bearing quartz lodes, and the specimens Mr. Eph Witcher has brought back are pronounced very rich. The party never saw an Indian while in the Hills.

Dawe seized the clipping back as though it were the key to a bank vault.

—Now, y'see? This is what folks are readin back east. If we don't skedaddle up to them hills, come summer this whole territory is goin to be flooded with fellas from New York and Chicago that aint et a square meal since the panic of 'seventy-three. Most of 'em will stage through Yankton. We got the drop on 'em because we're here and they aint.

—I don't expect Cora would take to this scheme.

—Surely you aint goin to let a woman run ye, Eb? She don't wear pants, last I seen. If she objects, you point at the stove and tell her to mind her own business.

—I'll take it up with Cora, see what she has to say. She's tired of all the traipsin around we been doin, wants to set still in one place.

—Aint nobody asked her to go traipsin. You do the prospectin, she can sit home and figure how to spend all that gold we're goin to find.

Eb didn't tell Cora about it until supper. He waited until she finished spooning beans onto his plate and the boys said grace, their identical heads bowed like chickens over a scatter of oats. Then Cora had to tell him about Bernadine Hagel, a neighboring woman who got up one morning and packed a valise and took the stage to Yankton to catch a steamboat back east, leaving her husband and six children to fend for themselves. When she was through, he cleared his throat.

—Samson Dawe says they found gold in the Black Hills.

—Who found gold?

—Custer.

—What was Custer doing in the Black Hills? Those hills belong to the Sioux by treaty.

—The government sent him to have a look-see.

—That doesn't make it right. The government is supposed to keep white settlers away from there, not invite them in.

—It's goin to be hard to keep folks away, now that they know there's gold up there. Thing like this can turn into a stampede. What you want is to be the first up there, ahead of the pack. Get the easy pickings before it's mined out and you have to turn to hydraulickin and knock down a mountain to find a solitary nugget.

—You're not thinking about going prospecting there. The Sioux won't allow it.

—I'm not thinkin a thing just yet, Cora. Samson says there's a bunch of prospectors gettin together. He wants me to throw in with them because I got experience in California.

—Sounds like one of Samson's no-good schemes to me.

—Anyway, I got a week to think it over. If I was to hit on a real strike, we could live like civilized people.

—We do live like civilized people.

—I could provide better for you and the boys.

—If it's us you're thinking of, you'll keep your scalp attached to your head, Eb Paint. That way the boys won't have to say their father died trying to snatch gold off Indian land.

—That aint how most folks see it.

—We're not most folks. We ought to know better. The Sioux were given those hills by the Laramie Treaty. Plain as day, spelled out in black and white.

—That deal was signed before anybody knew there was gold up there.

—Yes, and it means that if there's gold there, it belongs to the Indians.

—They don't care two whoops for gold.

—Then leave the gold where it is and let them be.

—Cora, that gold is goin to get got. If it aint me that gets it, it'll be fellas like Samson Dawe gettin rich and once they have the money, they'll run this territory. Fellas that aint struck it rich won't have no more say in what goes on than a chipmunk.

They argued for a week. Eb had the gold fever as bad now as when he'd struck out for California as a boy of nineteen. Cora tried to remind him that all he brought back from California was a lame foot but he was not in the mood to listen. When he couldn't persuade her with his own arguments, he turned to the popular press. One evening after the boys were asleep he read to her from the Yankton *Press and Dakotaian*, which damned the Laramie Treaty that had handed the Black Hills to the Sioux in the strongest possible language. "This abominable compact is now pleaded as a barrier to the improvement and development of one of the richest and most fertile sections in America. What shall be done with those Indian dogs in our manger? They will not dig gold or let others do it."

—Indian dogs? How can you bring that filth into our house?

—It aint filth. It's right here in the newspaper.

—And you with a wife with Sioux blood standing right before your eyes. Shame on you.

Eb would listen neither to reason nor to anger. He would lower his head and let Cora say her piece and when she was done he would be as unmoved as ever.

Samson Dawe had lit a strange light in Eb's pale eyes, so that for the first time Cora could imagine how it was that Eb Paint had crossed a continent to California in 'forty-nine. At times now he reminded her of Augustus Connell, with that same streak of madness. Connell was God-addled; with Eb it was gold. Before them she had married Hobart Landry, who could not resist the beat of the war drums. Men liked to think of themselves as sensible creatures in comparison with her sex but from her experience, if there was any steadiness to be found in a family it was provided by the woman. She had always thought Eb the most calm and reasonable of men; now it was as though he had lost his mind overnight. Gold fever in this manifestation appeared to her as a disease as virulent as the smallpox, because a man struck down with it would wreck just about anything in his path for gold. Finally she was reduced to pleading for him to postpone his departure.

—Can't it wait until summer?

—No, it can't, woman. Can't y'see, that's the whole point? To get there first.

To finance the expedition, Eb sold what was left of his freight business except for one mule team and a wagon to haul the prospecting gear to the Black Hills. When Cora objected, he argued that the freight business was dying anyway, what with the railroads poking into more and more corners of the territory. He left Cora a hundred dollars to cover expenses for herself and the boys until he returned and invested the rest in a partnership with Samson Dawe and six other men, each holding equal shares in the El Dorado Prospecting & Mining Company. It was little consolation to Cora that each man insured his life with the Missouri Valley Life Insurance Company out of Leavenworth: In the event that Eb was killed by Indians or died of other causes, she was to receive one thousand dollars.

The night before he left, Eb tried to reach up under her shift. Cora would not allow it. They spent a sleepless night lying back to back, wrapped in silent, unyielding anger. An hour before dawn, Ezra cried and Cora took him into their bed, where the boy lay like a reproach between them. When Eb harnessed the mules and left, she did not give him the satisfaction of weeping.

Eb had been gone barely a week when a band of about two hundred Sioux from the Spotted Tail Agency came down to attack the Ponca south of Fort Randall. The commander at the fort decided to leave a party of woodcutters and the fort's herd of cattle unprotected and to set out in pursuit of the raiding Sioux. When the warriors saw the cavalry ride away from the fort, they quickly changed their objective. The troopers were slowed by the small cannon they had in tow; the Sioux baited them, laughing and baring their buttocks just out of range to lead the soldiers on until they were a half dozen miles south of the fort. Then they rode over a hill, peeled away to the west, and circled back to steal the unguarded cattle. They might have gotten away with it except that driving the cattle slowed their war ponies down enough for the troopers to catch up to them in the wooded country directly across the Missouri River from the Paint homestead.

Eli and Ezra were helping their mother dig the garden when they heard shots fired and the boom of a little three-pound cannon echoing across the river. Before Cora could shoo them back, the boys ran up a little rise overlooking the river and flopped on their bellies to watch the battle. Cora would have ordered them in immediately, but the skirmish was far away and they seemed in no danger. She watched anxiously from the kitchen window as she peeled potatoes, ready to dart out and snatch them to safety if the battle came any closer.

The Spotted Tail chief led his warriors into a stand of thick timber in a little canyon, with cover from the trees where they could fire at the troopers without being seen. The boys saw several soldiers tumble from their mounts, including one who had his foot caught in the stirrup and was dragged away by his panicked horse. The cavalry mounted three charges on the Indians in the timber, and three times they were driven back. Their only effective weapon against the well-concealed warriors was the cannon, but once they had fired a half dozen shots they ran out of ammunition. The Sioux crept through the woods to outflank the cavalrymen and the troopers were taking it on all sides from the concealed warriors. The Wagon Box Fight in Wyoming had taught the Sioux that to charge bluecoats armed with Henry repeating rifles was suicide; instead they remained hidden, picking off soldiers with accurate fire from their old needle guns.

The battle turned when some of the troopers, who had taken shelter in a log cabin that was under construction, found a keg of heavy-cut nails. They loaded the three-pound cannon with the nails and fired off a charge that stripped the young foliage from the cottonwoods, making a sound like a great reaper tearing through the timber. The frightened Spotted Tail warriors ran like deer, leaving the cattle behind. As they fled, a wild shot from one of the needle guns carried across the river and shattered the doorframe of the cabin. Cora ran outside, grabbed both boys from their vantage point, and dashed with them back to the house, where she turned the big wooden table on its side for protection from more stray bullets. She threw herself on top of her sons, determined to stop a bullet with her own body if necessary. They wiggled and squirmed, wanting to get back to watch the skirmish, but Cora would not relent until long after the firing ended. When she let them up, the boys wanted to dart back outside to see what had happened, but Cora refused to allow them even to open the door until near dusk, when she had to go out to milk the cows while the boys fed the chickens and pigs.

The next day Cora paid the ferryman to take them across the river to explore the woods where the skirmish had taken place. The boys hoped to find dozens of arrows but both sides had fought with rifles, and all they discovered were a few empty cartridges and some flattened chunks of lead, which they dug out of the trees with the point of a pocketknife. Still, they could crouch in a grove of ash and maple and imagine what it had been like with the bullets whizzing through the branches, the acrid odor of gunpowder in the air, the war cries of the Sioux and the moans of the troopers. Cora had never seen the boys so excited, but the incident added to her store of bitterness toward Eb. What if one of them had been struck by a bullet while he was away? What would he say then? That it was all worth it for a few dollars' worth of gold dust?

Even before the early birds of the El Dorado Prospecting & Mining Company out of Yankton arrived in the Black Hills, white prospectors were pouring into the territory. Some were striking it rich, panning for flecks of gold the size of a pinpoint in streams and creek beds from Belle Fourche to Rapid City. If the hills did not yield nuggets the size of turkey eggs, an industrious prospector willing to squat all day in a cold stream could still pan out five dollars an hour and some could find more underground. Already the Black Hills were pocked with shafts ten feet deep dug with pick and shovel. Prospectors were building sluice runs of four or five consecutive wooden sluices lined with riffles designed to catch gold dust so fine that the favored pouch to store it in was a bull's scrotum, because the cloth did not exist that was woven so fine the gold would not sift through.

For the men of the El Dorado company, the trouble started almost before they rode out of Yankton, and it started with Samson Dawe, who got crosswise of all the other members of the party. After two months traipsing from claim to claim with little success, Dawe's quarrel with Jeb Enochs grew so bitter that Dawe said he would rather prospect alone than put up with Enochs for another day. He took a horse and two mules and struck out on his own, still swearing at Jeb over his shoulder as he departed. The others watched Dawe ride off to the southwest and shrugged; the man went against the grain. Four days later, Enochs himself stumbled across Dawe's body while they were searching for unclaimed slices of land north of the Lost Mining District. The Sioux warriors who killed Dawe had left his scalp intact but severed his arms and legs and crisscrossed them next to his body. Eb understood what they were trying to do: if Samson Dawe should make it as far as the Happy Hunting Ground, he was so maimed that he would be unable to hunt. Enochs made up his mind that day that it was time to return to Yankton. Wilfred Starkey decided to go with him, leaving only five members of the original company to carry on. On a frigid morning in late November, Martin Frackleton tried to climb onto a frisky horse that did not want be ridden and was thrown onto a sheet of ice. The fall broke his neck and Frackleton was dead by the time the others reached him. Two weeks later, Barney LaRhett died of dysentery, which was as common as theft in the crowded mining camps. Eb sat in his white tent and struggled to compose his weekly letter to Cora:

My dearest Cora,

Have worked south 3 mile from spot where I last rote. Going is steep. Riding down sloap we had to get off and lead the horses, which all skined their knees and the pack mules worse. Didn't expect such high mountins as they call them the Black Hills after all, but they are mountins all right. Set up a sluice run here and like to broke our backs at the shovel, took maybe forty dollars of dust out of the riffles the first week but it is hard going. If she don't improve will move to another claim a mile down the creek. There is more and more prospecters poring in here the livelong day, pretty soon there won't be room for one more pick and shovel. Give my love to yourself and the boys.

Eb

Cora tossed the letter into the stove in disgust. If it was love Ebenezer Paint felt, then he should be at home, not gallivanting about the Black Hills in hot pursuit of his own demise. Of the deaths of Samson Dawe, Martin Frackleton, and Barney LaRhett, Eb had said not a word, but Cora heard the news anyway from relatives of the dead men. She tried to picture him returning to her and found that she could not, nor could she imagine him dead. The boys were so young that he was already a vague figure to them, half-remembered and growing less substantial by the day.

Eb and the Halbert brothers, Ned and Tom, soldiered on until cold and snow made prospecting impossible. Then they began to work underground, tunneling and shoring up shafts that might begin to yield significant gold once it was warm enough to work the mines. Eb was careful after his experience in California; Ned and Tom were not. They tunneled in haste and several tons of gravel collapsed on them. Ned managed to dig his way out; Tom did not. It took Ned and Eb working together two days to recover Tom's body.

Alone in his tent south of Deadwood, Eb smoked his pipe and considered his prospects. His crippled foot hurt more with every passing day, he had angered Cora and he had little to show for it. He wanted to return to the homestead on the Missouri but he did not want to go back empty-handed. Finally, he struck on a scheme; during the summer and into the fall, some miners had taken as much as thirty thousand dollars' worth of gold dust out of a single claim. Eb had been unable to light upon such a lode but it might be possible to convince a newcomer that he had; all it would take was a little ingenuity. He moved three miles farther south, staked his claim, and proclaimed its brilliant future with placards posted at all four corners: the El Dorado Rainbow. Three weeks later, he sold the Rainbow mine to a Chicago newspaperman turned prospector for the sum of one thousand dollars. He would not return home empty-handed.

. . .

Cora was hanging out the wash when she spotted his mule team a mile off. The boys saw the wagon too and went pelting off to greet their father for the first time in nearly a year. Cora stuck to her task. She heard the wagonwheels creak, the shouts as the twins climbed down from the wagon bed, his boots as he limped to join her. On an impulse she spun and slapped his face.

—That was for leaving your wife and children.

—I didn't leave nobody.

—Yes, you did. You went to a place where all those other men managed to get themselves killed. You did it with me begging you to stay. If you plan to take off again, you'd best stay gone, because we will not be here when you get back.

—My prospectin days are over. Sold the last claim for a thousand dollars and will never stake another. I did my damnedest but it wasn't enough.

—I could have told you that before you left and spared us all a deal of trouble. I thought I had married a man who had a lick of sense. You told me a long time ago that you learned in California that prospecting for gold was a fool's game.

—I know I should a listened. But a man gets a dream in his head, it aint easy to ignore.

—It's going to take me a very long time to forget this, Eb Paint. And longer to forgive.

The twins were more welcoming. Eli listened, Ezra did the questioning:

—Did you strike gold, Pa?

—Some. Not enough to make us rich.

—Did you fight any Indians?

—Nary a one, though the Sioux did catch up to our old neighbor Sam Dawe. They left him a awful mess.

—Did they scalp him?

—Nope. But they cut off his arms and legs.

Cora interrupted.

—Ebenezer Paint! You cut it out now or you'll have them terrified of Indians.

Ezra had a story of his own.

—We had a Indian fight right across the river. The troopers from the fort were chasing the Spotted Tail and the Sioux got into them woods and they was shootin and a bullet hit the door and Ma threw us down under the table and laid on top of us so we wouldn't get kilt.

Eb looked up at Cora.

—Is that so?

—Yes. The cavalry went out chasing the Ponca and the Sioux came in and tried to drive off the cattle herd from the fort. They killed five or six soldiers before someone loaded nails in the cannon and scared them off.

—You didn't write me about that.

—I didn't want to worry you. I figured you had enough to worry about.

Cora was still angry but that night she welcomed him in her bed and into her body. She had been too long alone, missed him too much to do otherwise. The next morning, she was not surprised when he announced that they were going to pick up stakes again and move to the Belle Fourche River at the western edge of Dakota Territory, just north of the Black Hills.

—That's ranch country, Cora. The wide-open spaces. We can buy some cattle, fatten them up on government grass and sell beef on the hoof to all those hungry miners down in the Black Hills.

She was too weary to resist. A month later, they had purchased a homestead relinquishment on Hay Creek just west of the Belle Fourche River, with a broad hay meadow and a ridge to the north and west to cut the gales of the worst winter blizzards. By the fall of 1877, there were enough settlers along the river to open a schoolhouse four miles from the Paint homestead. Eli and Ezra plowed through the first and second readers but in the spring of 1878

Eb lost most of the calf crop to a late spring blizzard and when it was time for them to go to school the next fall he didn't have the money to buy new shoes for their growing feet. Cora spent the winter cooped up indoors with them, giving them lessons in reading and ciphers herself.

By the following spring, Eb felt he was beginning to get the hang of the cattle business. He had a good bunch of healthy calves and he was able to sell one of his two purebred Hereford bulls for a decent profit, enough to buy new shoes for the boys and to lay in sufficient staples to take the family through another winter.

During the long winters by the fire, Eb told stories. He told the boys about Lucian Quigley and running a storeboat on the Mississippi River, about joining the 'forty-niners in the Gold Rush to California and getting his foot crushed by a falling redwood tree. He told of watching two vaqueros, one a Mexican and one a freed slave like Lucian, fight a duel with twenty-foot Australian kangaroo-hide whips.

—The Mexican, he lost an eye and the other fella, he almost lost somethin worse than a eye when the Mexican caught him right between the legs with that whip, sliced him wide open. My friend Virgil Saleen, he got sick and couldn't watch no more but it didn't matter because the fight was over. Somebody passed up a bottle of tequila and the two of 'em sat down together and passed that jug back and forth until they was drunk as skunks and then the sawbones went to work on them. Mexican lost the eye but the rest of what wounds they had was sewed up. Somebody said they was both back workin cattle in a week and they was best friends after that. Anyhow, that's when I decided to get myself a bullwhip. I worked it and worked it until one day I got Virgil to stand with a cigar in his mouth and I popped it right out from twenty feet away without touchin him, only Virgil wet his pants so we didn't try that trick no more. I figure it's always better to settle a argument with a whip than a gun. Somehow, a whip seems to scare a man more—fellas that aint afraid of dyin don't want to get all cut up. All the muleskinners and bullwhackers we get workin out here, plenty of them handy with a whip, so it pays to learn it your own selves.

In the spring, Eb set up a row of tin cans on fenceposts and spent hours showing the boys how to use a bullwhip. They were taught that a muleskinner could kill a horsefly on a mule's ear without touching the animal, that the best skinners never actually hit an animal with a whip because whip cuts drew flies and infections; the purpose was strictly to get the animal's attention. Ezra had trouble getting the hang of the bullwhip but he was a far better shot with Eb's Whitworth. Despite the awful kick of the old rifle, he was accurate with it up to a thousand yards. Eli could never top Ezra as a marksman but he went at the whip with grim determination; after a week he could make it pop like a firecracker and hit the tin cans nine times out of ten.

✥ CHAPTER 12 ✥

On a hot July morning in 1880, Eb harnessed the team to the buckboard at sunrise and took Cora to call on Alvah Harrison, a neighbor with an ailing wife and a pair of Hampshire shoats to sell. Before they left, Eb made a list of the day's jobs for Eli and Ezra: They were to cut and trim a half dozen lengths of lodgepole pine to replace the corral poles splintered the night before when lightning spooked a bull and he turned the old timbers to kindling. First they had to muck out the corral and then get the new poles up and lash them in place with rawhide strips. Then they were to take the hoe to the weeds in Cora's vegetable patch and pump a dozen buckets of water from the well and tote it to water her turnips, carrots, and potatoes. Once they had done all that, it would be time for the evening chores if Eb and Cora were not yet back. Before the wagon was out of sight, the boys went to work with hatchets and in half an hour they had a dozen lengths of lodgepole pine stripped of their sparse branches and ready to rebuild the shattered corral fence. Before the rails went up, they forked steaming clumps of straw and manure from the corral, releasing hundreds of no-see-um flies that flew into their noses and mouths and a ripe, choking, sulfurous odor. After two hours Ezra stopped and leaned on his pitchfork.

—I could use a dip in the swimming hole.

—So could I, but we got a awful pile of work to do.

—I aint saying a long dip. We jump in, get cold and wet, get back to work. That's all.

Eli lugged another forkful and lifted his hat to wipe away the sweat that was running into his eyes.

—We better catch them horses and go quick. Pa will hide us if we aint done these chores when he gets back.

—He never hides us. He only *says* he's goin to hide us.

—Just the same. If it aint him then Ma will be sending you for a willow switch and you know she'll use the danged thing.

They packed biscuits and ham for lunch, grabbed halters from the barn and caught the fat white mare and the big old bay gelding. They rode bareback down to the river, their legs stretched wide by the broad backs of their mounts, their britches sweaty and matted with hair, their pace no quicker than a slow walk. A mile along there was a sharp bend in the river and at the apex of the bend a deep hole the water had carved out beneath the roots of a tall, spreading cottonwood. They left the horses to graze and stripped off their clothes, climbed naked to the highest bough they could reach and swung off in unison, dropping into the river in a glorious double cannonball that sent arcs of clear white water flying into the air. They climbed the tree again and again, plunging headfirst, doing bellyflops, knifing into the water and diving as deep as they could go, trying to find the muddy bottom but never quite reaching it.

Eli had no idea how long the three Sioux boys had been watching. They simply appeared, as though the dust had given them birth, slender brown twigs sitting all in a row astride the spine of a spavined, slat-ribbed old horse. One by one they dismounted, stripped off breechclouts and moccasins, swung off the same high limb, plunged into the water and came bobbing up with their long black hair plastered to their necks, solemn and wordless until Ezra spoke to them in Lakota. Then the five of them spent the afternoon climbing high in the tree to plummet into the water, diving under to see who could stay down the longest, racing upstream against the current, arms brown and white flailing in the water, splashing one another with long arcs of water that flashed rainbow colors in the sunlight.

In late afternoon, with the shadows beginning to lengthen, they flopped on the riverbank, drying in the sun, talking softly in Lakota. Ezra was almost fluent, Eli could get by but he let Ezra do the talking anyway. The boys were *Ite Sica*, Bad Faces. The oldest was Spotted War Bonnet and his friends were Crossing Rivers and Bad Heart Bull. Their band under Chief Lone Feather spent winters at the Rosebud Indian Agency and every spring, with the Indian agent's permission, left the agency to hunt, sometimes working their way north along the White River and then west along the Belle Fourche, sometimes riding east to the Dakota River and then north all the way to Devils Lake.

When Eli and Ezra got back to the homestead, it was well after dark. Eb had returned to find the chores undone, the corral poles still down, and the unwatered vegetable garden dry and withering in the sun. Ezra saw the coal-oil lantern from a half mile off and cooked up a long and elaborate excuse for their absence, which involved chasing a runaway calf and getting lost on the way back. Eli went into the house first while Ezra fed the horses. Eb was waiting.

—Where were you?

—I don't know. Wherever Ezra says we were.

Eb laughed but he still reached for the saddlecinch hanging on a nail by the door.

—Bend over and let down your britches. You've got a lickin coming.

—All right, Pa. It don't matter. It was pretty near worth it.

After that day at the swimming hole, Spotted War Bonnet, Crossing Rivers, and Bad Heart Bull spent so much time around the Paint cabin that Eb said he hadn't realized he had five sons, not two. The boys rode, hunted, fished, and swam together, and when Eli and Ezra had work to do, the Sioux boys pitched in and helped. War Bonnet was the one boy who could wrestle Eli without losing. He was older and a bit heavier and adept at Sioux wrestling tricks Eli had never seen before—but he held his own mostly because he was possessed of the same determination and unbreakable will; if he couldn't quite get the better of Eli, neither could Eli defeat him. They would wrestle each other to exhaustion because neither would give up. War Bonnet's friend Bad Heart Bull disdained wrestling; he liked to draw, so Cora got him paper and pencils and he drew pictures of the five of them on horseback riding after deer and buffalo and portraits of the boys in a group, seated around a fire in a tipi.

Two summers after they first met, Spotted War Bonnet rode by one morning to say the Ite Sica were about to break camp and follow the Dakota River north to Devils Lake. Eb was away again, receiving cattle for one of the big outfits to the north. Once again, Cora was angry with him: If he could be forever "journey-bound," then so could she. As soon as War Bonnet brought the news that the band was leaving, she drove the buckboard to their camp and spoke with War Bonnet's grandmother, Iron Cloud. The wars against the white man had left Spotted War Bonnet an orphan; Iron Cloud had taken him into her own spacious tipi and was raising him herself. If there was room for them, Cora told the old woman, then she and her sons would like to travel with the band to Devils Lake so that the boys could learn more of the Ite Sica ways. Iron Cloud smiled her toothless smile: It would do her old heart good to have so much company.

Eb had taken on two reliable cowpunchers to help run the ranch, Luke Golding and a man who called himself Kansas Bob. Cora told them she was taking the boys to Sioux Falls to visit her old friends and that she was leaving the cowpokes to look after the ranch. She didn't dare mention that she was taking the boys on a hunting trip with the Indians. Cora chose two horses each for the three of them and prepared light kits for their journey. The note she left for Eb told the truth; by the time he read it, it would be too late for him to follow, and in any case, Eb had never discouraged her efforts to teach their sons about the life of her mother's people.

They broke camp on the first day of *wipa zunka wa'ste wi,* the moon of Juneberries, at the hour Iron Cloud called *antpa niya,* when the first glimmer of light strokes the prairie. The women struck the tipis; within minutes they were down and the lodge-poles transformed into travois or pony drags to carry all their belongings. The more agile young boys, Eli and Ezra among them, were sent to round up the ponies. Dogs barked and quarreled over stray scraps of meat, ponies freed from their hobbles bucked and kicked. Within an hour the horses had been subdued and the drags loaded and they were on their way north, strung out across the prairie in a long, dusty caravan. Cora rode her trusty white horse while the boys darted around bareback on Indian ponies, ranging far out from the main party with War Bonnet and Bad Heart Bull, Eats Ponies, Crossing Rivers, and Red Horse, hunting small game for the pot with bows and Eb's old scattergun.

Each night when they made camp, it took the women a little more than an hour to set up the tipis again. Cora learned to help with the task, but her fingers were never as deft as those of the Indian women. At night in Iron Cloud's tipi, they slept like the spokes of a wheel, in a circle with their heads to the embers of the fire in the center. The women, exhausted from the labors of the day, always fell asleep as soon as they stretched out on their blankets; Eli and Ezra and War Bonnet stayed awake as long as they could, watching the slow-wheeling drift of the stars framed by the cone of the lodgepoles high above their heads. Then it was light and the fire was going again and Iron Cloud was at her kettle muttering to herself, something between a chant and a monologue. At first Eli and Ezra thought her half-mad; then they began to catch the glint in her hooded eyes, the toothless smile that made them understand that what they took for madness was the sly wisdom of an old woman who has seen too much and forgotten nothing.

By early July, the month Iron Cloud called *canpa'sa wi*, or the Moon of Red Cherries, the Paint boys were hobbling around because their old boots had worn to nothing. The soles flapped loose, the heels came off, they pinched growing feet until the toes had to be cut open. Iron Cloud made careful tracings of their feet on deerhide and cut moccasins that fit like a second skin, decorated with porcupine quills and colored a brilliant royal blue with a dye made by crushing the blue petals of spiderwort flowers. Ezra and

Eli wore blue moccasins the rest of that summer and into the autumn, feeling light and swift as antelope.

Traveling with the Ite Sica were a dozen Minneconjou including Fears Hawk, a warrior now forty years old who had taken part in the Custer Fight. On the hottest night of the summer, Eli and Ezra listened by the fire with the other boys as Fears Hawk told what happened in *Pehin Hanska Ktepi*, the year they killed Long Hair on the Greasy Grass, the river the whites called the Little Bighorn. Fears Hawk took a long, solemn puff on his pipe, gazed up at the stars, and began:

—You should know the truth about what happened on the Greasy Grass. Many lies are told, but you young ones can tell people what really happened because you heard it from one who was there. I have known white men who say that we set a great ambush for Custer but that is not true at all. It was Long Hair who surprised us after we had a fight with Crook on the Rosebud. We beat Crook and it was a great victory. After that we thought the soldiers would leave us alone. There were dances and some of us danced all night. We danced until our feet bled. It was light when I went to bed. I was still asleep early in the afternoon when I heard women screaming, saying that the bluecoats were coming. There was no time even to paint myself for battle. I pulled on my shirt and grabbed my coup stick and my rifle and rushed out of the tipi. All the women and children were running and screaming and the men were trying to get them out of the camp and up into the hills before the soldiers came because we knew what the bluecoats would do: They always killed the women and the young ones first before the warriors could find their guns or catch their horses. It was the biggest camp we ever had, maybe three thousand tipis all along the river there. At one end of the camp I could see the soldiers had already set two or three tipis on fire and there were dozens of warriors from all over the camp heading that way and I could hear shots being fired. I had trouble catching my horse but then my cousin came along on horseback and he was leading a second horse, so I rode that one and we went to the fight as fast as we could ride, but we got there too late. The soldiers were running through the woods and up a hill, away from the fight. We found out later it was not Custer who ran, it was Major Reno with his men. We were about to chase them when someone said soldiers were coming to attack the other side of the camp, so we let Reno go and raced back the other way to fight Custer. Now we had hundreds of men on horseback ready for the battle and some on foot still trying to catch their horses. Everywhere you looked you could see warriors going that way, running to the battle. I saw the *Shyela* Yellow Nose and I saw Two Moon and Gall and Runs the Enemy but I did not see Crazy Horse, although I know he was there. We went up through a ravine to get behind Custer and his men and when we got there we could already see many of the bluecoats were dead and one company was trying to get back to another company, the men on the white horses. The white horse men were firing too much and we had to retreat and find another way to charge them. All around you could hear people shouting: *Hoka-hey! Hoka-hey!* and blowing the eagle-bone whistles. *Hoka-hey! Hoka-hey!* A soldier on a sorrel horse tried to run and for a long time it looked like he would get away, but then he was hit and went down. *Hoka-hey! Hoka-hey!* The soldiers with the white horses had them tied together in fours but the horses went crazy with all the gunfire and the soldiers couldn't hold them. The horses ran down toward the river and our people caught most of them before they could cross. There were clouds of dust everywhere and sometimes you could only tell where the fight was by the dust. My horse was very fast and I ran right at a soldier firing from his knees and touched him on the shoulder with my coup stick and rode right on through to the other side, where a *Shyela* lifted his lance to show that he saw what I had done. *Hoka-hey! Hoka-hey!* We saw Yellow Nose ride in and grab one of the flags from the soldiers and gallop away with it. He was very brave, Yellow Nose. He made us all brave, and we attacked from every side. *Hoka-hey! Hoka-hey!* The soldiers were falling one after another like trees in a high wind. Some of them fought very well and some were so frightened that they shot themselves with their own guns. When it was over, all the soldiers were dead and our women were stripping their bodies. We lost many warriors too. Twenty, maybe thirty. Some of our people brag that they counted coup on Custer or they saw Long Hair with slashes in his arms and thighs. It isn't true. We didn't even know

Custer was in the fight until later. We thought it was Crook, that we killed the great General Crook.

Fears Hawk paused for breath and relit his pipe.

—It was a great victory and we danced again to celebrate but because of that victory we lost everything. After that the soldiers were everywhere and always there were more coming. They chased us and we never had time to rest or hunt. The little ones had empty bellies and the women were crying and asking why we had nothing for the children to eat. Finally we had no choice: If we wanted to eat in the winter, we had to come in to the agencies and beg the white man to feed us. We have to ask permission from the white man even to go on a little hunt like this, killing geese and ducks because the white man killed all the buffalo just for the hides and left the bodies of our brother *tatanka* to rot on the prairie, feeding no one but the crows and the buzzards. Now we live only for our children. Someday, there will be no more white men on this land. They will all vanish like the snow. This will happen, in the same way that Custer died on the Greasy Grass.

Fears Hawk fell silent. An owl hooted, bats darted out of the darkness chasing invisible things that whirred in the night air. When the fire crackled, Ezra jumped as though he had heard a shot and the Ite Sica boys laughed because Fears Hawk's tale had made him nervous. When they returned to the tipi, Cora and Iron Cloud were asleep but Ezra and Eli lay awake a long while, whispering between themselves, wondering how much of what Fears Hawk said was true and whether whites like themselves would one day vanish from the prairie like winter snow. In their dreams for months after they saw the whirling dust of the battlefield on the Greasy Grass and heard the eaglebone whistles and the war cries of the Sioux: *Hoka-hey! Hoka-hey!*

The Ite Sica camped for more than six weeks at Devils Lake. The hunting was good and there were fresh duck eggs to eat every morning. The boys swam in the lake and practiced with their bows, exploring the country on horseback while Cora stayed close to the camp. One hot, dry day followed another and for a time it almost seemed they could go on like this forever, hunting and swimming and lazing around the camp. They could see the sky change to a deeper shade of cobalt; the nights were cool, birds were beginning to fly south. Soon it would be time for the band to return to the agency and for Ezra and Eli to go back to the Belle Fourche with Cora. For now there was only the hunting and fishing in the day and the campfires at night, Lone Feather and Fears Hawk telling tales of battles and daring expeditions to steal horses from the hated Crow.

On a cool evening in late August, the boys returned from hunting to find the camp had white visitors. They were five men in African pith helmets and high laced boots, part of a crew surveying a road from Red Lake in Minnesota west to Fort Clark. Ezra and Eli trotted into the camp and nearly found themselves in the midst of a skirmish when the surveyors spotted them, decided they must be white children who had been kidnapped by the Ite Sica and grabbed their rifles to free the twins from their captors. Fears Hawk and two dozen warriors surrounded the surveyors, who were persuaded to put down their rifles. Lone Feather motioned for Ezra to join him and stepped forward to parley with the leader of the surveyors, with Ezra translating.

—Tell him you are hunting with us and that your mother is here and we did not steal you.

Ezra repeated Lone Feather's words in English. The surveyor stared: Ezra was an odd sight, a twelve-year-old white boy wearing a breechclout and blue moccasins, his long hair braided Sioux fashion, speaking Lakota as though it were his mother tongue. The surveyor listened in disbelief.

—How did you end up here? You sure these redskins didn't haul you off from someplace?

—They asked us if we wanted to go goose huntin, so we came. Me and my brother are friends with that boy over there, Spotted War Bonnet. We met him and others back where we got our homestead, on the Belle Fourche River. That's almost to Montana.

—The Belle Fourche is five hundred miles from here. Maybe more.

—Yep. We come a long way. We're headin back right soon. Ma wants us in school. We got to go to the fourth reader.

—You sure these savages aint holdin you prisoner?

—Nossir. Not a bit. We're havin the time of our lives, is what Ma says.

—Can one of you fetch her? We'd like to hear that from her. Hard to believe a white woman would take up with this bunch.

—Ma is part Minneconjou.

The surveyor turned to the other whites.

—Sounds like the mother is a half-breed squaw.

Eli went pelting off to Iron Cloud's tipi but Cora refused to come out. She was afraid the surveyors would do something rash, take her for a white woman and touch off a fight with some of the young Ite Sica. The surveyors had already lost interest: They didn't care how many half-breed Indians were traveling with the band. Both sides relaxed, Lone Feather offered to share some rabbit and goose and the white men squatted on their heels to eat next to the fire. One of them went rummaging in his kit and came back with two bottles of whiskey, which circulated between white and Sioux. Cora, watching from the shadows next to one of the tipis, saw the danger and whistled to the boys, who slipped away to join her.

—I want you two away from those men. They're drinking whiskey with those warriors and that never leads in any good direction. You come with me and we'll get to bed. War Bonnet too. You tell him Iron Cloud wants him in the tipi.

Late that evening, after four bottles of whiskey had been shared among the surveyors and the Ite Sica, the surveyors left in the company of a dozen of the younger Sioux, who went along to guide them back to their camp. It was just before dawn when Eli stepped outside the tipi to pee and saw the warriors who had accompanied the surveyors returning to camp with a wagon and a team of horses, all of them decked out in pith helmets and other bits and pieces of the clothing the surveyors had been wearing. Some of them were carrying shiny new Henry repeating rifles. The noise of their return roused Cora, who wanted to know why they had the white men's gear. Coyote Tooth, one of the young men in the pith helmets, spat on the ground near her moccasins.

—We traded buffalo robes for these things.

—But you had no buffalo robes when you left here.

Coyote Tooth laughed and ignored her. He was about to turn away when Lone Feather, who had emerged barefoot from his tipi, felled him with an enormous clout to the jaw.

—What have you done? You have put all of us in danger. Now tell the truth. What happened to the white men?

Lone Feather was standing over Coyote Tooth, holding a broad knife in his hand.

—They were drinking. They grew angry and shot at us, so we killed them.

Lone Feather kicked him hard in the stomach and turned on the others.

—You are fools. You will leave us now, all of you. You are no longer part of this band.

The young men did not argue. Within an hour they were gone, taking the white men's team and wagon with them as they rode north. By the time they left, the women were already striking the tipis. Lone Feather hoped to return to the reservation before someone discovered the dead white men and came after them, but sixty miles north of Yankton, the band was intercepted by a detachment of cavalry out of Fort Randall. The cavalry captain said the surveyors had been slaughtered and scalped and Lone Feather's band was responsible. Lone Feather refused to put the troopers on the trail of the young men. After a brief standoff, Lone Feather, Fears Hawk, and a half dozen others who had nothing to do with the killings were arrested, despite Cora's protests, and taken in chains to the prison in Yankton to be tried for the murder of the surveyors at Devils Lake.

By the time Cora returned to the Belle Fourche with Eli and Ezra, Eb was home again. He knew of the arrest of the Sioux and he knew that Cora and the boys had been with Lone Feather's band when the surveyors were murdered. He was furious; Cora didn't see what the fuss was about.

—When you get the urge to light out, you go. Not so much as a by-your-leave, not ever. The boys had a chance to learn about the way my mother's people live so we took it. I didn't want you to go off prospecting in the Black Hills. You didn't listen to a word.

—I won't stand for it. This is different. You went off with the Indians.

—I'm part Indian. Remember? So are your boys.

—I aint forgot none of that. Taint right, is all. Them surveyors gettin killed.

—We had nothing to do with that. Some very good men are in jail in Yankton right now and they had nothing to do with it either.

—They was there.

—Not when those men were killed, they weren't. It's wrong to put innocent men in prison and you know it.

Eb was so angry that he threw his hat on the ground, picked it up and stomped off to the corrals. The woman had the ability to render him tongue-tied and apoplectic; no matter what he said, she had an answer for it.

They fumed and feuded for a week. In the end, they seemed to wind down like spinning tops. Eb said he was married to the most bullheaded woman in the territory; Cora said there was never a man born so contrary or so set in his ways. Finally the night came when Cora allowed him under her shift, letting him know that she was weary of their squabbling.

A week later, they were at it again. It started over breakfast when Eb looked out over the Belle Fourche River and said he would miss seeing it in the morning.

—Miss it why?

—Because there's a chance in Fort Pierre I can't miss. The mines is usin heavier and heavier machinery, building big stamping mills and sinking shafts two thousand, three thousand feet down.

The machinery comes in over the Pierre Trail from the Missouri River, same way you come home with the boys. They's a big outfit or two haulin already but they's room for more. Somebody who knows how to outfit bullwhackers and muleskinners could do right well. We got enough here we could sell up, make a start.

—We've finally settled here. I thought we were building something. The boys have the school, the country is pretty as can be. I like it here. I thought you did too.

—I like it fine, only a man can't make no money runnin cattle unless he can put at least a thousand head on government grass.

—You've been all over this territory, Eb. You've run sawmills and freighted and run cattle and worked as a rep for other men and tried gold mining yourself. Don't you think you might have gotten farther if you had stayed at one thing?

—I always had a good reason to go. You see the size of the equipment they're freightin through Pierre, you'd see this is the best chance I ever had. The Homestake Mine alone needs thousands of tons and one outfit can't haul it all. You got Fred T. Evans and the Merchants Line but there's room for a shotgun freighter if a man knows what he's about.

—If you go, you go alone, Eb Paint. I'll stay here, keep the ranch going with the boys and a couple of cowpunchers. I'm not moving again.

A smart fellow who knew the freighting business could make good money hauling mining machinery from Pierre to the Black Hills— if he had the money to invest in dozens of wagons and animals, which Eb did not. When the trails were turned to a kind of gruel by spring rains, he hauled with six or eight teams of cloven-footed oxen hitched to a single heavily loaded wagon. When the trails were dry and hard, he moved freight with quick-footed mules, hauling to both the DeSmet and Homestake mines. The big freight companies moved eight-thousand-pound Blake crushers and hundred-pound stamps by the dozen. They took a ten-ton flywheel apart and moved it in sections. They hauled in equipment for an entire mill. They were earning three to five dollars per hundred pounds of goods hauled, but a small shotgun freighter like Eb Paint had to settle for the leftovers and at that he had to deal with the big outfits trying to force him out of business every chance they got. Still, it was the life he liked best, on the move, listening to the crack of the whips, the bellowing of the oxen, the curses of the whackers, hunkering down with their rough company at night and listening to tall tales while the fires crackled and beefsteaks sizzled in the pan. He missed Cora, he missed Eli and Ezra but soon the boys would be big enough to whack bulls or skin mules alongside their father.

Eb made it home in time for Christmas. He spent a week at the ranch, helped patch up the roof for winter, horsed around with the boys. He and Cora, tired of quarreling, spent a few tender nights in their narrow bed. On New Year's Day, 1883, he left before dawn. The weather was cold but dry, good freighting weather. Cora usually let him go with a peck on the cheek, but this time she felt an odd sense of foreboding. She held him for a long while, her arm locked around the back of his neck, her heart pumping. He promised to be back in the spring and rode out with a last wave to the boys.

At the end of February, Cora received a letter from a friend in Yankton. Lone Feather and Fears Hawk had been released on the basis of Cora's written testimony and the word of the respected Ite Sica woman Iron Cloud. The two men, thin and haunted from their ordeal, were allowed to return to live out their days at the Rosebud agency, where Lone Feather said that the only difference between life at the agency and life in prison was that on the reservation you could not see the chains that bound his people.

⫷ CHAPTER 13 ⫸

Cora rose early that morning in late March. Spring was in the air, meadowlarks along the fenceposts sang each to each, she could feel the dark weight of winter vanishing with the warmth of the rising sun. She boiled coffee, ate a little cornbread slathered with butter, winked at Eli when he tumbled out of bed with his eyes half-closed. She warmed more cornbread in a frying pan on the stove, handed it to him stuffed with six slices of bacon.

—Get on the outside of this and then you can do the chores.

—What about Ezra?

—He's a slugabed. He's going to miss a fine spring day. He'll do the evening milking alone. Be careful with Bess, get the hobbles on tight or she'll kick over your bucket.

—I know that, Ma. It only happens to Ez. She gets the better of him.

—But not you, is that it?

—Never.

Eli pulled on his boots and an old sheepskin jacket of Eb's that was only a bit too big for him, tugged his hat down to his ears and headed out to do the chores, a boy a week short of his thirteenth birthday with the wide shoulders and long-striding gait of a man. She could feel it coming, this impending manhood. It would be hard to hold them. Eb was talking already about putting the boys to work on the Pierre Trail after spring roundup. Cora thought it too soon for them to be with the teamsters, as rough a lot of men as you were likely to find. Let them grow a little first, help on the ranch, stay close to her. Perhaps that was all it was: In protecting them she was protecting herself from that jolt of departure, the day when they would go wandering off, journey-bound like all the Paints, leaving her to invite toothless Kansas Bob in for supper because she had no other company.

She opened the door and stepped out into March sunshine. The light bounced off the snowbanks, wrapping her in a lazy warmth as seductive as a feather pillow. It was not a day for indoor chores; she would have to find some reason to be out. It was a perfect washday except that it was a Thursday and she always did her wash on Wednesday. What then? Too early for gardening with the ground still wrapped in snow. There was Esther Harrison, who was ailing again. She could pay a call on the Harrison homestead, take the poor woman a couple of loaves of fresh-baked bread, perhaps help with some of her chores. She thought of asking Eli to harness the team or catch her old white horse but the roads would be a muddy mess. Better to go afoot on such a beautiful day, four miles there and four miles back, a pleasant stroll around the lake with the world turning to spring. She packed a basket of bread, tossed in a pound of churned butter and a half dozen jars of preserves; the Harrison woman had been too ill in the fall to do her canning.

Cora woke Ezra before she left, pointed to his breakfast getting cold on the table and set forth feeling virtuous and perfectly in harmony with this world. She hummed as she walked, skirting the small lake north of the Paint ranch before striking the trail that led downhill to the Harrison place in a swale to the northwest. There were redwing blackbirds on the frozen stalks of last year's cattails, circling hawks rode currents of breeze, a half dozen grazing antelope dotted a far hill. She listened to the meadowlarks and the trickle and rush of snowmelt on all sides, felt the basket light in her hand as she picked the driest path she could find. She was still a half mile away when Alvah Harrison saw her coming and rode out on a pale horse to greet her.

—What brings you all the way over here afoot, Mizz Paint?

—It's a fine day for a walk, so I thought I'd look in. How's the missus?

—Poorly, I'm sorry to say. She'll be happy to see you. Awful shame to see her this way. Used to be she was strong as an ox.

—Have faith, Alvah. She was strong before, she'll be strong again.

—I surely do hope so.

Inside the cabin, Esther Harrison lay under a beautiful quilt on the big brass bed the Harrisons had carted all the way from South Carolina. Cora had not seen the woman since Valentine's Day and in that short time Esther had simply wasted away. Once she had been a robust woman who was heavier than her husband by fifty pounds; now she looked hollow and gaunt, her lips dry and cracked and her brow feverish to the touch. Cora bustled about, trying to get Esther to eat something, tidying up her kitchen, opening curtains to let a little more light in the room. She tried to be cheerful but the most she could coax out of Esther was a wan smile. In midafternoon, with Esther fast asleep, Cora told Alvah it was high time she was getting back to the ranch. Alvah walked out with her, squinted up at a hazy sky, sniffed the air, noted that the breeze had picked up and shifted to the northwest.

—Storm comin.

—Don't be silly. On a beautiful day like this?

—She's comin all right. I can smell her. Maybe you ought to take a horse, get home quicker. Or hunker down with us until she passes.

—I'll be fine, Alvah. Even if there is a storm coming, I'll be home before it hits.

—You'd best step lively, then. She's comin quick. I'd feel a sight better if you'd take that horse. One of your boys can ride her back tomorrow.

—Muddy as it is, I'll get home as quick on foot. You look after Esther now, I'll come back in a few days to see how she's doing.

In the time it took Cora to walk the first half mile, the breeze had turned into a stiff northwest wind, the temperature had plummeted twenty degrees and the haze had darkened into threatening storm clouds. Cora shivered and chastened herself for having forgotten the way Dakota weather could shift from fair to foul in minutes. She looked back at the Harrison cabin, thought of turning back, rejected that notion as soon as she thought it. She did not want to leave the boys alone and in any case she would be home in less than an hour.

Within another half mile, the wind was so stiff it made her eyes water and the darkening sky began to spit snow. It was now well below freezing, and the mud puddles left from the morning melt wore a glaze of ice. She quickened her pace again, fighting down a rising panic as the stinging, isolated crystals of snow thickened into a real storm. *What a fool you are, Cora. What a fool. On horseback you'd be home by now. If this gets any worse, you'll be lucky not to freeze to death.* A horse would also have known the way back to the barn no matter how heavy the snow; already, Cora was having trouble seeing more than a few feet ahead. A trail that in bright sunshine seemed as familiar as her own kitchen now appeared alien and threatening. Was that the big cottonwood where the track bent to the south or the cottonwood that marked the western boundary of the big Tumbleweed outfit to the east? Why was that stand of ponderosa pine trees on her left when it should have been on her right? *Calm yourself, Cora. Calm down. Worst thing you can do now is to panic. You've been through worse. Yes, but when? Well, you must have been. Sometime.*

She could feel the beginnings of frostbite on her fingers and toes, her nose and ears and cheeks. Oh, my. It would take a while for her to thaw out after this. The boys would have to melt snow for her. She would have to start with her feet and hands in cold water and ease up to lukewarm water or the pain would be too much to bear. *Silly, silly woman. How did you get yourself into this fix?* She floundered on through deepening snow, now completely unsure of her direction. She calculated that she had been walking thirty minutes at least, so she ought to be coming to the lake at the north end of the ranch but she could see nothing at all now. The snow fell so hard that she could barely distinguish the air from the ground, the wind tore at her linsey-woolsey dress. She fought her way through a drift nearly as high as her waist, found herself going steeply downhill. *Yes, this must be the rise that leads down to the lake. Now if I can just bear left here and circle about a hundred yards that way, I can find the fence line and I'll be as good as home.*

The path leveled out and for the space of a few seconds the wind eased and she could see exactly where she was: a dozen feet out onto the thin ice of the lake. When she turned to make her way back to shore, she heard the ice crack as it gave way and she fell through, plunging nearly waist deep into frigid water. *Oh no. Oh no, you stupid woman. This is awful.* The brief respite in the storm had at least given Cora her bearings: she half-swam, half-walked to shore, breaking the ice ahead of her with her arms. As the storm renewed its fury, she found a weeping willow and tugged on its branches to pull herself out, weeping with the pain of her freezing legs. The skirt of her dress and her underthings were now solid ice, she had no feeling at all in her feet and she felt a sudden horror of losing her feet or her legs.

She wanted desperately to quit, to give up and lie down and let death take her. Somehow, she forced herself to keep walking, circling what should have been the edge of the lake, looking for the fence line. *Don't panic. Don't panic. Just find that old fence and you're as good as home and the boys can thaw you out.* It seemed that at least another thirty minutes had passed since she dragged herself out of the lake and still no fence. Perhaps the snow had drifted over the fence and she had crossed it without knowing? Or she had passed through the gate at the eastern edge of the ranch and she was almost to the cabin? Then where was the river? The river ought to have been near but there was nothing at all, just white and drifting white. She felt weighed down by an irresistible fatigue. There was no point going on like this, frozen solid to the waist. Best to lie down, rest a little, gather strength to go on. She stumbled onto a clear spot in the snow, sank to her knees and rolled over onto her side, wrapped the shawl around her as best she could, curled up and closed her eyes. A little rest and her strength would come back. Just a little time and she would get up and walk to the cabin and everything would be fine.

—*My fine strong boys. Eli and Ezra. So proud I am of both of you. You will know what to do, you will get your foolish mother out of this fix. I'm afraid I'm going to be under the weather for a time.*

Cora thought she heard someone coming, heard a voice at her side. Lifted her head, realized it was just the wind, let herself rest again.

Eb, Eb, Eb. If you could see your wife now. What a foolish woman I have been. I do love you, Eb, in spite of it all, I do. These last years have not always been easy, I know that. But I cared for you as for no other. I do love you, Eb.

Alvah Harrison found Cora's body the next morning. He had worried all night while the storm raged and set out shortly after dawn, rags tied around his eyes, squinting through the narrowest of slits at the glare of brilliant sunshine off white banks of snow. He saw what looked like a bundle of old clothes cast into a dry patch where the wind had scooped out the snow and rode up for a closer look. She was fifty feet north of the lake and appeared to have been circling back toward his cabin when she froze to death. She was curled up on her side like a child, a thumb oddly in her mouth, her curly hair frozen into ropy icicles. *By sweet Jesus, what a awful thing this is. She come to help my Esther and now look. Them boys has lost their mother.* Alvah dismounted to have a closer look but there was no doubt. Cora Paint was dead, had been at least twelve hours by the look of her. *At least the animals haven't been at her. Thank God for small mercies.*

In the distance, Alvah saw two riders picking their way through the snowbanks a mile off. The Paint boys, had to be. He spread his coat over Cora and rode to head them off: It wouldn't do for them to see their mother like this. From a quarter mile away he waved at them to stop. They sat their horses like born cowpunchers, calm. Their mother had gone missing but they weren't going to lose their heads, young as they were. Alvah trotted up to them, removed his hat.

—Boys, I've got some bad news. I found your ma back there a ways, froze to death. She left our place yesterday, wouldn't take a horse when I smelled that storm comin. I prayed all night that she made it through before it got too bad but it looks like she got lost around the lake and might've fell through the ice.

One of the boys, Alvah thought it was the one called Eli although there was no telling them apart, walked his horse forward a few paces. Alvah thought they would both go to bawling but this one was calm as a rock.

—We thought she had likely stayed over at your place but when she didn't come back this mornin we knew better. Where is she? We got to bring her home.

—I think it's best you don't see her like this. I thought I'd take her back to our place, get her thawed out so we can bury her proper.

—She's our ma. We'll take her home, Mr. Harrison. That's where she'd want to be.

—If you're sure about that, I'll help you. We'll ride to my place and hitch up the team. Easier to carry her on the sled.

The three of them retied the rags around their eyes against the glare, rode to where Cora's body lay curled up, thumb still in her mouth. Ezra dismounted and knelt beside her, pulled the coat off her to look, wrapped his arms around his mother and held her a long time. Eli sat on his horse, not saying a word. Alvah gazed at him but you could not read the boy, what it was doing to him. Alvah reached a hand out but Eli shook his head, not wanting to be touched.

—Just get the team and the sled, please, Mr. Harrison. Leave us be with her.

When Alvah returned, he found Ezra still holding his mother, Eli still on horseback. Both boys helped lift Cora's body onto the sled. Ezra climbed up beside her. Eli rode on ahead, leading Ezra's horse and not looking back. Alvah felt about as bad as a man could feel, blaming himself for not keeping her safe and dry in his cabin until it blew over. At the Paint ranch, they laid Cora out on the table in the kitchen. Alvah asked again if the boys were all right alone with her and left them to ride into Belle Fourche and fetch the undertaker, Oscar Nye. Before they left town, Alvah sent telegrams to Eb everywhere he might be found: to Pierre, Deadwood, and Lead.

It would take a week for a telegram to catch up with Eb; when a Methodist minister performed the service and Cora was laid to rest in the cemetery at Belle Fourche, Eb Paint was midway between Pierre and Lead with a bull-team caravan hauling mill implements to the Homestake Mine. He was in a hot bath in the back of a livery stable in Lead when the telegraph boy found him and by the time he arrived on the Belle Fourche, Cora had been three days in her grave. Eb harnessed the team and rode to the cemetery with the boys, stood hat in hand on a warm April morning, and cried like a baby. Ezra clung to his father but Eli stood apart, gazing not at the grave but off into the middle distance. When it was time to go, he led his father by the elbow back to the wagon and took the reins himself to drive them home.

Without Cora, Eb sank into a state he called "somewhere between hell and utter confusion." He managed to collect the boys to pay daily visits to Cora's grave for a month but beyond that he wasn't much use to anyone. It wasn't that he was mourning, exactly; he simply didn't know what to do with himself. Day and night he felt as though he had wandered into a room in search of something and couldn't for the life of him remember what it might be. Finally, he sat down with the boys and asked what they wanted to do. Ezra spoke up.

—I don't want to stay here. Seems we'd be thinkin on it all the time, what happened to Ma. I'd like to go back to Sioux Falls. Always seemed to me that's where things was best for us.

Eb turned to Eli.

—You feel the same way?

Eli nodded.

—Sioux Falls would be good. We can go freightin with you.

—All right then. I expect you're old enough to pitch in. We'll sell up here and get a place in Sioux Falls. Maybe I'll freight out of there to Yankton and such, get off the Pierre run. Aint makin a damned dime haulin to the Homestake. Competin with the big outfits don't pay.

The boys stayed with the Harrisons while Eb traveled to Pierre to sell the wagons, oxen, and mules; he was so in debt to the banks for the money he had borrowed to finance the venture that he barely broke even. Back on the Belle Fourche, he sold the ranch to a big Wyoming outfit for enough money to give them a fresh start, paid one last mournful visit to Cora's grave, and made the move back to Sioux Falls with two wagons, Eb driving one, Eli and Ezra taking turns driving the other.

As they neared the falls, Eb decided to take the boys on a detour to visit his old friend E. L. Biggs, the man who sold him his first freight business. Eb had not laid eyes on Biggs since the day the big man rode out for the place he called Emanija, bound and determined to corner the market on the future capital city of the great state of Dakota. They found the junction of the Split Rock and the Big Sioux all right, but there was not a sign of anything called Emanija or of E. L. Biggs, apart from a tumbledown stone cabin whose roof had long since collapsed. Eb and the boys poked around the rubble for some sign of what had become of Biggs. They found a writing table with bound volumes of the account books from the days when Biggs ran the freight business, the pages yellowed and mildewed. There was a narrow bed and an engraving of a Mississippi steamboat on the wall for decoration and a few rusted kitchen utensils near a rusty stove but there was no sign of Biggs. Eli wandered out behind the cabin to escape the musty air inside. He stopped at the johnny with the door dangling by one hinge and swatted away the spiderwebs with a roll of old newspaper. When he had done his business, he walked another fifty feet along a path that made a long loop back toward the Split Rock. The lumped earth on the grave had settled into a shallow depression. Someone, possibly the occupant himself, had lashed two planks together to form a rough cross on which was carved the epitaph:

HERE LIES
E. L. BIGGS
WOT DIED
OF FALURE

Eb stood at the grave for a long while, hat in hand. It appeared that Cora and Biggs had died at almost the same time. With two of the anchors of his life in Dakota Territory gone, he felt like an unmoored steamboat afloat on the Mississippi in a December flood, unable to see or recognize a single landmark between Cairo and New Orleans. If not for Eli and Ezra, he might have decided at that moment to return to the Mississippi, to find a way to resume the life he led on the *Marielita*. Looking back, he felt that he might as well have stayed put on the big river. A man could put in a great deal of living if he chose, but for all the difference it made, he had just as leave spend his days on a towhead in the big river, running a trotline for catfish and watching the sun go down over the Arkansas bank through a fog of Lucian Quigley's tangle-foot whiskey.

⇥ CHAPTER 14 ⇤

Within a month, Eb had moved back into his old freight office in Sioux Falls with the sign now faded and swinging in the wind: EBENEZER PAINT & SONS, FREIGHTING AND HAULING. He plowed what money he had left into the business, but freighting wasn't what it used to be. The railroads had pretty much taken over, with spur lines running in all directions. About all that was left was hauling freight from the railheads, usually through rough country. Still, Ezra and Eli loved the life, the sound of the bullwhips, the creak of harness leather and the jangle of the trace chains, sleeping out under the stars. They were with Eb most of the time, working shoulder to shoulder with their father, feeling his pride in their strength and skill. With the bull trains, they went on hauling right through winter. Nights brought a frost so severe they sometimes heard porcupines whimpering with cold but they were warm enough, wrapped in buffalo robes near the fire, swapping yarns with rough bullwhackers who knew no other life.

Early in March of 1886, they were home again to shift the freighting from bull trains to mule trains but first the mules had to be shod. The blacksmith was Hugo Oser. Hugo was to start shoeing mules before sunup on a Saturday morning in late April but he sent his boy around just after first light to say that he was sicker than a dog and would not be able to swing a hammer before Monday at the earliest. It might be the Sabbath but Eb would count it as a workday lost if he didn't get shoes on those mules, so he started in with Eli and Ezra helping. He was no more than half as quick as Hugo Oser but by ten o'clock a half dozen fresh-shod mules milled in the holding corral, new metal gleaming on their hooves. Eli roped the seventh, a big brindle jenny missing half an ear, and dallied the rope around the hitching post in the middle of the corral. Eb, who was always careful to keep well to the side when handling an animal with a kick like a shotgun blast, grabbed the hoof nips and went to hoist the jenny's left rear leg. As he stooped, he slipped on wet manure and stumbled awkwardly, directly into the path of her back hooves. She launched a two-footed kick that caught him in the stomach so hard he sailed eight feet across the corral and landed in a pile of wet manure. The boys hovered over their stricken, gasping father. Eli turned to Ezra.

—Go for water, fool.

Ezra ran. He came pelting back with a full bucket of water and hurled it in Eb's face like a man trying to put out a barn fire. Eb mouthed silent curses, water pouring off the ends of his mustache, his face purple. Five minutes went by, the boys standing there terrified and silent, until he rolled onto the thickly patched knees of his trousers and puked his breakfast: two slabs of Canadian bacon, a half dozen biscuits and gravy and three eggs fried sunny-side up.

—That was a damned fool thing you done with that water, boy.

Ezra stared at the ground, chastened. Eli tried to grab Eb's hand to help him into the house but Eb pushed him away and staggered to his feet. He puked again, found his hat, dusted it off, reached for the hoof nips, and went back to work on the jenny, her left front leg tucked across his thighs. When she was shod, he decided to call it a day. He still couldn't talk above a whisper.

—That has to be a Missouri mule. Only a goddamned stubborn Missouri mule would possess a kick like that.

That night after supper, Eb started spitting blood. He said it wasn't nothing but a little tap under the ribs, no worse than any man took a half dozen times a year working around livestock. The next morning, he went back to shoeing mules. By noon he was done, bent over in pain so fierce he was unable to speak. The boys helped him into the house and up the stairs to bed and Ezra went to fetch Doc Finnan. Finnan was a drunk, but he was the only sawbones available. He came by, clucked his tongue, took Eb's pulse, clucked some more, said that mule must pack a wallop, prescribed a little laudanum for the pain, and that was it. By the end of the week, Eb was failing badly. Doc Finnan visited every evening but seemed to do nothing except help himself to Eb's whiskey. When the doctor left the house, he was usually in worse shape than his patient. Every evening as he staggered out the door, he said the same thing:

—That mule busted him up somethin awful. Somethin in his innards aint right. He might pull through and he might not.

After three weeks Eb called Eli to his bedside late one afternoon. Eli wasn't in the habit of sitting but Eb pointed to the rocking chair next to the bed, so he sat. Eb stared out the window at the setting sun. Eli waited. He was a quiet boy himself, so it never worried him when a fellow took his time getting ready to speak. Finally Eb cleared his throat and put his hand on his son's knee.

—I tried to lick this country. Tried my damnedest.

—I know you did, Pa.

—Came close too. Had her runnin downhill before I took a notion to sell up and light out for the goldfields. Never quite got it back after that. Can't blame your ma for bein mad at me. Once a notion like that takes hold of a man, it don't let go. When your ma died, it took the wind out of me worse than that mule. I kept chewin on it, how I loved that woman but I was always off somewhere when I ought to been at home. If I'd been there, she might not have died.

—She would have gone to the Harrisons afoot whether you were there or not.

—I expect you're right. She was ever a bullheaded woman.

Eb paused for breath.

—You're a strong young fella, strong as a man.

—Same as Ezra.

—True enough, but you're strong another way too. You're strong the way your mother was strong. You got a power inside you, I saw that from the time you was maybe one year old. Other people see it too. You weren't more than five years old when you could make kids two, three years older do what you wanted 'em to do, and damned if I could see how you did it.

Eli said nothing. Eb gazed out the window again. The sky to the west was lit amber and red. A groan rattled his teeth and he shifted his weight in the bed. Eli started to fuss with his pillow, but Eb shook his head, grabbed his arm in a grip like a blacksmith's vise.

—You aint like I was.

—Like what?

—You got too much sense to go poundin around the hills lookin for gold. Hell, I ought to had more sense than that. I seen what happened in California. Only folks that made a dime were them who was sellin goods to the miners, not the men breakin their backs lookin for gold. I lay here thinkin of all the things I aint got time to teach you. You got to know that to get anythin started, you got to have a stake. I hoped to leave you with somethin but there aint goin to be scarcely a thing. I borrowed to buy more mules this spring, so we're in a hole again and if I can't freight, we got no way out. I expect the bank is goin to want their mules back and most of the rest of it too. That's their way, y'understand: They're all for you as long as you're payin up the first of every month but if you miss a payment they'll swallow you whole—remember I told you that about banks. Don't get into debt to a bank, whatever you do. Them smilin vultures will pick you clean. They don't see no purpose in the ordinary man except to rob him blind.

Eb groaned and shifted his weight, winced at some awful pain inside him. It was near dark but he didn't ask Eli to light the lamp.

—This is hard country, Eli, don't ever think it aint. Reason I'm tellin you, you're the one bullheaded enough to make a go of it. Ezra is a fine boy, none better, but he's too easygoin. He looks to you to lead. Always has.

—Yessir.

Eb paused for a breath and a long sip of whiskey. A sudden chill rattled his bones. He couldn't seem to get comfortable. Eli reached for the pillow again, helped him settle. He was quiet for a while, looking out the window, watching it get dark.

—You're young to be orphans, not yet sixteen.

—We're most grown. We'll do all right.

—I expect you will but I need you to understand two things. First, don't be a fool like your pa. Get your feet set solid underneath you, get a good woman, don't go gallivantin off all the time. The second thing is, look after your brother. You're born to lead and he's born to follow, nothin wrong with that. Just keep him out of harm's way. Promise me that?

—Yes, Pa. I'd do that without bein asked.

—I knowed you would. I just wanted to say it clear. Now I aint got much to give you, apart from your saddlehorses, which you already got. I want you to take my bullwhip because you're the one mastered that and I'm goin to give Ezra the Whitworth because he's about the best shot with it I ever seen.

—Yessir. Thank you.

—Aint no need to thank me. Taint much and I know it but it's what I got to give. Now send your brother in. I got to have a talk with him too. I'll tell him to watch after you when you get too damned bullheaded and don't have sense enough to let go of a thing.

Eli grinned a little at that, went out to fetch Ezra, buttered himself some biscuits, ate them in the kitchen listening to the murmur of his father's voice talking to Ezra.

Ezra was dozing on the rocking chair in the wee hours of the night, when Eb woke and sat bolt upright.

—Goddammit, Lucian. You take my meaning and get it all twisted up.

Ezra jumped. Eb looked at him like a man seeing a ghost, let out a groan like a rusty nail yanked from an old board, fell back onto his pillow and died.

* * *

The meeting at the bank went pretty much the way Eb said it would. Three bankers sat in a semicircle with their hands folded over their spreading guts, clucking in sympathy over the plight of two boys orphaned so young. The fattest of the bankers explained that, by the terms of the mortgage, most of the worldly goods of Ebenezer Paint were now the property of the Dakota First State Bank, including the mules, wagons and harness, the house and barn and corrals. The boys had two saddlehorses apiece and a couple of spavined pack-horses the bank didn't want anyway; they had their own tack and shotguns and Eb had made sure that his bullwhip was to be given to Eli and his Whitworth rifle to Ezra. The fat banker finished saying his piece and extended a smooth pink hand to Eli.

—Now is there anything else I can do for you boys?

Eli took the man's hand in a grip that made him wince.

—I reckon not. You pretty well picked us clean. I generally prefer if a man is going to rob me that he sticks a gun in my ribs instead of a pen in my hand.

The day Eb was buried in the Sioux Falls cemetery, Eli cantered up beside Ezra as they rode back to the house.

—I imagine we're orphans now.

—I expect so.

—You want to stay around here?

—Not much.

—Me neither. We're the same as men now. We got no choice but to look after ourselves.

—Where we headed?

—I always wanted to be a cowpuncher, ever since we was out on the Belle Fourche.

—Me too.

—What do you think? Texas? Head to Ogallala, see if we can't catch on with a trail drive outfit goin back to Texas?

—Sounds about right.

BOOK 3

Powder River

Wyoming, 1886–1887

⚜ CHAPTER 15 ⚜

I n the swimming hole on the Belle Fourche where the river bent southwest to Wyoming, Eli dove too far into black water looking for something that had fallen off the skiff, something lost. A Barrow knife. Eb's pocket watch. A tortoiseshell comb that had belonged to his mother. A silver dollar Eb had retrieved from the poker table in Deadwood where Wild Bill Hickok slumped and bled. The lost bauble glittered in the sunlight and slipped through his outstretched fingers: a knife a watch a comb a coin changing as it fell until it broke the surface of the water with a clean, delicate splash and vanished, down and down over silt and riverworn rocks. Down and gone. He had to climb naked to the highest branch of the old cottonwood and dive for it, deep into the clear, cool water. Ezra rowed the skiff and pointed: *There it is. No, over there. It went down there. You got to get it. I can't go that deep. Get it or Ma is goin to send us for the willow switch.* The water was a cold shock on sunwarmed skin as he went in straight and clean. It was so clear underwater that he could see the scales on a trout lazing in the heat and count the pebbles on the riverbed as he pulled himself deeper and deeper into the river until the light vanished. He let go and rose seeking bright air and blue sky until the faintest trace of sunlight streaked the water, climbing a trail of bubbles until he could make out the bottom of the skiff, holding his breath until he thought his ears would burst, fighting toward a surface distant as the Pleiades. At last he rose to light and air with his arms gone limp, a dead thing rolling belly-up in the current.

He always swam out of the dream the same way: clutching at his chest, gasping for air, panicky and flailing at shadows. There were long scratches on his skin where he had clawed himself with his fingernails. His lungs heaved, his heart skittered. He was unable to shake a searing, oppressive vision of Eb and Cora in their graves, boxed and airless under an infinite weight of earth. He missed Cora, longed for her in a way that made him writhe like a man trying to escape a terrible beating.

Mama. Goddammit, Ma, this cannot be. I am not ready. I am too damned young. I still see you froze to death and that goddamned mule that killed Pa, I ought to shot the sonofabitch. I want to go back to the Belle Fourche and hear the rooster in the goddamned morning and wake up and smell coffee and buttermilk pancakes and hear Pa telling us that time's awastin. I want to sit by the fire at night and watch you at your knitting and Pa over the paper and Ez and me playin checkers and find everything not gone so goddamned wrong. I aint ready, Ma. I just aint ready for it to be me and Ez and nobody else.

Ezra snored on with his head tucked under the quilt. The birds outside chittered in the morning dark, the first rooster's crow set the others crowing at the Baxter place and on down the road. Eli fumbled into his bluejeans and shirt, pulled one suspender over his shoulder, toted his boots out of their room and sat at the kitchen table to pull them on. There were two cold biscuits and an apple left on the table. He ate one of the biscuits and stuck the other with the apple in his pockets, went out the door and stood shivering to pee in a corner of the corral. The dozing horses separated into dark shapes as the sky to the east faded from inky black to dark blue. The smell of horses was a comfort, like the sound of their whuffling in the dark, a deep, rippling *whunh-hunh-hunh-huh* as Monty recognized him and came for his treat. Eli wrapped his arms around the big sorrel's powerful neck and leaned heavily on the horse while the big teeth crunched the apple. He sobbed without making a sound until his shoulders shook and he had to bend double like a man who has taken a mule kick to the stomach. At last he caught his breath with a long, ragged gasp, stood up straight and set himself square for the trail.

They rode out through the heart of Sioux Falls: west along Ninth Street, north up Phillips Avenue past Johnson's Flour Store, Obert's Millinery, Bungenheimer's Meat Market, Kinkade's Bankrupt Store, Gillett's Farm Store, the Masonic Temple, the Cataract Hotel, and the sign swinging in the breeze that still read EBENEZER PAINT & SONS, FREIGHTING & HAULING, time slipsliding away with the chipped paint, the cracked and spiderwebbed windowpanes, the dust that ran in little dunes under the doorsill and the door now sagging on leather hinges, their lost father pale but visible to a certain cast of eye in the warp of bootworn planks and the rusted clawfoot stove where Dakota winters had vanished in wads of Mickey Twist and the yarns of men now wasting unmarked in graves where the spring runoff leached the earth of secrets close-held and guarded, a beggar's hoard of the vanished. Ezra had purchased a big, floppy two-dollar black hat new for the occasion; he reined up his little roan mare to allow himself a lingering glance at the old office. Eli, astride Monty, rode on without looking back.

It had rained for three days, and the fresh-shod hooves of the horses moved in sprung rhythm through the mud as the news went up and down Phillips Avenue: The Paint boys were leaving. By the time they reached the outskirts of town, they had a number of outriders, mostly boys who were younger than themselves. Johnny Borgmuller, who had lost a hand in the fall when his rifle blew up while he was trying to slaughter a den of rattlesnakes, declared that he was ready to ride to Texas but Eli wouldn't allow it.

—It's because I aint got but the one hand, aint it?

—No, it aint. It's because you're young and your ma needs you.

—You two aint but sixteen your own selves.

—We aint got no ma nor anyone else. You look after her and when you're growed a bit, you can come after us.

—How am I goin to know where to find you?

—We'll be in Texas.

•   •   •

Nights on the trail they slept rough and ate worse, hardtack leavened with the occasional jackrabbit or prairie chicken singed black on the outside and left raw on the inside over poor fires. They crossed the Niobrara River between Fort Niobrara and Valentine, passed through Simeon, Oasis, and Kennedy in Cherry County, crossed the North Loup River, camped a night on the Dismal River south of Norway, bore west through Omega before passing through Largo and Lilac in McPherson County, spent a last night on the trail outside Keystone northeast of Ogallala and duded up a little before they rode the last thirteen miles into a famous cowtown that was quiet as the tomb. They arrived in Ogallala expecting to find thousands of longhorns milling and bawling in the cattle pens and drunken cowhands dashing up and down Railroad Street. Instead there was no one about except a few settlers loading supplies onto their wagons, the occasional tradesman and a couple of oldtimers swapping lies on a bench outside the mercantile. They stabled their horses and mule at the near-empty livery and strolled the boardwalk past a long row of shuttered saloons as far as the Cattleman's Rest, where they ordered two sarsaparillas and asked if there was anyone around they could talk to about hooking up with one of the big cattle drives.

—That business is almost dead but if you want to jaw, that sonofabitch hangin on the whore's titty at the end of the bar is the man to ask. He's drinkin whiskey.

Ezra paid for a glass of whiskey and slid it down to a snaggletoothed cowpuncher who looked a good deal older than his forty years.

—How do.

—How do your own self.

—Like to stand you a drink.

The cowpoke held the glass up to the light like a jeweler gazing at a diamond ring, drained it, belched, slammed it on the bar. Ezra motioned the barkeep to fill it again. When the glass hit the bar a second time, he introduced himself.

—Name's Ezra Paint. This is my brother, Eli.

—Teeter Spawn. This here prime slab of American woman-hood is Miss Hattie Bettis. I do thank you for the whiskey, boys. If it's about Miss Hattie, she aint for sale.

—Beggin your pardon, miss, but taint that. We come down from Sioux Falls lookin to catch on with an outfit trailin longhorns from Texas. Barkeep says you're the man to ask.

Teeter drained another glass of whiskey and squinted at Ezra.

—Now what was it ye wanted to ast me?

—Trail drives. Where a fella might hire on.

—Tell ye what, it's too crowded for a confab in here. If ye'll stand a man to a mite of grub, we can talk to your heart's content.

Teeter Spawn had a walk like a scarecrow blown over plowed ground. He led the way to a table at the Ogallala House, the last establishment before Railroad Street turned into cow trail. The Paint boys followed, gawking at glass chandeliers, white table-cloths, gleaming silverware, polished brass spittoons, and a twelve-foot painting along one wall that showed a strangely magnified George Armstrong Custer firing his pistol at a swarm of Sioux as a muscular warrior drew back a spear to pierce Custer's heart. Ezra gestured with his chin.

—Ever seen a Sioux warrior hold a spear in your life?

—Nope.

—Me neither. Guess whoever painted that thing wasn't there. Up close, the Sioux fought with war clubs. The Cheyenne carry a skinny little lance, but it don't look nothin like that spear.

Teeter stared at a painting he had never noticed before.

—How come you boys know so much about Indians?

—Our mama was half Sioux.

—Orphans, are ye?

—We are.

—Figured as much. We don't see many your age when they got folks at home.

The menu at the Ogallala House gave the boys indigestion: a six-dollar porterhouse steak, prime rib at five dollars, roast beef four dollars and fifty cents. They both settled for biscuits and ham at a dollar and a half but Teeter guessed he'd have the porterhouse steak. The waiter when he returned from the kitchen staggered under plates the size of stock saddles with fluffy white mounds of mashed potatoes, green beans, and slices of fresh bread two inches thick. Teeter washed it down with his second ale and ordered a wedge of apple pie and coffee.

—Now what was it again you fellas wanted to ast me about?

—Longhorns and trail drives.

—Longhorns and trail drives. Well, I expect they don't have newspapers in Sioux Falls, otherwise you'd a heard tell of the Texas fever that has just about put a end to the longhorn business. Texas fever don't bother your longhorn, bastards can live on prickly pear and drink sand and there aint the disease made could kill 'em. Trouble is, the ranchers here brought in blooded bulls, Black Angus and Hereford and Galloway, pastured their stock next to the longhorns and the breed cattle startin dyin off from what they call Texas fever. We always called it the Spanish fever or red-water fever but I guess it depends who you want to blame. First the state of Kansas told the Texas drovers they couldn't pass through, then Nebraska done the same.

—That explains why it's so quiet.

—There was a time two, three years ago there'd be outfits drivin six miles a longhorns in here, dust clouds you could see all the way to Denver. Two hundred cowhands with every outfit and hellzapoppin up and down Railroad Street every night. Now it's so quiet you could hear a horsefly fart. If you was to ast me about it, you didn't miss out on a damned thing, because trailin longhorns from the Pecos is the most miserable task a man could set hisself, short of eatin ground glass with a pitchfork.

—How many times you make that drive?

—Couldn't say. Fourteen, fifteen times maybe. Takes a ridin fool. Don't know why they call it a drive, because if you've been around stock at all you know you don't drive cattle. That would be like tryin to push a rope. What you do is you get the lead stock goin the way you want and the rest follow like water runnin downhill. Then ye don't have nothin to worry about except rattlesnakes, prairie fires, wolves, rustlers, Indians, and blizzards on the Fourth of July.

—What keeps you around here if there aint no more cattle drives?

—I started winnin at poker and I just couldn't seem to stop. But I got the itch to be back on the trail, figure to head up to Wyoming, try to catch on with a outfit ahead of spring roundup. You boys are welcome to tag along if you decide you can get through life without Texas.

The bill came to better than twelve dollars. Eli was about to reach into his jeans when Teeter slapped a twenty-dollar gold piece on the table.

—The deal was we was to stand you dinner if you'd tell us about longhorns.

—And I aint told ye a cussed thing about longhorns except that they don't get Texas fever. You boys got a long ride to somewhere. Best hang on to your money.

—Thanks, Teeter. That was decent of you.

Ezra glanced at Eli, got the nod he was looking for.

—If you don't object, we might tag along to Wyoming then.

—More'n welcome. Get tired of talkin to myself on the trail.

—When do you figure to head out?

—You be ready to ride at first light.

Eli and Ezra followed Teeter across the street. They rented a room for fifty cents a night and paid ten cents apiece for a bath. Ezra was in a brown study when they turned in for the night.

—We're too late for every damned thing. Missed the War Between the States, too late to fight Indians, we never got to run a steamboat on the Mississippi, and the buffalo's mostly dead. Now we can't even chase longhorns. Might as well go work in a danged bank.

—You might had your legs shot off by Johnny Reb, or got scalped by Crazy Horse, or burned alive when a steamboat blew its boiler, or run over in a buffalo stampede. They's plenty fun left out here. We'll follow old Teeter Spawn up to Wyoming, see if we can't catch on with a big outfit up there.

—We could always go back to Sioux Falls.

—Now that's the one thing we aint goin to do. I might go back one day, but I aint goin back with my tail between my legs. We can't give up just because there aint no more trail drives from Texas. Look at Pa: When he was nineteen years old, he went clear to California lookin for gold. He got his foot all busted up, but he never quit tryin. This is a big new country, Ez. It's like a apple tree bustin with fruit. If you lay down under the tree, maybe a apple will fall on your head, maybe not—if you get up and climb that tree and shake it, you might fall and bust your head, but you might find yourself a dozen bushel of apples.

—Between us we could homestead three hundred and twenty acres. That's a fair start.

—I don't want to bust ground with no plow, Ez, not when we don't have a stake. You start that, you're goin to spend a good part of your life lookin at a mule's hind end, hopin it rains and the grasshoppers don't come and eat your harness and the handles right off your plow. At least we're on the move. A homesteader is tied to his patch. Some of 'em are livin in dugouts, that's all they got. No windows, no rugs, no nothin but a hole in the ground and a borrowed plow. I heard of this Swiss feller got hisself a mail-order bride from back east. She took the train all the way to Nebraska, married this crazy old coot in Rushville, rode in his buckboard a hundred and fifty miles to her new home. When they got there, she found out her new house was a hole dug into the dirt on the side of a hill. The only furniture he had was a wood chair and a smelly straw tick on the ground for sleepin. Had coyote and wolf pelts hangin from the walls and a big old pig he butchered for her was danglin from the ceiling right in the middle of the room. Well, don't she sit down on that straw tick and cry for a week. Must a broke her heart.

—She stay or go?

—Stayed. Spent all her money gettin there, what else was she goin to do?

❧ CHAPTER 16 ❧

They followed the Oregon Trail west and northwest, climbing steadily into gumbo badlands and tall bluffs dotted with mesquite, yucca, and ponderosa pine, the pine bent to the east by the eternal wind that barreled through the gullies and ravines of land sculpted by a river that was now wide and flat as a wheatfield. The wagon rut in some places was deep as a tall man's head, shallow troughs to either side of the ruts where men and boys had walked to Oregon and California while the women drove the teams, their passage marked along almost every mile with a trail of graves that began west of St. Joe's and did not end until the settlers and prospectors ran out of country on the Pacific coast. The dead were buried in shallow graves dug in haste by grieving family members afraid of falling too far behind the wagon trains, the occasional legend carved into a rough board still legible after thirty years:

LAVINIA WYATT
B. SPRINGFIELD APRIL 4, 1846
D. THIS PLACE JUNE 30, 1851
R.I.P. OUR GIRL

The landmarks loomed one by one, bluffs visible for miles in flat country that rose as prairie soared to mountain. They passed the narrow spire the Indians called Elk Penis; the settlers deferred to the delicate sensibilities of their women and called it Chimney Rock. Beyond that there was Courthouse Rock and Scotts Bluff, where the fur trapper Hiram Scott had died of an arrow wound. East of Scotts Bluff, they hit wind and wet weather. They pulled on canvas dusters, wrapped scarves over their noses and mouths and rode on. Bursts of rain mingled with the dust brought the smell of sage and the wind kept the horses cool. As they rode, they flushed pheasant and sage hens, jackrabbits and cottontail. The country was treeless except for cottonwoods and willows down by the river, scattered ponderosa and lodgepole pine on the bluffs, an occasional box elder. Bunchgrass and buffalo grass were mixed with prickly pear, soapweed, yucca, mesquite, juniper. As the ground rose toward the Wind River Mountains far to the west, it was as though the lower layer of sky peeled away to reveal a vault so pale blue it was almost white. Ezra said he could see why they called it God's country. Teeter begged to differ.

—If I was God, damned if I'd pick a spot where it's a hundred degrees in summer and fifty below in the winter and the wind blows pretty much all day long. If you ever been to Tennessee, that's a fit place for God to put down His rockin chair. Nebraska aint nothin but a way to make a man appreciate bein someplace else.

When they made camp, Teeter showed them the best way to make a cook fire in this country, dragging mesquite into a narrow trench to build a low fire that wouldn't ignite the whole prairie if the wind picked up. He stewed jackrabbit in a kettle held above the trench on a rod supported by forked sticks at either end, seasoned it with sage and scrapings of rock salt, and served it up with cold springwater. Ezra and Eli said it was the best thing they had tasted since the day Cora Paint died.

—Secret is your mesquite fire. If you can find it, you always want to burn mesquite. In a pinch you can use sage but sage goes up quick and you don't get no regular flame. Hard as hell to cook anything without turnin it to charcoal. If you can't find mesquite, the old buffalo chips have been here twenty years or more, so they're cured, but your real buffalo chips are gettin scarce, so cow chips will do. If the shortgrass is dry enough, you can pull bunches and twist it tight for a fire. Sage is your last resort.

At night, once they had finished their stew and hunkered back on their heels, Teeter sipped his whiskey and talked about the great trail drives or his experience as a teenage southerner in the War Between the States.

—My people back in Tennessee were blacksmiths. Didn't own no slaves. Never had, never would. When the shootin started, they just wanted to keep clear of both sides. They might a stayed out of the whole thing but I had two cousins who shod a bunch a horses one day for the Confederate guerrillas. That was all it took, shoein horses for the wrong side. The Federals came in and hung 'em both from a big old oak tree right in the middle of town. Said if anyone else helped the Confederates, they'd find themselves hangin from that tree. I wasn't much more than a kid when that happened but I couldn't sign up with Johnny Reb quick enough. By the time I got myself into the ranks, we could see there wasn't no sense in it and no way of winnin but we kept on fightin anyway because we didn't know what else to do. I knew men who swore they must a killed a thousand Federals all by themselves. Didn't matter how many we killed, they kept a-comin. They never run out of ammunition and they never run out of men. Them Union generals was idiots, mostly, but when you got enough men and enough guns, it don't much matter if your generals is dumber than dirt. At Cold Harbor we was dug in behind works you couldn't blow with dynamite and they just come marchin up big as life, and we shot men and boys until the gun barrels was so hot you couldn't cool 'em with a bucket of piss. Didn't matter how many died, the next bunch was chargin right up after 'em, climbin the bodies of the first wave. We shot them too and the next bunch after that and still them officers didn't learn that you can't send men into defended works. It's like pourin water down a snake hole.

Teeter talked until he was done and when he was through talking there was no use prodding him. He would stare into the fire like he was seeing ghosts and then he would pull out his harmonica and play until the fire flickered out and they drifted off to sleep watching the Big Dipper slipslide across a sky that was seeded with stars thicker than a field of new oats.

West of Cheyenne they veered north again over shortgrass prairie greening with spring, crossing streams still ice-choked in mid-April, difficult and dangerous to ford. Everywhere there were cattle back in the draws. They cadged a meal off a chuckwagon or two but jobs were scarce. Once or twice a foreman offered to hire Teeter but wouldn't take a chance on hands as green as Eli and Ezra and Teeter wouldn't hire on unless there was work for all three. They veered back to the northeast, crossed the Belle Fourche not more than fifty miles southwest of the cabin where the boys had passed a good part of their childhood, turned west again and camped a night at the foot of the Devils Tower. Near the fork where Crazy Woman Creek runs into the Powder River, they finally found what they were seeking: A toothless old hand named Pappap Morgan was out back of yonder trying to help a wild-eyed cow with a difficult birth. The calf's front legs were already out, so Teeter wrapped them in leather and Eli got his lariat around the legs in a double half hitch and backed Monty off nice and slow while Teeter and Pappap eased the calf from the bawling cow. After both calf and cow were saved and the calf was nursing its first milk, they crouched on their bootheels around the fire and drank coffee and ate cold biscuits. Pappap said this spread was the O-Bar, a hundred-thousand-acre ranch owned by a British lord, Sir Humphrey Doane. Doane's cousin Moreton Frewen owned the 76, one of the biggest and most powerful outfits in Wyoming, but Frewen had pulled up stakes in 1885 and gone home to England and Doane himself never left the old country.

—Damnedest thing I ever seen. He built a big house, had windows shipped clear from Chicago. Married his bride and was fixing to bring her out here, but they say she left him for a fellow had a place in Africa. Guess she figured Africa was better than Wyoming. Doane was too broke up to care about ranchin, so he hired a fella named Dermott Cull to run this place for him. Cull is about one hundred and sixty pounds of pure mean. He calls himself a Texian, carries that short Texian rope. He don't believe in cuttin critters no slack, nor men neither. I expect he come up here because he done killed half of Texas. He aint no cattleman, I know that. Far as I can make out, he aint nothin but a hired gun for the Stockmen's Association.

—Hell's the Stockmen's Association?

—Stockmen's Association is all the big outfits bunched together. They run the legislature, they blackball any cowboy running his own stock. They got it all sewed up. They run the whole state for about three dozen rich men and leave the rest of us to suck the hind tit.

Teeter pointed to the slat-ribbed cow nursing her calf.

—That cow is in pisspoor shape.

—They're all in poor shape. These big fellas don't do a damned thing to keep their stock alive winters. Put 'em out and let 'em freeze and starve, then wonder why the calf crop is so thin come spring. Dumb sonsofbitches overstock the range, then they wonder why they aint makin money and blame it on the cowboys. Word is they want to cut pay five dollars a month, so top hands making forty dollars is dropped to thirty-five, and hands like these young fellas here is to make thirty.

—We might have to take what they're willin to pay. We're lookin for work.

—You come to the right place. Between Dermott Cull and the association, they run off most of the hands young and strong enough to handle a big roundup.

—Where can we find Mr. Cull?

—Installed himself in the big house belongs to Sir Humphrey Doane, if you can believe that. Don't lack for cheek, Dermott. Livin like a lord and him nothin but tumbleweed trash blown up from Texas. Got a Mexican *señorita* with him, don't look more'n twelve years old. They say he won her in a poker game in Juárez. Got a old Mexican lady with her, she looks after the both of them. If you want to hire on, I'd ride over there, catch him at the big house.

They rode the last five miles to the house Sir Humphrey Doane had ordered for his wandering bride and found Dermott Cull still abed at eleven o'clock in the morning. Two big wolfhounds came snarling down the lane but hushed at a word from Teeter, who pounded the brass door knocker and wouldn't let up until Cull came stumbling out to meet them, strapping pistols over long johns that had gone pink in the wash. The girl trailed behind him, smiling shyly over Cull's shoulder. She was a pretty little thing, small-boned as a hummingbird. Teeter did the talking.

—I didn't figure on a fella still abed when it's almost high noon.

—For six bits I'd shoot any man rousts me out of bed. State your business or ride.

—We heard you was in need of cowhands.

—We're hirin men, not boys. I got bunions older'n them two children.

—And I got whiskers older than that girl behind you. The boys are young, but you won't find better hands between here and Texas.

—We're shorthanded or I wouldn't look at any of you twice. Thirty-five a month and found for you, thirty a month for them two wet-behind-the-ears puppies.

—We aint workin for Stockmen's Association wages, Dermott. Forty a month and found. Thirty-five a month for the boys. Cheap at the price.

Cull chewed it over.

—Forty and thirty-five it is but if them boys want work they'll be nighthawkin till I see if they're worth a damn. Bunkhouse is yonder past the barn, you'll find some bunks aint took. Most of the boys is out catchin up their horses after winter pasture. Plenty of wild ones out there too, especially up in the high country. You'll need ten head apiece for roundup. Rule is the same for horses as it is for anything else you find loose: If it's got hair on it, you brand it O-Bar.

—That apply to women and cowhands or just livestock?

Teeter grinned a snaggletoothed grin to show he didn't mean anything by it. Cull let it ride, turned on his heel and pushed the girl back into the house ahead of him. She flashed a white-toothed smile over her shoulder at the Paint boys.

They watered the horses, slipped on rope hobbles and turned them out to graze, washed up in the stock tank and toted their gear into the bunkhouse, a long narrow building cobbled together out of lodgepole pine and bits and pieces of whatever scrap lumber lay to hand when the big house was finished, with two slits that passed for windows facing due west. At one end was a blackened stove, a chimney pipe and coal scuttle and two chairs. A dozen straw ticks were scattered helter-skelter on the floor, some with bedrolls and some without. The straw ticks closest to the stove were occupied, so they dropped their bedrolls at the far end. Once they had stowed their kits, Ezra asked Teeter what Cull had in mind when he said they would be nighthawking.

—Keep track of the horses till daylight. Aint hard. Got a good horse, you can do it while you sleep. Wrap the reins of your horse real tight around your hand, then you can nod off. If the other horses start to move, your horse will move with 'em, and the tug on the reins'll wake you quick enough. Horses that's been broke aint likely to ramble too far, less there's wolves or coyotes around or they get spooked by lightning. What you got to watch for is rustlers. Any stock gets rustled, that sonofabitch Dermott Cull is apt to hang you first and go after the rustlers after.

—He don't seem all that hard.

—Neither does a bobcat, till you got one with its teeth in your balls. You boys give that one a wide berth. A man like him, you're just beginnin to wonder if there's goin to be a fight and he's cleanin his pistols and fixin to dump you in a shallow grave. Aint no point crossin him.

—We wasn't raised to run from nobody.

—That's exactly what worries me.

Eli changed the subject.

—Where we goin to find extra cowponies?

—I think we'll go huntin mustangs. I was up this way two or three years back, I remember big herds up in them mountains.

❧ CHAPTER 17 ❧

An hour before first light, they were up drinking coffee and chewing biscuits and hardtack around a crackling mesquite fire. By sunup they were in the saddle yawning and shivering, giving the horses plenty of rein and letting them pick their way along a rocky trail that followed a shallow creek bed due west from the Powder. They rode most of that day, camped another night on high prairie in the shadow of the mountains, rode out the next morning toward a hogback that was little more than a black slash on the western horizon. At noon they changed mounts in a shady copse at the foot of the switchback that led up to the ridge, dismounted and led the horses in a last belly-scraping scramble up the final thirty feet to the summit. They paused to let their trembling mounts cool, gazing openmouthed at the chain of mountains lifting west and farther west until the last peak vanished in mist, the sun gleaming off the snow on its southern flank. From the divide, the ridge dropped in an easy grade into a long narrow valley that fanned out to the south in a glacial moraine, gravel and rock and boulders as big as a house all tumbled down by a slow and solid sheet of spreading ice that came and went thousands of years before the first men reached the Bighorns. Teeter plugged along, quieter than usual. In the high country it was difficult to get enough air in your lungs to speak a whole sentence; even the boys felt a little giddy from the altitude.

In late afternoon they reined the horses north, away from the open country into thick alpine forest. Shrill magpies scolded from bare branches, deer bounced away in a flash of white tail, an owl's wings whuffed in the gloom. Eli spotted a mountain goat watching them from a crag a half mile up and they paused to wonder that any creature could climb so deft-footed where the rock offered no purchase. Dark came early once the sun slipped behind the mountains. Teeter called a halt where the creek petered out into a narrow gorge clogged with balsam and quaking asp that grew almost to the base of a cliff, a hundred feet of striated granite where there was scarcely a handhold. They made camp with the cliff to their backs, the fire between them and the wolves that would howl all night long. Ezra and Eli hung the saddle blankets over branches near the fire to dry, gave the animals a quick rub with currycombs and brushes, got them watered and staked to picket ropes to graze. Teeter fried beans and they dipped the hardtack in beans and molasses.

—In case you boys been wonderin, we come up this high because the mustangs here aint been chased and picked over. They should be grazin out on them western slopes early tomorrow mornin. Once it gets hot they'll work their way down into the trees and it'll be hell to pay to bust 'em out of that brush. What we want is to catch them out in the open, get 'em bunched and headed this way fast so they don't notice they're runnin out of room. Where it's narrow enough to hold them, we'll string a triple strand of ropes. Leave the ropes slack until the mustangs is past, and then if we got it set up right, I can pull the whole shebang tight with one good yank. The ropes ought to hold them where it's open, and they sure as hell can't shinny up this cliff.

The campfire played on the dark, swaying branches of lodgepole pine and cast their shadows in long ripples up the rock face. Teeter and Eli tucked into their bedrolls and slept. Ezra lay awake watching the fire, listening to the wolves, thinking that, if a man were to die up here, the wolves would have the meat stripped off him by sunup. He shivered, pulled Eb's old Whitworth a little tighter to his chest, its weight a comfort as he tried to sleep. When he woke, the sky above the cliff was a color somewhere between black and rose and Eli and Teeter had the fire going. Ezra rolled onto his stomach and covered his face with his hat. Eli prodded him with a booted toe.

—C'mon, little brother. Places to go and things to do.

Ezra sat up. The coffee tasted worse than it had the night before, thick and bitter. He strained a sip or two through his teeth and reached for his boots.

—Let's ride.

They left the spare mounts and mules loose-hobbled and rode stiff in the saddle, waiting for the sun to rise far enough to warm their bones, following the gravel fan north of the creek with the horses stumbling now and then in semidarkness. They pulled their hat brims low against the rising sun and followed Teeter's lead, expecting to find mustangs grazing where the gorge opened into a tall-grass meadow dotted with wildflowers; they found plenty of sign but no horses and rode on through the meadow with the dew-damp grass soaking the horses to the knee and down the slope to where the gorge opened into a wide gravel fan of rocks and boulders. Here ancient ice had probed and retreated, leaving behind a three-mile stretch where there wasn't enough forage for a billy goat. Teeter reined in his horse.

—I'll be damned. Why would a animal want to graze on gravel, anyhow?

There were two dozen mustangs strung out along the creek bed for a mile or more. Teeter motioned for the boys to spread out to flank the horses and get them headed back up toward the gorge.

—We can't move without them seein us. Go easy and maybe we won't spook 'em.

Eli and Teeter splashed across the creek and started working their way to the fringes of the moraine. Ezra headed the opposite direction. They had picked their way a quarter mile through the rocks when Teeter reined up again and pointed at the nearest horse.

—Hold up. Somethin aint right. What do you boys see on that dapple gray filly?

Eli leaned forward in the saddle.

—All I can see is somethin hangin off its forelock.

—Aw, hell. Somebody's been up here already, fixed them poor devils with pounders. That's why they aint up in the trees and they aint run from us yet.

—What's a pounder?

—Hunk a metal. Railroad spikes, mostly. Tie it to the forelock, and every time that horse moves the spike will pound him right between the eyes. It's a thing only a cruel and lazy man would do to a wild horse to keep it from running off.

Eli whistled to signal Ezra to join them and they turned back, crossed the creek again and worked their way toward the gray filly slow and easy. When they got to within a hundred feet, they could clearly see the railroad spike dangling between her eyes. She had run some in spite of the pounder, enough for the spike to rub her face raw. Eli shook out his rope and approached her at a slow walk, talking low. Teeter held up a warning hand.

—Whoever done this won't like us messing with their animals.

—I aint leavin a horse in that fix.

—Suit yourself.

Eli dangled the lariat down his right thigh until he was in range and threw in one easy motion without twirling the loop to spook the horse. He caught her clean around the neck and dallied the lariat in a quick half hitch around the saddle horn as Monty backed to keep the rope taut. The mustang didn't struggle; all the fight had been beaten out of her. He dismounted and approached her on foot, talking softly. She was half-crazy with pain, her eyes wide and rolling, white flecks of foam around her mouth, nostrils flared. Eli slipped an arm around her neck.

—Whoa, sis. Gimme half a chance, I'll cut that damned thing off you.

When she had calmed some, he took the forelock in his right hand and a clasp knife in his left, cut the pounder free and tossed it aside. Ezra came up easy from the other side with a tin of purple horse salve and rubbed some into the cuts left by the spike to keep the flies off. When he was done, he loosened the lariat and tugged it free. The horse shuddered, wheeled away from the men, scrambled back to the meadow and went to grazing as though nothing had happened.

It took most of the day to catch all the horses and cut the pounders loose. They found twenty-six animals in all, including a half dozen mares with foals at their sides. One shaggy pinto had to be shot because the pounder had put out one of his eyes and he had broken a foreleg struggling on the rocks. The others headed shakily uphill toward the shelter of the trees. Ezra had just roped the last horse, a chestnut mare, when Teeter spotted four riders approaching from downstream.

—Here they come, Ezra. Can you get that old rifle up quick?

—Quick as need be.

Ezra slashed the pounder free, patted the horse on the rump as it spun away, pulled the heavy Whitworth from its scabbard and sighted over the pommel of his saddle, feet spread wide to steady his aim. Teeter shook his head.

—I know those boys up front. Big fella in the lead is that good-for-nothing O. T. Yonkee that likes to brag how he used to ride with Quantrill. The skinny one with the red hair and no teeth, that's Thaddeus Shank. They aint nothin but two-bit thieves. I don't know the other two but they got to be more of the same.

Ezra tried to swallow and found nothing in his throat but a big ball of cotton. He tightened his grip on the rifle and tested the wind with a wet forefinger. Yonkee was a target wide as a grizzly bear. The oblong bolt of the Whitworth would blow a hole in the man you could drive a fencepost through. Teeter saw his trigger finger tighten.

—Leave him be, won't you? Put that thing on the ribs of that skinny sonofabitch and if he so much as sweats, you open him up some breathin room. Don't worry bout the other two. They aint none of 'em goin to make a move unless O.T. moves first.

Yonkee ignored the Paint boys and rode straight at Teeter. Eli slid Monty a little to his right, opening space between himself and Teeter. Up close he could see Yonkee was built short but wide, way too much man for his struggling pony to carry. Head like a cannonball under a wide-brimmed black hat, greasy hair lank to his shoulders, a broad face and little pig eyes not much more than a rumor between a curly black beard and the hat. He stunk of grease and blood and worse and looked like he wouldn't take a bath unless his horse happened to throw him into a creek full of lye soap. Yonkee spat a wad of chewing tobacco the size and color of a horse turd and glared at Teeter.

—You fellas done a damned fool thing. Them's my horses you turned loose.

Before Teeter could answer, Eli spoke up.

—Any man treats a animal that way don't deserve to own one.

Yonkee rolled his head around on his massive shoulders like a grizzly bear about to swat a collie pup, took in Eli, decided he wasn't much account and returned his attention to Teeter.

—Teeter Spawn, aint it? Used to ride with the King outfit outa Texas? You ought to of stayed in Texas, Teeter. These children don't know better but you're old enough not to mess with a man's stock. Now me and my boys are goin to sit in the shade a spell while you catch up them horses for us. Then we'll be on our way peaceful.

—We aint catchin jackshit for you, O.T. What you done here is dumb and vicious and it would save us a lot of trouble if you'd turn that pony around and ride on down the mountain.

Eli figured Yonkee to pull his Colt Navy right then but Yonkee crossed them. He vaulted off the wrong side of his horse and came at Teeter on the run, crouched low like a bull after a bastard calf. Ezra had the Whitworth up but with Teeter's horse between them, he couldn't pull the trigger. Teeter got a hand on the five-shot Colt he carried but before he could get it free from the holster, Yonkee grabbed the reins, yanked the horse around with sheer brute strength, lifted Teeter out of the saddle with one paw and pitched him into the dust. Teeter's Colt went skittering away.

Yonkee followed with a booted kick that caught him under the jaw and spun him like a top. When Teeter lifted his head, Yonkee chopped him again and again behind the ear with a fist like a maul, slow and deliberate as a man killing a rabbit for the pot.

Ezra thought someone had fired a shot until he saw that Eli's bullwhip had torn a gouge the size of a turkey egg out of Yonkee's right biceps. Yonkee squealed like a castrated pig and turned toward Eli as the whip cracked a second time, ripping a gash in his thigh. The big man roared and pawed for the pistol with his left hand but a third strike from the whip caught his gun hand three inches above the wrist and broke it like a twig, leaving a jagged edge of bone poking from Yonkee's hairy forearm. Thaddeus Shank saw Yonkee getting the worst of it and went for the old cap-and-ball pistol he carried in his belt; the two riders behind him spread out, looking for a way to get a clean shot at Ezra, standing behind the roan. The Whitworth roared once, and Shank's hat sailed off his head, lit on a branch of a lodgepole pine, and did not come down, a fist-size hole through the crown. Shank raised his hands with care, like a man poking his fingers into a beehive. Ezra motioned with the rifle again and he raised them a little higher. The two riders behind him imitated Shank. Ezra let the big barrel of the Whitworth range back and forth from rider to rider. If they charged, he would get no more than one but that fellow would be missing most of his chest.

O. T. Yonkee was all chewed up but he wasn't done. He lowered his head and charged. Eli reversed the whip to get a short grip on the handle, which was weighted with a pound of lead. Before he could swing it, Yonkee bowled him over and they rolled in the dust, punching and gouging. Eli had a bare-knuckle heavyweight boxer's build and disposition but he was giving up a hundred pounds in weight and twenty years of experience. Yonkee staggered to his feet, dragging Eli up with him. Somehow, Eli hung on to the whip, and he swung the lead-weighted handle like a club, pounding Yonkee's ribs and back as the big man spun him around. Eli heard Yonkee groan as the pain of cracked ribs made the huge body shudder. He tangled the fingers of his left hand in Yonkee's greasy hair and pounded at his face with the weighted handle but Yonkee had his arms locked around Eli's back. Eli could feel the wind driven out of him as a brown mist began to sift down over his eyes and his body sagged. With all the strength he had left, he brought a knee up hard into Yonkee's groin and felt the man's body go limp. He got the whip handle fastened under Yonkee's beard and put all his power into it, his biceps straining as he tilted the outlaw's chin back, trying to crush his windpipe.

Ezra hollered the warning just in time.

—Knife!

Eli leapt back as Yonkee jabbed with the bowie knife he had pulled out of his boot, slashing in an upward motion that would have gutted Eli like a deer. Eli dodged out of range of the blade, reversed the bullwhip, and went to work. The whip cracked and cracked again. Yonkee ducked and rolled, pawed at the whip with his hands, tried to grab and missed every time, buried his face in his shoulder to protect his eyes. The lash gouged his buttocks, tore the back of his neck, ripped his shirt open, and split his calf. Eli cracked the whip without mercy until his arm ached. At last he tossed the whip aside and kicked the man in the belly with a booted toe, then a second time full in the face to be sure, feeling cartilage give way as Yonkee's nose shattered. The outlaw rolled over onto his back and lay bleeding and spent. Ezra waved the rifle at Thaddeus Shank.

—Maybe you'd best doctor him up.

Shank eased himself out of the saddle.

—Might be easier to doctor a grizzly bear.

—That aint my concern.

Teeter sat up, looked around like he was trying to remember who these people were, then vomited between his boots. Eli picked Teeter's pistol up off the ground and pointed it at the two younger riders.

—You two get down slow and take off your gun belts. I don't want no accidents. My brother is awful accurate with that rifle.

They did as they were told. Closer up, it was clear they weren't much more than boys, about the same age as Eli and Ezra. Eli saw the family resemblance: The fat one belonged to Yonkee clear enough, the skinny one had to be Shank's kid.

Yonkee groaned and tried to spit at Eli, ended up with a gout of blood in his beard.

—You little pissant. I ought to whup ye like a cyclone whuppin' a outhouse.

Eli kept his peace. Let the man talk. They waited until Shank, who seemed to have an idea what he was about, finished ripping up an old shirt to bandage Yonkee's hurts. When he was done, it took some heaving and pulling but Shank and the boys managed to heave Yonkee back onto his horse, the man screaming in pain every time they shifted his weight. Yonkee gritted his teeth, glared.

—Next time I'll kill ye first and think about it after.

—Aint goin to be no next time and you know it. You'll ride off down off this mountain and not look back. You're the same as every bully I ever knowed. Scratch deep enough and there aint nothin but purebred coward underneath.

Yonkee snorted and wheeled his horse after Shank. An hour later the boys could still see them riding down a switchback far below. Above them, buzzards flew in lazy circles on the updrafts from the valley, their dark wings little more than pencil scratches on a clear blue sky.

⊰ CHAPTER 18 ⊱

For six weeks they worked the North Powder Roundup in a frenzy of bawling cattle, shouting cowpunchers, sizzling cowhide, and galloping horses, never quite free from the stench of sweat and cowshit and burning hair. They rode from the first glimmer of dawn to the last faint evening twilight day after day until the toughest hardbottom cowboys were cramped with saddlewolf, the quality saddlehorses were worn out and even the wiry, tireless little mustangs stumbled with fatigue. Twenty outfits based around twenty chuckwagons worked together valley to valley. Sharp-eyed reps tried to spot their own brands among a thousand head of milling cattle, so that deft cutting horses could sort the 76 stock from the O-Bar, the Flying-W from the 2-Lazy2-P. Eli and Ezra Paint worked as a three-man team with Teeter Spawn: Ezra to rope, Eli to throw and hold, Teeter to brand and castrate. The spring calves were roped and earmarked and branded, the bull calves castrated, ears notched to conform with the brands.

The foremen for the various outfits pushed them hard. It didn't seem to matter if they missed a quarter of the stock hidden up rocky draws or lost in thick timber along the hillsides. Teeter reckoned that a man could put a decent herd together from the cattle left behind in the race to sweep from one valley to the next.

The prairie was so dry that the roundup horses stayed on the move all night long, pushing farther and farther away in search of fodder and fresh water. Within two weeks, it was obvious to veteran cowpunchers that the winter count was far below what the absentee ranchers would expect. Investors back in Chicago and New York and London calculated the number of cattle they expected to see in the spring by a simple formula: They had the cowboys count the cows on the range and then doubled the number, making no allowance for wolves, accidents, or the uncontrolled breeding that meant too many cows were giving birth in midwinter, when the calves had little chance of surviving until spring.

The rain had stopped falling before the roundup began. The grass greened early, then went brown and stayed brown. The overgrazed pastures turned parched as buffalo bones and cracks opened in the dry land as wide as a man's fist. When the wind picked up, they ate dirt for breakfast and dirt for supper. They worked with bandannas over their faces to keep the dust out and still chewed grit day and night, their eyes red and watering and half-blind, eyelids stuck with gummy black dirt from the endless blowing dust. As the prairie dried out, the cattle drifted miles beyond their usual range, searching for a blade of grass or a creek that hadn't run dry, gnawing at greasewood and sagebrush when they could find nothing else. The punchers battled through the hot, dusty summer to get them to grass and water but at the fall roundup they came in slat-sided and bony anyway, bawling and exhausted and underweight. As the earth dried and cracked and the cattle turned to skeletons on the hoof, Dermott Cull turned mean. He staggered into camp one night just as the O-Bar cowpunchers were crawling into their bedrolls and started ranting about the short count on the spring calves. He was toting a mostly empty bottle of Blackfoot rum in one hand and a rope in the other, and his eyes were red from dust and drink.

—We aint got half the cattle we ought to have. Some of you goatfuckers is stealing livestock. If I catch any of you with so much as a cross-eyed heifer, I will hang your sorry ass from anything that will hold a rope.

Cull parked his Texan boots and Mexican spurs in front of Eli, who sat next to the fire with Ezra. With practiced fingers, he tied a hangman's knot in the lariat and made as though to loop it around Eli's neck.

—Don't play at that.

—I'm foolin with ye. I don't think you're the one rustlin stock anyways.

—Don't matter. You don't put a rope around a man's neck unless you mean to use it.

Cull tried to drop the noose over Eli's head but Eli grabbed the rope and hauled himself to his feet with such force that he pulled the Texan offbalance and stood glaring down at him.

—If the day comes that I get hung, Dermott, it won't be for a couple scrawny steers.

Some of the men behind Eli scrambled to get out of the way in case Cull started shooting, but he seemed to forget what he was about. Eli let go the noose. Cull undid the knot, coiled his rope, and wandered away. Somewhere in the darkness they heard the creak of leather as he swung into the saddle and rode off.

Ezra and Eli saddled up and rode out to their nighthawking. Teeter said he wasn't tired and would ride with them in case Dermott Cull came back. Coyotes started their *yipyipyip* over the low brown hills close and dark. A bitten, cloud-smeared moon sailed from the east. All around them they heard the whuff and plod of horses, dark forms grazing from one isolated clump of wiry yellow grass to another or standing three-footed and fast asleep and farther off, the pitiful bawl of a cow whose sickly calf had been torn apart by coyotes. Teeter cantered out to head off a dozen horses making for the mountains. Ezra stayed with Eli.

—Don't know what you're lookin for with Dermott, but it can't come to no good.

—Only way to get him to back off is to call his bluff.

—What if he aint bluffin?

—He aint bluffin. I aint neither.

●　●　●

The first day of December the O-Bar quit paying wages until spring. Half the punchers stayed on in the bunkhouse. By Christmas there was still no snow on the ground and the plains were bare and brown all the way to the blue curtain of the Bighorns. There were stories of blizzards up in Montana but Wyoming stayed dry. The cook, an Austrian named Theodore Herzl, chopped half-rotten potatoes into his nameless stew while the punchers played poker on the horse blankets, where they lost their wages to Teeter Spawn. When Herzl ladled it up, the cowboys took their tin plates outdoors and hunkered down on their heels. Ezra showed his plate to a cowpoke called Honest Abe.

—You know what meat this is, Abe?

—Prairie dog. Prairie dog stew for Christmas. That German says it's jackrabbit but it's prairie dog. Watch you don't break a tooth on his buckshot.

Herzl followed them outdoors. He sniffed the weather.

—That is rabbit, Mister Honest Abe. I want to shoot prairie dog, I shoot prairie dog. Is no good for the pot. Be happy we got anything to eat with no rain. No snow this winter. This is not a place for snow anyhow. Back in Austria, we have snow. Real snow, real mountains. This Wyoming is a place for little girls. No snow, mountains a little girl could climb. We don't see one damned snowflake this winter, you watch. Dry as my old woman.

—Thought you left her back in Germany.

—Austria, you ignorant goddamned fools. Not the same thing. Germans was living in trees when the Austrians have already Vienna.

Ezra scanned ribbons of stars in the early winter dark.

—The Lakota call this the Moon of the Popping Trees.

—What's that mean?

—I dunno. Cold as a witch's left tit, I guess.

—Is no real cold here. Back in Austria, we have cold.

Eli woke sometime after midnight to a howling outside like a thousand wolves camped at the door of the bunkhouse. He crawled off his tick in his union suit and stocking feet to see what was going on. Before he could get to the door, he slipped on a long ribbon of snow and fell on top of Ezra just as a great hammer of wind blew the bunkhouse door open. It took four cowpunchers to close it and by the time they managed to push it shut, half a foot of snow had drifted onto the planks of the floor. They pushed one another aside to peer through the tiny windows. All they could make out was a solid wall of snow whirling in the feeble cone of light from a kerosene lamp. Beyond that raging wind and dark. Teddy Herzl threw more wood on the stove, doused it in kerosene and struck a match and they sat listening to the rattle of the snow in the stovepipe until the wood caught. When the stove glowed red, they huddled around, rubbing their hands and cursing the wind that found every chink in the walls. Teeter Spawn struck a match on the seat of his pants and lit a cheroot.

—Might as well go back to bed, boys. Aint a damned thing we can do for horse nor cow in this. Winter calves don't stand a chance, cattle should be all right if the blow don't go on too long. Horses ought to scrape through, they generally do.

They put out the kerosene lamp and sat in the dark watching the red glow of Teeter's cheroot. Teeter finished the cheroot and stubbed it out on the floor and went back to sleep. Ezra lay on the bunk next to Eli and listened to the storm.

—Ma died in a storm like this one.

—I know it.

—Makes you think how it was.

—I know that too.

Daybreak when it came was little more than a fading of the dark. They dressed in mackinaws and sheepskins, tied their hats down with mufflers and heaved through the bunkhouse door into the storm. It took most of the morning for men bound together with lariats to stomp a path a hundred feet to the corral, where their shaggy mounts stood heads to the wind. They took axes to chop holes in the foot-thick ice in the stock tanks and forked icy hay into the corral. Eli found Monty and tucked a bag of oats around his neck. While the big horse ate, he tried to rub some of the ice off his coat. There was nothing they could do for the cattle out in the open. They managed to run a rope trail of lariats from the bunkhouse to the corral and the outhouse. It was dark by the time they fought their way back inside, peeled off layers of cold, damp clothing and tried to rub the feeling back into fingers and toes. Teeter laughed at Theodore Herzl standing with his fanny almost in the fire.

—Still don't think much of our Wyoming winters? Wish ye was back in Germany, do ye?

—I am Austrian. One winter back in the Tyrol we had snow above the rooftops.

—Aw, shut it. And watch you don't light your private parts afire.

Teeter took up his harmonica and tried to play above the howling of the wind. Pappap Morgan sang an old tune from the Mexican War. Herzl said they had to conserve kerosene, so they kept but one lamp lit and in the half-light they retreated each to his own nook as the blizzard sealed them off like men in a dungeon.

By noon of the next day, the snow was four feet deep on level ground and as high as a two-story house where it drifted. A rider who made it in from Sheridan said there was snow in the mountain passes forty feet deep and Teeter said he wanted to meet the man who had crawled up there to measure it.

It was four days before Dermott Cull left his tender Mexican girl to venture down to the bunkhouse and tell the cowhands the O-Bar was paying wages again.

—Soon's this storm breaks, I want y'all out there scourin up cattle, makin sure they's all right. Take some pony drags and get hay out to them, see if you can turn up any winter calves. I expect this is our winter right here, and when it's done, it's done. Taint long till spring, anyhow.

Teeter threw down his harmonica.

—Taint long? This here is January, Dermott. You expect to be pickin daisies next week, do ye? Your winter calves, they're makin a nice dinner for some starving coyote right about now. The older cattle, might be we could keep some out of the draws and off the fences where they're goin to freeze to death or smother under ten feet a snow. Aint much else we can do.

—Are you sayin you don't want to work?

—Hell no I aint. We been workin every day as it is, pay or no. Didn't ask a red cent from you or the O-Bar. But you might want to ask the folks who run the Continental Cattle Company why they dumped thirty thousand head of southern cattle on this range before winter. They'll be lucky if they got three steers left when this is over. Their stock is crowdin ours, makin it tough on everybody.

—Cows is tougher than you think.

—Yeah, and this blizzard is worse'n you think.

Cull glared around the room. The punchers sprawled on their ticks, played cards, mended boots and frayed ropes and caulked chinks in the timbers. He pushed his way out the door. In his wake the storm seemed to rise in its fury. Wind ripped at the bunkhouse and the timbers groaned. Ezra thought he could hear wolves howling in the night, a gathering wolf pack closing on the bunkhouse. He shivered and tried to cover his ears with his bedroll. If this wasn't hell, it would sure enough do.

It was two weeks before the first train broke through to Douglas on the nineteenth of January. Broke through and stayed, unable to move forward or back. In northern Colorado, a Union Pacific train was blown clean off the tracks. West of Ogallala, dudes riding the westbound train had to climb out in their suits and patent-leather shoes and grab sticks and chunks of coal to help the trainmen drive thousands of desperate, starving cattle trapped in the railroad cut between enormous snowbanks. Somehow the men pushed fifty thousand head of dying cattle seven miles to a break in the cut where they could escape. The ranchers among them had no doubt what they would find when they reached the high country of Wyoming.

The storm went on for ten days without pause. When it broke, the temperature plummeted and the men of a thousand cow outfits from Colorado to Montana thawed saddle blankets on bunkhouse stoves and saddled up and rubbed stove charcoal or lampblack from the lanterns around their eyes to cut the glare and rode out into brilliant sunshine where the icy wind blew plumes of snow gritty as sand off snowbanks sculpted like sand dunes. They tied scarves around their faces against the glare and still a man from Arkansas went half-blind and sat moaning on his tick with a wool cloth dipped in snow tied over his eyes to ease the pain of his singed retinas. After three clear days, the next storm hit, and two green Missourians rode down into a coulee in the blizzard and couldn't ride out. They were found huddled over a dead fire, frozen stiff as their horses. Abe and Teeter tied their bodies over packhorses and lugged them back to the bunkhouse, where they had to be left in a snowbank for burial in the spring. A kid from Montana died trying to free trapped cattle in forty-below weather, the manner of his death fodder for a bunkhouse argument. Pappap Morgan said the kid worked too hard and the frigid air seared his lungs; Teeter Spawn thought he smothered after his muffler froze to his skimpy beard. It mattered little to the Montana kid, whose body was added to the pile in the snowbank.

The punchers when they piled back into the bunkhouse in frigid dark at the end of another day filled the clawfoot stove until it glowed red and gathered round peeling away layers of wet and frozen clothing to hang on lines thawing pungent and steaming. They helped one another shuck wet boots, one straddling the other's leg and tugging while his partner planted a bootheel on his behind and shoved. Wool socks doubled in wet boots came away clumped and frozen from cracked and bleeding feet. They doctored fingers and toes with reeking horse ointment and fell on their ticks exhausted, the long, perilous slog of winter now a tunnel without beginning or end. A heavyset Virginian had his toes frozen so solid that two of them snapped off as he tried to pull his stockings from his feet. The man said he felt nary a thing but when he plunged his feet into a bucket of cold water, his screams echoed over the snowbanks and the ribbed carcasses of dead cattle.

After a four-day blizzard in late January, the weather broke for two days. A mild chinook blew, the snow thawed some and puddles of water formed between the drifts. They hunted cattle lost behind snowbanks and piled into dead-end coulees and draws where every last heifer and steer ought to have perished but some lived yet, thin and half-frozen as they were dragged from drifts twice the height of a tall man. After the chinook, the freeze when it came was so hard that a horse could travel over the crust without breaking through. The temperature plunged again, as far as fifty below. Cattle that had somehow survived the first ten-day blizzard and the series of storms that came howling after it now had no chance of breaking through to what fodder might be left beneath. Some slipped on the ice and died where they fell, too weak to get up. In places where they did break through the ice, they scraped all the hide off their legs so that the punchers could have trailed them by following the blood in the snow, but if they did their horses would have suffered the same fate.

When they ran low on oats and hay, Eli and Ezra showed the others an old Indian trick to feed the horses. They took axes, chopped away the outer bark of cottonwood trees, and shaved the tender inner bark. The horses ate and kept their strength up, but horses fared better than cattle anyway. The half-wild mustangs captured in the spring would paw through the snow to get at the grass beneath or fight their way into the wind to find shelter on the lee side of slopes, while cattle unable to find a spot where the wind had swept the winter grass free from snow would drift with the wind until they piled up against fences or struggled down into the draws where the snow was deepest. They died standing up, buried in twenty-foot drifts.

One night in February, the O-Bar hands woke to find a dozen head of cattle gnawing at the bark on the corral poles and the logs of the bunkhouse itself and nibbling at a pile of garbage and horse manure west of the bunkhouse. In the morning, when the punchers headed out to find fodder for the poor devils, Ezra heard a crackling noise underneath and dug down and found the carcass of a steer that had died within six feet of the house. Some of the cattle survived snow and cold and starvation but went crazy with thirst, drifting downhill and out onto river ice in search of an air-hole where they could drink. The leaders were pushed into the hole by the desperate cattle behind and drowned under the ice and the next rank stepped up to be drowned in turn.

By the end of February, the nine men still alive in the O-Bar bunkhouse were fractious and bitter and exhausted, every last one suffering from frostbite or worse. On two consecutive nights, the thermometer outside the big house hit sixty below zero. The old Mexican woman living with Cull and his señorita went mad listening night after night to the howling storms and was found stark naked and frozen to death in the corral, her mouth stuffed with hay.

On the first day of March, Ezra and Eli rode out early in search of a dozen surviving cattle sheltered in a draw within two miles of the bunkhouse. The day was overcast, not much more than thirty below but still whip-cold and threatening more snow. They found the cattle piled up one behind the other, dragged them out one by one, and tried to point them in the general direction of the bunk-house. Eli paused and looked back over his shoulder.

—You ever seen nothing like this?

—Can't say I have.

—Any idea what it is?

—Ice fog, must be. Heard of it. Never seen it.

—You still got a clear notion which way it is to the bunk-house?

—Not much, but I can see the trail all right.

Within thirty minutes they couldn't see even that much. The fog was on them, an impenetrable sheet of freezing white mist. Eli held his hand out and wiggled his fingers. He could barely make out his own hand.

—Maybe we better give up on the rest and head back.

—I'm with you, brother.

They tied Eli's lariat from the saddlehorn of his big sorrel to the saddlehorn of Ezra's roan mare. Eli thought they should let the horses pick their way back, figuring that they could find the bunkhouse and the corrals by instinct. It was strange riding, floating in deathly white, unable to see the hooves of the horses as they picked their way along the trail. They had gone less than half a mile when Ezra felt himself choking.

—Can't breathe this stuff. It's goin to freeze my lungs solid.

—Keep your scarf tight over your face, try to heat the air a little before you swallow it down. Aint no other way.

They rode with their reins drooping loose, the horses walking slow through the mist. Eli felt something like real terror. It was one thing fighting something you could see, like O. T. Yonkee. This was a menace that could not be seen or fought. If the horses weren't on the right trail, they were dead: They would freeze to death long before anyone found them. Even with the roan's nose almost on Monty's tail, he couldn't see Ezra behind him. The only way he knew he wasn't alone in the fog was the sound of the roan's steel-shod hooves ringing on ice. Then he heard a chuckle.

—Say, we coulda stayed home in Sioux Falls, y'know.

—I know that, and I'm sorry, brother. I dragged you a pretty ways to get into this.

—I aint a bit sorry. We seen some things.

The sound began as a panting out in the mist.

—*Hufh-hufh-hufh-hufh.*

—What is that?

—I dunno. Somethin out there.

—*Hufh-hufh-hufh.*

—Who's there? That you, Teeter? Abe? Who the hell's there?

They listened, heard nothing but the panting, like the sound of a huge dog at the end of a long run. Through a slender crack in the fog, Eli saw a dark loping shadow.

—Wolves!

—Dammit. Where are they?

—All around, by the sound of it.

—*Hufh! Hufh! Hufh!*

—My holy Lord. They're gettin awful bold if they're down here after us.

—Easy pickins for them here. Maybe they can smell that we're lost.

—Jesus. Are we lost?

—Must be. Should have come to that bunkhouse by now if we're on the trail.

—How long has it been?

—No idea, little brother.

Monty slipped on the ice, stumbled, and almost went to his knees. Eli had all he could do to keep from being pitched over the horse's head into the snow. As the big horse struggled to recover his balance, Eli saw one of the shadows knife in out of the fog to nip at the sorrel's heels. He tried to peel off a mitten to get at his pistol but by the time he reached it, the wolf had disappeared. He looked around wildly, searching for a target. Ezra's voice came from somewhere off to the right.

—Sonofabitch! One of 'em just went at my horse!

—I know. I had one after Monty when he stumbled there.

—Where in the Lord's name are we?

—Could be in Hades for all I can say.

The bloodcurdling howl was so close it sounded as though the wolf was riding double behind the saddle. Monty shied and skidded sideways, nostrils flaring in terror. Eli felt the skin tingle on the back of his neck. The wolves seemed to be coming from all directions at once.

Ezra felt a thud as one of the wolves struck the roan in the flank. The force of the blow staggered the strong little horse enough that Eli felt the tug on the lariat.

—You still there, Ez?

—She's all right but one of 'em hit her like a cannonball. Another shadow danced in out of the mist and slipped between the roan's front legs. All around he could hear the wolves panting as they closed in.

—Hufh! Hufh! Hufh!

Somewhere off to the right, they heard the roar of a big shot-gun.

—Eli! Ezra! Over here! This way, boys!

—Teeter Spawn. I'll be damned.

—Here, Teeter! We're right here!

—Keep comin as you are, comin steady. You're headed right at the corral.

—We got wolves on us, Teeter. Be careful, and keep that scat-tergun handy.

Monty walked almost into the rails of the corral before Eli saw Teeter, shotgun in hand.

—Where are these wolves?

—Right on top of us.

—I don't see no wolves.

—That's because you can't see your own pecker in this.

They dismounted and turned to face the wolves. Eli decided he'd rather die with Eb's bullwhip in his hand, so he undid the whip and held it and Ezra got the big Whitworth out of its scab-bard. When the wolves attacked, he would get at least one of them. They waited in a tight little circle with Teeter in the middle.

—Hufh! Hufh! Hufh!

—You hear that, Teeter?

—Sure as hell do.

A long, quavering howl came from somewhere out in the mist, and then another and another. It sounded as though the wolves were closing in, still hidden by the ice fog. Eli tightened his grip on the whip and waited but the wolves did not appear. He had no idea how much time had passed before he realized that the only sounds he could hear were coming from Ezra and Teeter and the horses.

—I don't hear the bastards no more.

Teeter shouldered the scattergun.

—Me neither. They must have cut and run. Too close to the bunkhouse.

Ezra let the heavy Whitworth rest at his side.

—Jesus. They scared me so bad I'd of pissed my pants if it wasn't froze.

They got the saddles off the horses and followed the rope lines to scare up oats and a currycomb, the boys nervous, waiting for the wolves to attack. In the bunkhouse they pulled off clothing that was frozen stiff, gasping to get warm air into their lungs. Teeter filled a basin with cold water for their feet.

—You sure them was wolves after you?

—Didn't you hear 'em howl?

—I did. But there's times when a fella hears things in a fog like this.

Ezra, shivering, shook his head.

—Nope. I felt one of them bastards hit the roan. Near knocked her plumb off her feet.

The next morning they followed the trail back to the draw in bright sunshine. The track of their horses was plain as day but there was no wolf-sign at all. Not a paw print, nothing. Ezra shook his head.

—What you suppose that was after us yesterday?

—I don't know. Ghost wolves, maybe.

—Ghost wolves.

—You got a other explanation?

—Can't say as I do.

—Well then. We was chased by ghost wolves.

Ezra gave his brother a serious look.

—Is that the yarn as you aim to tell it?

—It is. Truth can be the strangest yarn a man ever hears.

❧ CHAPTER 19 ❧

On April Fool's Day of 1887, the Paint twins turned seventeen without noting the date. At dawn they were squatting on their bootheels on a patch of high ground swept dry by the wind, watching the ice break up on the Powder River in the company of Pappap Morgan; Teeter Spawn; Honest Abe, whose real name was William Parker; the foreman, Jim Brower; and Roy Titus, a short, red-haired, quarrelsome kid who had turned up after the last blizzard and decided to stay because there was nowhere else for him to go. All with faces peeled, lips cracked and bleeding from snowburn, winter ache in every limb and muscle, defeat in their gaunt cheeks and death-weary eyes. The feathery spring breeze carried the reek of carrion and below them the ice broke in rapid pistol shots like a man fanning a sixshooter. Wagon-size blocks of ice tumbled and rolled in the thaw-swollen river and at intervals a frozen tail or a calf's head or the water-bloated body of a brindle steer surfaced before it was swallowed again as the river's share of the great die-off mingled with the riven ice, the detritus of catastrophe borne by the rushing spring current. The watching cowpunchers noted the magnitude of their failure with each hoof, hock, and horn.

Ezra plucked a blade of grass.

—The Lakota call this the Moon of the Tender Grass.

Roy Titus sneered.

—You and your goddamned Lakota. Like they was anythin but stinkin ignorant savages.

Ezra grabbed Roy by his shirtfront and hoisted him off the ground with one hand.

—I'd be right careful the way I talked if I was a pip-squeak like you, Roy.

Eli was about to come to Roy's rescue when Teeter spotted Dermott Cull a mile off with a second rider.

—Hush, boys. That's Dermott's horse and I believe it's Perceale Pike with him.

Cull had taken on a new sidekick in Pike, a tall Texan of cadaverous mien who favored a sawed-off scattergun and a bowie knife for his dirty work. Pike rarely spoke but he had a habit of sizing a man up like he was trying to imagine how the fellow would look in a coffin. Cull reined up and got right down to business.

—Mr. Humphrey Doane sent a wire to the telegraph office in Sheridan yesterday. Says I'm not to pay one thin dime to cowpunchers who set around all winter on their sweet behinds and let his stock die off. I told him we'd be lucky to bust a thousand head out of the brush and Mr. Doane and his investors, they aint happy.

Teeter Spawn spoke up first.

—That's purely horseshit, Dermott.

—Be as may, taint my decision. Doane hears most of his cattle is dead, he aint happy.

—A wage is a wage. Wasn't nothin said about keepin those cows alive. It was about *tryin* to save as many as we could, and we done that. Busted our backs and nigh froze to death all winter, lost five hands killed tryin to save O-Bar livestock. You needed punchers in the middle of a blizzard and now you don't want to pay what's owed.

—If any of you was worth a cuss, you'd have your pay.

Teeter took a step toward Cull. Pike swung the sawed-off scattergun so it was pointed right at Teeter's gut, sneering like he hoped Teeter would step into a load of double-aught buckshot and leave his innards on the prairie for the magpies. Cull came up with his Colt Navy so quick it was like a strange metal creature birthed there in the wink of a hummingbird's eye. Before it was too late for the bunch of them, Eli stepped between Teeter and Cull.

—Whoa now. No call for trouble here. Dermott, you know every man at the O-Bar is owed three months' wages. You come down to the bunkhouse yourself in January, said we was back on full pay if we wanted to drag calves outa snowdrifts. You give your word and we done our best.

—Your best wasn't worth a heap a buffalo shit.

Eli feared Teeter might walk into a shotgun blast out of pure spite but Spawn took his fury out on his hat instead. He flung it on the ground, stomped it, picked it up, dusted it off with a couple of backhand wallops, stalked back to his horse and paused for a parting shot at Cull.

—I happen to know you and that scarecrow killer holdin the scattergun is paid detective's wages from county taxes, because that's the way the Stockmen's Association fixes things. You're drawin two hundred and twenty-five dollars a month from the association for wavin that gun around and the O-Bar is payin I don't know how much more atop that, and a honest working puncher can't collect the forty a month he's owed. If we don't get our wages, you might find yourself awful short on cowboys come roundup.

—If you're too lazy to round up what stock is left, there is punchers out here who will. North Powder Roundup starts a week Monday. If I was you, I'd put a string together and try to find ponies with some bottom in them this time.

He and Pike rode off, Pike half-turned in the saddle to keep the scattergun leveled at Teeter. Eli waited until they were out of sight before he drew Teeter away from the rest.

—That was not the time to pick a fight, Teeter. Not with Perceale Pike holdin that scattergun. You want to square things with Dermott and the O-Bar, we're goin to have to wait our chance and hit 'em when they aint lookin.

—I'd just as soon go after the bastards right now.

—This aint the time. You go at 'em direct like that and you'll start a war. There has to be a better way but we got to take time and think on it.

Teeter took in the set of Eli's jaw.

—How old did you say you was?

—I believe we just turned seventeen.

Teeter nodded. He had known men like Eli in the War Between the States. They didn't say much, but they had a way about them, and when hell itself opened up, other men looked to them instinctively. There were some who led because they had gold braid and stars on their epaulets and there were others who led because of some inner compass and strength that no rank could confer. With men such as Eli Paint, age did not matter. They could be fifteen or fifty; they were birthed with such a quality or they were not, and it was not a thing a man could acquire any more than he could acquire those strange pale eyes. Even between twins, the ability to so move and command other men did not distribute itself equally, so that Ezra could be of a size and strength and manner identical to his brother and yet not be the one to whom other men would turn when they feared their last hour was upon them. Teeter had pondered it often since his first encounter with the Paint boys and yet he understood it no better than he understood the wind; Eli had a gift of command, the gift had likely been his since the cradle, and in this conflict with Dermott Cull and Perceale Pike, as in all other situations, Teeter would without a second thought trust Eli's judgment despite his tender years.

—Well, you let me know when it's time, because I would bet my weight in gold that Mr. Humphrey Doane never said not to pay us. Them cocksuckers decided to hijack our pay for themselves, so the quicker we take it back out of their sorry hides the better.

—I know it. We have to wait till the wind is right.

At first it wasn't a plan at all, just loose talk around mesquite campfires after a long day in the saddle during the North Powder Roundup, which mostly involved counting the carcasses of the dead. Teeter and Eli talked cattle, but the few cattle that had made it through the winter were down to ribs and hide and hoof. Then they talked horses, especially the tough and shaggy little mustangs that had proved their worth by surviving the winter. Horses could move farther and faster than cattle, and a well-broke saddlehorse would bring two hundred dollars, provided you could convince the buyer that your ownership was legitimate. The O-Bar had its breaking corrals near the middle prong of Crazy Horse Creek and from there it was a short ride to Montana, where Teeter knew the country and Eli had a buyer in mind.

—You remember that half-Blackfoot fella Joe Kipp up to Fort Benton? Runs liquor to the Indians. We met him on that trip up the Missouri, the time Pa and Niall McPhee sold him all that Blackfoot rum. Joe runs liquor up to Canada. He needs good horses to outrun the U.S. marshals and a man in his line of work can't be too particular where they come from.

When they got down to the fine points, Ezra tried to say that stealing horses was a good way to end up on the wrong side of a rope but once they got the bit in their teeth, Teeter and Eli weren't about to let go. The O-Bar owed them for a winter's wrangling in snow and bitter cold and the O-Bar was going to pay—one way or another. Ezra asked Eli what he would do about the O-Bar brand, which was known from Denver to the Yellowstone.

—Every critter for twenty miles around is branded O-Bar. Even if we put a gun to his head, I don't see Dermott signin a bill of sale.

—I thought a that. We got to get over to Sheridan and register us a new brand.

Eli drew his clasp knife and sketched the new brand in the dust, showing how easy it would be to alter the O-Bar brand to the 8T by adding a second loop to the O and a vertical band beneath the bar to form the letter T.

—Any man half decent with a runnin iron ought to be able to do that quick as a wink. Give 'em a month to heal, won't a man anywhere be able to say for sure whether that livestock belongs to the O-Bar or the Eighty.

Ezra took the knife and added another 8. A dust-borne brand and a new partnership, carved in dust: 8T8.

—Two eights for you and me, the Paint boys, and the T for Teeter. The eighty-eight. Has a ring to it.

—How many head of horses you think we could manage, Teeter?

—The three of us? Almost any number you care to name. I heard of a fella up in Dakota made off with two hundred head of prize Percherons all by his lonesome. Would be better if there was four of us, though. That way if we have to split up, there's two riders with each bunch.

Ezra still didn't like it.

—That's a deal of horseflesh. If we take that many horses, Cull will hang us twice.

—Aint but the first time that matters. If we're goin to run the risk, we might as well make it worth our while. I'd rather get hung for a couple hundred horses than a Shanghai rooster.

—So who's your fourth man?

—Honest Abe. Got to be. He knows Montana.

It took a week before Abe in his slow-talking way decided to throw in with them. He did know Montana, especially the country north to Fort Benton. He sketched a map in the dirt.

—They's a place called the Pinnacle, shaped long and skinny like a porcupine's peter, just above where the Little Powder meets the Powder. Long, spiny thing, high as hell, you can't miss it. Rough country around there, deep coulees where Custer could a hid his whole army if he'd had any sense. Whoever gets there first could lay up until the rest of the bunch gets there. From there we head north and west to Fort Benton. There's ways we can keep to rough country where we won't run into much but outlaws and Blackfoot all the way from the Pinnacle to Benton.

When they were alone, Ezra tried to persuade Eli to change his mind.

—We wasn't raised to be horse thieves.

—No, we wasn't. But we can keep on workin for the likes of

Dermott or we can strike out on our own. This way, maybe we'll have somethin to show for all that hard ridin.

—Or maybe we end up in a shallow grave, waitin to get dug up by coyotes.

—Maybe we do. Least we took a chance at bein something more than cowpokes or sodbusters all our lives, the kind of men end up more broke than they started out. That's how I see it, but I aint goin to force you to stick your head in no noose.

—I'll make like you didn't say that.

Eli wished Eb was around, wished he could sit in the rocking chair at his bedside and talk this through, see if the old man would have another angle on things. He remembered the conversation at Eb's deathbed, the way his father had urged him to look after Ezra and to set himself up in such a way that he wouldn't have to depend on banks or railroads. The way Eli saw things, if that meant taking a great chance, then you squared your shoulders and you took it. Eb had risked everything repeatedly and if he had not exactly failed, he had not been successful either. Given this opportunity and the way they had been treated by the O-Bar, Eli was sure that Eb would elect to roll the dice. He was about to do the same.

That night Eli was nighthawking with Ezra on the far side of the remuda. A sliver of new moon sashayed over the Bighorns and thin cloud streaks ran across the moon like antelope over pale sand. The horses were calm, worn out after being worked hard in the big corrals all day. Eli rode easy and quiet, rocking to the sounds of creaking saddle leather, the nightrush of owls, the run of the Powder River slipping over worn rock. The fatigue of the winter and a long day in the saddle caught up to him and he fell into a deep sleep with the reins wrapped tight around the saddle horn. What moon there was dodged behind a cloud and the night went dark. When the cloud drifted east, the moon had changed color from bone to blood orange and Spotted War Bonnet stood before him astride a pinto war pony, wearing his father's scalp shirt and holding a war club adorned with eagle feathers. At first he was like the boy they'd met at the swimming hole; then he was a medicine man with the head of a buffalo and the body of a grizzly and his voice came from the mouth of a blood orange moon. He spoke in Lakota, saying that the grandfathers had warned him of thunder and lightning, a forked tree, many horses at the river. Before Eli could ask what it meant, the moon went dark again, like a lantern plunged into a lake. When it slipped out from behind another cloud, War Bonnet stood in the watery light wearing a pith helmet like those the Ite Sica had taken from the dead surveyors at Devils Lake. He spoke with a tongue of forked lightning and thunder in the rumble of his voice but the language was incomprehensible. Then he vanished like smoke. In the distance Eli could make out a pack of white wolves bounding over rags of dirty snow, pursuing shadowy figures that might have been deer.

A horse whinnied in the herd they were watching. Monty whinnied back. Eli woke with the vision of War Bonnet running through his mind. He shivered. The night had turned cold, and sunup was three hours away. He lifted Eb's bullwhip coiled in its leather thong on his saddle opposite his lariat, something of the old man still in its heft and feel, a talisman for the long, hard ride ahead.

Near dusk the next afternoon Teeter and Eli squatted with Honest Abe in the shade of a cottonwood, going over last-minute details, with Abe drawing and redrawing the map in the dust. When a twig snapped, Eli rousted Roy Titus out of his hiding place behind a knoll where the prairie sloped down to the Powder River. Roy came out with his hands up.

—Don't shoot! I didn't hear nothin about rustlin no horses.

—You little sneak. I ought to take a bullwhip to you right now.

—Maybe you ought, but you'd be losing a man. I can be some help.

—Help how? You aint nothin but a boy, and a scrawny one at that.

—I can ride as hard and long as ary man and stick like a sand-bur to ary horse.

Eli drew his clasp knife in frustration, stuck it point first in the dirt next to his boot.

—What do you say, Teeter?

—I say shoot the little peckerwood and feed him to the coyotes.

—You aint going to shoot me down in cold blood, are ye?

—No, I'm going to shoot ye in hot blood. What call you got snoopin?

—I don't want to be left behind, is all. You boys is the only ones decent to me.

—Well you're a sorry case then, because we got no more use for you than we have for a egg-suckin dog. But I don't see we got a choice. We got to kill you or take you along and I aint got the stomach for killin today. Long as you can keep up, you might be some use.

CHAPTER 20

That night Eli persuaded Teeter to drag out his last two bottles of Tennessee skullpopper to sedate any curious cowpoke inclined to wonder why they were saddling up in the middle of the night. Among the half dozen new riders Cull had hired for the North Powder Roundup was a Mexican vaquero who had come as far as Wyoming with a Texas cattle drive and forgot to go back. The Mexican took a long, gurgling pull on the whiskey bottle, made a face like he was swallowing weasel puke, went to his kit and brought out a bottle of fiery, clear liquid with a worm at the bottom. Teeter's whiskey circulated one way and the mescal went the other and somebody located a couple of bottles of Blackfoot rum. They whooped and hollered and argued and danced the Virginia reel and sang songs about Texas and the war and the girl back home.

Finally they keeled over and fell asleep one by one where they lay. Eli kept a close eye on his crew, especially Roy Titus. They took the odd sip to keep up appearances as the bottles went round but Eli had sworn he would take the bullwhip to any man who got drunk. By midnight they had passed out, all except the Mexican, who seemed to get livelier the more he drank. Finally he drained the last of the mescal, saddled his horse, and rode off to the south, singing in Spanish at the top of his lungs. Ezra looked at Teeter.

—Where the hell you suppose he's going?

—Mexico, I imagine.

Eli loaded his gear on an albino packhorse, Ezra got the rest onto a swaybacked bay mare. Teeter and Roy and Abe looked after their own animals. When they were ready, Teeter gave a low whistle and they nudged the slumbering horses into a kind of motion that was like water running down the slightest grade, the mustangs no more than gliding shadows in the night. The splinter of moon gave just enough light to silhouette riders on the dark plain. They signaled one another with their hands and whistles and rode like ghosts until three hundred and twenty-eight O-Bar horses were headed north for Montana. Teeter got a long rope on a lead mare up front knowing the others would follow and Abe rode to the east, crowding the animals tight to the riverbank, while Ezra and Eli swept the rear for stragglers and Roy Titus tried to show he could ride as hard as anyone.

They rode all night and at first light had traveled thirty miles on a line north-northeast following the lazy bends of the Powder. With daylight to work by, they turned the herd in to a shallow side creek for three miles to throw off trackers. The coats of the winded horses smoked as they splashed up the riverbank out of the water, their nostrils flaring after the long night's walk. The whistling riders drove them north to a rise where, with the sun lifting clear of the prairie to the east, they paused to look back at a horizon empty of pursuers. There they split up. Teeter and Ezra crossed the river to drive half the herd along the west side of the Powder while Eli with Roy Titus and Honest Abe veered away from the river with the rest of the horses for a dozen miles and then turned due north to meet up with the river again where it looped to the east on the far side of the Montana line. Eli hoped that Dermott Cull and the vigilance committee he was sure to collect would not notice they had divided the herd and would lose one bunch or both in the river or on the hardpan to the north. After some argument, Ezra persuaded Eli to take Eb's old Whitworth rifle, because if Cull picked up a trail, it was more likely to be Eli with the main bunch east of the Powder.

—I can't shoot this thing worth a damn.

—Don't matter. If you got riders after you, fire into the bunch.

It will carry a mile and scare hell out of 'em if nothing else. After your second shot, you'll have to use the ramrod to get them bullets down but I molded aplenty last winter. You won't run out. Don't forget to allow for your windage and squeeze her real slow. She kicks like a mule.

—Maybe that's why I never took to the damned thing.

Ezra tipped his hat and rode off after Teeter. When he looked back, Eli was riding hard to catch up to Abe and Roy.

After four decades working stock, Pappap Morgan had been bucked, kicked, shot, clawed, and bit so many times that his carcass felt like it was held together with chewing gum and binding twine. Along with the rheumatiz, lumbago, piles, cataracts, and a tendency to list to the left because of a mule kick that had shattered his shinbone, he had a bladder the size of a withered pea. He had passed out for no more than an hour when he was awakened by a need to piss. He rolled over onto his back and squinted at the night sky. The Milky Way was a mare's-tail cloud of stars riding the spring breeze a knuckle or two past the lee side of the Bighorns, which would make it two o'clock in the morning or thereabouts. His head felt like a blacksmith's anvil, he had the cottonmouth and an evil rumbling in the gut that would mean half a day wasted crouching in the weeds. He staggered away from the fire, found a likely spot to unzip and pissed in rusty little dribs and drabs. When he was done, he sniffed the wind out of old habit and found in it a dearth of horses. He knew who was to blame. *Sonofabitch goddamned Mexican. The bean-eatin horsethief done run off to the Rio Grande with our livestock.*

Morgan's head throbbed so that he wanted nothing except to crawl back into his bedroll and let the missing horses wait until morning. Had he known Teeter and the Paint boys were involved, he would have pulled a blanket over his ears, slept till high noon and kept his secret until the Second Coming but he had no use for Mexicans, with their fancy boots, their faces you couldn't read, that fast jibber-jabber they talked all day long. He pulled on his boots and rousted Jim Brower and they booted to life sleeping cow-punchers who woke one by one cussing and puking and so liquor-befuddled it took some time to get the point across: They were short one Mexican horsethief and better than three hundred head of horses. The hands saddled up drunk and rode out in darkness and no man among them paused to notice that they were short five of their own.

The sun was up by the time they reached the main house and roused Dermott Cull, whose mood brightened when he learned that a Mexican had run off with the horses. He and Perceale Pike conferred quickly and agreed that in all probability a theft that size involved a whole gang of Mexican horsethieves waiting to run the herd south to the Rio Grande and that it was a sweet day when a man found out before breakfast that he had a chance to string up a whole gang of Mexicans; Cull was not one to allow the presence of a sweet Mexican girl in his bed to interfere with his loathing of her race. It took the rest of the morning for him to put together a vigilance committee composed of nineteen men willing to ride out after the horsethieves, who were assumed to be headed south for the Colorado line and beyond. By the time they were ready to ride, Cull was in such a state of boiling and venomous anger that he also failed to note the absence of five men from the posse.

When Perceale Pike mentioned that the Paint boys were not in their company, Cull concluded that the sneaking, thieving Mexi-cans had crept up and slit the throats of the nighthawking boys, adding murder to the list of capital offenses that would make it a pleasure to hang the bean-eating sonsofbitches. They spent the rest of the day trying to pick up the trail, riding in great, looping circles to the south, encountering other roundup outfits here and there but no herd and no Mexican horsethieves. Cull did not give up until they had ridden all the way south to Pumpkin Creek. By that time it was too dark to find a trail had there been one to find. It wasn't until they made camp that he got around to counting noses.

—Anybody seen Honest Abe? How about Teeter Spawn? That redheaded kid?

It was Pike who put the question to Brower.

—Jim, you didn't see no dead men out there nor follow no trail? You didn't find them Paint boys with their throats slit?

—Not a bit. Twas dark night when we broke camp.

—You don't know for a fact them boys is dead?

—Well, no. Pappap said it was Mexicans took the horses and the Mexican was gone.

—So it could be the Paint boys throwed in with the Mexican. Or it could be the beaner has nothin to do with this and it was old Teeter and Abe and them boys all along.

Brower spoke up.

—None of them struck me as the type for rustlers.

Cull spat into the fire.

—I've seen just about every type of man there is hung for a rustler, includin a Adventist preacher in Waco was strung up for stealin a Appaloosa stud horse from a second cousin of Sam Houston. They aint no type for a rustler, Jim. You ought to know that. Greed and opportunity is all it takes to make a horsethief. If it's Teeter and Abe took them horses, you can bet they went north. They both know Montana, Abe in particular. We spent a whole damned day ridin the wrong direction because you didn't have the sense to look for sign. Now they got a whole day's start on us.

The men turned in for an uneasy slumber, knowing that come sunup they would be riding hard after their own kind, looking to put a noose around the necks of five men who had done something they all thought of doing at one time or another. It was still moondown dark when Cull rousted the members of the vigilance committee out of their bedrolls and pointed them north. They had made ten miles before an angry red sun rose in a cloudless blue sky, a perfect day for a hanging. The trail when they came upon it due north of the breaking corrals was plain as the road to perdition. They picked it up at a canter, riding too hard to notice where the Paint boys had split the herd, nor did a single rider note that half the horses had crossed the Powder at the ford and that they were now in pursuit of the bunch that had swung east away from the river, chasing Eli, Abe, and Roy Titus driving two hundred horses while Ezra and Teeter ran the balance of the herd due north.

At midmorning Roy panicked and fired his rusty six-shooter to head a rawboned bay mare inclined to go her own way. That scared the rest and the three of them had to wear their horses nearly to nothing running them down. By the time they were on the trail again, Eli spotted riders far off to the south and knew what was coming; they would never make the rendezvous at the Pinnacle without a fight. They tried to push the mustangs harder, but their own mounts were now too worn down to keep up. The alternative was to let the rustled stock get away and make a break for it. As far as Eli was concerned, that was no alternative at all. When the trail ran through soapweed, yucca, and sage and between two fair-size gumbo buttes, Eli imagined that he saw a way to be sure the bulk of the herd made it at least as far as the Pinnacle. He signaled a halt to talk it over with Abe.

—One man up there with a good rifle could hold them vigilantes off the livelong day. I got the Whitworth, I'll find a likely spot to keep Mr. Dermott Cull entertained while you and Roy push them horses far and fast. If I can hold 'em off until dark, I can sneak off and meet up with you at the Pinnacle.

—That don't amount to much of a plan.

—It's all we got.

Eli watched Abe and Roy chase the herd out of sight. He tied Monty and the albino packhorse to a scraggly pine hidden behind the butte and found himself a good flat spot in the shadows with some protection from a flange of boulder he could use as a gun rest. With the Whitworth ranging at near two thousand yards, he figured he could hold off an army for an afternoon. He tossed up a handful of dust to check the wind direction, adjusted his sights, squeezed off a test round, watched where it kicked up dirt a half mile away and a little off to the right, adjusted the sights again and settled in to wait.

☙ CHAPTER 21 ☙

They came on like a sandstorm, nineteen vigilantes in a whirling cloud, shapes shifting as they edged into focus and vanished again behind the curtain of dust. Eli wiped his eyes with a bandanna: The riders were moving fast and there was little but the occasional glint of sunlight on a bit or buckle as a guide to sight the rifle propped in the notch of a gumbo rock. The thing to do was to shoot the horses, draw a bead on the broad, lathered chest of the nearest animal and squeeze off a shot and hope the tumbling hooves would bring down two or three more and leave their riders scrambling for cover. But Eli Paint could no more shoot a healthy horse than he could level the Bighorn Mountains with a spade. He waited until the riders were under fifteen hundred yards and drew down on a jouncing rider who might have been Dermott Cull or Perceale Pike or anyone else and squeezed the trigger. He peered into the dust and saw the riders still coming. He fired until he thought he saw a rider slump over his horse's neck but it might have been a man crouching low in the saddle like a jockey. He was ramming another hexagonal ball down the muzzle of the Whitworth when he saw the vigilantes pull up and drop and scatter; Cull and his men were diving for cover, dismounting to use their horses as shields.

Down below, Dermott Cull had tumbled to the earth in a swale with Perceale Pike next to him, holding the reins of their jittery horses while they tried to locate the source of the shots.

—Anybody hurt?

—Brower took one in the elbow. Made a mess outa his arm but he'll live.

—Ought to let him bleed to death. Where the hell are they, Pike?

—Got to be in the shadows under them bluffs. Awful hard to spot them from here. Figure they got five men up there with rifles, maybe more, and they got the cover and the high ground. I know one of them Paints has got himself a big old Whitworth rifle and knows how to use it. We aint got nothing can range that far.

—I'll hang every last one.

—We got to catch 'em first. We'll have to circle around.

—That's a five-mile ride through badlands.

—You got a better notion?

A bullet kicked up dust and gravel a foot from Cull's boot, followed a second or two later by the boom of the big rifle.

—Goddamn! The bastards are gettin the range. You take four, five men. We'll give you two hours and then we'll open up to keep them busy.

It was high noon and the sky was empty except for the distant specks of a circling red-tailed hawk and its mate. An hour passed and another. Eli watched the vigilantes pull back, thought at first they were going to cut and run, then saw them settle into better cover three hundred yards back. He still had three canteens full of water so he took time to belly-slide back to where Monty and the albino packhorse were tied to a scrub pine in the shade of the bluff, filled his hat with water, and let them drink. Back at his post he tried to count the men below. There were a dozen at least, with twice that many horses. Fresh mounts, not worn down like Monty was after a long night pushing mustangs. The vigilantes had come equipped for a long chase with a hanging at the end of it. He adjusted the sights again and fired a couple of rounds, probing, saw them kick up dust well short of their targets, and settled in to wait again, but with his eyes burning from exhaustion and dust and the effort of keeping them trained on the distant men, he succumbed to a weariness so complete that he fell sound asleep with his eyes still open.

Eli woke with a start to the sound of a jangling spur. Someone was scrambling up the gumbo rocks to his left. He grabbed the Whitworth, slithered and tumbled down the slope, slipped the rifle back into its scabbard, grabbed the albino's rope, and vaulted into the saddle just as Perceale Pike's black hat peeped over the edge of the shelf where he had been concealed a moment before. Eli heard Pike's shout, the pop of a Colt Navy, the whine of a ricochet. He drew his pistol and fired back, Pike's curse telling him that he had come close. Monty sensed his tension and didn't require spurs to shift gears into an easy gallop. He was a better horse than any the vigilantes rode, but he was worn down. The chase lasted three miles. Pike had left three men on horseback at the base of the easternmost of the two bluffs; they made a dash to head off Eli, who had to veer toward the river to avoid running right into them. Farther back, Cull and the rest of the vigilantes heard the gunfire, mounted up and charged straight through the gap in pursuit.

Eli had no chance. He tried to get more speed out of Monty but when he had to swerve to avoid a steep gully, Pike cut the distance between them to a dozen feet. Before Eli could get the pistol free from the holster again, Pike had a rope out and his left-handed toss caught Eli clean around the waist, yanked him out of the saddle at a dead gallop. He tumbled and rolled over a yucca plant. The others caught up and surrounded Eli, guns drawn. Dermott Cull pulled a knife from his boot and held it to Eli's throat.

—Which one are you?

—Eli Paint.

—Where's the others?

—North. They're ahead a me, on the other side of the river.

Cull grinned.

—Bastard's lyin' through his teeth, boys. That means the rest are headed south. Where's the Mexican?

—What Mexican?

—The one stole these horses.

—Mexican didn't have nothin to do with it.

—Well, it don't make no difference. All right, boys. Let's get him strung up.

Theodore Herzl, the plump Austrian cook whose winded horse stood splayfooted under his weight, pointed a stubby finger south.

—We pass a big cottonwood back that way, maybe three mile.

Cull wheeled his horse.

—Let's ride, then. That's our hangin tree.

—Maybe we should get a judge first, *ja?* Hang him with proper law.

—You stick to killing men with your stew, mister. Let me worry about the law.

Cull left the job of bringing Eli along to Pike, who wedged his loop under Eli's armpits and set off while two of the other hands led Monty and the albino. For a mile or so, Eli followed Pike's horse at a slow jog. When he stumbled and fell, Pike kept going without looking back, dragging him over prickly pear and cowflop, mesquite brush and yucca. Each time Eli managed to struggle to his feet something else would take him down, so that by the time they made it to the cottonwood, he was barely conscious enough to know he was about to hang. In the shadow of the tree, someone kicked his feet out from under him, and he fell facedown, Pike's rope still tight around his arms. Nobody wanted to waste a good lariat on a hanging, so a young vigilante donated thirty feet of worn sawgrass rope from his saddlebag. Two men with short-handled shovels in their kits scraped out a shallow grave. Cull tied a hangman's knot with a flourish. A skinny cowpoke they called Skeeter climbed into the fork of the tree and made the rope fast and Eli was boosted half-conscious into the saddle astride Monty. Pike thought it was a sloppy way to go about a hanging.

—We ought to tie his hands at least.

—No point. He's half-dead already.

A puff of breeze cooled the sweat on their backs and the pale, hot afternoon changed keys, the shift abrupt as a whipcrack. Black thunderheads bore down on them like a highballing freight train.

Lightning semaphores flashed across the plateau signaling cloud to cloud and a line of dark rain streaked down to shortgrass prairie still green from snowmelt. The men saw the fury of the lightning and peeked around to see if the others were as scared as they were: They all knew someone who had been vaporized by a bolt of lightning, reduced to a twisted heap of burned cinders not fit for a grave. Cull squinted into the distance and saw hail scything the prairie not a mile away.

—Let's get a move on, try to see if we can't make that sheepherder's shack yonder before the lightnin catches up. Give this horsethief a short drop. I don't want to bust his neck and make it easy. If we leave him to dangle long enough, maybe that hail will beat him to death.

Cull was about to slap Eli's horse when a bolt of lightning cracked so near that he could smell the singed air. Monty didn't flinch but Cull jumped and turned pale.

—We'd best ride, boys. He don't need our help to die.

Cull gave Monty a whack with his hat and the horse lurched forward three or four steps. Eli's feet slipped off the big horse's rear and the rope stretched taut, leaving his toes dangling two or three inches above the ground. Cull leapt onto his pinto without pausing to admire his handiwork. He raked the horse's flanks with his spurs as a matched pair of lightning bolts crackled on either side of the cottonwood. The vigilantes did not require another invitation. They were off at a gallop, a hundred feet behind Cull. Jim Brower, gritting his teeth against the pain of his shattered arm as he rode hard in Cull's wake, had time to savor the gunslinger's terror: The sonofabitch was afraid of something after all.

Brower glanced back at the scene they had left behind: the lightning bolts merging into a single, incandescent flash, the dead cottonwood black against a blacker sky, a dangling man, dying slow. The vigilantes had covered a mile on bone-tired horses when the hail caught up to them, rolling across the plains with the great booms of thunder that shook the earth itself and the constant zigzag of lightning bolts from clouds dark as the devil's outhouse. They strung out across the prairie with Cull on the fastest horse trying to make it to the sheepherder's shack ahead of the lightning.

Eli felt the rope tighten like an iron bar on his gullet and heard the crash of thunder.

—*Ah, God, this can't be. The bastards leavin a man to die slow like this.*

He could see the dust under his toes turning to mud. With each flash he could almost taste the lightning, swallow its sulfurous fury with a cold gulp of rainwater.

—*Except I can't swallow because I'm choking to death.*

He grasped the rope with his hands, tried to claw it away from his neck, strained his powerful biceps to lift the tension. He could manage it for only a few seconds at a time, but when he did, oxygen rushed to his brain, a sweet release that was shorter each time as he weakened. He began to saw his weight back and forth like a child on a swing, trying to build enough momentum to bring the branch down, knowing that he couldn't possibly last more than another minute or two before he blacked out and strangled just as Cull intended.

—*Save me, sweet Lord. Let this damned old tree bust before it's too late.*

Dermott Cull did not look back. He reached the old shack on the dead gallop, piled through the open door followed by his men coming in one on top of the other to huddle in the dark with the spiders, the mice, and the rattlesnakes. The tin roof wasn't good for much except to make a fearful racket while cold rainwater sluiced down their necks. The last to arrive was Jim Brower, cradling his shattered arm in a makeshift sling with a tourniquet above the wound to keep him from bleeding to death.

—Y'all see what happened to Skeeter? Lightnin got him. Just plumb made him evaporate, him and that white pinto he was ridin. One minute he was poundin along, next minute he was just a puff of gray smoke and gone.

—Jesus Christ.

Herzl crossed himself.

—Ja. Lightning got him. Horse too. Judgment of God, *ja?* For hanging a man without a proper judge, *ja?* He was the one tied the rope to the tree, *ja?*

Pike spat his chaw at a rustling noise in a dark corner thinking it might be a cornered rattlesnake, hoping the bastard hated the taste of Brown's Mule.

—Aint no God of yours nor mine had a thing to do with it. Damned fool was out in the open in a thunderstorm and got what he had coming to him for pure stupidity. That's what happens to a man dumb enough to ride a white horse in a thunderstorm. It's always the lightest colored horse gets hit.

Herzl poked his head out the door, saw another flash of lightning and ducked back in.

—We got to go back for him. Maybe he has family. We must gather the remains for proper burial and notify his relations.

Pike laughed.

—Skeeter? If he got hit by lightnin, there won't be enough left to bury in a tobacco tin. We have more rustlers to catch. Somewhere out there is all them stolen horses too.

Cull shook his head. He had lost his stomach for hanging.

—Hell with 'em. We hung one, that's enough to teach the rest a lesson. After a gullywasher like this, there won't be no track left to follow in any direction. You fellas want to go on a wild-goose chase, you go without me, because I'm headin back to the ranch and my sweet little Mexican. We hung a horsethief and Skeeter got himself burnt up like a goddamned three-cent cigar. I'd say that's about a day's work.

Eli felt himself losing his grip on the slick sawgrass rope. Every time his hands slipped, the noose pulled tight. His body sagged, his strength was gone. There was nothing to do but make his amends as best he could.

I done a bad thing, Lord, but these are desperate times.

Dark washed over him, a merciful, enveloping, all-encompassing night. An instant before the darkness became eternal, he reached toward a beckoning light, radiant as the heart of the sun. A single spike of blue lightning from the black heart of the sky split the old cottonwood and tumbled the dangling man into a shallow grave half filled with water. The storm swept past, the wind died, the shortgrass prairie glistened damp under the arc of a distant rainbow. The big sorrel horse grazed nearby, his damp coat steaming in the sunshine.

⊱ CHAPTER 22 ⊰

Twenty miles to the northeast, Ezra Paint sprawled with his head propped on a saddle in the shade of a willow tree on the river-bank. His skin felt hot as a griddle. He was wrapped in his own bedroll with Teeter's bedroll atop that and he was still shivering. The two herds had met up just north of the spot where Eli waited to hold off Dermott Cull but Roy Titus had vanished. The first thing Teeter wanted to know was why Abe was riding alone. Abe shrugged.

—Eli, he figured he could hold Dermott long enough for us to get away.

—That's a damned fool plan.

—It's what he wanted to do. Once he gets his head set on a thing, there's no turning him.

—What happened to Roy?

—We were comin through the rough country and I looked around and he was gone. Just plumb vanished on me. I imagine he got scared and just lit out alone.

—No point jawin about it. We better put some more distance betwixt ourselves and Mr. Cull. Let's ride.

Thirty minutes on, Ezra was so exhausted that he took a pinch of Teeter's tobacco, half-chewed it and rubbed the juice into his eyes to stay awake, then vaulted off his horse and plunged his head into the Powder River up to the neck. Teeter thought the boy had gone loco.

—Hell's wrong with you?

—I tried rubbin tobacco juice in my eyes.

—Now why ever would you pull a fool stunt like that?

—Read about it once. Story said the old pony express riders used to do that.

—Story writ by a man was never west of the Mississippi. I told you about them newspaper fellas. They's not to be trusted.

—I see that now.

—Lucky you see at all, doctorin your eyes with chewin tobacco. Lucky ye aint blinded.

Within three more miles Ezra was reeling in the saddle.

—You're plumb wore out, Ez. Maybe we should make camp right here.

—Taint that. I feel like somebody poured kerosene down my neck and lit it afire. I'm burnin up, Teeter.

Teeter brushed his hand across Ezra's forehead and felt a searing heat.

—You're sick as a bluetick hound swallowed a pound of butter. We'd best make camp.

—I can ride as long as you nor anybody in this world.

They pushed on as far as Baking Powder Creek, where Teeter saw there was no way Ezra could ride any farther. In any case, it was better to ride at night, when the dust from the herd wouldn't attract attention. Teeter and Honest Abe put out picket pins for a dozen of the more troublesome horses, figuring the rest wouldn't stray too far. Ezra dismounted and fell asleep almost under the hooves of his horse. Teeter dragged him to a better spot and left the boy to sleep while he kept watch. Abe tilted his hat over his eyes and declared he would catch forty winks but Teeter had passed through fatigue into a state that was like the way he felt when he had been drinking so long that he had drunk himself sober. The next thing he knew, Ezra was thrashing around and babbling about mules and sarsaparilla. One moment his teeth were chattering so bad he sounded like an angry rattler, the next he had thrown the bedroll away and was trying to tear off his clothing because he was burning up. Suddenly, Ezra sat straight up and pointed in terror at the empty prairie.

—What the hell's that, Teeter?

—Hell's what.

—*That.*

—Nothin at all except maybe three hundred miles a buffalo grass.

—You don't see it?

—I see a whole lot of Wyoming off yonder.

Ezra pointed again.

—That big black bird. Plain as day.

Ezra saw a monstrous dark bird wide as a hundred bald eagles flying wingtip to wingtip, flapping across the prairie, its wings trailing fire. He saw it and he heard the sound of its wings:

Whuff! Whuff! Whuff!

—There it comes, Teeter. Head like a buzzard and feathers black as a crow. Must be a hundred feet across. Them wings is going to light the whole prairie afire.

—Son, I don't see a thing out there but prairie.

—Here it comes, Teeter. Black as midnight in Hades. Comin right at us.

Teeter tilted a canteen for Ezra to drink. Most of the water slopped down his neck.

—You settle down now, get some sleep. You're seein things.

—I aint seein things. The bastards got Eli. That bird is Eli's soul flying off to perdition.

—Don't get yourself all chafed up over a thing that aint there.

—Hell it aint. Dermott Cull got him and strung him up. I can feel it. Aint nothin happens to Eli I don't know about it. We're close as two peas in a pod.

—I know you are but it don't matter. You're wrong. Eli is about three times as smart as Dermott. I don't know what you're seein out there, but there aint no birds around here except meadowlarks and magpies, maybe a couple killdeer.

—You hear that awful shriekin sound? Hear it? Sounds like a

tornado rippin a tin roof? I know that sound, Teeter. That's a man's soul bein dragged right out of the socket.

—They Lord. Aint no big fiery bird out there, son, and they aint no soul bein tore from its socket.

Teeter tried to pour more water into the boy's mouth but his lips were shut tight, his eyes red-rimmed and fixed on a point in the distance where the great fiery bird bore down on him.

Abruptly, he fell asleep again and Teeter was not entirely sure whether he was alive or dead until the boy moaned as he rolled over, trembling and soaked through with sweat. Teeter covered him again and resumed his vigil, scanning the rolling prairie to the south. There was still no sign of anything out there, least of all a great fiery bird.

A couple of hours before midnight, Ezra's fever broke and he managed to climb back into the saddle. They pushed on in darkness, driving hard, Abe ahead to lead the way because he knew the country, Ezra doing his part although he was still weak as a kitten. At dawn they were still going, north past the forks of Line Creek, Bradshaw Creek, Rough Creek, Trail Creek, Thompson Creek, Flood Creek, and Spring Creek until the Pinnacle loomed in the distance. Ezra hung on as far as the coulee Abe had sketched in the dust back at the O-Bar. He even managed to help Teeter and Abe tie ropes from one lodgepole pine to the next to make a lariat corral. And then they settled down to wait.

The first thing Eli Paint saw when he came to was the freckled face and jug ears of Roy Titus. Roy was bending over him, pouring water from his canteen onto Eli's face.

—Dang. You're alive sure. Scared me near to death. You look like a porcupine been run over by a freight train.

Eli tried to speak, pointed to his throat, finally managed a croak.

—I feel some worse than that.

—I expect you do.

—What happened?

—You been drug and hung.

—Hung dead. I felt it when I went. The whole world went light. Then it was over.

—No, it weren't. You aint much to look at but you aint dead.

—You sure I aint gone to hell?

—Nope, because if you are, I'm in the same fix.

—What are you doin here? You was supposed to ride with Abe, keep them horses movin.

—I know I was but I got to thinkin Abe could drive them horses alone and you might need some help, so I snuck off. I got back too late to help but I seen the whole thing from that ridge yonder. Seen them string you up, seen them ride off, seen that lightnin bolt hit this tree, bust it up into kindling. When the storm blew up, they rode off south. They was tearin along hard as they could ride and another lightnin bolt got one of them, I think it was that fella they call Skeeter, ridin a white horse in a thunderstorm. The rest made it to a old sheepherder's shack and I hunkered down till the storm was done. Then I seen them come out and I figured they'd try to pick up the trail again, but they rode off south like they wasn't lookin for nobody.

—Why would they do that?

—Damned if I know. Maybe they got discouraged after Skeeter got turned into a puff a smoke.

—We got to ride.

—I expect so but first let's get some water in you.

Eli managed to choke down a little water and sat up. Roy had removed the noose but his neck was raw. He was bruised and battered and stuck full of cactus spines but as far as he could tell, nothing was broken. Eli drank again and Roy washed a little of the blood off his face and caught Monty and led him over. Roy was a hundred and ten pounds soaking wet and Eli was better than two hundred pounds but Roy managed to boost him into the saddle. Eli's voice had improved from a whisper to a croaking rasp.

—I got to say, Roy, you got more sand than I figured you for.

Now let's see if we can't find that doggoned Pinnacle. I've had about all of Wyoming I can take.

By sundown they were riding north, Roy Titus leading Eli's albino packhorse over glistening rainwet prairie, bound for Montana.

Teeter was the only one awake when Eli and Roy rode in.

—If you two aint a sight for sore eyes.

Eli shook his head. Roy grinned.

—Never thought I'd be so happy to see an old cuss like you, Teeter. I got the saddlewolf so bad I feel like I rode a armadillo bareback.

—Hell happened out there?

—Tell you the whole story, Teeter, but first I got to eat. And Eli here, he needs some tending to. The man has had a difficult couple of days, what with gettin hung and all.

Teeter helped Roy get Eli out of the saddle and laid him next to Ezra, who had slept soundly for a dozen hours and was still out cold. Roy squatted on his bootheels by the fire, washing beans and biscuits down with bitter coffee, telling the story of the hanging on the Powder River with only a little embellishment. Teeter was skeptical.

—You wouldn't kid a old cowpoke, would you?

—That's the God's truth as I live and breathe. Take a look for yourself. You can see the rope burns on his neck. Maybe it was just a odd stroke a luck saved Eli and maybe it was somethin or Somebody else.

Teeter opened a bottle of rye and pointed to Eli and Ezra sprawled sleeping by the fire.

—Aint they a pair, now?

—Aint they.

—I say it's a goddamned miracle.

—I expect it is.

⚔ CHAPTER 23 ⚔

Thirty-nine days later they rode into Fort Benton trailing two hundred and ninety-six head of O-Bar horses now artfully become the property of Eli and Ezra Paint and Teeter Spawn, proprietors of the 8T8 outfit down in the Powder River country, so proclaimed by the brand on the left shoulder and the swallowtail notch in the right ear of each animal. They found Joe Kipp at his general store.

To meet with Kipp, they had to walk right past a U.S. marshal leaning on the hitching post outside. The marshal had spent two years trying to catch Joe running liquor to the whiskey forts north of the Canadian border, forts that bore the names Fort Whoop-Up and Fort Kipp, the latter after Joe himself. Joe's father, James Kipp, had inherited a block of real estate right in the heart of Montreal, but he left it all to strike out for Montana, where he married a pure-blood Blackfoot woman and fathered Joe, who inherited his mother's complexion and his father's head for business. He figured that if white men could make a fortune peddling liquor to the Indians, there was no reason a man with Blackfoot blood in his veins should be barred from profiting as well.

The marshal was after whiskey runners, not horsethieves. Six weeks earlier, on their last sortie from Fort Benton, he had arrested Joe Kipp, attempting to cross the border with three wagonloads of whiskey. Joe pointed to three border stakes, did some calculating, and convinced the marshal that they were four hundred yards north of the Forty-ninth

Parallel, in Canadian territory and out of the marshal's jurisdiction. Back in Fort Benton, the lawman found out that Joe's surveying was as faulty as his Blackfoot rum, but by that time the liquor had all been sold and most of it had been drunk as well. The marshal was left to hang around Joe's place like a no-good drifter, while Joe cursed him for running off respectable trade. Because Kipp and his whiskey had eluded him so often, the marshal didn't have an eye for another thing. Day after day, Teeter and the Paint boys went in and out of Kipp's store without drawing a second glance from the marshal.

Joe had the cash and the boys knew he could be trusted; the delicate part was negotiating a fair price. Joe had an advantage because he knew the horses were stolen but he found the horsethieves drove a hard bargain. At first he assumed he was dealing with Teeter Spawn because Spawn was the oldest and did the most talking. Then he decided the boss was the talkative Paint boy, the one they called Ezra. Once he figured out who was in charge, he and Eli sat down elbow to elbow, Eli with a glass of buttermilk, Joe with the jar of good whiskey he kept on hand for special occasions. Within ten minutes they agreed on a price: fifty dollars per head for trained saddlehorses, thirty dollars a head for those that weren't broke. It came to better than twelve thousand dollars. Joe paid the sum in cash he had on hand in his safe and at dawn the next morning, a Métis cowpuncher named Donald LaChance arrived with three Blackfoot riders and two Canadian cowboys to drive the horses across the border, where most were sold to the North West Mounted Police.

Eli split the money evenly five ways. It worked out to better than twenty-five hundred dollars each. Their business done, they put up at the Grand Union Hotel and after long, soapy baths stood rounds at the Break of Day and Moses Solomon's Medicine Lodge. Near dawn they stumbled after Teeter to the Cosmopolitan, where Eli alone declined the company of the working girls and waited downstairs with his buttermilk.

After a week they had seen more than enough of Fort Benton—all except Roy, who decided he liked living within hailing distance of several hundred whores. Honest Abe took his share from the sale of the horses and rode west with four mules and a cross-eyed Dutchman, looking for San Francisco. The day after Abe rode out, Teeter rose early in his room at the Grand Union Hotel, dressed and shaved and roused the others. After breakfast, he declared that it was time to hit the trail.

—Where to now, Eli?

Eli's voice was still a rasp, so that you had to stand close to hear what he had to say.

—I don't know. You fellas decide.

BOOK 4

On the Niobrara

Nebraska, 1888–1915

⚜ CHAPTER 24 ⚜

The rainbow rose in a long, shimmering arc across the bruised sky. It was born from the limbs of a gnarled ponderosa pine clinging to the edge of Monroe Canyon, rode the trail of the vanishing thunderstorm to the southeast, and came down in a long-legged glide like a sandhill crane landing on still water. Livvy Stanton tiptoed from the door of the cabin where she had taken refuge during the worst of the storm. She was soaked through, her dress clinging to her legs. The thunderstorm with its rain and hail and lightning had swept off to the east, leaving no sound behind except the rush of water running off the slant roof of the cabin and down every course along the grade running south into Prairie Dog Creek. Somehow all this had erupted out of the pale, dusty heat of an August afternoon, so that even her heartbeat felt like something new and novel, as though the electricity in the prairie sky had ignited her and set her in motion. She inhaled a deep breath, drinking in the rich scent of sage on the damp air, and wandered on down to Prairie Dog Creek, transfixed by the rainbow, watching dozens of cliff swallows leave the rain-soaked gumbo bluffs to wheel and dip in pursuit of the clouds of buffalo gnats that came out after the rain. The wet earth squished between her toes, the tall grass soaked the hem of her dress. On the banks of the creek she undid the buttons of her dress, folded it neatly, unbuttoned her underthings, folded them on top of her dress and slid into the creek naked for her first real bath in a month.

The water in the creek was up half a foot after the storm but it still wasn't deep enough to do much more than dog-paddle along the surface. She preferred to float on her back, watching the sky while she let the current carry her down and around the bend. There she turned and started back on her belly, working her way against the force of the water by pulling herself along, feeling the soft mud of the creek bottom against her breasts and thighs where the water was shallow, wishing she had thought to bring a hunk of strong lye soap so that she could really wash. She turned onto her back again and drifted, watching a hawk ride the breeze so high up it was barely a speck in the sky. She was still drifting when she heard a horse whinny and another horse answer and a metallic sound like the faraway jangle of spurs. She paid no attention and went on paddling, drifting naked in the creek, thinking how different it all seemed after the storm, with the awful dust subdued and the sky a deeper, gentler blue and the afternoon now so cool that she felt goose bumps on her bare skin. Then the horse whinnied again, and she heard men's voices up toward the cabin and, in a sudden rising panic, realized that she had ignored her father's urgent instructions never to go more than twenty feet from the cabin without the scattergun cocked and loaded.

She took a few deep breaths and decided the first thing was that she had to get her clothes. Whatever her fate, she was not going to meet it naked. She clambered up the muddy bank, keeping the willow with its low-hanging leaves between her and the cabin. Her hands trembled so that she could not do the buttons; she bit her lip, took three deep breaths, buttoned the dress halfway up, discovered that she had started the row of tiny buttons in the wrong place, started over. Once she was dressed, she worked her way upstream to where she could get a view of the cabin. She could see two horses, a big sorrel and a smallish roan mare, ground-tied near the cottonwood. Good horses, good saddles, a little work-scuffed. Rifles left in the scabbards on both saddles. There was nothing for it but to face them. Courage in battle, her father always said, did not mean that you weren't afraid: It meant that you squared your shoulders and faced your enemies and kept your fright to yourself. To steady herself, she sang her mother's favorite hymn under her breath as she marched toward the cabin:

> —*Onward, Christian soldiers, marching as to war!*
> *With the cross of Jesus going on before . . .*

If she could reach the cabin before them, she could dart inside, grab the loaded scattergun and come up firing. She would be like the Sioux warriors her father so admired. What was it the Sioux always said before going into battle?

Only the earth and the sky go on forever. It is a good day to die.

Livvy was not more than thirty feet from the door when he stepped out of the shadows on the east side of the cabin, a man large and rough as the badlands. He was the first true desperado she had ever seen, with a red bandanna around his neck and a floppy old gray hat pulled low over his eyes. She caught the glint of a pistol tied low on his left thigh and felt her legs go watery with fear. She turned to run, took three steps through slick, wet grass, and fell heavily onto her face with something hard and malevolent tangled between her legs, rolled onto her back kicking at it furiously until she saw that she was in mortal combat with an old scythe left to rust, the worn and curved wooden handle a trap for a panicked girl now at the mercy of a cold-eyed killer. She saw his relentless boots moving toward her, Spanish scrollwork tooled into the leather, jangling silver spurs dulled to the color of lead from hard use. *Janglejanglejangle*, those long-striding boots one of the last things she would see on this earth. *Janglejanglejangle* the last thing she would hear, the man with the spurs coming to take her before he cut her throat.

He would not get her without a fight. Her grandfather Owen Stanton, a crusty old tyrant and a veteran of the Mexican War, had taught her the proper way to use a scythe back in Illinois before she was ten years old, taught her to pull it toward her in long, smooth arcs, letting the blade do the work. She scrambled to her knees, grabbed the scythe with both hands, yanked its rusty blade from the earth and went at those boots like a harvest hand cutting oats, pulling the scythe low to the ground with a mighty swing that carried her completely around and dropped her on her fanny as her tormentor skipped nimbly over the blade. She was up and at him again, a firm grip on the wooden handles, carrying the blade high overhead this time and slashing down with it as she descended on him in a blood fury, aiming at the red bandanna around his neck, hoping the point of the scythe was sharp enough to slash all the way to the jugular. The scythe fell on him out of the red ball of the afternoon sun, his weight shifted slightly, his hand came up quick as a rattlesnake and he caught the curved wooden shaft. His white teeth gleamed through a week's growth of beard.

—Whoa now, girl. Whoa now. Easy. We don't mean you the least harm.

—I'm not a horse! Whoa yourself, you pirate.

She pulled away from him, her weight low, trying to twist the scythe out of his grip.

—You better get! I am Livvy Stanton from Moultrie County, Illinois, daughter of Captain Jack Stanton the Indian fighter. I can slice you to ribbons with this thing.

He skipped back a step or two, light on his feet for such a powerful man.

—I can see you're a bobcat for fightin, miss, but I don't believe this old scythe would cut a boll of cotton. If you'd just ease up now, maybe you'll see taint strictly necessary to kill us.

She ignored him and tugged at the scythe, using it to pivot on one foot and aim a low barefoot kick at his groin that came up a foot short. The ease with which he deflected her sorties made her madder than ever. She pushed hard on the handle, trying to drive it into his belly, then yanked back. He waited until all her weight was pulling away from him and let go. She fell heavily but bounced up with the scythe again, heard footsteps closing on her, spun and swung the scythe blindly. This time she almost hit what she aimed at, the blade missing by no more than an inch the worn red suspenders stretched over a broad chest. She pulled the scythe back and crouched on the balls of her feet, ready for another slash. Then she saw his face: It was the same man. Somehow he was in front of her and behind her all at once. She lowered her grip to the butt of the handle and spun around and around in as wide a circle as she could reach, forcing them both to keep their distance. They backed away a respectful step or two. The one she had seen first spoke again, still sounding like a man trying to calm a skittish horse.

—Easy now, sister. Easy. We aint goin to hurt you, now. Easy. We got a little homestead claim up Squaw Creek and we heard there was new folks on the old Amundsen place, so we come down to say howdy. We're tryin to do the neighborly thing if you'd give us half a chance.

She took another halfhearted poke at his chest with the scythe and stood panting, gazing from one to the other. Twin desperadoes.

—I don't care where you come from. Go back to Squaw Creek and leave me be.

—If we meant you harm, we'd of grabbed you when you was swimmin down at the creek.

—You were spying on me.

—We wasn't spyin. We saw there was somebody down at the creek, is all. If we was spyin, we would have rode down for a better look. If you want us to go, we'll go.

—You better go. My father will be back with the whole family any minute now. If he sees the pair of you hanging around the house, he's apt to come in shooting.

—If he's half as feisty as you are, he might at that. We'll come back when your pa is home, introduce ourselves proper.

He backed off toward the horses, still facing her in case she decided to make another charge with the scythe. His twin circled in the same direction, hands up as though she had a pistol leveled at his belly. She let the blade of the scythe drop to the ground. He doffed his hat politely and she got a good look at him for the first time. Straight black hair that needed cutting, the barest wisp of beard, eyes a strange pale shade somewhere between gray and blue. Much younger than he seemed at first but possessed of an infuriating assurance, as though he had never found anything difficult and never would. That there should be two ruffians like this, identical as a pair of wagon wheels, struck her as an affront to nature.

The one with the bandanna swung into the saddle on the tall sorrel and the other mounted the roan. She hesitated. Her father had left her with contrary instructions: First, she was to be wary of strangers and keep the scattergun with her at all times. Second, it was the law of the West to be hospitable and never to turn a stranger away from your door. These men were armed with pistols, knives, rifles, lariats, and a bullwhip. They could have taken advantage of her, despite her rusty old scythe. Big as they were, they were little more than boys, not much older than she was. She had been rude and inhospitable and tried her level best to kill them. They were about to wheel their horses away when it occurred to her that, more than anything, she did not want to be left alone again after dark.

—Wait! Don't go. You gave me a fright, that's all. Perhaps if you climb down we can introduce ourselves properly?

—You sure about that? We can come back later when your folks are here.

—No, it's all right. If you wanted to hurt me, I expect you could've done so already.

He swung down from the saddle carefully, holding out a gloved hand.

—Eli Paint. The ugly one there, that's my brother, Ezra.

She noticed a rasp in his voice, as though he had something

caught in his throat. She took his hand, aware that she was blushing deeply. The curse of red hair and pale skin.

—Olivia Stanton. Everybody calls me Livvy. I'm sorry, but Pa took the spring wagon to the railhead at Rushville to get Ma and the little ones. He said to be careful while he was gone.

Ezra stepped down cautiously and shook her hand. As they stood shoulder to shoulder, she peered from one to the other, trying to find some way of distinguishing them. Other than some vague difference in the way they carried themselves, she could see no way to tell them apart.

—You gave me a fright. I'm sorry.

—No call to be sorry. We oughtn't to scared you. This country aint no place for a girl alone.

—I'm not a girl. I'll soon be seventeen years old and I know how to take care of myself.

—Well, we're eighteen and I aint certain we've figured that out yet. Was Ezra's idea to ride out for a visit when you could see plain that a real gullywasher was comin. If we hadn't crawled into a old sheepherder's hut north of here, that hail might've knocked some sense into him. Looks like it knocked your stovepipe off kilter. I'll just shinny up there and fix it.

Before she could object, Eli swung onto the back of the sorrel, rode the horse up next to the cabin, stood in the saddle and hoisted himself onto the roof. He slid the stovepipe into place with a deft twist and eased himself back down onto the horse, which was so well-trained it hadn't moved an inch.

—That ought to do it. C'mon, Ez, we ought to go, stop scarin this poor girl half to death.

—I was about to fix potatoes and bacon and I have corn dodgers and molasses and coffee if you care to eat. If one of you boys could milk that old cow, I could get supper on quick.

—If you're sure it's no trouble. Rattlesnake would taste better'n our grub.

The two of them went off to do the chores. In half an hour they had finished tasks that would have taken her two hours to do, washed up in Prairie Dog Creek and slicked their hair and come in for dinner looking much less like ruffians. They found her kneeling next to the stove, struggling to get a fire going with green cottonwood twigs. Ezra ducked outside, returned with twists of bunchgrass for kindling, and showed her how to start a proper fire.

—We usually burn cow chips or buffalo chips in them things. If you use wood all the time, you'll find there aint enough trees around here to keep you supplied with fuel.

—Cow chips must stink something awful.

—They do if they're fresh, but dry cow chips don't hardly smell at all, and they burn steady. If you pick up the dry stuff and get a good pile before winter, you should make it to spring.

—Oh, I'm sure Florence won't have cowflop in the house.

—You get used to it.

When the stove top was hot, Livvy sliced the potatoes thin and fried them on the griddle with a dollop of lard. When they were almost done, she tossed a slab of bacon in with the spuds and put the corn dodgers on the stove top. She hadn't had time to churn butter, so she served up the dodgers with molasses and apple jelly carted all the way from Moultrie County. Livvy made them wait while she said grace before they dug in. They ate like starving men, almost polishing off their plates in the time it took her to put a little jelly on a biscuit. When they were through eating, Ezra tilted his chair back.

—So how is it a young lady from Illinois finds herself out here on the far side of nowhere?

—Because my pa was fighting Indians on and off for ten years and he just couldn't get it out of his head that he wanted to live in the west. He was a brevet colonel before he went back home to Illinois after the war, see, but then when he came out here to fight Indians again, he was a captain. He lost an eye at Fredericksburg, and he was at Fort Randall for a while, and at Fort Laramie and in Montana with General Crook after the Custer massacre. Then he was two years at Fort Robinson, but our mother died so he came home to Illinois to take care of me and my brother, Sherman. Then he married another woman, Florence is her name, that's my step-mother, and now I have another little brother and a little sister, and they're coming too because Pa says a man can't breathe in Illinois.

She paused to catch her breath, aware that she was nervous and because she was nervous she was talking too much. The Paint boys didn't say much and when they did, the one called Ezra did all the talking.

—Happens we lived a time at Fort Randall. Pa was a freighter from Mississippi, Ma was part Sioux. We've been orphans since we was fifteen.

—Oh, that's awful.

—We made out all right. We worked a ranch up in Wyoming for a time but I have to tell your pa, it aint easy to make money runnin cows. You can do it but it aint easy. I expect most folks is in the business just because it beats slavin in a bank or a cotton mill but there's miles of beautiful country out here, more than enough for everybody.

—Is there? I don't find it beautiful, I find it hot and dusty and bare. I can't see what it is my father found to like out here. It's awful country in the summer and I hear the winters are worse.

—They are. But it grows on you.

—I can't imagine how. I won't stay long enough to let that happen.

—That's a pity. You might come to like it.

—I did find the storm rather thrilling. You don't get storms like that back in Illinois.

—I expect not.

When Eli stood to go, Ezra got up to follow. Livvy walked them out to their horses. It was not yet fully dark but already the night sky was splashed with great handfuls of stars.

—Did you know the man who owned this place, Amundsen?

—He come by once before he left. Set a spell, didn't say a word. Drunk a cup of coffee and took a biscuit when he left and that was it. Man had his own ways, nothin wrong in that.

—I can't imagine what he was thinking with all these tin cans.

The cabin was lined, inside and out, with hundreds of tin cans pounded flat and nailed to the walls.

—I guess Crazy Amundsen thought you couldn't have too much of a good thing. He run four miles of fence posts in all directions but he had no bobwire to string, wondered why cattle kept goin through his fence.

Ezra wheeled his horse and cantered after Eli, who had already vanished into the darkness with no more than a tip of his hat. Livvy watched them ride out of sight, then hurried back into the cabin because she didn't want to be caught out alone after dark. Already she could hear the coyotes starting up, that awful *yipy-ipyip* that went on all night so a person couldn't sleep. She chided herself for her foolishness: If she had asked, the Paint boys would surely have spent the night. They could have slept in the lean-to next to the house. Now she was alone. She dragged the chair over to bar the door, decided that wouldn't be enough, took a hammer and in a fit of panic banged in a dozen twopenny nails to fasten the door shut.

Alone in his cabin, she feared that she had begun to hear Amundson's song in the wind, to see his shadow between the cabin and the chicken coop, to feel his presence as she sat rigidly in her chair with the scattergun pointed at the door and the triggers cocked. Was Amundsen mad when he left Norway? Or was it this land that made him take leave of his senses? They said it happened to settlers every winter, especially to women left alone. They would find the poor things in the spring, hanging from ropes tied to the roof beams. Livvy did not intend to linger and wait for such madness to claim her. She would stay long enough to help the family get settled in. A year, two at the most. She finally lulled herself to sleep by imagining the train journey to Illinois, the telegraph wires dipping and rising and dipping and rising as the train rolled by.

⊰ CHAPTER 25 ⊱

Livvy spotted them away off toward the Cotter place, plodding through a cloud of dust the color of buttermilk. Florence drove the spring wagon with Annabelle and little U. S. Grant Stanton on the seat beside her. Sherman trailed on a long-legged bay so dark it was almost black, with the captain farther back astride his big gray, a liberated cavalry horse. They were a hundred yards from the cabin when Flo shrieked as though a ghost had jumped into the wagon. Her scream panicked the team, which took off and swept past the cabin with Annabelle and U. S. Grant clinging to the wagon seat for dear life. They were shambling draft horses so they couldn't run very fast, but they were headed straight for the badlands when Stanton thundered up beside them, riding like he was again leading the charge at Fredericksburg, leaning out of the saddle to grab the lead horse and seesaw the team to a halt.

—Whoa! Whoa! Whoa! What set that off, woman? Did you step on a rattlesnake?

—Tin *cans*!

—How's that?

—Tin *cans*! Our house is made out of tin *cans*! We're living in a *tin-can* house!

—It aint a tin-can house. There's tin cans tacked on the outside, is all. Fella called Crazy Amundsen, he pounded them cans on there to keep the weather out. I'll take them off just as soon as I get six minutes. It aint but temporary quarters anyway.

—I wouldn't let a family of rats live in that, temporary or not.

—Folks out here has to make do, Flo. We'll have a better house before winter.

Florence wasn't persuaded. She gave her stepdaughter a curt nod, went straight to her bed, and refused to move. Livvy took Sherman and the younger children in tow and walked to the brink of the badlands, warning them a dozen times to watch for rattlesnakes. Sherman looked pale and exhausted but he was excited by everything he saw.

—Isn't this a grand adventure, Livvy? Isn't it beautiful? Have you seen any Indians yet? We saw a few wrapped up in blankets at the railroad stations, but they didn't look like much. I want to see real, wild Indians on horseback. Can you believe this is our home now?

—It doesn't feel like home to me. It was awful these past nights, staying here alone while Papa went to get you. I thought I'd be fine, but as soon as it got dark, I was terrified. I didn't sleep a wink, and we had an awful storm, and these two cowboys came by, and I thought they were going to kill me. They turned out to be all right, but I sat up all night every night with the scattergun. I don't want to be frightened like that again and I don't want to live where there's nothing but dust.

Captain Jack Stanton, alone in the early morning dark, boiled his coffee and stepped outside before dawn, with a tin mug so hot it singed his palm. He could hear turtledoves somewhere, meadowlarks starting up far out on the prairie. He sipped his coffee and watched the rising sun send long, rose-colored runners of light into a sky that would open like the gateway to heaven itself. He took a deep breath and shivered. This was why he had come west again: for the sky. He had explained it all to Flo in terms of dollars and cents and cattle raised at so much a head and sold at so much a pound, covered long sheets of paper with his chicken-scratch calculations intended to prove that ranching in the West was a can't-miss proposition. It was all a lot of twaddle. What was true was that, after a dozen years at various posts from Camp Robinson to the Little Bighorn, he found that the sky back in Moultrie County was too close and suffocating, too like a familiar patchwork quilt filled with the same old household odors year after year. In the West, a man could stand as he was standing now, in awe of a firmament that leapt toward eternity. It was reason enough to uproot his family and to make his stand here while there was still room for a man to spread his wings and soar.

Stanton finished his coffee and tossed the dregs aside. He was about to turn back in to the house when he saw two riders far out to the east, their long, wobbly shadows rippling like water where the wind stirred the grass. By the time they were a half mile off, he could tell that they sat their mounts in exactly the same way. Twins. They would be the boys who'd paid a call on Livvy while he was away. He would see to it their suspenders were snapped for that particular error in judgment: There would be no saddle tramps hanging around his daughter. Stanton drew himself up to his full height and held the scattergun loose in the crook of his arm as they approached.

Ezra was in the lead. He swung out of the saddle, ground-tied his roan mare and stepped away, keeping his hands where Stanton could see them.

—How do.

—How do your own self.

—Fine mornin.

—It is that.

—Ezra Paint. That there is my brother, Eli.

—That visited my girl some days back.

—Bein neighborly.

—I expect so. Best to come by when her father is home, you want to come callin.

Stanton felt that he wasn't scaring these boys the way he usually had with the young men who'd come sniffing around Livvy back in Moultrie County. He noticed Ezra peering at him queerly: Somewhere between Prairie Dog Creek and Rushville, Stanton had lost his jaunty black eye patch. Flo had fashioned him a new one out of what came to hand, which happened to be an old calico dress. He felt a damned fool, meeting strangers with a piece of a woman's dress flapping where his eye used to be. It put a man at a disadvantage.

The Paint boys stepped up and shook hands. Hands the size of dinner plates, strong boys. With their hats off, they lost about five years. They looked rough as a corduroy road but he had commanded men who looked the same, men you would trust with your life. Stanton decided on the spot that these were men he could trust.

—I understand my girl gave you boys a warm welcome.

Ezra chuckled.

—She did at that. Like to took Eli's head off with that old scythe.

—That's my Livvy. She got all the sand, that one. I wish Sherman had her gumption.

There wasn't room for so many big men to sit in the cabin, so they sat in the shade of the cotton tree and talked until Livvy came out to ask if anyone was feeling peckish. Twenty minutes later, they were digging into plates of ham and biscuits washed down with more thick black coffee. When they were finished, Stanton hollered for little U. S. Grant Stanton and his sister Annabelle to collect their plates while the men squatted back on their bootheels, squinting at the far horizon, where the sunlight had already washed out the contours of the ground. Ezra snapped off a blade of grass to pick his teeth.

—Your daughter says you're fixin to ranch here in Sioux County.

—That would be about right.

—Late in the season to make a start.

—Took longer to locate this spot than I thought. Time I was able to persuade the mizzus we ought to move west, we got a late start, then that locator out of Rushville run us all over the state looking at places where a dog wouldn't stop to piss.

—That's a locator for you.

They talked sawgrass, buffalo grass, grama grass, shortgrass, tall grass, black wool and slough grass, tick fever and Texas fever and Spanish fever and whether they were the same thing, blackleg and coyotes, government grazing and private land. Mostly they talked water. Ezra spelled it out for Stanton.

—First thing is to get three or four windmills up, because you can't keep haulin barrels to feed more than a few head of stock and that creek is apt to run dry any day. Figure a cow will need eight gallons of water a day and a workin cowhorse more'n that. Before you start buyin cattle, you got to have water enough to keep 'em from dyin of thirst, less you want to drive a spring wagon over eight miles of rough country to buy your water from old Stan Sarcowitz on Sowbelly Creek. If you start buyin water, you'll be like the sod-busters who find they got no time to dig a well. They're too busy haulin water.

Before they left, the Paint boys offered to help Stanton get the place ready for winter.

—I won't turn you down. I could manage to pay forty a month for a couple of good hands, and Livvy gets a good supper on the table.

—We wouldn't take it. Least we can do, bein neighbors and all.

Stanton watched them ride off, wondering how neighborly they would be if not for Livvy. They seemed like good young men but they would bear watching: He liked them all right, but he still wasn't going to have his daughter married to a saddle tramp.

The first frost came without warning. They were only a few days into September, and Jack Stanton stepped out of the cabin at dawn into a world where the buffalo grass was frost-slick and the tumbleweeds lining Crazy Amundsen's old garden fence were coated with a delicate, shimmering tracery of ice. There was hoarfrost on

the north side of the cabin and the shady side of the fence rails
and a real snap in the air. Stanton had spent enough winters on
the high plains to know that the first storm could come any day.
Before the weather turned colder, the Paint boys turned up with
an older cowpoke named Teeter Spawn to help patch the chinks
in the cabin and shore up the sagging roof. They took two spring
wagons and hauled lodgepole pine from fifteen miles away for the
cabin, stripped the tin cans off the walls, put up a new double wall
of logs chinked with clay, and added on a much larger room connected to the east side of Amundsen's original cabin. They built
a smokehouse, dug a root cellar, helped butcher three hogs and a
yearling steer, cut down the cottonwood tree and pulled the stump
with a mule team, shored up the well, gentled two of the Stanton
horses that were too rough to ride, and insulated the henhouse
with straw. Before the first snow fell, they'd endeared themselves
to Stanton by locating an old Swiss farmer who swapped them a
barrel of black-cherry wine for a load of logs.

Livvy would never be able to say just when she began to feel
an odd connection to this barren place, when it took hold of
her, when she started to feel her spirit soar each morning as she
stepped out of the cabin into a world vast and radiant at dawn.
Because she could not leave, she set out to make the best of it.
She went to the square dances, where Eli watched from a quiet
corner while she danced with Ezra. She took her cheerful part
in a quilting bee. In October, she agreed to teach in a one-room
schoolhouse four miles from their cabin. Annabelle and U. S.
Grant would attend the school with a dozen other students, ranging in age from five to seventeen. Livvy would earn little more
than pin money for teaching, but she had graduated from high
school in Moultrie County, which made her a rarity among the
settlers, and she was delighted to have something to distract her
from the routine of life on Prairie Dog Creek. Four days a week
she made the hike to the school and back in darkness, sometimes
towing the little ones on a sled. Eight-year-old Annabelle was the

brightest of her students, so bright that she could tutor one of the large, sullen teenage boys in his sums:

—*Now repeat after me, Caleb: Two plus two is four. Three plus three is six. Four plus four is eight.*

When the winter dark began to fall a little after three and the snowbanks built up outside, Livvy would stand in front of the glowing stove with her McGuffey reader, reciting the lessons while the stove scorched her behind and left her nose so cold it was numb. Still, it was her first paying job, and she got a little thrill every time one of her students mastered a new word or worked his reluctant mind around the concept of long division. The long walks to and from the school revealed a prairie that was, however bare it might have seemed at first glance, home to an infinite variety of flora and fauna. She watched circling hawks and crouching rabbits with their winter coats almost white; she breathed the fresh pine scent of the evergreens and the crisp, clean air; she gloried especially in the sky, that enormous vault she had first taken note of the day of the awful thunderstorm. She was not quite ready to admit it to anyone, not even to Sherman, but each day she thought less about returning to Moultrie County. In spite of herself, she had come to love Nebraska.

On a January afternoon, as Livvy was trying to explain to some of the older students the difference between the Civil War and the Revolutionary War, Eli Paint came bursting through the schoolhouse door without bothering to knock. It was a crisp, clear day, just beginning to look a little hazy. Without a word to her, he began giving instructions to her pupils.

—There's a storm comin. Everybody get bundled up now before it hits. You boys got your horses outside, saddle up and ride. Arne, you ride double with your brother. Lewis, you take Chester there, his place aint but a quarter mile from yours. Fred, you take Paulina. Be sure to take the Fort Robinson cutoff to her place, it's a whole lot quicker. Once you're home, get the saddles off them horses and curry 'em down, don't put 'em away hot. You young-sters come with me. I've got Old Man Cotter's team and sleigh outside, and we're goin to try to haul every last one of you home before it hits.

Livvy was furious.

—You can't just walk in and tell my class to leave.

—There's a blizzard comin.

—How do you know?

—I can smell it.

—I'm supposed to close the school because you think you can smell a blizzard when the sun is shining?

—That's right. And it aint half so sunny as it was. It's gettin hazy already.

—These children are my responsibility.

—Well then, tell them it's time to go home. We can't stand here jawin.

—Aren't you the lord of the manor!

—I never said I was lord of a solitary thing. Only there's a time to talk and a time to do. Help me get these young ones where they got to go and then we can argue it all night long.

The older children were already on horseback and the little ones were pulling on their coats. Livvy, still so angry that her cheeks were flaming almost as red as her hair, helped Eli pile them into the sleigh, where they all burrowed under two big buffalo robes. Eli grabbed the reins, whistled to the pair of shaggy bay mares in the traces and they were off. Livvy peered at the sky, but still she could not see what the excitement was about. It wasn't as though huge dark clouds were on the horizon; the sky had shifted subtly from cobalt blue to a pale gray hue that seemed to thicken by the minute, like gravy in the pan.

Eli reined the team away from Prairie Dog Creek. He planned to make a big circular swing to drop the Pollard brothers at their cabin before taking Katie Jewell to her soddy, a journey of close to ten miles in all. The first leg was easy. Bess Pollard waved from the door as the boys hurried in; from her manner, Eli figured she had been into her husband's store of corn liquor again. Katie's father, Henry, was more anxious; he had seen what was coming and met them a mile down the trail. He squinted to the west while Eli boosted the girl up behind his saddle.

—I thought if there was any chance of a bad blow I ought to get the child here to home.

—You thought right. Best you hurry on back and buckle down tight.

—Much obliged to you for bringin the girl home.

The last child under the buffalo robes with Annabelle and U. S. Grant was Arthur Gabriel Poulton, a tall, awkward twelve-year-old boy who always wanted to be addressed by all three of his names. Eli got him to within a quarter mile of home and ordered him to leg it from there as fast as he could go. Livvy watched him flying down the hill with his schoolbooks, all elbows and knees and feet.

—Just like Ichabod Crane.

—Who?

—A character in a novel. Ichabod Crane.

—A novel. You mean a story that aint true?

—Well, kind of.

—Never could see the point of that.

They were still three miles from the house when it started. The wind shifted from dead calm to a stiff breeze that seemed to knife through the buffalo robes. The first snow when it came streaked into their eyes like gritty summer dust. Eli popped his whip to hurry the mares into a brisk trot and the sleigh bumped and swayed over rough ground. Annabelle and U. S. Grant in the back were bouncing like rubber balls, giggling as though they were enjoying the finest adventure of their lives. Livvy sneaked a peek through the snow at Eli: He was unsmiling, hunched over the reins, unable to see more than twenty or thirty feet ahead. Already the snow was eddying and drifting around the sleigh, the runners no longer dragging over the grassy patches. Livvy heard a sound coming through a stand of aspen and pine and thought at first that wolves were on their trail, until she realized that what she heard was the howling of the wind. The shaggy coats of the mares were turning white with snow and ice, although the horses were so hot from exertion that their haunches were steaming. Livvy wound her scarf around her face, leaving a narrow slit for her eyes. Eli seemed somehow to know where he was going, although to her the trail ahead had become a solid, unvarying sheet of white bounded on either side by the occasional ghostly tree. When the sleigh hit a bump on the trail, she was thrown heavily into him and had to fight to regain her balance against the tilt of the slippery bench seat, grabbing his strong right arm with both hands to right herself. Once she caught her balance she tried to shrink farther away from him, but it was hopeless with the sleigh bouncing her back and forth. Finally she tired of fighting it; when she was thrown into him again, she let her shoulder rest against him and then held his arm to keep from being flung out of the sled. She could not understand why, but she trusted him. She did not like him one bit but she trusted this rough young man to get them home.

The wind shifted to the north and seemed to blow even harder. Livvy tried to look back to be sure the children were all right but couldn't see a thing; she had to reach back and fumble through the buffalo robes to reassure herself they were still there. The horses plodded more and more slowly, picking their way. The wind was deafening, and the temperature seemed to have plunged forty degrees since they had left the schoolhouse. Now Livvy was genuinely frightened, more so when the horses plodded to a halt and would not move even when Eli cracked his bullwhip. He handed her the reins and pulled her close so he could shout in her ear.

—I'm goin to have to get down and lead 'em or they won't move. You hang on to these reins in case I need you to guide them. Don't pull back, because the idea is to keep them movin forward. If we get to goin quick, just give them their head.

He climbed down and stumbled through the snow to grab the halter of one mare in each hand. He coaxed and heaved and they stumbled forward, with Eli dodging to stay clear of the heavy front hooves. The sleigh was moving again but the cold was paralyzing, the reins between Livvy's gloved fingers stiff as boards. Above the howling of the wind, she could hear Annabelle crying; the children no longer thought this was a lark. Livvy wanted to console the girl but she couldn't make herself heard above the wind and she didn't dare let go the reins. She saw Eli stumble backward and fall into the snow, but he bounced up between the mares, apparently unhurt. They were moving faster, apparently on a downhill grade. The snow came more heavily then, a solid white wave. This was how they would be found, engulfed in an enormous drift miles from home. The children, Annabelle and U. S. Grant, and their older sister, Olivia Stanton, all of Moultrie County, Illinois, and a local cowboy named Eli Paint, their frozen bodies discovered by a troop of cavalry out of Fort Robinson.

—Whoa!

The sleigh stopped so abruptly it almost threw Livvy out of the seat. She wondered what had possessed the man, but then he was boosting her down, reaching into the sleigh for the children, bundling them all in their buffalo robes, and pushing them toward the cabin, fighting to get the door open so they could burst in on a tearful Florence and a stove that glowed red-hot, with Jack Stanton feeding more logs into the fire.

—Flo, you take care of them while I get the harness off them mares and get 'em into the corral. Captain, you want to help me get them horses unhitched?

It made Livvy want to spit in his eye, the way everybody jumped when he spoke. He could order the others about if they chose to kowtow to him but Olivia Stanton would never allow herself to be commanded in that fashion. She was grateful for the rescue but that was no call for Mr. Eli Paint to get uppity. The fact that he was right about the blizzard just made her more angry.

The first storm lasted more than four days, the second one a little less than two. In all, eight days passed before Eli could make it back to his own cabin. He stayed on with the Stantons, sleeping at night on the pine-plank floor next to Sherman's tick, rolled in his buffalo robe with his saddle for a pillow. Florence was happy to have him around, to have another capable man and another strong back to help her husband fight through the drifts to look after the livestock. Livvy felt uneasy at his presence. She would never have told a soul, but her feelings stemmed from an odd recurring dream: She and Eli were alone under the buffalo robes, the sleigh careening through an endless, snowy landscape, his powerful body rolling onto her at every turn. The second time she had the dream she woke to find that her hand had slipped down under her winter woolens and that her thighs were slick and wet, her abdomen taut with a need more powerful than anything she had ever known. She rolled out of bed, prayed until her toes were all but frozen on the icy floor before crawling back under her quilt, where she lay trembling and cold until daybreak.

The next day, even more than most days, she disagreed with everything Eli said, corrected his grammar fussily, ordered him not to eat with his elbows on the table and not to chew with his mouth full. When at last the storms eased enough for Eli to carve his way through the drifts back to his own cabin, Livvy watched him ride away on his big sorrel horse. He didn't look back. When Flo saw her watching him, Livvy blushed.

—That young man has too fine an opinion of himself.

—I wouldn't know about that, but he has a fine opinion of you.

—Eli? He doesn't know I'm alive.

—Yes he does. You're his shining star. I'm surprised you haven't figured that out yet.

⊰ CHAPTER 26 ⊱

In the spring of 1889, Ezra Paint left with Teeter Spawn to work the roundup on the big Jim Dahlman ranch a hundred miles to the east. On the way back to Squaw Creek in late May, Ezra stayed three days at Fort Robinson, where a cavalry captain persuaded him to sign on as a scout. The Dakotas were on the verge of statehood but the Sioux were angry over the Dawes Act that sold a huge chunk of their remaining land in the Black Hills to the U.S. government and the Ghost Dancers were frightening white settlers with their talk of an Indian Messiah and ghost shirts that would make them impervious to the white man's bullets. The cavalry was charged with persuading bands of reluctant Sioux under Sitting Bull, Big Foot, and other leaders to give up their way of life and come into the Indian agencies. The troopers were in desperate need of men who knew the Lakota language, the lay of the land, and something of Indian ways. When he got back to Squaw Creek, Ezra explained to Eli that he felt it was his duty to offer his services as a translator and scout.

—Folks are all worked up. They think they're goin to see a big Indian attack. The Sioux aint got enough weapons left to put up a real fight but that don't mean they can't make trouble.

—I thought we was goin to stay here until we turned this ranch into a goin concern.

—Well, that's more your interest than mine. There's somethin about wakin up to the same view every mornin that bothers me. I get to wonderin what's goin on over the next hill.

—Just like our pa. Journey-bound.

—Maybe. I know them troopers ride far and fast, cover a lot of ground. That suits me fine. I aint ready to sink a deep well in one place just yet.

—I'll be sorry to see you go.

—You're welcome to come along.

—I can't do that just now.

—I know it. I aint ridin off forever. When I'm done, I'll be back.

On Livvy's eighteenth birthday that September, Eli showed up just after breakfast riding Monty and leading a dapple-gray two-year-old filly. Annabelle ran out to meet him and he pulled her up onto Monty and let her ride behind, holding on to his waist.

—Mornin, Livvy.

—Good morning, Eli. That's a pretty little horse you're leading.

—I'm glad you think so. She's a birthday present for you.

—For me? I couldn't accept her.

—Well, you'll have to. I held on to her until I could get her workin real nice for you.

—She must have cost a fortune.

—Nope. Her mother is a little mare belongs to Ezra, stallion is Teeter's. We've had her since she was a foal. Little small for us but she's just right for you.

—I don't know what to say.

—Aint no need to say a thing. We'll saddle her up, go for a little ride.

—What's her name?

—I call her Wildflower but you can name her somethin different if you want.

—No, no. Wildflower is a beautiful name for her.

They rode that day and the next and most Sundays after that until the cold weather hit. When they were riding, Eli said little but Livvy found that he could be good company even when he was silent; when he said a thing, it was never foolish. He spoke with an assurance that had annoyed her at first, but she had come to understand that it was the assurance of a man who thought before he opened his mouth.

On Christmas Day, Eli rode through a snowstorm for a ham-and-potatoes dinner with the Stantons. He brought little gifts for every member of the family except Livvy, which left her a little miffed. She sat opposite him at the dinner table and counted his words: He said exactly ten, of which "Please pass the spuds" were four. After dinner, he and Jack Stanton went outside, stood in the lee of the cabin and braved the snow for a smoke. With their cheroots half burned down, Eli said his piece.

—Captain Stanton, I've come to ask your daughter's hand. I want to marry her.

—I hope you've thought it through, son. You don't paddle up that creek but once.

—I have or I wouldn't be here now.

—No, I expect not. You aint one to jump off a cliff without lookin first to see a haystack where you can land. There's no man I'd rather have for my daughter. I know what you are and I got a fair idea where you're headed. Livvy couldn't find a better man, son, but she's got a head of her own and I pretty much give her all the slack she needs. If she wants you, I'm not one to stand in her way.

They shook hands on it, tossed their cheroots in flaming cart-wheels of sparks into the snow, and Stanton went back inside. A few moments later, Livvy stepped out with a shawl around her shoulders.

—What is it? Papa said you wanted to talk to me.

Eli reached into his pocket and pulled out an opal necklace.

—Here it is, then. I didn't give you a present before because I wanted to hand this to you private. This was my ma's before she died. I want you to have it.

Eli fumbled with frozen fingers to put it around her neck, gave up, and let her complete the task. He looked at her straight and steady with those pale gray eyes.

—I aim to make something of myself in this life, Livvy. I don't have no education to speak of, but I'm a hard worker and I'm good at turning a dollar. Give me another ten years, I'll have a spread where it will take you half a day to ride Wildflower from one end to the other. I wondered if maybe you might like to come along.

—You want me to go somewhere with you?

Eli kicked at the hitching rail with the toe of his boot.

—You're foolin with me. I'm askin if you would consent to be my wife, Olivia.

It was the first time he had called her by her given name. He had doffed his hat and his hair was turning white with snowflakes. She laughed and brushed some of the snow away. He thought that in all his life he would never again see anything as beautiful as Livvy at that moment, with the opal necklace around her long neck, her face lit by the kerosene lantern shining through the cabin window.

—Well, if I don't say yes, I'm afraid we'll both catch our death out here. First I want you to understand that I will never be a wife like some. I will not walk two paces behind any man. I will not be ordered about, and I will have my opinions heard. You are not marrying some empty-headed dullard because you're in need of a work mule for the house. As long as you understand all that, I would be pleased to marry you, Eli Paint.

—I understand you clear. I knew what I wanted first time I saw you, swingin that scythe at us, tryin to kill me and Ez. I took my time about it because I aint one to rush into things.

Livvy felt a rush of unexpected tears. To hide her emotions, she put an arm around his neck and pulled him to her. It didn't appear he was going to kiss her, so she would have to kiss him. She turned her mouth to him, and then he was kissing her, lifting her off her feet with those powerful arms. Livvy felt her legs weaken. She felt as though she had just consented to leap off a mountaintop in the arms of a whirlwind. When he finally let go, she had to breathe deeply before she could speak.

—Oh, my.

• • •

Eli Paint and Olivia Stanton were married on the twentieth day of April 1890. Ezra left off riding with the cavalry and came to stay for a week before the wedding. It was the first time he and Eli had been separated for any length of time and Eli found Ezra strangely quiet.

—What's eatin at you, brother?

—Nothin at all.

—C'mon, Ez. You know that I know better'n that.

—There's a bit of ruckus with the Sioux.

—This Ghost Dance thing?

—I guess you heard.

—People aint talkin about much else. How much do you know?

—I went huntin three days with War Bonnet. He told me the Indians have got a messiah. Name's Wovoka, comes from the Paiute people out in Nevada, the ones the Lakota call the Fish-Eaters. Anyway, this Wovoka has 'em all believin that the white man is about to disappear and that everything is goin to be like it was. The buffalo will be back and the streams will be full of fish and the people won't be hungry anymore. They do the Ghost Dance until they collapse, fall down like they was dead, and when they wake they'll be in heaven, only it aint heaven, it's right here without the whites.

—What does War Bonnet think about all this?

—Well, he don't like the Dawes agreement, I can tell you that. He believes the Black Hills are sacred territory. He thinks the Indians was robbed, and the land is somethin you can't give away, that it's supposed to be for all. He doesn't believe a man was born to work and nothin else. He thinks it's a crime for a Sioux warrior to bust sod and shovel horseshit when the Great Father put plenty on this earth to live by, so's a fellow doesn't have to do that kind of labor the livelong day. There's somethin to that, if you stop to think about it.

—Aint the way we was brought up.

—No, but that don't mean we've got it right either.

—What about Wovoka? Is War Bonnet doin the Ghost Dance with the rest?

—Not yet, far's I know. I can see War Bonnet don't strictly believe in the things this Wovoka is sayin, but he wants to believe it. He's seen a lot since that summer we went up to Devil's Lake and he don't like a bit of it. He says everybody is waitin to see what some of the leaders are goin to do, especially Sitting Bull. They got the army and the Indian agents nervous as hell, I can tell you that much.

—Aint no reason for anybody to be nervous. Not unless the Lakota got Henry repeaters and five-pound cannon.

—I know that and you know that, but some folks think it's still 1876, that Crazy Horse is about to come whoopin out of the Black Hills with ten thousand warriors behind him.

—That's foolishness.

—Sure it is, but you can't always tell people that. I'm afraid there's bound to be trouble.

—Maybe it's time for you to get out of there, get back here to Squaw Creek.

—No, this is the time I got to be there. If there is any way to stop the trouble, I got to find it, because if it comes you know who will lose. The Sioux have lost enough, had enough stole from them already. I got to do what I can to keep this from turnin into a shootin war that the Indians can't win.

—Well, I expect our ma would be proud of you.

—I'm proud of you, brother. Livvy Stanton. Prettiest girl in Nebraska and now she's goin to be Mrs. Eli Paint.

—It's your turn next. Time to find you a wife, little brother.

—No, it aint. Once we get this Ghost Dance business settled down I thought maybe I'd ride out to California, take a peek at what our pa saw out there. Get me a look at the Pacific Ocean before I settle down.

—Journey-bound.

—Aint it the way, though?

•   •   •

The evening before the wedding, Livvy saw Eli for the first time without the bandanna around his neck. When they were alone, he removed it deliberately in the light of a single kerosene lamp and turned so that she could get a clear view of the scar that circled his neck.

—Before we go through with this thing, I want you to see this so's you know the truth. There's a story some are tellin around that I was caught as a horsethief in Wyoming and got myself hung from a old cottonwood tree. Some say I wouldn't be here except a bolt a lightnin split the tree.

—I've heard that.

—And you thought it was a tall tale.

—I did.

—Well, it aint. It's the God's truth, Livvy. Me and Ez and Teeter stole them horses, with Roy Titus and a fellow we called Honest Abe. The whole thing was my idea. We took them horses from a outfit called the O-Bar up on the Powder River, because a foreman named Dermott Cull wouldn't pay us our wages after we most froze to death tryin to save his cows in the winter of 'eighty-seven, the time they call the great die-off. Wasn't just cows and horses that died either. We had five dead cowpokes at the end of that winter, and Dermott, he didn't want to pay the rest of us as made it through. It aint for me to judge if it was wrong or right what we done, but we done it. We might a got away clean but we didn't. Ezra and Teeter, they was split off with one bunch a horses, and Roy and Abe, they was with me with the second bunch. When I saw Dermott and his vigilance committee was on our tail and ridin hard, I stayed behind to hold off them vigilantes so the rest could get away. Held 'em up a while too with Pa's old Whitworth, though I aint half the shot with it that Ezra is. But some of 'em circled around me and Cull's sidekick, killer name of Perceale Pike, he caught up to me. Roped me right off my horse, drug me three, four miles, hung me from a big old cottonwood tree. Didn't give me a big drop because Dermott, he wanted to let me choke to death slow. I would've too if it wasn't for the awfullest storm you ever seen. Come blowin up with lightnin crackin so's you could smell the sulfur. Scared the vigilantes, they took off and left me to die.

Livvy had never heard Eli say so much. She was entranced and frightened at the same time. Until that moment, she felt, she had never known the man she was about to marry.

—My goodness! That is awful. What happened?

—I didn't exactly see. I was busy dyin at the time. But Roy Titus, he circled back and saw the whole thing. Said that right after them vigilantes went ridin off, a bolt a lightnin hit that old tree, split it right in two. Dumped me on the ground. That's where I was when Roy found me. Wasn't for that lightnin, I wouldn't be here now.

—That does sound like a tall tale.

—I know it does, I'll grant you that. Sometimes the truth is the tallest tale you'll ever hear. I wouldn't feel right without you knowin the truth before we get hitched. Happens I've still got some money put away from them horses we stole, which is why we have a chance to make it with our own spread where other folks wouldn't. Roy, he already spent most of the money he made off them horses on whores up in Fort Benton, but I held on to just about every penny of my share. One day, that money will come in handy. When that day comes, I don't want you wonderin where the money come from, and I don't want us to talk about this again. You want to call off the wedding, I won't kick up a fuss. I ought to told you this at Christmas. It just didn't seem like the right time, is all.

Livvy ran her fingertips over the scar. She found it appalling and oddly exciting at the same time. Her first impression had not been entirely wrong: Eli Paint was a bit of a wild man.

—It must have been horrible for you.

—It was some worse than horrible. I think I was dead for a while there.

Livvy pulled him down closer, put her lips to the scar, took a deep breath to give herself a few moments to think about it. In the end it was a simple decision. Hanging or no hanging, she had never known a man like Eli Paint. She would be proud to be his wife.

—Hush now. If you stole those horses, I'm sure you had a good reason for what you did. Now that's enough talk about hangings. We have a wedding tomorrow.

Teeter Spawn dug out a frock coat he hadn't worn in twenty years, stuck a pasqueflower in the lapel for the occasion, and rode over from the Dahlman outfit. Settlers and their wives and children arrived by spring wagon and buckboard from twenty miles away, bringing baskets filled with fresh-baked bread, sliced hams, apple cake, and black-cherry wine. The Reverend Hollis Applewhite, a circuit rider out of Rushville, performed the ceremony at Livvy's favorite spot near the creek. The preacher had dipped into Jack Stanton's store of blackberry wine that morning and was very nearly unable to perform the ceremony. He went off on a long and flowery disquisition about a bride's duties on her wedding night, which he choked off with an embarrassed cough when he caught a glimpse of Jack Stanton's red face and glaring eye.

When it was over, they ate and drank and danced to the best fiddler in Sioux County well into the night, and most of the wedding guests fell asleep in the backs of their wagons. Almost no one noticed that, shortly after dark, Livvy and Eli tiptoed away and rode horseback to his cabin on Squaw Creek for the night. The next day they took the Stanton buggy with Wildflower between the traces and rode to Rushville, where they were photographed standing solemnly in their Sunday best, their hands resting together on the edge of an enticing water fountain that was no more than a photographer's prop. Eli had shaved and persuaded Flo to cut his hair for the wedding; his dark hair was parted in the middle and slicked down. He wore a brown suit with a vest, proudly displaying a real gold pocket watch. Livvy wore her best pale green shot-silk dress, with her hair in a long braid that reached almost to her waist. When she saw the photograph, she was surprised that the braid made it look as though her hair was cut short like a boy's and disappointed that the black-and-white picture did not show how well the dress matched the green of her eyes.

That night they slept in the best hotel in Rushville. Their room was above a billiard hall and they could hear the click of balls and occasional shouts. Livvy feared that the rough men below could also hear the rhythmic creaking of their bedsprings at intervals through the night, but Eli chuckled at her embarrassment and tangled his fingers in her hair.

—Aint one of them wouldn't give his eyeteeth for five minutes of your company. Let 'em suffer. Any man who'd waste the life the good Lord give him shootin pool don't deserve better.

Livvy felt him swelling against her belly again. She was tired and sore, but her body responded to him in ways she could not control. From the day Eli had rescued her and the children from the blizzard, she had dreamed of this, and now she could not get enough, even though she teased him for the way he was after her.

—You're incorrigible, Eli Paint.

—No, I'm not. I got money in the bank and a wife at my side.

She let it go without correcting him. As gently as she could, Livvy vowed to help complete his education. She would begin by explaining that *incorrigible* did not mean *insolvent*.

A month after the wedding, Eli broke the news to Livvy.

—We got to have better land. I've got in mind the country along the Niobrara. Ezra and I come through there on our way to Wyoming. Grass is knee-high, and there is plenty of elbow room left. If I head out soon, I ought to be able to stake us a homestead claim and get a soddy up by fall.

Livvy stared at him, her green eyes telling him no.

—There's grass enough around here when it rains and you and Ez already have your land.

—Yes, we do. But there aint grazing enough here for one man's herd, let alone two. What moisture we get, the wind blows it all to Iowa before it can sink into the ground.

—All I want is you safe and sound right here with me. I've got that now.

For a week they carried on a silent argument, Livvy stiff and unyielding, Eli with his jaw set, ready to strike out alone without her approval if that was what it took. Eli wasn't much on explanations but he managed to tell Livvy what he was thinking: If she stuck by him, they would have a big ranch, a fine house, a brace of sons.

Livvy finally gave her consent. She had only one condition.

—I want you to try to find a place near the railroad so I can visit my people any time I want.

—I wouldn't think of doin otherwise.

⊰ CHAPTER 27 ⊱

For almost two months that summer, Eli Paint rode east under a sky that rained light. He had three saddlehorses and the albino packhorse, a big collie dog named Skeeter, and enough experience with cow outfits to know what he wanted: good grassland, fresh water, a hay meadow of some size, a spot for a cabin with some shelter where the force of the winter blizzards would be blunted by hill country or tall trees, and a town near enough so you could make the round trip for provender in a day but not so near that town fools would be driving their buggies over your range on Sunday afternoons. Now and again, he stopped and made camp for two or three days at a likely spot, only to move on because there were too many settlers in the neighborhood, or because the water in the creek tasted alkaline, or because he just didn't like the lay of the land.

He was as free as a man could be, sleeping outdoors every night, traveling each day as far as he wanted to travel and no farther. Along the way he shot grouse, pheasant, sage hens, and once when he was hungry, a stray pig. Everywhere he encountered settlers, most barely staying alive. There were Swedes and Bohemians, Germans, Swiss and Dutch, a cluster or two of French homesteaders from Quebec. What towns there were looked as though they'd been picked up a hundred miles away and dropped where they were by the last tornado. Shacks and soddies had been thrown up helter-skelter, abandoned or added to in random fashion, some gussied up with a coat of paint on one side or a window that had long since shattered, most with nothing better than wax paper for windows if they had windows at all.

Fifteen miles east of Rushville, he hauled out the scattergun late in the afternoon and shot a half dozen prairie chickens, then stopped at the dugout of a Swedish farmer and his wife and three children. The man hadn't even put up a soddy, just moved into an abandoned dugout on the side of a hill with a cracked door dangling by a single hinge from the timber framing the entrance. He was plowing with a slat-ribbed horse while a slat-ribbed cow grazed on the roof and his four slat-ribbed children stood outside staring hungrily at the brace of prairie chickens dangling from Eli's saddle horn. The Swede was tall and pitchfork thin, his wife not much older than Livvy but so worn and haggard she looked ready to pitch headfirst into her grave. She perked up some when she saw the birds. Eli helped pluck them, and she made a passable meal, although apart from the prairie chickens they seemed to have nothing to eat but cornmeal mush, which the children scooped into their mouths with rusty spoons. The farmer gnawed a drumstick and talked about how much he wished they had stayed in Minnesota.

—I don't know why we come to Nebraska. It's crazy country. The cattlemen want to kill us. There is no law. Breaking the ground almost break my plow and my back.

When he went out to feed his scrawny pigs after dinner, the woman waited until he was out of earshot, then turned to Eli.

—You call me Ingrid.

—All right. You call me Eli.

—You find me pretty, yes?

—You're a good-lookin woman.

—Please, I need help. He beats me. I leave him. Take me. I'll do anything for you.

Eli stared at the dirt floor, embarrassed.

—I got a wife back on Prairie Dog Creek.

Trembling, she stood next to the table, lifted her skirts to show Eli that she was wearing nothing underneath.

—Please. I will do anything if you take me from here. I don't ask to be your wife. All I want is help. Let me go with you to a town where there is railroad. Anywhere not this place.

—I'm sorry, ma'm. I can't do it. It aint right. It aint right that he hits you neither. If you want, I can talk to him about that.

She reached down and tried to unbutton his trousers, but Eli pushed her hand away gently. Abruptly, she dropped her skirts and turned away as though she had expected no other reaction. She went back to the washing up, stooped over an empty lard can on the dirt floor filled with filthy water, her weary back a silent reproach to Eli for his refusal. He tiptoed out the door, avoiding the stares of her wide-eyed children as he rode off without saying good-bye, and camped alone on the prairie, spending a sleepless night thinking about poor Ingrid stranded in that dugout. He could have stepped out to talk with the man about the way he treated her, but that might have brought another beating after Eli was gone. The railroads had enticed thousands of these desperate homesteaders onto this inhospitable prairie; stranded and broke, they were so desperate that their women offered themselves to passing strangers who might offer a way out. It wasn't right, but it was not a thing a man could fix all by his lonesome.

Eli never doubted that he would have something better. The ranch he would have somewhere in Nebraska was a clear vision that never wavered. At night he would lie on his back watching the stars wheel overhead, planning everything, right down to the location of the main house, the outbuildings, even the concrete dipping tank where the cattle would be treated with creosote to kill the ticks that he was sure were responsible for the spread of blackleg. Because it was all so clear in his mind, he never doubted that he would know the spot when he saw it. He would top a rise one day and there it would be, spread out before him like a picture in a book.

Alone on the trail, Eli lost track of the days. He passed through Rushville and Valentine and from Fort Niobrara followed the north shore of the Niobrara River through Keya Paha County east as far as Butte, where he forded the river and doubled back to the west through Holt and Rock counties, still not seeing what he wanted, although he was convinced that the place he sought would be within twenty miles of the Niobrara, one way or the other. The big river was the heart of the country. Simply fording the river, he felt it like an undertow, the Niobrara inviting him to come and settle.

In Brown County, two hundred miles east of Prairie Dog Creek, Eli stopped for the night in the town of Ainsworth. It was nearly August and he was running out of time if he wanted to establish a claim and put up a sod house before the snow fell. He was beginning to think that he might have to return to Squaw Creek and try again the following summer when a drunken locator in a tumbledown hotel told him free of charge that there was a place that might appeal to him six miles south and a mile east of Ainsworth.

—Pretty spot, aint sure why it aint took. Calamus Trail runs to the south and west so you get the military tramping back and forth, but they aint much of a nuisance. That claim has been filed on three times and nobody who filed stuck as much as a month. Last one said the mosquitoes drove him out. You let a mosquito bother you, you aint fit for this country.

Eli rode out before first light the next morning. He topped a low ridge and there it was, where a nameless creek meandered across the prairie toward the Calamus River, another ten miles to the south. The ridge to the north provided shelter from the wind and a line of big cottonwoods formed a natural windbreak for a house. Even now, at the end of a dry month, there was plenty of shortgrass for pasture and a natural hay meadow. As far as he could make out, there were no current claims on the land and there was plenty of government pasture to the south and west. No other houses, no shacks, no fences, no wells, nothing. Untouched homestead country, ready for the claiming in a county with good access to the world. The Fremont, Elkhorn & Missouri Valley Railroad had reached Neligh by 1880 and pushed on as far as Long Pine, just east of Ainsworth, by October 1881. Now the railroad would take Livvy west as far as Chadron when she felt the urge to visit her family and Eli could ship his cattle from the railhead east to Omaha and from there on to Chicago.

Still, he was a cautious man. Before he filed a claim on the land, he camped out for a week, getting the feel of the place. He paced out the locations for the house and barn. It took a great deal of casting about but he finally found the section markers left by the government surveyors and took down the numbers he needed to file a claim at the land office on one hundred and sixty acres of land in section 24, township 29, range 22. The numbers fairly sang in his mind. For lack of anything better, he scraped a patch of bark off a cottonwood tree and scratched a message with his pocketknife: "This be the land of Eli Paint." After pacing it one last time, Eli had to ride all the way back to Valentine to file his claim. The government agent, a bald gnome with a beak like a buzzard, peered over his spectacles.

—You don't look like much of a farmer, and that land aint much good for farmin.

—I aint a farmer. I aim to ranch it soon enough.

—Hundred and sixty acres? Won't graze a dozen head, that.

—One hundred and sixty acres the homestead, one hundred and sixty the timber claim I'll be back to file. Don't worry about me. You just take care of that claim.

The claims agent spat a stream of tobacco juice in the general direction of a spittoon.

—Many a man has said that and many a man has failed to get through the first Christmas. But you're welcome to try. Aint no skin off my nose if you end up as coyote food.

—I aint makin no meal for no coyote. That's the place.

—If that's what strikes your fancy.

Eli shrugged and walked out thinking about what the man had said. The place did strike his fancy, so he would call it the Fanciful. As for the homesteaders who had failed for hundreds of miles all around, he didn't care a whit. He had some things they didn't have, energy and experience and his ace in the hole, cash money from the sale of a herd of O-Bar horses to one Joe Kipp of Fort Benton, Montana, wrapped tight inside the rain slicker he never wore. He stayed in Valentine long enough to register in Nebraska the brand they had stamped on the O-Bar horses with a running iron: 8T8. Before he was through, he was sure the 8T8 would be the biggest ranch in Brown County.

Before he left Valentine, Eli bought paper at the general store and spent the better part of the morning scratching out a letter to Livvy:

My dear Olivia,

I had a good coming of it. As I thot there were no Soo on the way nor many other Indians, thogh plenty of despirate farmers in the panhandle, where they have tryd growing corn and taters on land that is good for ranching and nothing else. I feel sorry for the poor devils, espeshly a Swede and his wife and kids I come across, all of them living in a dugout and near starving. I am vowed that will never hapen to us.

I have found our home. It is on the 24th section south of Ainsworth, about two hundred miles from Prairie Dog Creek as the crow flys. It has good grass and a crick for runing water and a stand of cotonwood trees for shelter. The water is fresh and swete not alkalli. I have filed the claim today in town, the 7th of August 1890. As it will be coming winter soon and there is no house on the property, it is not a good time for you to come. I will set out today building us a sootable house which I aim to finish before the first snow. By spring it will be outfited comfortable and I will come to get you. It is less than ten miles to the post office in town here, the same distence for supplys. I will ride in once a week so you can rite care of the United States Post Office Ainsworth which I hope you will do reggular. I know this is hard for the pare of us, but I will make it worth the waiting. I will be back to fetch you come spring.

Your loving Eli

Livvy's nightmares came from dime novels that had belonged to her uncle Horace, consumed when her mother wasn't looking: Eli scalped and staked naked to an anthill under the broiling sun with molasses poured over his body. Eli dry-gulched by road agents, shot in the back and left for the buzzards. Eli thrown from his horse and forced to crawl miles with a broken leg. When his letter from

Ainsworth finally arrived at Squinty McNab's post office and general provisions store in Crawford, she wanted to dry-gulch him herself. Other than a three-line note scrawled in Valentine on the Fourth of July, she had not heard from him for most of the summer. Now he was telling her to wait an entire winter before she saw him again. She read the letter aloud to her father, then set her jaw:

—I am going to take Eli's spring wagon to Brown County. My place is with my husband.

—Not by yourself, you're not. He said wait, so you'd best wait.

—I told him before we got married I was not going to be ordered about.

—He doesn't want you taking chances. There are road agents and every manner of riffraff between here and Brown County, not to mention the Ghost Dancers. Now if you were to ride the railroad, it would be different.

—That would be ridiculous. Eli needs that wagon and everything it can carry.

—Maybe if you were to take Sherman along, you'd have some protection.

—Sherman? But you need Sherman here.

—We're pretty well set, thanks to Eli and his brother. I can spare him until next spring. I won't have you out on the trail alone.

Livvy started to argue that she could make it by herself but Captain Jack shook his head.

—You take Sherm and I will outfit you for the journey. You can have the bay team and you can take Bess for milk and you'll want to take Wildflower. Take as many hens as you want and that scrawny one-eyed rooster, because if he starts crowing at three in the morning one more time, I'm going to grab the scattergun and turn him into a pile of feathers. A full wagonload ought to give you a start. Better three of you than Eli alone, although he is bullheaded as they come and no doubt thinks he can do it all himself.

A week after Eli's letter arrived, Livvy was on her way with Bess and Wildflower tied to the wagon and Sherman riding back and forth like Daniel Boone himself, keeping his eyes peeled for Sioux warriors while Livvy did the real work of driving the team. The wagon was heavily loaded; as a parting gift, her father had presented her with a brand-new Home Comfort potbellied stove, bought in Chadron, which would burn wood, coal, or cow chips. The stove would keep the soddy warm until they could build a real house, and Livvy would be able to grill pancakes, boil coffee, and fry corn dodgers on the stove top. It was Stanton's way of making allowances for her husband's cowboy habits.

—Eli is apt to think he's just fine rolled up in a buffalo robe on a winter night, but I'm not going to let any daughter of mine freeze to death.

Before they set out, Livvy wrote to Eli care of the post office in Ainsworth:

My dearest Eli,

I received your letter a week ago and I have been in a state since. You can't imagine my joy, knowing you were alive and well and that you have found the place we will call our home. That joy, however, was matched by sadness at the prospect of spending a long winter without you, worrying about you alone out on the prairie facing all the trials you have to face alone. Therefore, I have decided to join you as soon as I can get there. Papa insisted that Sherman should come along as well. We are to leave at sunup tomorrow.

You can't imagine how eager I am to see our new home; the cottonwoods and the willows along the creek, to taste the sweet water and to be again with you, my darling husband. I am bringing the bay team, Bess the milk cow and Wildflower, a rooster, some hens, other things you may need. We will travel as quickly as we can without wearing out the horses. Papa says it should take about two weeks to travel that distance, so I will see you shortly after this letter arrives.

Your loving wife,
Olivia

In Ainsworth, Eli read the letter slowly, his lips moving as a blunt finger traced the delicate progress of Livvy's handwriting. When he was sure he understood her plain enough, he cursed and kicked a wall in the post office.

—Damned fool woman. I give her instructions, plain as day. Stay with her folks until I get a house built. Couldn't have been plainer. That's just plain disobedience and I won't stand for it.

Eli couldn't waste time worrying about Livvy. He had a house to build and the first piece of equipment he needed was a grasshopper plow to cut rectangles of sod for the house along with mule team to pull it. He asked around Ainsworth, found an old farmer whose eyes were too weak to hunt and swapped the use of the plow and the mule team for a brace of prairie chickens and a pheasant he had shot. The grass on his claim, a mix of bluestem, wire grass, and prairie cord, was perfect for sod. The grasshopper plow cut the sod into strips a foot wide and four inches thick. At first he tried cutting the strips into three-foot lengths with a spade but found that a corn knife worked better. Even with the plow, it was slow, backbreaking work cutting the wedges out of the sod, hauling them to the site he had blocked out for the house and stacking the walls in overlapping sections to make the structure more or less watertight.

Near noon on a sizzling day near the end of August, Eli heard the squeak of a wagonwheel a half mile away. He was guiding the grasshopper plow through the tough blackroot that held the sod together, the mules pulling fitfully to the rhythm of his curses. Striped brown deerflies hard as buckshot would land on his face, neck, and arms and bite, leaving tiny cuts that stung from the sweat and darting away from even the hardest slap. When he heard the wagon and saw Skeeter take off at a dead run, he knew who it was without looking up. He let the plow heel over, unhooked the harness, slipped the rope hobbles back on the mules and turned them loose. The surprised animals ambled to the creek for a long, noisy drink.

Eli watched Livvy and Sherman come down the long slope from the ridge, Livvy driving the team, Sherman on horseback,

Skeeter bouncing around them like a tumbleweed. She drove the wagon to the edge of the plowed strip, Sherman beside her holding the Winchester to show how well he had protected his sister. She wrapped the reins around the brake lever, jumped down and scrambled over the rough ground, her face flushed, her arms out to embrace him. Eli's voice cracked like a bullwhip.

—That's far enough, woman. I wrote you plain enough to stay in Dakota until I come to get you. My writin aint that good but your readin is just fine. So all I can figure is, you decided that a clear instruction from your husband don't mean no more than a drop of water in a hailstorm.

Livvy did not take a backward step. Eli had assumed that, at the first hint of his displeasure, she would be teary and apologetic. He had miscalculated by a wide margin. As he turned, determined to stalk away and leave her to ponder her transgressions, Livvy grabbed his shoulder to spin him around.

—Eli Paint! If you walk away from me now, don't you ever turn back. I have come two hundred miles to be with the man I married. If that is not what you want, then I will climb back on that wagon this minute and you will never see me again. If you cannot offer me a civil greeting when we've not seen each other in all this time, then I will not be your wife.

Eli scuffed the dirt, anger like a dark bubble in his chest. The night before, Livvy and Sherman had stayed in the only hotel in Ainsworth. She'd had time to wash and change from the old calico frock she had worn on the trail to a pretty cream-colored dress, which set off her green eyes and red hair. In her anger she had whipped off her sunbonnet. Now, as she stood facing him with the wind in her hair, her bosom rose and fell in anger. Her pluck was enough to make a fellow weak in the knees. She was no more afraid than if he was kneeling before her holding a bunch of daisies. Still, a man could not afford to back down. If not for a sudden gust of breeze, the two of them might have stood there all afternoon, stubborn as army mules, refusing to bend. The breeze cooled the sweat where the suspenders cut into Eli's back, and it blew Livvy's dress between her long legs. He felt a lump in his throat and a tightening in his groin, stared at the sod, kicked it with the toe of his boot.

—Aw, hell. You come all this way.

—Don't cuss.

The breeze was up again, the dress taut between her legs. At that moment, Eli would have declared himself a three-headed chicken with a prize goiter if it would have ended this quarrel and led to something sweeter.

—I think we're clear enough. Only you ought to asked my opinion before you left.

—Well then, in future I will ask your opinion, as you may ask mine. But there will be no ordering about. I will never speak in that way to you, nor you to me.

He reached out for her. She hesitated, then stepped forward and pressed her face to his chest. He was in terrible need of a long bath but she allowed him to hold her anyway. When at last he kissed her, she was sure he understood: They would go forward as partners or they would not go on at all.

Eli spent the rest of the afternoon showing Livvy and Sherman the lay of the land. The walls of the soddy were three feet high and rising, frames for the door and two windows already built. There were scuffed traces in the dry earth where he had sketched out the corrals, a small shed near the house for chickens, a barn, a smoke-house, a pigsty. He took them on horseback up to the ridge and pointed from one horizon to the other, the breadth of his vision.

—If I can get Teeter and Ezra to partner up with me, we can have ten sections of land in this valley in another ten years or so. We just got to put it together one piece at a time. Over to the east there, we have a couple of homesteaders still hangin on, but I expect they're looking to prove up their homestead claims so's they're free and clear and sell for the profit. South as far as the Calamus River the settlers are precious few, and them as stuck would sell at the right price.

Before sundown, Eli went out on horseback and shot and skinned two jackrabbits. Livvy slid the meat into his greasy pan and fried it over the fire, mixing flour, milk, and baking soda to make biscuits in the fat. While she was cooking, Sherman picked a bucket of buffalo berries down by the creek, and the three of them sat cross-legged watching the sun go down, happily eating biscuits and rabbit and berries with their fingers. When it was time to turn in, Sherman went to stretch out his bedroll next to the creek because he liked to hear the running water as he slept. Livvy and Eli slept inside the walls of the soddy, on the spot where she would spread their straw tick when the house was finished. He barely gave her time to unbutton her dress before he was on her, his face buried in her neck as her legs locked around his waist. When it was over, she tangled her fingers in his long hair, her lips tight to his mouth. They stayed that way for a long time, rocking gently. Finally, she nuzzled his ear.

—If you hadn't been so rude to me this afternoon, I would have told you right away. I have some news for you, Mr. Eli Paint. I am with child. Come March, you'll be a father.

Eli threw his head back and let loose a Lakota war whoop. Down on the creek, Sherman heard and moved his bedroll farther away. Livvy had obviously married a wild man.

There were times during those first weeks on the Fanciful when Livvy would see Sherman stumbling and red-eyed with fatigue and whisper to Eli that the boy needed a rest. Eli would hand him the shotgun and tell him to go scare up a rabbit for dinner, or maybe drop a fishing line into the creek to see if he couldn't catch a few perch. Sometimes, Livvy feared Eli was going to push so hard he would kill them all. He slept no more than four or five hours a night, rested in fifteen-minute snatches once or twice during the day, and somehow managed to work even while he was resting. It was not in his nature to order her or Sherman about or even to frown if they weren't working as much as he was, but he went at it so hard that if she dozed until six o'clock in the morning she felt like a slugabed. As long as she was working, Sherman felt that he should be too, whether his constitution was up to it or not.

The soddy went up more quickly than Livvy would have thought possible. The house was fourteen feet by sixteen, two feet larger each way than the size you needed to prove out on a homestead claim to the satisfaction of the government inspectors. Above the window frames they left four-inch spaces filled with rags and grass to allow room for the sod to settle without shattering the windowpanes. Eli had managed to scare up a cedar ridgepole and timbers to hold more sod for a roof and he did his best to seal all the cracks with mud mixed with straw. Every time he went into Ainsworth, he bought all the newspapers and Livvy used the papers to line the walls as both insulation and decoration.

Before the ground froze, they managed to dig a rootcellar, where Livvy was able to store the jars of sauerkraut, butter pickles, and crab-apple jam she'd brought from Prairie Dog Creek and to put up more jars of chokecherry and buffalo-berry jam before winter. Sherman helped her gather dry cottonwood leaves for their mattress ticks. They had no straw handy and she found the leaves worked better anyway; when they were fully stuffed, the ticks were more than four feet high, although they would sink gradually so that by spring the sleepers would be almost down to the dirt floor. One day, Eli promised, they would sleep on a real mattress on a real brass bed. Until then, the warm, dusty smell of the leaves made her sneeze. Eli and Sherman got the stove in and ran the stovepipe through a corner of the roof, then sealed the hole with mud. Livvy gathered cow chips with a wheelbarrow; by the time they needed the stove for warmth, she had six full gunnysacks of the stuff piled almost to the ceiling in one corner of the room. It smelled less than one might have expected, but she still looked forward to the day when they wouldn't have to burn cow excrement to keep from freezing to death.

In late October it began to rain, and it rained without pause for a week, a sullen, leaden downpour. For the first two days, the roof of the soddy held up well enough, with only a few leaks. By the morning of the third day of rain, the sod was soaked through and water poured into the house faster than Livvy could find buckets to catch it. Worse, it wasn't simply leaking water; gritty mud was falling in clumps that got into everything, the pots and pans, their clothing, the ticks and quilts where they slept. No matter how much fuel she put on the stove, it was never warm enough to dry anything; even the cow chips in the gunnysacks stored by the fire were soaked, and runny manure poured onto a hard-packed dirt floor that had turned to a pool of mud four inches deep. Eli brought in planks for them to use as walkways, but the planks slipped and slid in the mud. At night they huddled shivering under rain slickers and still they could not stop shivering long enough to sleep.

Finally Eli broke out his canvas tarps and they pitched a kind of tent next to the stove, with another tarp on the floor to sleep on and just room for the three of them to stretch out if no one rolled over. On the seventh straight night of rain, Livvy tried to make ham and biscuits, but mud kept dripping into the food, and if she stretched the tarp over the stove, the smoke made her gag. She gave up and the three of them, all sick with hacking coughs, huddled under the tarp and chewed on cold jerky to keep their strength up. After a few bites, she felt a sudden desperate urge to visit the outhouse, which meant sliding along a muddy path under a bone-chilling downpour and then sitting on dark wet boards with rain pouring through the slats on the roof while spasm after spasm tore at her belly. On her way back, she fell twice in the mud and before she could get her outer things off to crawl back under the tarp, a great wad of wet sod slid from the roof down the back of her neck. She shrieked and beat at it as though it was a living thing. Eli and Sherman tried to help but succeeded only in getting in her way. Livvy finally ordered Sherman to turn his back while Eli unbuttoned her dress and wiped the mud away with a rag that was cold and damp. After he finished buttoning the dress again, she sat cross-legged next to the stove and wept. Neither Eli nor Sherman could console her; she curled up on her side, her shoulders shaking. In the wee hours, she told herself that if the rain kept up for another day, she would saddle Wildflower, start riding east, and not stop until she came to Illinois.

The next morning, the first of November, dawned sunny and fair and unusually warm, warm enough for Livvy to spread their damp things to dry. She heated water and washed the mud out of everything, the bedding first. She left the door open to allow the mud inside the house to dry, then lined the ceiling with muslin. Muslin wouldn't keep water from dripping into the house but it would at least hold back the mud.

The last leaves fell from the cottonwoods, the temperature dropped, the wind shifted to the north. Eli worked himself and Sherman to the bone, the two of them trying to cut enough hay with scythes to see the cattle through until spring. When there was no more hay to be cut, Eli took Sherman to the railhead in Ainsworth for the trip back to Chadron; Livvy was sorry to see him go. Her brother's weakness and lack of independence annoyed her at times but he was a chatty companion and a good listener. Sherman found more to say in an evening than Eli would say in a month; she would miss him if only because he kept her mind from dwelling on the silence.

In December, Livvy stitched a new quilt filled with wild duck feathers for their tick. If she spooned up tight to Eli in the wee hours, she could keep from shivering, although the sound of the prairie wind howling around the little house made her feel a terrible, bone-chilling cold. She wrapped her arms around her belly, felt the baby move, pushed up closer to her husband, tried not to imagine that the howling of the wind was a wolf howl echoing long and lonely over the snow.

⚜ CHAPTER 28 ⚜

Near the Forks
Christmas Day, 1890

Brother Eli,

Ten days now riding hard with the Sumner Command and it is as cold as the winter of '87. The folks that run this army are afraid of a Sioux war after the killing of old Sitting Bull by the Indian police at Standing Rock these three days past. I was with a detail of troops camped here at the fork of the Cheyenne and the Belle Fourche when Sitting Bull was killed. By sunup the next morning runners from Standing Rock were at Cherry Creek, ninety miles away. They reported the fight with troops from Fort Yates and they said a lot of Indian Police and soldiers was killed and that 2000 warriors were coming, altho it now appears no part of this was true except the death of Sitting Bull. This caused a lot of excitement as you can imagine. Lt. Evans was in command and he sent a detail of soldiers with myself as a guide to go and meet these Indians to find out how many there were. All the scouts wanted to push hard because we were promised three months pay if we could be the first to meet up with Big Foot and persuade him to come in and surrender. We went up Cottonwood Creek and on north from there until we crossed Bear Creek and camped on the Moreau River but we didn't see any Indians. We started again at daybreak next morning and found that the Indians had crossed the river at the mouth of Thunder Butte Creek, six or seven miles above us, the night before. We followed the trail back to Cherry Creek and found that instead of 2000 there were only about 160 Indians but Fort Yates had already wired to Fort Meade that soldiers were needed. The troops marched all night and the next day they disarmed all the Standing Rock Indians but they found only a few old guns. If the Sioux have more rifles they got them hid pretty good. They're sick and starving so it dont look to me like they have good guns at all.

The second day we were on the trail we came within two miles of the Big Foot Camp. Captain Hennessy told the Indians they would have to go on to the Forks but Big Foot said they did not want to go any further. He was so sick he was spitting up blood and he was home now, his horses were tired, his women and children were hungry and besides, his friends the Standing Rock people had come to pay him a visit. After talking for about two hours Big Foot said he would not go that day but he would come up to the soldier camp the next morning with his head men and they would hold council. In the meantime a Standing Rock Indian started abusing an Indian Scout named Ree for helping the whites against his own people. Eventually he drew a gun and shot at Ree, missing him but killing his horse, a fine black-and-white pinto for which Ree got $150 from the U.S. Army. By this time things were getting lively. It looked as though we were going to have to fight or run so we ran. The commanding officer took Big Foot at his word and we went on up to camp about 10 or 12 miles away. Big Foot did not come the next day but sent word he was not feeling well.

The following day the message was the same and some of the Indians said Big Foot was dying. We sent word again to Big Foot and he said he would come up to dinner but when he did not show up we started after him. I wanted to travel quick with the Indian scouts but the captain said we had to take two hundred soldiers and a wagonload of ammunition in case of trouble and that slowed us down. We had some cold weather and although riders had been crossing the river on horseback, when the soldiers tried to cross it with a six-mule team and that wagon, the ice broke through. The water was only about three feet deep and they were able to cut the ice so we could pull the wagon out. It was almost dark by the time we got to Big Foot's camp and we found only five or six old women and a bunch of dogs. A dispatch was started to General Carr at the mouth of Rapid Creek telling him that Big Foot and his band had started on the warpath and were heading for the Bad Lands and that they should be headed off.

We had to make a detour to warn some settlers to clear out in case of Indian trouble and that trip put us fifty miles away from Big Foot, so tomorrow at sunup I will take about ten Indian scouts and see if we cant reach him before the army gets there and get him to give up, because them soldiers is drunk half the time and apt to shoot first and ask questions after. The government has fifteen thousand troops now between Chadron and Standing Rock, enough to fight the War Between the States again if they had a mind to, and still they cant seem to locate one sick old Indian chief with a bunch of women and children and old men. It is hard riding in the snow backtracking up and down in rough country and we have been generaly miserable, tho I expect the Indians is worse off, being sick and half-starved and wore out from us chasing them over hell's half acre. Right now it seems like Big Foot just vanished right off the face of the earth. Now we have to ride hard or we will never find him. Once we get him to come in peaceful to the Agency I am bound to light out of here because I've had about enough of dumb officers and wormy hardtack. The pay is good but it don't make up for the things that drive a man half crazy.

Give my love to Livvy, you got a good one there.

Ezra

Ezra's second letter arrived in early February.

Prairie Dog Creek
January 30, 1891

Eli,

Do not share this letter with Olivia, brother, as what I mean to do here is to tell you the truth of what they call the Battle of Wounded Knee and it is not a thing fit for a woman to hear.

First you will be surprised to know that I am back home and staying with Capt. Stanton and family as a part of the roof of our old cabin is colapsed, I guess that would be with the load of snow that was on it because we had no stove burning to melt it. I got what we left behind moved out of there and packed it in a big trunk which I will leave with Flo Stanton.

As I expect that you might have heard by now some false account of the Battle of Wounded Knee Creek, I thot it best to tell you the truth as to what hapened. I want you to know that I did not take part altho I did come upon the site at Wounded Knee one day after the fact, so what I know is part based on what I saw with my own eyes and part what others told me such as Phil Wells, the breed scout you will remember. Phil most had his nose sliced off by a cheese knife in the hands of a medicine man. If anyone has cause to be mad at the Indians it is Phil, so I have to think his acount is true. Wrong inteligence or maybe you could say no inteligence at all is what started this. What happened was because people said Big Foot had 2000 warriors, as I told you before, and that they was on the warpath but this was also not true.

If you got the letter I sent Christmas Day you know I was to take ten Indian scouts and go after Big Foot and his people. We trailed them south across the Black Hills road the next morning. They were headed for West Pass and were a long distance ahead of us because we lost time with that wagon that broke through the ice. This was the 26th of December and the next day I was sent up to Lt. Casey's camp at the mouth of Spring Creek. Casey had 200 Indian scouts with him but a big bunch like that moves too slow, so we rode out ourselves the next morning. I thought we had some chance to catch up to Big Foot in a day or two but the snow made it slow going for two days. The 28th the weather was like spring and warm which gave us all a rest from winter except it made the snow heavy and wet and the going slow, which I will regret to my dying day because I will always wonder if we could have put a stop to what happened if we got there a little quicker.

On the morning of December 30 an Indian scout found us before we broke camp. He said there was no more need going after Big Foot because Major Whitside and his men had killed most of the Big Foot people. What happened was that the troops caught up with Big Foot at the mouth of Wounded Knee Creek and all hell busted loose for no reason at all. Big Foot didn't try to fight, he was so sick with the noomonia he was coughing blood and almost dead and he put up a white flag to surrender. He had 120 men but almost no rifles and with him was 230 women and children. The troopers had taken all the weapons from Big Foot's band and searched the tipis and were searching the wariors when that Medicine Man began to act up. This is what I know from Phil Wells, who said the Medicine Man was painted up and he was doing the Ghost Dance and saying, "Ha! Ha!" meaning he had lived long enough.

The Indians say the trouble started then with Black Coyote, who did not want to give up his rifle because he needed it to hunt, but the cavalry had orders to dismount the Indians and take their horses and their guns and some did not want to go along with that because they said their young ones would starve. Phil says it was no more than five or six young warriors who had rifles hid under their blankets. Everyone seems to think it was Black Coyote who fired a shot in the air and that caused all hell to break loose. That was when the Medicine Man come at Phil with the cheese knife and hacked his nose. Phil knocked him down with his rifle and killed the man, then Phil went to finish pulling his nose off but a lieutenant yelled at him not to do that because his nose could be stitched back on, which it was that afternoon. Phil says he shot the Medicine Man in self-defense and I know that is true because I saw his face and it aint a pretty sight. But no one can claim that the rest of what hapened after that was in defense of anything at all. The army had Hotchkiss guns all around the Indians and when they heard that shot they opened up from all sides and it was the most terrible slaughter. I don't know if the troopers panicked or what but they aimed to kill every Indian on that spot and they came close to doing it. They say 25 of the Blue Coats was killed but the fellas who was there say the troopers was almost all killed by their own men shooting into the Indians from all four sides, so they was caught in their own cross fire. Plenty of the Indians that wasn't killed had it bad. They say a woman name of Blue Whirlwind was hit fifteen times and lived but I do not take that as fact because I did not see it with my own eyes.

We rode hard all day and when we got there they was digging the trenches for a common grave. It was a sight I do not wish to behold again and I have been sick in my heart ever since I laid eyes on it. Some 260 was dead and more than 100 of these was women and children. It had gone cold again and the bodies was froze stiff the way they died. Some was leaning against trees, some was holding their babies and children, many of them was all twisted up. It was imposible to straiten them out froze as they were so the trenches had to be wide and it was a helluva job to dig in ground that was froze solid. The dead was fitted into the trenches with the children sort of chinked in between the bodies of the older people. The trench was about half dug when a blizzard hit, what I call a Powder River blizzard, you will know why. It was so bad we had to wait three days before we could get back to the burying. The troopers done the digging with pickaxes in frozen ground but I was ordered to the burial detale which was the most awful detale I have ever done in my life and if there is ever a worse I swear I will not do it. We was dragging frozen children and old folks that was all shot up and throwing them into the pit and while we was at it some of the troopers was drunk and braging what they done. Now some say the soldiers are in line for medals which makes no sense at all. I thought there ought to be a court martial for them killing women and children but of course there wont be none.

On the way back to camp we found a Sioux woman almost a mile off from the rest with just her foot sticking out of a snowdrift, dead where they run her down on horseback and shot her in the back. Under her was her baby. It looked like she just fell there and tried to protect the baby with her own body but he froze to death. After all the bodies we drug and buried, them was the two bothered me the most, that mother trying her best to keep her baby alive. I heard later some of the bodies was took down to Fort Robinson where they was put in a church where it was still writ in big letters above the alter "Peace on Earth" for Christmas, as though folks ought to give thanks for the *killing of so many Indians. I wonder how much peace on earth they figure Big Foot's people got.*

When it was all done I rode out and did not wait to collect my pay. I found Teeter drinking hard and winning money at poker at Fort Robinson, pretty much the same thing he was doing down in Ogallala and don't that seem like a million years ago. Come spring if he aint drunk himself to death we will come to join you and see what we cant make out of the Fanciful. I expect it will do me some good to have hard work again. The things I have seen come at me nights and I dont sleep good without a coal oil lamp turned up high to keep out the shadows. You take best care of your Olivia and the baby that is to come because this life is a sacred thing.

Your brother,
Ezra

❧ CHAPTER 29 ❧

Eli had been up until long after midnight with a sick mare. He crawled onto their tick somewhere in the wee dark hours of a February morning, so cold that his skin through his long woolen underwear bore the chill of a dead dark world. Livvy had to steel herself to allow him to curl shivering into her bare flank, to let him seek warmth there and to slide spoonwise into her until she felt herself opening. She heard herself moan as though it were a sound coming from someone she barely knew. He stiffened and gripped her tightly with one arm wrapped around her breasts so that for an instant she could not breathe, and then his body went slack and he was asleep. She pushed back into him to hold them together a bit longer, her rump fused to his groin until he slid out of her and rolled onto his back, already snoring. She slept little and rose before him to stir the fire and boil the coffee. She lit a single candle to save on coal oil and sat nibbling a cold biscuit and waiting for sunup.

A brittle moon hung low over the southern horizon, lighting the February snow toward the Calamus River and beyond. South of the sod house, where the land curved down to a big dead cottonwood a half mile off, a dozen black gliding figures appeared as the merest shadows, a trick of the moonlight. She wet her fingers and doused the candle to see them better as they spread out, coming straight to the house. They moved in a steady, rippling trot, and as they came nearer she could see the puffs of vapor when their crystalline breath met the frigid air, their long, tireless legs propelling them like wind or water. No more than a hundred feet from the house they came to a halt and stood in a semicircle still and panting. Now she could see plainly they were wolves, not dogs. She went to stoop over the tick where Eli was sleeping like a dead man, one arm thrown over his face to shield his eyes from the light.

—Eli! Eli wake up, there are wolves out there.

She had only to whisper it and he was up and reaching for the Winchester rifle on its pegs above the table. He threw the door open and stepped through in his stocking feet. She watched from behind his shoulder as he swept the expanse of snow with the rifle, searching a target.

—Where?

—There. Just past the woodpile. Not a hundred feet from the house, looking right at me.

—They aint there now.

He stepped back inside to put on his boots and sheepskin coat.

—I better see if I can't hunt 'em. I thought the wolvers got most of 'em with the strychnine, but it's been a hard winter. They must be after the stock.

While Eli searched, she sat shivering, staring at the spot where the wolves had gathered to watch her. The fire glowed in the stove. It was not cold within but she had been chilled by Eli's body in the night and the wolves had terrified her, bringing back the awful loneliness of her nights in Crazy Amundsen's cabin on Prairie Dog Creek. It was there she heard the tale of Clementine Yost, a settler woman who fought off a pack of wolves trying to come right through the window of the cabin where her babies were sleeping. The Yost woman, they said, had only a pitchfork to defend herself, but she had killed two of the creatures, impaling one with his powerful body wedged halfway through the window before her husband came home and drove off the rest. The apparition of the morning had chilled Livvy so that she felt it still like ice in her belly, where the baby turned and kicked as though it felt the chill as well, felt the wolves as dark messengers from a darker world.

To banish such silly thoughts she swept the floor, even though she had swept it the evening before. Then she looked for washing up and found none to be done and instead put a bucket of water to boil on the stove and filled it with Eli's stiff wool stocks and his one extra pair of long wool underwear. When the water was hot enough, she would rub flakes of lye soap on the washboard, scrub them hard, rinse them out, and hang them over the stove to dry, something to keep her busy until he returned.

In an hour he was back.

—I can't find no sign. Not a track. Nary a thing.

—They were there.

—I aint sayin they weren't. Be as may, there aint no wolf sign I can see. There's a crust on that snow froze so hard I suppose a wolf could glide right over it and not leave a trace. Maybe a Indian tracker could find them but I can't. Could be they smelled that sick mare.

—Can they do that?

—Wolf can do most anything. They're part bear, part dog, and part ghost.

—Don't say that. They frighten me enough as it is.

—Well, maybe they can't quite do all that, but you ask anyone has tried to trap one and they'll tell you a wolf is the smartest animal there is. Any chance a fellow could get a little breakfast before noon?

—Is that all you can think about? Your stomach? With your wife frightened to death?

—Last time I seen you scared, you was swingin a scythe at me and Ezra, tellin us you were the daughter of Jack Stanton the Indian fighter. Them wolves is lucky you didn't get real scared or you'd be out there runnin 'em down with a pickax.

Eli grinned and poked her in the ribs and she let him get away with it because for a month or more he had been far too quiet.

There had been a letter from Ezra that he claimed to have lost before she could read it, and after that he'd got real quiet and stayed that way for two weeks, brooding and working himself to exhaustion. She guessed that the letter had something to do with the Battle at Wounded Knee. The papers were full of stories about the heroism of the troopers and there were even reports that one of them might get a Congressional Medal of Honor for his deeds. On the winds of rumor was a different tale, of women and children slaughtered. When she broached the subject with Eli at the supper table, he gave her a look she had never seen before and said that it was not an affair for women, nor would he offer one grudging word beyond that.

For three days after Ezra's letter came, he rose in the early winter dark and spent the day alone, cutting slabs of ice from the Calamus River and towing them to the icehouse by horse-drawn sled. His hands were cut and bleeding from wrestling with the ice but when Livvy wanted to bandage them, he waved her away. As the long winter closed around the sod house, he worked so much and talked so little that Livvy wished Sherman had stayed to provide a little company. On frigid mornings when the flat winter sunlight ricocheted off the snow, he left the house at dawn and rode out to check on the livestock with scarves wrapped tight around his eyes, peering through a tiny slit to avoid snow blindness, battling the elements, knowing that all their labor so far had won no more than the merest toehold on a cruel and capricious land, a grip that could easily be loosened by drouth, hail, prairie fire, disease, grasshoppers, or the fluctuations in markets thousands of miles from Brown County.

Now he had relaxed just the tiniest bit, enough to laugh with her. His laughter did not cancel the fears stirred within her by the apparition of the morning wolves, but she took it as a sign he was coming back to life, a harbinger of spring in the dark heart of the winter.

The snow piled high against the soddy, the wind blew hard from the north, the blizzards alternated with spells of cold when they had to scrape the frost from the windows with a butter knife just to peer out. By the end of February, it seemed that spring was a secret the Lord had decided to keep for himself, hidden forever behind a shroud of storms. Through the worst of it, the company of other settlers kept Livvy sane. Even a loaded spring wagon could be hauled over an ice road; buggies were lighter, sleighs were better still. Settlers thought nothing of traveling to come calling on a Saturday night; ranchers stopped for Livvy's biscuits and to talk cattle with Eli; wives from struggling homesteads came with fresh-baked bread or pea soup to ease her tasks in the month before her time. On the last Saturday of the month, Sewall Gandy stopped with his jug and his fiddle, and word went out that there would be a winging at the Paint house. By nine o'clock the soddy was so full of neighbors there was no place for anyone to sit except Livvy, who perched on one of the two chairs at the table and watched, her face flushed and excited, as Sewall's jug circulated one way and Bo Stanly's blackberry wine the other, and couples whirled around the dirt floor to the "Virginia Reel" or "Turkey in the Straw." They whooped and danced until well past midnight, when those who had only a few miles to travel harnessed their teams and went plodding home by moonlight, while those with farther to go bedded down on coats or buffalo robes spread on the floor, their mingled snores a comfort to Livvy, sleeping fully dressed next to Eli on their tick.

Sunday mornings were the one time during the week when Eli made a concession to powers greater than himself. After the chores were done, he would harness the team to the buckboard, hoist Livvy onto the seat, wrap her in a buffalo robe and drive the eight miles to the First Congregational Church in Ainsworth, where he would remove his hat and sit in silence, his mind far from the pulpit, where it was so cold the minister's breath rose in puffs of spidery vapor to the heavens. The Reverend Chester Cubbin, a pudgy, timid little preacher from Pennsylvania, had nothing to say that Eli hadn't heard before. Certain undertakings, however, had been made on Eli's part while his neck was in a noose in Wyoming.

His presence was intended to fulfill his part of the bargain; anyway, it was in church that he got his best thinking done. While Reverend Cubbin perspired despite the cold and worked himself up to what he thought was a suitably dramatic conclusion, Eli would sit with his wide-brimmed black hat dangling from his knee, deciding how much to pay for sixteen Hereford cows belonging to the nearly bankrupt Asa McBride. During one such sermon-inspired reverie on a sunny morning in March, Eli felt a pressure on his arm and looked to see Livvy smiling up at him. She mouthed the words silently:

—It's time.

Octavia Olivia Paint was born shortly after noon on March 7, 1891, after a labor that was so brief Eli barely had time to fetch Clara Hardesty, the midwife. Pale early spring sunshine spilled over the dirty snow outside and a squall of sparrows blew against the window as Livvy fell back, too weak to reach for the child, barely hearing what the Hardesty woman had to say.

—I hope you aint too disappointed. She's a she, but she's a big strong girl.

Then Eli's voice from somewhere off to the side where Livvy could not see him:

—Aint disappointed one bit. I'll make her a hardbottom cowhand, same as any boy.

He kissed Livvy's damp forehead, a gesture not common for him in the presence of others, and asked if she was all right. When she nodded, he said he had chores to do and left. She raised her head, watched the woman bathe the child, her child, waited until she was wrapped in a bit of blanket and handed up, a package surprising in its weight, solid and already unyielding—or perhaps it was just that Livvy imagined her so because she was Eli's daughter. Clara put more water on to boil.

—What will you call her?

—She was to be called Ezra after Eli's twin brother but I don't think that will do now, will it? Perhaps Octavia, after my mother.

She died when I was two, so I would like this child to have her name. We'll call her Tavie.

A month passed before Livvy stopped feeling that she had stepped out of her body the day the girl was born and couldn't quite step back into it. She felt weak, she tired easily, she started to do something and forgot what she was about and the baby at her breast seemed to gobble all her strength before she could make use of it herself. Neighboring settler women passed from time to time with baskets of food and stayed to help sweep out the soddy and do the washing up, but they had their own burdens, troops of children and worn-down men all but beaten by the land. Often the women were caring also for ailing mothers or fathers under the same roof, where dying and the endless procession of babies went on in lockstep, often in the same room, always with the women in attendance to wash the sick, clean the babies, comfort those in pain, and shroud the dead, while the men stood about with their callused hands dangling helplessly at their sides like rusty tools, the purpose for which had vanished in the mists of time.

Eli at least was not too proud to help with the washing up or even to clean the baby's bottom when he was home but that was not often, what with cows calving out on the prairie, fences to mend, more sod to break, alfalfa to plant, milking and feeding and roughing out the two yearling fillies he had purchased the day before Tavie was born. He would come in weary and hungry and Livvy would feed him and force herself to eat something to keep her strength up. They would sit briefly by the fire as she nursed the baby and then shed their clothes and fall onto the tick, the cradle near enough that Livvy could reach out to rock the baby during the night. She would sleep with Eli's thick forearm wrapped around her strangely flat belly while she dreamed of wolves, strange dark beautiful loping tireless creatures whose significance she never quite understood. In her dreams the wolves were no longer frightening; they brought her neither fear nor comfort but a hopeless yearning for something infinite, something always just beyond her reach or ken. After such dreams, she would sometimes awaken to find her cheeks wet with tears, whether of sorrow or exaltation she could never quite recall.

The first warm days brought her strength back. She liked to take a chair outdoors in the morning and lean back against the soddy, letting the sun wash over her while the growing child tugged at her breast and the meadowlarks sang far out on the prairie. On Sunday afternoons after church, she made meat sandwiches for a picnic, and Eli harnessed the team and drove to the banks of the Niobrara, where she spread a cloth for them on the ground and they ate and talked and played with Tavie and felt about them a luxuriant optimism, their lives without boundary, Eli for a few precious hours willing to put aside the quest that drove him in order to linger with his young wife and baby. On those sweet Sundays, all things seemed possible: The Fanciful would extend all the way to the Niobrara, they would build a large white house with a broad veranda to the south, they would have a dozen children, they would persuade Captain Jack to pull up stakes on Prairie Dog Creek and settle in Brown County so the entire family would be together.

As Tavie slept and the shadows lengthened on one such afternoon beside the river, Livvy pulled Eli atop her and opened to him as her fingers dug into his shoulders. They rolled over once and again and finally off the old quilt that held the baby and the picnic basket, Livvy's auburn hair spread on the newly green grass, her head down the sloping bank toward the Niobrara. She heard the distant honking of a long, wobbly flight of geese headed north, breathed the fragrant earth, looked and saw that Eli was watching her with infinite tenderness as he moved inside her. He finished with their eyes locked, promises offered and received at that moment deeper than any wedding vows, her unspoken prayer given wing under that impossible vault of blue sky. *Let it never change. Let it never change, O Lord, let it never change.*

CHAPTER 30

Ezra Paint and Teeter Spawn arrived on the Fanciful in June. They turned up in time for supper, as though they had sniffed ham and biscuits on the wind and dropped by like grub-line riders wanting to brand a few calves in exchange for a meal. Ezra had thinned some and Livvy saw or imagined that she saw the shadow that had passed over him at Wounded Knee. He had always been a gentler soul than Eli but now he was less talkative and he seemed more watchful, although he had the same easy grin. When he grabbed her and held her shoulders, she felt the way he seemed to need her, as though no one had shown him pity or kindness in years.

Over the coming weeks, Livvy tried several times to draw Ezra out on the events of late December at Wounded Knee Creek but he refused to be drawn. He would cloud up like a winter sky, shake his head, look off across the swale where the land swooped down toward the Calamus, and mumble something about how a man had different feelings when he had a little Sioux blood sown against the grain.

—If something is eating you inside, you ought to talk.

—Aint nothin. Things happened that oughtn't to happen, is all.

While Ezra was subdued, Teeter kept everyone entertained with his card tricks and his storytelling and his observations on just about everything from rainmaking to the administration of

President Benjamin Harrison. Within two weeks he and Ezra had filed claims on two homesteads adjoining the Fanciful. Six months later they bought another entire section of homestead relinquishments, so that, with Eli's holdings, the three of them already had almost two sections of land.

Teeter met Livvy's every request, even to the point of refraining from his habit of chewing tobacco everywhere he went and spitting into a tin cup next to his dinner plate. In Livvy's presence, he waited to bite off a fresh chaw until he was outdoors again. He took to Tavie as if she were his own daughter, hovering around when she took her first steps, spoiling her any time he was given the opportunity. Visitors to the Paint house became accustomed to the odd spectacle of the stove-up old cowboy, his remaining teeth stained brown with tobacco, seated in the rocking chair with the baby girl on his knee.

A dry fall followed a long hot summer. The grass turned brown and brittle, and they sniffed on the wind the acrid smell of a prairie fire forty miles to the west where two young boys had died, suffocated as they crouched among the cattails in a shallow pond when the fire swept over them and drained the air of oxygen. Livvy watched the sky and slept fitfully at night, wondering how she could get Tavie out of the path of a roaring prairie fire. They plowed fireguards around the sod houses belonging to Eli and Ezra and around Teeter's shack, with burned strips in between to keep the fire from spreading if it came their way. Two days of rain in late October doused the fire threat but did not do much to put Livvy's fears to rest.

Their second winter on the Niobrara came and went in more comfort than the first. In the spring Livvy's belly was large again but there was almost no rain. The land greened briefly and turned brown again. Eli's prudence meant there was some hay left from the winter but not enough to keep his growing herd if there was no rain. Bit by bit, he had spent what he thought of as his "black money," the money left from the sale of the O-Bar horses to Joe Kipp, on livestock and land. Once or twice Livvy had even questioned him about it, wondering if he really ought to buy another twenty head of cattle or a new horse or another half section of land. Now there were no more questions: The money was gone. He had risked everything and if it did not rain, he would lose everything. He watched the skies, muttered to himself, slept less than ever. A drouth was a biblical thing, like a blizzard or a flood or a grasshopper plague. There was little a man could do but pray, and Eli put precious little stock in prayer, though he prayed dutifully enough on his church Sundays, just in case.

The drouth did not ease. By the time Livvy gave birth to Marguerite Florence, in November 1892, the oldtimers were calling it the worst drouth they had ever seen and predicting dire and terrible consequences if it did not rain. Settlers saw the crops they had planted in the spring, their neat rows of corn and alfalfa, lettuce and radishes, wither and die except for the tiny patches that could be watered from a good deep well. They cultivated deep, hoping the soil would hold the moisture, but there was no moisture to hold. Corn grew six inches and died, wheat refused to head out, oat fields held nothing but the white skeletons of the dead stalks. Families poured years of work into their plots of land, then lost it all to the eastern loan companies that financed their plows and seeds. Some of them stopped at the Fanciful on their way back east, because the word was out that Eli never turned away a hungry family. They ate well at his table and moved on under the tattered canvas of the wagons that held their few remaining possessions, their bony children gazing wide-eyed at the receding prairie.

As the drouth got worse, traveling preachers held revival meetings and baptized whole towns in scummy lakes that were nearly dried up. The newly baptized emerged singing and praying and stinking of the muck, but still the most they could summon from the sky was the occasional thunderhead, which would water one farmer's field while leaving his neighbor's crop bone-dry. The preachers took up their collections and moved on, rain or no rain. In their wake came the rainmakers. Some were wandering Indians who would do an impromptu rain dance; others would roll into a town like carnival barkers, driving gaudily painted wagons, toting smoke-making machines, and promising the sweet release of a week's steady, soaking rain in return for a few of the hard-earned dollars the settlers could scrape up.

When Teeter heard that a rainmaker by the name of Julius J. Ragsdale had set up shop in a whistle-stop town and was promising rain in exchange for one hundred dollars, he rode the one hundred and fifty miles west to see what the excitement was about. He arrived early on a Sunday evening to find the unfortunate Ragsdale, a potbellied little man with a few scraps of hair on a bald dome and a stutter that might have been brought on by his circumstances, surrounded by an angry mob of settlers and small cattlemen determined to lynch him, because after a week of smoke machines and folderol and pocketing their money, he had not delivered a drop of rain. Ragsdale attempted to talk his way out of his predicament and might have succeeded, except that his stutter made it impossible for him to get out more than a few words. A husky man egged on the crowd, claiming to have seen Ragsdale bilk another town.

—He done the same thing in Sidney. Took the money and run. Only way that lyin sonofabitch could make rain is if he drunk a barrel a beer and pissed on our crops. The man ought to be tarred and feathered and run outa town on a rail. These is hard times and them as attempts to cash in on another man's misfortune is lower than a egg-suckin weasel.

Someone found a bucket of tar and set it to heat in the fire. A dozen men surrounded the rainmaker and ripped his clothes off. When he came up wailing and still in their grip, he had been bloodied from head to toe. A cry went up for feathers; hot tar alone would not do.

—Tar and feathers, boys. Got to be tar and feathers. Can't do a proper job with tar alone.

—Bertha Waite got all the feathers you need right acrost there at her henhouse. Run tell her what it's for, she'll give you a pillowcaseful.

Teeter had seen such mobs in action a half dozen times in his life, and he knew that getting in the face of one was as futile as trying to halt a stampede with a mouth harp. There were a hundred men gathered round, armed with everything from pitchforks to shotguns. They were not to be denied their revenge, even if no one present was out more than a single dollar for the services of the rainmaker. A teenage boy went pelting away and returned with a bag of feathers to find the mob had already pulled the bucket of hot tar from the fire. They tried to pour it over Ragsdale's head, but it was not yet hot enough to pour, so they settled for daubing at it with sticks and smearing it over his naked body from head to toe. At every touch of the tar the man screamed, but his screams just seemed to spur them on. It wasn't quite as Teeter had always envisioned it, with the victim evenly coated in tar all over his body, but by the time the tar bucket was empty, the huckster had enough smeared here and there to hold most of the chicken feathers after the bag was shaken out over his head. Once that job was done, they got Ragsdale up on the rail three times, and three times he fell off. Someone finally managed to hogtie him to the rail by his hands and feet, exactly like a hog on a spit. He was hoisted again, and this time they got him going at a good run, his privates slamming hard against the rail at every step. As they swept past Teeter, he caught a glimpse of the man's tar-smeared face, the eyes wide with fear. A half mile out of town, the energy seemed to go out of the mob and Ragsdale was cut loose from the rail and left to fend for himself, naked and still covered in the mess of tar and feathers. He staggered off into the darkness and the mob stumbled back into town.

At dawn Teeter rode out on Ragsdale's trail, fearful of what the August sun would do to a man on foot and covered with tar. He found a thin trail through the dry and brittle grass running a few hundred yards up a slope away from the river. Then the trail simply vanished at a dried-up lake bed where the clay had baked too hard to hold the track of a barefoot man. Teeter could see for miles in any direction but there was no sign of the rainmaker. When Teeter told his tale back at the Fanciful, Ezra speculated that perhaps a merciful God had intervened to save the man. Eli shook his head and spat in the dust.

—If there was a merciful God, I expect He'd a made sure it rained by now rather than see all them starvin kids and their folks with their pockets empty and their hearts broke.

There was no mercy to be found in the high-vaulted sky. Season followed season, clouds formed and passed and formed and passed again, and still it did not snow in winter or rain in summer, not enough to matter. Phantom rain streaked down from distant clouds but no man or beast could find the cool, wet place where it touched down. Two years into the drouth and following the economic crash of 1893, the Fanciful was in trouble. No amount of hard work, cultivation, and prayer could make up for the lack of water. Eli had to cut back on the size of his herd and cut back again because the bare, windswept prairie would support so few cattle. By the time Velma Viola Paint was born, in January 1894, the Paint family had three daughters to feed from land that would turn to desert if it did not rain.

Ezra left early that winter to visit Spotted War Bonnet at the Pine Ridge Agency. War Bonnet was trying to make a living the white man's way, running a small ranch on the northwest corner of the reservation, not far from the Black Hills. He lived in a comfortable, tightly chinked log cabin with his wife and two young sons, his apparel, language, and habits an odd hodgepodge of white and Lakota. War Bonnet was mistrustful of any white man, even Ezra, but after a supper of fried cottontails, the two men talked well into the night. The Indian agent Dr. D. F. Royer, nicknamed "Man Afraid of Indians" by the Sioux after his panic helped create the atmosphere that led to the Wounded Knee massacre, had been replaced by the acting agent Captain George Leroy Brown. Brown was no Valentine McGillycuddy, the one agent who understood the Sioux and spoke their language, but he was a soldier and he was not given to panic. Captain Brown tried to encourage native ranchers like War Bonnet, mostly because he felt that if they took up white ways they were less likely to attempt another rebellion. He was also trying to supply the Lakota people with enough beef to get them through the drouth. War Bonnet himself was looking for good breeding stock, a Galloway herd bull and a dozen purebred heifers. If Eli and Ezra could provide War Bonnet with quality stock, he would swap some of the wild horses they were still capturing all the way west to the Black Hills; the Paint brothers could break the horses and sell them at a nice profit back in Brown County. They sat staring into the fire, getting comfortable with each other again through long silences. Finally Ezra said what had to be said.

—You ought to know I was workin as a scout for the Sumner command out of Camp Robinson a few winters back. Tryin to find Big Foot, get him to come in before the troopers found him first. I got to Wounded Knee Creek all right, but I got there a day late and a dollar short. It was a awful thing, and it ought never to have happened. They killed women and children and old ones along that creek for no reason at all.

—The whites were afraid. They had nothing to fear from us, but they were afraid.

—Yes, they were. They were afraid, and frightened people do stupid and vicious things. Which don't make it right. They were afraid of the Ghost Dance.

War Bonnet got up to put more wood on the fire.

—The Ghost Dance was like a dying buffalo. The buffalo has an arrow through the heart, but he stands anyway, pawing the earth. Sometimes he stands like that for a long while. But he always falls in the end. At the time of the Ghost Dance, we Lakota and our friends the Cheyennes were already shot through the heart, but we didn't know enough to fall over.

The next day, Ezra went with War Bonnet to meet Captain Brown. Brown wanted beef contracts and he was willing to pay top dollar, but he did not want to buy cattle in small lots. If the Paints could supply a thousand head in the spring, he would buy them at two dollars a head, more than they could get in Omaha. Ezra tried to persuade him to accept five hundred head as a first consignment but the captain would not agree: It was a thousand or nothing. Ezra left that day and rode back to Brown County to put the proposal to Eli.

Eli didn't hesitate. He simply said yes and wrote to Captain George Leroy Brown agreeing to supply the Pine Ridge Agency with one thousand head of mixed steers and heifers no later than May 15, 1894. Livvy questioned his judgment.

—Where are you going to get the money to buy all those cattle?

—I'll talk to the bank.

—Mrs. Whitman says her husband tried that and they wouldn't give him a dime.

—Well, that's him. I've got to give it a go. There aint no other way.

—What if something goes wrong and you can't get the herd to Pine Ridge?

—Then they foreclose. Same as if we give her up now.

—Except if we give up now we'll have some things to sell. We can make a new start.

—If we give up now we aint half-tried, Livvy. We got to try.

—You always said your pa told you not to get mixed up with banks.

—He did. He absolutely did. But he also taught me that sometimes you got to take a risk to do a thing, and far as I can tell, this is one of those times. I try to talk to Eb about it, make out what he would do, and near as I can tell, he'd swallow his pride and go talk to the bank.

—All right. I trust you, Eli. You know that I trust you, right?

—I know that, girl. That's why I got to make this work. I got to make it work or we're done here.

CHAPTER 31

Bly Olp, the man the settlers called Foreclosure Olp, sat with his boots propped on his massive oak desk watching the March wind start a tumbleweed parade down Main Street in Ainsworth, ignoring the little drifts and fantails of dust that worked their way under the windowsill and eddied along the floorboards. He was a big man with a walrus mustache, a red drinker's nose, and a spreading gut nurtured on roast beef, mashed potatoes, sweetcorn, and Tennessee whiskey. Times were hard and business was slow: Olp pared his nails with a six-inch clasp knife and toyed with the double-barreled shotgun he kept dead center on his desk. It was aimed at the rickety chair provided for supplicants seeking a loan, in case some quarrelsome settler should take it into his head to raise a fuss over a foreclosure. The howl of the wind was the only sound Olp heard most of the day, other than the noise Gus Schrautz made sucking the holes in his teeth while he sat counting and recounting the money in his cash drawer.

—Gus, could you please goddammit stop that.

—How's that?

—I said could you please goddammit stop.

—Stop what?

—Stop suckin your goddamned teeth all the goddamned day.

—Can't help it. Got holes in 'em. Need a dentist. Can't afford one on what you pay me.

—Goddammit, Gus, I am not goin to get into another goddamned salary dispute with you. I am talkin about your goddamned
teeth, not your goddamned pay. Stop suckin them chompers or I
am goin to take holt of a pair of pliers and yank every last goddamned one right here and now. That ought to relieve you of the
need for a goddamned dentist pretty much for goddamned ever.

The clerk's mouth clacked shut. His bony behind squirmed on
the hard stool. One of these days he would stroll over to Olp's desk,
turn that shotgun around, shove it in Olp's belly, and trip both triggers. The thought made Schrautz feel so good he sucked a back
molar as he squinted down Main Street.

—Company comin.

Bly Olp peered out the window.

—Well I'll be goddamned. Them two is Eli and Ezra Paint.
Never thought they'd be fool enough to come to a bank.

—These is hard times. The drouth and all. Grover Cleveland
back in the White House.

—Yes, they are. But one man's hard times is another man's
profit, Gus. You remember that: One man's hard times is another man's profit. And them folks as blames the President of
the United States for their troubles is just too lazy to see a opportunity when it whacks 'em upside the head. Now you sit back
and watch how it's done, Gus. This ought to be fun, takin candy
from these babies.

For no good reason Olp could see, Eli Paint was toting that bullwhip right into the bank. The man never seemed to go anywhere
without it. It made a fellow feel less than comfortable sitting down
for a chat with a fellow carrying a bullwhip. Olp eyed the shotgun,
swiveled his chair to where he could reach it quicker if it came to
that. But Eli took the whole setup apart and kicked the chair out
of the way with one booted toe so he could sit on the edge of Olp's
desk. Ezra went to the far side, took his perch directly opposite Eli
with his hip on the desk so that his freshly oiled Colt Navy poked
out of its holster, the barrel angled southeast, in the general direction of Olp's privates. Olp didn't even leave off paring his nails.

—Mr. Paint and Mr. Paint. What reason do you boys have for wasting my time today?

Eli picked up his hat, rose, and started for the door without a word, Ezra trailing. Olp waved the clasp knife to beckon them back.

—Whoa, whoa, whoa. Just a manner of speaking, young fellas. A manner of speaking. I assume you came here for a reason. You have a proposal for me, maybe?

Ezra did the talking while Eli stared out the window.

—We need money.

Olp guffawed.

—Of course you do. Show me a person in Brown County who don't need money and I'll show you a horsethief.

—It aint the usual thing. We got a contract to deliver a thousand head of beef on the hoof.

—So deliver 'em. I aint holdin you back, am I?

—Three of us together, me and Eli and Teeter Spawn, we got about four hundred head right now branded 8T8. That leaves us six hundred short of that contract.

—So you want enough money from me to buy six hundred cattle?

—That's about the size of it.

—From what I've seen of the goddamned cows around here, the man holds your contract wouldn't want any part of 'em. Just hide and bones. Goddamned drouth and all, y'see.

—I expect we know pretty much all there is to know about the drouth. Our cows are some better than most because we had a good deal of hay put up. Cut the brome and wheatgrass and planted some alfalfa, left the shortgrass for winter pasture, kept our cows from starvin to death. But we got to buy six hundred head more from Unc Slater and Dale DuChamp in Valentine, trail 'em from there.

—What do you figure? Twenty dollars a head for yearlings?

—That's about it.

—That's twelve thousand dollars.

—We can do cipherin just fine, Mr. Olp. It's twelve thousand dollars and we can turn five thousand profit on that money in a month's time.

—If it's such a lead-pipe cinch, what's to stop me just buyin those cows?

—Not a thing, if you know how to get a thousand head of cows to go where you point 'em and you already got a contract for beef.

—You know banks out here is going under left and goddamned right. Three out of four banks in Rushville is dead already, and it aint much better here.

—If you aint goin to lend money, what are you doin here?

—Well, to give you a safe place to keep your money, one thing.

—A safe place to keep my money is where I can keep a eye on it.

—A lot of folks believe that. You have to think of all the things that can happen. Fire and flood. Thieves in the goddamned night.

—That's our lookout.

—Yes, it is. People around here seem to think you fellas are sound as this here oak desk, which counts for somethin. But let's say I did want to make you the loan, there's a problem. There's a rumor you boys are part Indian.

—Indian.

—That's right. You know. Redskin. Savages.

Ezra started to speak but Eli cut him off.

—It happens we aint part Indian, we're part Jewish. Our mama was a Jewish lady. Come from a family in Chicago.

—Well, that might change things. They say Jews is good with money.

—I wouldn't know.

—But if you're part Jew, then maybe you're worth the risk.

—We aint no risk at all. We borrow money, we pay it back. We drive these cows where we got to drive 'em, we come back with the money, we pay off the loan, and we're quits. We'll put up everything we got, the whole shebang. Three houses, two sections of land, outbuildings, horses, hogs, plows, mules, two pretty good whiteface bulls, and one top-notch Galloway bull.

—All that together aint worth a tinker's damn the way things are now.

—It is, because if we don't get them cows through, you'll foreclose on the lot. Might take you a while, but you'll double your money sooner or later.

Olp sucked his lower lip. If Eli could make a decent dollar now, he might survive the drouth and when it was over he could be a rich man and a rich man beholden to the bank. If he didn't, then the bank would own a fair-size chunk of prime ranchland.

—You'll have to sign some papers. You'll have to put up every last stick you own, animals and all.

—Well, let's get to signin then. We got cows to move.

Perched on his stool, Gus Schrautz watched it all unfold, grinning and sucking his teeth. These Paint boys still wet behind the ears had just marched into the Pioneer Bank and shook twelve thousand dollars out of Foreclosure Olp. If you lived long enough, there was pretty much no solitary thing you would not see, sooner or later.

By the time they had a thousand head of cattle ready for the trail, it was the first week of April. They managed to hire on nine pretty fair riders, four with trail drive experience, and pointed a herd of eleven hundred cattle northwest toward the Niobrara and beyond on the ninth day of April. Ezra watched the cattle strung out for nearly a mile along the valley of the Niobrara and grinned at Eli.

—Aint that about the prettiest sight you ever saw? And all them cows belongs to us.

—Belongs to Bly Olp, more like. Unless we get 'em to Pine Ridge and get the deal done and pay that bastard, most of them is his cows.

—We'll do it. Only thing we got to worry us now is quicksand on the White. Teeter says the Dixon outfit lost two hundred head tryin to cross the White in a quicksand year. If that sand swallows them cows, we might as well call it bust right now.

—I aint losin no herd to quicksand.

Teeter rode ahead to scout the river and came back with the news Eli expected: The White was as low as anyone had ever seen it.

—That quicksand would bog a saddle blanket. We're goin to have to water 'em in a creek first so's they don't stop to drink, because any cow that stops is bogged. If we can find a spot with some solid trees on the far bank, we can get out some of that heavy corral rope and run it to the trees, give us a chance to haul 'em out of the bog if they get stuck. She's bound to be a bitch no matter how we go at her.

They brought the herd to within a half mile of the White River in the middle of the afternoon. Eli ordered a halt; there was no point pushing the cattle into the river before daybreak because they would need every minute of daylight to rescue any animals that got mired. They spent the rest of the day scouting and planning. There was no ideal ford but some spots were better than others. Eli and Ezra agreed that Teeter had lit on about the best spot that could be found.

They were up well before dawn the next morning to water the herd at a creek that branched into the White a half mile up. The cattle balked at the river's edge, but when two oxen were brought up and led into the river, the steers followed as the cowhands urged them on with piercing whistles and short rawhide whips. The light-footed cowponies crossed and recrossed the river without difficulty but the heavier steers were no more than forty feet into the stream when the leaders sensed the treacherous footing underneath and tried to turn back. Within thirty minutes nearly a quarter of the herd had bogged down along five hundred feet of river. Those who were able to cross were mostly heifers and the lighter steers; the rest sank to their bellies and stuck, their pitiful bawling echoing up and down the river.

Eli left the animals that were safely across with the horse wrangler and led the way to rescue the rest: the cowhands stripped off their boots, pants, and pistol belts and waded into the river. They found that as long as they kept moving they were all right but as soon as they stopped, their own feet would begin to sink. First they ran corral ropes from the trees on the far bank to the horns of the animals, who were caught so fast that it took four men to pull their tails out. Once a steer's tail was freed, it was coiled and tied up with a rope hobble. Then the men rolled the steer over as far as possible and burrowed until they could tie up one foreleg and one hind leg with the rope hobbles, then tip the steer on the opposite side in order to tie up the other legs. Once all four limbs were secured, lariats were tied to the heavy corral ropes and four cowponies worked together to pull; the men in the water swung the steer back and forth to give it a start and then heaved as the horses on the bank strained to haul the steer free.

One by one, the bogged steers were hauled out. The trickiest part of the job was to free the cattle on the far bank; it took only a few seconds to undo the ropes but once they were high and dry, the animals were angry and ready to fight. By the end of the day a half dozen cowboys had been bruised and battered and one of the cowponies gored in its flank.

While the cowboys labored, a group of Lakota boys watched from a nearby knoll, talking among themselves, smiling now and then. Ezra suspected that they found it all very funny, the white men nearly killing themselves trying to rescue a bunch of cows. The sun was fierce, men and animals alike were dogged at every step by deerflies, horseflies, and no-see-ums. The boys would see such labor the way War Bonnet would see it: white man's foolishness that was beneath the dignity of a Sioux warrior. With his hands cracked and bleeding and the sweat stinging the deerfly bites in his neck, Ezra felt the Lakota boys were probably right.

At sundown they were still at it, half-deaf from panicked cattle bawling in their ears, soaked through, their hands bleeding and cracked, backs aching, heads spinning from lack of food. Teeter finally stumbled up the bank and sat down heavily on a hummock of grass. Eli, feeling spent himself, bent over and vomited from exhaustion, then dumped a canteen of water on his head. Teeter groaned.

—I'm just about played out. I don't think I can haul on one more steer. If they wouldn't fight it so, we'd be done in a hour.

—Maybe you ought to talk to them steers. Tell 'em they're goin about it all wrong.

—I would, but I never knowed a steer to listen worth a tinker's damn.

They worked until dark, lit torches and carried on, cursing a moonless and cloudy sky for the inky darkness that threatened to swallow everything—cows, ponies, boots and ropes and saddles, the mortgage on the Fanciful, and life itself if a man was not careful. By midnight they had freed all the cattle they were going to free. Eli estimated they had lost about a dozen head.

The next morning Eli left Ezra in charge of getting the herd pointed to the Pine Ridge Agency while he took two punchers and went back, intending to drag the dead cattle to shore and skin them for the hides. The half-starved Sioux had beaten him to the carcasses; the cattle had been pulled from the quicksand and picked clean. But they had crossed the White River with the herd pretty much intact and the worst part of the drive was now behind them. Eli tipped his cap to the Sioux boys still watching from a respectful distance, their stomachs now full of Fanciful beef.

Livvy was at home with the girls when Bly Olp came calling in a high-wheeled buggy with a matched team of chestnut pacers. She had Maggie on her hip, Velma asleep in a cradle in the sunshine, Tavie helping to plant snap beans in the garden patch behind the house. Olp toyed with his watch chain as he stomped on a row of new planted carrots.

—Mizz Paint.

—Mr. Olp.

—I just come to check, Mizz Paint. If you had any news of that husband of yours.

—Not a word.

—Nor have I. Which is why I've come to call. I am owed a sum of money your husband borrowed against the Fanciful here. The first payment comes due Friday, and I don't know a soul has seen hide nor hair of the Paint boys. Some is guessing they might have got themselves swallowed by quicksand along the White River, or maybe they been scalped by wild Indians. Or maybe they just decided to leave these parts without repayin a loan. Now if that is the case, or if they didn't get them cows through, we may have to foreclose here, and I don't like to take a piece of land without seein what it is I'm about to get.

—As far as I know you're not about to get a thing except payment on your loan.

—Be as may, a man has to keep an eye on what might be his. I have taken the trouble this morning of makin a little circuit of your husband's property, ma'am. If this drouth ever ends, this could be the best place in the county. Might be able to make somethin of it, you run it right.

—My husband runs it right.

—Sure he does. Only you aint heard from him and I aint heard from him.

—He's got four days before the first payment. Then you'll have your payment in four days.

—Pardon me, Mizz Paint, but you could be makin that pledge on behalf of a dead man. Or a fella who lost the whole goddamned herd tryin to cross the White River.

—There's no need for cussing. My husband is neither dead nor has he lost his cattle.

—You know this for a fact.

—I do.

—That's some faith you have in a fella so young.

—It is. If you knew him, you would know that he'll be back with your money.

Livvy hoisted Velma from her cradle with one arm, held the squirming Maggie with the other, motioned to Tavie to follow, and walked to the house, wishing she had worn her corset. She hadn't been expecting company, and Bly Olp made her feel naked. She could feel his eyes on her all the way inside the house. Even after the door was closed, she felt him staring still. Finally she heard the pop of his whip, and she watched from the kitchen window as the buggy bounded on the ruts along the trail to the front gate and the Ainsworth road. The nerve of the man. She felt a sudden, awful weariness along with a fear she had not been able to admit. What if Eli failed? What if he didn't come back at all? What if they lost everything and had to start over?

Bly Olp was on his favorite subject, the Fanciful and his plans for the ranch once he had foreclosed. Gus Schrautz sucked his teeth and listened. He had never known Olp to take such an interest in a piece of property, although it was plain that it was not the ranch itself that interested him but the wife of the current owner. Olp would start out talking about pasture and cattle and how the place would be if this goddamned drouth ended and the next thing you knew he would be back on Livvy.

—Now if they wanted to work things that way, I would sure enough take that Livvy woman in lieu of a foreclosure, say. That red hair. The way she walks. You ever watch her walk, Gus? The way them hips move, like a Kentucky thoroughbred. Hell, let Eli keep the goddamned ranch. I would not hold a grudge. He offers up the woman, we're square.

Gus Schrautz was so preoccupied that for a moment he forgot to suck his molars. The Paint boys were striding up Main Street walking tall, Teeter Spawn trailing with that funny bowlegged walk. Olp was about to launch into another disquisition on Livvy's finer points when the door swung open and Eli and Ezra strode in while Teeter stayed behind like the lookout for a bank robbery, although the cash was going the other way. Ezra toted a gunnysack to Olp's desk and dumped a pile of greasy bills in front of the banker. Olp acted as though it was the only thing he expected on this fine May morning, a customer dropping in to repay a loan.

—Count it, Olp. Count every goddamned dime.

—Aint but the first payment due, boys.

—We'll be paying you in full right now. I will not be beholden to such as yourself.

They waited while Olp counted, right down to the last seventy-two cents in change, which Ezra hauled out of his pocket.

—We'll be needing a piece of paper now to say we're quits.

Olp had Gus bring him the papers on the loan, dipped his quill pen and signed with a flourish, pointed Ezra and Eli to where they were to sign. When they were finished and Ezra had folded the documents into his hip pocket, Eli swatted Olp's scattergun to the side and leaned over the desk, the coiled bullwhip in his hand.

—We are now quits, Mr. Olp. You gave us a helpin hand and I appreciate that but we will not be doing business with this bank again in the future. If you bother my wife again, I will take this whip and flay every square inch of hide off your sorry carcass, is that clear?

It was so quiet in the bank they could all hear Gus sucking his teeth. Eli stared until Olp nodded and then turned on his heel and walked out, Ezra trailing. Olp glared at Gus.

—What are you lookin at? You got no books to do, take the mop and get some dust off this floor. I could a shot the three of 'em anytime, if I wanted to.

—Oh, I expect so. They looked like they was plumb scared you would do just that.

—I've had just about goddamned enough of you, Gus Schrautz. You're fired. Get your bony ass out of here right now.

Gus dumped his inkpot over the ledger in front of him, reached his frock coat off the peg, and left without looking back.

That Saturday night they had a party at the Fanciful. Neighbors got word that Eli was putting on a feed and came from miles around. They managed to scrape up three fiddle players, and Teeter Spawn showed how to make a mouth harp sound like the angel Gabriel. They dug pits and roasted three steers and six hogs and drank blackberry wine and danced to "Turkey in the Straw" and "The Virginia Reel." Gus Schrautz, newly hired to keep the books for the Fanciful, danced with the widow Upjigraf, three hundred pounds if she was an ounce, and the two of them were later seen spooning out back of the barn. Sleepy children nodded off in the haystack, the grown-ups followed them hours after midnight and woke the next day feeling like the devil himself was going at their eyeballs hammer and tongs. But it was worth it to see one of their own making good in such hard times, one who wasn't going bust and pulling up stakes to return to Indiana or Pennsylvania or North Carolina. It made them feel they could all do it, even if they didn't have the strength of the Paint boys or their luck or Eli's knack with a dollar.

While the others danced that night, Ezra and Eli perched on a top rail of one of the corrals and talked. Ezra waved a hand, vaguely taking in everything around them.

—Looks like you done it, big brother. You set out to have yourself a place like this, and you done it. We aint but twenty-four years old and you got what you always wanted.

—Aw, I aint half-started on that.

—No, I expect you're not. But you have a good enough start you can do without me for a spell. I got a proposition from George Sperling over in Spearfish. He wants me to ride to Arizona with him and bring back a herd of buffalo.

—A herd of buffalo.

—That's right. They got upwards of eight hundred head in Arizona. He wants to bring 'em back north, put 'em on a reserve in Wyoming, where folks aint allowed to hunt 'em.

—I thought we were just fine right here.

—Well, we are. But I don't think you need me like you did, and I aint seen Arizona.

—How long do you expect all this will take?

—I don't know. A couple months, anyway. I wasn't strictly figuring on comin back.

—Why not?

—I always got to see what's on t'other side of the next hill, you know that. I don't think I was built to settle in deep like you done here. I thought I might scout ranchland up in Montana, look at some of that country we went through on our way to Fort Benton.

—What about your spread?

—I got my share from the cows we sold at Pine Ridge. I'll sign the rest over to you for one dollar.

—I won't stand in your way, if that's what you want. You don't have to sign over a thing to me. I'll stay here and look after the whole shebang if you want. If you're determined to sell, you won't get away without takin a fair price from me. I'll miss you, you know that. We've been like peas in a pod since we was born. Almost like we was twins.

Ezra laughed.

—I know. I can't figure it myself. I get the itch to move on, and it's got to be scratched.

—Journey-bound.

⤝ CHAPTER 32 ⤞

A week before Christmas of 1899, Livvy and Eli Paint loaded all six children onto a sleigh and drove into Ainsworth to have their portrait taken by Jackson Edwards, a young man who had come out from Philadelphia to photograph the West before it was overtaken by industry. When Edwards was not trying to capture the expanse of the prairie or Indian chiefs in full regalia, he did portraits of the citizenry to keep body and soul together. The exposures took most of the morning: They stood stiffly, Livvy and Eli in the back, Tavie in front of Livvy holding the baby Daniel with two sisters to her left and two to her right. Livvy wrote the date in one corner of the eight-by-twelve-inch print Edwards made and carefully noted the names and ages of her children on the back: "Octavia Olivia, 8 years old; Marguerite Florence, 7; Velma Viola, almost 6; Ruby Elizabeth, age 4; Katherine Abigail, age 2; Daniel Boone, age six months."

When they were through sitting for their portraits, the girls were taken to the soda parlor across the street and allowed to buy one candy cane each for the ride home; then they were loaded into the sleigh and driven back to the Fanciful, now a ranch that stretched over more than five thousand acres of Brown County. When they piled out of the sleigh, they walked up the path to a two-story white frame house with a wide veranda around three sides. South of the house were a half dozen corrals, a good-size red barn, more than two dozen windmills pumping water day and night to as many cattle tanks, a long bunkhouse with one ten-by-fifteen room walled off with a separate stove as the abode of Teeter Spawn.

On Christmas morning, the girls came piling into Livvy's bed long before daybreak, begging her to come downstairs so they could open their presents. Eli had already been out for more than an hour doing his chores. Livvy had nursed Daniel and fallen asleep again with him at her breast; Tavie carried him downstairs to give her mother time to get dressed. Marguerite brought a basin of hot water from the kitchen, and Livvy took her time washing herself as she gazed out over the expanse of snow that led down to the Calamus River. She never tired of the view. It was one thing she'd insisted on when Eli began building the frame house the year after Velma was born: She had to have a bedroom on the second floor with a large window and a view of the prairie. That vista, so appalling to her during the first summer the Stanton family spent on Prairie Dog Creek, now held her spellbound. She never tired of it, although the changes were few and subtle from season to season. The grass greened in spring and browned in late summer and fall; the snow fell and melted. A stand of sandbar willow down toward the creek spread slender, olive green leaves in April and shed them in October. The sky stretched toward the infinite all year long. If it was cloudy, it was usually because a storm was building; days when the clouds hung low and gloomy over the Fanciful were rare.

Velma came back up the stairs to see what was taking her mother so long. Of Livvy's five daughters, Velma was most attached to her mother. Even four-year-old Ruby loved the horses so much that Livvy could see already that she would be like Tavie and Marguerite, a cowgirl first and a help around the house second. The two older girls had their own horses and Tavie, who was like Eli in almost every way, was already helping with the spring and fall roundups; Eli said she could ride as well as any boy in Brown County. Most men would have pined for sons and been more disappointed as each daughter arrived in turn; Eli simply taught the girls to ride and rope and expected them to work like any cowboy. Velma was the only one who also enjoyed being in the kitchen with her mother, rolling out a piecrust or helping to churn the butter. She was also the only one who had inherited her father's black hair and dark skin; during the summer she looked like a Lakota girl, especially when she was on horseback. Velma also had a questioning intelligence behind those dark eyes that Livvy found appealing if sometimes exasperating.

—Papa's coming back from the corrals. Does that mean we get to open our presents now?

—Soon. He'll be hungry, so we'll all have breakfast first.

—Tell me what my present is and then I won't mind waiting.

—If I do that, it won't be a surprise.

—Tavie got a new saddle, didn't she?

—I don't know. I guess we'll just have to wait and see.

—When do I get a new saddle?

—When you're old enough.

—Will you still be here when I'm old enough?

Livvy looked into Velma's dark eyes.

—Well, of course I will. Why do you ask?

—Because Mrs. Manson died having a baby.

—How do you know that's how she died?

—Tavie's friend Betty Manson says her ma died because she had too many babies. I don't want you to have too many babies and you've already got six.

—Honey, it's awful about Mrs. Manson, but I'm healthy as a horse. Don't you worry about me. You go on downstairs now, and I'll be down in a minute.

Velma went. She was slender and inclined to be a little sickly, which was perhaps one reason Livvy felt drawn to her; as much as anyone, Velma reminded her of her brother Sherman, who had been so sickly as a boy.

Livvy pinned up her hair and glanced at herself in the mirror. She thought she looked a little worn but any woman with six children was bound to be worn out. Still, it was a wonderful life:

She did not wish to trade places with any person in the universe. Again she mouthed the silent prayer that had never been far from her lips since the day when Tavie was a baby and Eli made love to her on the banks of the Niobrara while she watched the geese fly overhead: *Let it never change, O Lord, let it never change.*

There were twenty-two people at the long pine table for Christmas dinner that afternoon, among them Teeter Spawn; the Reverend Cubbin from the church in Ainsworth and his spindly son Rafe; the permanent cowpunchers Lonesome Pete Yeager, Gizzard Hopkins, and Roy Titus, a cocky little redhead who was hired on that summer because he had some vague connection to Eli from the old days up in the Powder River country; Livvy's brother Sherman Stanton and the young woman, Susanna Deegan, to whom he was betrothed; a settler couple down on their luck whom Livvy invited with their children because she was sure they would eat no Christmas dinner otherwise. For dinner they had roast beef, a pair of roast geese, a turkey with all the trimmings, mashed potatoes with gravy, three kinds of pickles, fresh-baked bread, and corn, carrots, peas, and beets put up in jars in the cellar. It was a joyful, noisy meal until the children went off to play and the adults sat back, groaning, to contemplate the inroads they had made into the steaming platters of food.

Teeter hauled a toothpick out of his shirt pocket and began poking at the remaining stumps of his teeth.

—That was some feed, Miss Livvy. When we was about froze to death up on the Powder River in the winter of 'eighty-seven, I never thought to see a feed like this. Never thought to see spring again, come down to it. Now taint but a dozen years later, and Eli here has the best house in Brown County and you folks can put out a spread like this. Shows you never know what's around the next bend in the river. Could be a waterfall or it could be the smoothest stretch of clear sailin you ever saw. Aint nothin a man can have in this life better than to sit himself down to a Christmas dinner like this one, amongst such company. It's enough to make you grateful to the Lord God Almighty.

The guests dutifully murmured "amen," although what Teeter had to say was not meant as a prayer. Livvy blushed and thanked him for his kindness. She looked down the long table at Eli, saw him gazing back at her. It still happened like this: He was busy and often weary himself, but when she least expected it, she would catch that look and know what it meant, the depth of feeling Eli Paint held for her, Olivia Stanton Paint, the girl from Moultrie County who had come west so reluctantly, only to fall in love with the land and to marry a cowboy and bear his children. It was like a story out of a book, almost too good to be true.

The girls went to school six months every year and worked on the ranch the other six months. The walk to the Hay Flat School was a mile each way if they cut across the fields, a ramble they considered the best part of the day. Livvy would watch them until they disappeared over the rise to the east—Tavie, Maggie, Velma, Ruby, and Kate lined up in a row, laughing and holding hands as they skipped along. All eight grades, twenty-three students altogether, were taught in the same room at Hay Flat, by Livvy herself for the first two years and then by Miss Nora Lee Reinhardt, a broad-backed young woman recruited from Iowa. At noon and recess they played hide-and-seek, run sheep run, pom-pom-pollaway, and baseball.

By the time Tavie was ten years old, some of the boys were bringing bats and balls to school, so the girls took up baseball with the same enthusiasm they brought to horseback riding. Tavie quickly established herself as the best pitcher in the school, a lefty who could get the boys out anytime she wanted. When Tavie struck out a big blond boy named Joey Dishman, he took a run at her and punched her in the nose. Then Velma and Ruby jumped on Joey's back, and two of Joey's buddies came to his aid. In the fierce battle that followed, the Paint girls gave as good as they got, and Joey went home with a black eye and a bloody nose.

Three days later, Joey approached Tavie as they were leaving school.

—I expect I should walk you girls back to the ranch, keep an eye peeled for rattlers.

Tavie laughed in his face.

—We've been walking this way since I was five years old and not one of us ever been bitten. We don't need any big stupid jughead boy taking care of us.

Joey slouched off, his head down. Velma felt she had to protest.

—You were mean to him. He only wanted to walk us home.

—Nope. Boys always want more than that. Sooner or later they want kissing, and I'm not doing any of that. Besides, he's dumb and he's ugly.

Velma thought her sister was cruel, but she had a point. Poor Joey was ugly and he was dumber than a lump of coal.

During the winter, the girls made a deal with the teacher to skip recess so they could have a longer noon hour. At lunchtime, they walked back across the fields to Eli's pond and went skating, or if there was enough snow on the ground they went to a hill south of the Hay Flat School and slid down again and again, using old school benches or scoop shovels for sleds. Then they would go trooping back to school for the afternoon with their dresses soaked through. Miss Reinhardt allowed them to huddle around the red-hot stove to dry while they wolfed down the lunches that were always left on a bench at the back of the room, a row of old syrup pails and grape baskets filled with meat sandwiches, pickles, apples, corn dodgers, and biscuits. Livvy always slipped a little extra into their lunches for the kids who had less. Boys like Joey would stand around looking hopeful and licking their lips until Velma or Maggie offered a pickle or half a sandwich. They knew it was no good trying to get food from Tavie, because she always ate all her lunch, and even if she didn't she would throw it to the birds before she would give it to the likes of Joey Dishman.

Tavie was hardly bigger than a sandbur on a horse's mane when she started to ride. When she was six, Eli found her a pair of tiny goat-hair chaps on a bull-buying trip to Cheyenne. After that she rode with chaps strapped over her long dress, because the girls were never allowed to wear pants, or even the divided skirts some horsewomen were already wearing. As each girl began riding in turn, she wore the same outfit, long dresses with cowhide or goat-hair chaps. Nor did they ride sidesaddle like some of the town women; like their mother, the Paint girls rode a western saddle and nothing else. Livvy sewed their skirts with extra material so they wouldn't be too tight to straddle a horse. The dresses were the only concession to the fact that they were female; beyond that the Paint girls were expected to ride and rope, flush stray cattle out of draws, crash through underbrush, brand, doctor, and separate bull calves from heifers so the males could be castrated.

Eli never forgot that they were girls, however, and he had strict rules. He made them look away when calves were being castrated. They could never say the words *bull* or *stallion* either. A bull was always called "Romeo," and a stallion was "the big horse." Eli tol-erated Teeter Spawn as a special case, but he was careful never to swear in front of his daughters, and if any of the other hands let slip a word as foul as *damn* in the presence of the girls, he would get a black look and a sharp word from Eli. In every other way, he expected them to be full-fledged cowhands. If they were tired or saddlesore, they bore their discomfort in silence, as Eli taught them, because a real cowgirl didn't complain. No matter how tough things were, he would always tell them that the winter of 'eighty-seven was worse and not to whine. As much as he would have liked a brace of sons, Eli said with pride and some truth that no boy in Brown County could ride with the Paint girls.

To prove his point, Eli liked to tell the story about the day when Ruby and Velma were saddling their horses outside the corral. Vel-ma's filly shied at a dust devil and took off across the open prairie at a dead gallop. Ruby finished tightening the cinch, vaulted into the saddle, and took off in pursuit of the stray. She caught up with the runaway three miles west of the Fanciful, when the horse finally slowed as it neared a group of roundup riders working a neighbor-ing ranch. A tall cowhand roped the stray and held it for Ruby.

—Only girl I've ever seen who could ride like that is Tavie Paint.

Ruby reached for the horse's reins and wrapped them around one hand.

—Tavie's my big sister. But I can ride better than she can.

The top of Ruby's pigtailed head barely reached the cowhand's belt buckle. The cowboy laughed so hard he insisted on riding back with her just so he could tell her father the story.

Evenings when the supper dishes were done Eli would sit in his rocking chair reading the Ainsworth *Democrat* or month-old editions of the Omaha *World-Herald* and the Denver *Post* while Livvy nestled on the divan with a book by one of her favorite novelists, usually Mary Augusta Ward, Eliza Lynn Linton, or Charles Dickens. The girls read or sewed or did their schoolwork, and when it came time for bed they always sang a Stephen Foster song or two for their parents. With five older sisters and a mother to look after him, Eli declared that baby Daniel was going to be spoiled rotten before he was a year old. Livvy smiled. Surely by now she ought to be permitted to spoil one of her children. They all worked so hard. So few families had such great good fortune; they would have to learn to enjoy it.

⚔ CHAPTER 33 ⚔

On a bright, fragrant day during the first week of May, Livvy saddled her chestnut filly shortly before noon, strapped little Daniel to her breast, and rode to the west pasture to take a basket of meat sandwiches for Eli, Lonesome Pete, Gizzard, and Cale Hutchinson, Eli's new partner in a company ranch fifteen miles to the west. The men had been out rounding up strays since before dawn, and they would be hungry. As she rode, she watched a spray of redwing blackbirds wheel into the sky at her approach, then settle a few yards farther along. There were so many that it seemed there was a bird for every cattail all along the creek, and there were even more down in the draws, where the snowmelt would run for another month.

It was a long ride out to the pasture on a ranch that seemed to double its size from one year to the next. Every year there were new outbuildings going up, and every year Eli needed more cowhands for the roundup, even with the girls able to do more and more of the work. He seemed never to tire, but as the babies had come one after another, Livvy felt herself wearing down like an old wagon. She rose at first light in summer and long before first light in winter, and sometimes she was fortunate to have an hour to read before bed, but there were never enough hours for everything that had to be done. There were always babies to be changed, hogs to be slopped, cows to be milked, milk to be separated into cream, butter to be churned, quilts to be made, tomatoes and vegetables to be canned, chickens to be plucked, sick children to care for, washing to be done, endless meals to be made. Most women with five daughters had plenty of help in the house, but for the most part Livvy had only Velma, and Velma only when Eli could spare her from other work. The Paint girls were cowhands first and everything else after; Livvy loved their strength, their independence, and their energy, but sometimes she wished for girls who cared about nothing except washday and getting a good roast on the table.

Just as Livvy spotted Eli and Hutch, she heard another horse coming up behind her. It was the comical figure of the pudgy little Reverend Cubbin from the church, bouncing all over the saddle at a slow trot.

—Mrs. Paint, Mrs. Paint! 'Scuse me, Mrs. Paint, I need to have a talk with you.

Cubbin was red-faced and sweating heavily.

Livvy turned her horse to face him.

—What is it?

—Mrs. Paint, I rode all the way out here because I've got some awful news.

Livvy's first thought was that Reverend Cubbin had somehow received news that one of her parents had died. After a couple of false starts, Cubbin finally managed to speak his piece.

—It's your brother, Sherman. I'm afraid he passed on this morning.

Livvy felt her limbs go weak. She righted herself by holding on to the saddlehorn.

—What are you telling me? That Sherman is dead?

—I'm afraid so.

—That can't be true. Sherman is not yet thirty. We just saw him at church on Sunday.

—That's so, ma'am. Sherman never said he was feeling poorly. But when he didn't come down to open the store today they went to check his rooms and found him dead. Doc Remy says he died of a sudden fever.

—No, no. This is wrong. Are you sure? Did you see him yourself?

—I did, ma'am. I saw him. He has indeed passed on. I'm sorry to be the bearer of such awful tidings.

Livvy looked around wildly, hoping for someone else who could say it was all a mistake.

Eli cantered over, wondering what would bring the preacher out from town.

—What's wrong here?

—Reverend Cubbin says Sherman's dead.

—Sherman? He can't be dead, he's just a boy.

—I know that, Eli. But the reverend says he's dead. They found him in his room this morning. Have you told poor Susanna Deegan? They were supposed to wed in the fall.

—I have, ma'am. The girl is quite shattered. She's with her mother now.

Livvy's mind was racing, thinking of poor Susanna, the letter she would have to write to her parents, the funeral arrangements. It was impossible; Sherman never had the strongest constitution, but to die of a fever overnight, that was one of those cruel quirks of fate that men like the Reverend Cubbin could never quite explain, especially when it came at such a time. With Eli's help, Sherman had purchased Red Woolsey's general mercantile, sure that some modern ideas would help the store grow into the biggest for a hundred miles in any direction. Sherman threw all his energy into the work in a way he never did with ranching. He was funny and smart and energetic and thrifty and well liked by everyone in town, even those who owed him money. Now, with no warning at all, he was gone.

Eli saw the stricken look on Livvy's face.

—We'd best get back to the house.

The hardest part was telling the girls that Sherman had died; they all adored him. The bad news could wait until they came home from school. Eli harnessed the buggy and they rode into Ainsworth to make arrangements for Sherman's funeral. Livvy wept all the way to town, where she sent a telegram to her parents, saying only:

—*Sherman has passed on. More later. Livvy.*

That night she sat down to write a long letter to her parents, but the words wouldn't come. In the end she mailed a single paragraph. Sherman was dead. There was no way you could gussy it up with fancy words.

Two days later, Sherman was buried in the cemetery at Ainsworth. The weather was warm and the funeral could not be held up long enough for the Stantons to come all the way from Sioux County, and in any case Flo was feeling poorly again. People kept shaking Livvy's hand at the wake and telling her what a wonderful, gentle soul he was, and Livvy kept wondering what good that had done poor Sherman. He had always been a shade too delicate for the rough-and-tumble of the frontier. A harder man, a man like Eli, who was as dry and tough as a thistle, that's what it took to survive out here. She almost wanted to blame Eli, as though his vitality sucked up all the nourishment in the land without leaving enough behind for the weaker stalks.

After Sherman's death Livvy felt lifeless herself, wan and fatigued and doubting the certainties that had been her compass since childhood. She had always kept her faith, but on those Sunday morning visits to Reverend Cubbin's church she found herself asking what sort of God would allow a fine young man like Sherman to die so young. Why was there so much suffering everywhere you looked? Hungry children, vicious men who beat their womenfolk, horrible diseases that robbed a person first of her dignity and then of her life. If God was capable of putting a stop to this, why didn't He? Because God was a man, of that much she was sure. A woman would have held in her soul more of the tender mercies, would have spent less time erecting cathedrals to herself and seen to it that living creatures did not suffer so.

By the following summer, Livvy became convinced that there was something wrong with Daniel. He was a year old and he did not see well. He bumped into things, he stumbled and fell, he had to fumble around when he was reaching for his food. After her son's first birthday, Livvy took him by train all the way to the School for the Blind at Nebraska City, where her worst fears were confirmed: Daniel was blind. Not completely blind, the doctor assured her. He could distinguish shapes and even colors if they were bright enough, but he would never be able to do most of the thousand things a ranch boy needed to do. On the train home, Livvy blamed herself. Pride goeth before a fall. She had believed her family spectacularly blessed, she had believed they were above the little tragedies that burden every family and she had always felt secure behind an invisible wall that Eli built for her. But not even Eli could protect his son from blindness.

Teeter Spawn met Livvy and Daniel at the railroad station in Ainsworth; he had allowed Velma to tag along. At the sight of her gentlest and sweetest daughter, Livvy felt a pang of remorse; here she was feeling cursed when she had five splendid, lively, energetic, and intelligent young daughters and a healthy little boy who was happy even if he couldn't see. She surprised Velma with the strength of her affection; for a moment Livvy held her so tight that she couldn't breathe. When she finally let go, Velma's cheek was wet with Livvy's tears.

—What's the matter, Mama?

—Nothing, sweetheart. I was just reminded of how much I love you all. Our baby Daniel is blind, and now I will need all of you to help me care for him.

Although they called him Blind Daniel, as he grew, the youngest Paint child learned to do more with his limited sight. He could see shapes and distinguish his sisters one from another before they spoke. He learned to ride Velma's Shetland pony, Midge, and to do chores for his mother like churning the butter or turning the handle on the separator. Despite his obvious intelligence, Livvy was obsessed by a fear that Daniel would somehow stumble into the river and drown. She fussed so much that during the summer of his fourth year Eli began taking the boy to the stock tank when

Livvy wasn't looking. He would hold Daniel by the waist and let him paddle and splash. After a week he let go and the boy sank to the bottom of the tank, then came up spluttering and laughing. Within a week, Eli called Livvy out to watch: Daniel could already swim the width of the thirty-foot tank.

—The boy was born for the water. He mightn't see much, but he can swim like a fish.

Eli had little time for small talk or strange notions, which was why the girls were all so giddy when Ezra turned up, as he did once or twice a year. Velma loved Ezra because she could sit and talk with him about any old thing and he always found it interesting. Early one morning during one of Ezra's visits, Velma tried to tell him what was on her mind as he sat whittling a wooden doll out of a hunk of firewood.

—Have you ever been out in the wheat early in the morning, Uncle Ez? I was out there on Midge one day and I saw this bright light sort of rolling through the wheat. Only if I tried to look at it straight on, it wasn't there. I had to catch it out of the corner of my eye or I couldn't see it at all. See, when I'm in church and Reverend Cubbin starts talking about God, that's the only thing I can imagine that comes close. I think God is like the light in the wheatfield that you don't see if you're looking right at it.

Ez nodded and worked the eyes into the doll with the point of his clasp knife.

—I know just what you mean, girl. The Indians know all that, things the white man can't get his head around. They know that sometimes the thing you're starin hardest at is the thing you don't see. If I catch your drift, that's what you're sayin. I can't say I've seen it in a wheat field, exactly. But other times, up in the mountains rounding up horses, say, I'd be startin a fire at sunup and see the light come pourin through the pine trees and know what I'm lookin at is more than just sunshine. But you can't hogtie it, a thing like that. You try to throw a half hitch round its hind legs, you'll find it's slipped away, left you with nothin but a hunk of rawhide and a notion that somethin you ought to understand just went right through your fingers.

—That's it, Uncle Ez. That's what I think about, sometimes. But if I try to talk to people about it, they think I'm strange.

Ezra finished the doll and handed it to her.

—You're a deep little girl.

—I'm not that little and I can ride as well as anybody.

—All right then, you aint little. But you're still deep.

Velma took the doll and bounced off to the house, where she would add it to her collection of corncob dolls. She let Daniel handle the dolls one by one, feeling their little corncob heads. The wooden doll she saved for last. Daniel rubbed it and waved it in the air.

—Know what, Daniel? Uncle Ez says I'm deep. Now what do you think about that?

Late in the spring of 1902, Livvy realized she was carrying her seventh child. It was a difficult pregnancy from the beginning. She had waves of morning sickness and lost her appetite. She bled at odd times and thought more than once that she had lost the baby. She had dark circles under her eyes all the time and she was losing weight even though she was carrying a child. Only Velma seemed to notice how sick her mother was. In the midst of plucking chickens, with steaming tubs in the kitchen filled with feathers, chicken feet, stinking brown entrails and chicken heads, Livvy would abruptly declare that she couldn't work another moment. She would stumble up the stairs, fall facefirst into bed fully dressed, and collapse into a deep slumber. Each time Velma asked if her mother was all right, Livvy insisted that she was just a little tired and that she would be fine as soon as this baby was born. Finally, Velma coaxed Eli to get Doc Remy to come out from Ainsworth. He prescribed regular doses of cod liver and castor oil and told Eli to let his wife rest as much as possible until the baby was born.

It was a terrible winter. Cold winds howled across the prairie from the north, blizzards piled snow in drifts a dozen feet high against the house. Livvy felt the weight of another child suspended in her belly as a burden that she dragged up and down the staircase through long, bleak nights when the frozen stars hung in the inky sky and the moon drifted, icy and white, through her dreams.

⚜ CHAPTER 34 ⚜

John Milton Paint was born during a blizzard in February 1903 and named for his great-grandfather. He was two pounds lighter than any of Livvy's other babies, yellow and jaundiced and thin as a skinned rabbit. He cried day and night and wanted neither Livvy's breast nor the cow's milk she warmed for him. He lived exactly one week. Livvy woke an hour before dawn to find the child dead at her side. When Eli came in from doing his chores, he found her sitting up holding the baby, rocking silently to and fro as the first gray light filtered into the room. He sat with her for a time in the winter dawn, then took the child from her, wrapped him in blankets from head to toe and had Teeter cobble a tiny coffin. Livvy would not allow the child to be buried as far from her as the Ainsworth cemetery, so Eli took three of the hands with pickaxes and shovels and dug a grave on a bare spot where the wind had swept the snow off a ridge overlooking the Fanciful. Eli read a passage from the Bible and said a few words, which Livvy did not hear.

For a month, Livvy scarcely left her bed. Eli was patient and unusually tender with her but he could not boost her spirits. Her only pleasure was in listening to Velma read from the works of Charles Dickens. Velma would sit beside the bed and read from *Great Expectations* or *Bleak House* for an hour at a time. Sometimes she was sure her mother had fallen asleep but when she stopped reading, Livvy would open her eyes and pat her daughter's hand.

In early April a stretch of warm weather convinced Livvy that it was time to start on her garden. She went to work with a rake and shovel, turning and combing the dark earth and preparing it for another season. She felt the sunshine would do her good; she had moped around long enough, even if she did not yet have quite all her strength; after an hour in the garden, however, she felt weak and clammy and out of breath and had to sit in the shade of the house for a time with a wet cloth pressed to her forehead. When Velma asked what was wrong, she said it was a bit of fever from working in the hot spring sun.

On the evening of April 6, 1903, a half dozen guests came to dine at the Fanciful, including a rancher who had traveled from Wyoming to buy a Galloway bull from Eli. After dinner Teeter played his mouth harp and the girls sang and Livvy joined them on "Swanee River." For the first time since John Milton's death, she seemed to be enjoying herself; her cheeks were flushed, her green eyes gleamed, she laughed often. Before the children were ready for bed, however, she complained that she was tired and feverish and went upstairs to sleep, leaving the girls to do the washing up.

The next morning Velma went upstairs early with a bowl of hot oatmeal for her mother's breakfast. Livvy didn't move, so Velma put the bowl down on the night table and went to open the window. Then she sat down next to the bed and touched her mother's arm to wake her. Livvy didn't stir and her hand felt cold to the touch. Velma squeezed it a little harder but Livvy still did not respond. Velma felt as though her stomach had tumbled right out of her body. She stood to reach her mother's cheek, but that was cold too; she grabbed Livvy's shoulders and shook her. There was no response. As Livvy's head rolled to the side, Velma saw that her eyes were wide open but that she did not see. She leapt to her feet, knocking the oatmeal onto the crocheted rug next to the big brass bed, shouting for Eli as she ran down the stairs.

Eli had finished his chores and was eating his pancakes and reading the Ainsworth *Democrat* in the kitchen. He took the stairs two at a time and dropped to his knees next to the bed. Velma waited in the doorway while Eli felt Livvy's pulse. He held her wrist for a long, long time, so long that Velma thought he was counting the beats of Livvy's heart. Then he shook his head, sighed a long, weary sigh and stooped to lift his daughter, his powerful arms wrapped tightly around her ribs.

—Your mama's passed on, girl. She won't be feelin no more pain and she's in a better place now. I don't want to see no cryin. Your ma wouldn't want you bawlin, now.

Livvy in her coffin was laid out on the big kitchen table, wearing the green shot-silk dress she wore on her wedding day. Her arms were folded in her lap, her hair plaited in a long braid down the back just like it was the day she'd married Eli thirteen years before. Eli gave them all what-for for crying and the others hushed, but Velma could not stop. She wished as hard as she could wish for Livvy to climb right out of that coffin, start laughing about it all, and sit at the table to help her daughters with their arithmetic. The night before the funeral she lay awake praying, but in the morning Livvy was still lying there, her eyes closed, lost to the world.

People came from all over the county to pay their respects. Maude Hutchinson said it was going to be the biggest funeral in the history of Brown County because everyone loved Livvy. Henry and Ingrid Sundstrom brought their organ on a wagon for the service. When Velma looked out the window, she saw at least fifty teams hitched to wagons and buggies, waiting for the ride up to the ridge where Livvy would be buried next to John Milton. Ingrid played the organ as the mourners shuffled in, all of them pausing to shake Eli's hand or to offer a few words to his children.

Before the service, Reverend Cubbin was nervous as a new mother. He preached on the theme "Through a Glass Darkly," a sermon he had worked on over the better part of two nights. Once he began to speak, however, his words seemed hopelessly inadequate. He had planned to be brief, but the more nervous he got the more long-winded he became; his mouth was parched, he rambled, in desperation he threw in long digressions that had nothing to do with the service he had planned. Eli was the richest member of the congregation and the donor who kept the church in hymnals and coal for the stove in winter; Livvy was considered the finest woman in the county. If the sermon didn't measure up, they'd send him to some awful place like the Running Water to preach to homesteaders who put sunflower seeds in the collection plate. Cubbin found it was impossible to read Eli's face. The man had now buried a son and his wife in a span of two months but through it all he kept the expression of a cigar-store Indian. It wasn't natural. When it was over, several of the female mourners had good words for Reverend Cubbin, but Eli went out to the barn to check on a heifer that had foundered on fresh spring alfalfa. It was no way, the preacher thought, for a man in mourning to behave.

Before they buried Livvy, Eli told his children that their mother was being laid to rest in the perfect spot.

—From up there on the ridge, your mama and little John Milton can see forever.

Velma thought about that. If her mother's eyes were closed, how could she see? How could she see anyway, inside that coffin? If you were dead, what difference did it make whether you were buried up on the ridge or down by the creek or in the Ainsworth cemetery?

The mourners gathered round the grave. Velma sang along with the rest as Maude led them in Livvy's favorite hymn:

> *O Beulah land, sweet Beulah land*
> *As on thy highest mount I stand*
> *I look away across the sea*
> *Where mansions are prepared for me*
> *And view the shining glory shore*
> *My heav'n, my home forever more . . .*

As they sang, Velma wondered where Beulah Land could be found. Somewhere west of the Wyoming line, most likely, up in the high mountains west of the Powder River country, where Papa and Uncle Ezra and Teeter used to ride. She pictured her mother in her green dress, standing on a peak looking out over a beautiful valley filled with mansions, holding John Milton on her hip. It was beautiful but the vision wouldn't hold in her mind; when it vanished, all she could see was cold black earth and all she could hear was the howling wind that blew over this ridge on long winter nights. It seemed like the loneliest place in the world for a mother to be buried, even if her baby boy was beside her.

The neighbor women wouldn't leave without doing the washing up, so it was near dusk when the last wagons and buggies rolled off toward town. For the one and only time in his life, Eli sent the girls off to bed early and sat alone at the table with a glass and a bottle of Tennessee whiskey. When the whiskey was gone, he crawled up on the table where Livvy's coffin had lain until that afternoon and passed out with his boots on. Velma found him there the next morning, curled up like a baby. When he smelled the coffee perking in the kitchen, he got up, drank two cups of thick black coffee with a dollop of cream, declared that he would skip the pancakes, put on his hat and boots and went to work without saying a word.

As far as any of the girls could remember, he never mentioned Livvy again, although he did order a pair of marble tombstones from Omaha. The larger one read:

IN MEMORY OF OLIVIA ALTA PAINT,
B. 1872 D. 1903.
OUR DEVOTED WIFE AND LOVING MOTHER,
MAY SHE REST IN PEACE.

Velma cut out the notices of her mother's death in the two local papers and pressed them carefully into her *Treasury of Beloved Poems*, a present from Livvy on Velma's ninth birthday. The first account was long and flowery. Velma liked best the last paragraph:

> The gathering of friends and acquaintances was the largest ever seen at a funeral in this part of the county. To the bereaved family and to her mother, brother, and sisters, the sympathy of a wide circle of friends and acquaintances go out to them in this, the darkest hour of sorrow.

The other newspaper account was brief:

> Mrs. Eli Paint was one of our noble women and much liked by the people of the community for her many good traits. She was an affectionate wife and kind mother, and her departure will leave a vacuum at the head of the family circle that will ever be held in sorrowful remembrance by the kind husband and children. The funeral was conducted from the house yesterday afternoon and the remains followed to the grave by a large circle of sympathizing friends. The bereaved husband and family have the sympathy of the entire community in their hour of deep affliction.

Velma loved the phrases from the newspapers, the way they sounded on her tongue, like the full bass notes of the church organ: "The darkest hour of sorrow." "In sorrowful remembrance." "In their hour of deep affliction." When her chores were done, she would stroll along the creek or walk up to the ridge where Livvy and John Milton were buried, whispering the words over and over to herself. Her mother, she was certain, had been the most wonderful woman on earth—strong, kind, funny, hardworking, beautiful, understanding. Velma knew that most children felt that way about their mothers but in Livvy's case it was all true; even the newspaper stories of her death said as much.

For weeks after Livvy died, Velma would find little Kate sitting on the back steps of the house, staring up at the ridge. When she asked Kate what she was doing, the answer was always the same: "I'm waiting for Mommy to come home." Velma mentioned Kate's strange behavior to Tavie, but her oldest sister just shook her head.

—I guess she'll get over it someday. I expect we all will.

Tavie, Velma thought, was too much like Eli. Velma knew better. Life on the Fanciful would never be the same.

⚜ CHAPTER 35 ⚜

Mourning was a luxury and Eli Paint had no time for luxuries. Within a week after Livvy's death he was driving himself harder than ever. He would be up in inky darkness even in high summer, boiling coffee and getting ready for the day's work. After supper late in the evening, the girls would find him sitting on a bench on the porch, tying knots in a half dozen lengths of rope. They all knew enough to leave their father alone when he was tying knots because that was his "figuring time," when he did his calculations and made all his important decisions. Other men liked to talk things over, visit a neighbor and lay out a problem, beat their gums about it while they sipped dandelion wine. Eli went at things alone, without saying a word to anyone until his mind was made up. Then his word was law. No one could argue with his success: Eli now had nearly ten thousand acres of ranchland of his own and another five thousand acres at the "company ranch" that he ran in partnership with Cale Hutchinson, fifteen miles west of the Fanciful.

In the spring of 1906, all six Paint siblings made the trail drive to Pine Ridge for the first time. The drive began as they all did, with a roundup that started as soon as the snow began to melt. They left Brown County with nearly four thousand head of cattle, bound as usual for the Indian Agency in Pine Ridge. Tavie was fifteen, Marguerite thirteen, Velma twelve, Ruby almost eleven, and Kate, the youngest of the girls, not yet nine years old. Even

Blind Daniel, nearing his seventh birthday, came along on one of the chuckwagons. They moved out on a May morning after three days of soaking rain had turned the grass green. Teeter Spawn and Gizzard Hopkins drove the chuckwagons, one loaded with feed, spare saddles, harness, hoof nips, currycombs, bits and bridles and other equipment, the other with a Dutch oven, water barrels, lanterns, bedrolls, earned goods, and food enough to last a month. Hobbles dangled from the sides of the wagons, along with a supply of rope and picket stakes for the horses. Eli's formula called for eight horses for each rider, so they were also driving a hundred and fifty horses.

Eli didn't believe in pushing cattle hard on the trail. He made a steady twelve to fifteen miles a day, leaving time for the stock to graze along the way so they would arrive in good shape and fetch top dollar. A wet April had left the grass tall and green but long before they reached the White River, Eli knew what they would find. The river would be high, so they wouldn't have to deal with quicksand, but what they would face would be worse. With heavy winter snows and a month of steady spring rain, the White would be in flood, a boiling caldron of muddy water.

Even with the looming obstacle of the White River, the drive for the first four days was easy and relaxed. On the fourth afternoon, they drove the cattle over the one narrow crossing on a nameless creek and made camp for the night, with the cattle on one side and the wagons on the other. The next morning, Eli took all the riders except Tavie and Velma to round up another thousand head for a rancher north of the Niobrara who had been crippled up when a horse fell on him. Teeter and Blind Daniel stayed with the wagons while Tavie and Velma headed out in May sunshine to keep an eye on the herd, an easy job with the cattle grazing or lying in the shade, chewing their cud. They were talking about Rafe Cubbin, the preacher's son, who had come along on the trip but had proved such a tenderfoot that Eli left him with the chuckwagon. The boy was Tavie's age but she disliked him intensely.

—I guess he's pretty to look at, but I'd rather spend time with Teeter. He's got no teeth and he stinks but at least he aint a sissy.

—I've never known you to like a boy, Tavie.

—Well, I've never known you not to like one.

—That's not true. I don't like Rafe. Much.

Tavie laughed. She might have said more but the wind had shifted abruptly. Now it was blowing from the north and blowing hard. Gray, low-riding clouds came in with the wind and the temperature began to drop so steeply that within minutes they were shivering. Tavie squinted into the wind.

—Looks like we should a brought our wraps.

Before they could think about riding back to the wagons, the clouds began spitting snow. A few steers began to stir and soon the rest followed, drifting upriver away from the wind. Tavie galloped to head them off and Velma followed. By the time they caught the leaders, it was snowing hard, a freakish spring blizzard blowing in over open prairie. The cattle were spread over nearly a mile and drifting steadily away from the wagons. Tavie shouted that she was going to ride across the front of the herd to turn them. She took off at a dead gallop, waving her hat and shouting to stop the herd from drifting further. Velma waited until Tavie had almost disappeared in the storm and then dug her spurs in and followed, shouting at the top of her lungs. When they reached the far side of the herd, they turned their horses and cantered back and forth in front of the leaders, hoping that the herd wouldn't stampede right at them. The cattle were still moving at a walk, so a little whooping and hollering and Tavie's earsplitting whistle was enough to turn them back south. The girls galloped after the strays until they were able to get them all headed in the right direction. By that time, their horses were about worn out and Tavie and Velma were half frozen, their hair caked with snow. Velma was used to taking orders from Tavie, but this time she made the decision for both of them.

—We've got to go back, sis. If we don't, we'll freeze out here.

—Pa will kill us if we don't hold the herd.

—He can't kill us if we're froze to death.

Velma turned her horse east toward the wagons. Tavie hesitated, uncertain whether she was more afraid of staying alone in the storm, or of Eli's wrath if any of the herd were lost. With Velma about to vanish in the snow, she finally made up her mind and galloped after. How Velma found the creek crossing again Tavie would never know; the snow obscured all the landmarks and whirled so hard in their faces that Tavie couldn't even tell which direction they were going. Somehow, Velma rode straight to the crossing and eased her horse into the stream, with Tavie right on her tail. From there it was another hundred yards to the camp. Teeter had kept the Dutch oven going in the chuckwagon, with wood scavenged before the snow fell. The girls crowded close to the fire, shivering and shaking the snow out of their hair. Rafe was sitting near the fire with a heavy coat over his shoulders and a shawl wrapped around his head. Rafe stayed where he was, looking miserable and cold. Teeter jumped up to help them with their horses.

—What took you two so long? I thought you'd be back as soon as it started to snow.

—We were afraid to let the herd drift. We were riding back and forth ahead of the cattle, but it got too cold. I don't know what Pa is going to say if we lose any cattle.

Teeter spat a chaw of tobacco on the dirt floor of the tent.

—Eli is a hard man, but he won't say a word if we lose them all. He might be a little vexed that you didn't come in right off. He might not show it, but he'd sooner lose a thousand cows than two daughters.

The storm was over by late afternoon. It left behind nearly a foot of wet snow, which the high winds had piled into drifts. After Velma and Tavie left them, the cattle again began to drift with the wind at their backs. By the time Eli returned the next morning and the riders caught up to the herd, they were scattered over three miles of prairie. It took two days' hard work to pull them together again and get back on the trail, but as far as Eli and Hutch could make out, they hadn't lost a single steer. Teeter was right: Eli made it plain that they should have returned to camp as soon as the weather turned.

—I ask a lot of my girls, but one thing I will never ask is that you risk your life for a cow. I've lost two of my own already and I don't aim to lose any more.

They resumed the drive to the White River, with Velma feeling certain of a thing she had doubted since her mother's death: Hard as he was, Eli Paint loved her and all his children. He didn't show it, but he cared for all of them and looked after them like a fierce old wolf guarding his pack. She would have liked it a whole lot better if he could show a bit of Livvy's tenderness, but Eli wasn't like that and he never would be. It was a fact she had to learn to accept, like spring blizzards and rivers in flood.

Eli ordered a halt a mile short of the White River and made camp to wait for the flood to ease. After four days the water was still as high as ever. The fresh water hauled in barrels on the wagons was running out, and everyone grumbled about the river water: the white mud that gave the White its name made its water almost undrinkable, even after it was left in barrels overnight for the mud to settle. The next morning a layer of mud would have sunk to the bottom of the barrel but anything boiled in the water—coffee, meat, beans—had a coating of white scum when it was done. The Paint girls did as the cowboys did: they drank the muddy coffee, chewed through beans covered with white grit, spat grit out of their teeth all day long.

As the days went by, Eli grew restless, anxious to be across the river before some unimagined disaster struck the herd. He rode twenty miles north and then twenty miles to the south, trying to find some way around the predicament. At last he found the solution in a small band of tattered Sioux camped next to an Indian school five miles upriver. The Indians had a little boat, which they used to ferry things across the swollen river. A frayed rope tied to trees at either end and passed through iron rings in the bow and stern of the boat kept it from being torn downstream. Eli reached an agreement with the Indians: He would give them twenty head of cattle and five horses in payment if they would ferry all the goods across the river; once the wagons were across, the cowboys could swim the cattle across the river.

The first thing was to replace the frayed rope with three hundred feet of good corral rope. Two of the cowboys went to help the Sioux change the rope while some of the men began breaking down the wagons and the Paint girls joined the rest in bringing up the herd. The cattle seemed to sense the peril of the crossing; they were jittery and restless and little bands kept breaking off from the main herd and trying to turn back. All the hands rode their horses to a white, foamy lather trying to keep the cattle headed in the right direction. After an hour of hard riding, a wild-eyed steer charged right at Tavie's horse, horns down and long streams of spittle dangling from its jaw. If Tavie had not stood her ground, the steer might have triggered a stampede. She reacted as Eli had taught her: She dug her spurs into her cowpony's flanks, waved a rawhide quirt over her head and ran right at the steer, hollering "yipyipyipyip" at the top of her lungs. Ruby cut to the left and galloped beside her and together they forced the steer to return to the herd. From the far side of the herd, Eli lifted his hat.

The wagons were taken completely apart for the crossing. The wheels, running gear, and wagon tongues were loaded on the boat and ferried across along with all the contents of the wagons, from water barrels to harnesses. With the water raging, Eli said that Daniel and the girls were to ride across two at a time with the first supplies. Tavie started to protest that she could drive cattle into the water and swim a horse across the river as well as any cowboy, but Eli raised a leather-gloved hand without saying a word and she bit off her complaint.

Velma crossed first with Daniel, the two of them crouched low in the boat, Velma's arms wrapped tightly around her brother. When the boat was halfway out in the stream, those onshore could still hear Daniel laughing; he thought the crossing was a wonderful adventure, possibly because he couldn't see the raging river. The two young Lakota piloting the boat pointed at him and joined in the laughter: The blind one was brave. The crossing had looked like it would be fun until Velma found herself in the middle of the river. It seemed the boat might tear apart from the strength of the current, or tip over, or simply break the rope and drift a hundred miles. The boys pulling the boat across with their callused brown hands on the rope were as calm as if they were standing in a shallow pool. The one at the back of the boat smiled at Velma, a big, toothy grin. He said something in Lakota that she didn't understand but she smiled back anyway, reassured the crossing was safe.

Velma was turning to wave to her father when the stump of an enormous cottonwood tree rose from the water and gave the little boat a thump that lifted it out of the water and dropped it back again. The boat tilted so sharply that the Sioux boys had to pull hard to keep it from capsizing. Velma fell onto her back in the bottom of the boat. As soon as the boat righted itself, she realized that Daniel had been thrown out by the force of the collision. She screamed to the boys that Daniel had fallen overboard. One of them pointed to her brother, already twenty feet downstream, his head above water as he paddled frantically toward the shore, where the waiting Sioux shouted to him as they waded in. Daniel was trying to swim toward the sound of their shouting but he was weighed down by his clothing and the current was strong.

Velma began pulling off her boots, although Daniel was a far better swimmer than she was. By the time she got them off, she saw it was hopeless; the current was carrying him away much faster than she could swim. He was now a hundred feet downstream, trailed by the Lakota running along the shore. Velma could see that he was making progress, fighting toward the sound of the voices on the riverbank, his little arms churning in the water, his head turning from side to side as he fought for air. If he could get close enough for someone to grab him before the river exhausted his strength, he might make it. Velma lost sight of him for a moment and thought he was drowned at last, but Daniel's head bobbed up again and there he was, swimming harder than ever. He was still five feet out in the river when the tallest of the Sioux men strode into the water up to his chest, made a grab for Daniel and missed his hand, made a second grab and caught his foot the instant before the boy shot out of reach. Daniel's head was under the water as the man pulled him back; then he was up, held out of the water by two strong arms as more reached to help them to safety.

The boys in the boat had been pulling steadily toward the shore as they watched the rescue. As soon as the boat came to a halt on the far bank, Velma jumped out and ran to Daniel. He was dripping wet and his chest was heaving as he tried to catch his breath, but he was otherwise unhurt. Velma waved to Eli to signal that Daniel was all right, then held him until she was as wet as he was.

When Eli finally reached them, he lifted Daniel to his chest and tousled his damp hair.

—That's about the toughest thing I ever seen a boy do, son. A blind boy swimmin in a river like that. You can do that, there aint nothin you can't do, you hear me now? Nothin. You want to do somethin, you go right ahead and try. I've seen plenty cowhands got perfect eyesight but they aint got half the sand you got.

Eli tracked down the Sioux man who had rescued Daniel, thanked him in Lakota, and told him that he could pick out a horse from the remuda as soon as they got the horses across the river. That was not going to be an easy task, persuading four thousand cattle and a hundred and fifty horses that they wanted to swim a swollen river. The oxen detached from each wagon were led into the river by Eli and Hutch, who were both accustomed to swinging off a horse's back as the water got deep and swimming the rest of the way while holding on to a stirrup. But Hutch was riding a green horse, a big, nervy sorrel gelding who was steady enough on solid ground but didn't take to water one bit. As soon as the sorrel felt Hutch swimming alongside, it decided that the prudent thing to do was climb Hutch's back to safety. Its left front hoof caught Hutch in the small of the back and dragged him under. He came up sputtering and coughing, flailing in a desperate attempt to get away from the horse, who was equally desperate to climb on his back. Eli saw Hutch go down a second time and a third, and was just thinking he might be lost when Hutch got the upper hand and pointed the horse toward the shore again.

With the cowpunchers pressing in on them from all sides, using short rawhide whips to keep them moving, the lead cattle followed the oxen into the water. Once they were headed into the stream, the cowboys flanked them, swimming alongside their horses. Despite their best efforts, some of the cattle gave up swimming and were caught by the current and dragged to their deaths, bawling in terror as they whirled down the river. There were moments when it seemed as though the whole herd would be lost along with half the cowboys, but somehow the vast majority scrambled up the far bank, where Velma had deposited Daniel on the chuckwagon while she and her sisters rode like demons to keep the herd from scattering. Once the cattle were safely across, the cowboys still had to go back and bring up the spare horses. When it was finally over, the sun was going down; exhausted punchers flopped facedown in the grass, their lungs heaving, unable to summon enough breath even to curse the river. Eli sat beside the soaked and shivering Hutch, his hand on his shoulder.

—Sonofabitch gelding kicked me right in the spine. I thought I was done for.

—I saw it. I oughtn't to let you take a green horse on a river crossing.

—I'm the damned fool took him into the water. Did the bastard drown at least?

Eli waved his hand toward the school.

—Nope. He's up there grazin like nothing happened at all.

—Good. Soon as I can breathe right, I'm goin to shoot the sonofabitch.

Hutch didn't shoot the horse. He had a black bruise the size of a dinner plate on his back and assorted other bruises all the way down his thighs and he would spit blood for a week, but he was all right. Daniel was safe and sound and still laughing over his adventure in the river. Eli couldn't be sure without doing a complete count, but he thought they had lost no more than fifty head while crossing the White River at flood time. He didn't like to lose a single cow, but there were times when you had to take what you could get.

The Paint girls spent the night with their brother in a supply building used to store buggies and grain and harness, and fell asleep breathing the mingled odors of wheat and leather. Daniel slept under Velma's blanket, his hard little body curled into hers. She held him all night long, unwilling to let go.

They reached the Indian agency late the next afternoon. Once the transaction was complete and Eli had the cash tucked into a money belt around his waist, he paid the temporary hands, turned them loose and went to buy wild horses from Spotted War Bonnet. They spent the next three days camped near War Bonnet's cabin. The morning they were ready to begin the drive back to Brown County, War Bonnet offered Eli a warning.

—These are good horses but you have to watch that shaggy sorrel mare. She's mean as a rattlesnake. If you give her half a chance, she'll head them all back to the hills.

—Thank you kindly. I'll watch her. And we'll be seein you next year.

It had rained during the night and the air smelled of sage and wildflowers. Redwing blackbirds wheeled in the air, pheasant were flushed with a whir of wings as the horses approached, a lone eagle circled high overhead, prairie dogs chirped from a prairie dog town. They were no more than ten miles along the trail, the Paint girls riding along the left side of the herd watching the prairie dogs, when a dozen horses broke from the herd, led by War Bonnet's shaggy sorrel mare. Tavie saw that the mustangs were hell-bent for a steep gully that loomed to the north like a rip in the earth. Eli, Hutch, and Gizzard were all caught on the wrong side of the herd and Teeter was driving the chuckwagon with Kate and Daniel beside him on the seat. Tavie saw that if the Paint girls didn't head them off, no one else could, and that the way the wild horses were running, there was nothing to stop them plunging off the edge into the gully and breaking their necks. She was riding a rangy black gelding, Ruby beside her on a quick little pinto, Maggie and Velma trailing behind on bay mares. Within four strides the black and the pinto were at a full gallop.

Eli reined in his horse to watch as the mustangs and their pursuers swept down through the valley to the badlands where the gully slashed through the prairie a mile away. His daughters rode low in the saddle, with their faces almost in the manes streaming in the wind. Everything he had taught them was caught up in this wild, desperate ride; from half a mile away, he could sense their muscles straining, see how smoothly they flowed with the horses, their spurs flashing in the sunlight. With a quarter mile to go, Ruby broke into the lead, bent low like a jockey as she closed in on the shaggy mare. She and Tavie leapt a clump of sage almost in tandem, skirted a sinkhole and broke to the left of the mustangs, working to force the wild ones away from the cliff.

Tavie kept one eye on the scrub that marked the edge of the gully and the other on the mare while she calculated their chances of heading the wild horses before they all sailed over the edge and ended up in a mass of broken legs at the bottom. Ruby was still gaining, the lightest rider on the fastest horse. When she drew head-to-head with the mare, she reached out and flicked her quirt at the mustang's nose, forcing her to turn. For several long seconds they rode with a dozen feet between them and disaster, Maggie now almost even with Ruby and the two of them squeezed between the mustangs and the chasm. Then Tavie's piercing whistle cut through the air and the mustangs changed direction again, wheeling away from the gully and calamity, turning in a long, looping circle that would take them back toward the rest of the herd.

Velma, following a dozen feet behind Tavie on her bay, tugged slightly at the snaffle bit and sat up straighter in the saddle to get a better look. She didn't see the rock thrown up by the pounding hooves of Tavie's horse but even if she had, she would not have had time to duck. The rock tore through the lid of her right eye and pierced the iris. The pain was so awful that she thought she had been shot by an arrow that had gone right through her skull. She dropped the reins and put both hands to her face, her scream lost in a rush of wind and the noise of horses in full flight. Somehow, she managed to keep her saddle, although for a few strides she leaned far to the left with her right boot out of the stirrup, like a trick rider about to grab a hat off the ground until she managed to grab the saddlehorn with her right hand and pull herself upright. The bay slowed to an easy lope, came to a halt and stood there blowing hard, her flanks heaving. Velma dropped the reins and slumped over the saddlehorn, her hands to her face. The others didn't even notice she was missing until they drove the breakaway bunch back to the main herd. By that time Velma had slipped off her horse and collapsed facedown in a patch of pale yellow wildflowers, clutching at her eye as blood streamed down her face. Even through the red curtain of pain, the name of the flowers came to her. Livvy had once told her what they were called, a lovely name she liked to say over and over: creeping jennie hereabouts.

By the time Tavie looked back and saw what had happened, there was blood on the blossoms and Velma Paint was blind in one eye.

Eli carried Velma, still wearing chaps, boots, and spurs but minus her sunbonnet, into the Pine Ridge Hospital. She was fortunate to be treated by Dr. James R. Walker, a dedicated young man who had transferred to Pine Ridge from Leech Lake on the White Earth Agency in Minnesota, where he had worked with the Ojibwa. Dr. Walker was the rare white physician who believed he could learn from the Indian medicine men; he gave her laudanum to ease her pain, but the poultice he applied to Velma's eye was a herbal concoction supplied by his friend Yellow Thunder, a Sioux medicine man. With the help of two Minneconjou nurses, he cleansed the wound, sewed the eyelid, examined her carefully and concluded that, although Velma would not lose the eye, she would not be able to see from it again.

Eli had to get the horses back to Brown County, so he left

Tavie to stay until Velma recovered and then escort her home. Dr. Walker said there was a stage they could catch from Pine Ridge to Buffalo Gap, where they could take the Fremont, Elkhorn & Missouri Valley spur to Chadron and change trains for Ainsworth.

On the morning of her second day in the hospital, Velma woke to the sound of Lakota all around her, a language that sounded to her like the rush of the breeze through the trees on a summer evening. The ceiling overhead was painted white, a white like blindness. The pain, a steady throbbing in her right eye, was a distant knocking at someone else's door, held at bay by the dreamlike drift of the morphia. She was vaguely aware that a rock thrown up by Tavie's horse had put out her eye. When she sat up and looked around, Velma realized she was the only white girl in a large, open hospital dormitory where all the others patients were Lakota girls and women, several of them consumptives in an area separated by thick white curtains that were pulled open during the day. She heard heavy, racking coughs, saw bloody rags piled next to some of the beds, watched as the thin shoulders of a girl about her own age shook with the effort of a cough that seemed too awful to be coming from such a tiny body. Velma felt a wave of pity for the girl. Surely it was much worse to have the consumption than to lose an eye, as long as you lost only one eye.

For the first two or three days, it all seemed like it was happening to someone else: the Indian nurses coming to bring or remove a bedpan, Dr. Walker making his rounds, Tavie appearing at her bedside as if by magic, tall and strong and confident, reassuring her that a cowgirl with one eye could be every bit as good as one with two eyes. When Dr. Walker stopped giving her laudanum the pain was hard to bear, but it eased each day. She began moving around the dormitory to get used to seeing with only one eye; it left her feeling dizzy and disoriented but she was sure she could get accustomed to it. If Blind Daniel could go through life seeing no more than vague shapes with both eyes, she could live with good vision in one.

The thin Lakota girl was named Susan Crow Dog. She had been

to the mission school, where the priests had soaped her mouth if she was caught speaking Lakota, so she spoke English well. Susan had just discovered that she had the consumption and was afraid it would be the death of her. To pass the time and cheer up her new friend, Velma told her all about the cattle drive, about crossing the White River, ending with her own mishap.

—We were just startin for home when this doggoned shaggy sorrel mare took off with a bunch of horses. Papa is friends with a Sioux named Spotted War Bonnet, and War Bonnet warned him that horse was trouble. Well, it sure enough was. I was runnin after my sister, and her horse threw up a rock and there went my eye. Things can happen to a person that quick.

Teeter Spawn met them at the railroad station in Ainsworth, driving the spring wagon so Velma could lie down in the back for the journey home. He had a jug of mulled wine under his seat, and he offered Velma a couple of swigs so the jouncing of the wagon would be a little less painful. Velma looked to Tavie, who urged her to drink. It wasn't the first time Velma had tasted liquor, but it was the first time she had felt grateful for the warmth that flowed through her limbs. Teeter took several long swallows himself, winked as he passed the jug to Tavie.

—Don't tell your pa. He'd take that blacksnake whip to my hide.

Halfway to the Fanciful and with the jug half gone, Teeter turned philosophical.

—Y'know, I been thinkin. Everything comes in cycles. When your pa first come to Brown County, he was on the up part of the cycle and every doggone thing he touched turned to gold. I never seen anythin like it. I have watched 'em come and watched 'em go, and I can tell ye, aint a man before him had his luck. Most settlers out here don't last their first winter but there wasn't a thing Eli Paint turned his hand to didn't come out right. Then he hit the calamity cycle. Daniel was born almost blind, Sherman died, then little Johnny, and Livvy, the sweetest woman in four counties.

I don't mind tellin you that it brought me low as a snake in the weeds when she went. After all that, Velma here lost her eye. As bad as it seems now, I do believe that was the end of your calamity cycle. Now things is bound to be on the upswing.

At home, Velma was happiest to see Blind Daniel. She held him in a long, long embrace. They shared something now, this blindness, although hers was restricted to the half of her vision that had vanished when the rock struck her eye. Still, it made her feel closer to him, more a part of his world. She kept turning her head, trying to see things on her blind side, jumping at unexpected sounds from things she did not see, lifting the back of her hand to her face to try to brush away the darkness. Because Daniel could not quite imagine sight, she fancied that they shared this world, a world in which perception was altered by misfortune, so that blindness itself became another kind of sight. She thought of what she had tried to tell her uncle Ezra, about the ball of light bounding through the wheatfield, a vision that always seemed to elude her because just as it was about to come into focus it would vanish. When Daniel was older they would have to talk of these things; she had often felt that somehow he saw things that the others didn't. Now that sense was stronger than ever, as was her boundless affection for the boy. As soon as she saw him, she vowed to use her remaining eye to watch out for him more than ever.

Velma went to bed that night thinking about Teeter and his calamity cycle. She was twelve years old, an age when calamity, to those who have suffered through it, means a death in the family. Or three deaths in a year's time, when the household never quite emerges from mourning. She knew of other calamities secondhand, like the grasshopper plague down in Kansas, hoppers six inches thick on the ground for miles, their wings blotting out the sun, hoppers coming through your windows, hoppers crackling under the quilt on your bed at night, hoppers stripping every blade of grass and every leaf, eating harness and hoe handles and anything that tasted of the sweat of man, leaving the ground and the trees bare as January, so that when the plague had passed everything, well water and hogs and chickens, all tasted like grasshoppers for months to come. That was another sort of calamity, like a prairie fire or a tornado or losing your eye to a rock thrown up by a horse. The only thing she could hope was that this calamity cycle had come to an end, that her losing an eye was the last of the misfortunes and that there were better times ahead. There was no way of knowing what was to come. Sometimes, there was just nowhere to hide.

ᘔ CHAPTER 36 ᘕ

Later, Velma would say that she saw Frank Hughes coming a mile off. April Fool's Day it was, 1909, the thirty-ninth birthday of Eli and Ezra Paint, the kind of early spring day when you just can't wait to get on the outside of breakfast and get a saddle on a horse. Velma was whipping pancake batter while Ruby tended the griddle. When she happened to glance out the kitchen window, she saw him top the rise and come prancing down through the north pasture toward the house riding a long-legged black horse.

—Best do another batch of pancakes. There's another one comin. I swear they can smell breakfast ten miles off when the wind is right.

Eli didn't look up from the month-old newspaper he was reading.

—Set another place. Anybody we know?

—Not this one.

—Lookin for work. We're full up. Feed the man and send him on his way.

Ruby spooned three more big pancakes onto the griddle.

—Gizzard is still all stove up from tryin to ride Giddyup. We could use another hand.

—I can't afford to hire every no-account saddle tramp between Montana and Missouri.

Velma poured a quart of buttermilk into the flour in the big mixing bowl and cracked four more eggs, staring out the window and paying less attention to her mixing than she ought.

—I don't know, Papa. This one sits a horse real nice.

—Every cowboy ever born looks good astride the right horse. Put him on the wrong horse, then we'll see how good he looks.

The stranger reined up at the stock tank. He wore oversize leather chaps with metal studs, hand-tooled Spanish boots with silver spurs that gleamed in the sunlight, a big, floppy black hat pulled low over his eyes so you couldn't see his face. Ruby clucked her tongue.

—That's one long, tall drink of water. I don't think I ever seen a man that tall.

Eli put down his paper, reached for his hat and went out to meet the man. While they talked, the stranger unbuckled the saddlecinch, hung the saddle and blanket over the corral fence, led the horse into an empty corral and turned him loose. Then he and Eli headed up toward the house and the girls scattered away from the window and went back to tending to breakfast. The man hung his hat on a peg and strolled across the floor, his spurs going *janglejanglejangle* with every long stride. He was much younger than he looked on horseback, not more than eighteen or nineteen, and he had dark hair and dark eyes and an easy grin. When Eli introduced him, all Velma heard was "Frank," and she let three pancakes burn before she got her mind back on breakfast.

—Frank here claims to be a broncobuster. Spent the winter workin for Ez up in Montana, and Ezra told him I might need a horseman, which I don't. But we're goin to feed him till he busts.

Only Tavie was bold enough to shake his hand.

—You're young for a broncobuster.

—I been ridin since I was three. If you got a animal needs gentling, I'm your man.

Eli tried his coffee, added another dollop of cream.

—It's too bad we don't need help, son. Aint no horse we can't handle ourselves.

Velma left the burned pancakes for the dogs and made three more fresh.

—We can't manage Giddyup, Papa. He's supposed to be my pony but he's thrown everybody comes near him. Gizzard tried again this spring and Giddyup like to killed him.

Frank paused before digging into his pancakes.

—If this Giddyup is a horse, I can ride him.

Eli held his mug out for Velma to fill it again.

—He aint a ghost, if that's what you're gettin at.

—Then I expect I can ride him.

Gizzard came limping in for breakfast followed by Lonesome Pete and Teeter Spawn. Teeter had the last word on Giddyup.

—A horsefly couldn't ride that little sonofabitch.

—I seen horses like that. How old is he?

—Three-year-old. Old enough to know better. Taint worth the trouble.

—He's young enough to learn. I'd like to try.

Eli thought it over.

—All right, son. I've put up with that animal eatin up feed to no purpose long enough. If you can ride him, I'll pay you two dollars a head to rough out the rest. Any broken bones is your affair.

The girls trailed Frank and Eli down to the circular corral where they worked the horses. Eli saddled up and he and Pete rode out to the pasture and hazed Giddyup back in to where Ruby held the gate open and slid it shut just as soon as the horse pranced through. Frank asked Eli if he could borrow the bullwhip. Eli turned on him like he'd been scalded.

—We don't whip horses here. If that's how you work animals, you better skedaddle.

—Never said I was goin to touch him with that whip.

Eli looked doubtful but he undid the leather thong that fastened a brand-new Australian kangaroo-hide bullwhip to his saddle. He offered the weighted handle to Frank, who ducked through the rails and sized up the horse, a white pinto with scattered black and ginger patches. Giddyup had a Roman nose and one blue eye and one black eye. The black eye was surrounded by a ginger patch and the blue eye was on the white side of his head, so that he looked like two different horses, depending which side you were on.

A half dozen cowhands settled on the top rail of the fence to watch. The Paint girls stood in a row on the far side of the corral. Eli swung himself up onto the rail next to Teeter.

—Aint he goin to saddle him?

—He says not yet. Looks like he's fixin to talk him to death.

Frank was already talking, circling to his right, forcing the horse to circle to his left.

—All right, son. You and me are about to have ourselves a little waltz.

Frank took a long step right at Giddyup. The horse whirled away. Frank flicked his wrist and the whip cracked, startling the men on the rail so that Gizzard almost tumbled backward. Giddyup whirled to face Frank, his flanks shuddering, head up, ears pointed right at Frank.

—Whoa now. Easy.

Frank took one short step. The pinto turned to bolt. The whip cracked.

—Whoa now. Whoa son.

Giddyup whirled away, the whip cracked, he whirled back. Frank took a step. The horse bolted along the rails. Frank cracked the whip, Giddyup spun to face him.

—Whoa now easy now whoa son.

Whirl and run, crack and halt.

—Whoa now, son. You want to run, you go right ahead. I can do this all day. I aint runnin a dang bit and you're workin your fool head off for no reason at all. Whoa now easy.

Velma had seen men who would take the whip to a horse and men who would just keep climbing back on until horse and rider both were worn out or busted up. She had seen every kind of rider, good and bad, cavalrymen and rodeo riders and the Lakota boys who could ride bareback at a dead gallop. She had never seen anyone go about it the way Frank did. She watched his long legs and the Spanish boots moving quick and fluid as he turned with the horse, the spurs' *janglejanglejangle*. The crack of the whip made her jump each time. By degrees Giddyup turned so as to keep that wild blue eye on his tormentor, whirling away and then whirling back ahead of the whip.

After half an hour the horse was heavily lathered, standing spraddle-legged in the dust, head down with fatigue. When he whirled away, it was halfhearted, a tentative movement instantly withdrawn, like a bad checker player in a tight corner. The space between them closed a foot at a time until Frank extended the whip toward the pinto's chin. The horse made to whirl away, the whip cracked. Frank thought he had given up but Giddyup was a stubborn animal. They had to do it again and again, a dozen more times, until finally he rubbed the whip gently along the animal's neck and down to his chin and back to his mane. Giddyup did not flinch.

At last Frank backed away a half step, the whip just touching Giddyup's chin. The gelding took a half step forward, coming with him. Frank backed and the horse did not follow. He cracked the whip and tried it again and this time the horse stepped along with him. Frank led the pinto in a long circle around the corral with nothing to hold him but the whip to his chin, then laid the whip aside and led the horse with his fingertips under its chin. When Frank changed directions, the horse stayed right with him. Frank asked for a bucket of oats, and Velma ran to the barn and came back with the bucket and Frank fed the horse from his palm, still talking and rubbing it behind its ears. He nodded to Eli.

—I think that's about it for today.

—You still aint rid him.

—That'll take three days yet, but he'll ride as easy as a old plow horse when I'm ready.

—That wasn't what we agreed.

—We said I'd ride him. We didn't say how nor when.

—You got your three days. It looks like you might know what you're about at that.

Three days later, Frank eased himself into the saddle and signaled for Teeter to open the gate. Around the corral, hardened cowpunchers held their breath and waited for the explosion. Giddyup sauntered out through the gate, balked and crow-hopped a little when Frank tried to neck-rein him, then eased on downhill toward the creek.

Mornings, Frank was up before the bluebirds. He would roll out of the bunkhouse while the other cowpokes were still snoring, splash a little water on his face out of the stock tank, put on his hat and go to work. He found a stretch of sandy bottom off the creek bed two miles south, a perfect place to work the devilment out of a horse. He would saddle up in the half dark, fumbling under the horse's belly for the cinch, waiting for the exhale of breath that would signal the moment to pull it tight so that a tricky animal couldn't roll the saddle off his back, working the curb bit into his mouth.

That early in the morning, he had to be ready for the double-hooved kick when Giddyup lashed out with his hind legs. It was like the horse had to show he still had some devilment in him before they settled down to work. Frank would slip into the saddle and ease him out the corral gate and down toward the creek with the *whoo-whoo-awhoo* of the turtledoves the only sound. They reached the creek in time to catch the first long riff of the sunrise, rose petals of light to the northeast, stars fading, a slender moon dropping behind the ridge like a fishhook into a pond. By breakfast time Frank would have spun the horse down on his hocks until his tail swept the sand, taking him left and right and left again. He could see that Giddyup was going to be the kind of cowpony that could walk into a herd, nose out a one-horned steer, ease up to its flank and walk it right out of there, a half spin ahead every time the steer tried to bolt. Eli was paying top dollar for Frank's services but the truth was that Frank would have paid for this, a chance to work good horses alone in the morning quiet, light-stepping through the dew.

Two weeks after he started work at the Fanciful, Frank stayed out so long one morning he missed breakfast, working a chestnut stallion Eli had purchased from a rancher in Cherry County. He was still at it when the new punchers taken on for the cattle drive rode out to meet him. Wade Tourtelotte, Cletus Mooney, and Buford Brooks were green as grass but they were better company for a young man like himself than crusty old hands like Teeter and Gizzard and Lonesome Pete or that cocky little redhead, Roy Titus. Frank took the biscuits from Cletus.

—Thank you kindly. Didn't know you had it in you to be such a sweet thing.

—Aint me. You can starve, all I care. It's that Velma girl made us bring 'em out. Keeps talkin about how nobody could ride that Giddyup horse till you came along. I think she's got her mind on you ridin somethin else.

Frank wasn't amused.

—Dammit, Cletus. You're goin to get me crosswise of her old man. Now are we goin to play poker or aint we?

Buford peeled the saddle off his horse, tossed its blanket on the bunchgrass and squatted on his heels as Frank dealt a hand of seven-card stud. Frank lost a couple of hands to keep everybody happy but they were such poor poker players, sometimes he couldn't help taking their money. Cletus had dealt him a pair of aces and a pair of sevens when Wade cursed and threw down his cards.

—Uh-oh, boys. Game's over.

Eli and Teeter rode up slow. Eli dismounted, came up behind Frank.

—Frank here has a pair of aces and a pair of sevens, fellas.

Frank threw the hand down in disgust.

—You got no call to break up our game like that.

—Who was it brought playin cards onto my ranch?

—Cards belong to me. These boys brought me some biscuits and bacon cause I been out here all morning workin that stud-horse you want so bad. He don't neck-rein worth a hill of beans.

—It's daylight and it aint Sunday, so these boys got work to do.

—That's between you and these fellas. It aint none of my business how you work them, but you pay me by the horse and I will break them when I damned well please. I've been out here since before sunup, and now I'm goin to take her easy for a while.

—Son, you're as good a horseman as I've ever seen. But I run a tight outfit here. Next time you sass me like that, you'll be pickin your front teeth off the grass.

During his last cold winter in Montana, Frank had braided eight narrow strips of cowhide into a perfect lariat, pulled taut and oiled so that the loop paid out easy and held firm. The rope was so well-made he could make it sing, twirling harder for the high notes, easing up for the low notes. After supper he would linger by the corrals, watching the horses and twirling the rope around his body in a circle a dozen feet wide, tightening it until the loop was barely large enough for his shoulders, letting it out again.

After the washing up was done, Velma said she was going down to the corrals to check on Giddyup. Instead she stood in the shadows by the barn, watching Frank do rope tricks.

—You're pretty good with that lariat.

Frank laughed, spun the rope up and over his head, and dropped it around her, twirled it a dozen times to pay it out wider, then brought it up and stepped into the circle himself, drawing the loop tighter until they were standing no more than a foot apart.

—Roy Titus says you had an argument with Papa about gambling.

—Don't know if I'd call it a argument. He didn't take kindly to cardplayin.

—As far as my pa is concerned, a person is supposed to work twenty hours a day.

—He's a pistol. I heard he'd horsewhip me if he caught me lookin at one of his daughters.

—He would too. But I'm old enough to make up my own mind.

—How old is that?

—I'll be sixteen in January. How old are you?

—Goin nineteen come October.

Velma moved a little closer inside the spinning rope, put her arm around Frank's neck, drew him down to her and kissed him on the mouth. For just an instant he felt the warmth of her pressed tightly to his abdomen. He let the rope fall and reached for her waist but she was gone, skipping back to the house before he could say a word.

Eli wanted to be on the trail for the cattle drive by the first of May, but it rained hard most of that week, turning the trails to mud. Eight days passed before he came pounding on the door of the bunkhouse near three o'clock in the morning, letting the punchers know they had thirty minutes to get ready for the trail. By first light, they were moving out, the best riders up on the point with the lead steers. It was the first time Frank had seen the Paint girls working together, and it was a sight to behold, these pretty girls in their long dresses and sunbonnets spinning their cowponies on a dime, running down strays at a dead gallop, whooping and hollering like Comanches. Frank kept an eye on Velma all that first day on the trail and decided that getting any closer to her was going to be impossible: As busy as he was, Eli always had an eye on his girls. The afternoon before they were to cross the Niobrara River, however, a Brown County sheriff's deputy rode into camp to say that Eli was needed back in Ainsworth to testify at the trial of a settler accused of diverting water from his neighbors, Eli among them.

Eli left Teeter Spawn in charge of the herd with instructions not to cross the Niobrara until he returned. While the other wranglers drove the horses down to the river to drink, Velma helped Frank fashion a rope corral around the wagonwheels. Being that close to him made her feel shaky and flushed. When she handed Frank the rope, their hands brushed and he squeezed her fingers. She glanced around. There was no one watching. He was kneeling at her feet in the shade of a big cottonwood tree on the riverbank, knotting the rope, his hat in the grass. Velma felt a wild urge to tangle her fingers in that dark hair.

—I'm sorry we haven't had much chance to talk, Frank.

—I feel like we're the chickens and your old man is the chicken hawk.

—He's like that sometimes. It isn't you. He doesn't trust any boy near his daughters.

—If I had daughters as pretty as you, I'd keep watch too.

—Marguerite's the pretty one. She looks like our mother. How come you're not after her?

—Because you're pretty as a picture and you got liveliness and spunk to boot.

—Not that pretty. I can't see out of this eye and it looks funny.

—Doesn't look a bit funny to me. Just makes you prettier.

Frank made the rope secure and stood up. He was so tall, she liked it better when he was on his knees. On his feet he made her feel like she was standing under a big old tree. He brushed the back of his hand over her cheek.

—It would be nice if we could find somewhere to talk tonight.

—It would.

Frank took a long look around. Upstream from the camp, the river ran due east for a quarter mile, then took a sharp turn to the north. A clump of three cottonwoods marked the spot where the river changed direction.

—You see them cottonwoods down by the bend in the river? Why don't you meet me down there after dark?

—I don't know, Frank. I don't want Papa to chase you all the way to Montana.

—It's up to you. Soon as everybody has turned in tonight, I'll head out like I'm goin to answer a call of nature. You hear me go, you wait fifteen minutes and then you come down to them cottonwoods. I'll wait a hour. If you aint there, I'll know you're too scared of your pa.

—If you cross him, he doesn't forgive and he doesn't forget. He scares folks.

—Well, he don't scare me.

After dinner, Frank paced back and forth, restless as a coyote.

Velma avoided his gaze. She knew when it was quiet he would go down to the cottonwood grove and wait for her; whether she would go to meet him was a mystery. Finally, Buford Brooks and Wade Tourtelotte went out nighthawking and the others turned in to their bedrolls. The Paint girls slept on one side of the wagons, the men on the other. Lying on her side, Velma could see the sleeping forms of the punchers and recognize Frank's long legs when he got up and tiptoed off.

Frank waited an hour, lying on his back in the tall grass. It was a clear, moonless night, the Milky Way an endless, glowing stream, like blue-white dust shaken out of a coffee can. He had almost forgotten why he was waiting when he heard a rustle of skirts. Frank took her hand and pulled her down to him. She stretched herself out on his long body so that she could feel his heart beat through her chest and the deep rumble of his voice when he talked.

—Are you scared?

—Of what?

—Papa. Somebody catchin us.

—Not a bit.

Velma said she wasn't scared either but her heart was pounding. She had never been like this with any man or boy, let alone a fellow as powerfully handsome as Frank, this long, tall mystery who came into her life on a big black horse.

—Tell me where you come from, Mr. Frank Hughes.

—Montana.

—I know that, silly. Montana where?

—Place called Alder Gulch. There's a mine there. My pa's a miner from Wales.

—That's funny. Our people are Welsh too. Well, except for the Lakota part. Ezekiel Paint, that was our ancestor. He came to Boston from Wales. He was in the American Revolution. Papa is very proud of that, because he says the Paints helped to create this country.

To stop her nerves, Velma covered his mouth with hers. She held it a long time, pressing her lips against his, not quite knowing what else to do. Then his tongue slipped between her lips and she opened her mouth a little and that was a whole lot better. She could feel him swelling against her, his pelvis starting to rock a little, his hands straying down where they oughtn't to be. She rolled off him and got to her feet.

—I'd best be gettin back before somebody notices I'm gone.

She vanished into the darkness. Frank shrugged and unbuttoned his jeans. If she wouldn't stick around, then there was a thing he would have to do for himself.

The next night they were back in the cottonwoods and the night after that. The second night they kissed for more than an hour and she let Frank slip a finger inside her. He coaxed and coaxed but she wouldn't let him do more. The third night she gave in. He had been touching her, had somehow unbuttoned her so that her breasts were free in the cool night air and then all her underthings were off and his fingers were stirring inside her and his tongue was in her mouth. She could see the long river of stars and hear a hoot owl somewhere and she wanted him as she had never wanted a solitary thing in her life. She reached down for him and felt it rigid, the heat surprising to her, her legs open and her hips tilting to him, whispering "Frank Frank Frank oh Frank" as his hands found all the right places. Then there was a small, sharp jab of pain and he was inside, the shock of his bare belly against hers and his wispy beard soft on her neck. She felt a long trembling come up from his strong legs and it was over.

She'd barely had time to catch her breath when he took her again, this time standing with her face brushing the bark of the cottonwood tree and Frank behind her, her legs shaking so that she thought they would give way as something long and deep and slow happened inside her. She pushed her hips back into him, breathed the spring air, felt his strong hands on her breasts.

❧ CHAPTER 37 ❧

On a chilly October morning, Velma woke feeling poorly. After breakfast, she went out back of the house and vomited until her legs shook and her eyes watered. Within an hour she was feeling steady enough to help around the house but she missed school that day and the next day and the day after. After eight days of morning sickness, she could hide it no longer. Roy Titus saw her throwing up behind the house two days in a row and said something to Eli and Eli, grim as winter, marched Velma to the buggy the next morning and drove her to Doc Remy's office. The ride took more than an hour and neither spoke a word the entire way. Twice, Velma had to ask her father to stop the buggy so she could be sick again. They had to wait nearly an hour while the doctor dealt with Alda Beechley, who was complaining of lumbago, arthritis, varicose veins, shingles, and piles in a voice that carried through the thin walls. Velma stared at her feet. Eli stood at the window, staring out at Main Street. All Velma could hear was the ticking of Doc Remy's grandfather clock and Alda's whiny voice going on and on. It was the longest hour of her life.

When the Beechley woman finally bustled out of the office clutching a bag of potions including blue vitriol, balsam copaiba, and tincture of iron, Eli went outside for some air. Velma removed her clothing behind a screen, donned a gown for modesty and slipped onto a narrow bed that served as the doctor's examining table. In her mind, she tried to take herself as far away from that bed and that room as she could. She imagined herself reading a book to Livvy, her mother's face beautiful and attentive by the light of a kerosene lamp. Far away, something metallic entered her body. Doc Remy clucked and hummed to himself. Finally he told her to get dressed, stepped into the anteroom and closed the door. While she was dressing, she heard him speaking to Eli in low tones. Velma wished she could just curl up on the rag rug and die. Anything but this, something strange and unwelcome growing inside her, her father's anger like the shadow of an approaching storm. When Doc Remy returned, she heard his words as though they were coming from somewhere off in the distance.

—I'm sorry to have to tell you this but you are going to have a baby, Velma. Your father has given me to understand that is not joyous news. The only thing I can help you with is your health. Near as I can tell, you will give birth in June. You're a healthy girl and you should be fine, but if you see anything unusual, especially any unusual bleeding, you get someone to bring you back to me.

Velma nodded. Doc Remy helped her up and she walked out into brilliant sunshine in a stupor. Eli strode to the buggy without looking back, uncoiled the reins from the brake lever and popped the buggy whip without saying a word or even looking to see if Velma had settled herself beside him. They rode nearly a mile with no sound other than the rattle of the trace chains and the thud of the horse's hooves before he spoke.

—I want his name.

At the sound of her father's voice, Velma began to weep, long, shuddering sobs shaking her body so that it was impossible to speak.

—I want his name.

Velma took a long breath.

—If I tell you, you'll kill him.

—You are fifteen years old and you did not get in this condition all by yourself.

Velma buried her face in her hands. Her shoulders shook with sobs but Eli couldn't get her to say another word. When they were home, Eli sent Ruby to fetch Tavie.

Tavie was now almost as tall as Eli himself, a wide-shouldered, confident cowgirl. She had already guessed at Velma's condition and she had a pretty good notion as to who was to blame.

Eli came straight to the point.

—Your sister has got herself in a family way. Now there's got to be a man involved and she won't tell me who he is, but I expect you know.

—I might. It would have to be Frank Hughes. Never saw her talking to anybody else much, except Teeter.

Eli nodded. Going over the hands in his mind, he had reached the same conclusion: It could not be anyone but the broncobuster. Eli found Frank working a filly in the corral.

—You turn that horse loose and come with me, son. We got to have ourselves a talk.

Frank thought maybe Eli wanted to talk about the horses. He was almost finished breaking the new stock; maybe Eli didn't want to keep him on for the winter, which suited Frank just fine. He had been thinking it was time to ride west to Wyoming, get a look at some new country. He took the hackamore off the filly and followed Eli to the stock tank, where Eli perched on the edge, staring off toward the ridge where he had buried a wife and a son.

—Doc Remy says somebody has been foolin with my girl Velma, and Tavie says that somebody would be you.

Frank started to protest but Eli held up a hand. He spoke so softly Frank had to lean forward to hear.

—Don't you deny it, because that's only going to make it worse. Now here's what's going to happen. As soon as I can fix things with the Reverend Cubbin at the First Congregational Church, you'll marry the girl. Once that's done, I'll give you a springwagon of supplies and a team to pull it. You can pick one milk cow and take that big Hampshire sow and a brace of chickens. I've got deed to one hundred and sixty acres just east of a wide spot in the road called Enterprise over in Keya Paha County, the other side of the Niobrara. There's already a house on it, so you have a sight more than I had when we started here. Once you get there, you and the girl are on your own and I'm shed of the pair of you. All you got to do now is nod to show you understand what I'm sayin here.

All Frank wanted was to be astride that big black horse on his way to Wyoming or California or just about anywhere that wasn't Brown County, Nebraska, but there was no way to run from a man as powerful as Eli Paint. He nodded.

Late that afternoon, Tavie found Velma curled up in the hayloft in the barn. Velma wasn't crying; she was empty and silent and spent. Tavie sprawled in the hay next to her sister and stroked her hair.

—It was Frank, wasn't it?

Velma nodded.

—I thought you had better sense, girl, but it makes no difference to me. You're still my sister and I'll stick by you. We all will. You know that much.

Velma didn't answer. The only thing she could imagine at the moment was a little soddy set in an endless stretch of flat, empty prairie, a barren world waiting for the life inside her.

—Did you talk to Frank yet?

—Not yet.

—He's a good man.

—I suppose he is. I don't want a man, though. Not yet.

—You should of thought of that before. Whatever are you going to do, little sister?

—I have no idea. I guess that's Frank's lookout now. I'll have to go where Papa says. He says he's giving us that old homestead in Keya Paha County, so that's where we'll be.

—Aint nothin there but an old run-down soddy and a hundred and sixty acres of nothin.

—Be as may, I guess beggars can't be choosers.

Velma wasn't angry with Eli or Frank, she was angry with herself. This slender body had betrayed her, first with the force of her lust for Frank and then by getting her with child. Now she was being cast out of the only home she had ever known.

—You'll come to visit me and Frank sometimes?

—Papa will change his mind. I'll talk to him. He'll change his mind.

—He won't. Not ever. Papa's like a river. Once he gets to flowing one direction, he won't change for anything. Not even you. He's more stubborn than the most stubborn Missouri mule.

—Mama could get him to change his mind. Only person who ever could.

—She could but she's gone. There's just us and now I'm going to have to go off with Frank and try to raise a baby. I won't be sixteen until January and I'm scared about half to death.

Tavie wrapped strong arms around her, pulled Velma into her bosom.

—Oh, my sweet little sister. There was nothing I could do about Frank. He just came along spinning that rope and riding that big black horse and stole you away, didn't he?

—I guess that's about it. I'm so ashamed of myself.

At the supper table, Marguerite, Ruby, and Kate sat with their heads down. After Eli said grace, not another word was spoken until Tavie came striding in from the barn. She had long since begun defying her father's edict that the girls were to wear nothing but dresses; she wore a man's trousers and a work shirt and vest and she still had her spurs on. She took her seat opposite Eli and stabbed three pork chops before she swept off her hat and set it down beside her plate. She ate two of them with a mound of mashed potatoes before she spoke.

—Papa, it's not right what you're doing to Velma. She made a mistake but that's no reason to run her off.

—It aint what I'm doin to her. It's what she done to herself.

—She isn't even sixteen years old yet. You can't send her off to live in a soddy.

—Your mama wasn't much older when we started here and we had to build our own house. Velma made her own choice, now she's got to live with it.

—You can't treat her like a dog. Velma has worked hard as any of us to take care of this home and to help build up this ranch. She even lost an eye when we chased down those wild horses. It's not fair to her, no matter what she did.

—All right, girl, I've heard enough. You spoke your piece, now that's an end to it. I expect you all to be there Sunday to see her lawfully wed to that saddle tramp Frank. After that, I don't want to hear your sister's name in my house again. Far as I'm concerned, it's like she never was born.

Tavie slammed down her knife and stormed out. A minute or two later, the others heard her horse as she cantered off toward the creek. Eli let her go: She would come back when she was good and ready. While the other girls did the washing up, Eli retreated to the bench outside the front door, where he kept a half dozen lengths of rope to help with his figuring. He sat there until long after dark, toying with the ropes, tying one knot after another. He tied the same knot over and over without thinking, his mind far away.

This was a day as bitter as any since the day Livvy died, taking the best part of him with her to that grave up on the hill. Of all his children, Velma was his favorite. Now she was gone to a no-account bronc rider whose one good quality in life was that he could handle a horse, and Eli could no more alter the course of things than he could fly pigs to market. It had taken a will as tough as blackroot to survive here, and now he was hogtied by the same bullheaded determination that had carved a thriving ranch out of this wild prairie. He might have been too harsh on the girl, but to go back now would be a sign of weakness. He was trapped as much as she was.

Astride that bench in the October dark, Eli Paint allowed himself no pity. After he had run through every knot he knew a dozen times, he tied a hangman's knot in a ten-foot length of worn raw-hide rope and left it dangling off a peg beside the front door, a noose in search of a customer. One of the dogs started barking at the clouds, a thin moon straggled into the sky, the wind out of the Dakotas carried a hint of winter. Eli felt a new stiffness in a leg broken by a horse's kick ten years before. If a man lived long enough, his life came to taste like Russian thistle.

CHAPTER 38

Frank Hughes and Velma Paint were married in Ainsworth on the sixteenth day of October 1909. Eli stood at the church door in case Frank got notions of backing out. Wade Tourtelotte stood up for Frank, and Tavie was at Velma's side. Reverend Cubbin was older and wiser, and he had no illusions about how difficult these young lives would be.

—Do you, Velma Paint, take this man . . .

She did, but later she could not recall: Had she kissed Frank? Had he kissed her? Did they sign something? Velma had Tavie ask Eli if she could have her dead mother's opal necklace, but Eli refused. There would be no gesture of kindness or sentiment from him to bless this marriage; Livvy's ring would go to the first of his daughters to marry with Eli's approval. Through it all, Velma was aware of Eli looking on like someone observing the wedding of a stranger. She wanted to go to him, put her arms around him, beg his forgiveness. Wipe away this thing that had come between them, change the set of his jaw, the tightly pressed lips, release the tension coiled in those powerful shoulders. She knew better, though. To anyone acquainted with Eli Paint, the warning was plain as the rattle on a snake: Don't tread on me. Instead, Velma turned away, took Frank's arm and strolled from the church with her head held high.

Frank had collected his pay in full up to the day Doc Remy

confirmed that Velma was carrying his child. He entered the state of holy matrimony with nearly two hundred dollars to his name, minus the fifty-eight dollars he insisted on paying Eli for the pregnant Hampshire sow, a Guernsey milk cow, a dozen Plymouth Rock hens, and a rooster that tended to crow at midnight. After the wedding, Frank and Velma left the church for their new home with Teeter's team pulling the wagon. Velma drove the horses while Frank rode alongside on his black horse. The milk cow was tied to the back alongside Frank's pack mule and Giddyup, who kept trying to kick the mule until Frank solved the problem by tying the milk cow between them. The sow was too big for the wagon, so Frank drove her on ahead, swearing that this was the one time in his life he would be caught herding a hog on horseback. The chickens were loaded in a crate on the wagon with an old set of dishes, spoons, forks, and knives enough for two. Velma had three dresses: the good dress she wore for her wedding, a calico riding dress, and an everyday muslin dress for housework or mucking out the corrals. There were two kerosene lanterns with a ten-gallon jar of kerosene, two gunnysacks of coal for the stove, a hundred pounds of potatoes, a fifty-pound bag of cornmeal, a hundred-pound bag of flour, a hundred pounds of chicken mash, twenty pounds of coffee beans, baking powder, a basket of maple sugar, a jug of molasses, a bucket of hulled corn hominy, sorghum, canned beans and tomatoes, a box of soda crackers, a dozen jars of plum jam, a hammer and saw and a bucket of penny nails, horseshoe nails and a come-along for stringing bobwire fence, a shovel and a pitchfork. There was a milk can and the old wooden cradle that had rocked Livvy's seven children.

After a summer without rain, the Niobrara was all but dry at the ford where they crossed. Because the Hampshire sow slowed them down, they had to camp overnight on the north side of the river, kept warm by a moldy old buffalo robe. The next day they followed Eli's directions north and east for half a day in bright October sunshine to a spot a mile south of the Keya Paha River and a mile west of the town of Enterprise, where Velma halted the team at a woebegone little soddy. It was ten feet by twelve, the minimum a man needed to prove out a homestead claim, and barely seven feet high. There was a single window covered with grease paper instead of glass and a wobbly door that collapsed in a cloud of dust when Frank tried to open the latch. Out back there was an outhouse with half the boards missing, a tumbledown corral missing a rail here and there, a henhouse with the roof fallen in and a rootcellar overgrown with weeds.

Velma sat in the wagon, reluctant to take a step toward the place. She felt the weight of it then, the weight of exile from the Fanciful and the only home she had ever known, marriage to a man she barely knew, this awful little house, the months and years of labor that would be needed if they were to survive here. A pair of sandhill cranes flapped south toward the Niobrara, their long, graceful wings stroking the air. She wanted to fly south with them, all the way back to the Fanciful.

Frank carried Velma to the door of the cabin. He had no sooner put a toe into the soddy than the wings of something small and frantic brushed her face. She thought it was a bat but Frank pointed to a stick-and-mud nest like a beehive on the windowsill; swallows had made the cabin their home. As their eyes adjusted to the darkness, they could make out the jumble of old furniture left behind by the original homesteader. A couple of chairs, a rickety table, a tumbledown cabinet, a rusty potbellied stove in the corner farthest from the door with the stovepipe collapsed beside it.

Frank took another step, still carrying Velma, and froze. The sound was unmistakable, the buzz of a rattlesnake. He carried her back outside and set her down a safe distance from the house, dug the shovel out of the wagon, dumped the potatoes out of one of the gunnysacks, and wrapped the sack around his left hand, hoping to lure the snake into striking at his hand so he could pin it with the spade. When he took another cautious step the rattler buzzed again, too close for comfort. Then there was another rattle off to the left. Two snakes, maybe more. One of the rattlers, Frank was pretty sure, was behind that stove. The other was a lot closer, off to his right. He took a step and then a second step and the rattler struck once and then again without coiling to strike. Frank felt the surprisingly powerful strike of the fangs on the toe of his boot and brought the shovel down hard, but the snake had already pulled back. The second strike hit the back of the spade, a metallic thud in the dim light. Now Frank could see the diamondback pattern of the biggest rattler he had ever encountered in his life. When it struck a third time he waited until it was fully extended and brought the point of the shovel down just behind its head and jumped back. The blow cut the snake in two. The rattle buzzed wildly as the body flapped and writhed. The fangs closed a half dozen times in the severed head before the snake was still.

Frank took a deep breath. He could hear his heart pounding as he moved back toward the stove. The second rattler buzzed a warning; it was in the shadows behind the stove. He held out the hand wrapped in the gunnysack, waved it back and forth a few inches above the ground. The snake went for it, a strike so quick he had no time to react. If not for the gunnysack, the fangs would have been buried deep in his wrist. Frank swung the spade a half dozen times. Hit, miss, hit, miss. The snake rolled toward his boots and he caught it one last time, right between the eyes, then drew back, panting and fighting the urge to vomit. At last he tiptoed cautiously around the cabin, sweeping back and forth with the spade. There seemed to be no more rattlers, although he would want to poke into every corner of the room to be sure before they moved in.

Velma watched from the wagon as Frank shoveled pieces of snake out the door.

—I hate rattlesnakes, Frank. I hate them. What are they doing in my house?

—Aint been nobody here for a long time. I guess they figure it belongs to them.

Velma had held it in for too long. Through that long buggy ride to Doc Remy's office and back with Eli. Through the night when he said that she would be marrying Frank and that she would be turned out of his home. Through the tense, wearying days getting ready for the wedding, seeing Frank only at a distance, feeling they were both sheep being led to the slaughter. Through the whispered conversations with her sisters, when they all promised to stick by her and do everything they could to persuade Eli to change his mind. She had borne up well through all of it, but this squalid little house and the rattlesnakes inside it were more than she could bear. She sat right down on the prairie and bawled and Frank could not get her to stop. She wrapped her arms around his knees and would not let go. Frank stood feeling helpless. She kept a death grip on his legs but her sobs subsided. Finally she wiped her eyes on his pants and reached up for him to lift her off the ground. When she was on her feet, she threw one arm around his neck and kissed him so hard his lower lip bled. When she stepped back, he could see Velma had made up her mind.

—All right, we'll have to make the best of it. But I am not sleeping in that house tonight. We'll sleep in the wagon, and to-morrow we'll clean that soddy out to make a decent place for you and me and the baby. Winter is coming quick, so we don't have much time. It's going to be hard but we can do it if we stick by each other. Are we going to stick by each other, Frank?

—You know we are, Velma. We aint got nobody else, now do we? It's just us two and that baby.

It was almost dark by the time they finished unloading the wagon. Velma refused to sleep in the house, so they slept in the wagon. Frank managed to get a campfire going so they could warm the ham and corncakes Velma had brought from the Fanciful. They washed it down with fresh water hauled in pails from the creek and made a reasonably comfortable bed in the wagon. In the darkness, she pulled off her dress and crawled in next to Frank in her petticoats. Velma adjusted her clothes, opened herself for Frank and held tight to his neck, watching the stars, feeling nothing at all except that she was a woman doing her duty to her husband. When it was over, they fell asleep with him still atop her, man and wife.

• • •

The sky said winter was coming fast: mallards and Canadian geese flying south, the pale blue of summer deepening as the air cooled, the rush of cottonwood leaves blown by a wind with real bite in it. Velma could not imagine spending a Nebraska winter in this place, but they had no choice. They worked hard to ready the gloomy, drafty cabin for winter. Velma filled the chinks in the walls with mud and straw, Frank repaired the door with a new wooden frame and metal hinges and drove the wagon all the way to Ainsworth for a real glass window. Velma spent a week scraping down the walls with the edge of the spade before whitewashing them with calcimine to brighten the place. Frank bought a wagonload of straw off a dryland farmer and Velma used some of it to fill their mattress tick. The roof leaked and needed stabilizing; the forked poles at either end of the cabin that held the ridgepole aloft needed reinforcing, and some of the old boards that held up the sod roof were on the verge of tumbling into the cabin itself. Frank strengthened them all and sealed the spaces between the rectangles of turf with wet clay.

Tavie, Marguerite, Ruby, and Kate rode up from the Fanciful every Sunday, bringing things from the big house to make the soddy feel more like home: a hook rug, cushions and doilies, pictures cut out of magazines for the walls, a rag doll for the baby. Velma enjoyed their visits, but when they left she felt more desolate than ever. Shortly after Thanksgiving her sisters braved the winter's first snow to bring the news: Eli had gone off to Denver on a cattle-buying expedition and returned with a wife, a broad-backed, no-nonsense woman named Ida Mae Pugsley, who had taken over the kitchen and begun bossing everyone around.

Tavie had taken a powerful dislike to the woman at first sight; the younger girls were inclined to be more charitable. Velma could not imagine why, after so many years without a wife, Eli had suddenly decided that he needed a woman in the house, especially if the description she got from her sisters was accurate. To them, Ida Mae was like a porcupine, except that her manner was rather more fierce. At least she could cook, which was a blessing because all the Paint girls agreed that a decent meal had not been served at the Fanciful since Velma left. More than anything else that happened after the move to the Keya Paha, Eli's marriage made Velma feel that she was truly exiled from the Fanciful. Every time the other girls stopped by with more complaints about Ida Mae, Velma laughed with the rest, but when they were gone, she felt more desolate than ever. This Ida Mae woman was cooking in her kitchen, she had replaced Livvy in Eli's affections, she was attempting to be a strict mother with the younger girls, and Eli had not even seen fit to inform Velma of his marriage. Obviously, he meant it when he said that she was to move in with Frank in the soddy and that he was shed of the both of them forever. Tavie still held out hope, but Velma knew there was no chance Eli would invite her back. Her life with Frank was her future now, and she would have to make the best of it.

The snow that winter started in late October and didn't let up, forcing ranchers to dip into their hay stocks six weeks earlier than usual. In mid-December, Frank came in from doing the morning chores to say that it had turned bitterly cold. The sky was gray, and the wind kept picking up. Around noon, Velma saw the first hard little pellets of snow outside the window. Within an hour she couldn't see as far as the corral. When Frank tried to go back out to check on the livestock, he found the door already blocked with a heavy drift and had to shovel his way out with the scoop they used to clean ashes out of the stove. When he made it back, his mustache was iced with snow, his eyes almost frozen shut. He was wet through. Velma peeled his shirt and undershirt off and hung them to dry, then helped tug off his wet boots, his socks, his pants and long johns. He stood naked in front of her, shivering, his back to the stove. Velma thought of a faster way to warm him. She stripped off quickly, guided him to the straw tick, pulled the quilt over both of them and straddled him, pressing her breasts to his chest, covering his neck with kisses, feeling his cold body tremble as nature took over and he slipped inside her. When it was over, she held him, feeding her breasts into his mouth as though he were the baby.

—I was scared. I was afraid you weren't coming back.

—That'll never happen. No matter where I go, I'll always come back.

It was three days before the storm let up enough to allow Frank to shovel paths from the house to the corral. Velma baked pies, sewed things for the baby, and mended some of Frank's clothing. While she worked, Frank paced from the window to the door, restless and impatient for the storm to end. With no other outlet for his energy, he kept dragging her back under the quilt or taking her bent over the table or up against a wall.

Cooped up in the soddy day after day, he became more talkative. For the first time, he told her about his life in Montana, about his father and the way he would get drunk and beat Frank and his mother.

—That must have been awful.

—It was. I knew one day I'd be strong enough to handle him. When I was, I beat the hell out of him and then I left. Told him if he ever touched her again I'd kill him.

—Did you ever go back?

—Nope. But I got a letter from Ma when I was workin up on the Powder River. She said he stopped beatin on her, but that was only because he got religion and quit drinkin.

Velma listened for a moment to the wind howling outside.

—Frank, does it bother you that we don't get to church?

—Tell the truth, I never thought about it.

—Do you want our baby brought up religious?

—That's what you do with kids, aint it? Teach 'em right from wrong?

—Is that what you learn in church? How to tell right from wrong? Some of the worst people I know are church folk and some of the best are like Teeter Spawn. He only gets dragged to church for weddings and funerals but Teeter does right by folks. That's more important than going to church, isn't it?

—I don't know. What's the point of church if you don't learn right from wrong?

—That's what I'm asking. Do you believe in God?

—Whoa, girl! You're gettin all serious on me here.

Frank was laughing. Velma was still on top of him, straddling his thigh, wet from both of them. It struck him as a funny time to be talking religion. She gave him a light peck on the mouth to stop him giggling and nibbled his lower lip.

—I just want to know what you think, is all.

Frank paused, stroking her hair. The wind was louder than ever; he felt enormous pity for the livestock out on the prairie, especially the horses, but there was nothing he could do for them now. There would be animals that would not survive this storm.

—When I was a kid, we had a sky pilot come round to do his revival meetin twice a year. All fire and brimstone, whoopin and hollerin and tellin us the devil would get us if we didn't put something in the offer bowl to save our souls. He used to scare hell outa me. Must a scared everybody else too, because them poor miners would dig deep to give the preacher money they didn't have. But when I got a little older, I start wonderin about this hell the preacher was always ravin about. Where was it? I'd been way down in the mines, and my pa had been down a lot farther than me, and we never ran into no devil, so hell must be awful deep. Anyway, one night I got to the tent meetin late, because I was workin a horse over in the next county. I could hear the choir singin gospel music, so I tied my pony on the far side of the preacher's wagon, one of those big, closed-in things all painted fancy to tell you who he was, with words from scripture writ all over it. I remember he had John 3:16 on one side. I was walkin toward the tent when I saw the wagon was movin funny like, so I went to check what was wrong. The back door was open and there was a coal-oil lamp inside, and here was the preacher with a bottle of liquor in one hand. He had Mizz Keppler, the big old wife of the mine foreman, bent over with her skirts up around her neck. She was moanin and he was huffin and puffin, and they was both goin so hard that whole wagon was shakin. It was about the funniest sight I ever seen, but that pretty well done it with religion for me. Here he was tellin us every night about the devil snaggin our souls, and it looked to me like the devil already had that preacher's soul, lock, stock and barrel. I aint sayin all preachers are bad. Some is and some aint, I expect, but that makes 'em pretty much like the rest of us. Some of your preachers, it might do 'em good to go out workin a horse in the mornin. I get out there and watch the sun come up, hear the meadowlarks out on the prairie, it makes you feel all— well, I can't exactly say what it makes you feel, but it's somethin a preacher could use.

—You mean it makes you feel humble?

—That's it. Humble. I aint met many humble preachers, although that little Cubbin fella that married us wasn't too bad.

Velma tried to get him to say more. It was the first time she had been able to get Frank talking, and she didn't want him to stop.

—So you don't believe in God?

—I wouldn't say that. If you've ever camped out on the prairie, you've got to believe in somethin. Up in Montana, I slept one night under this big old cottonwood out in the middle of nowhere, the only tree you could see for twenty miles in any direction. There were a million stars at first, and then the moon came floatin up. There was a little breeze in that tree, just rustlin the leaves a bit. I laid there awake the longest time, lookin at that tree and them stars and the moon and the wind and all, and I thought, That's where God is, whatever He is. In that cottonwood. Almost like you could reach out and touch Him, a living thing right close by in the tree and far off in the Big Dipper all at the same time, if you catch my drift.

—I know what you mean about somethin out there you don't quite see, how it could be up in the Big Dipper and in that old cottonwood all at once. I tried to tell my uncle Ezra about it once, about things that are just outside where you can look at them straight on. I saw it one morning when I was a kid, out in the wheat stubble. It was cloudy and then the sun broke through, and the light was bouncing through the stubble, almost like the wind was blowing it. Then the clouds came again and the light was gone. I sat there a long time almost freezing to death, waiting for it to come back. It never did, but I always thought that was God, a ball of light bouncing over the wheatfield.

Frank didn't say anything. Velma was grateful he hadn't laughed. She shifted her weight a little and reached down for him and the second her fingers were on him, he began to stir like he always did and she shifted again and took him inside and rocked back and forth on him the way you would rock a baby. Something about the wind howling outside made it better, the two of them snug in this little world, like they weren't living in the loneliest cabin in the sandhills anymore because they were all tangled up together so you couldn't tell where one left off and the other started.

The fourth day after the storm began dawned with snowblinding brilliance, the sun ricocheting off an endless white curve of drifts in every direction, fenceposts and landmarks all lost. Velma and Frank emerged lightdazzled, opened the door and poked their heads out like curious prairie dogs, peering over the snowbanks at a world gone white. Velma felt a bit dazed and resentful because the sunshine had dissolved their little cocoon. The days when they were snowed in had a sweetness to them that made her believe she and Frank could make a go of it on their little parcel of this earth. Most of what she would ever know about him she learned during that blizzard. When the snowstorm ended, he clammed up and stayed that way, as though he thought talk would waste his soul.

On Christmas Day, Tavie turned up with Maggie and Kate, apologizing because Ruby was in bed with the flu. She brought a warm jacket she had sewn for Velma and a knit wool hat for Frank: The girls stayed only two hours because they wanted to get back to the Fanciful before dark. Velma had hoped that Eli would send word inviting them to the big house for Christmas dinner but he did not. She killed and plucked one of the hens and made a roast chicken instead. The chicken was cooked dry because it was almost impossible to regulate the heat on a cookstove fueled with corncobs, but Frank liked it well enough and sat back after he had finished, cracking the bones to suck the marrow and then using the splintered ends to pick his teeth. That started the worst fight they had that winter.

—You have the manners of a starving coyote. We have tooth-picks, you know.

Frank looked at her and kept picking his teeth with the bit of bone.

—You want a toothpick, use a toothpick. I find a chicken bone works better.

—It isn't polite.

—It aint polite? You got me stuck in a sod house in the damned middle of nowhere and you're goin to worry at me over what's polite and what aint?

—It's not good manners to pick your teeth with chicken bones. Just because we found ourselves in a difficult position doesn't mean we oughtn't to mind our manners.

—Why? For your father? So he'll be civil to us again?

—This doesn't have a thing to do with Eli. If you get invited to Sunday dinner at a nice home, are you going to pick your teeth with a chicken bone?

—Maybe I would and maybe I wouldn't. As long as there aint nobody here but us, I'll pick my teeth with a chicken bone any time I please.

—Not if I have to look at it, you won't. If you do, I won't roast any more chickens.

—Well, starve then and see if I give a damn.

He got up and pulled on his coat and boots and started out-side.

—Where are you going at this time of night?

—Check on the livestock.

He slammed the door. Ten minutes later, Velma heard him riding off. She wanted to run after him, but she was too stubborn to make a fool of herself. She did the washing up and tried to sew. At every sound she jumped, sure it was either Frank coming back or wolves at the door. It was nearly midnight when she gave up and went to bed. She dozed on and off but couldn't fall asleep because it felt like her spine was tied in knots. She wanted to have him back so she could tell him that he could pick his teeth any way he pleased, as long as he promised never again to abandon her. Around sunup she started to worry about what she would do if he never did come back. He had ridden out in darkness and bitter cold; it was possible he had frozen to death, leaving her alone with a baby on the way. Or maybe he would just keep going, back to Dakota or Montana or anywhere he pleased. Around noon, Frank came striding into the cabin without taking his boots off, tracking snow all over, not saying a word about where he'd been or where he'd slept during a cold winter night in the sandhills. He sat at the table and waited.

—I'm hungry, woman. Get some feed on the table.

It went against her grain to let herself be ordered around. She had coffee boiling on the stove. It would be the easiest thing in the world to throw the pot in his face, and if it blinded him it was no more than he deserved—but she couldn't bear another night without him. With her back to him to hide her fury, she warmed some of the chicken and potatoes and poured him a cup of coffee. Frank ate without saying a word and went out again but this time she could hear him outside, whistling while he fed the livestock. Inside her, she felt the baby move.

They didn't fight again that winter, but they didn't talk much either. When her sixteenth birthday came in January, Velma didn't even mention it because she didn't want Frank to feel like he had to make a fuss over her. That day she felt as blue as she had the day Eli dragged her in to see Doc Remy. It was no way for a girl to turn sweet sixteen, alone most of the day and night with no sound but the wind, scrimping on the portions she dished up for herself because they had barely enough provisions in the rootcellar to last them until spring.

The mule and all but one of the hens died in a cold snap in February, when the thermometer went down to thirty below and stuck. It was worst on days when the wind picked up, finding every crack in the soddy, turning their breath to ice. The sky held clear but what light they got was thin as a scarecrow, filtered through blowing snow. Frank, muttering through blue lips, said a sun like that was no more use than tits on a boar. Even with the stove going day and night they could not keep warm; the air within five feet of the stove was so hot they could hardly breathe but the walls on the far side of the soddy were still covered with frost. The only thing to do at night was to throw every bit of clothing they owned atop the quilt, strip down and crawl underneath and let their combined body heat work like an oven.

After the cold snap, Frank got steady work skinning dead cattle all over Keya Paha County for fifty cents a hide. He did the work with a hunting knife, his fingers stiff from the cold, searching for cattle whose death was recent enough that he could jam his hands into the warm intestines to stave off frostbite. Once the cutting was done, he would work metal hooks attached to leather straps through the hide, tie the straps to the saddlehorn, dig the spurs into his horse and pull, the half frozen hides making an awful ripping sound that echoed over the snowbanks. There were so many dead cattle that winter that the hides piled at the railhead for shipment to the shoe factories back East were higher than a man's head. Frank hated the work, hated the death all around him, hated using a good saddlehorse to tear the hide off another animal. Most of all he hated Eli Paint, because the way he saw it, Eli had put him in this mess. They ought to be welcome at the big house, Velma carrying Eli's grandchild, Frank working Eli's horses, sharing the bounty of the Fanciful—but Eli had made it plain they were as welcome as an alkali well. Frank was sure they would have a difficult spring. He couldn't work Eli's horses, and the other ranchers had lost as much as half their stock. Ranchers were going to hang on hoping for a better year, and a broncobuster would be a luxury most of them couldn't afford.

When Frank was away skinning hides, it was the quiet that bothered Velma most, because the only sounds day and night were the pop and sizzle of the fire and the howl of the wind outside. The only change in her routine came when her sisters visited on Sunday afternoons if the roads were open. Maggie kept bragging about the new Edison phonograph Eli had ordered at the big house and all the wax records they could play, more music than you could listen to in a week. Saturday nights, settlers were coming from as far as twenty miles away just to listen to the phonograph and dance. Hearing about the music and the dances made Velma feel more desolate than ever: If the silence began to gnaw at her, she would sing gospel music and spirituals. When Frank was restless and moody, her singing seemed to soothe him. He never asked her to sing, but when she did he would stop pacing the house like a restless coyote and sit and toy with her hair or stretch out on the bed with his head in her lap.

In March the weather began to turn. There was a hot day when they woke to the sound of the spring runoff, the sun beating down on the snow, the sound of water trickling everywhere. They had survived a winter on the Keya Paha. It was a beginning.

⊰ CHAPTER 39 ⊱

Frank was the first to spot the lone rider more than a mile away on the prairie to the north. One man, two pack mules, and a half dozen saddlehorses coming straight for their homestead. He threw a saddle on the black and rode out at an easy lope. Velma watched Frank shake hands with the rider, who looked vaguely familiar, although at that distance she couldn't tell who it was. It was a little past noon and she had a bit of stew on the stove, so she sliced in more carrots and onions and turnips and waited for them to work their way down the long slope to the house. In the pasture to the north Frank and the other rider dismounted and Velma saw they were putting rope hobbles on the spare horses, a sign the stranger meant to stay a while. It was a brilliant May day, so she stepped outside and waited for them. They were still two hundred yards off when she recognized the visitor; if she hadn't been heavy with child, she would have run out to greet him.

—Uncle Ezra!

The little chestnut horse broke into a canter. As he turned in front of the house, Ezra dropped the reins and swung out of the saddle.

—Aint you the little beauty! A little beauty about to have a little beauty.

Frank led the chestnut and the black to the corral while Velma stood chatting with her uncle, trying to shake the odd feeling that she was really talking to her father, they looked so exactly alike.

—What are you doing here, Uncle Ezra? I thought you were in Montana. I wrote you about marrying Frank and all but I never heard back. I wasn't sure you got my letter.

—Well, I aint much for writin, honey. I was married for a time to a Blackfoot woman but she died last fall. We didn't have any kids and I got tired bein way off in Montana with my people down here, so I'm headed back to Brown County. Aim to settle down for a time, take a piece of the Fanciful where I can raise horses. Don't have any interest in the cattle business but horses are another matter.

—Does Daddy know you're coming?

—Naw. We don't write much and I wasn't goin to send a telegram. He's kept a piece of the ranch for me all the while I been gone, says all I have to do is put up a house. I aint ambitious and I aint lookin to own half of Nebraska. Raise a few horses, you don't have the worries Eli has, about the drouth, calves got the scours, the price of beef and wheat, whether the new bull is any good, whether the cowhands you hired are rustlin cattle on the side. A man like my brother, he can drive himself like that and never stop to breathe. I aint made that way.

Velma laughed. For the rest of the afternoon, she and Frank listened to Ezra's stories. When Frank went out to do the evening chores, Ezra lingered to talk with Velma.

—Honey, I'm ridin on to the ranch tomorrow. I don't know if it will do any good but I'm goin to speak with my brother, see if I can't do somethin about all this.

—All what?

—Him bootin you off the ranch and all. Tavie wrote to me once or twice, said I ought to write him a letter, persuade Eli he ought to take you back. I thought it would do more good if I talk to him man-to-man.

Velma felt her baby move and cradled her belly in her palms.

—It's sweet of you to offer, Uncle Ez, but I don't think it's going to do any good. His mind was made up as soon as he knew I was in the family way. You know how stubborn he is: I don't want him getting mad at you because you're taking my side.

—That part is my lookout. Wouldn't be the first time Eli was mad at me, and it likely won't be the last. God, how we used to fight, go at it the whole afternoon. Both of us tryin to get the upper hand and nobody wantin to quit.

—Have you ever once known him to change his mind?

—Not that I can recall, but it aint right, you bringin up this baby way off here when your daddy is one of the richest men in Brown County. I'd like to take a whip to Frank myself for gettin you in the family way. What's done is done: The thing to do now is to make the best of it and get the pair of you back on the ranch.

Velma saw Frank coming back from doing his chores and changed the subject. She was not about to get her hopes up. Once her father had made up his mind, he would never change it.

Ezra found Eli late the following afternoon. It was not yet suppertime but when Ezra rode up the long path from the gates of the Fanciful, Eli was already seated on a porch swing on the veranda, doing some figuring. Inside, Ezra saw a broad-backed woman who had to be Ida Mae bent over the stove. Eli rose to greet him and called to Ida Mae, who shook his hand in her brisk way.

The girls were out on horseback. Within half an hour they had all trooped in. Ezra had to rise again and again to say hello to his nieces. Tavie was the last in, a young woman now, nearly as tall as her father and uncle, dressed like any of the cowhands on the Fanciful in boots, spurs, men's trousers, a work shirt, and a big floppy hat. Before they sat down to dinner, Teeter strolled in and Ezra jumped up to shake hands. Teeter was a little thinner and a little more stooped but apart from that he never seemed to change; he had looked old the first time the boys laid eyes on him in Ogallala and he still looked old.

All the girls except Tavie helped Ida Mae get dinner on the table. Ezra decided that her cooking must have been what attracted Eli, because the woman was plain as an old shoe. Once he got on the outside of two plates of roast beef with all the trimmings and a slice of steaming apple pie, Ezra leaned back and picked his teeth and listened as the girls all talked at once, telling him what had happened since his last visit to the Fanciful, mentioning everything except Velma's exile. It was pretty clear that Eli wouldn't allow such talk at the table. Ezra waited until the girls went to do the washing up and he and Teeter joined Eli for a smoke on the veranda. Teeter finished his cheroot and headed back to the bunkhouse and Ezra decided that the best way was just to plunge right in.

—I stopped in to see Velma and Frank on the way.

—I figured you might.

—She's awful big. Looks as though she might have that child any day now.

—That aint my concern.

—Oh, yes it is. That baby is your first grandchild. Don't matter the circumstances. That little baby needs you and Velma needs you and turnin her out like that is a harsh punishment.

—I give her a hundred and sixty acres with a house on it. That's more than you nor I started out with.

—Yes, it is. And you could of given them a section of land and a hundred head of cattle and missed it no more than you would miss a pared fingernail. It aint the givin that matters, anyhow. It's havin your own within reach, where you can see 'em every day. Give them a talkin to if need be, but have 'em around. I always thought that was why a man had a family.

—You aint got one.

—Not yet. I got time. I was always more restless than you are. But if I ever set still long enough to have kids, I hope to God I'm going to stick with the job until they's full raised.

—Are you accusin me of turnin my back on my own?

—Only that one.

—She turned her back first. She knew the rules all along. She knew what was expected. She knew that bein a Paint girl is not like bein any tumbleweed trash that comes along, and yet she went and tumbled for that broncobuster—the one you sent along, by the way.

—I did, and I will regret that until my dyin day. He's a good man with a horse, and I thought he would be smart enough to steer clear of your daughters.

—Better he stuck to breakin horses in Montana and stayed out of Nebraska altogether.

—It would have, at that. It's a damned shame what happened. I told Velma I wanted to take a whip to Frank myself. But that don't do no good once the thing is done. You don't have to like the man, but you can bring him back and let him break horses for you and have Velma and her baby right here on the Fanciful, which is how things are meant to be.

—Ezra, you're my brother and I would just about walk through goddamned fire for you. We done all this together, or most of it. The hard part of it we did before either of us had a damned dime to our name. I aint forgot that and I never will. You want to run a horse ranch out here, all you got to do is to say the word. But don't interfere in the way I raise my family. I will listen to you on any other subject and you can disagree to your heart's content, but them girls is mine and so is Blind Daniel, and how I handle them is my concern and nobody else's. Velma is gone to me, she don't exist anymore. What she does with that broncobustin sonofabitch and his baby is none of my concern, and I'll thank you not to say another word on the subject.

—I can't say I'm surprised. You was always a stubborn cuss. But you're plumb wrong when it comes to Velma. She's a good girl— hell, she might be a month from havin a child but she's still a girl. Aint no reason at all she couldn't raise that child right here.

—I got five other children to raise, and I can't let that one set a bad example.

Tavie, who had tiptoed out the back to eavesdrop from the shadows, bit her lip in frustration. She had not really expected that Ezra might be able to change her father's mind, but Ezra was the last chance: If he couldn't persuade Eli to allow Velma and Frank to return to the Fanciful, no one could. Ida Mae might have helped, but she had made it clear that she would oppose any kindness granted to Velma, so now it was down to Ezra, and Ezra had failed.

Ezra rose and put on his hat.

—You've become a hard man, brother. Too hard. The way you treat that girl is just a damned shame and I want no part of it. She aint no outlaw that needs to be whipped for tying pounders onto mustangs. She's just a little girl that made a mistake, and that's no excuse for you to be a stubborn goddamned fool.

Eli was still in a crouch, halfway up off his chair, when he drove a fist into Ezra's midsection that lifted him off his feet and sent him sprawling into the dust below the veranda. Ezra had barely rolled over onto his knees when Eli was on him, throwing punches with both hands. Ezra came up underneath, lifted Eli in a bear hug around his waist, and drove him into the edge of the veranda so hard that Tavie thought it might have broken his back. Eli spun away and circled, took a hard left to the jaw, and threw one of his own that made Ezra's nose bleed. They closed again, rolling over and over in the dust. Ida Mae was screaming, the other girls had come out to watch from a safe distance on the porch. Tavie shouted at them to stop, but it was like trying to stop two bulls from tearing down a section of fence to get at each other. She ran for the bunkhouse to fetch Teeter Spawn, the one person who might be able to put a stop to it.

Somehow, Ezra had come out on top as they rolled in the dust. He held Eli down with his left hand on his throat, his right fist beating a steady rhythm on the left side of Eli's face. They battled on in silence, except for the occasional grunt and the sound of punches landing. Their shirts were torn and bloody and they were so covered in dust and blood that it was impossible to tell them apart. Just as Ezra drew back to try to finish it with one mighty blow, Eli got a hand inside his belt buckle and managed to muscle him over onto his side and spring clear. They were up on their feet and circling again, looking for an opening, when the roar of a shotgun put an end to the battle. Teeter stood between them, the double-barreled scattergun pointed at the stars. He glared back and forth from Eli to Ezra.

—Damned if you two aint a sight. Fightin like kids in the schoolyard. You're done now. I got one more load a rock salt in this here gun and I'll put it in the behind of the next one throws a punch. You're both too old to act like such damned fools.

As if by common agreement, Eli and Ezra both bent forward to catch their breath, hands resting on their knees. Eli was the first to start laughing.

—It's been too long, brother. That was a heckuva fight. You near got the best of me.

—Would a had you, Teeter hadn't come along with that scattergun.

—Naw. I was just lettin you win a little to make you feel good.

—Hush now, or we're goin to go again.

With Ida Mae clucking and scolding, the brothers went to the stock tank to clean up. Their shirts were torn strips, so Ida Mae had to find fresh shirts for both of them. It looked as though Ezra's nose was broken and Eli's left eye had already swollen shut. When they had washed off the blood, Eli wrapped his arm around Ezra's shoulders.

—Damn. It's good to have you back, brother. Stay with us a while now, will you?

—That's the plan.

—Good. I expect we're gettin a little old to scrap, though. You stick to runnin your own affairs and we'll get along just dandy.

—I had to try.

—I know you did. Now you tried, and that's an end to it.

Ezra rode back to the Keya Paha the next day to give Velma the bad news. She shrugged.

—My God, Ezra! What happened to you?

—Your father and I had a little difference of opinion.

—Oh, no. You didn't fight over me?

—We did, but it was overdue. We used to battle like that two, three times a week. I miss it, tell you the truth. Keeps a fella in tune with himself.

—This is awful. What are you going to do now?

—Same as I was always goin to do. Turn part of the Fanciful into a horse farm.

—Papa will let you do that?

—Of course he will. We had a good laugh about the whole thing, but I couldn't get him to change his mind about you. Done my best, but he wouldn't budge an inch. I could spend the whole day whackin him over the head with a two-by-four, wouldn't change a thing.

—I can't say it's a surprise, Uncle Ez. That's about what I expected. Papa is as stubborn as they come. We'll be all right, me and Frank. We'll look after this baby ourselves.

—You're a strong girl, honey.

—I don't have a choice. I can lie in bed and cry all day, but that isn't going to help.

⊰ CHAPTER 40 ⊱

On a brilliant June morning, Velma heard the meadowlark almost before her eyes were open, clear as a piano in the next room. Two descending quarter notes followed by paired triplets in descending thirds. Then another meadowlark farther off and another way out on the prairie. It was delicious to lie on the cool mattress, feeling the morning light spill in through window and door, knowing she should get up to fix Frank's coffee and breakfast, reluctant to move. There was a fullness to the light as though even the sunbeams were with child.

Frank hovered nearby. She caught his eye and smiled.

—What are you watchin me like that for, Frank Hughes? You'll make a woman nervous.

—You're so close to your time, I don't know if you should be up like that.

—I'm perfectly capable of being up and about. I have chores to do and you know it.

—I think I should go get that Bohemian midwife.

—Don't be silly. No point bothering her till it's time. Do you hear those meadowlarks? Isn't that a beautiful sound?

It had rained through most of April and with the rain and the runoff from the snow, the prairie grass was high and lush. Frank had collected a half dozen eggs from the chicken coop, so Velma cracked them with a dollop of milk into her bowl, whisked the eggs smooth, poured the mixture into a lard-greased frying pan on the stove. When they were done, she scooped the eggs onto a plate for Frank with four slices of bread from one of the loaves she had baked the day before. She was pouring his coffee when the first pain took her low in the abdomen. She fell onto a chair and waited but the pain didn't come again. Frank finished his breakfast and went out to saddle the black. He had promised to ride to the Ebsen place ten miles off to help with the branding.

—You sure you're going to be all right?

—I'll be fine.

He cantered off. He was a quarter mile down the trail when she felt a gush down her thighs and that twist of pain in the abdomen again. She shouted at Frank, but he was too far away to hear. In desperation she rang the bell Frank had mounted on the doorframe so she could call him to dinner, rang it and rang it until another wave of pain forced her to lie down where she was. She closed her eyes tight and curled up, holding her belly, gasping for air. She was about to get to her feet when another spasm took her even harder. When the spasm passed and she opened her eyes again, Frank was standing over her. She smiled at him.

—I think it's time.

—I know. I never went to the Ebsens. This here is Vera, from over at the Bohemians. She's the midwife.

The women smiled. Vera and Velma. Vera's English was halting, but they understood each other well enough. Together, they would get through this. Frank wanted to stick around but Vera told him to go on and help the Ebsens with the branding because he would just be in the way. When he returned two hours after dark, he found Velma sweating and exhausted, Vera still tending to her. Emaline Olivia lay beside her, tiny and wrinkled and with a black topknot like a Pawnee warrior. Velma held the girl to her cheek.

—She's going to have a good long life. I knew that when I heard the meadowlark this morning. You should have heard her yowl when she came out. What a holler.

Frank had a hard time seeing a good long life in such a wrinkled little thing, and he had a harder time still figuring what the meadowlark had to do with it. He supposed that, after all the pain she had been through, the woman had a right to say things that sounded a little odd.

Velma had a sweet summer with Emaline. She was a calm, quiet baby. Frank was more attentive than usual and even managed to bring some of the horses he was breaking home so that Velma and the baby could watch him in the training corral. Velma did her gardening with the baby strapped to her chest, Ezra came to visit every few weeks, Daniel was home for the summer from the School for the Blind and he came for Sunday visits with her sisters, who took turns spoiling the baby. At home on the Fanciful, Ida Mae was now in the family way. Tavie said it had mellowed her some, although Tavie still had to keep an eye on her: At every opportunity, Ida Mae bullied Ruby and Kate and treated them like scullery slaves. She was afraid of Tavie, however, so they maintained an uneasy truce in the household.

Despite the hard times, word got around that Frank had a rare gift with horses, that he could handle the most difficult animals. He was hired even by ranchers feeling the pinch of hard times because there was no replacement for a good horse. He would saddle up and kiss Velma and Emaline good-bye, ride off for two or three days or a week, and return with cash in his pockets and little presents for them, soap for Velma or a rag doll for Emaline. When he was away, she did the chores and tended to the livestock, worked in her garden, put up dozens of jars of pickles, beets, and chokecherry jam, looked after Emaline and Benjamin Franklin Hughes, who was born in August 1911, fourteen months after Emaline. Velma and Frank weren't thriving, but they managed to stick. Through Vera, Velma got to know some of the Bohemian women. They were her nearest neighbors, a dozen families in a single enclave two miles east of the homestead. Sometimes when Frank was gone, she would saddle Giddyup and ride over at a slow walk with Ben tied in an apron she had resewn to carry a baby and Emaline behind clinging to her waist. Emaline played with the Bohemian children so much that she was learning to say a few words in Czech. Velma sat at their kitchen tables and gossiped with Vera and the other women, and they made sure she never went home hungry.

Velma couldn't say when she felt Frank slipping away from her. It was so gradual she hardly noticed until he was all but gone. He was home less and less, then he was barely home at all. At first she was pleased there was cash money coming in, but then she realized that having money to buy a few things was not the same as having a man who was home at night. The year Emaline turned three, Frank was gone most of the summer, breaking horses for some of the big outfits in Cherry County. He would come home at unpredictable intervals, stay a night or two, leave a little money for Velma and ride out again, headed for a ranch whose bronc rider had busted a leg or vanished over one of the sandhills. While he broke horses, most of their own land lay fallow because Frank refused to touch a plow. When she tried to persuade him to change his ways, they quarreled.

—Why don't you stay home some and try to make something out of our land instead of running off to work other people's stock all the time?

—I'm a horseman. I aint no farmer. Don't know a thing about farmin and don't care to know. Anyway, it aint our land, it belongs to your pa. We could break our backs here and that mean old man of yours could kick us out any time he pleases.

—He wouldn't do that.

—He run you off the Fanciful, didn't he? Lost your eye chasin wild horses for that man, and what good did it do you? As soon as you crossed him, he gave you the boot.

—He's a hard man, but he wouldn't run us off from here.

—How do you know that?

—He wouldn't, that's all. This place is all we got in the world.

—And damned little enough it is too.

—Don't curse. It's the same as what he and Mama had when they started out. A hundred and sixty acres and a baby, only they didn't have a house.

—You're always holdin me up next to that man. Maybe I don't do some of what he does, but I wouldn't turn my own daughter out to starve neither.

—We're not starving.

—Close enough. If I couldn't work horses, your belly would be empty and then maybe you'd see what a old sonofabitch that man really is.

—Frank!

—Well, he is. A sonofabitch and a mean old sonofabitch at that.

—Don't talk about my father that way.

—I'll talk about him any way I please. He's the reason we're in this fix. Aint no reason at all we couldn't of stayed on the Fanciful, where he'd have his grandkids right next door. He's got enough horses to keep me in work all year round, I wouldn't have to go joggin off all over the sandhills lookin for work and I wouldn't have to listen to you moan about it.

She kept at him, but if she said a bit too much, he would pick up his hat and his kit and ride out without another word, leaving her in an agony of fretting until he returned. They went on like that until August, when Frank was gone for a month. In early September he showed up right at suppertime, sat down at the table, and didn't say a word. He wasn't drunk, but even at the stove she could smell the whiskey on him. Emaline clung to his leg but Ben hid behind Velma, scared of the stranger. When Frank was through eating, he went out and looked after the horses until dark. Velma could see him through the window currying a bay horse. She could feel the tug of him like a strong current in a river, pulling at her. Then she heard him at the bootjack and he came in the front door, peeled his clothes off, rolled into bed, and was asleep before she had finished the supper dishes. The kids tiptoed around as they always did when he was home, afraid of his temper. They went to bed without a whimper and Velma crawled in next to him, drew the quilt up to her chin, tucked herself into his back. She pulled the nightshirt to her waist, naked underneath.

—Frank?

He was motionless as rock.

—Frank?

She let her fingers wander to his thigh and then farther up until his hand locked around her exploring wrist, held her in a vise until her eyes watered, then pushed her hand away.

—Can't you see I'm all in?

He turned to her and she caught the odor, as unmistakable as leather or onion. Woman smell. The smell of a woman, not her. It was all over him, in his mustache, on his chest, lower, everywhere. As though he bathed in that smell.

—Who is she, Frank?

—Who?

—You got someone! I can smell it on you.

—I got nothin on me but the sweat of hard work and horses and a little whiskey.

—You've been with someone. I might be young, but I am not stupid. I can smell it all over you. Who is it? The Ebsen girl? I know you're sweet on her because you talk about her every time you're over there. Is that why you leave me here, weeks on end? Is that why you don't want to have anything to do with us?

—Velma, all that aint nothin but your imagination. You're as crazy as your old man. Now leave me alone. I got to sleep.

He rolled onto his side, and in seconds he was snoring again. She tried to wake him but he was out cold from liquor or exhaustion or both. Velma climbed out of bed, too upset to lie quietly beside him. Ben was whimpering, so she lifted him out of his crib and paced the floor with the baby on her hip, listening to the rattle of Frank's snores. She wanted to take the rusty old rifle he kept around for varmints and shoot him while he slept. She was not much more than a girl but she was a Paint girl and she could look out for herself and her babies.

Once Ben was quiet, she returned him to his crib and slipped beneath the quilt again. She cried silently, her face buried in a feather pillow. Somehow, she fell asleep; when she woke, late-summer sunshine was spilling through the window, Ben was jumping up and down in his crib, Emaline was playing with her rag doll. Frank wasn't in bed but when she glanced out the window, she saw that he was feeding the stock. She got the stove going, put coffee on to boil, and fried toast in the pan. If Frank wanted eggs, he could gather them himself. When he came in, he sat down at the table, chucked Emaline under the chin and tickled Ben as though nothing was wrong. When she set his fried toast and coffee in front of him, he lifted his plate and made a big show of looking underneath it to see what was missing.

—We got·no eggs this morning?

—You have no eggs. If you want eggs, gather them yourself. Fry 'em yourself too.

Frank slammed his palms on the table so hard his coffee spilled.

—Dammit, woman, hard as I work I expect a square meal in the mornin.

—Expect what you want. You want to go gallivanting after women all over three counties, you can learn to cook your own breakfast. And don't curse in front of the children.

—What do you want a fella to do? I got to ride half the horses in Nebraska to make a living. A man out on the trail all the time has his needs.

—So it's true, then? You're telling me that it's true. A man needs things? What about your children, Frank? They need you.

As though to emphasize the point, Ben began to squall.

—How do I know they're mine? They could belong to Cletus Mooney, far as that goes. Or maybe Teeter Spawn. I always thought that old man had a eye for you.

Velma went at him with the cast-iron frying pan hot off the stove, swinging it one-handed right at his jaw, putting all her strength into it. He ducked and the pan clipped his ear. When he came up he caught her wrist, bent her arm back and twisted hard. She heard something snap, felt a jolt of pain as her entire body went limp. The pan dropped on his toe. Frank cursed and kicked her legs out from under her. She fell heavily onto her broken arm and screamed, the pain coming in waves. She felt sick to her stomach and turned her head to vomit. The children were screaming, Frank was still cursing her. She tried to push with her good arm to get up but the pain was too much; she blacked out, and when she came to Frank was bending over her. Too late, he realized that she was badly hurt.

He wrapped his arms around her waist to help her up, Velma near blacking out again as he carried her to the tick. With his face near hers, she smelled it again, the mingled scent of whiskey and a woman's sex. The smell and the pain made her vomit again. Frank held her good hand and she felt absurdly grateful for his touch. Then she passed out again. When she woke he was gone. Ben was in his crib, holding on to the rails and hollering at the top of his lungs. Emaline was beside her, her large dark eyes round and scared. Velma squeezed her hand.

—Honey, can you get me a glass of water? I'll be okay. I just need a glass of water.

Emaline climbed on a chair to get the water pitcher, poured a glass half full and brought it to Velma, her chubby hands just big enough to hold it.

In an hour Vera was there with her husband, Ivan, who was so big he had to turn sideways to squeeze through the door. She managed to explain that Frank had come by to say Velma was hurt and needed help and then rode off without saying where he was going. Ivan made her understand that he would take her to Doc Remy in Ainsworth while the children went to stay with the Bohemians. Ivan lifted her as gently as he could in his powerful arms and carried her out to the wagon.

The trip was a blur; each jolt of the slow-moving wagon caused a lightning bolt of pain to shoot from her arm to her spine. They had traveled only four miles toward town when a shiny new Model T driven by a cousin of Ivan's caught up to them. They managed to transfer Velma from the wagon to the automobile, and she made the first car trip of her life the rest of the way into Ainsworth at a dizzying twenty miles per hour, with only one stop to change a flat tire. Petr was a cheerful, talkative young man who chatted all the way in heavily accented English; Velma tried to concentrate on what he was saying to keep her mind off the pain in her arm, but every time the Model T hit a bump on the deeply rutted road, she came close to blacking out.

Doc Remy was sitting at his desk by himself writing notes when they arrived. Petr helped guide Velma to the table and stood by while Remy administered a healthy dose of laudanum before setting her arm. The doctor said the ulna was fractured and displaced but it hadn't broken the skin, which was good. With help from Petr, he managed to slip it back into place; Velma fainted but when she came to the laudanum had taken effect and she was able to bear the pain as the doctor worked her into a plaster cast. When he asked how she had broken her arm, Velma told the truth:

—It was my fault. I was arguing with Frank. I took a swing at him with a frying pan and missed and he grabbed my arm and twisted it and that's how it broke.

Petr got his supplies at the mercantile while Velma was having her arm set. He came whistling back with a bag of candy for her children and helped her into the Model T for the ride home. She was overcome with weariness and slept most of the way. When she woke, she was at Petr's cabin and his enormously fat wife was helping her out of the car. Inside, Emaline and Ben were playing with Petr's four children. Vera was at the stove making soup in an enormous pot. When she smelled the soup, Velma realized that she was desperately hungry.

Petr poured her a tiny glass of some kind of clear liquid.

—Here, drink this. All at once, like this.

He demonstrated with a larger glass of his own. Velma did as she was told. It went down like liquid fire and left her choking, her eyes watering.

—Oh my? What is that?

—Schnapps. I make, from pears. Here, one more. Drink. Feel better.

Velma braced herself and swallowed the second glass. The fiery effect wasn't quite as bad. This time she felt the warmth spreading through her limbs. Ivan came into the kitchen. He said something to Vera in Czech and she translated.

—Ivan will feed your stock, milk your cow. Everything good. No worry.

—Did he see Frank?

Ivan shook his head. Frank had not returned. The alcohol and the hot soup warmed her entire body. Emaline was at her side, her chubby hands squeezing Velma's skirts. Benjamin was bouncing on Ivan's knee. The children seemed to have forgotten the quarrel. Vera was feeding Ben a pulped mixture of apple and carrots, Emaline was sipping a bowl of soup. Velma smiled, thinking, *This is my world now, these are my people.*

Doc Remy was a subscriber to the wildcat telephone system Eli had first installed to keep in touch with Hutch at the company ranch. Once they had the phone working, other ranchers wanted to tap in, so Eli had his hired hands run more line to nearly thirty outfits all over the county, stringing the phone wire along the barbed-wire fence lines and even into Ainsworth. It was called the rubberneck line because anyone who subscribed to the service could listen in on anyone else, but it worked. Doc Remy was connected for free in case anyone needed his services. The evening after he set Velma's arm, he used the gadget to contact Eli. The doctor could never get over it: Six miles away and the two men could hear each other like they were standing in the same room.

—Eli, it's about your daughter, Velma.

⊰ CHAPTER 41 ⊱

Eli Paint rode through the gate at the Ebsen place at dawn and struck off along the mile of dirt road to the main house, trailed by Teeter Spawn and Roy Titus. First they stopped in Luke Ebsen's kitchen for ten minutes to make sure he would not interfere, found him boiling his coffee and pushing cold biscuits at them. Roy and Eli chewed the biscuits, Luke and Teeter shared a plug of Teeter's tobacco and made good use of the spittoon next to the kitchen table. Luke spat a thin stream of brown juice. It was all Teeter could do to keep the old man from putting a load of double-aught sure-kill buckshot in his 12-gauge scattergun and going after Frank himself. Cass Ebsen opened her bedroom window and tried to holler a warning to Frank, who was working a spooky little bay horse in the training corral. Frank was too far off to hear but he saw them coming and went on with the horse until Eli vaulted the top rail of the corral.

—Drop that lounge line now, son. We got to have us another little talk.

—What's on your mind, Eli? Aint often you pay me a visit.

—Aint never. Rather it had stayed that way, but you busted Velma's arm.

—Her arm was broke? Gee, I didn't know that. She like to took my head off with a fryin pan. She's got a crazy mean temper, that daughter of yours.

—You aint doin yourself a bit of good, talkin like that. Velma was ever the gentlest of my girls. Wouldn't hurt a fly, unless she had cause. From what I heard, you gave her cause to smack you with that fryin pan. What will happen now is you will pack your kit and take what horses is yours and ride. North, east, south, west, it don't matter as long as you don't set foot within a hundred miles of here again.

—I'd like to oblige you, but I can't do that, Eli. I got work here. Got horses to break for Mr. Ebsen, got a dozen more outfits waitin for me to get to their horses.

—Mr. Ebsen no longer requires your services. If you ask around, you'll find that no rancher within three days' ride of here will hire you. Now I have asked you nicely to leave.

—Or what, old man? Or you'll whup me? Or was you goin to sic that half-pint gunslinger Roy Titus on me, have him shoot me in the back? Where I go is none of your concern.

—I don't like to hurt a man unless I have to. You left me no choice, son. When we're done here, just you remember that.

Eli nodded to Teeter, who tossed him the whip. The first strike bit into Frank's rib cage, the second wrapped around his ankles and yanked him off his feet, the third left a long slash across his back. Frank screamed and tried to crawl away, but Eli caught him with a booted toe under the chin and sent him sprawling.

—You had enough, young fella? I can do this all day long.

—Go to hell.

Eli stepped back and the whip cracked again, the lash ripping Frank's shirt open across his belly. The next strike caught him in the same spot and left a trail of blood. Eli cracked the whip four more times, then stepped up and stood with his boot on Frank's neck, grinding his face into a pile of horse manure.

—Are we done? After what you did to my girl, I'll kill you if I have to.

—We're done.

—You're goddamned right we are. Now when I let you up, you're goin to get your things and ride. Next time I won't be so polite.

Eli stepped back. When Frank tried to stand, he brought up his breakfast. Cass Ebsen came running from the house, still trying to do the buttons of her dress. Eli climbed out of the corral, fastened the whip to his saddle, and rode off without looking back.

It was midafternoon when Eli ground-tied the big sorrel horse, the third incarnation of Monty, outside the soddy in Keya Paha County, walked around back of the house, and found that Velma had some-how managed with one arm in a sling to drag a washtub outside in the sunshine. She was down on her knees scrubbing Benjamin's short pants with lye soap. When she saw his black boots, the spurs coming at her *janglejanglejangle*, she thought at first it was Frank, but the stride was shorter, heavier, more bowlegged. Then she thought it was Ezra: She rocked back on her haunches, covered her eyes to look up at him. He was standing with the sun at his back, his face in shadow, his hair ringed with a fiery red halo. Hat in one hand, resting it against his thigh, like a man come courting. She had never seen him look so awkward, did not know the appropriate response. Heart pounding, wanting to hug him, slap him, run into the house and slam the door and refuse to open it, collapse in tears.

—Papa.

—I see you're still up to housework, broke arm and all.

—No choice. Two little ones to look after here.

—I imagine they're a handful. Anyhow, I come to tell you that you won't have no more trouble with Frank because I run him off this morning.

—Oh, Papa. You didn't.

—I won't hold with a man hurtin one of my girls. You done things you oughtn't, but that don't mean he can go and break your arm.

—Did you hurt him?

—Some.

—You didn't take that bullwhip to him? Tell me you didn't use a whip on Frank.

—No more than I had to.

—My God, Papa. You could kill him with that thing.

—I'm more or less exact with a whip. If I meant to kill him, I'd have killed him.

—He's my husband.

—He was your husband. What I understand, he already took up with that Ebsen girl.

—He would've come back.

—I don't believe so.

—It wasn't your decision to make. Frank is my man. What happened was between us.

—He broke your arm.

—You didn't even ask what happened. I took a swing at him with a frypan first and that's when he twisted my arm. If I hadn't clipped him with that thing, he wouldn't have hurt me. I could see it in his face, how bad he felt.

—If it bothered him all that much, how come he lit out on you? Doc Remy says it was some of them Bohemians had to bring you in so he could set your arm.

—It was Frank went to fetch them.

—Went to fetch them and left you to their care. His own wife. Not carin your arm was broke nor stayin to look after his own children. Now he's gone, you and your babies are welcome at the Fanciful.

Up close she could see the way he had aged, the gray at his temples, the spiderwebs of crow's feet around those gray-blue eyes. For years she had imagined this moment. Now that he was three feet away, the only thing she wanted was to have the same frypan she had swung at Frank, to let it rip, do all the damage she could do.

—Damn you.

—No need for that kind of talk. I'm still your father.

—Are you? You threw me out of the house when I wasn't but fifteen years old and I had a baby on the way. For one mistake, the kind any girl could make, and there are plenty as do. You wouldn't even let me show my face at home. You've never laid eyes on these babies, your own grandkids. Now you run my man off, then you come to tell me it's all right if I want to come crawlin back, is that about it?

—No, that aint about it. You were my favorite daughter, did you know that? When you took up with that saddle tramp, it cut me to the quick. I thought we raised you right.

—It wasn't anything to do with how you raised me. I was young and I lost my head. Anyway, you had pretty much quit raisin us except for the work you wanted us to do. We were handy cowgirls to have on a cattle drive until I crossed you, and then I was no more to you than a weasel in a henhouse.

—There isn't a word of truth in any of that, but I aint goin to stand here and argue with you. You can't go on all by your lonesome, not with two kids and a arm that's broke.

—I don't see why not.

—I don't think you have a choice.

—I have a choice. I'm a grown and married woman with two children. I've made it so far with precious little help from Frank. I can look after my own.

Eli gazed off into the distance, put his hat back on.

—So you aint comin back?

—I am not.

Ben was still in the house taking his nap but Emaline had wandered out and stood near her mother. Eli saw some of Livvy in her, more of her mother in those serious dark eyes.

—This would be your little girl.

—That's right. This is Emaline. Emmy, this is your grandpa.

—I don't have a grandpa.

—Yes, you do. This is him. He lives on a big ranch called the Fanciful.

—Are we going to visit Grandpa sometime?

—I don't think so, honey. Grandpa is a busy man.

Eli put his hat on and turned toward his horse.

—I expect I'd best be going, then.

—I expect you had.

—Pleased to meet you, Miss Emaline. You're a pretty little thing.

—Bye, Grandpa.

Velma watched him ride out of sight, scooped up Emaline and carried her into the house, curled up on her tick between Ben and Emmy and tried to cry. She was empty as a dry well. Any tears she had to cry for Eli Paint had long been shed, the tears she had for Frank Hughes wouldn't come. She was on her own now, and her only man was Benjamin Hughes.

By late August 1914, the Bohemian community on the Keya Paha River was in an uproar. The war had begun in Europe. Czech and Slovak soldiers were already fighting for the Austrian emperor and some of the younger settlers were talking about going home to enlist, debating whether they would have time to make it to the front before the tyrannical French, English, Russians, and Italians were forced to surrender. Even Petr was talking about going to fight, though he and his wife had three children in America. The papers were full of war news, although it was plain that the United States would never be drawn into a war on the European continent. Still, people were choosing sides, some with the English and French and Italians, others with Germany and the Austro-Hungarian Empire. The Germans were already almost at the gates of Paris. Velma tended to side with the English and French, but she knew little about the war or what had caused it. From the way her Bohemian friends talked, Velma doubted that Eli would make any money off the hundreds of acres of wheat he had planted in anticipation of a European war and soaring wheat prices. The war would be over by Christmas, long before American wheat could make much difference to anyone. It was just as well she had no money to buy seed: If the price dropped, the wheat would be worthless anyway; now she could cut the brome- and wheatgrass to put up enough hay to see the livestock through the winter. She only hoped that men like Petr would not go off to war.

Velma worked herself to exhaustion, helping Ivan and Petr

with the haying on their land, driving the team to pull the mower that cut the prairie hay on her own land and on another quarter section of unfenced government land to the north. She handled a rake and pitchfork as well as some of the men. Ivan, the strongest of them all, remarked on her endurance.

—I never see woman so strong. You make somebody good wife.

—I made somebody a good wife. He's gone now.

—Frank is fool. We write to Europe. Find somebody better. I have a cousin, good Czech boy, wants to come to America. He's only fourteen years old now, but soon he will grow.

—So now you're marrying me off to a fourteen-year-old boy? Maybe you better ask how he feels about an old lady with two kids.

Velma paused from forking hay into the stack, unwound the scarf she wore in her hair to mop off the sweat and hay from around her neck. In an hour, Vera would bring them meat sandwiches for their lunch. Emaline and Ben would come with the Bohemian children, Emaline eager to tell everything that had happened during the endless morning, Ben pelting around after grasshoppers while the haying crew sat in the shade of the stack to eat or nap.

On a warm Indian summer day, Velma left Ben with the Bohemians and took Emaline for a wild gallop on Giddyup, thundering up and down hills lit gold with autumn leaves, the girl clinging to her waist and giggling with every stride. She had not been so completely happy since before the day Eli dragged her into Ainsworth to confirm that she was with child. She felt free and unfettered, young and full of ideas and energy, and capable of managing her own fate. If she could make it through a Nebraska winter alone with two small children, she could do anything.

The next time her sisters came to visit, Velma talked it over with Tavie and Marguerite, who helped persuade her that it was time to divorce Frank so she could start looking for a new husband. Marguerite drove her to the Brown County Courthouse in

Ainsworth in Eli's eighteen-horsepower Rambler. Earl Neese, the county clerk, filled out the documents with Marguerite acting as the witness to Frank's disappearance. Unless Frank returned to contest the divorce within a year, Velma would be a free woman. From the way Earl stared at her chest, Velma thought he might be the first to come calling. When they climbed back into the Rambler, Velma took a coughing fit that lasted halfway back to the homestead. It was so bad that Marguerite wanted to turn around and take her to see Doc Remy. Velma refused.

—Vera is looking after the babies, and she'll be tired by now. It's just a cold, Maggie. You worry about me too much.

⊰ CHAPTER 42 ⊱

By March 1915, Velma had a dry, hacking cough that kept her awake night after night. At first she blamed the dust of a dry month. Then it rained most of April and the cough got worse. It was time for the planting. Mornings when she should have been out plowing a few acres with Ivan's team she was in bed instead, unable to overcome the weariness that seemed to consume her bones. Half the time when she managed to prepare something, she was too tired to eat. Vera fussed over her and brought pots of cabbage and potato stew, which she claimed her own family could not eat. When her sisters arrived with an entire carload of provisions, Maggie was shocked to see how much weight her sister had lost; she tried again to persuade Velma to see Doc Remy about that cough; again she refused.

Throughout that summer Velma tried to keep working the land. Crops were doing well, the war was still on in Europe, the farmers who were able to grow wheat were getting a good price. She did not want to be left behind because of a silly cough, but now it was more. She often felt feverish; the fever made her cheeks bright red, a false sign of health. At night she would wake bathed in sweat, so wet she had to crawl out of bed and change nightshirts. Day and night she was so exhausted that even the smallest tasks seemed daunting. Gradually, the cough changed. It became a hollow rattle in her chest that brought up a thick green mucus occasionally tinged with blood. Twice in one week she woke with blood trickling from her nose and mouth. Her swollen joints ached, and sometimes when she allowed herself to sleep on a Sunday morning, she would awaken long after noon to find that Emaline and Ben had eaten cold porridge from the day before and spent the day playing quietly so as not to disturb her.

Finally, on a Sunday in August, she did not get out of bed at all. When she woke it was past sundown, the cow was bawling because her bag was full, and Vera was standing over her, lighting a lamp. She held a hand to Velma's forehead.

—You are like a prairie fire, child. It's going to burn you up and you will die in this flame. It is not a cold, this I know. You have to listen to me. We will use Petr's telephone, I will call doctor. You are very sick. You can't go on like this.

—I have work to do, Vera. If I don't work, we'll starve.

—You can't work. What good are you to your children if you work until you die? I have seen this in Europe. It is possible you have the consumption.

—It can't be. My family is healthy.

—I don't know your family. I know this disease. I saw it, the way it eats people until they are nothing but skin and bones. In this rich country, they can find a way to make you better. Perhaps it is something else and you are very lucky. I will pray for you. Now you will eat some soup, try to keep up your strength until the doctor can visit you.

Velma was too weak to resist. After two days that were little more than a feverish blur, with Vera, Ivan, and Petr coming and going and the children sleeping at Vera's, Doc Remy arrived in the Chevrolet Roadster that had replaced his horse and buggy. Velma, lying bathed in sweat on her tick, could hear the car coughing and wheezing a mile away.

The doctor was slow and deliberate. He took her temperature, pressed his stethoscope to her chest, listened, listened again, shifted it to another spot, listened again, making little puzzled sounds in his throat.

404 ᴗ **Jack Todd**

—Do you have any idea where you might have gotten this, Velma? Have you been in contact with anyone who had the consumption?

Velma tried to think back.

—Only when my eye was put out. I was in the hospital on the reservation. There were some Sioux girls there who had it.

—That could be where you contracted TB: This disease can linger for a long time before you have any symptoms. Or you may have gotten it from someone else—there's no way of knowing.

With Vera's help, the doctor turned her onto her stomach and listened again, the metal stethoscope on her ribs sending icy jolts through her fevered body. She repeated her symptoms: exhaustion, swollen joints, coughing up green mucus and sometimes blood from her lungs, night sweats, fever, the endless, racking cough, a lack of appetite. From the way her clothes fit, she thought she had lost twenty pounds, possibly more. The doctor returned the stethoscope to his bag, produced three small cups, and held one beneath her chin.

—I will need a sample of your saliva.

—My mouth is too dry.

Doc Remy waited while Vera brought a glass of water so that Velma could produce a specimen.

—You have all the symptoms of tuberculosis, but to be sure I'll need this to take back to Ainsworth. We should test the children too, if you can persuade them to spit in separate cups. In my office I'll use an acid stain; then I can put it under the microscope. If the bacillus shows up blue, it will confirm what I hear in your chest.

Velma had no idea what a bacillus was but it sounded bad, a small evil thing of enormous, hidden power. She had to drink three glasses of water before she could summon enough saliva for a sample. Vera helped to persuade Emaline and Benjamin, wide-eyed and solemn, to provide their specimens. Doc Remy gave Velma a dose of laudanum to help her rest and promised to return in two or three days with the results. In the meantime, he cautioned her to avoid coughing near the children and to keep the young ones away from the rags that accumulated beside her bed through the night, stained with green mucus and blood.

It was four days before the doctor returned, this time with Marguerite beside him in the roadster. When Velma saw her sister standing over the bed, she knew that the doctor had bad news. Marguerite sat with Ben on her knee while the doctor discussed the results.

—It's not good, Velma. The bacillus was blue, which pretty much means you have TB. A lung X-ray would confirm it, but we don't have an X-ray machine here, and with the other symptoms it's a sure diagnosis anyhow. The only good thing I can tell you is that neither of the children have it, at least not yet, although you're going to have to take precautions around them. Meantime, we've got to find a place for you.

—My place is right here.

—Well, it is, Velma. It is. But you have tuberculosis, and the place for someone in your condition is a sanatorium, where you can be looked after proper.

—I don't need to be looked after. I have to look after these children.

—You can't look after them when you can hardly get out of bed. Your joints are so swollen you can barely walk, you have the fever night and day and you don't stop coughing. If we don't get help for you, I don't think you'll live through the winter. Some of these sanatoriums are better than others. I have a young friend who got into the medical school at the university on my say-so, and now he's one of the smart young doctors at a place in Denver that has to be one of the best in the country. Fellows like him, they know more when they come out of school than this old country doctor will ever figure out. The sanatorium is called the National Jewish Hospital for Consumptives. It would be perfect for you.

—But I'm not Jewish and I don't have the money to pay.

—You don't have to be Jewish. Their first patient was a Swedish woman. Their motto is "None may enter who can pay—none can pay who enter." It's not a hospital for the rich, it's for people like you. Obviously, it's not easy to get a place there, but I will send a telegram to my young doctor friend and see what we can do. Given the state of your health and your circumstances, I think we can have you admitted.

—I can't leave here. I can't leave my babies.

Marguerite put her hand on Velma's forehead. She felt singed as though she had touched a fire.

—Honey, I don't think you have much choice. You can't take care of these children by yourself. I'd take them myself if I had a place of my own.

—Who's going to look after them, then? Papa wouldn't take them on the ranch, and I don't want to go begging for his charity anyway.

—I know that, honey. I've already looked into it: They can go to the St. James Orphanage in Alliance. The nuns there run a good school, and the children get a decent education and three meals a day.

—It isn't right for a woman to leave her children.

—You wouldn't be leaving them. You'd be going where you can get better so you can care for them.

Velma tried to argue, but she was out of breath and strength.

—Do what you have to do. If they have a place for me in this sanatorium, I'll have to go.

Doc Remy left more laudanum for Velma and repeated his instructions for her to avoid spitting or coughing near the children; he said that he hoped to have her on a train for Denver within a week.

—You're a strong young woman, Velma. With the right treatment, you have a chance. Sometimes TB patients live for years or even decades.

—And sometimes they don't, right?

—I won't lie to you, Velma. Sometimes they don't.

Velma left the house in Keya Paha County for the last time in September 1915. Because her trunks were too heavy for Eli's

Rambler, he sent Teeter Spawn with a wagon to drive her to the railroad station, with Marguerite along to help with the children. Velma was so sick that she had to lie down in the wagon bed with the bags holding everything they owned piled around her, Emaline and Ben seated on her trunks. She had just strength enough to lift her head one last time to look back at the soddy, the tall stand of sunflowers in front of the house nodding in the breeze, her thriving garden.

Teeter was almost seventy but he could still handle a team of horses. As he drove with Marguerite beside him, he talked over his shoulder to Velma in the back.

—I never thought your daddy was fair to you, girl, and now it looks as though life aint turned out fair either. Young as you are and sick as you are, it aint right.

—Thank you, Teeter, but there are folks have it worse.

—I expect that's always true, but that don't mean a body can't complain now and again.

At the station, Teeter and Marguerite had to lift together to get Velma out of the back of the wagon. Ben jumped down and fell, skinning his knee, but he was so awed by the occasion he forgot to cry. Marguerite got Velma and the children settled while Teeter paid a big layabout four bits to wrestle her trunks onto the train. When everything was aboard, Teeter came and stood awkwardly beside her seat, hat in hand.

—You'll see the mountains, first time. Always looks like somebody painted a lake up in the sky. Then you get closer and they're like blue clouds. Finally, you can make out that it's mountains you're lookin at, and it just about takes your breath away. Denver is pretty enough, but you want to get up to see the Bighorns, the chance ever comes.

—I'll remember that, Teeter. You've always been so good to me, ever since I was a little girl. I'm going to miss you.

Teeter squeezed his hat and squirmed with embarrassment, trying to think of something else to say.

—Train ought to be movin soon.

—Yes, it should.

—Now you take care and get well quick.

—I'll do my best.

Teeter bowed his way off the train and stood on the platform, waving his hat until the cars clicked and lurched, Ben and Emaline on their knees waving back. Marguerite touched Velma's forehead. The fever was a living, devouring thing, consuming her sister.

They took the train together as far as Alliance. It was late in the evening when two nuns from the orphanage met them at the station. Their parting took most of Velma's remaining strength. Emaline wept quietly and held her hand, but Ben screamed and clung to her neck and refused to go. The nuns waited, tight-lipped and impatient, until one of them simply grabbed the boy and towed him away. Velma wrapped her arms around Emaline and held on for dear life herself until the girl had to be pulled from her grasp. The nuns and the children disappeared into the darkness, and Marguerite helped Velma back onto the train.

—This is as far as I go. The conductor said he will look after you as far as Cheyenne, where you have to change trains. Someone from the sanatorium will meet you in Denver.

Velma nodded. Through her fever, Marguerite looked so much like Livvy that she wanted to cry "Mother" and ask to be held like a little girl. Instead she slumped with her face against the cool, soothing glass of the window. She was seized by a terrible coughing fit as the train pulled out of the station, soaking three handkerchiefs with bloody mucus before she could stop. Outside, a chubby orange moon rose in the prairie sky. Velma wondered if Emmy and Ben could see it. At last she fell asleep and didn't wake again until they arrived in Cheyenne, where two porters came with a stretcher and carried her into the station.

After a dozen stops, including one in Fort Collins that lasted three interminable hours, Velma arrived in Denver at dawn on the thirtieth of September. She was met at the station by two patients whose tuberculosis was in remission, gaunt, bearded men

who had fled the ghettos of Eastern Europe to find themselves
dying of the consumption in America. They spoke English with
accents she found hard to understand, but they were not without
a sense of gallows humor: She was loaded into the back of a wagon
that smelled of sour milk from the sanatorium dairy and taken on
a back road to the National Jewish Hospital for Consumptives on
Colfax Avenue, past a cemetery that was larger than the entire
town of Ainsworth. She peered through a steady drizzle at the long
rows of gray crosses, obelisks, stone pillars wound with the husks of
dead flowers. Between coughing fits, she noted odd details: Leaves
floating in a mud puddle and a rain-soaked black cat that curled its
way through and through the rusty iron bars of the graveyard fence
like furred ivy, keeping pace with the slow-moving wagon. Three
gravediggers leaned on the wet wooden handles of their spades,
smoking cigarettes cupped against the rain in callused palms as
water dripped from their hats. Row upon row of graves, and in that
vast city of the dead where time had been extinguished was the
balm for her affliction: to be laid in the cool earth, proof against
wind and weather.

The right rear wheel of the wagon needed greasing. She listened to its monotonous creak, to the *thwuck thwuck thwuck* of
shod hooves sucked out of the mud by the heavy-hocked horses,
to the faint dripping rain on the canvas over her head. The journey
ended inside the gates of the hospital, with two orderlies lifting
her out of the wagon onto a stretcher. They carried her on a long,
twisting passage to her bed, their soft-drawling voices echoing
along the dim corridors.

—She don't weigh hardly nothin.

—Most gone already, this one.

—I make her eighty pounds, eighty-five the most.

—Could be, Abner. Don't seem hardly worth it to fetch her to
a cot, just goin to have to drag her out in a day or three. Watch
that post now, easy now, don't drop her.

—Here we are. She's number twenty-four. All right, miss, we're
goin to lift you onto this here bed, now one two three up you go.

Now you rest, honey. A nurse will be right along, give you somethin for the pain.

When they were gone, she raised her head, pressed her cheek to the cool pane of glass behind her cot. The window looked out on a courtyard where stood a quaking asp, its dark, damp branches stirring as the wind blew a slurry of rain against her window. When she let her head sink back into the pillow, she saw him. He was waiting on a high-backed wooden chair beside her bed, black hat balanced on his knee, his silver spurs jangling when he moved.

—*You are here at last. I have been waiting for you a long while. Now they have brought you to me. It's time.*

BOOK 5

Little Goose Creek

Wyoming 1916–1925

⚜ CHAPTER 43 ⚜

In the void of midwinter darkness, Velma heard the grandfather clock at the nursing station toll four times, each strike of hammer on bell vibrating along the polished wooden floors and up the metal frames of the cots where worn-out women coughed and waited: *Bong . . . bong . . . bong . . . bong . . .* echoing down the corridors past the sleeping women each in her narrow room. She felt the night reach far down and turn itself inside out like an old wool sock reversed to hide the stitches of the darning needle, a rebirth snatched from eternal darkness, a miracle delivered each night at the moment when she was certain that the light would vanish forever, that the tide of darkness had finally swallowed the sun, that star on star and world on world to the edge of the universe had been extinguished as surely as a lit match dropped into a torrent. She closed her eyes for a time, and when she opened them the clock tolled six times and somewhere out there the cold dark world shook itself awake and dawn poured down the slopes of the mountains until the quaking asp was lit black against the pale snow. She found him waiting in his chair, patient and upright, heard his spurs when he moved. *Jangle jangle jangle jangle.* Reminding her. *Time time time time time time time.*

—*Not yet it is not time.*

—*Yes. Time time time time time time time.*

—No.

Down the hall, the clock tolled again. Seven o'clock, and she could hear the orderlies bringing breakfast. She glanced toward the window, toward the pale light. When she looked back at the chair, he was gone.

In the evening after the nurses made their rounds, Velma hoisted herself onto a corner of her narrow cot with three thin pillows to prop her head, pressed her cheek to the cold pane of the tall window, and turned until she could see the moon dance through the branches of the tall quaking asp. She watched the moon until it vanished, leaving nothing but a faint blue light that clung to the bare black trees and the shadowy brick buildings across the courtyard.

She was young and she had been strong. Now she coughed blood and sputum and lay wasting away like the others, and her life had the liquid texture of a dream. When the weather turned cold, there were nights with no moon at all, and the falling snow was lit by the gaslights in the courtyard. She lay awake and watched the snow and listened to the women weep and cough into their rags. She heard the soft tread of the night nurses, their starched white dresses and their stockings hissing *shhhh-shhhh-shhhh-shhhh* as they hurried through the ward where the dead were borne away by whispering orderlies with their dark strong arms.

Mornings the same cheerful soft-drawling men came through at daybreak, their faces masked against the plague. During the night, the patients in the Women's Pavilion coughed into rags and dropped the rags into cloth bags that dangled from their bedposts, and at dawn the overflowing bags were plucked by the orderlies with gloved hands, hauled downstairs, and dumped into great dustbins pulled by horse carts. The carts were hauled to the fire pits beyond the dairy barns and the bins emptied into an enormous pile. The men started a fire with hot coals and dry branches, then labored with pitchforks to heft into the blaze the rags soaked with blood and green phlegm and salt tears. The flames crackled into showers of sparks, and from their beds the women could see the tall, thin pillars of drifting black smoke, their nightly struggle consumed in cleansing fire. As the rags burned, the men stood warming their hands in the blaze, talking of boxers and women and racehorses.

Bit by bit, Velma's lungs emptied of breath and time. He waited in the stiff-backed chair at her bedside, hat on his knee. His spurs jangled when he shifted his boots. She listened through a laudanum haze.

Are you ready? It's time please. Come. We'll follow the river, one river or another, all the rivers that flow to the sea. It's time. You've lingered long enough. Come with me. It's time. Time time time time time.

It would be so easy. All she had to do was to let go. Let go as she had when she was a child, perched on the bank of the Niobrara on a warm June day. The river had undercut the bank, and while she sat nibbling buffalo berries, the earth gave way beneath her and her stomach was left in the air as she plunged into sun-warmed water where the river bent south at the cottonwood tree. She laughed like a child on a carny ride and let herself go with the water. Her skirts spread out, her long dark hair flowed behind her, and she spun with the current round and round like the hands of a clock, head to toe, head to toe around the bend and out of sight, down the river to the sea.

On a winter morning so cold there was a sheen of frost on the floor near the windows, Velma woke to find a new patient in the next room, separated from her own bed by three or four feet and a thin partition. Her name was Bessie Moon. She had arms like hams and a voice that boomed even now, and although she was not yet fifty years old she had buried three husbands and all three of her children. She was reckless and profane and funny, and the women in the ward loved her because Bessie would curse for all of them and apologize to no one, least of all to the Lord God in Heaven, who had condemned them all, Jew and Gentile alike, to such a cruel fate.

On rainy days in this place, even Bessie would get weepy and shed tears for her lost babies, her lost husbands, her lost youth.

—Don't be like me, girl. Not if you can help it. If you ever make it out of here, try to manage it so as to catch on to a run of luck and hold it. You're young and pretty still, so maybe things will turn out different for you. I had chances aplenty, but it was always like tryin to grab a greased pig. I'd catch it by the tail and squeeze for all I was worth, but it always got away. Then just about the time I thought I'd finally figured the whole thing out, I come down with this here consumption. It's a thing you got to know when you're young, because when you're old it's too late to learn. There are times when you have to grab hold of what you got and never let go. You got smarts and gumption aplenty, so if you ever get luck on your side, maybe you can hang on, make something out of this hard old life. There is people who was born with luck, and people who was born without it, and if I had any luck at all it was bad. Story of my life. Every time I fell I managed to land butter-side down.

Velma was less frail and more stubborn than anyone imagined, unyielding as blackroot prairie. Every night that winter they expected her to go, and every morning she was still there. In the spring they were surprised to find her with them still, ghostly perhaps but not yet a ghost, pale as the drifting plumes from the cottonwoods sailing breeze-borne over the lawns, her bony hands clinging to the edges of the wooden wheelchairs they rolled outdoors rain or shine. Dr. Kleinmeyer was in charge, and he believed that you treated the white plague with fresh air, even on rainy days, when the patients lay with quilts tucked to their chins under canvas umbrellas breathing new-mown grass, purple lilac, white columbine, woodsmoke, fresh manure, wet stone, rain on damp earth, and all the shrieking buds flinging themselves from brown to green over row upon row of the haggard, the weary, the dying.

Bessie Moon recovered and was released. She returned to Montana, and she wrote one letter a week. Velma tied the letters with a bow and put them in the drawer at her bedside with the letters from Tavie, Marguerite, Ruby, and Kate, all wrapped in ribbons of various colors. She had two postcards from Ezra, and no letters at all from her father.

Her gentleman caller did not come at all in the summer of 1916, but when it rained for eight cold days in November and the rain turned to snow he was back. He had changed. Now he behaved like a jilted suitor. He was impatient and fidgety, toying with the razor-sharp rowels on his spurs that still came *jangle jangle jangle* down the long corridors.

    —*You disappoint me.*

    —*For that I am truly sorry.*

    —*I waited for you. By the river.*

    —*I know.*

    —*You did not come.*

    —*I did not.*

    —*You seem to think you can elude me forever.*

    —*Not forever. For a time, perhaps.*

    When she woke the next day he was gone and he did not return. She understood that something had changed. Somehow she had survived those dark winter nights; she thought of the Denver cemetery, how she had once almost yearned to be interred with the quiet dead. Her hold on life was tenuous, but she was alive. It was enough.

America entered the war in Europe on the side of England and France. The patients at the sanatorium were bitterly divided; those of Russian or East European descent cheered the U.S. entry into the war and predicted that the kaiser was going to get his comeuppance at last; those who came from Germany or Austria-Hungary insisted that America should have remained neutral, and that it was only the perfidious diplomacy of the English and French that had persuaded Woodrow Wilson to go to war. Velma was baffled; she felt only that war itself was wrong, that anything that slaughtered so many people and wrought so much destruction could not possibly be good, no matter whose side you were on.

As Velma's health improved, she grew anxious and restless, eager to be with her children again. Her anxiety grew almost to a frenzy after Emaline was hurt in an unexplained accident at the orphanage; somehow a heavy pot filled with boiling water had fallen on the girl's right arm. The arm was badly burned and broken and it had not healed well. Although she wrote several letters to the nuns, Velma never received an explanation as to how such a thing could happen to a child in their care. The result was that the arm was permanently bent, and Velma worried about Emaline day and night. If not for this infernal disease, she would have been there to protect her daughter. Not for the first time, she cursed her own body; somehow it seemed to betray her, again and again. She worried about the war but the war was a distant thing; her daughter's misfortune was not.

By the spring of 1918, Velma had recovered to the point where she was ready to be released. She received careful instructions from Dr. Spivak, who said there was no reason she couldn't survive another decade, or perhaps much longer, if she took care of her health and avoided undue exertion. Under the circumstances, she couldn't possibly consider a return to the Keya Paha, and in any case Eli had leased her little farm to another tenant. Tavie was living on a dude ranch outside Sheridan, Wyoming, where she worked as a wrangler for her friend Amelia Arbuckle, whose father owned the ranch. Tavie urged her to come with the children and stay at least for a while; with few other choices, Velma agreed. She wrote to the nuns at the orphanage in Alliance to arrange for Emaline and Ben to meet her in Wyoming. The mountain air would be good for all of them.

The day before Velma was to be released from the sanatorium, she heard the solid thud of something striking the tall window of her room. At first she thought one of the orderlies playing baseball on a distant field had struck a ball impossibly far, but when she ran out to see what it was, all she found was a dead robin, its neck broken. The poor thing had apparently mistaken the reflection of the sky and clouds in her window for the sky that soared overhead, flown full tilt into the unyielding glass, and died. Even though her own release was at hand, the death of this solitary, unlucky robin affected her to an absurd degree. She collapsed to her knees, held the robin to her breast, wept over it like a lost child, finally dug with her fingers a small grave for it in a flower bed, and whispered words of solace as she covered it with earth, repeating the phrases that had been written on the death of her mother, stringing them together over and over again in a kind of prayer: *In sorrowful remembrance in their hour of deep affliction the darkest hour of sorrow in sorrowful remembrance in their hour of deep affliction the darkest hour of sorrow . . .*

It was all so capricious and unpredictable. One moment you were a robin in spring, flying through the clear blue sky. The next moment you crashed into a pane of glass and died. Or you were dying, ready to embrace death, and in the next moment you were flying away, free to rejoin the living, unable to believe your good fortune. She remembered Teeter's speech about the calamity cycle, wondered if perhaps her own calamities were over at last, if she might find a better life in Wyoming—or whether, like the robin, she would be soaring one moment and broken and dead the next.

❧ CHAPTER 44 ❧

Caleb Wheeler, the white-haired son of a slave, drove Velma to Union Station in a high-topped and noisy Willys-Overland, which belonged to Dr. Spivak, the physician who had granted her release. A 1915 model, Caleb informed her with some pride. Almost new, built the year she entered the sanatorium. Velma sitting tall and proud beside him in the front seat this time, not stretched out in the back of a milk wagon for a grim and ironic detour past a cemetery in the company of two consumptives who were themselves little more than skeletons. Perhaps Caleb possessed no sense of irony, or perhaps he simply found the life of a black man in America too ironic to require embellishment. In any case, he made no such graveyard detour. He drove instead directly along the muddy track of Colfax and through the crowded streets of downtown Denver, detouring along Arapahoe so that she could gawk at the twenty-story Daniels & Fisher Tower, at three hundred and thirty feet the tallest building in Denver, on the way to the station on Wynkoop Street. Caleb drove with an unlit pipe jammed between his teeth, greeting with a friendly smile and a lift of his slouch hat the impatient drivers who sounded their klaxons when they found their passage blocked by the Overland doing a stately three miles per hour through the mud. After three days of rain and a sudden, plummeting frost, the day of her release dawned sunny and warm, the buds bursting on the trees, the air floral and fragrant until they pulled out onto Colfax and plunged into city streets reeking of the mingled odors of gasoline fumes and horse manure. All around them cars and trucks roared and backfired and slithered in the mud, trolley bells clanged, newsboys hawked their wares. She marveled at the chaos and energy on all sides, wondered how a person caught up in the whirl of this human torrent could remember where she was going or why, or how her driver could find his way to the railroad station. Caleb, calm in his goggles and leather duster, insisted that piloting an automobile was a good deal easier than running a boat on a river.

—Everybody worry too much about everybody else. Trick to it is you pay no attention to nobody but your own self. You get to listenin and worryin about everybody blowin they horns and gettin theyselves in a fuss, that's when you forget what you're about. That's pretty much true of life, if you ponder on it. Keep yourself set on a thing, you'll get there by and by.

—Life aint necessarily like that, Caleb. Once upon a time I was set upon a thing. I was going to have my own ranch, and show everyone what a woman can do if she puts her mind to it. Trouble was, I got interrupted. One day I could put in my twelve hours in the fields just like a man, and the next day I could hardly get a bowl of porridge on the table.

—I still don't see no reason you can't start up again now.

—No, I can think of a thousand reasons. Back then I had our hundred and sixty acres and a house, at least. Now I have nothing except the clothes in that valise, and the homesteads are pretty much all taken. And I'm a lunger. No bank in this wide world will loan money to a lunger. That's the way it is with the consumption. No one wants to take a chance on you.

—Every time you go thinkin like that, you *know* it's goin to get you again. You got to be sure you done outrun it. Then you just keep movin fast, and we won't never see you in that hospital again.

—I'm not going to be back again. Now that I beat it once, I'm not ever going to let it catch me again. The doctors told me how to take care of myself. Long as I do what they tell me, I can live to a ripe old age, just like you.

—Lordy, girl, that's what I want to hear. A little pluck is all it takes.

—Oh, it takes more than that. Takes luck too, but I figure I'm due some luck.

Velma would have liked to pursue the conversation but they slewed through the mud round a corner, and Union Station loomed in front of them with its three high-arched glass windows and its famous clock. Caleb found a spot between a truckload of chickens and a pile of what might have been refuse that stirred mightily as though tunneled by voracious raccoons before yielding a derelict wino who emerged from his heap of belongings, cursing the automobile that had disturbed his resting place, and begging Velma for a nickel to buy a cup of coffee. Caleb stepped down, shouldered his way between the bum and his passenger, deftly palmed the man a nickel, handed down her valise, and accompanied her into the station. He swept off his hat and took his leave with a low bow.

—Every chance you get, you send a postcard, Velma. Let us know how you're doin. Listen to what the doctor told you and don't overdo now, hear?

—You take care of yourself, Caleb. Thank you and God bless. It was very kind of you to give me a ride to the station. I felt like a queen.

He grinned a wide, gap-toothed grin and vanished into the crowd, leaving her to wish that she had begged him to stay a while to keep her company. She had been too anxious about missing her train: Now she faced a two-hour wait in a station that was like an army base, with hundreds of doughboys fresh out of boot camp awaiting transport to places like New York City and Newport News, where they would ship out for the killing fields of Europe. They sprawled sleeping on their kits, sat in little circles smoking cigarettes and shooting craps, stood like predatory birds watching for the flash of an ankle or a Clara Bow smile, paced up and down the bricks with their sweethearts, saying stiff good-byes, constrained by the presence of so many onlookers. Some of the soldiers wound and re-wound their puttees, others squatted on their heels in the shadows away from the crowd. Velma felt enormous compassion for these young men, most of them anxious to get across the Atlantic before the shindig was over.

She stood clutching her valise in the center of the vast, cav-ernous station, staring at the board overhead with its long list of departures for distant places like Chicago, Salt Lake City, Santa Fe, and Los Angeles. Halfway down she located the train to Chey-enne. She found a place on one of the benches and sat down, trying to make herself as small as possible. She felt awkward, frightened, out of place, especially around the confident women in the station and on the platform. Everything about her cloth-ing was wrong, from the black calf sixteen-button high-cut shoes that cost $2.39, ordered new from the 1914 Monkey Ward catalog, to the hobble skirt ($3.99 in the same catalog and the best thing she owned) that came all the way to her toes. Her old coat was now worse than threadbare and smelling of mothballs. She had regained some weight at the sanatorium but her clothes still hung off her bony shoulders like hand-me-downs from a much larger woman; it made her feel simultaneously like a little girl dressing up in her mother's clothes, and an emaciated survivor of some nameless tragedy.

There were many young women her age bustling in and out of the station. Compared with them she felt ancient as the Rockies, a weathered old thing who had endured far too much. At the same time they seemed to understand this modern world so much better than she, to know how to move and behave and dress without any of her annoying clumsiness. The young women waiting for trains or bidding good-bye to their soldier beaus were ordinary working girls, most of them, and yet their skirts were at least a foot shorter than hers, full and belled toward the calves to give them a freedom of movement she lacked; more than once, Velma saw a flash of knee when a woman sat down or twirled on the platform. Some, probably on their way to work at some factory, wore peg-top trousers with web belts like the soldiers wore. They wore strange little round hats and their lips were rouged and they flirted with the soldiers in an open, easy way she found scandalous. One pretty, dark-haired girl, her slender body pressed tightly to a private who was bidding her good-bye, peeked over his shoulder and winked at another doughboy farther up the track. He grinned and blew her a kiss.

Five minutes later, the same soldier appeared at Velma's elbow, hat tucked under his arm, offering her a cigarette.

—I'm sorry. I don't smoke. I'm a lunger. It isn't good for us.

He took a step back, leaving her to wonder why exactly she felt compelled to say that.

—A lunger? What's that?

—The consumption. I've just been released from the sanatorium.

The soldier looked as though he had just found a rattlesnake in his kit.

—Excuse me. Sorry to trouble you, then, ma'am.

He turned on his heel and rushed away, bound to offer the same cigarette to another young woman sitting primly on a bench and staring at her nails. Velma stared at the black-and-white pattern of the tiles on the floor, her face burning. Despite her sallow complexion and her very unfashionable clothing, this young man had been bold enough to speak to her, and she had chased him away by saying immediately that she was a consumptive. If she was ever to entertain another man, she would have to learn not to blurt her entire sad story on first acquaintance. After she had driven him away, the other soldiers seemed to realize that she was not to be disturbed and left her alone, even though she was clearly without a chaperone. By the time the conductors were bellowing "all aboard" for the train to Chicago, most of them had already boarded the train. She wondered how many would return. If the conflict was anything like the war some of the patients in the sanatorium had heard about from their relatives, they were bound for a murderous hell that consumed body and soul alike. In some ways, the war was like the sanatorium: The number of souls entering those doors was always significantly greater than the number who returned. She sat thinking of all those she had known who had died, so many in such a short time. She supposed herself lucky to be among the survivors, but the survivors also carried the burden of memory.

The train to Sheridan was half empty, all the heavy traffic flowing in the other direction with soldiers bound for Denver from the training camps in Wyoming and western Nebraska. Velma sat with her face pressed to the window on the left side of the coach, so she could stare out at the Rockies looming blue-black on the horizon. A corseted matron who smelled heavily of rosewater sat next to her as far as Cheyenne, complaining ceaselessly about the overheated car and the dirty fingernails of the conductor. Velma watched the telephone wires swoop and rise, swoop and rise, listened to the deep, churning rhythm of the train, watched the high-wheeling hawks in that impossible blue sky, coughed now and again softly into her kerchief, wanting to be alone with her thoughts. She felt like a returning prisoner released after a long confinement. Everything was so new it glistened, every slightest object had meaning, every passing sight brought a lump to her throat: a towheaded boy near Longmont chucking a rock at the train, a long string of cirrus clouds like white cotton candy, the endless vistas of sagebrush leading to the distant blue of the Rockies, a stand of quaking asp like the tree she watched so many nights from her window in the sanatorium, a big old longhorn south of Cheyenne, standing in a pasture all by itself, as though stranded and forgotten after one of the great trail drives from Texas. Nothing in all that landscape appealed to her more than the horses: She saw mares with their spindle-legged colts, a lone palomino stallion, and a herd of thirty or more yearlings almost keeping pace with the train as they bolted over an even stretch of prairie, manes flowing in the wind.

After Cheyenne, their passage was painfully slow, the train a genuine milk run. They stopped every few miles, often at towns that were not towns at all, but merely signposts beside the track:

Horse Creek, Iron Mountain, Chugwater, Wheatland, Glendo, Orin. Sometimes a passenger or two would step down; sometimes they would simply sit and wait and after thirty minutes or more resume the journey again without explanation. With nothing else to do, Velma read a volume of poetry by Walt Whitman, a farewell present from another patient. Whitman's rhythms were like the train running over the rails, long and loose and open as the West itself, leaving her to wonder whether he had ever visited this part of the country. She stopped reading to watch the glory of a Rocky Mountain sunset, luxuriated in her freedom, enjoying even the weariness of travel. The earth at dusk was still vast. Some of it, at least, remained untrammeled, a world where a slender young woman returning from a long sojourn in a lung hospital could still dream. She felt a pang of guilt over friends who were unlikely ever to leave the sanatorium. They would live there and die there, imprisoned by this awful wasting disease. Through a miracle of rejuvenation, recovery, and rebirth, she had been granted world enough and time. The task now was to savor it like cool spring-water, drop by drop. She would hold her children, she would ride a horse again, she would bake pies in her own kitchen. Perhaps, if there was any land left to claim, she would file on another home-stead and try again to build her own ranch, this time with Emaline and Ben to help. The possibilities were so limitless they left her a little giddy.

Long after dark, she was half dozing with her cheek pressed to the cool glass of the window and watching a pregnant moon rise over the Bighorns when the conductor came striding through the car.

—Sheridan coming up. Next stop Sheridan, Wyoming. Sheridan in five minutes. This is the end of the line, folks.

CHAPTER 45

It was near midnight when Tavie met her at the station in Sheridan. Velma did not realize how near she was to complete exhaustion until she stumbled and all but fell into her sister's arms. When she recovered, she saw that Tavie was dressed like some of the women at Union Station in Denver: peg-top trousers, a wide web belt, high lace-up boots, a flannel work shirt that might have belonged to a man. They embraced on the platform, Velma aware that she was little more than a bag of bones held tight in Tavie's powerful arms. She thought for a moment that those arms would crush the last breath out of her, but Tavie finally pushed her away and held her at arm's length for a good look.

—You're still looking a little peaked around the edges, but a lot better than the last time I saw you. How long's it been?

—Nearly a year since last time you were in Denver.

—Time flying like it has wings, going to fly us all right on out of here one of these days. Looks like they made you some better, anyhow.

—Some. Tell the truth, I never thought I'd walk out of that place alive.

—Tougher than they thought, I guess. Us Paints are hard to kill. Now, if we don't stop jawing we're apt to get old standing right here, and Amelia will be waiting a late supper for you.

—It's past midnight.

—You don't think we'd send you to bed without a feed, do you?

She swept up the heavy valise under one arm and set off for her automobile, striding long-legged like a man, a woman six feet tall, narrow in the hips and wide in the shoulders as any cowpoke, Velma in her old-fashioned hobble skirt struggling to keep up. Tavie swung the valise into the mother-in-law seat of a 1909 Model T Ford that looked as though it had been run through every creek in Wyoming, took Velma by the elbow and almost lifted her into the passenger seat, set the magneto and spun the crank with a single ferocious twist and they were off, the narrow dirt road barely lit by a single functioning headlamp. The Arbuckle Ranch was on Big Goose Creek, fifteen miles of winding dirt track to the south and west of Sheridan. Even with the moonlight, the road was dark and treacherous but Tavie drove fast, saying little, wrenching the Model T over loose gravel and sudden, jarring bumps. Velma twisted her hands in her skirt and bit her lip to hide her anxiety; she did not want to survive consumption only to die in an automobile accident the first night after her release. Over the backfiring engine and the hiss of the tires spinning on gravel, she tried to carry on a conversation to take her mind off pending disaster.

—I'm proud of you, sister, running your own ranch up here.

—It isn't mine, honey, and it aint much of a ranch. Anyhow, it doesn't belong to us, it belongs to Amelia's father, Leland Arbuckle. He bought it five years ago. Philadelphia lawyer, doesn't know a gelding from a hackamore, but somebody convinced him he needed to move out here for his health, so he bought this little spread, then figured out he didn't know how to run it. There isn't enough land to run cattle, so we raise a few prize horses and keep the plugs around for the dudes to ride in the summer. We even hired a couple of guitar-playing cowpokes to play "Red River Valley" and serenade the rich ladies around the fire, make 'em forget they're saddlesore after a three-mile ride. Those drugstore cowboys can hardly sit a horse, but as long as they can strum a chord and wear a big old cowboy hat, the eastern folks think they're the real thing.

—Doesn't sound like you to put up with a bunch of tourists.

—You get used to it. Country is beautiful and the work isn't too hard. Me and Amelia get along real good. Beats trying to get steers across the White River in a quicksand year.

A deer loomed suddenly in the middle of the road and Tavie spun the steering wheel hard to avoid hitting it. The deer scampered into the darkness, but for an awful moment they leaned out over what Velma was sure was an infinite chasm, although she could see nothing at all below. Tavie gave it more gas, the left rear wheel bit into gravel, and they were on solid ground again, Tavie giving no sign at all that they had survived a close call. Velma wished they were on horseback, where a person felt some sort of control. Automobiles seemed to her like so much hurtling metal, apt to go off in any direction at any moment without warning. By the time they skidded to a halt in front of the house, she was gripping her seat so tight it was hard to let go. There was a kerosene lamp burning in the window and Amelia Arbuckle was waiting up for them. When Tavie first mentioned her close friend Amelia in a letter, Velma imagined a large, pallid, horse-faced character with hair the color of dishwater. Instead, Amelia was small and lively and almost pretty, with too many freckles and curly red hair. She served up roast beef with gravy and mashed potatoes and all the trimmings, an odd meal for the wee hours of the night. Velma was surprised at her own voracious hunger; it was her first home-cooked meal in three years and she ate like a young wolf. She polished off her plate, drained a big glass of milk, and stumbled off to her narrow bed in the loft, sleeping for the first time in nearly three years without the background noise of women coughing, choking, crying. She feared the silent darkness of the mountains at night would be unnerving, but the big, soft feather pillow embraced her. She pulled the quilt to her throat and went spinning down into its depths, asleep before she could think how sweet it was to be away from the land of the dying.

The sun had been up for three hours and Tavie had long since finished her chores when Velma finally rose to the smells of coffee and frying bacon. Amelia was at the stove, Tavie in a chair at the table, reading a three-day-old edition of the *Sheridan Press*. Amelia set a huge plate of bacon and eggs in front of her, while Tavie outlined their plans for the day.

—You get on the outside of that breakfast, then we'll give you the tour. Some of the most beautiful country you'll ever see, and the air is a sight better than it is down in Denver.

While Velma ate, Tavie gave her the latest news from the Fanciful. For nearly three years, she had followed the progress of her family through the letters of her sisters, now neatly bound in separate ribbons according to the sister and the year: Marguerite's letters, Ruby's letters, Tavie's letters, Kate's letters. Taken together, the letters were like one of the big old novels by Charles Dickens or William Makepeace Thackeray from which she had once read to her mother. Her siblings began to seem like characters in a novel. She knew that Marguerite had just married Custer Johns, the wealthy rancher's son from Cherry County; that Ruby was now wed to Wade Tourtelotte, one of Eli's cowpunchers who had begun building his own spread on Sheep Creek near Torrington, a little Wyoming town near the Nebraska state line; that Kate was studying pharmacy in Lincoln. Daniel had gone to live with Wade and Ruby in Torrington, and convinced the town authorities to hire him as a lifeguard and swimming instructor at the new municipal swimming pool, after demonstrating that his eyesight was good enough to detect a floundering swimmer, and that he could dive to the rescue more quickly than lifeguards blessed with perfect sight. Both Ruby and Marguerite were now able to take in Emaline and Ben, but there was no longer a need with Velma out of the hospital.

The one person who had never been mentioned in the letters was Eli's second wife, Ida Mae. When Velma asked, Tavie made a face.

—If you can imagine it, that woman with five children of her own. Ida Mae loathes all of us, you know that. When I see her, I get the feeling she's trying to put a hex on me. But Papa thinks she's wonderful because she can make a perfect apple pie and she dotes on him.

—How is Papa, anyway?

—He's pretty much like always. Works seven days a week except for church Sunday morning. Never lets up. Between the Fanciful and the company ranch, he has twenty thousand acres now, but he says he's going to give up on Nebraska as soon as the war is over, because then there won't be any money in wheat. He's got so much money he doesn't know what to do with it all.

—And Uncle Ezra?

—He's raising prize Appaloosas on the Fanciful. Wanted to help us do the same here, but I don't think we're ready for that just yet.

Velma finished eating and tried to help with the washing up, but Amelia wouldn't allow it and Tavie was anxious to get out on horseback and show Velma the ranch.

—How long has it been since you rode a horse?

—More than three years. I was too sick to ride before I went into the sanatorium.

—Let's go, then. I've got four good cowponies that the dudes aren't allowed to touch. The rest have been pretty much ruined to where even Frank couldn't straighten them out.

Velma dressed in a pair of Tavie's trousers, rolled up at the cuffs and held up by a pair of man's suspenders over one of Tavie's plaid shirts. Tavie saddled a big, rawboned roan gelding for herself, and a compact little black filly with one white stocking for her sister. Velma was so excited that her hands trembled as she slipped her toe into the stirrup and swung into the saddle. Tavie had done the breaking herself and the filly was beautifully trained; Tavie said it might be the fastest horse at a quarter mile she had ever seen. Velma hadn't been in the saddle for a long while, so she held the filly to an easy walk. They rode past the outbuildings and a bunkhouse now outfitted for the dudes who would be arriving in June, through a stand of tall pine, and into a long, green meadow that provided pasture for a couple of dozen shaggy plugs that would soon be caught to give the dudes the illusion they were riding real western cowponies. The black wanted to run and Velma could not resist. She leaned forward in the saddle, gave the filly a squeeze with her thighs and the mildest tap with her heels, and felt a surge as the horse gathered its powerful hindquarters and they were off, Tavie's long-legged roan thundering along behind. Velma could feel the spring sunshine on her face, the clear mountain air coursing through her lungs, sense every bone and sinew of the little horse straining as they flew over the long grass, startling a pheasant into a whirr of flight, clipping through columbine not yet in bloom, the rush of wind making her eyes water. They ran nearly a mile at a dead gallop before the roan began to catch up and Velma tugged the filly to a halt. She was laughing so hard that tears ran down her cheeks as Tavie pulled up beside her.

—Oh. Oh. Oh. That was wonderful. I never thought I'd be able to do that again. What a splendid horse. What a beautiful place.

Velma slid out of the saddle and sprawled in the grass, the reins wrapped loosely around her hand, the feel of the spring greenery luxuriant against her back. Tavie dismounted and squatted on her heels next to her sister, chewing a blade of grass.

—It's a fine place to live, isn't it? I never thought I'd end up wrangling dudes for a living, but it could be worse. If they were around all year they'd drive me crazy, but for a few months I can just about take it. And I'm lucky to have Amelia around, because I don't do a lick of housework.

—You never did housework before, I don't know why you'd want to start now.

Tavie stuck out her tongue.

—I didn't have to do housework, because we had you around, little girl. You're the only one of Mama's children could get a meal on the table without lighting herself on fire.

—But we were good at trailing stock and chasing wild horses, weren't we? I was never so happy or so proud in my life as the day we ran down those horses in Dakota, at least until that rock hit my eye. That kind of took the fun out of it.

Tavie paused to listen to a meadowlark.

—What are you going to do now, honey? Where are you going to live? Have you thought about it?

—I haven't had much time. It's only two weeks since I found out I was going to be released. I might file a homestead claim, except the doctors say I'm supposed to be very careful about over-doing it, and when you're trying to make your own place work, it's hard not to overdo. Anyway, I imagine most of the good claims were taken a long time ago, at least around here. I wish I could have gotten more schooling. There are things I'd like to do but you have to go to college to do them, like Kate studying pharmacy.

—You could have done anything, Velma. Mama always said you were the smart one. She thought you would go to university and be a lady writer or a doctor.

—I might've, if not for Frank.

Tavie sat up and pulled her hat low over her eyes to block the glare from the sun.

—Even with Frank around, it would have been different if Mama was alive. You know that. If Mama hadn't died, a lot of things might not have happened. She wouldn't have stood for you being booted out of the house because of Frank, for one thing. She would have helped care for her grandkids, because that was the way she was. When you got sick she would have looked after you, and she would have looked after your babies.

Velma stared off into the distance, to the gray-blue peaks coiled on the horizon like the shoulders of the gods, the deep snows gleaming in spring sunshine. *Beulah land. Sweet Beulah land. As on thy highest rock I stand.*

—Well, there isn't much use fussing over it, is there? What's been has been. Now I have to make my way, same as anybody.

—You could stay here, help Amelia in the kitchen when the dudes come.

—I couldn't take your charity.

—It wouldn't be charity. We could use the help. It's a good place for kids to be.

—You don't have room for all of us in that little house.

—We'd make room.

—All the same, I don't like to be beholden. We were raised to make our own way.

—Bullheaded. Just like your father.

—Just like all of us.

—I expect so. But you think on it.

—I will. But after all that time in the hospital, other people looking out for me and the kids too, at the orphanage, I want to be able to look after myself now.

For supper they had venison from a deer Tavie had shot up in the high country, with sweet potatoes and peas. They drank black-cherry wine and laughed in the glow of the kerosene lamp, Amelia fussing over them both like a mother hen. At ten o'clock Velma climbed, still giggling, to her loft bed and collapsed facedown on her pillow, giddy from the first wine she had touched since Frank ran away. She woke to an odd sound in the night, and thought at first she had been dreaming of Frank and that accounted for the noise. She couldn't quite place it, except that she knew it had nothing to do with coughing and dying, and yet it sounded a little like dying. She sat up and tried to get her bearings: She was not at the sanatorium, she was in the loft bed at Tavie's and Tavie and Amelia were asleep in the bed they shared off the kitchen, separated from the rest of the house by a heavy quilt hung from the ceiling. Or not asleep: The sound was rhythmic and a little harsh, bedsprings squeaking, sounds like the sounds that she and Frank used to make in the night, a high-pitched moan coming from a throat that had to be Amelia's, then silence, movement, a rhythmic sound building again.

Velma lay awake, heart pounding, hands trembling, trying not to listen, listening in spite of herself, feeling an odd sort of excitement that made her feel flushed and embarrassed. She pulled the feather pillow over her head but could not block out the sound. My God. Tavie. She had known of such things between women at the sanatorium, had even thought she heard women making love once or twice, but this—her own sister. The sounds grew louder, until a voice that was unmistakably Amelia's rose in a long, quavering cry. There were other brief noises, bodies shifting, then silence and finally a different but familiar sound, that of Tavie snoring. There was no chance she would be able to fall back to sleep. She stared into the darkness, thinking hard. In this tiny house, there was no way that Emaline and Ben would not hear, and Emaline was old enough to understand what was going on. It was a forbidden love and whatever her own confused feelings, she had to think first of the children. She could not imagine a way that she could explain it to them. As the first pale light began to filter into the room, Velma made her decision: She would have to go.

⊰ CHAPTER 46 ⊱

LeRoy Weldrum could hardly believe his good fortune. He had been up long before dawn, loaded the crates bearing two hundred and twenty-seven squawking fryers onto the wagon, harnessed the best mule team on Big Goose Creek, instructed his wife Luella not to let any goddamned strangers into the house in his absence, and set out for Sheridan, not expecting for one moment to encounter this apparition of a young woman shuffling along the road alone and toting a heavy valise while sunup was still a rumor. A pretty thing at that, although she could do with a square meal. So weak that Weldrum had to climb down to hoist her valise onto the wagon before he took her elbow to boost her up. The fact that she did not complain about the pressure on her elbow encouraged him. For two miles he was content to chat about the weather and the price of chickens. Then he made his pitch in the most elegant manner he knew.

—I don't suppose that you would suck a man's pecker, now would you?

Velma had expected something of the sort from the moment Weldrum halted his team.

—I would not.

—That aint very sportin of you.

—I am not going to trade favors for a ride on a wagonload of chickens. If you want to be a friendly and neighborly soul, that's fine. If you want otherwise, I'll walk, thank you kindly.

—I was only funnin you.

—No, you were not. You thought to make a lewd suggestion to see if you could get away with it. It aint so dark I can't see what you have out of your overalls. You can stick that thing back in your pants, mister. Honestly, I don't know how you can get up to such things with the stink of these chickens trailing after you. Even if I was inclined to bed you, which I'm not, I wouldn't do it within smelling distance of all that poultry.

Weldrum grumbled but tucked his penis back in his pants. He left her alone after that, drove his team with a clucking tongue and the occasional "gee," "haw," and "you there, Hannibal, quit slingin your head like a damned fool." When he worked up nerve enough to ask what she was about, it turned out that he knew of a cook's job in town that might be open. It was full daylight when he dropped her on South Main Street in Sheridan and pointed to the Blue Hawk Diner.

—Fella you want to see in there is Wesley De Weese. If you can cook, he'll give you employment at a fair wage. And if you can make a decent pie I'll be a regular customer. My wife, that's Luella, she can't bake worth a damn.

—Thank you, Mr. Weldrum. And please convey my sympathy to Luella. She has been highly misfortunate in her selection of a man.

Weldrum lifted his hat.

—No hard feelins, huh, miss?

—The next woman gets that near to you might not be so un-derstanding. You keep wavin that little thing around, somebody is apt to take a poke at it with a knittin needle.

Weldrum pulled the hat down low over his eyes, clucked to his team, and drove off. Velma strode into the Blue Hawk Diner, thanking Bessie Moon under her breath for teaching her how to deal with the likes of LeRoy Weldrum. Ten minutes later, she had worked out a deal with Wesley De Weese. He would pay her thirty-five cents an hour for ten hours a day, six days a week—and she could have the narrow furnished apartment above the diner free for herself and her children. She did not mention that she had just been released from a sanatorium where she was undergoing treatment for tuberculosis and he did not ask. He handed her off to Nellie Dorenbecker, who showed her the ropes, and she had the first paying job of her young life.

It was near suppertime when Tavie tracked her down and came bounding up the steps two at a time, throwing open the door without knocking. Velma was sitting on the tattered davenport, weary from her first shift in the diner. The room reeked of bacon grease from the diner, the wallpaper was peeling, a spider the size of a tennis ball dangled by a thread from the fly-specked kitchen ceiling, and a steep set of rickety steps led from the back door to the ground, where the winding path to the outhouse was so overgrown with weeds that a woman would need a scythe to cut her way through. Tavie spun a chair around and straddled it, arms folded across the back.

—Gosh, you are an impulsive woman. You could have waited two hours, I'd have driven you to town. I thought you were asleep till I came in from doin the chores and found your note.

—I didn't want to disturb you.

—You're fresh out of the hospital. The doctors said you have to take things easy.

—That isn't the same as taking charity.

—I swear, you can be as bullheaded as Papa.

—It's not being bullheaded. I spent the last three years in a place where I couldn't do things for myself. When I went in there, I couldn't even wash my own body. I had to just lie there like an old dishrag and let other people do things for me. Now I don't want to be beholden.

—Could this have to do with somethin you heard in the night?

—It could. It doesn't really bother me, Tavie, except I don't want Emaline and Ben to hear.

—I'm sorry. We ought to been more quiet.

—Why? I hope you aren't ashamed of what you are, if that's what you are. I just can't imagine what it would be like if Papa found out.

—He doesn't have anything to do with his first family anymore. He talks to Marguerite some, because she married Custer Johns and Custer has money, but that's pretty much it. He doesn't know who I'm with, and I aint likely to tell him.

—I guess not.

Tavie looked around at the bleak furnishings in the apartment.

—So this is your new quarters, where you're going to start your new life.

—I expect so.

—And you're going to cook for Wesley De Weese? That bald-headed, cackling old fool? He run the last cook off squeezing her behind while she flipped pancakes, did you know that?

—If he touches my behind he'll get a black eye. Nellie Dorenbecker says he's not a bad sort as long as we don't let him take liberties. So far he's been a gentleman to me. If he isn't, I know how to deal with him, same as that chicken farmer this morning.

—What happened?

—Nothing I couldn't take care of myself.

Tavie stood to leave.

—I'm disappointed you couldn't see fit to stay with us, honey. If you have any trouble at all, we have the telephone. You just pick up the phone in the diner and ask the operator for the Leland Arbuckle ranch, and she'll put you through. And we'll expect you to come out every Sunday. Only this time, you wait for me to come get you.

Velma nodded, figuring she had done enough to prove her

point. Tavie hadn't even removed her spurs before coming to town. Velma heard them jangling all the way down the stairs.

Emaline and Ben arrived on the Elkhorn, Fremont, & Missouri line from Alliance a week later. They were so big that Velma almost didn't recognize them when they stepped off the train. Emaline was nearly eight years old, and you could see in her face the woman she would become; Ben was taller than Emaline and he looked so much like his father that Velma could almost see Frank's long-striding shadow in his walk. Em spotted her first and ran to her mother. Velma fell to her knees, holding on to her daughter like a drowning woman gripping a cottonwood bough in a flood. She reached out for Ben but he hung back, shuffling his feet and staring at the platform, gratified but embarrassed by her show of emotion. Emaline stared at her mother with dark, serious eyes, running her fingers through the white strip in her mother's jet-black hair. Velma read her mind.

—My hair just turned this way after I got to the hospital, honey. It turned because I missed you two so much. Another year and it would have been all white.

—Will it change back?

—I don't think so but it doesn't matter, the fellas who eat at the diner tell me it looks mighty attractive. They say I look like a skunk, but a pretty skunk.

—You don't smell like a skunk, Mama. You smell pretty.

—Thanks, honey. Now let me see your arm.

Emaline slowly brought her right arm out from where she was hiding it, behind her back. Velma gasped when she rolled up the sleeve: The arm was badly scarred from the wrist to the shoulder and so thin it was little more than skin and bone. Emaline could straighten it a little more than ninety degrees, but that was as far as it would go. The girl was staring at the ground as though she felt ashamed of her crippled arm.

—What happened, Em? How could they let this happen to you?

—It wasn't anybody's fault, exactly. I was scrubbin the floor in the kitchen. This big pot fell on my arm and scalded me.

—I can see that, but why were you scrubbing the floor? Did you have to do that every day?

—No. Only when they caught me wavin at Ben. We weren't allowed to socialize with the boys.

—Not even your own brother?

—No, ma'am.

—So your punishment was scrubbing the floor, and that's when you got hurt?

—Yes, ma'am.

—My God. My poor child. You'll be fine now. Your mama will take care of you. I'm so sorry I had to leave you to them.

—It's all right, Mama. You were sick.

—I was, but I'm better now. We all are.

Velma took two days to get the children settled into the apartment. There was barely enough room for the three of them to turn around and it smelled of frying grease from the diner, but it was warm and dry and there was a roof over their heads. It almost seemed like home after Velma spent her spare hours for weeks sewing curtains and tidying up to make the place a home. Ben was rebellious and difficult at times, but Emaline was the most serious eight-year-old Velma had ever seen, quiet and helpful. Sunday mornings Tavie came in the Model T to pick them up and they spent the day at the dude ranch, learning to ride and care for the horses, to gather eggs from the hens for Amelia, to fork hay to the calves and feed the pigs. They chased grasshoppers, rolled a hoop from an old wagonwheel uphill and down, played hide-and-seek in the barn, rode Tavie's ponies, and tried to rope the cats with lariats. Velma watched from the porch, letting the sun bake the weariness from another week at the Blue Hawk Diner from her bones, watching them grow.

The armistice came in November, the boys came home from Over There, the Spanish flu epidemic started in the trenches in Europe and took its toll in Wyoming as it did all around the world, but left Velma's tiny family and the wider Paint clan untouched. The Volstead Act brought in Prohibition and made liquor illegal; Wesley De Weese toasted the occasion with gin from a flask he kept in his pocket and predicted that the new law would make a lot of smart fellows rich.

The letter from the War Office in Washington, when it caught up with Velma at last, had been forwarded from Montana to Ainsworth to the town of Enterprise, from there to the National Jewish Hospital for Consumptives, and finally to her apartment over the Blue Hawk Diner in Sheridan. It informed her that Corporal Frank Hughes of the United States Expeditionary Force had been killed in June of 1918, fighting with the Fourth Marine Brigade against the Germans at a place called Belleau Wood. Velma was stunned and saddened; the war was over, she hadn't even known that Frank was in France. The years in the sanatorium had not hardened her to the pain of unexpected death: She grieved for Frank, for their youthful passion and all that it had cost her, for the long-legged young man who knew how to perform magic with horses but did not possess the magic that would keep him alive in war. She sat the children down, explained that their father had died a hero. Ben looked puzzled; he had no recollection at all of this man Frank Hughes, though he was willing enough to imagine his father a hero. Emaline listened wide-eyed; she had vague memories of her father, but felt no attachment to him. Still, it seemed odd to her not to have a father somewhere in the world. Velma wondered what the man who died in combat was like. Braver? Wiser? Or still the same old Frank, chasing every mademoiselle in France? She wondered if he had given any thought to her or the children before he died, or if they were all simply gone from his mind, an incident in his youth that was already forgotten. She had not forgotten him. He still strode through her dreams, long-legged and handsome, the sound of his jangling spurs in the kitchen on the Fanciful the day he rode down from the north while they were making pan-cakes, her future for better or for worse astride a tall black horse. She thought of Livvy's death and the phrases tolled again in her mind: *In sorrowful remembrance, the darkest hour of sorrow.*

There was another truth that came to her with age and loss: Life goes on. Sometimes, that's the saddest part of all.

CHAPTER 47

It was Tavie who found Ora Adolphus Watson. Their paths might never have crossed if not for a thirsty homestead claims inspector named Emmitt Spangler. On a cold October afternoon, Spangler chose to linger over a whiskey-and-whiskey lunch at the Sheridan Hotel saloon while his horse was poorly tied to the hitching post outside. A backfiring Packard spooked the horse, which bolted along North Main Street with Spangler's old rattle-trap buggy bouncing along behind. Amelia's father, Leland Arbuckle, on one of his infrequent visits to Wyoming, happened to be crossing North Main when he saw the horse and buggy bearing down on him. Arbuckle's enormous bulk and weak lungs made it impossible for him to move quickly. A more agile man might have skipped out of the way, but Arbuckle had just enough time to wonder which way he ought to jump before he was trampled. According to the account of the incident in *The Sheridan Press*, Arbuckle died instantly, after receiving a blow to the back of his skull from one of the horse's steel-shod hooves. The reporter described the runaway horse as a "steed" for alliterative effect, the kindest thing that had ever been said about Emmitt Spangler's swaybacked, Roman-nosed, splayfooted plug, which broke a leg and had to be shot the same afternoon.

Arbuckle was a widower and Amelia, his only child, was too shattered by her father's death to cope with the funeral arrangements, so Tavie stepped in. She was directed to Ora Adolphus Watson, an upholsterer who had branched out into coffin making. Watson lived in a cabin up Little Goose Creek, and was said to be a man of impeccable manners whose craftsmanship reflected his personal character. After driving a hard bargain on the price, Watson agreed to make Leland Arbuckle's oversize, brass-trimmed oak coffin, complete with burgundy velvet upholstery. When Tavie visited the workshop on his homestead up Little Goose Creek, she began to wonder whether the coffin maker might not make a fine husband for her poor, consumptive sister Velma. Watson struck Tavie as a fine, sensitive creature. He was a slender, fastidious man of less than average height, with a high forehead, thinning blond hair, vague blue eyes, and long, thin fingers that performed the most delicate work with precision. He owned his cabin, his workshop, and a Model T truck he used to haul lumber and deliver coffins and ottomans. What attracted Tavie to him, at least on Velma's behalf, was his sadness. He was forty if he was a day, but he had a gentleness in his manner that seemed to stem from some hidden tragedy.

While they fussed over the specifications for Leland Arbuckle's coffin, Tavie extracted Watson's story from him a phrase at a time. He had sold a thriving upholstery business in Chicago and drifted to Wyoming because he found the idea of the wide-open spaces of the West irresistible. He learned too late that the outdoor life didn't appeal to him, at least not when it involved such things as sixshooters, rattlesnakes, and road agents who would bushwhack a man for his hair tonic. Hired to help a drunken coffin maker who was falling behind in his work, Watson showed a flair for both precision carpentry and for the delicate stitching required for the upholstery of the interior of a proper casket. Eventually, he took over the business. With a reliable trade established, it was time to find a wife. Unlike most men in Wyoming, he was looking for something more than a woman with a strong back and a handy way with a skillet. Watson lured his eighteen-year-old bride from the Chicago neighborhood where he grew up; he had known Ada Torgensen's mother and father and remembered her as a lively kid who loved his mother's jam. Four years and dozens of letters later, Ada agreed to become his wife and in the spring of 1914, she boarded the train west. Watson met her at the station in Sheridan and they were married by a justice of the peace. After two nights in a hotel, Watson took his new bride for her first look at the Bighorns and his home on Little Goose Creek. Life was good: The mountains were beautiful, his bride was beautiful, his work was not too taxing. He looked forward to their first child.

Within six weeks, Ada was dead of a fever. He tried to explain it to Tavie.

—The West didn't agree with her, I guess. They say this is a healthy climate, but it don't please everyone.

—It didn't do much good for Leland Arbuckle either. Came out here for his health, and got himself run over by a claims inspector's buggy.

—It's not for us mortals to see what fate has in store.

Tavie felt that Velma ought to be drawn to the man. Watson had grown up in the city and he had city manners. He didn't have to be told not to track cow manure into the house, not to blow his nose on his fingers and wipe it on his pants, not to spit tobacco juice on the floor or break wind at the table. If she smelled booze on his breath, she could hardly blame the man. He had suffered a terrible loss. With a new wife by his side, he wouldn't need to drink. Velma and Watson had both endured pain, they had both been married before. If there was any man who was likely to accept a tubercular woman with two children as his wife, it was Watson.

—Velma, the man is positively afflicted. The poor devil laid his wife to rest four years ago and he's still pining like an eagle that has lost its mate. A man who could feel that deeply for a woman is hard to find. Most fellas, when they wear out one wife with childbearing they go right to looking for another one to bear their children and cook their meals.

—Sounds to me like he's too far gone over his dead wife to pay attention to another woman, let alone a one-eyed woman with the consumption and two children of her own.

Velma tried to laugh it off, but once Tavie got the bit in her teeth, she was not going to be reined in. A month after Leland Arbuckle was buried in the Sheridan cemetery, she asked Watson to come by the ranch on a Sunday afternoon to settle the account. Velma happened to be in the kitchen when he arrived. Tavie brought him in and introduced him like a horse trader trotting out a prize stallion.

—Velma, this is Mr. Ora Adolphus Watson. Mr. Watson, this is my sister Velma.

—You can call me O.A., please. Nobody but my mother ever called me Ora.

Velma shook his hand and got one of those wet-fish grips, just enough pressure so that you could say there had maybe been a handshake there, and stepped back and eyed the man. She was not impressed. Pale eyes, pale eyebrows, pale thinning hair, pallid skin. A pale shade of a man, his conversation as pallid as the man himself, so that the children fidgeted and squirmed until at last he put on his hat, mumbled something about three pine coffins to finish, and ducked out the door. He was still turning the crank on his Model T truck when Velma started giggling. She couldn't help herself. The man was strange as a goiter on a goose.

That should have been it for Watson, but the man was persistent. After that first meeting he came by the Blue Hawk Diner every time he was in town for chicken-fried steak and a slice of Velma's blueberry pie. If she wasn't too busy, Velma would come and drink a glass of milk while he sipped his coffee and tried to persuade her to come to the moving pictures.

—There's a new picture show in town.

—There's a new one every week.

—This one is *Amarilly of Clothes-Line Alley*. Mary Pickford.

—I can't go to the pictures. Who would look after my babies?

—They aint babies. You leave Emmy to watch Ben when you're at work.

—Where I'm right downstairs and all they have to do is holler.

—This aint but right up the street. She could fetch you if anything goes wrong.

They went to *Amarilly of Clothes-Line Alley* and Velma sighed over Mary Pickford. They went to see Charlie Chaplin in *Shoulder Arms* and to *Tarzan of the Apes* with Elmo Lincoln. They went to see Mary Pickford again in *Stella Maris* and they laughed over Fatty Arbuckle and Buster Keaton in *Out West* even though the picture-show version of the West did not seem like anything like the west that they knew. She always felt a little blue after these outings, remembering how Frank could brush his fingertips over the back of her hand and make her feel a tremor in her soul. Watson's dry, long-boned hand was just a hand, and nothing he might do with that hand was apt to stir much in her body or her heart. Tavie had to keep reminding her that her feelings had nothing to do with this; she was a lunger with two children to raise and the bigger they grew, the smaller those rooms over the Blue Hawk Diner would seem. Watson had the means to take them out of there; in Tavie's eyes, nothing else mattered—but Tavie did not have to marry the man.

In early December, with the snow holding off and the roads clear, Watson persuaded Velma to skip her usual Sunday visit to the Arbuckle ranch and to bring the children to see his place on Little Goose Creek instead. They were to head out Saturday afternoon and spend the night at his house. Watson came to get them in his Model T truck and they drove nine miles south from Sheridan to the town of Big Horn and then due west, up the rough, winding road that followed the course of the creek, a spectacular vista opening behind them as the truck labored up the mountain in first gear until at last Watson braked at a well-made log cabin that backed onto the creek.

—This here is my spread. The Watson place, everybody calls it now.

He opened the door and led them into the house. It was as neat as Tavie promised. Velma had never known a man to keep house like Watson did, with curtains on the windows, a beautiful quilt on the bed, the kitchen spotless. Watson had made every bit of furniture in the house, from the bed frame to the kitchen table, a comfortable rocking chair and another for the shop, and a beautiful blue silk ottoman with cushions he upholstered himself. After Emaline and Ben were asleep on a cot in a room separated from the parlor by a drawn curtain, Watson poured her a tiny glass of rye whiskey and himself a big tumbler. He drank his down, poured another, and drank that and a third tumbler even before he sat down to talk. The liquor loosened his tongue and he began talking, telling her about life in Chicago, about taking the El, living with the booming noise of the big city day and night.

—Chicago is a great town, but I could never go back. I got to like the quiet up here.

—I'd love to see a city like Chicago someday. The only big city I've been to was Denver, and I didn't see much except the sanatorium.

—That must have been pretty bad, that hospital.

—The bad part was being sick. They were good to me there. I made friends with lots of city people. There was a famous Jewish poet there who read poems in Yiddish.

Watson's face darkened. He drained another whiskey before he spoke.

—I don't care much for Jews.

Velma poked him and tried to make a joke of it.

—That's because you don't know them. The doctors and most of the patients at the sanatorium are Jewish. Wasn't for them, I wouldn't be alive today.

—Only people I dislike more than Jews are the Indians.

—Then you won't like me much. My grandmother was half Sioux.

—You don't say. Why didn't you tell me this before?

—You didn't ask.

—It didn't occur to me you were descended from murderin savages and no-good drunks.

—The Sioux were a great people, Watson. We stole their land. We didn't leave them much choice. If you hate the Indians, we're never going to get along.

Watson downed his whiskey and poured another large tumbler. His eyes were watery and unfocused. He seemed to have lost the trail of the conversation, as though he had something else to say but could not imagine what it might be. Abruptly, he tried to kiss her. Velma allowed it with her lips tight shut, but when he slid his hand to her thigh, she moved it away firmly and he did not complain. He eased back, poured himself another tumbler of rye, and drained it. When he kissed her again the smell of the whiskey made her eyes water. He tried to force her mouth open with his tongue but she resisted. When he bent her back with his weight and tried to force her legs open, it was too much. She slapped his face, hard. He sat up, startled, rubbing his cheek.

—What the hell did you do that for?

—Because you are taking liberties I won't allow. If you keep this up we're not going to stay the night. I don't care if we have to walk back to town.

—Walk if you please. It's the middle of the night and that walk is near twenty miles. Don't know why you're so tight with what you got to give. Aint like it would be your first time.

—Speaking to me like that isn't going to help. You're drunk, Watson. I'm going to sleep on Emaline's cot. I'll speak with you in the morning, when you've had time to sober up.

—Aw, don't take it so hard. There's things a man needs.

She ignored him, curled up next to Emaline, and tried to sleep. She thought Watson might try to follow her into Emaline's bed, but in less than a minute he was snoring. *Lungers can't be choosers*, Tavie kept saying. *Watson has steady work and always will, as long as people keep dying. He'll care for you and the children, get you out of that diner. Don't be proud.* Velma did not want her pride to stand in the way of a better life for her children, but putting them in the path of Watson's drinking might be worse. She had no feelings at all for the man to begin with, and his drinking didn't help.

The next morning Watson was so hungover he could barely manage to drive them back to town. Velma was too angry to talk, and Watson needed all his concentration to drive through a thundering headache. She thought that might be the end of it, but three days later, he turned up at the diner after the lunchtime rush.

—We have to talk.

—I don't see why.

—I know I didn't act real good the other night.

—I'd say you didn't behave well at all.

—I know that. I get into the liquor, and I say things I don't mean. I'm mighty sorry.

—Not sorry enough to get me back, I'm afraid.

—You can't hold it against a man what he does when he's drinking. You said yourself I'm a fine fella to be with.

—When you're sober, maybe. I don't like the man I saw when you were drunk.

—I swear, Velma. I'll quit. All I need is a little woman like you to give me a reason.

He came back the next day, and the day after that. He brought her little gifts: a tiny doll for Emaline, a carved wooden soldier for Ben, a tiny wooden box for her jewelry, lined with satin, all made in his shop. In the end, Velma relented to the point where she promised to think it over. He was back the next afternoon and the next, and finally she agreed to go to the picture show with him again. He didn't smell of whiskey this time, and he was as kind and mild-mannered as he had been at their first meeting. When he brought her home, Velma let him kiss her on the cheek.

—If you can stay off the rye, Mr. Watson, I will continue to see you. Sober, you are a gentleman. Stinko, you are another creature altogether. I will not abide a man who keeps ranting about how much he hates the Jews and the Indians. I'm part Indian and I will not allow you to make me feel ashamed of it.

Watson stared at the floorboards.

—That aint me. Aint me at all. I get along with all kinds of people, except when the drink is in me, and then I'm apt to say any kind of thing. Hell of it is, the next day I don't hardly remember a word, but folks hold it against me and I guess I can't blame 'em. I'll do my best to see it don't happen again.

Watson followed her around. Helpless, infatuated, hat in hand, pleading. She begged him to wait, to give her time. He waited like a hungry puppy. On Valentine's Day, he proposed.

—Look, I know I'm not much of a catch for a beautiful young woman, being a widower and all. But I've got my little business, and a house and a truck, and I'll do my best to look after you and the kids. I know some men would be anxious about you bein a lunger and all, but it don't bother me none. From what I can see, you've got the consumption beat.

—Nobody beats the consumption.

—Then you've learned to live with it.

—I suppose I have.

—Them kids need a father.

—I don't know, Watson. I'll have to think on it. Stop hounding me.

She held him off for another month. He had a home and a steady income. She couldn't keep the children living above the diner forever. Up on Little Goose Creek, they would have room to run as she had run growing up on the Fanciful. She was twenty-six years old, and her first responsibility was to care for her children. Most men would bolt like a skittish horse when they found out a woman had kids; the fact that Watson seemed to like the children stood in his favor. If she could keep him off the bottle, it might work out. In the end, she agreed to marry him because she was too tired to say no.

The ceremony was performed by a justice of the peace in Sheridan on March 13, 1920, with Watson looking pale and a little lost in a shapeless brown suit, Velma half smiling in her best blue dress, Tavie thinking that she had never seen her sister look so weary. After the ceremony, they threw on a feed at the Arbuckle ranch and invited friends and neighbors from twenty miles around.

There was supposed to be no alcohol on the ranch, because Amelia was strictly temperance, but Watson found a bottle somewhere, got drunk, and insinuated there was something improper about the relationship between Tavie and Amelia. A rancher friend of Tavie's said that was about enough and floored Watson with a left hook, then helped Velma load her unconscious husband into the passenger door of the Model T. With much grinding of the gears, Velma drove him home to Little Goose Creek, where with some effort she managed to revive him enough to get him into the house. When he attempted to consummate the marriage, he fell asleep on top of her, and Velma spent the second wedding night of her young life alternately holding ice to her husband's jaw and telling herself he would be a fine man, as long as he wasn't into the liquor.

The next morning Watson did manage to perform his marital duties, though not in nearly as energetic or spirited a fashion as Frank would have. Emaline and Ben, who had stayed on the ranch to give the newlyweds some privacy, moved in a week later and they settled into a comfortable routine: Velma cooked and baked and canned, Emaline did the chores in the house, Watson worked in his shop upholstering furniture, building the occasional coffin, happily sawing and stitching, gluing and polishing. Ben milked their two little shorthorn cows and slopped the pigs and helped Watson with odd jobs in the shop, where he loved the smells of wood and sawdust and the way Watson hummed while he worked. The children had a four-mile hike to school but they had fresh air and room to roam, and at dawn the view to the east from high up Little Goose Creek made Velma's eyes grow misty: It was too much beauty, a beauty that made you ache inside.

Early that summer, they all piled into Watson's Model T truck for a camping trip in the Bighorns: Amelia and Tavie, Watson and Velma, Benjamin and Emaline. Ben liked to fool around with Amelia's big box camera, so she let him take their picture: Amelia with her arm around Tavie's shoulders, Velma in front wearing a cap and a heavy white sweater, Watson in the middle with a rueful smile. Emaline, wearing the same dark cap as her mother, sat off to the side, her dark, watchful eyes peering out from under the bill of the cap. Watson was delighted with the picture and had it mounted in a frame over the fireplace. Velma didn't care for it much; she didn't like the way Watson was leaning into her, clinging to her, didn't like the shadowed, haunted look in her own eyes, didn't like the weakness around his mouth, didn't like the way poor Emaline sat apart from the rest, watchful, her crippled arm hidden behind her back.

Watson's physical attentions were mercifully infrequent. Once or twice a month at most, and then only if he was somewhere between moderately drunk and insensate. He was effective enough, however, because the boys were born eleven months apart: Robert, named after Watson's father, Robert E. Lee Watson, in February 1921, William in March the following year. They were Bobby and Billy, the Watson boys. Even Bobby had Velma's black hair, but Billy took after his father. He was fair-skinned and blond with blue eyes and a wide, expressive mouth. He was a slightly built child, small for his age, light as a feather when Emaline hoisted him into bed or the boys rough-housed with him, rolling him back and forth on the floor. Velma spoiled him, the older children spoiled him. Watson spoiled him most of all, never returning from the shop without carving a little toy for Billy—a wooden Indian, a tiny wagon with wheels that turned, another livestock car for the choo-choo train that circled the parlor floor. Billy was too young to understand jokes, but if someone said something funny at the supper table, all it took was one giggle to set him off. His infectious, high-pitched laughter, Watson liked to say, would draw a chuckle out of a coffin maker. Velma loved to watch the boy wake in the morning. He would be lying completely still, and suddenly those blue eyes would pop open, then he'd look around for an instant and laugh and jump out of bed, wide awake and ready to go.

To Velma, the children were everything. A blessing in exchange for the years in the sanatorium. A comfort and joy, cheerful company and hope for the future. As long as Watson cared for them all, she would tolerate his many weaknesses. She loved them all, but deep inside she knew that she loved Billy most. She couldn't help it; he was such an attractive, happy child. If she never bore another she would be content, because Billy was as marvelous a little boy as a mother could raise.

For Billy's second birthday, in March 1924, Watson bought him a red wagon, the first store-bought toy any of the children ever had. It was for all of them, really, because Ben and Bobby would spend hours out in the road pulling Billy back and forth. Planing fresh pine in his shop, Watson would hear Billy's laugh floating through the window and grin to himself, thinking that little red wagon had been worth every penny.

CHAPTER 48

Billy took sick the day after Christmas 1924. It had started to snow that morning, a scattering of hard, wind-driven pellets that turned into thick, heavy flakes by noon. Watson had made the children a sled out of a board that cracked as he was nailing it to a coffin, adding wooden runners and a rope so the boys could tow it uphill and rails on the side so the little ones wouldn't fall off. By midafternoon there was six inches of fresh snow on the hill above the cabin and the snow was still falling hard. There was no holding them. Velma let Emaline and Ben skip their chores, Bobby and Billy were bundled from head to foot, and Ben grabbed the rope to tow them uphill. All afternoon, Velma could hear them whooping and hollering while Watson worked in the shop and she baked in the kitchen. When the wind picked up and the mountain faded to dark, Velma called them in for hot chocolate and cookies. They shed wet clothes, boots and scarves and stood by the coal stove baking in the heat. Emaline dried the younger ones with an old towel, and they trooped still laughing to the table.

Two hours later Velma called them to a supper of meat loaf with gravy, potatoes and canned peas she had put up in the fall. Billy barely touched his but Velma assumed it was because he was tired from their day on the hill. After supper he curled up on the rag rug in front of the stove and fell sound asleep with his thumb in his mouth. Ben lifted him into his cradle and rocked him while Emaline and Velma did the washing up. When they finished, Emaline noticed that Billy was roll-ing back and forth in the cradle and whimpering. He had tossed off his blanket, and his cheeks were flushed. When Velma touched his forehead, it singed her fingers. Billy kept arching his back and twisting his head.

Watson was reading an old copy of *The Sheridan Press*.

—Watson, maybe we ought to take Billy down to Big Horn while we can still get through, see if Doc Newell will take a look at him. He's pretty sick.

Watson didn't even look up.

—Aw, the boy will be all right. He's made of tough stock.

When he finished his paper, Watson claimed that he had some work to do and headed to his shop, although Velma suspected the only work he would be doing would be on a bottle of rye whiskey. It had started again a month before and was getting worse by the day. While Watson was out, Billy got steadily worse. Velma was ac-customed to children with fever but she had never seen anything like this.

When Watson came back an hour later, the wind was ripping at the house and the snow was falling hard. Velma could smell the liquor on him as soon as he stepped through the door.

—It's turnin into a real howler out there. Could be we'll be stuck here three or four days.

—We can't afford to be stuck. You're going to have to take the truck and try to get through for the doctor. Billy is in bad shape.

—Helluva night to send a man out into a blizzard.

—Billy needs a doctor. You should have taken him before the storm got worse. Now you sober up and go get the doctor.

Watson cursed under his breath but reached for his coat. She heard the truck start, but five minutes later he was back. This time the wind was so strong he had to fight to push the door closed be-hind him.

—Truck's stuck in a snowdrift high as the cab. Nobody's goin to make it up or down that road, not in this.

Velma slammed her hand on the table in frustration.

—You should have gone when I asked you two hours ago.

—Why? Doc would never make it back up here anyway. I don't know why you're carryin on so. The boy will be fine.

Velma and Emaline finally coaxed Billy into taking a spoonful of laudanum and another of castor oil by promising him a candy cane. He made an awful face but choked the medicine down and fell asleep with the candy still in his mouth. Velma set it aside and put her hand on his forehead. It was like touching a stove top. He moaned and twitched in his sleep and she pressed her lip to his cheek. His skin burned her lips. Never had she felt such a fever in a child. No doctor, no way to get a doctor, and the storm raging outside. There was nothing to do but wait and hope the fever would break. She wrapped him up to the neck in her best quilt and put him back in the big wooden cradle, which was still his bed because he was so small he hadn't outgrown it. When she checked on him an hour later, Billy had bright red blotches all over his body and his fever was higher than ever. He woke briefly and complained that his neck hurt and the light hurt his eyes, then fell asleep again. Velma, weeping with frustration, lit into Watson for his failure to have a telephone line run to their house.

—It is nineteen hundred and twenty-four. People have telephones. If we had a phone, I could at least ask a doctor what to do for him.

—The boy will be all right. It's just a fever.

—It is not. Look at this rash. Have you ever seen anything like that? It's not the smallpox and it's not the chickenpox, because I've seen those, and it sure isn't tuberculosis because I know what to look for with the TB. This is something else Billy has. Something quick and awful.

Velma told Emaline to run outside and fetch a bucketful of snow. They tried to pack snow around Billy to bring down the fever, but he kept fighting his way out of the cradle. Watson, paralyzed with fear for his son, did nothing to help. Billy was crazy with pain and slippery and wet with snow that melted the instant it touched his skin. His neck was stiff, he complained that his head hurt, and he vomited until his little body quivered.

—Do something, Watson! Do something! My baby is dying and you are standing there watching. Do something!

—I aint no doctor. You act like I'm a doctor. I aint no doctor.

He pulled a metal flask of rye out of his pocket. He was sweating, his hair and eyes wild, his face gray in the light of the kerosene lantern. He screwed the cap off the flask, took a long pull and then another. Emaline kept holding fistfuls of snow to Billy's face and the back of his neck, but he was so hot the snow melted. There was blood coming from his nose and he kept crying for his sister, "Emmy Emmy Emmy Emmy," the words bubbling out of his mouth. He would hush for a minute, his body pinwheeling on the floor, then he would cry for her again.

—Emmy Emmy Emmy Emmy.

—I'm right here, Billy. It's all right. You're going to be all right.

—Emmy Emmy Emmy Emmy. It hurts, Emmy. Stop it hurt.

—I'll try Billy, I'll try anything. What do you need?

—Emmy Emmy Emmy Emmy.

—Oh, Billy, please get better. Please get better.

—Emmy Emmy Emmy Emmy.

Velma could bear it no more. She turned on her husband.

—Watson, you are the most useless man was ever born. Your own son and you wouldn't even drive him down to a doctor. Do you still think he's going to be all right, you drunken fool?

—I won't be talked to that way in my own house.

—You don't want to be talked to that way, act like a man. Look at this poor baby. Look at him. He's dying and you are not doing a damned thing about it. My baby is dying right in front of my eyes and you are letting it happen.

—Emmy Emmy Emmy Emmy.

Emaline was on her knees, holding Billy as tightly as she could.

—What can I do, Mama? Tell me something to do for him and I'll do it.

—I don't know, child. We can pray to the Lord. That's all that's left.

Religion had pretty much left Velma in the hospital but she knelt with Ben and Emaline and prayed, her hand on Billy's forehead, touching pure fire.

—Dear Lord, hear my prayer. Spare this child that he may live. Dear God, I could not bear it. Spare my baby, do not take him. Take me if you must, Lord, I have the TB in my lungs anyway, I almost went those years ago, take me now and spare him. Lord God, please spare my child.

—Emmy Emmy Emmy Emmy.

—Please, sweet Jesus, do you hear me? Spare my baby boy.

—Emmy Emmy Emmy Emmy.

It ended just after dawn. Velma thought Billy might be getting better because he grew quiet and remained that way for an hour or more. His eyes were open but it appeared that his neck was so stiff he could not turn his head and he was in a stupor; when she moved her hand in front of his face he looked right through her. Then a tiny spasm seemed to pass through his torso and he was still. Velma pressed her ear to his bony chest. She sought a heartbeat, heard nothing but the seashell tidal wash of her own blood humming in her ears. Emaline threw her arms around her mother. Ben and Bobby sat motionless, side by side on the ottoman. For a few long moments there was no sound but the ticking of the grandfather clock, and then Velma let go a prolonged wail, her voice breaking as she collapsed in sobs, lifting Billy to her as though he might find in her breast some solace that would coax him back to life.

Watson stood by the wall, an outcast from the tight little circle of death. He tipped up the flask again and drank deep. It was his second flask in two hours, but it had no effect at all. In the pitiless light of that little room, he had drunk himself sober. His son was stone dead, his wife screaming. *God why doesn't she stop that hollering it aint goin to do a goddamned thing hollering like that you're not going to bring him back now no matter how much you scream and carry on. The boy's dead, any fool can see that, and once you're dead you're dead, as a doornail, as a crow, as a hooked carp in the bottom of a boat. Dead dead dead.* He knew himself for what he had always been: a coward and a weakling, of no more use in a crisis than a jaybird.

Velma held Billy to her breast as though somehow she could squeeze the life back into him. Ben stood waiting for someone to tell him what to do. Bobby stroked his mother's hair the way she stroked him when he had skinned his knee or stubbed his toe. Finally Emaline sent Ben to fetch another bucket of snow. She melted it on the stove and waited for the water to warm, then pried Billy from her mother's grip. She undressed him and washed his body with care, then wrapped him from head to toe in his favorite blanket, laid his body on the table, dragged the rug out into the snow to be washed later and scrubbed the pine floor until the traces of blood and shit and death were gone.

Watson didn't move until Velma turned on him.

—Get out. Get out, Watson. You are no man at all. Take your bottle and get out of my sight or so help me I will take a butcher knife to you. You can sleep in your shop with your whiskey. It's where you belong.

Watson went. He started a fire in the cast-iron stove in his workshop, broke the seal on a fresh quart of bootleg rye, and sat in his rocking chair, pouring ninety-proof whiskey straight from the bottle onto a wound that would never heal.

The day was radiant, bright slivers of golden sunshine reflecting off the white mountain. Pine boughs shed cascades of wet snow onto the hill where the children had yelped and tumbled the afternoon before. Velma stared out, expecting Billy to come pounding to the door at any moment, ruddy-faced and runny-nosed, begging for hot chocolate. The afternoon before he was a lively little two-year-old; by dawn he was dead. She had wept herself dry. She had mourned enough, mourned all the ghosts and mourned herself, the consumptive Velma Watson, stranded in a little house on a

Wyoming creek with a drunken coffin maker for a husband and a dead child laid out on her kitchen table. The mourning this time would be without end.

Watson's truck sat where he had left it, hood-deep in a snow-drift at the edge of the road. Another drift rose more than six feet in the middle of the road. The only way into Big Horn would be by snowshoe; there was nothing to do but wait for the horse-drawn snowplows to work their way up the pass. Every hour she checked the other children for sore throats, fevers, the ache of contagion. Emaline said a girl she knew down in Big Horn had died the same way as Billy the week before school went out for Christmas. They said it was something called meningitis, and meningitis was contagious.

—Why didn't you tell me before?

—I only thought of it after Billy was gone.

—So that was it. Meningitis. We ought to have had a doctor.

—I don't know, Mama. The girl down in Big Horn, they took her to the hospital in Sheridan. She died anyway.

Late in the afternoon, Velma could hear Watson hammering and sawing. He was working on Billy's coffin, had to be. When Emaline was sent over with a plate of food, she found him wild-haired and red-eyed, a fresh bottle of rye at his side, carefully hand-stitching blue velvet upholstery to fit inside a tiny coffin. He butted the cord ends and overlapped the welt precisely, working the warp and woof of the cloth between long, needle-callused fingers. He stared at her as though he had never seen her before in his life, hefted the bottle and poured a long string of urine-colored fire down his throat. Emaline set the plate down on a coffin lid and left without a word.

When the coffin was finished, Watson took Ben up the hill and they worked all day with a pick and spades, digging a grave. At dawn the next morning they filed up the hill for the little funeral, Ben carrying Bobby on his shoulders, Watson half-drunk. Emaline read from the Good Book. *The Lord is my shepherd. I shall not want.*

He maketh me to lie down in green pastures. He restoreth my soul. A white magpie flapped to a branch on a lodgepole pine, then rose and flew off toward the rising sun.

When Velma woke the next morning, Watson was gone. No letter, nothing at all. Vanished as Frank had vanished. Velma was too numb to care. She kept busy mending, baking, sweeping, washing up, getting meals on and off the table. Every day when they weren't snowed in, Emaline and Ben walked the four miles down to the schoolhouse, leaving her alone with Bobby and too much time to think. Billy's death was a judgment on her, surely, wages for sins past and present, for the sin of Frank. Voices in her mind telling her that a woman should find a way to keep her child alive no matter what, that his death was on her head. A thousand tag ends of thought, each with a barbed hook of guilt. She had plenty of anger left over for Watson. Now the man was gone: a no-account drunk to the end.

The raging fever that had taken Billy left the other children untouched. Emaline as always was quiet and watchful, attending to her mother and her younger brothers. Benjamin was more obedient than usual, Bobby was quiet but sweet and affectionate. Velma envied him; he was too young to carry the load of grief that was coiled in her belly.

❧ CHAPTER 49 ❧

In April, Tavie and Amelia left Wyoming for Pennsylvania. Amelia's mother was alone in the city, her health was failing, and she refused to come to Wyoming on the grounds that it was too dangerous: Look what had happened to her husband, poor Leland Arbuckle, struck down by a runaway team on the street in Sheridan, may his soul rest in peace. Amelia did not want to leave Wyoming, but she felt that she had to care for her mother; she was going to use the money left by her father to open a riding academy in Philadelphia, where Tavie would teach children to ride. Velma could not imagine Tavie in such a place.

—I never thought you'd leave Wyoming, sis. Back east, they ride with those flat pancake saddles, don't they?

—They do. I expect I can ride that saddle as good as any. Riding is riding.

—But there aren't any mountains in Philadelphia. Won't you miss them?

—I will. I'll miss most everything about Wyoming, especially you and your kids. But Amelia—well, I pretty much got to go where Amelia goes, and right now she has to be with her Ma.

—She means that much to you?

—She does. I love her, Velma. Different kind of world, I'd marry her. We can't do that, but there isn't anything could stop us being together. I know it's strange to you, but that's how I feel. I wrote to Papa. He doesn't understand why I'm going back east. I said I want to see the world before I'm too old to travel, and there's some truth in that too.

—It doesn't seem strange to me, honey. I've kind of gotten used to the idea, you with Amelia. Heck, you get along better than most married folks I know. Better than me and Watson, for sure.

—I feel awful about Watson. I didn't use good judgment there. I should never have pushed you to marry the man. You were better off without him.

—It's not the man, sis, it's the drink. You were right when you thought that Watson would make a pretty good husband. Sober, he's a decent man. Drunk, he's pretty awful.

—Well, he's gone now.

—He is, and I hope he stays gone. But I'm going to miss you something awful. I can't imagine Wyoming without you. Other than the people from the diner, we don't know a whole lot of folks out here.

—I know that. I hope you'll be all right.

—We'll make out. We always do.

Velma tried to hide her anxiety. Tavie was like a mother, father, best friend, and big sister all rolled into one. In a crisis, she was the first person Velma would turn to, and now she was leaving.

Watson had left his Model T truck behind. Velma learned to drive it well and made the rounds, collecting what Watson was owed from various customers. It came to more than three hundred dollars, and she found another three hundred in the safe in his workshop. She took in sewing, sold vegetables from her truck garden, survived without him. It was a skill she had learned after the departure of Frank Hughes, and she had missed Frank a good deal more than she missed the absent O. A. Watson. Life was not perfect, her sorrow over Billy's death gnawed at her night and day, but experience had taught Velma not to expect too much. She had her children, they had a beautiful little home in the mountains. It would be foolish to ask for more.

They might have gone on that way for years, Velma and the children living in Watson's cabin up Little Goose Creek, but six months after Watson left, he was back. Velma heard a crash in the middle of the night, a kerosene lantern hitting the floor in the sitting room, and rose to find Watson lurching and fumbling in the dark, so drunk he could barely stand. She lit another lantern and saw his face, blotchy in the lamplight. He seemed both angry and baffled, as though he had no idea where he was or how he got there. He smelled as though he hadn't had a bath in all the time he had been gone. He had lost a dozen pounds from his already thin frame, his clothes were stiff and unwashed, his hair uncut and full of hay; he had obviously been sleeping in a haystack somewhere. When she stepped toward him, he greeted her with a backhand slap that caught her on the left cheekbone and sent her sprawling. Before she could get up, he kicked her in the ribs, then fell on top of her, grabbing her hair with one hand and punching her face with the other. Velma got a hand under his jaw and bent his head back, then rolled away. Watson tried to get to his feet to follow her, but he was too drunk to stand. She ran to the kitchen for a knife and waited with her back to the sink, ready to fight for her life. He didn't come after her, so she tiptoed back to the sitting room. He was passed out where she had left him, sprawled on his face, a spreading pool of urine filling the room with a sharp, acrid odor. Velma was still standing over him with the knife still in her hand when she realized that Emaline and Benjamin were watching from the bedroom door.

—You kids go back to bed. Watson is home, but he's had a little too much to drink.

Emaline ignored her and stepped closer to get a better look at her mother.

—What did he do to your face?

—We had a little disagreement, honey. That's all. Now you go back to bed.

—Why do you have that knife?

Velma stared at the knife, wondering how it happened to be in

her hand. Emaline took it from her, like a mother removing something dangerous from the hand of a child.

—Your nose is bleeding.

She led her mother to the sink. Emaline poured cold water
from the pitcher onto a cloth and wiped her mother's face. Velma
was trembling, all the strength gone out of her, her eyes beginning
to close.

—Mama, we can't let him do this to you.

—He's a fine man. Really, he is all right. It's just the drink,
turns him into another person. I expect losing Billy just about
killed him. He loved that boy.

—So did you. That's no excuse.

—No, I suppose it isn't.

Before they went to bed, Velma found a cushion and slipped it
under Watson's head. She and Emaline mopped up the urine off
the floorboards and Velma tossed an old blanket over him.

—He'll be all right in the morning. He's always real sorry the
next day.

It was near noon before Watson woke. He rolled over and
sat up with his head between his knees, then blinked around the
room, trying to figure out where he was. Emaline and Ben were
gone to school. Velma sat with Bobby on her knee, watching him
carefully.

—How'd I get here?

—You came stumbling in here in the middle of the night and
beat the hell out of me. I'm not going to stand for it, Watson, not
in front of the kids, not any time. I know you're broken up over
Billy, but that doesn't make it right.

Both her eyes were black, the left eye swollen almost shut. Her
ribs where he had kicked her felt like they were broken. Her nose
was puffy, her lip split in two places.

—I did that to you?

—Who else? I didn't run into a door. You came in and just
started whaling on me for no reason at all. It won't do.

—Oh, Jesus, Velma. I'm sorry.

—Don't bring Jesus into it. You're not near sorry enough. My daddy always said that a man who would hit a woman was the lowest kind of cur. He like to killed Frank for breaking my arm, and that was the only time Frank ever hurt me. If he knew you did this to me, he'd kill you with his bullwhip.

—Eli Paint? He doesn't even talk to you. Doesn't send money either. Why would he care?

—Oh, he'd care about something like this, right enough. Not that I mean to tell him. But I won't stand for more.

—You won't have to. I promise. I came back. That counts for somethin, don't it?

She sat and glared at him.

—Where have you been the last six months?

—Ridin the rails. Here and there. Montana. Utah. Idaho. Colorado some. When Billy went, that took me hard.

—So you just dove down into your bottle and decided not to come out. You're a coward, Watson. You think losing Billy didn't just about kill me too? But we stayed. We stuck without you. Every day I walk up that hill, put flowers on Billy's grave. And where were you? Drunk in some hobo jungle in Montana. Isn't that the truth?

—I guess that's about the size of it.

—I won't stand for it. Not the drinking, not being left, and especially not you hitting me. The children need a father but I won't stand for you hitting me.

—It won't happen again. I swear. It won't happen again. I'll quit the drink.

—If I had a dollar for every time you told me that, I'd be the richest woman in Wyoming.

—I mean it. I know I got to straighten my ways.

—Why should I believe you this time?

—Velma, I'm a changed man. I mean that. All them nights ridin the rails, thinkin how much I missed you and the kids. You give me a chance, I'll show you.

—You showed me last night, and what you showed wasn't very pretty.

—That was because I had to get myself liquored up to get the courage to come back here. I guess I overdid it.

—I guess you did. You were so drunk you wet yourself.

—I know. I want to make a new start.

—Your business is pretty much all gone. You'll have to start over.

—I can do it. I have my craft if naught else. But I don't have a thing if I aint got you.

—I'm not deciding anything right now. You're not sleeping a night in this house until you bathe. You stink like a goat. Bathe and get yourself some clean clothes. I don't want you around the kids looking like somethin slept in a garbage dump.

—Thanks for keepin care of the place while I was gone.

—I did what I could. The bills are paid and there's some garden in. The rest is up to you.

—You can count on me, Velma.

For most of the summer, Watson worked hard in his shop. Because few others had his knack with wood and upholstery, he found customers. He was kind and quiet with her and the children, although she could not bring herself to open her legs to him again. Four-year-old Bobby worshipped his father and tagged after him everywhere; that was enough. Emaline and Ben did not need Watson, Velma could barely tolerate him, but Bobby needed the man. For that she would put up with a lot.

Watson fell off the wagon on Labor Day and came home drunk but did not hit her. He slept it off, and although she barely spoke to him for a week, he went back to work as though nothing had happened. In October it happened again: one drunken night, no abuse. Velma thought they just might make it. Watson could make a good living if he could stay off the drink. Little Goose Creek was a beautiful place, Emaline and Ben liked the school down in Big Horn, Bobby seemed happy for the first time since Billy's death. There was no reason to disrupt their lives.

A November snow fell outside. Velma cowered on the bed. Watson was standing over her, holding the wide leather saddlecinch he used to strap her, his flaccid penis dangling inches from her mouth.

—You goddamned squaw. You goddamned little squaw whore. I married a redskin cocksucker, that's what. I'll bet that's how you got that TB you're so proud of, aint it? Fuckin some big Indian buck in his tipi. Aint it? I bet you done a couple dozen of 'em up on the reservation.

—Don't, Watson. Please. I haven't tried to hurt you. Don't say these things. I know you don't mean them, and you'll hate yourself for it in the morning.

—Hell I don't. I mean every goddamned word of it.

—Don't do this. Please. How do you get these things in your head? How can you speak such filth with children in the house?

She tried to placate him, to hush him, to get him to fall into a drunken stupor before he killed her or one of the children. She let him take her any way he wanted, the roughest ways, making her bleed, swallowing the pain if it would buy them a night of peace. She could hear the children, hear Bobby crying. She knew they were waiting to see if she could get him to stop or if it would end with her bruised and battered, with Ben weeping in frustration because he was unable to help, with Watson warning Emaline that she would be next.

Watson was red-eyed, wobbling on his feet, his face flushed, the liquor fumes rising off him so powerful it made her eyes water. He had vanished at the end of October and returned in this state, looking as though he had spent his nights in a gutter. She knew him well enough to know that the only thing that could settle him now was the act of love that had become the most hateful thing in her life. She took him in her mouth, fighting down the urge to retch.

She tried to take her mind somewhere else. It didn't work. She was with Watson, and if she didn't satisfy him, he might kill her. She tasted bitter semen and forced herself not to gag or spit it out because that might set him off. He shoved her away and collapsed facedown on the bed, trousers still around his knees. She put her nightgown back on and went to the kitchen to wash her face. Emaline slipped up behind her, quiet as a shadow.

—We have to go, Mama. We can't do this anymore.

—I know, baby.

—Really. No more. I can't listen to it anymore. Nor Ben, nor Bobby. We should go now. Tonight. While he's out. We should take the truck and go.

—I know, baby. You're right. You and Ben help. We'll pack everything we need and we'll load it in the truck. I'm not sure I can drive it down this mountain in a snowstorm, but I'll have to try.

Ben dragged their trunks down from the attic. He and Emaline packed the children's things while Velma packed her own, working quickly, terrified that Watson would wake and see what she was doing. They were halfway through packing when Velma heard a strange sound from the sitting room and went to see what it was. Watson was standing in the middle of the room, wild-haired, his face flushed and sweating, gleefully urinating. When Velma tried to stop him, he turned the stream on her. She pulled away, but he followed, backing her into a corner and holding her there. By the time he finished, her gown was soaked. Watson tangled his fingers in her hair and held her face inches from his. He drew back and slapped her hard with his free hand. Once, twice, three times. Velma tried to fight back. Over Watson's shoulder she could see the children standing at the door to their room.

—Emmy! Take the boys! Go!

Watson looked over his shoulder at Emaline.

—Don't you move, you little bitch. I'll get to you in a minute. Soon's I get done with your ma, you and me are goin to have ourselves a party.

His threat gave Velma a surge of wild strength. She twisted away from him and ran to the rack above the front door where he kept the .22 rifle for skunks and raccoons. She whirled, pointed the gun right at his forehead, and pulled the trigger. There was a dry *click!* and Watson collapsed in crazed laughter.

—Damned fool woman! You think I'd keep a loaded rifle in the house with kids? I ought a beat you to death for tryin that.

Before she could reach the box of shells he kept on the shelf, he twisted the rifle out of her hands and punched her in the stomach with the butt end, leaving her writhing and breathless on the floor. He stood over her and lowered his trousers. Velma gathered herself and brought her knee up hard in his groin, but Watson twisted away and caught the blow on his thigh. He retaliated with a hard punch to her stomach and another to her face, and then the two of them were wrestling on the floor, Velma clawing at his eyes while he tugged her urine-soaked nightgown up around her waist.

—Open your damn legs now or I'll choke you to goddamned death.

His hands closed around her throat. She tried to squirm away as he tightened his grip and forced her legs apart with his knees. Velma gathered enough breath to scream:

—Stop it. You're killing me!

Somehow she got a hand free and jammed her fingernails into his eyes.

—You crazy whore! You coulda put my eye out!

Velma got as far as her knees before the punch caught her flush on the jaw and knocked her flat on her stomach. Watson got to his feet and reached for the saddlecinch he kept on a peg on the wall in case one of the kids needed a strapping. This time he turned it so that the heavy metal buckle faced down and swung it hard from the leather end, catching her in the kidneys with the buckle. The next blow opened a cut on her thigh.

Emaline watched it all from the door of the bedroom with the boys behind her, keeping her body between them and Watson. The scream when the buckle hit Velma between the legs spurred the girl into motion. She pushed Ben and Bobby back into the bedroom.

—You two get in there now. Crawl under the bed and don't come out unless I tell you.

Ben led Bobby by the hand into the bedroom, locked the door behind him and dragged his half brother under the bed. As soon as Emaline heard the bolt slide shut, she couldn't watch anymore.

She slipped across the floor in her bare feet and grabbed the kerosene lantern by its wire handle, using her crippled arm to support her good arm. Watson had Velma's hair twisted in his left hand. With his right hand, he was furiously trying to get his penis erect. Velma tried again to get him to stop.

—Please, Watson. Don't do this here. I'll go in the bedroom with you.

—What's wrong with you? You ashamed of me? Is that it?

She was too weak to fight. Watson shifted his grip from her hair to her throat again. Emaline heard her mother choking and saw her face turning red. Choking Velma seemed to excite him. He thrust his stiffened penis into her. She tried to roll away but he tightened his grip on her throat. Emaline crouched three feet behind Watson. She was young and lithe and desperate. She took a long, shuddering breath for courage, spun completely around once with the lantern held at arm's length, spun again harder as the lantern crashed into the back of Watson's head. The glass shattered and Watson's head was engulfed in burning kerosene, his long hair a halo of fire. Watson rolled on the floor and scrambled on his hands and knees toward the door, howling with pain. Glass and kerosene splattered Velma and three little fires caught on the rag rug. Emaline stomped them out, cutting her feet on the glass as she hauled her mother to her feet. She pushed Velma, choking and gasping for air, toward the bedroom.

—Go, Ma, go! Ben! Get Ma, now!

Ben grabbed Velma's elbow and pulled her into the bedroom. Watson tore the kitchen door open and ran outside, his hair still on fire. Emaline slammed and bolted the door and watched from the kitchen window. Watson ran into the winter night, flaming kerosene trailing off his shirt, and plunged headfirst into a snowbank. The plunge put out the fire but it did not ease the pain; he was still howling like a mad, wounded beast. In the lantern light from the window, Emaline could see blood pouring from a gash in the back of his head. She picked up the .22 rifle where Watson had tossed it, found the box of shells, and loaded three into the magazine, just as he had taught her to do when there was a coyote after the hens. She watched as Watson staggered out of the snowbank, clutching at his blackened scalp. The mingled scent of kerosene and burned hair was so powerful it made her eyes water. She propped open the window, crouched on her knees with the barrel of the rifle resting on the windowsill and drew a bead on him. If he came toward the house, she would put all three bullets into him.

Watson grabbed fistfuls of snow and rubbed them into his face and hair. Emaline could see that his eyebrows had vanished and his face was a pale, twisted mask. He roared an incoherent threat. Emaline tightened her finger on the trigger, aiming right at the middle of his torso, where she couldn't miss. She would let him take one step toward the house, two at most, and then she would fire. She drew her breath and held it the way he had taught her, her cheek welded to the stock of the rifle, her right eye closed, the sight perfectly centered on Watson's heart. Abruptly, he spun away from the house and staggered to his truck. She watched him set the magneto and turn the crank until the engine coughed and caught. He climbed back into the cab, adjusted the spark, ground the transmission into first gear and set off down the hill, careening from one side of the road to the other until he vanished in the snow. She listened until the drone of the motor faded, then called to Ben that it was safe to come out. She handed him the rifle and told him to use it if Watson came back.

While Ben kept watch, Emaline and Velma tended to each other. Velma had to pour some of Watson's rye down her throat before she could control her trembling hands enough to remove the slivers of glass from Emaline's feet. She had black-and-blue marks around her throat from Watson's hands and bumps and bruises all over. The smell of kerosene was making her sick, but she was alive. Emaline still had that strange calm, even as Velma was pulling the glass splinters and doctoring her feet.

—I don't think he'll be back tonight. I think I hurt him bad.

—You had to, baby. He was hurting me. The mood he was in,

he might have killed us all if you hadn't taken that lantern to him. Made an awful mess, but at least he's gone.

—I don't want to live here anymore.

—None of us do, honey. We'll get out before he comes back. The way he looked, he's going to have to get to a hospital, so he shouldn't be back for a day or two. We'll go to Isaac Gunderson's place tomorrow and get him to take us down to Big Horn.

—We have to keep watch with that rifle anyway. All night. We can take turns. Two hours each, Ben first, then me, then we'll wake you. You get to bed now. This is too much for you.

Velma nodded and did as she was told. As she drifted off to sleep, she wondered at what point along the way it had happened that Emaline had taken charge of the family. Fifteen years old and a woman already. Real strength in her, the kind of strength Velma had once seen in Eli, that thing inside that you couldn't scare or push. If Watson did come back, she hadn't the slightest doubt: Emaline would shoot him dead.

⊱ CHAPTER 50 ⊰

Before he stepped out of the car, Sheriff Gale Gupton paused to polish his badge, lift his hat and slick back his hair. The Watson woman had borne four children but she was still a looker, so a man had to be prepared. He strolled toward the front door of the house, sheepskin coat open to show the badge, trying to walk with that long, rolling cowpoke stride, although the truth was he had always been scared to death of horses. He stood for a moment, composed his face to look appropriately solemn, and hammered on the door.

—Mizz Watson? You home? It's Sheriff Gupton.

She was in there with the girl. He had seen movement at the window just as he pulled in, as though someone had been watching, waiting. What was the girl's name? Emma? Evelyn? Something with an *E. Evangeline?* Nope, that wasn't it either. Young, but she was a comer. A girl to keep an eye on, anyhow. Once she filled out, she would be a girl for a Saturday night dance and what came after, the type a lawman's star might impress.

The door opened a crack. Velma Watson.

—Yes?

—I wonder if I might step in for a moment, Mizz Watson.

—You might. Is there a reason for this visit?

—There is, ma'am, although I'd rather not talk through the door.

—Come in then.

The door swung wide and he stepped through, waited for his eyes to adjust to the inner dark. When he could see clearly, it was plain the Watson woman had been beaten up some and had bruises on her throat. There had been rumors that Watson was knocking her around but Gupton made it a point never to interfere in domestic squabbles—a man had a right to keep his wife in line. Gupton eased his bulk through the door, cradling his Stetson in his palms.

—What is it, Sheriff?

—Mizz Watson, you might want to sit down. I got some bad news to bring you.

She sat primly, waiting for him to speak his piece, an attractive woman once you got past the bruises. Thirty years old, maybe. The sheriff wasn't a man to complain but Watson ought to have been a little more strict with the little lady about her housekeeping: Gale Gupton prided himself on his reputation as the bloodhound of the sheriff's department. This room smelled of urine, kerosene, and burned hair. Nothing a little soap and water wouldn't cure.

—Ma'am, I got to say, you look like you been hit some. Was your husband roughin you up last night?

—We had a little argument, is all. He had too much to drink.

—Uh-huh. Your Mr. Watson had a habit of drinkin a bit too much now and again. I know he caused trouble in town a time or two.

Velma changed the subject.

—You said you had bad news for me, Sheriff Gupton?

—I'm afraid I do. It's about Ora, ma'am.

It took Velma a moment to understand that Gupton was referring to her husband; she had called him Watson for so long that she had forgotten he had a first name.

—A couple of cowpunchers was out lookin for a stray horse this mornin. They found his truck down at the bottom of the canyon where Little Goose Creek bends due east, must of fell about a hundred feet pretty much straight down. Probably had a full tank of gas because the truck caught fire and burned up pretty bad, him along with it. There was a empty coffin fell out of the back appears to be of his making, so we think it must a been him.

—So my husband is dead? Is that what you're telling me?

—He is, ma'am. I'm awful sorry to say, but Mr. Watson has passed on to meet his Maker.

She nodded, taking it calmly.

—So what happened last night, ma'am?

—He took off, I suppose he went to get more liquor. I never knew where he got it.

—I think he was gettin the stuff from Wade Babcock, has a still north a Sheridan.

—He never told me. I know the prohibition didn't slow his drinking one bit.

—Soon as we plug one leak they find another one. Too many folks wantin liquor and not enough law. Don't do nothin but make our job harder, prohibition. Well, here I am chattin about the prohibition when your man has passed on. I'm terrible sorry.

He glanced at the girl, perched on a kitchen chair, watching. She didn't show any emotion at all, just sat there staring with those big, dark, serious eyes. Hard to figure how folks were going to react when you told them someone was dead.

—Well, ma'am, I'd best be goin. His body's at the morgue in Sheridan. You'll be wantin to make arrangements for the funeral, I guess.

—I will. I guess he can be buried in one of his own coffins.

Velma waited until he was gone to talk to Emaline.

—You know it isn't your fault, honey.

Emaline nodded, staring out the window.

—You were just trying to protect me. Nobody in this world is going to blame you for that.

—I hope not, but even if they do, I had to do it. I wasn't trying to kill him.

—You didn't kill him. He killed himself, trying to drive that truck down the mountain in winter when he was dead drunk.

—I saw him in front of the house. Right before he climbed in the truck. His eyebrows were burned off. He looked like some kind of crazy animal. I was going to shoot him, but he didn't start back for the house. If he did I would've shot him.

—He was crazy when he was drinking.

—Do you think that sheriff will figure out what happened?

—Gupton? Honey, that sheriff is so dumb he's lucky he can button his pants.

Velma wrapped her arms around Emaline. She remembered Watson choking her, how close she'd been to blacking out when Emaline swung the lantern at his head. Rescued by a fifteen-year-old girl, and how had it all come to that?

Finally Ben and Bobby came in, hungry, and Velma got up to fix them something to eat. When they were finished eating, she took a deep breath and sat down to tell them that Watson was dead. Bobby listened wide-eyed.

—Does that mean he's not goin to hurt you any more, Mama?

—That's right. He's not going to hurt any of us. But I don't want you to think bad of him, Bobby. He was your father, and he was a good man when he was sober.

Bobby nodded. Ben said nothing at all. After they finished their lunch and ran back outside, Emaline was still at the window, staring out at the snow.

Watson was buried in the cemetery at Sheridan, in a coffin he had made himself. There were a dozen mourners, most of them Watson's drinking pals. It was a cold, overcast day, snow in the air, a preacher from a church Watson had never attended presiding. Only little Bobby cried, and that was mostly because his toes were freezing. Emaline stood off to the side, expressionless, watching.

The day after the funeral Velma went into the cashbox Watson kept in his workshop and found almost nothing left. Before Billy's death he had been a dependable craftsman; after the boy was gone, he'd failed to complete orders on time, forgotten them altogether, botched his work because he was too drunk to plane a board or stitch upholstery. Although he had long since proved out on the original hundred-and-sixty-acre homestead claim, Watson had twice mortgaged it since, first to equip his shop and then to pay the debts incurred during his six-month drinking binge. W. J. Porter at the bank in Sheridan told her the bank had no choice but to foreclose. The house, shop, farm animals and all Watson's equipment went on the block at the sheriff's sale, with the auctioneer Arthur Roby presiding. Friends and neighbors bought everything that could be hauled away. Once all Watson's debts were paid off, Velma had eighty-two dollars left.

By the time they moved back into the apartment over the Blue Hawk Diner and Velma went back to baking for Wesley De Weese, she had little more than she had when she and Watson married. Except for little Bobby and the bruises on her body and soul, it was almost as though she had never met the late Ora Adolphus Watson, although after his death she felt an odd sympathy for the man. It was a terrible thing, drink. It could take control of a man and turn him into something he wasn't meant to be. The shame was that the Prohibition hadn't put a halt to the flow of liquor; if anything, it seemed people were drinking more than ever.

Before the columbines were out, Velma had another suitor in William Hobart, a slender, balding clerk for the Great Western Insurance Company, who lived with his widowed mother in a little yellow house on the edge of town. With Nellie Dorenbecker married and gone to Nebraska with her husband, Velma baked during the morning and doubled as a waitress for the lunchtime crowd. At five minutes past noon each day, Hobart would take his place and wait for her to bring his coffee. He tried to make bright conversation, but the man was dull as dishwater. Velma paid him little attention. To her, exhaustion began to seem like a normal way of life. She rarely slept more than four or five hours a night. The narrow band of white hair over her right temple spread into a solid stripe two inches wide. Velma made the skunk jokes on herself, but Hobart, mooning over a second cup of coffee at the diner in hopes she would finally consent to go out with him, said it made her more beautiful than ever, and would she like to come to the dance over at the Elks Lodge Saturday night? Velma thanked him and cut him a second wedge of apple pie on the house, but she turned him down.

—You're a sweet man, Hobart, but I've had two husbands who left me with nothing but children and grief. I'm my own woman now and I aim to keep it that way. Besides, you don't even have a roof over your head.

—I do so, and it's all mine when Mother passes on. Really, Velma, you shouldn't torment a man so.

—What you mean is that your home is your mother's, not yours. I will not live with any man's mother, nor will I be party to waiting about, in the hope that someone else will improve my lot in life by consenting to die. Any torment is strictly of your own making, William Hobart. I have done nothing but my job. Now eat your pie and leave me be.

Hobart did not discourage easily. He was back every lunch-time, punctual as churchbells. Even when Velma started coughing again, he kept coming back. At first he was sympathizing with her over that cold she couldn't shake; after a while, even Hobart realized it was something more than a cold. She hid it as well as she could, coughing into her apron at first, then into rags she brought from home, but you couldn't work long as a cook with a cough like that. Within a month, her joints were swollen, her bones ached, at times she barely felt able to get out of bed in the morning. She knew what it meant but she kept working. Emaline watched her with those wide, dark eyes.

—You're sick again, aren't you, Mama.

—No, I'm not. I'll be fine. I just caught a little cold.

—It's been a month now. I hear you cough all night. I'm afraid they're going to put you back in that place.

—Nobody is going to put me anywhere. I'm with you and this is where I'm going to stay.

—Promise? I don't want to go back to that orphanage.

—You won't, honey. You're older now, we can find a better place for you, even if I have to go back to the sanatorium, but I won't. I'll get better. It's just that it's winter now. The weather is awful and I'm tired from Watson and everything. I'll get better.

She said it and crawled into bed, her bones alive with fever, shaking, exhausted, coughing thick green mucus through the night, knowing that somewhere Emaline lay awake listening, frightened, waiting.

On a rainy afternoon at quitting time, Velma stumbled out of the diner and headed for the pharmacy down the street to get more laudanum. She made it two doors down before collapsing in a coughing fit. She was leaning against a brick wall coughing blood when Hobart found her.

—My goodness, Velma. I think you must have pneumonia. You'd best stay home.

—It's not pneumonia, Mr. Hobart. I've got the TB.

—You wait here. I'll go get my car and drive you to the hospital.

When she woke in the hospital on Saperton Street, it was near midnight and Emaline was asleep on a chair next to her bed. At first Velma thought the girl was her gentleman caller from the sanatorium, back with his boots and spurs, waiting. She lay awake, heart pounding, desolate. A shaft of moonlight through the window lit Emaline's sleeping face. Velma felt a wave of tenderness for the girl. So young, and she had been through so much, and now there would be more. It was inevitable. Velma would have to go back to the hospital. That or die. The children could not be allowed to return to the orphanage. It was time to swallow her pride, time to ask for help. When the night nurse came padding through the room, a white ghost trying not to wake Emmy, Velma whispered to her. A pen and paper, would that be possible? Something with which to write?

She wrote to Nellie Dorenbecker—who had married Bose Hubbard and left her job at the diner to move with him to Nebraska—asking Nellie if Emaline could come to live with her and Bose, so that she could go to high school in Scottsbluff. She wrote to her sister Ruby and Wade Tourtelotte in Torrington, asking them to take in Ben and Bobby. Finally, near dawn, she began the letter she had waited years to write. Imagining him on the Fanciful, sitting at the long pine table, reaching for his spectacles, recognizing or perhaps not recognizing her handwriting, opening the letter, reading the words:

—*Dear father . . .*

She sat up much of the night writing the letter. At dawn she read it over carefully from top to bottom, then tore it into very small pieces and threw it into the wastebasket at the foot of the bed.

BOOK 6

Valley of the Shadow

Nebraska 1926–1933

⊰ CHAPTER 51 ⊱

Emaline woke to a sky the color of smoke, reached for the bedside water pitcher, poured a glass, and found it gritty to the taste. A hard March wind was blowing outside and the snow had peeled away to dirty strips left in swale and shadow, the plowed fields not yet planted, no roots of growing things to stop the brown fields from lifting as the hard wind stole the topsoil. She reached automatically into the drawer next to her bed and ran her fingers over the bundle of letters from Velma, neatly tied with a ribbon. She read all the letters each evening but in the morning she merely touched them. The letters were a talisman, reassurance that Velma would recover again as she had before, that the day would come when she and Velma and Ben and Bobby would live together again. Satisfied that the letters were still in their proper place, she slid the drawer shut and lay back on her thin feather pillow, listening to the rattle of grit on the windowpanes. The dusty air made her sneeze. She sneezed three times, tried to sneeze again and could not. Most times she liked the delicious little thrill of a sneeze, but not this morning, not with dust sifting under the doorsill, dust in the corners of her eyes, dust in her nostrils, dust in the corners of her mouth, grit in the sheets of her bed. Awful. This dry, awful, place in the North Platte Valley. She yearned for Little Goose Creek, narrow and tumbling in white springfroth, running clear and cold between aspen and tall pine, sunrise gleaming off

white snow on the tall peaks to the west, the way you could see forever to the east where the creek, lively as a toddler, rushed down
into the valley. Here, the North Platte River was at almost any season a muddy, lazy old thing, wide and flat, mud brown where it ran
between cottonwoods and cattails through a channel a half mile
across, bearing southeast toward its confluence with the South
Platte, then on to the Missouri and the Mississippi, so that a willow
twig dropped into the stream here might end up one day in New
Orleans. To Emaline, that was the only magical thing you could
associate with the Platte. Once upon a time, her great-grandfather
Ebenezer Paint had run a storeboat on the Mississippi; how wonderful it must have been to rise at dawn on a great river far from
this dusty, dreary place.

She drew back a dusty curtain and peered out the window.
Through a haze of dust, she could barely make out Scotts Bluff,
the one redeeming feature of the landscape. It rose on the far side
of the Platte southwest of town, like an abandoned castle thrusting
its battlements to the sky. On clear days, Emaline fancied that she
could make out a giant crouching buffalo in the vegetation that
grew on the bluff's north side. She would never have told a living
soul, but sometimes she had conversations with that huge, gentle
buffalo. She confided her fears, told her buffalo about Velma in
the hospital, confessed that one day she would like to get away
from all this and see the world. Chicago, New York, even Paris and
London. Perhaps the buffalo could climb down from the bluff and
amble off with her, like Babe the Blue Ox with Paul Bunyan. They
would be famous: Emaline Hughes and Billy the Green Buffalo.

It was a Saturday. No school, a day to help Nellie clean the
house. Even above the wind, she could hear Bose Hubbard. His
snores shook the house, tore at the walls like the wind itself. If he
did not work the night shift at the sugar factory, she and Nellie
would never catch a wink; he came home at seven o'clock in the
morning, had a couple of belts of whiskey, and went to bed. He
would sleep until three or four in the afternoon, so if the housework was done, Emaline could escape before he woke. She did

not want to be there when Bose crawled out of bed, grumpy as an old wolverine, and sat at the kitchen table in his undershirt grousing about everything from Nellie's gravy to the administration of Cal Coolidge, which had no sympathy for the working man. Bose weighed near three hundred pounds. He was bald and always sweating and he never wore anything in the house but his undershirt and his OshKosh B'Gosh coveralls because he complained it was too hot, even when she and Nellie were shivering next to the stove. He had a hairy back like the pelt of some large and dangerous animal, and Emaline thought that living with Bose was like sharing a cave with a grizzly bear. You tried to make yourself small to stay out of his way, but you always felt that if you crossed him you would feel those jaws on your neck, feel the power of him crushing the life out of you. Nellie insisted that his bark was worse than his bite, but if Emaline was in the kitchen washing up, she would feel those beady little eyes on her and turn to find Bose staring in a way that made her feel naked no matter what she was wearing.

When they were living above the Blue Hawk Diner, Emaline had always loved to go down to the restaurant to chat with Nellie Dorenbecker, because Nellie was easygoing and happy and funny. Around Bose now, Nellie seemed thin and shrunken, frightened and submissive. Every evening after the supper dishes were cleared, Bose would point one thick finger toward the bedroom, and Nellie would put her head down and lead the way, after carefully turning up the volume on the radio so Emaline wouldn't hear too much. But she heard anyway, even if she covered her ears. The big man chugged away like a freight engine, and Nellie moaned so that Emaline couldn't tell if it was because she liked it or because he was hurting her. As long as it lasted, Emaline sat at the kitchen table with her hands over her ears, trying to concentrate on her arithmetic or her essay on Alfred Lord Tennyson, her face flushed, trembling. She would find herself twisting her skirt in her hands, holding her breath, covering her ears, willing it to be over. Then Bose would roar like a lion, and in another moment or two he would come out of the bedroom and make a show of buttoning his fly. Then he would splash a little water from the kettle on the stove into the washbasin and dab at his face and shoulders and armpits, before putting on his work shirt and boots and heading out to play checkers before his shift began at the sugar factory. Nellie never left the bedroom until he was gone; then she would tiptoe out and make coffee and sit quietly while Emaline finished her homework in silence. Those were the best times, the two women alone without Bose, comfortable in the quiet house until Nellie put the radio on.

Emaline remembered that if she wanted to escape before Bose was up, it was time to go to work. She dressed, ran a brush through her hair, and found Nellie seated at the kitchen table with a cup of coffee, watching the grit blow against the window.

—Nellie, it's awful out there. I never saw so much dust.

—I know it is, child. That's March in Nebraska. We get it like this from time to time. Especially this time of year, when the fields are plowed but the crops aren't in. Nothin to hold the soil. Makes me miss Wyoming somethin awful. There's nothin like a Nebraska dirt storm to make you wish you were somewhere else. Old Mrs. Suffolk swears there was a windstorm out here, blew one of her hens backward so hard she laid the same egg three times. That's why I made Bose gather the eggs when he came home this morning. Light as I am, I could hardly stand up in that wind. You want me to fry up a couple eggs?

—I can do it. You rest.

—I hate to say so, but I need it. My feet are sore and my back hurts.

—What are we doing today?

—Nothin that means goin out in that dust. Bose will sleep most of the day and wake up mad, but it can't be helped. I'd sooner face Bose than a dust storm.

Nellie bit her knuckles, a habit she had when she talked about Bose.

—He wasn't always like this, hon. I want you to know that.

—Like what?

—You know how he gets. Mean. Just plain mean. Mad at everybody, not a good word to say. He wasn't a bit like this when he was courtin me up in Sheridan, but after we came down here he worked himself just about to the bone. Then we lost the farm when the bank failed, and he had to start carryin a lunch pail to the sugar factory and lucky to have a job at all. He hasn't been the same since. Says a man can't live like a man ought to live on this little ten-acre patch of dirt, says his mama always told him that any man has to carry a lunch pail and punch a clock for a living is no better than a slave. Like it's all my fault that he's gettin paid by the hour, and he aint his own man anymore.

—I guess things happen, they change people. That's what happened to Watson. Little Billy died, and he started with the drink, and then he was like somebody you never met before.

—I know, honey. I know how hard it was for you, but Bose, he don't get like that. Thank God he don't hit me, because if he did he'd break me right in two. With him it's just that mean streak, the things he says. Says I'm uglier than homemade soap, and if he knew I was goin to be such a ugly woman he wouldn't of married me. I know he don't mean it, because now and then he says the nicest things, but when he starts talkin like that, he makes me feel about a foot tall. Specially when he talks about my barren womb, and how I haven't provided him a son. That's the worst of it. When we were courtin up in Wyoming, he said he wanted to have six, seven kids. He wanted a whole slew of little ones, and so did I, but it seems we can't have a solitary one.

Emaline, embarrassed, listened to the mingled sounds of grease popping on the griddle and grit blowing against the windowpane outside. Nellie sipped her coffee and made a face.

—I swear there's dust in the coffee. It gets like this, you can't keep it out. You eat dust and breathe dust and sleep in dust. I expect you've heard enough about Bose, honey. He is not your cross to bear.

—I wish I could be more help. Mama wanted me to come down here and be a help to you.

—You are, child. If you only knew. Sometimes I think I'd just about wither up and die if I didn't have you. That, or I'd have to pack my things and get on a bus and leave Bose for good. If I had to sit alone in this house day after day with him like he is, I'd get so blue I couldn't take it.

Emaline flipped the eggs onto a plate, cut herself a wedge of bread, spread a little strawberry jam, and sat down next to Nellie, putting her arm around the older woman's shoulders.

—Nellie, if Bose was a good man once, he'll be a good man again.

—I hope so, baby. I hope so. It's been a year now that he's been like this, and it just sucks all the pleasure right out of life. I wake up in the morning, I feel just as tired as when I went to bed.

—If it would just stop blowing and turn spring, I think you'd feel better. This wind can drive a person about crazy.

An hour later, the wind died suddenly and the dust began to sift out of the air. By noon, blue sky poked through here and there. Nellie lifted herself from the table.

—Well, if the wind is done, I suppose we'd better try to get some of the dust out of this house. The next time I get into town, I'm goin to ask Bose for a dime to buy some tape at the Woolworth's. If we could tape all the windows and doors shut tight, we wouldn't have this mess every time it blows.

By noon they had finished sweeping up all the dust that could be swept. They shook it out of the sheets and curtains, swept inside the closets, wiped and dusted every surface where dust could collect. To keep from breathing dust while they worked, they tied bandannas over their faces. Emaline pointed a finger at Nellie.

—This is a stickup, mister! We're a couple of desperadoes and we want you to fill this here bag with cash!

Nellie laughed. Emaline smiled behind her mask; it was good to hear her laugh.

—Maybe we should try it, Nellie. What do you think? We'll stick up a bank, and get wads of money, and move to California to be in the moving pictures.

—No, I think we should stick to robbin banks. They'll call us the "flapper bandits," and we'll be in all the papers and the radio.

Nellie sighed. It was sweet to think of such freedom, but what they had was this: a white frame house with the paint almost entirely peeled off and the gray clapboards exposed to the weather. A weedy ten-acre patch of ground with tumbledown fences. Bose snoring so the walls shook. Weather so dry the trees were bribing the dogs.

What troubled her most was that they also had a mare in foal.

—We'd best go check on the mare. She's going to drop her foal any day now, and if we lose that colt Bose is going to take a conniption fit.

Emaline tucked a handful of sugar cubes into her apron.

—I'll do it. She's sweet, that mare.

—Bose thinks he can get fifty dollars for that colt. Anything happens, he'll blame us sure.

—Don't worry, Nellie. I'll look after her.

The mare was round as a barrel, but otherwise showed no sign she was about to foal. She nuzzled Emaline's apron, looking for the sugar, and Emaline slipped two cubes into her palm and let the horse eat from her hand. She stroked its nose, looked into the round, dark eyes.

—We need you to have a healthy colt, sister. Bose, he needs the money real bad, and he's mean and nasty when he don't have money. You have a healthy colt, and maybe things will look better around here.

Emaline forked hay to the horses and scattered slops in the pig trough. Strong as he was, Bose never did more than half the chores. Sometimes she would hear the milk cow bawling and know that Bose had neither milked nor fed her, or she would find the sheep in the garden and know he had left the gate open. Even Emaline with her crippled arm could outwork the big lug. A good thing too, because if she couldn't, the livestock would starve. On the way back to the house, she stopped to pump a bucket of water at the well. Pumping water was her favorite chore; she found the well cool and mysterious, the water that emerged from its depths clear and cold. Bose had let the primer bucket run almost dry, but there was a cupful of murky water left, and Emaline managed to get it going with that. She pumped out at least a bucket of rusty water before it ran clear, filled both buckets and set them aside, then dropped to her knees, slid one of the planks aside a few inches, peered deep into the well. The well frightened and enticed her at the same time; sometimes she wanted to fall in, to curl up in its depths where the world could not reach her. At other times, she thought how awful it would be, trapped down there and unable to escape, closed up in a hole that would become your coffin. The fear made her want to run, but the well held her with a magnetic attraction, turning her legs to water. She wondered how you could be drawn to a thing and fear it so at the same time.

She was still gazing into the well when Bose came up behind her and startled her so that she had to brace herself to keep from falling in. His voice was harsh and thick.

—What you lookin at down there?

—Just the well. Trying to see what makes it work.

—Water is what makes it work. Aint got no water, you aint got no well.

—I mean the pipes and all, what draws it up. It's all so mysterious.

—Don't see what call a woman has to fuss over such things. A man digs a well so's a woman can pump water. All there is to it. Now get up off your hands and knees and find somethin useful to do around here. A fella sees you down in that position, he's apt to get peculiar notions.

Emaline got up and walked to the house, feeling the eyes on her back. She thought Bose would follow, but he went to check on the mare for himself. She popped into the house long enough to say good-bye to Nellie, then jumped on her bike and rode to Lucinda Nye's house. Lucinda's father had a Dodge truck, and he had promised to run them into Scottsbluff and treat them to a cherry Coke in the afternoon if their chores were done. They crowded into the cab of the truck. Emaline squeezed in between Lucinda and her father, the shift lever bumping her shins and knees when he changed gears. Luke Nye was a quiet man with an easy laugh, a sweet, reassuring man to be around, so gentle he apologized every time he hit her knee in the crowded cab. He was nothing at all like Watson or Bose Hubbard. Emaline thought that it was unlikely she would ever marry a man, but if she did, he would be a man exactly like Luke Nye.

They were still three miles from town when Luke had to brake at a crossroads to wait for a funeral procession to pass. There were a dozen rusty jalopies at the front of the procession, several barely in running condition, farmers and their wives seated stiffly in their Sunday best. One woman looked straight at Emaline as they passed. Her cheeks were rough and red from wind and weather, in her eyes a weariness so infinite that Emaline felt it like the weight of an anvil on her heart. The woman was thin-faced and thin-lipped, and Emaline wondered if she had ever been a girl, or if she had been born like this, a dried-out weed clinging as all these farmers clung to a parcel of earth that was always too small, too dry, too beaten down by hail and drouth.

The hearse crawled by, a plain pine coffin in the back. Luke shifted the truck into neutral, leaned out the window, and spat into the dust.

—Bound to his final resting place, he is. That would be Clem Sprague, or what's left of him. Singin loud at church last week, now he's bound to his grave. Appears he had a heart attack in the pigpen, and his own Poland China hogs ate him. Them hogs was his pride and joy. Wife found him, now they say it's turned her peculiar and she might never get over it. Helluva thing.

⊰ CHAPTER 52 ⊱

On the first warm Sunday in April of 1926, the lawyer Rafe Cubbin took his bride Clara for a drive in his open-topped 1923 Buick Roadster. They had finished their picnic lunch and were following a rough track parallel to the Niobrara when Rafe heard a loud bang and the car lurched to the right. He groaned; it was the third flat tire of the day and he was weary of the endless labor of jacking up the car, removing and patching the tire, inflating it, and tightening it back on the wheel. While down on his knees fumbling with the jack, Rafe spotted what looked like a scarecrow dangling from an old box elder tree in a deep draw that cut southwest from the river. He finished changing the tire and left Clara to gather wildflowers while he strolled over to investigate. When Clara looked to see what was keeping him, she saw Rafe down on his hands and knees puking his lunch. When she started to run to his aid, he yelled for her to stay back; she returned to the Buick in a sulk, angry that he had been cross with her for the first time in their three-week marriage. Rafe waited until she was back in the car before risking a second look at the tree.

The corpse, by the look of him, had been there at least a week. Birds, probably magpies, had pecked out his eyes and left a trail of birdshit down the front of his flannel shirt. His black tongue protruded, his neck was twisted awkwardly to the side, and his hands had been bound in front of him with bobwire. He was bootless, probably because his boots had been stolen by whoever tied the flawless hangman's knot in the tight-woven lariat that left him dangling from a heavy branch. The tattered remnants of gray socks clung to feet that had rarely been washed in life, and his ankles had also been bound together with bobwire. The sweet stench of the body lingered in the draw, made worse by the warm May sunshine. Rafe picked up his straw hat, jammed it back on his head, and stumbled to the car, gasping for breath and jabbering.

—Dead man. Dead man. Oh God, Clara. Somebody has hung a man from a tree back in that draw. It's awful. Awful thing. He's tied up with bobwire and the magpies have pecked out his eyes.

—Oh, I want to see.

—Clara!

Before Rafe could say another word, she had jumped down from the Buick and was running toward the dangling corpse. Rafe had grown fat as a Christmas goose while his law practice prospered; he lumbered after her, but couldn't gain ground on his slender bride. When he finally caught up to her, she was standing almost directly beneath the dangling man, gazing openmouthed at the corpse. Unlike Rafe, she had no trouble keeping her lunch down.

—I know this man. I know those red suspenders, Rafe. It's Herman Ostheimer. He owned a little place just west of ours.

—I know all about Herman. He's in court more than I am, but how do you know it's Herman? He's been dead a while, and lots of men wear red suspenders. If it's Herman, I wonder how come nobody noticed he was missing.

—Herman doesn't have a wife, and he was never sociable. I don't expect anybody would miss him much, but it's him, all right. He's short and he has that bushy hair. I wonder what happened to his boots?

—Forget the boots, and don't touch him. We've got to get back and tell the sheriff.

Rafe managed to drag Clara away from the corpse. In the Buick on the way back to Ainsworth, he calculated his chances of making something out of this: The fact that he had been the one to find the body would enhance his reputation in town. Herman Ostheimer had feuds going with half the big ranchers in the county, but his feud with Eli Paint was especially bitter. Ostheimer's place was due north of the Fanciful, and Ostheimer kept diverting water from the creek that ran through Eli's land. Eli had helped many of the small farmers in Brown County get their start, but Ostheimer was an exception and he and the farmer did not get along. There were even rumors that Ostheimer had rustled some cattle from the Fanciful. Rafe found that difficult to believe, because almost everyone in the county was afraid of Eli and his bullwhip.

Rafe knew from personal experience that Eli could be a hard man; he had once accompanied the Paints on a cattle drive to the White River, and it had almost been the death of him. Ever since that cattle drive, Eli had made no secret of his contempt for one Rafe Cubbin. Rafe thought this might be his chance to get even. Say Eli was mixed up in the death of Herman Ostheimer; Eli did all his legal business with old Bob Simmons, so he wasn't going to hire Rafe for his defense. However, among Rafe's duties in Brown County was the occasional prosecution of transgressors who broke the law. He had prosecuted rustlers a time or two, but he had never had a chance to try a man for murder, certainly not a man as prominent as Eli Paint. Trouble was, if he tried to prosecute Eli and lost, he was likely to be run out of the county on a rail. Evidence was going to be a problem too: Apart from the fact that Eli and Ostheimer had clashed in the past, there was little to go on. A body that had been hanging in a tree for at least a few days, a victim who was about as popular as drouth, no eyewitnesses, unless someone came forward now that the body had been found. No, it wouldn't do: Rafe would dump this mess in the lap of Sheriff Luther Beckwith, and if Luther could build a solid case against Eli or anyone else, Rafe would try it. In the meantime, he would do his bit by demanding justice, without saying exactly what form justice might take in this case.

Rafe found Luther at home, sitting on a rocking chair on the front porch, drinking a glass of iced tea. He left Clara sitting in the

Buick and climbed the steps, panting from the exertion. Luther invited him to have a seat.

—Don't leave the little lady settin in the car, Rafe. She aint likely to feel comfortable there by her lonesome.

Rafe motioned to Clara to join them, waited politely until she sat on the porch swing, and then squeezed in beside her. Luther looked at the pair of them. She was half of Rafe, if that. It was hard to see what she saw in the man, other than his bank account. Luther leaned through the screen door to ask his wife to bring two glasses and more iced tea and returned to the rocking chair.

—How's married life treatin you?

Luther addressed the question to Clara, but Rafe answered.

—Just fine, Luther. Just fine. A man doesn't know just how sweet life can be until he gets himself hitched, long as he finds the right little woman.

—I expect that's so. Me and the mizzus been together twenty-eight years, never a harsh word between us.

Estelle Beckwith brought more glasses and a big pitcher of iced tea. Luther waited until she had poured the tea and perched on a chair next to him before he got down to busienss.

—I don't suppose you came all the way out here on a Sunday just to chat about marriage. What's on your mind, Rafe?

—We found a body.

—A body.

—That's right. A body. Hangin from a rope. Down in a draw by the Niobrara. Looks like it's been there a few days. Maybe longer.

—Anybody we know?

—Herman Ostheimer.

—You don't say. Well, I guess Herman irritated enough people, it was bound to come to that sooner or later.

—That's no way to talk about the dead.

—I suppose it aint, but half the work I had the past five years was runnin after some problem or another had to do with Herman Ostheimer. I aint goin to miss him, truth be told.

—But what are you going to do about it?

—Do? Well, today's a Sunday. I'll likely ride down there with a couple of deputies tomorrow, take a wagon, and bring the body back so we can bury him proper.

—You're not going to arrest anyone?

—Well, who would you like me to arrest, exactly? Half the ranchers in this county wanted to shoot that man, one reason or another. We'll poke around down there, see what we see. But a body been out there that long, what do you suppose I'll find? Maybe somebody took a jackknife and carved a message in that tree: *My name is Joe Smith and I done hung this fella.* Short of that, I don't imagine we'll find much that would do you good if you're lookin to prosecute, do you?

—I never said I was looking to prosecute anybody.

—Then what's your interest, other than you findin the body and all?

—I'm just a citizen, Luther. Looking to do what's right.

—Well, I expect you done your duty, then. Me and the boys will go out and find out what we can, ask around a bit. But unless we find somebody seen who done it, I don't know there's much more we can do.

—You could at least ride out and ask him about it.

—Ask who?

—Eli Paint. It's him has had the most trouble with Herman.

—It aint like Eli to take part in no secret hangin. He gets mad enough, he's likely to go after a fella with a bullwhip, but he does it right out in the open. He aint the sort to go creepin round the county at night lookin for somebody to hang. Anyhow, that's as good as my job, askin him questions about a murder. I'll be lucky he don't take that whip to me.

—Could be as good as your job if you don't ask him, Luther. Me and all my people backed you for election three, four times now. We could back Augie Payne or Sam Piety, just as easy.

—I get your drift. Thing is, I would talk to Eli no matter what, y'see. What I don't like is you tellin me how to do my job. Now if you folks are done with your iced tea, I got a sick colt to look after.

—You'll let me know what you find out?

—Wouldn't think of doin otherwise, Rafe. But until you run for sheriff and win, you'll let me handle things my way, thank you kindly.

Luther waited until the orange Buick with the black fenders bumped its way back down the road, then he patted Estelle's knee.

—That Rafe Cubbin rubs me the wrong way.

—He'd rub a saint the wrong way. Now I guess you got to go find this fella that was hung.

—I guess I do.

Three days later, Luther Beckwith paid a call on the Fanciful. He had known Eli Paint since he first arrived in Brown County back around 1900, when Eli was already one of the more successful ranchers in the area. That was twenty-six years ago, a lot of miles on the both of them since. Eli was as tough as they come, but Luther couldn't see him mixed up in a thing like this. For one thing, there was that rumor that would never go away, folks saying that Eli had been hung as a horsethief up in Wyoming, that he had somehow survived and made a pile of money off the stolen horses and that was why he was a rich man today. Luther thought that sounded like the kind of tall tale envious people tell about a successful fellow, but if it was true, he couldn't imagine a man who had once had a rope around his neck being a party to a hanging.

All in all, Luther figured that it was getting near time to give up his badge. The country was changing. Bankers and lawyers and the railroad men and the big ranchers had always run things to suit themselves, but it seemed it was getting worse than ever, or maybe it was just that the people were worse. Old Bly Olp would rob you blind, but at least he did it pretty much out in the open. Rafe was the kind who was always tiptoeing around, so that you never quite knew what he was up to. When things reached the point where a man found himself running errands to please the likes of Rafe Cubbin, it was time to look into another line of work.

He drove up to the big gate at the entrance to the Fanciful, with the 8T8 brand pieced together with bent cottonwood branches in letters three feet high, rolled over the cattle guard, and drove the last mile to the house along a winding trail that ran between two neatly planted rows of Chinese elm trees. Ida Mae served him three slices of cherry pie in the kitchen while they waited for Eli to get back from the company ranch. He had a new partner named Mick Darnell, and he and Mick were settling some business ahead of the spring roundup. When Eli returned, Luther stood to shake his hand. Eli still had a handshake that made a man feel he was wrestling a bear. Like Luther, he had more than a few gray hairs, but he was as lean and tough as ever. Since the first time they met, Eli had always reminded Luther of a big old hawk, circling on the breeze real quiet, waiting for his chance to pounce. Was he capable of hanging a man? Luther didn't think so, but it was hard to predict what a man would do in a particular set of circumstances. About the only thing a sheriff could do in this situation was to let a man talk and rely on instinct to figure out if he was telling the truth.

They chatted for a time about the weather and beef prices. Luther sucked hot coffee through his teeth.

—It's a shame about Herman Ostheimer.

—It is.

—You and him had a dispute or two over the years, over the water and all.

—We did. That was a long while ago.

—Not that long. He was in my office to complain not three months ago. Said some of your cowhands was givin him a hard time, especially that little fellow, Roy Titus.

—Nobody ever said nothin to me about it. Herman was ever the sort of man would complain if you hung him with a new rope.

—That aint funny under the circumstances, Eli.

—Was it a new rope they used to hang Herman?

—Good quality cowboy lariat, I'd say. Surprised a puncher would waste it on a hangin and leave it behind.

—That don't sound right. I teach my men to hold on to what's theirs.

—I know you do. But there are folks say Eli Paint is behind all this, sayin I protect the big outfits to their detriment.

—I'm surprised at you, Luther. You were never one to listen to chitchat.

—It's worse than chitchat. I got a few farmers say if I won't bring you in, they will.

—On what grounds?

—Well, Herman Ostheimer was hung.

—You have anything resembling evidence a man could present in court?

—There was a whole lot of horse tracks around where Herman was hung. Ground was wet. Looks like a bunch did it, six or seven at least.

—Luther, this is ranch country. There are horses everywhere you look. And cowpunchers too. I can name you three dozen people had disputes with Herman Ostheimer, one time or another. He was ever a disputatious man, but I did not build the Fanciful worryin about the likes of him. With all I got, why would I risk puttin my own neck in a noose over some stubborn farmer who don't know no better than to divert a man's water? Ostheimer wasn't worth the powder it would take to blow him to hell. Anyhow, what I know of them other farmers, it aint them sayin I done it, it's Rafe Cubbin. My boys say he's been drivin around, goin farm to farm in that orange-and-black car looks like a big old pumpkin, tryin to stir up trouble. I wouldn't even think about hangin a man for stealin water, Luther. That's an end to it.

—What if he was rustling 8T8 cattle? I know you wouldn't stand for that.

—I wouldn't. But I wouldn't stand for no vigilance committee justice neither. If we caught him rustlin, we'd of brought him straight to you.

—All right, Eli. I believe you would. That's about all I have to say. You understand I had to pay the call on you or some folks would never shut up. I'll be talkin to everybody else that had trouble with Herman as well. I aint singlin you out.

—That's a good thing, since I can't see any reason you would.

Luther stood, put his hat on, thought of one more question.

—I was wonderin if you could tell me anything about that fella Roy Titus, used to work for you? Apparently he aint been seen around for a month or more.

—He aint. He still works for me. I sent him up to Fort Benton to pay a call on a fella named Jim Kipp, has a stud horse I'm lookin to buy. Time was we did a little business with Jim's daddy and Roy, he has a lady friend up there. Could be a while before he gets back.

—All right. You hear anything about this business, you let me know.

—We got a telephone, Sheriff. I'll call you quick. As long as we're still in Brown County, anyhow. But we're fresh out of elbow room here, so I'm lookin to move to Wyoming.

—You don't say. Kind a sudden, aint it?

—No, I been ponderin it for ten years. Thought I would go a year or two after the war, when the wheat prices dropped. But by that time we had five kids, me and Ida Mae, and little Leo was on the way, and it just didn't seem like the time to go.

—Where are you headed?

—Somewhere in Powder River country, most likely. I got my eye on a spread or two, both of them a lot bigger than the Fanciful. One of 'em is a place we used to work, me and Ezra and Teeter. Called the O-Bar.

—Well, I'll be damned. Never thought you for a fella to leave Brown County.

—Aint no more room to grow, Luther. I've poked around and talked some with other ranchers but they're all set. It's time to move on.

—Ezra too?

—Yessir. He can raise Appaloosas up in Wyoming as good as he can here, and you know Ezra. He gets restless easy. I'm surprised he has stayed here as long as he has.

Luther looked hard at Eli. For the first time, he was beginning to wonder if maybe Eli Paint didn't have something to do with this hanging after all. Otherwise, why would a man with thirty-six years' work invested in a place take a notion to sell up and head to Wyoming? It was a good thing Eli was not a gambler, because he was not a fellow you would care to meet at the poker table. Hard as he tried, Luther just could not read the man.

—Well, Eli, I'd best be gettin along.

—Thank you, Luther. And thanks for comin by. Give my best to Estelle.

—I'll do that.

CHAPTER 53

After the last day of school in May, the bus dropped Emaline on the south side of Erwin Beckman's hay meadow, a mile from Bose Hubbard's place. She could have followed the county road another mile south and a half mile west, but the land was greening after a week of rain and she felt giddy and triumphant. In her lunchbox, she carried a gold medal from the spelling bee and her two blue ribbons from the school track meet, where she won the girls' fifty-yard dash and the broad jump, and a red ribbon for second place in the high jump. She ended the school year second in her tenth-grade class, behind Percy Willis, and Percy was a doctor's son. Her most delicious triumph came in the spelling bee; she and Percy reeled off thirty words without a mistake before she spelled *Jugoslavia* correctly, with a J, not the way Percy spelled it, with a Y. Percy was sweet, shaking her hand and telling her that the better man won. Lucinda Nye teased her about him: She was convinced that Percy was sweet on Emaline, but Emaline refused to believe it. A doctor's son would never fall for a girl from the wrong side of the tracks. Still, she thought about Percy as she walked, his sweet smile and the cowlick in his hair that he could never seem to smooth down.

Emaline could see storm clouds building in the west, but she was certain she could beat them home, and she couldn't resist a stroll through the budding alfalfa and sweet clover in Beckman's field. Even if she did get a little wet, nothing could spoil this day. It seemed there was a meadowlark on every fencepost, the lilt and trill of their song lifting her heart as it always did. A bright yellow aeroplane, perhaps the mail plane from Cheyenne, flew directly overhead and the pilot tipped his wings to her, flirting from a thousand feet up in the sky. She waved gaily; even a machine could play a part in this glorious day. She leapt a narrow irrigation ditch, climbed through the barbwire fence at the edge of the Beckman farm, taking care to hold the strands apart so that she did not tear her skirt, detoured around a stand of cottonwood where a small herd of Holsteins grazed around a cattle tank, topped the rise a mile north of Bose Hubbard's little white house, and started downhill, skipping a little as she walked.

The first drops of rain felt cool and fresh on her skin. Still filled with energy from her triumphs on the track, she ran most of the way across the last hayfield as the sky opened up and it began to pour, her quick, slim legs slashing through wet alfalfa already higher than her ankles. A quarter mile from the house, the pelting rain turned to hail and she put her head down and ran hard, as hard as she had run on the track, her thighs burning and lungs straining for air as she stretched her limbs, until she felt as though she was flying across the meadow. She burst into the back porch gasping for breath and let the screen door bang shut behind her. Her bosom was heaving and she was soaked through and her dark hair hung in ringlets down her face and neck. She was laughing, a little dizzy from a lack of oxygen but fully alive, her skin fresh and tingling, aware of every living cell in her slender body. She stooped to unbuckle her shoes, peeled off her wet socks, stepped barefoot and dripping wet into the kitchen, and came to a halt so sudden it was as though she had slammed into a brick wall.

Bose Hubbard was installed at the kitchen table, wearing his OshKosh B'Gosh coveralls and no shirt. Emaline stood motionless on the cold linoleum floor, suddenly conscious of the way her wet clothes clung to her body. Bose reeked of cheap whiskey, sugar-beet pulp, cowshit, and sweat. When he drank, he always had a shot of whiskey and a bottle of beer for a chaser, and there were five empty bottles of bootleg beer lined up on the table, so Emaline knew exactly how much liquor he had in him. Bose was a big man and it took a lot to get him drunk; five whiskeys and five beers were just enough to turn him nasty. As she watched, still fighting to catch her breath, he poured and drained another whiskey, opened another beer, chugged it without pausing for air, wiped his chin with the back of his hand.

—'Bout time you got home. Where you been?

—It was the last day of school. We had a spelling bee, and a track meet after class.

—*It was the last day of school. We had a track meet after class.*

His tone was sour and mocking. His eyes were fixed on her breasts.

—School lets out at three, you're supposed to be home by four. You got chores to do.

—It's only this one time I was late because of the track meet. School's out now, and I won't be late again. I know I have chores to do. I'll start right away, soon's I change out of these wet clothes. Where's Nellie?

—Seein some damned sick neighbor lady at the hospital. Said she might stay the night. Off playin do-gooder, when she ought to be at home fixin supper for her man.

Emaline felt uneasy; she had never been alone with Bose. She decided to try to jolly him out of his sour mood.

—It doesn't matter if Nellie isn't here, Mr. Hubbard. I can cook supper.

—Don't sass me. I aint asked you to cook.

—It wasn't sass. I was just saying that I can get supper on if you're hungry.

—If I want supper, I'll say I want it and you'll cook it. You'll do any goddamned thing you're asked to do, because I sure as hell am not the one invited you to come waltzin in here, sashayin your little ass around like you owned the place.

—I don't act like I own the place, Mr. Hubbard. I work hard

for my keep. I know it's hard on you and Nellie, another mouth to feed, so I try not to be a burden.

—You're a burden all the same. Eat too much and don't do half enough.

—If that's how you feel, I'll leave. I'll ask if I can spend the summer with my aunt Ruby up on Sheep Creek.

—Don't sass.

—I'm not sassing you. I thought that's what you wanted.

—What I want is my supper.

—All right. Just let me change out of these wet clothes and I'll get supper on.

—Aint no need for you to change. I like you just like you are. Them wet clothes is hangin just right, so you get started and I'll set right here and watch.

Emaline put her lunchbox down on the table. The cardboard had soaked through, and now her gold medal for the spelling bee, her ribbons from the track, and the letter from the principal commending her for finishing second in her class seemed pointless and forlorn. Nothing she accomplished in school would change this: With her mother in the TB hospital, she was virtually an orphan, she was dependent on the goodwill of Nellie and Bose Hubbard, and right now she was his prisoner. Her only choice was to do as he asked. Usually when he got like this, he would eat and then fall asleep for a few hours before waking for the night shift at the sugar factory; all she had to do was to keep him reasonably content until he went to bed. She lit strips of paper to start the coal fire in the stove, grateful for its warmth because she was shivering and wet and Bose wouldn't let her change. She found pork chops and potatoes already boiled in the icebox, began slicing the potatoes while the soapstone griddle warmed.

Behind her she heard Bose open and swallow another beer without pausing for breath. He belched and slammed the empty bottle down on the table. She could feel his eyes boring into her and wished she had been able to change into something dry so that her clothes didn't cling to her body. Her hands trembled and she cut her fingers twice with the paring knife. Neither cut was deep; she washed off the blood in the washbasin and kept working. She put on four pork chops for Bose and one for herself and listened to them sizzle. Cooking was the most soothing thing she could imagine, especially on a rainy day. She browned the pork chops on one side, turned them to brown on the other side, shook on a little salt and pepper.

With the sound of the rain outside and the popping of the spuds and chops on the grill, she did not hear Bose move. He was in his stocking feet and he was behind her before she had a chance to run. A hand as hard as steel cable closed on her throat and spun her away from the stove. With one hand on her neck and the other between her legs, he lifted her away from the stove and threw her over the table. Emaline screamed as her head struck the bottles, knocking one off the table. She heard it smash on the linoleum, tried hard to struggle out of his grasp. She was a strong, athletic girl, but against Bose she had no chance at all. He twisted her neck around and she smelled something like sour bread dough as he pressed his mouth to hers and forced his tongue between her lips. She tried to bite him, but he pulled back and leaned all his weight on her, crushing the air out of her lungs. His voice was a low, menacing growl.

—You'll want to hold real still now. You pull another stunt like that, and you don't know what's liable to happen. Your neck's apt to get broke.

She froze. This must be, she thought, how it was when an antelope found itself helpless in the jaws of a lion; all the strength went out of her and her limbs turned to jelly, like they did sometimes when she was staring down into the well and the fear came over her. Bose lifted his weight slightly and the air rushed into her lungs a moment before she would have blacked out, but he didn't turn her loose. With his left hand still on her throat, Bose tore away her skirt and her slip, caught her undergarments with one thick thumb, and ripped them open. Emaline felt his hand cold on her buttocks, a thick finger slipping inside her.

—Aint that a pretty sight. Pretty as a picture you are, all spread out like that. You're makin old Bose hard as a rock.

He thrust harder with his finger. Emaline screamed with all the power in her lungs. Bose laughed.

—Scream all you please, girl. Holler good and loud. Aint nobody goin to hear you way out here. It's rainin buckets, and there aint nobody within a mile of this place. Nellie aint comin home neither, so we got us the whole night to play.

Emaline tried to scream again, but his hand tightened on her windpipe and choked her into silence. She felt him step back and pull the straps of the OshKosh B'Gosh coveralls off his bare shoulders, heard them drop to the floor. She braced herself; girls at school talked about this, the awful moment when you lost your virginity, the sharp pain when you were first penetrated by a boy's penis and the blood that followed. Except that this was a man, not a boy, and if Bose's penis was as large as the rest of him, it was going to hurt something awful. She tensed, holding her body rigid, waiting. Wishing she could simply float away before he touched her. Instead of his penis, she felt something cold and hard and wet: a beer bottle. He was toying with it, slipping it into her an inch or two and pulling it out. She imagined the thing breaking inside her, tearing her up.

—Please, don't. Please, not that.

—How's that, little girl? You don't take to that beer bottle? You'd rather have Bose's old prick, is that it? Well, that's just fine with me, honey. That's real sweet of you.

He flung the beer bottle away and she heard it smash against the wall over the stove. His hand tightened again around her throat. He was moving back and forth, rubbing himself on her bottom, and then something hot and wet splashed on her buttocks. He groaned deep in his chest and released his paw from her throat.

—Damn. Aint that a shame. You got old Bose so worked up, I lost it before we could get to the real thing.

He tossed her a dishrag from the sink.

—There. Wipe that off your ass and get my dinner on. Got to get my strength up if we're goin to have a second go-round. This time, you aint goin to be no virgin when I get done.

She thought wildly of the paring knife, plunging it into his eye, or using the butcher knife to slit his throat, but there was nothing within reach. Even if there was, if he saw her coming he would snap her arm like a twig before she got near enough to hurt him. He lurched away from her, clawing at his coveralls, pulling them up. He slapped her bare bottom once, hard.

—Now get my dinner on, girl. I'm so hungry I could eat that mare out in the corral, right down to the hock and hoof.

With her body quivering like a cottonwood leaf in a high wind, Emaline did as she was told. She wiped herself lightly and rinsed the cloth, pulled up what was left of her drawers and drew her slip and skirt up, and pinned the skirt fast; scooped the pork chops and potatoes onto a plate for him; and stood, trembling, waiting for a chance to bolt for the door. He watched her while he ate, his little pig eyes suspicious.

—Aint you goin to eat?

She shook her head.

—Suit yourself. More for me that way. Have a beer, at least.

He popped one open. Emaline shook her head again.

—I don't drink beer.

—Drink the goddamned thing. Do as I say, or I'll put you over my knee and whack you like you never been whacked in your life. A beer will calm you down a little, so's you'll enjoy it more next time. You look like you just seen a ghost.

Emaline took the bottle and drank. She made a wry face; the stuff was awful. He motioned for her to drink again and she did and felt it first cold and then warm in her belly, then a spreading warmth that relaxed her stiffened muscles ever so slightly. She drank the rest a few swallows at a time, forcing it down, wanting to feel something that would take her away from this place, this most awful moment of her life. When the bottle was empty, she felt a numbness in her limbs, as though the dull feeling might protect her from further hurt. Bose finished his plate, wiped it clean with a crust of bread, belched again, and pushed himself away from the table.

—Now I'm goin to rest a bit, girl, and when I come to, we'll have us another round. You'll get to like it plenty, I aint ever seen a one that didn't. Women is all alike; you all pretend like havin a man's peter up inside you is nasty as castor oil, but once you get it, you can't get enough. Now you see to it the cow gets milked, and the livestock gets fed, and look after that mare, and clean up this kitchen where you smashed them beer bottles. Don't you think about lightin out for town or nowhere else; if you do, I'll come after you in the truck, and when I catch you there'll be hell to pay.

Emaline stifled a sob, not wanting to give him the satisfaction.

—Don't go bawlin now. You had it comin. You been teasin me since you moved in here. Startin now, you're goin to take care of old Bose regular. Nellie, she don't know how to keep a fella happy. Girl like you, you could do a man real good, you put your mind to it. We can start practicin on it, soon as I get a little nap.

She stood numb and helpless. Bose nodded, as though they had reached some satisfactory contractual agreement, grabbed himself another beer, and headed for bed, scratching his crotch as he walked. Within less than a minute, his snores were shaking the house. Automatically, a girl in a trance, she took the dustpan and broom and swept up the broken glass and mopped the linoleum. She slid past the bedroom where Bose snored, closed the door of her own room and turned the key in the lock, peeled off her wet clothing and her torn underwear, took a cloth and the pitcher of water and washed herself until she was raw, then dressed in her chore clothes, trousers and boots and a flannel shirt, and trudged up the path to the outhouse. The smell released what she had held down until that moment; she vomited the beer along with the cocoa and cookies the school served after the track meet, then sat with her trousers down around her ankles, trembling and terrified in the chilly outhouse, biting her thumb to keep from crying, reliving every moment. His breath that smelled like sour dough. The crushing weight of him. Her terror of the beer bottle and what he might do with it. She tried to imagine Nellie coming home, what she would say. Surely Nellie would sense something was wrong.

Nellie knew Bose; she would ask questions, maybe find out what had happened. Perhaps she would blame Emaline. He had promised her that if she stayed it would happen again. And again. *Next time. Next time.* If she stayed, Bose would use her as hard and as often as he wanted, like a man mistreating a horse. She had no choice: She would have to run and hope he didn't come after her.

She tiptoed back into the house and threw her clothes into Velma's old cardboard suitcase in a frantic hurry. Bose was still snoring, but she was terrified that he would wake up and catch her trying to leave. With shaking hands she wrote a short note for Nellie and left it under the teapot, where only Nellie would find it, saying only that she was going to spend the summer with Wade and Ruby on Sheep Creek. She took the money she had saved for new shoes, three dollars and thirty-five cents, most of it in pennies, and she was out the door before she remembered her neatly wrapped bundle of Velma's letters from the hospital. She tiptoed back into the house, froze when she did not hear Bose's snores, listening to the sound of her beating heart. Then he mumbled something in his sleep and went back to snoring and she tiptoed past his door, snatched the letters, and left.

It was eight miles to town. She cut again across Beckman's hay meadow so that Bose couldn't follow her on the road, taking the same path she had followed only a couple of hours earlier, in a time that now seemed a century ago. When she reached the county road, she turned east toward town, keeping to the edge of the gravel, where she could duck out of sight in a hurry. She hadn't gone a half mile when she heard the noise of an engine and slid down into the barrow pit with her suitcase. She was about to try to hide in three inches of muddy water when she realized the sound wasn't the labored wheeze of Bose's old truck. She clambered back up onto the road and stuck out her thumb. The driver of a nearly new Nash braked to a halt and rolled his window down.

—Where you headed?

—Scottsbluff.

—Climb in. That's right where I'm headed.

The driver was a traveling salesman on his way from Cheyenne to Scottsbluff. Emaline didn't ask why he wasn't taking the highway; maybe he had a load of hooch in the back and was trying to avoid a run-in with the law. It wasn't until she pulled off the old cap she wore to keep hay out of her hair that he glanced at her and almost ran off the road.

—You're a girl.

—Yes.

—I took you for a young fella.

—These are my chore clothes.

—Late for a girl to be goin into town.

—I got a friend I want to see.

After that she said nothing. The chatty salesman went on talking about Cal Coolidge, and how he had put money in General Electric, and the stock market was going to make him a rich man, how it would make all Americans rich, if they just had sense enough to put their money in Wall Street. When they reached Scottsbluff, he asked where she wanted to go. Until that moment, she had no thought of an actual destination; she was simply heading toward town and away from Bose. She named the first place that popped into her head.

—The Eagle Cafe.

—The Eagle Cafe it is, then. I'd join you for a cup myself, but I've got to get my shuteye. Crawford, Chadron, and Gordon tomorrow. No rest for the wicked.

At the cafe, Emaline started to get her suitcase out of the backseat but he wouldn't allow it. Instead, he ran around and opened the door, lifted the case out and carried it into the restaurant for her, and tipped his hat to her when he left, a simple kindness that brought tears to her eyes.

—Ellis Einsel's the name, girl. If we bump into each other again, I'll buy you a Dr Pepper. You have a good night now and chin up. You look like you lost your best friend.

Emaline tried to smile. He was a nice man and he had been good to her, but the hardest thing for her to take at this moment was kindness. When the waitress came, she ordered a glass of milk because it cost only a nickel, and asked if she could use the cafe telephone to place a call to her aunt Ruby and uncle Wade in Torrington.

—Well, I'm not supposed to let folks use the phone for long-distance calls, honey, but if you was to leave a nickel it would be all right.

—I can leave you a nickel. I just need somebody to come get me.

—Oh, forget it. You go ahead and call, sweetheart. If my boss asks about it, I'll put in your nickel myself.

Emaline picked up the telephone and asked the operator to connect her to the Wade Tourtelotte ranch outside Torrington. When Ruby answered the phone, she had to fight to keep from crying again.

—Aunt Ruby? This is Emaline down in Scottsbluff.

—Well, hi, honey. Your brother Ben was just wondering how you are doing.

—I'm not so good, Ruby. Truth is, things aren't working out too good with Bose and Nellie and I was hoping I could come stay with you for a while.

—Sure you can, Emmy. Did you want to come now?

—If that's all right. I can see if there's a bus to Torrington.

—Never mind the bus. Wade will come get you right now.

An hour later, Wade found her sitting alone at a booth in the back of the Eagle Cafe. Her face was white and drained and she was shivering, although it wasn't cold. He wrapped his sheepskin jacket around her shoulders and led her to his truck. On the drive back to Sheep Creek, Wade asked her one question.

—I expect you don't want to tell me what went wrong at the Hubbards?

—No, I guess I don't.

—All right, then.

Wade was a quiet man by nature and Emaline was in no shape

to talk, so neither of them said a word over the bump and rattle of the old truck the rest of the way. When they reached the house, Ruby was waiting. She had hot potato soup on the stove and cornbread baking in the oven. Ben and Bobby met her at the door. The first thing Emaline noticed was that Ben was now taller than her, tall and lean like his father. Bobby was jumping up and down because he was so excited to see her. Ruby had three children of her own, six-year-old Alta and twin boys a year younger, David and Daniel. Emaline moved through all the confusion in a dream, her shattered self watching from a dark corner as she nibbled at soup and cornbread. She wanted a long, hot bath more than anything in the world, but baths were for Saturdays only.

While she ate, Ruby watched her carefully but did not ask questions. When they finally went to sleep, Emaline shared Alta's narrow bed. In the night, she felt the girl's bony arm around her waist as she lay staring at the ceiling, fighting back waves of nausea. The smell of Bose Hubbard clung to her nostrils, the stench of pungent sweat, sour bread dough, and something darker, something like the abyss at the bottom of the well.

⊰ CHAPTER 54 ⊱

It was Emaline's silent summer. She spoke so little that when she did, her voice sounded odd to her own ears, like the voice of a dummy on the knee of a ventriloquist. She could go whole days nodding and smiling, without saying a word. Wade and Ruby kept a close eye on her, but made an unspoken decision not to interfere. After trying one evening to get her to talk over a cup of tea, Ruby figured it was best to leave the girl alone; she would open up when she was ready, if ever. Ruby said only that her niece was smart and strong; she would work things out for herself if you gave her enough room. She guessed that Emaline's abrupt departure from Nellie Hubbard's home might have something to do with Bose, but the girl clearly did not want to talk about it, so Ruby let it ride; if Emaline had something to say, she would say it in her own good time. At first she burst into tears for no apparent reason, jumped at loud noises, and had an odd habit of scrubbing at her face with the palms of her hands, as though she was trying to wash away some invisible blemish. Sometimes in the night, Ruby would hear the girl walking restlessly in the kitchen and get up and join her for a glass of warm milk, the two of them quiet at the table until Emaline wiped her mouth, wrapped her arms around Ruby's neck, kissed her on the cheek, and tiptoed silently back to bed.

In the end, it was work that saved her. She rose with the sun and went wearily to bed after the supper dishes were washed and put away.

She worked hard all day long, helping Wade with the haying and the milking and fence mending, wearing a boy's coveralls and boots and one of Wade's old shirts tied up at the waist, so that she looked like a shorter version of Ben. Emaline had arrived in Wyoming looking pale and frightened, but with every passing week she seemed stronger and more confident. Her hands grew hard and calloused and her muscles taut; even with her crippled arm, she could do nearly as much work as her brother. With her hair cut short and her skin a dark brown from the sun, she looked so different from the slim young girl Wade found in the back of the Eagle Cafe in the spring that a visiting rancher thought Wade had taken on an Indian hired hand.

Wade Tourtelotte called his place a ranch mostly because it was too dry to farm the land. He and Ruby had a single section of land, barely enough for even a modest herd of cattle. He wanted to do as Eli Paint had done and build the place into a spread covering thousands of acres, but after eight years of hard work, he had pretty much what he started with, which meant they had just enough to get by with a lot of scrimping and saving. He raised a few sheep, a few hogs, and a few dairy cattle, sold butter and cream and wool, and dreamed of the day when rising prices for his livestock would make it possible to acquire at least another half section of land. Meanwhile, the ranch depended on the annual turkey crop to stay afloat. As far as Wade was concerned, herding turkeys was a woman's job. He and Ben would look after the horses, cattle, and the other livestock; he left the task of caring for the annoying birds to Ruby, who enlisted Emaline's help to fatten the gobblers and keep them out of harm's way. Ruby teased that it was because he didn't want her on horseback; she still rode in the Cheyenne rodeo every year, and even Wade admitted that she could outride him.

Emaline found that running after the turkeys kept her slim and fit. Sometimes she imagined she was back on the track in Scottsbluff, her legs flashing as she sprinted to a blue ribbon; she was only three or four months removed from that day, but it seemed that had all happened in another lifetime, a life of spelling bees and

Percy Willis and essays on Lord Tennyson. The girl who won the fifty-yard dash and the spelling bee was someone she recognized, no more than that: Now she was a slim, brown, hardworking ranch hand with no time for Tennyson and Jugoslavia. When fall came, Ruby asked if Emaline wanted to go with Ben to the high school in Torrington so she could finish her degree. Emaline refused, saying she was needed on the ranch. The truth was that the thought of school was all bound up with Bose Hubbard and his sour dough breath and his thick fingers probing inside her, the fist at her windpipe, gagging and fighting for air, his weight on her back.

Through the worst of the cold weather, when there was little they could do outside except look after the livestock, Emaline helped Ruby care for the little ones indoors. She seemed much better, but whenever Wade asked if she wanted to come along on a trip to Nebraska, she refused. When Wade asked for her help to get twenty-two Hampshire hogs to the auction barn in Scottsbluff on a glorious day in May, Emaline helped to load the hogs but declined to make the trip. Wade shrugged; if the girl wanted to avoid the town that badly, she must have good reason.

With the proceeds from the hogs, Wade bought a three months' supply of groceries and enough rolls of barbwire to fence the north pasture. He started with Ben and Emaline just after first light the next morning, digging the post holes, setting the posts, and tamping the dirt in tight before Emaline used the come-along to pull the wire taut so Ben could drive the U-shaped nails. Even a pair of Wade's old winter gloves didn't entirely protect her hands from the barbwire, and after three days of fencing her hands were scratched and bleeding. At night Ruby treated the cuts with iodine to prevent infection and the next morning Emaline was up and ready to go again. It was hard, hot work but Emaline loved it. They were outdoors, the meadowlarks were singing, Bose Hubbard's sour breath on her neck was a receding memory.

They were still stringing fence when Velma's letter arrived. Ruby sent little Bobby out on his pony to bring her the letter; he was still a quarter mile away when he started calling.

—Emmy! Emmy! We have a letter from Ma!

At that distance all Emaline heard was "Ma" and her first thought was that Velma had died in the hospital. She fumbled to tear it open, read it through once to herself, and then cleared her throat and read it aloud:

Denver

May 19, 1927

My Dearest Emaline, Ben, and Bobby,

I am so happy to be able to tell you they are letting me go from this prison at last. I have finally convinced them I am better, or perhaps they just got tired of me telling them all the time that I miss my beautiful daughter and my two handsome sons and that it's time to turn me loose. Dr. Spivak says that as long as I don't take a turn for the worse, I can leave here on June 1. I planned to go back to Sheridan, but Nellie Hubbard has found me a job as a cook at the Wardman Hotel in Scottsbluff at better pay, and Emaline can work there too as a waitress, so as soon as we are settled I will ask Wade to drive you down from Wyoming. I know you won't want to stay with Nellie and Bose, although they'd be glad to have us for a time, so I will try to rent some little place before you come down. I had to promise the doctors here that I had someone to live with who can take care of me if I get weak again, so I told them my daughter who is so strong and smart would take care of me. Ben and Bobby will have to stay with Ruby until we get settled, but I'm hoping they can join us in a year or so once we get a little money put away. Anyway, Sheep Creek is so close we can probably see them most every Sunday.

We will have so much to talk about. Now I must go and tell my friends here I will be leaving them soon for a much better life. Please give my love to Ruby and Wade and the other children and know that soon we will be together again.

Your loving mother,

Velma

Bobby turned his pony around and trotted back to the house. Emaline did not want Wade and Ben to see her cry, so she folded the letter and slipped it back into her pocket, then walked quickly across the pasture as far as the stream, where she found a rock under a big willow tree and sat there alone and wept. She had spent a good part of her young life waiting for her mother, worrying that she would not survive, imagining their life together once her mother was out of the hospital, but now the news of Velma's pending release filled her with dread. She loved the ranch, she had found peace with Wade and Ruby after the horrors of life with Watson and Bose Hubbard, and the last thing on earth she wanted was to return to Scottsbluff, a small town where she was bound to run into Bose sooner or later. Nellie Hubbard was Velma's best friend. Velma would want to see her, and how could Emaline stay away? If she told Nellie and Velma what Bose had done, would they believe her? A girl of seventeen talking that way about a grown man? She chided herself as a selfish, ungrateful daughter, but she couldn't help it. The thought of leaving the wide-open spaces of Wade and Ruby's ranch for a place in a town where she might run into Bose at any moment was almost more than she could bear. She tucked the letter in her pocket, wiped her eyes, pulled on her gloves, and went back to fencing. She had no choice: She would have to join her mother.

Emaline spent her seventeenth birthday on the ranch with Wade and Ruby and Ben and Alta and the twins. Ruby baked a cake and gave her a sweater she had taken months to knit, and they all sang "Happy Birthday." She wished she could stay on at Sheep Creek forever, but a week later, Velma called from Scottsbluff. She had started work in the kitchen at the Wardman Hotel. Emaline could also work as a waitress in the restaurant, so between the two of them they should earn enough to pay the rent on the tiny house Velma had rented on the outskirts of town.

Wade drove them all down, so Bobby and Ben could spend a Sunday with their mother before she and Emaline started work.

Bobby and Ben rode in the back of the truck while Emaline sat up front with Wade, feeling nearly as blue as she had the night Wade rescued her from the Eagle Cafe. Once they neared Scottsbluff, she became watchful, as though she expected Bose Hubbard to reach out and grab Wade's little truck with one powerful hand. Wade seemed to sense her reluctance. He had to clear his throat three times before he thought of something to say.

—Your mother is a wonderful woman. You two will get along fine, but you're always welcome out to Sheep Creek, the both of you. Don't feel like you have to be stuck in town.

Emaline nodded, staring out the window.

—I'll miss the ranch, Wade. I really like it out there.

—I know you do, honey. But your mother needs you, you know that.

Emaline knew it only too well. They bumped along the road, through the valley of the flat Platte, onto West Overland, where Wade located the little yellow house with its single forlorn elm tree in front. It was a damp, chilly morning and Velma's face, looming through the glass of the kitchen window, seemed ghostly and detached. Ben and Bobby leapt out of the truck and ran to their mother while Emaline hung back until Wade lifted her bag out of the back and walked her to the door. Velma wrapped her arms around the girl and clung to her, fighting tears.

—My girl, you've grown. I do believe you're taller than me.

Emaline had been taller than her mother since she was twelve years old. She knew that Velma was just making conversation. She looked so tired and drawn that Emaline wondered if she should have been released from the hospital at all. Velma finally gave up trying not to cry and wept into Emaline's shoulder; Wade turned away to light his pipe.

The house was even smaller than Emaline had imagined, just a tiny kitchen with a table big enough for the two of them, a living room big enough for a couch and one chair, and a bedroom with one narrow bed and a sitting room. With Ben, Bobby, and Wade in the house, there was barely room enough to turn around. There was a stove with two settings—on and off. Velma had done what she could to make the house cozy before Emaline arrived, but the linoleum on the floors was cracked and bare, there were stains in the wallpaper, and what furniture there was looked as though it had been rescued from the county dump. Velma's attempt to brighten the place with a bunch of spring flowers in a cracked vase only made it look more pathetic. Even in this place, Velma managed to cook a decent meal; she made pork chops and mashed potatoes and chatted happily with Wade and the boys. She didn't notice that Emaline didn't touch her pork chops and at the first opportunity slid them off her plate onto Ben's.

After Wade and Ben left, Emaline did the washing up and when she was done, she perched next to Velma and leaned her head on her mother's shoulder. Velma stroked her hair.

—Honey, I think you ought to tell me what happened that you decided to leave the Hubbards all of a sudden.

—I can't say, Mama.

—It had somethin to do with Bose, didn't it?

—I guess so.

—I knew that. Nellie says he turned real mean after they moved down here.

—Yes.

—Well, whatever happened, I'm sorry about it, honey. I wish I never had to ask you to go live there. It's a shame I just got down here and now Nellie is leaving, but maybe it's better that way.

—What do you mean?

—Didn't anybody tell you? Bose and Nellie sold their place. He got a job with the railroad, pays better than the sugar factory. They're moving to North Platte.

—Really?

—Their truck's all loaded. I was out there a while this morning, I think they're leavin at first light tomorrow.

Emaline took a deep breath and put her arm around her mother. She had to fight to keep from crying, but she felt that an enormous weight had lifted from her shoulders: the weight of Bose Hubbard.

. . .

They started work at the hotel the following Monday. Velma was one of two cooks on the staff, and it was her job to do all the baking while Emaline ran her legs off trying to wait on hungry customers and figure out how to juggle plates with her crippled arm. They left the house at five o'clock every morning and had their own hasty breakfast standing up, with Velma frying eggs and flipping pancakes. Velma did her baking after the breakfast rush was over, while Emaline helped with the washing up. It was hard, numbing work, with little of the satisfaction of ranch work, but most of the customers left her little tips, and the nickels and dimes added up.

The hotel was a popular lunchtime spot for lawyers and bankers and doctors with offices in town. The second week she was at work, Emaline was horrified to see Percy Willis and his father at one of their tables. She looked away as she took their order, hoping Percy would not recognize her in her uniform with the net on her hair. It didn't work.

—Emaline, is that you? I was wondering whatever happened to you. We were all disappointed when you didn't come back to school last fall.

She stared at the floor, wishing it could swallow her whole, aware that her cheeks were aflame.

—I moved up to Wyoming for a while and then back here with my mother.

—Will you be back in school in the fall?

—I don't think so.

—That's a shame. You were the smartest girl in the school.

—Oh, it's all right. I have to work now to help my mom. Can I take your order, please?

Emaline scribbled their order and hurried back to the kitchen with it. Velma saw the stricken look on her face.

—What's wrong, honey?

—There's a boy I knew from high school out there with his father. I had to take their order.

—So?

—I feel so ashamed. We were the best students in tenth grade, and his father is a doctor, and he's going to be a doctor too, and I'm just a waitress in a hotel.

—That's nothing to be ashamed of, honey. Never be ashamed because you're working hard. Are you sweet on him?

—No, I am not. He's rich and he's stuck-up and he doesn't care a bit about me or what happens to me.

—If he doesn't care, then there's no reason to be embarrassed. Now take their plates out to them. Meat loaf with mashed potatoes and ham with home fries, right?

Emaline took the plates, noting that Velma had heaped them even higher than usual. She wanted to dump the plates and simply walk out of the restaurant, but she did what she had to do. When she went to clear the table after they left, she found a twenty-five-cent tip Percy had left under his plate, the largest tip she had ever received. She took the quarter in her hand, squeezing it tightly, walked out the back door of the kitchen into the alley, and sat on the steps and cried. When Velma came out to see what was wrong, Emaline could do nothing but shake her head and repeat over and over:

—I don't know, Ma. I don't know.

❧ CHAPTER 55 ❧

Eli Paint left the Fanciful on August 30, 1927, at the head of one of the last great trail drives: ten thousand head of purebred Galloway and Hereford cattle bound for the hundred thousand acres of what had been the O-Bar ranch on the Powder River, rechristened the 8T8 under the ownership of the Paint brothers and Teeter Spawn. It had taken three years of negotiations for Eli to pry the ranch loose from the English company that still held title; there were other sizable spreads that could have been had for less, but he had set his sights on the O-Bar and nothing else would do. Even the absentee owners in London and Edinburgh seemed to see him coming: He had never been beaten on a deal in his life, but this time he overpaid by at least a dollar on every one of those hundred thousand acres. To close the deal he sold his share of the company ranch to Mick Darnell, who had taken it over after Cale Hutchinson was gored by a bull so badly he was no longer able to work. He sold all but two sections of the Fanciful itself, and met in town with Gus Schrautz, who still looked after his money, and the lawyer Bob Simmons to set things up so that those two sections would remain in the Paint family forever. Gus found it odd that in Eli's mind that did not seem to include any of the six living children Eli had with Livvy; they had been left out of Eli's will, apparently because Ida Mae wanted it that way, and Gus didn't think it was right. He knew better, however, than to argue with Eli. It was easier to argue with a cyclone.

For the drive to the Powder River, they had a new hand along to help Ezra with the Appaloosas. Teeter Spawn had spent the month of June visiting Ruby and Wade on Sheep Creek, and had come back convinced that Ben Hughes was going to be a horseman like his father. It took some doing, but he convinced Eli to take Ben on as a wrangler. Eli agreed, on the condition that Ben earn his keep like everyone else.

When they started working the horses to get them ready for the trail, Ezra perched on a rail of the training corral next to Teeter and saw the shadow of Frank Hughes in the way Ben approached a horse: the way he let the horse come to him instead of forcing things, how he seemed to anticipate what an animal was going to do long before the horse thought of it himself. He was long-geared and easy in the saddle like Frank, but he lacked Frank's swagger and had an air about him that could only have come from Velma, quiet and serious. When they were done with the horses for the day, Teeter worked to teach the boy the things a man ought to know: how to deal a crooked poker hand, weave a rawhide lariat, tie a proper hangman's knot, and follow a trail if you were trying to catch up to rustlers or Indians or a runaway bride.

—When you're trailin a man, don't waste your time pokin around on the ground, tryin to find bent twigs and all what them dime novels will tell you. What you want to do is you look far off, far as a hawk can see. In dry country, you watch for buzzards because the buzzards will always follow a man for the things he leaves behind. You can see 'em miles off, circlin high. If you can't make out the buzzards, then watch the dust, watch where it rises. Watch the birds they flush. That way you can ride hard, hard as the man you're chasin. Don't tell me a man is hot on the trail when he's down on his knees pokin around in human shit, tryin to figure if his quarry is eatin corn or beans. He aint doin nothin down there cept wastin time, and tryin to pretend he's onto a trail, pokin along because maybe he's *scared* to catch up to whatever it is he's chasin.

Teeter paused, got onto the subject of their last hand of poker.

—Now son, you dealt that ace off the bottom of the deck and I seen you plain. You want to cheat at poker, that's the only way to win. Trick is, you can't get caught. My eyes aint what they once was, but I seen you do it. You got to work until you can deal that ace off the bottom slicker'n otter snot. Learn that good before you start playin with them cowpokes, or you'll lose your shirt and you'll be lucky to hang on to your drawers.

Teeter broke out the deck and Ben laughed and tried again. Teeter watched and shook his head. There were some things the boy got straight from his father, but dealing a crooked poker hand was not one of them.

Once or twice, Eli dropped by for a time to watch young Ben work horses. He never said a word, but once when Ben pulled up a gelding, turned it to the fence, and then back out to get it on the right lead as he swung into an easy canter, Eli nodded slightly and rode off with a grin.

That last morning on the Fanciful, Eli rose before dawn to pay a visit to the graves of Livvy and little John Milton on the ridge overlooking the ranch. He dismounted and doffed his hat and stood in silence for a long while, looking off to the east, where the sun cast long pink tendrils up the clouds. The night before, he thought he ought to say something to Livvy, explain why he was leaving, but once he was next to her grave he couldn't think of a solitary word. At last he put his hat back on, swung into the saddle, and rode off without looking back.

When they rode out, Ben was back with the remuda alongside Ida Mae's two oldest boys, Calvin and Seth. Ida Mae was going to stay on the Fanciful with her girls, Jenny, Mabel, and Anna, and the youngest boy, Leo, Eli's favorite. Eli and Ezra rode point with their new rep Willie Thaw, the herd spread halfway across Brown County by the time they were properly on the trail, most of them yearling steers and heifers not yet with calf. It was painfully slow going: Eli had struck deals with other ranchers most of the way to allow his livestock to pass over their land, but a dozen cowpunchers still had to take down sections of fence and put them back up again once the herd had passed.

The trail west followed the same route Eli had taken in the summer of 1890 when he was looking for the ideal spot of land to build a house for his young bride: through Cherry and Sioux Counties, past Valentine, Gordon, Chadron, skirting the southern edge of the Black Hills, bound for the Devil's Tower and Powder River country. It was a dry spring. There were rattlesnakes everywhere along the trail and by the time they reached Crawford, three horses had been bitten on the nose so badly that they went half mad, standing with their grotesquely misshapen heads in the water tanks or crow-hopping across the prairie and bucking as though to shake off the poison.

They completed the last twelve miles to the O-Bar a month after they left Brown County. Once the herd had been turned out to pasture and the hands who were only along for the drive were paid their wages and released, Teeter and the Paint brothers went to have a look at the house where they had come calling on Dermott Cull and his Mexican girlfriend. Cull had long since moved on, no one knew where. There were rumors he had been dry-gulched and dumped in a shallow grave, other rumors that he was installed as the overlord on a plantation in Cuba. Eli didn't much care what had happened to him as long as they didn't meet; if they did, even after four decades, someone would have to die.

For its entire existence as a working ranch, the O-Bar had been managed from afar. The great house Sir Humphrey Doane had once built as a home for the bride who jilted him now provided shelter for owls and rattlesnakes, mice and nesting birds. Parts of the roof had collapsed, leaving the parlor a crisscrossed jumble of rafters. The chimneys were clogged with nests and an elegant divan, now weather-stained and rotten, sprawled on the warped cherrywood boards of the dining room. The dining table itself had been chopped up and burned as firewood by the occasional shepherd who took refuge here during the worst winters. They strolled through the remnants of the house, taking care not to wander where the roof appeared in danger of further collapse. Ezra shook his head: He hated waste.

—I expect the only thing to do is to salvage what you can and build somewhere else.

—Nope. I want the house right here. They chose the right spot to build. We'll have to put up a new roof and put in new floors, but if we go about it the right way, it will be a heckuva place.

—If it suits you. I've looked around some, but I think I'll build somethin about a quarter this size. There's a good stand of cotton-woods the other side of that ridge, and a creek that runs most of the year. We're both of us goin to need a place for the winter.

—There's two small houses must have been built for the reps about two miles south. They can be fixed up before winter good enough to get us through. The rest can wait.

That night they sat around a bonfire a hundred yards from the big house. Teeter played the mouth harp while Calvin and Seth sang. Eli sat next to Ezra, the two of them still as alike as two peas, at least on the outside. The mouth harp went silent and Ezra launched into a yarn about the time he helped drive a herd of buffalo up from Arizona to Wyoming. Teeter noticed Ben on the edge of the circle around the fire, listening, not saying a word. He had handled himself well every step of the drive, but Eli had said no word, nor given any indication that the boy was other than a wrangler hired on for a cattle drive, that he was of Eli's flesh and blood. Teeter saw him watching now and then, knew that at times Ben reminded Eli too much of Frank and that at other times he saw in him a grandson who might have more of what he wanted in a man than his own sons Calvin and Seth and the youngest boy, Leo, the one child to whom Eli seemed to grant the tenderness and affection of the father.

When the others all turned in, Eli threw another log on the fire. Ezra waited. He could always tell when Eli had something on his mind; he would talk when he was ready.

—It's been a rough year for Ida Mae.

—I thought somethin just wasn't right.

—It aint. She has spells. One day she'll be fine, the next day she's at me about somethin odd, like the devil is in the radio and I have to get rid of the thing, she won't have it in the house. So I'll move it out to the barn and the next day she comes down to breakfast and wants to know what I've done with the radio.

Eli paused.

—I didn't want to leave her with the young ones, but Maude Hutchinson came to stay, so they'll be all right. I told Maude she might have her difficulties with Ida Mae, but Maude figures she can handle it. Like as not, Ida Mae will take to her bed and stay there for a week. Then she'll jump up and go to cleanin every pot in the kitchen at three in the morning.

—You talked to Doc Remy about any of this?

—I have. He says that if the human body is a mystery, the human mind is a far greater mystery. Says doctors are just gettin a start on figurin out what happens with the mind, but that if it gets any worse I might have to take Ida Mae to the state hospital for treatment.

—What can they do?

—A whole lot that aint too pleasant, I'm told. Electric shocks and such. Not a thing to which you'd condemn one of your own, if you had a choice.

—You know if there's anything I can do, I'll be happy to do it.

—I know it, little brother. I just can't think what you or anybody else can do. Maybe she'll snap out of it.

They were silent for a time before Ezra brought up a subject that had been troubling him.

—Y'know, I wonder sometimes what we done out here. If it wouldn't of been better if the white man stayed back east, left this part of the country for the Sioux and the Cheyenne and the Crow. If Pa never left the Mississippi River.

—If we'd all done that, you wouldn't have no railroads, no banks, hardly a thing except tipis that could be picked up in a hour and put on the move.

—That's just about my point. Ride around Wyoming some and you'll see these coal mines, looks like the devil decided to just plumb tear the earth apart. We killed off most of the buffalo and the other game, killed the Indians with disease and drink, tore up the land to plant crops where it ought to have stayed prairie, now we're runnin roads every which way. Now I know your preachers and your men of business will say that's progress, but it seems to me it might be progress in the wrong direction. That's why I'm askin what exactly it is we done out here since the old man left the Mississippi.

Eli sat looking into the fire for so long that Ezra thought he may have forgotten the question. At last he spat into the blaze.

—That's what we did. We stuck.

Teeter Spawn died before he saw another Wyoming winter. He was in his eighty-first year, although no one he knew could have given his age with accuracy because he didn't strictly know himself. By the time of his death Teeter was attracting the occasional journalist, writers who wanted to talk to genuine cowboys from the Old West while there were still a few around. Teeter was one of the few who had made the great trail drives from Texas to Dodge City and Ogallala; he was also a Civil War veteran, even if he fought for the wrong side, and he loved to tell a yarn. He convinced one long tall drink of water from the *Philadelphia Inquirer* that he had once stopped a longhorn stampede by holding up the Good Book and telling the runaway steers to obey the word of the Lord.

All but one of Eli's children were at Teeter's funeral in Sheridan. Marguerite came with Custer Johns and her children, Kate from Lincoln. Wade and Ruby brought Blind Daniel with them. Tavie and Amelia had just moved back to Wyoming after the death of Amelia's mother, but they left the new dude ranch they were setting up in Jackson Hole to pay their respects to Teeter. Ida Mae came by train with the younger children, which meant that only Velma was missing. Tavie thought of saying something to Eli about Velma's absence, but decided it would be disrespectful to Teeter.

Although she didn't often get worked up about things, Tavie cried, and she and Marguerite held each other, and Ruby and Kate comforted the children. Tavie imagined that Teeter himself would have been a mite embarrassed to see all the fuss being made over one stove-up old cowboy, but there were not many people she would miss more.

After the funeral, Ben left with Wade and Ruby and went back to Sheep Creek. Ezra told him he was turning into a fine horseman and would be missed, but Eli paid him his wages and said good-bye. Ben didn't know if he expected anything more from Eli, but if he did, he wasn't going to hear it. At one point during the trail drive to the Powder River, Eli had hinted that he might give Ben a new saddle for his work with the remuda, but it seemed to have slipped his mind.

Late that fall, during the last week of his last term as sheriff of Brown County, Luther Beckwith left his Ford where it was parked next to the house, saddled his little buckskin mare and rode out to the draw along the Niobrara where Rafe Cubbin had found the body of Herman Ostheimer dangling from a box elder tree. Luther hadn't come to look for a solitary thing; for reasons he did not care to explain to a living soul, he could not feel shed of the job without coming to this place, the site of the only murder he had failed to solve during his tenure as sheriff. The leaves were gone, the branches were bare. Three magpies sat high on a branch of the old box elder; Luther wondered if they were not waiting still for another feast like the meal they had made of poor Herman's eyeballs. A horse whinnied somewhere far off and the buckskin answered. The old sheriff swung down out of the saddle, aware that it was no longer a thing he did with ease, and dropped the reins to ground-tie the mare. He could hear the Niobrara running its course, cattle lowing on the far side of the river. A long, wobbly formation of geese honked their way south, scuttling along as though afraid they had departed too late and had too far to go.

Luther walked one slow turn around the tree and then another, tried to imagine the sound of many hooves on the night Ostheimer was hung. It had to be night; a hanging in broad daylight would have drawn too many prying eyes. At one time or another, he had talked to all the big ranchers and half the cowpokes in the county and he had picked up no hint of a witness. Rafe Cubbin was still barking about the case, but Luther paid about as much attention to Rafe as you would to one of those round bits of fur that rich women liked to hold in their laps. Even without Rafe, little things stuck in his craw: Roy Titus had never set foot in Brown County after Ostheimer was hung. Now Eli Paint had left and was unlikely to return unless he was forced to do so by the law. A month before Ostheimer's body was found, a man over the line in South Dakota claimed to have met up with a fellow with a German accent, who was trying to sell a prize Morgan stallion bearing the 8T8 brand of the Fanciful. When Luther went out to the ranch, the stud horse was in his stall. Eli said he had never been missing, but Luther wasn't so sure.

The wind picked up and Luther turned up the sheepskin collar of his jacket. Winter was coming, he was about to hang up his badge. Somewhere in his carcass he could feel every kick and punch he had ever taken, and a gnawing pain in his side that might be something he didn't care to think about. He was about to mount the buckskin again, when something up in the tree caught his eye. It dangled from a branch ten feet off the ground that went out at a ninety-degree angle from the tree where Ostheimer was hung; it had probably never been noticed before because Luther and his deputies had come when the tree was bursting with green leaves. There was a time when he would have shinnied up the tree after it, but that was a long while ago, so he unbuckled his lariat and gave it a lazy toss and a strip of leather about a foot long drifted down from the tree.

Luther picked it up, turned it one way and another. He was no expert on bullwhips, but unless he was far wrong, this was from the business end of one of those Australian kangaroo-hide bullwhips, the kind Eli Paint always carried. Eli and three or four other men in Brown County, he reminded himself. It depended on which angle you wanted to take on a thing. Given half a chance, Rafe Cubbin would seize on this, and bellow to the heavens that it was proof positive of Eli's complicity in the death of Herman Ostheimer, and Bob Simmons with no more effort than it would take to shoo a housefly would sit in a courtroom and make of that pompous young lawyer such a fool that with two dozen sworn witnesses, Rafe would still lose the case.

The buckskin nuzzled Luther's pocket, looking for an apple he had forgotten to bring. He rubbed her nose, gathered up the reins, got a booted toe into the stirrup, swung into the saddle, and let her pick her own way south toward home. For a mile or more he carried the strip of leather he had found until finally, still within sight of the river, he cast it aside. It was not a thing to be taken to Rafe Cubbin or anyone else. As he urged the buckskin into a trot, Luther understood at last why he had come to the river: because there was a thing he had to know for himself. Now he knew, and that was an end to it.

CHAPTER 56

The Great Depression came like a sneak thief to the North Platte Valley, hurting people in small ways rather than smashing them as it did in the cities, in the industrial heartland, and farther to the south, where the great duststorms would start the heartbreaking migration to California and Oregon. By the time the stock market crashed finally and thoroughly, in October 1929, farmers had already suffered through a decade of privation and falling prices for their produce. The last time most of them could remember anything like prosperity dated back to the end of World War I. The high wartime prices had collapsed long before the Treaty of Versailles was signed, and while the rest of the country danced through the Jazz Age on the artificial profits of Wall Street, farmers went broke and lost their farms. A man worked until his back broke and his limbs felt like they would melt and promised his family the bounty of his effort: a new tractor, a new house, a trip to California. Then prices fell and he found himself hoping for a laying hen in good health, a well that drew clear water, a roof over his head, enough fuel for the fire in winter. When even those hopes were too much, he saw his front door padlocked and watched the auctioneer put everything he owned under the gavel and tried to explain to his wife and kids why all they had left was a rickety Model T and enough gas to get to the state line. Farmers were prepared for the Great Depression when it came, because they had already been living it for a dozen years.

Velma read the October headlines in the Scottsbluff *Star-Herald,* but for the most part the Depression left her untouched; she had never had money, so the disaster affected her less than some. Two of the Wardman Hotel's regular customers, the banker Bowen Kendall and the insurance man Russell Niver, committed suicide within a month of the crash. Kendall shot himself when it was clear his bank would fail, Niver hanged himself after losing thirty thousand dollars in a single day when the market collapsed. When she learned of their deaths, Velma was puzzled. How could money mean so much to people? She had spent fifteen years clinging to life by a thread, she had seen so many good people die that she could hardly remember all their names, the one thing she craved more than anything else was simple good health. Kendall and Niver were plump, healthy men in the prime of life, and yet they preferred to end it all rather than face life without money. In her steaming kitchen in the Wardman Hotel, Velma made two fewer meals at lunchtime, but life went on.

The Swedes came to eat at the Wardman Hotel in Scottsbluff every Thursday at lunchtime, regular as clockwork. They went to the sale barn in the morning, had their lunch at the hotel, paid a nickel each for haircuts at Gooch Lester's barbershop, and bought supplies for another week before heading back to their farm south of Lyman. They were brothers, Jim and Lee Lindquist, the quietest two men Velma had ever seen in her life. Big-shouldered, blue-eyed, thick-fingered, their round blond heads fresh-cropped by Gooch's clippers. When they perched on their stools at the lunch counter, Emaline would stroll over and stand hipshot with her pad waiting, and after studying the menu intently they would each say in turn:

—The usual.

—The usual.

Velma would dish up meat loaf, carrots, mashed potatoes, and peas, and ten minutes later Emaline would be back for their pie and Jim would have two pieces and Lee one and she would fill their coffee cups half full to leave room for milk and four teaspoons of sugar. When they were done eating, they would leave a nickel tip on the table for Emaline, and Jim would stick his head in the kitchen and say, "Good pie," whether it was apple or cherry or gooseberry or lemon meringue, and Velma would say, "Thank you," and when they were gone Emaline would say, "The one called Jim is sweet on you," and Velma would grin and pat her hair.

—If he's sweet on me, he's got a funny way of showing it. Those two have been coming here for six months and the only thing I've ever heard from him is just that: "Good pie."

—Still, they're good-looking men.

—If you like big, strong Swedes.

—They strike me as good men. Never trying to look down my dress. Wouldn't hurt a fly, big as they are.

—Big as workhorses.

—Clydesdales. I thought that the first time I saw them.

—People say they've got a good farm.

—They do. They're not gettin rich, but who is these days?

—How old do you think they are?

—Forty if they're a day. And neither of them married, although they say Lee buried a young wife in Sweden before he came over.

—I guess by the time we get to a certain age, we've all got people we buried somewhere.

—You shouldn't be dwelling on that, Mama. Jim has his eye on you, and if I were you, I wouldn't turn him down. He's a hard worker and he's quiet and kind and I don't think he'll ever treat you the way Watson did. You can just see it in his eyes, he's a gentle man.

Velma and Emaline went to the carnival on the Fourth of July, and there were the Swedes, Lee and Jim, watching solemnly as country boys tried to knock down stacked bowling pins with lopsided base-balls that refused to fly true. Finally Jim walked over and paid his nickel to try it, and he took the baseball in those hands like dinner plates and squashed it a little to take the lop out of it so that it was almost round again. When he threw, it was like the ball came out of a cannon. He knocked down the pins once, was handed another lopsided ball, worked it into shape with one squeeze, dropped another set of pins. The barker handed him another ball, this one so flattened out that it looked more like a pancake than a baseball, and Jim shaped it true as he could and threw so hard the ball knocked one set of pins flying and knocked down the set next to it. The carny barker tried to hold back the prize because Jim had knocked down two batches of pins when the sign said right there the prize was for knocking down one stack of pins, not two. A ripple like distant thunder went through the crowd that had gathered, and the barker, afraid he would be tarred and feathered or worse if he held out any longer, reached back and handed Jim a stuffed bear.

—All right now, you got your teddy bear, move it along. Goddamn dumb Scandahoovians. I oughta knowed better than to take your nickel.

Jim turned and looked at him, rolling those big shoulders. Velma thought he was going to reach over and put a thumb on the fellow's Adam's apple and throttle him with one hand, but he let it go and turned holding the bear under one thick arm and saw her and extended it like he was handing her a sick baby to hold.

—You want this? I won it.

—Oh, I couldn't. It's yours.

—What am I going to do with a toy bear? I've got no kids, got no wife.

—Well, in that case I'll take it. Where'd you learn to throw a baseball like that?

—Minnesota. I was maybe going to pitch for the St. Louis Cardinals, but a Holstein bull got me in a corral and knocked me down. My knee wasn't so good after that.

He was so matter-of-fact about it that Velma decided it must have been true. He didn't seem like a man to exaggerate as some would. They wandered down among the tents, inhaling the smells of cotton candy, popcorn, peanuts, and the stale sweat of the vendors tempting the crowd to part with their hard-earned nickels. Lee dropped back with Emaline so that Velma was walking alone with Jim. It felt reassuring, having this big, strong man beside her, even if you had to pry a word or two out of him with a crowbar. She realized they had never been properly introduced and extended her hand.

—I'm Velma.

—Jim.

They shook hands.

—My real name is Jens, but when I played ball they called me Jim, so now it's Jim. Easier for Americans.

—You like my pies.

—Yep. You're a good cook.

—Thank you.

They were married on the first day of September 1929. It took three weeks for Jim to propose and three more weeks for Velma to accept: Before she could take another step she had to caution him that she suffered from tuberculosis and that she could suffer a relapse at any time. He listened and nodded solemnly.

—You're a good woman. I figure if I only get ten years of you, that's better than no time at all, right?

—If that's the way it looks to you. I hope I have ten years more to give.

—You will. I'll take care of you.

He did. For once, Velma told anyone who would listen, she'd married the right man. Big as he was, Jim Lindquist was the kindest man she had ever known. He was so gentle that if she had not taken charge herself, he would never have got around to doing what she wanted in the room at the Wardman Hotel where they spent their first night.

The Lindquist brothers farmed three hundred and twenty acres of land fifteen miles west of Scottsbluff and four miles south of a town called Stegall, a wide spot in the road with a gas station and a general store. The tiny white farmhouse was down in a sheltered swale among a long stand of cottonwoods a half mile off the county road. From the house the ground rose to the north and west, and when she was hanging the wash, Velma would see one of the brothers on a tractor, his broad back framed against the horizon. They had dug a deep well, their fences were taut and tidy, the barn and corrals were a good distance from the house so that the smell of livestock in summer was not overwhelming. After she married Jim, they put up a one-room shack for Lee a hundred feet away, and Bobby left Wade and Ruby's ranch on Sheep Creek to come live with his mother while Ben stayed on the ranch to help with the horses.

Velma had visited Bobby almost every Sunday while he lived with Wade and Ruby, and she loved him as she loved life itself, but with him she was always pulled two ways, the tug of poor lost Billy behind that tousled blond hair, so that when Bobby moved his head a certain way or when he smiled, she saw a sketch of what Billy would have become as he grew and sometimes the pain of it almost took her breath away. Each day when she said grace before dinner, Velma remembered to be grateful that her boys had each found a father to replace Frank and Watson. Wade Tourtelotte in his quiet way had taught Ben how to shear a sheep, birth a calf, rebuild the carburetor on a Model A Ford. Jim was already a father to Bobby and a much better one than Watson had ever been.

Velma had Jim cultivate two full acres for a vegetable garden in a sunny patch north of the house, and from April to September her days were spent tending her sweet corn, tomatoes, carrots, turnips, peas, onions, and strawberries. There was the radio to listen to in the evening. Ben wrote once a week from Wyoming, dutiful brief notes about weather and horses signed "Love, Ben."

Velma's only disappointment was that she was unable to give Jim a child. The doctors had cautioned that another pregnancy might kill her, but Velma wanted it for him anyway, wanted Jim to have that portion of immortality a child represents. The seasons came and went, however, and the child did not come, and in the end she let go of that hope. It was enough that when she rose in the morning Jim already had the fire going and the porridge on the stove for himself and Bobby, that when she woke in the night his slow, heavy breathing lulled her back to sleep, that when she was bent over her sewing next to the fire in the evening he would sometimes come beside her and stroke her hair, running his blunt fingers through the white strip in her hair and gazing at her with such tenderness that she would put down her handiwork and rest her cheek against his hip, feeling all the weariness of the hard years flow from her body.

Late on a hot afternoon in June 1932, Velma took a pitcher of lemonade and went to sit with Jim in the shade of a Dutch elm tree south of the house. Velma had squeezed out six lemons with plenty of sugar to make lemonade for Bobby and Lee and Jim after a long day in the fields, but Lee was still tinkering with the tractor, so Velma sat with Jim. He had washed up in the basin outside the house. It was so hot he didn't bother to towel-dry but sat instead with the water from his hair trickling down his face and neck. He had spent the day wrestling with the cultivator in the corn and was still breathing hard, but he was grinning a little, the way he did after a good day's work.

It was Velma's favorite time of day. When she was not too busy in the kitchen or the garden, she liked to sit in the shade and watch the sun going down while she listened to the *woo-wook-wookoo* of the mourning doves in the willow trees by the creek and watched the cattle plod single-file downhill along the familiar path toward the stock tank. Jim had planted a hundred acres of flax in the field nearest the house because Velma loved it so. The stems were a shade of green unlike any other crop, and when it bloomed, the flowers waved in a pale blue sea in the slightest breeze. When it ripened, the stems turned brown and the brown bolls atop each stalk were filled with brown seeds the size of an apple seed. Velma always borrowed enough flaxseeds from the crop to keep a few jars in the kitchen;

she made flax tea sweetened with honey for colds, and when her chest was congested she found that a flaxseed poultice helped. She used the same poultice when Bobby got a sty on his eye, and when Jim and Lee came in from the fields with their eyes full of dust, she persuaded them to slip a flaxseed under the eyelid; the seed cleansed and soothed the eye. Seeing the field right next to the house where she could watch it grow and bloom was like healing itself; it soothed her heart and gave her hope for the future.

As they sat quietly side by side sipping their lemonade, Jim saw Bobby top the rise a half mile off and start down toward the house on foot with his rifle over his right shoulder, trailing a jackrabbit by the ears. Bobby had become a crack shot, and when he wasn't needed in the fields, he roamed the badlands four miles to the southeast of the farm with his rifle. Jim pointed to the boy with some pride.

—Looks like he got another rabbit. Before Bobby came, I used to go out there three, four times a week. Never hit a thing. Bobby, if he sees it, he shoots it.

—We have pork for supper tonight, but we'll have rabbit tomorrow. It makes things easier when we have Bobby to hunt.

Velma saw that Jim's glass was empty and filled it again, leaving enough in the pitcher for Bobby and Lee. She watched him drink and wipe his mouth with the back of his hand. When Jim had first asked her to marry him, Velma did not feel love for the man, not the way she had been in love with Frank, but through their quiet years together she had come to adore him so that every slightest gesture touched her heart: the way he brushed the cowlick of his hair back from his eyes, the way he drank his lemonade, the way he squared his powerful shoulders before he headed out to work at dawn every morning. She reached out and touched him, combed her fingers through the thin blond hairs that stood out on his bronzed and muscular forearm.

—You're a good man, Jim Lindquist. A very good man. I have known some bad ones, but you are a good man and I love you very much.

Jim blushed. She could see his forehead turn red above the line where he wore his cap in the fields.

—Aw, Velma.

—You are wonderful, Jim. You are honest, you work hard, you don't drink. You treat me like a queen. I wish I could be here forever.

—You will be. We take care of you. Queen of the farm forever.

Velma felt herself tearing up. She wiped her eyes on her apron and turned to him and buried her face for a moment on his broad shoulder. The breeze picked up, stirring the flax. Never in her life had she felt so absolutely, completely happy. Everything around them made her happy: the doves, the cattle, the flax, Lee in the shed with his tractor, Bobby with his rabbit, this good, strong man. She kissed Jim four times on the neck and felt his wide, powerful hands holding her, and when she looked up, Bobby was strolling into the yard, holding the bloody rabbit by the ears. Jim got up to take the rabbit.

—I'll skin him and leave him in the smokehouse. He'll be good for tomorrow. Where did you get him?

Bobby went to the basin to wash up.

—Down on the hardpan. It was a hard shot. He was maybe two hundred yards off and I was up on the ridge above him with the sun in my eyes. I knew I'd only get one chance at him and I had to make it good. I didn't miss.

When Bobby was through washing up, he came and sat in Jim's chair. Velma tousled his hair.

—How did you get to be such a good shot, honey?

Bobby shrugged.

—It's easy, Mom. You just got to have good eyes and stay real calm and quiet.

—Jim is calm and quiet, but he isn't a good shot like you. Now if you're all washed up, we'll go in for dinner. I made mashed pota-toes the way you like them.

Bobby trailed her into the house and helped set the supper table, Jim finished skinning the rabbit and washed again and joined them, and Lee finished with the tractor. Jim said grace as they sat with their heads bowed, and when he was through Velma passed the potatoes and gravy, pork chops and peas and pickled beets. Jim and Lee spoke a little in Swedish, making their plans for the next day, and Bobby marched through one big plate and half of another before he came up for air. Velma winked at him.

—Be sure you leave room for pie, honey.

—I always got room for pie.

—You always *have* room for pie.

—Yes. I always *have* room for pie.

Velma watched Jim all through dinner. When they were through, Bobby would help with the washing up while Lee went back to his house and Jim sat with his *National Geographic*, reading the issue carefully from cover to cover.

Velma felt as good and strong as she had ever felt. There was no way of knowing how much time she had; she was still a lunger and a lunger never knew, but she had all this, and for the bounty of this life she felt like the luckiest woman on earth.

On November 8, 1932, they all gathered around the radio at the farmhouse to listen to the election results. Franklin Delano Roosevelt defeated Herbert Hoover in a landslide. Velma and Emaline had always been Democrats; Jim had voted for Cal Coolidge in 1924 and Herbert Hoover in 1928, but Velma had finally persuaded him that the Republicans were the party of big business and that FDR was the only one who would give the working man a fighting chance and pull the country out of this awful depression. Velma went around for weeks humming the song of FDR's campaign: "Happy Days Are Here Again." Surely Franklin and Eleanor Roosevelt would put the country right again. All those poor men out of work would find jobs, farm prices would rise, and the nation would be strong again. She hoped only that her own strength would last that long.

❧ CHAPTER 57 ❧

Velma collapsed on the first day of January 1933. They spent New Year's Eve as Jim always spent it, praying in the new year with a marathon that began a little past suppertime and went on so long Velma's legs went numb from the hard wooden pew. Velma listened only at intervals; the preacher hated Franklin Delano Roosevelt and kept veering into tirades against the incoming president, who was to be inaugurated on March 4. Velma thought that Roosevelt was still the best chance the country had to pull out of the depression and that a preacher ought not to get into politics anyway. She mouthed her own silent prayers: that Roosevelt would have the strength to carry on, that she herself would survive another year. She prayed for Emaline and Ben and Bobby, for peace so that her boys would never have to fight and die in a foreign war as Frank had. At last, with more than her usual fervor, she prayed for lungers everywhere. Jim, bless his quiet heart, slept through much of the service, which was probably why he did not find it such a trial to remain so long. Every two hours the congregation took a break to nibble at the pies and cakes and casseroles prepared by farm wives; because Velma was the best cook in the county, she always worked to outdo herself. She had labored steadily for three days making angel food cakes and lemon meringue pies and shortbread cookies, and by the time they dressed for church, she was coughing heavily and complaining that she was worn out through and through. She kept coughing in church, but her neighbors thought nothing of it: It was winter and half of them were fighting colds themselves.

When the service was over at last, Jim drove the four miles home in the unheated truck. Velma was so cold her legs turned blue, and she feared that her shivering would shake her body to pieces. That night she had a fever, tossing and turning and tangling the sheets before the fever broke and she sweated so that they had to climb out of bed while she toweled off and changed the sheets. She recognized all the symptoms: her cheeks were red and flushed, her swollen joints ached, her cough brought up green mucus tinged with blood. Still, she crawled out of bed before dawn and tried to make breakfast for Jim and Bobby and Lee, who were all out on this frigid morning doing the chores. She was flipping pancakes on the griddle when the room began to spin around her and she fell heavily, face forward onto the rug she had crocheted to cover the cold pine floor. Jim came in from doing the chores to find his wife lying where she had fallen. He dropped to his knees, turned her over, and heard her breathing. Blood was pouring from her nose, which had been broken in the fall. Bobby and Lee came in a moment later, and Bobby stood white and pale beside the stove, watching as the Swedes wrapped the unconscious Velma in blankets and Lee helped carry her to the truck. Jim told Bobby to stay with Lee, Lee cranked the engine to life to speed things along, and Jim drove to the hospital in Scottsbluff as fast as the old truck could bump along the icy roads, unaware that tears were streaming down his face and all but freezing in the cold.

The ride into town took forty-five minutes, but it seemed to last for hours; he pulled up in front of the hospital with the truck wheezing and jumping as it ran out of gas, scooped Velma's bony frame out of the seat, and carried her inside. Someone located an elderly doctor, and Jim explained that his wife suffered from tuberculosis. The doctor nodded; a nurse found an empty bed in an empty room, someone administered morphia, Velma slipped into a troubled sleep while Jim sat stiffly at her side listening to the strain of her ragged breathing, his thick hands resting on his coveralls, frustrated that all his strength left him so utterly helpless. When he was certain she was asleep, he found a telephone and called Emaline. She arrived ahead of Doc Baker, and they all stood around in a solemn circle as he explained that Velma's condition was grave and that he was afraid for her survival.

—What we'll have to do is to get her back to the National Jewish in Denver as soon as she's able to travel, but if we tried that now, the trip would kill her, so we're going to have to care for her as best we can right here. She's a strong woman, and she's been through this before, so we can say our prayers. Maybe she'll pull through.

Ruby called Eli in Wyoming to tell him that Velma was back in the hospital. Her father sounded weary; Ida Mae was having one of her spells again, this time so bad that Eli was about to drive her to the state hospital in Evanston; Eli was having his wife committed. Her madness had finally become too much for him to handle. Ruby explained that they were all waiting for Velma to improve a bit, at least enough to return to Denver.

—Papa, I really wish you'd come see her. I think it would cheer her some.

—I'm not so sure about that, girl. Last time I saw her, I guess this was around 1914, when we run Frank off for good, she didn't want to see hide nor hair of me.

—That was almost twenty years ago. Things have changed.

—All right. Let me get Ida Mae settled in Evanston, make sure the kids are all right here, and I'll drive down to see her.

—She might be at the National Jewish by then.

—That's fine. I'll call you when I get back, you can let me know how Velma is doing and where to find her.

—Do that, Papa. Don't forget. It would be nice to see you.

—I know, girl. Older I get, more I miss my girls. All my girls and Daniel too. Don't see near enough of you.

—It's been that way for a long time.

—I know, honey. I'm gettin old, but I got Tavie nearby in Jackson Hole now, and once I take care of this business with Ida Mae, I'm going to spend more time with my own, Velma included. That's a promise.

Velma was not doing well, especially at night. She would wake with parched lips, her skin on fire, her joints swollen and aching so that every smallest move made her want to scream. On one of the worst of those nights, she woke to find her gentleman caller sitting high-booted on a stiff-backed chair next to her bed, his spurs jangling as he tied and retied knots in a length of rope, doing his figuring. She had not seen him for so long that she had to turn on the bedside lamp to be sure it was him come to call.

—Papa?

He looked up.

—*Sorry, girl. You ought to know better by now. Are you ready? It's time to come to the river.*

—*What river?*

—*Does it matter? The Belle Fourche. The Yellowstone. The White River. The Missouri, the Big Sioux, the Mississippi. The Tongue.*

—*The Tongue? That's a funny name for a river. Laplaplap. The Tongue River.*

—*Yes, it is. We can go there if you like.*

—*I don't want to go to the river.*

—*You must. It is time. Come to the river. Time time time time time.*

Velma's condition did not improve. The fever did not diminish, the cough was getting worse, her joints were still swollen, and she kept losing weight. Jim visited daily between his farm chores, silent and dependable as rock. He would sit with the square, blunt fingers of his square, blunt hands smoothing the creases in his trousers, gazing at Velma as she slept, sometimes stroking her face. What a pity it was, Emaline thought, that her mother could not have borne her children with this man instead of Frank or Watson.

After Velma had been in the hospital four days, it was obvious she was not getting better. Ruby came on Saturday afternoon and was appalled; as soon as she and Wade got back to the ranch that night, she called Eli, but he was still in Evanston. That night, Velma had the worst coughing fit Emaline had ever seen. It was near midnight, everyone else had gone home, and Emaline was sitting alone next to her mother's bed. Emaline rang for a nurse, and the two of them held Velma until it seemed she would cough her life out. When the coughing subsided, the nurse gave her another shot of morphine, and Emaline held her hand and she drifted into something like sleep. In her dreams in the long dark hours of the night, Velma heard the jangling of spurs and knew that he would come long-striding *jangle jangle jangle,* his boots ringing on the polished black oak of the corridor. When she woke, he was standing in the shadows, beckoning to her with an outstretched hand.

—*Come. It is time. Come to the river.*

Emaline watched Velma stir in her sleep and heard her say plainly: "Come with me now. Come to the river." Emaline stood for a long while peering out the window. A gaunt and fibrous moon rose in the winter sky. The great shadow of Scotts Bluff loomed on the horizon, moonlight basting its gumbo flanks the color of old bone. Somewhere out there between willow and cottonwood was the muddy trickle of the flat Platte, iced with winter. She heard her mother's desperate breathing, more words muttered in her sleep: "The river, the river."

Velma woke for a few minutes just before dawn, saw Emaline asleep, and rang for the night nurse. The nurse gave her something to sleep but she did not sleep, and as the sun came up she watched the great bluff to the southwest lift from darkness. In her darkened hospital room, a wave of light. Dancing wheat fields, a summer breeze. In the wheat, bouncing spheres of light, weightless as soap bubbles. She had no difficulty seeing them now. They were as plain as the wheat itself.

He took her hand.

—*Come with me now. Come to the river.*

She rose and looked out over the valley, past the North Platte

River and Scotts Bluff. The river and the bluff in the first light of dawn.

The birth of the world. It must have been like this, no? Nothing at all, then light on the horizon. Mountains rising from nothing, hurled to the sky. Time the force that moved the universe. Not a thunderclap, simply the long heave and thrust of time creating life from nothing. All this life out of nothing, light from darkness. See it in the light in the wheat fields in the morning, that ball of light, dancing. Light that is alive. Look away and you will find it, the light in the wheat, in the breezeblown grain. Grain waving in the breeze, light waving in the grain. All of life a yearning for the light, for the thing unseen, the mystery of the dancing light.

When Emaline woke, a dim midwinter light trickled into the room. Something was missing: The room was silent. She could not hear the sound of Velma's ragged breath. She stood and leaned over the bed and pressed her cheek to her mother's bosom. There was no sound, no slightest motion. She gripped Velma's shoulders and held her.

—Oh, no, Mama. Please, Mama. No.

⊰ CHAPTER 58 ⊱

Eli Paint parked on Front Street and returned in winter afternoon dark to the Hotel Evanston, his sheepskin collar turned up against an icy wind, decades of weariness in his bones. He felt himself to be an empty husk, hollowed out from the inside by the long, failed struggle with Ida Mae's madness. Each day at the hospital he sat waiting on hard polished wooden chairs while nameless things were done to her in nameless rooms, and then by her side where she slumped with a quilt on her lap, a woman he did not know and perhaps never had. A woman who might have carried this thing within her from birth. At home the girls Jenny, Mabel, and Anna and the boys Calvin and Seth displayed at times what he took to be signs of the same ripples beneath the surface that had consumed their mother. Or perhaps he simply took any slightest tremor as a sign, as evidence that her perverse and contrary nature, the sudden tantrums, had all been passed from mother to child. Only the youngest boy, Leo, seemed utterly free of what Eli had come to think of as a biblical curse, a curse visited upon him for sins of the past too numerous to contemplate. Now Ida Mae was like a bogged heifer in quicksand, impossible to free, and as she sank he had sunk with her, until his spirits were as flat as January sunlight.

Eli arrived in the hotel lobby at the same time as Lew Clancy, a cigar-chewing railroad man of slight acquaintance who was about as talkative as Eli himself. They unlimbered themselves of hats and coats and sunk into the deep plush of the chairs with a little more than a nod and a mumble.

—Cold as hell.

—It is that.

Eli sat letting the warmth of the furnace seep into his bones, thinking of Ida Mae and how it was they had come to this pass. He had married her because he needed a wife, thinking that with her square-backed strength she would look after the kitchen and care for the needs of himself and his six children, and that she would make no claims on that chamber of his heart where he nourished still a love for Livvy Stanton that was as strong as it was the day she tried to take off his legs with that rusty old scythe. Ida Mae took over the kitchen and made no claims on his heart, but she crashed into a feud with Livvy's children, separated him from them as neatly as a cutting horse working a steer out of a herd. She had enforced and hardened the expulsion of Velma, making it nigh impossible for him to offer a kindness to his most-loved daughter. She battled Tavie until Tavie bloodied her nose, and one by one all Livvy's children, even Blind Daniel, put distance between themselves and Ida Mae, until they were all gone and he was left only with this brittle woman and her unpredictable offspring, children who, apart from little Leo, seemed as different from Eli as the moon from the sun. Now she had gone to a place he could not follow, into the cold brick battlements of the state hospital, and he was left to while away his evenings alone in this hotel, brooding over paths not taken.

He was still seated in the armchair next to Lew Clancy, wondering if it might not be near time to wash up for dinner, when a bellboy sidled up sheepishly with a telegram five days old. Eli glanced at it:

ELI PAINT, C/O HOTEL EVANSTON, EVANSTON WYOMING
VELMA FAILING. COME QUICK. RUBY.

He looked again at the date, glared at the boy.

—What happened?

—The night boy went to take it to your room t'other night, sir. You was out, so he brought it back and it got stuck betwixt two ledgers. I found it just now while I was looking for my pencil.

Eli uttered a curse word that rarely passed his lips, rose to his feet, and swept up his hat and coat with a nod to Clancy.

—Got a sick daughter. Looks like I got some drivin ahead a me.

—Watch your step. That black ice is a she-bear bitch this time a year.

Five minutes later, Eli was back in the lobby with his valise, tapping a booted toe impatiently and still glaring at the bellboy as he waited for his account to be settled. Outside it felt as though the temperature had dropped ten degrees in half an hour, but he tossed the valise onto the seat of the big 1925 Cadillac V-8 Custom Suburban with the white doors and the black roof and drove too fast on icy roads, the tall car swaying over the bumps in the Lincoln Highway like a sailing ship on a high sea. By daybreak he was near Cheyenne, having traveled a distance of three hundred and fifty miles over the continental divide. In Cheyenne he stopped for three cups of coffee, drove sixty-five miles to Kimball over the Nebraska line, hung a left and drove north a whit less than fifty miles, made it to Scottsbluff a little after nine o'clock in the morning, with all that he would say to Velma rehearsed over and over in his mind. He stopped to buy flowers, came long-striding down the hall with his bootheels ringing off the tiles, stopped a harried nurse to ask for the room of Velma Lindquist. The nurse looked at him oddly, as though he had eyes of different colors.

—I don't believe Velma is with us anymore.

—How's that?

—Let me find Doc Baker, sir.

Five minutes later, she was back with Dr. Baker. Eli shifted the flowers from his right hand to his left in order to shake the man's hand.

—I'm lookin for Velma Lindquist.

—I understood that. I'm sorry. I have bad news for you, sir. Velma passed away five days ago. I believe another daughter and your granddaughter were trying to contact you. They didn't know where to find you.

—They sent a telegram to Evanston. Somebody lost track of it and I got it too late.

The doctor saw Eli turn the color of coal-stove ash, tried to find words that would comfort.

—She died in her sleep. She went peacefully.

Eli had to reach out to steady himself on the windowsill.

—She's gone, then?

—Yes, sir. Passed Wednesday morning.

—I should have got here sooner.

—I think she would have liked that.

—Can't be helped now.

—No, sir. It sure can't.

The doctor returned to his rounds. The nurse took Eli by the elbow and guided him to a room with two chairs and an empty bed. She brought him a glass of water and he handed her the flowers that were for Velma, suggested she give them to someone who was yet among the living. He sat staring out the window at that great, looming bluff across the river, wondering if anyone else found that it looked as though a buffalo crouched on its flank. Without thinking, he reached into a pocket of his sheepskin coat and drew out a length of rope. For two hours while nurses came and went, he sat tying and retying knots. His fingers worked through the rolling hitch and fisherman's bend and the stevedore's knot, through half hitch and timber hitch and the hangman's knot. Thinking of the lost daughter, the way he had shut her out. There was time for thought now. Time to parse the years, sift for nuggets of truth. Alone with a self he was not disposed to like, left in solitude to gaze into the dark mirror of his soul. A hard man testing himself, striking flint on flint and wondering at the sparks that flew.

Here you are, Mr. Eli Paint, alone with what you have wrought. Owner of better than a hundred thousand acres of ranchland in three states, worth better than a million dollars and this your own daughter lost to overwork and neglect. The sins of the father, visited upon the daughter. Mistakes a man can make when he sets his jaw too hard, when he hunkers down thinking he's got it right and won't listen to a living soul. It's true a man can't be a leaf blown this way and that by every passing breeze, but he must have in him something other than flint, he needs a little give, a little slack in the rope. Thought to be doing the right thing throwing her out like that, but a fellow always thinks he's right. I had lessons to impart. Needed to make an example of her lest the others drift as she had drifted, seduced by another tall dark stranger. Did my damnedest and they all turned out pretty good, but then so did she. Took care of her children in spite of all hell, and what more can a body do? Would not take help from me and now it's too late. Room for kindness there might have been. Right back to the day when I drove her to see Doc Remy in Ainsworth and took the news like a wet dishrag in the face. How hard I was then, how unbending. Obdurate, I think that's the word. Livvy would use a three-dollar word like that: obdurate. Hell yes. Goes back to the day dangling from that old cottonwood tree. Learned then never to yield. Don't give the sonsofbitches an inch or they'll take a mile. Built something of a fortune in that manner, a spread where a man could ride all morning and never leave his own land. But to treat a child thus, that was harsh. For that you will be judged. Keep to the straight and narrow or drown, that was the rule. My rule, her drowning. It was her chose to drown, was it not? Made her bed and must sleep in it? Chose that long, tall drink of water with his rope tricks and his way with a horse. But hell, I could have handled it better. The Old Testament unbending righteousness of a hard man, will made of steel and tempered at the end of a hangman's rope. There it was, the nub of it. No mercy at the end of a rope. Lesson a man learns hard and does not forget if he lives through it. What would you have done, Livvy? Yes, I know what you would have done. You trailed forgiveness like perfume, held it in every least tone and gesture. Always quoting Shakespeare at me when you felt my rules held my girls penned in like a bobwire fence: The quality of mercy, you used to say, the quality of mercy is not something something. Never had a head to remember poetry, although I can tell you to the penny what a shipment of cattle brought at the railhead in 1896 or 1903. Livvy, do you hear me? Perhaps it is not too late. I have held mercy always for Daniel, been merciful with him in his blindness. Mercy for Daniel, but from the sighted I have demanded too much and given too little. Can a man find his other nature? Is it within him, or is he caught in the web of self and old sins like a horse tangled in bobwire, never to be free? Expect my gentler nature went to Ezra at birth. Half to each. The half I was born with is stone and thistle, a desert upon this earth. No comfort there, no place for a man to take his ease. And now this. Velma gone and no way to get her back, too late even for the goddamned funeral. She always pulled through before. Thought she would again. Thought we had time, and now there is no time left. The glass has run out of sand, they used to say. Nobody has use for a hourglass anymore. Useless as an old cowboy.

He dropped the hangman's noose back into the tote bag and looked around for someone who could tell him how to find Emaline. A switchboard operator said that she had gone out to keep house for Jim Lindquist for a while. She gave him directions: Due west to the Stegall post office, turn left, go three miles and you'll pass a big red silo, and the Lindquist farm is just opposite. The farmhouse is down in a swale in a grove of trees.

It had been snowing all morning, and there was a foot of snow on the ground and a cold wind blowing when he got out of the car holding his Stetson to his head. Emaline saw him from the kitchen window, thought it was Ezra, opened the door and invited him in. It wasn't until he peeled off his sheepskin coat and held out his hand that she knew.

—I'm your Grandpa Eli, hon. Haven't seen you since you were a little girl.

—I thought you were Uncle Ezra.

—People have been known to confuse us from time to time. I'm sorry I didn't make it for the funeral. Had a little problem with my wife. Been in Evanston with her, drove all night.

—Mama died five days ago.

—I know she did. Her husband around?

—Jim? He and his brother went to help a neighbor with a sick cow.

—That's too bad. I'd like to meet him.

—He's a good man. I wish you had come to see her. She wanted to see you. She forgave you, you know.

—That's what Ruby told me.

—I wouldn't have forgiven you in her place.

—Maybe you're not like her.

—I'm not.

—Does that mean you won't forgive me?

—I will not.

Eli's wide shoulders slumped.

—Don't seem like I have much left. Ida Mae's in the state hospital in Evanston. Just seems everything has pretty much gone to hell at the end, except for Ezra and me. We just keep on keepin on. Sometimes I aint sure why.

He seemed smaller than Emaline would have expected, as though shrunken by time and tragic events. A man who had made much and lost a good deal more. A Denver newspaper had called Eli "one of the builders of the West," and yet he was sitting here in her kitchen looking like a man who had reason to doubt everything he had ever done.

She poured his coffee, and he stirred in cream and two heaping teaspoons of sugar and blew in the mug to cool it.

—I'd like to go out to the cemetery. Pay my respects to my girl. If you don't mind, I'd like you to show me to her grave.

—It would have been nice if you had come to show your respects while she was alive.

—I was always a busy man.

—Busy and hard. I've always wondered how a man could be so hard to his own daughter.

—We can talk all that until we're blue in the face and it aint goin to change a thing. Velma is gone and I didn't get to see her before she died. She was my favorite, you know. The apple of my eye. Now she's dead and I want to visit her grave. If you don't want to come, I'll find it on my own.

Emaline gave him a long, hard look and made up her mind.

—Finish your coffee and we'll go.

• • •

It was snowing again when they left the farm, snowing hard when they arrived at the cemetery north of Scottsbluff, where the ground rose to the north and east, toward the sandhills where Velma was born. Eli stopped the Cadillac on a lane that cut through between the long, straight rows of gravestones, and Emaline got out with him, led the way to Velma's grave, and brushed off the snow on a slab of pink marble laid flat on the ground. The flowers Emaline had left three days earlier were covered with snow. Eli read the inscription:

VELMA LINDQUIST, 1894–1933
BELOVED WIFE OF JIM LINDQUIST
MOTHER OF EMALINE, BENJAMIN, ROBERT, AND WILLIAM

Nothing said about her being the daughter of Eli and Livvy Paint; no reason there should be. Especially not Eli Paint, who stood now shoulder to shoulder with his granddaughter, the girl whose birth had driven a wedge between father and daughter, opened a distance that could never be closed. The wind picked up and the snow was falling so hard they could barely see. They could feel their toes turning numb and yet neither of them made a move to leave. The trees moaned and bent under their load of snow, a magpie flapped off a low branch and startled Emaline. Eli reached out and put his arm around her shoulder and pulled her closer to him. As the wind rose, Emaline could feel the tears beginning to freeze in the corners of her eyes. She turned her face into the sheepskin collar of his jacket and wept.

Author's Note

Twenty-five years ago, I received a thick package from my mother in Nebraska. Inside were two family memoirs: One was written by her great-uncle Eb Jones, the son of one of the first pioneers in South Dakota and a noted frontier character who had been a cowboy, a scout for the U.S. Cavalry at the time of the Wounded Knee massacre, and an adventurer who helped drive a herd of buffalo from Arizona to Wyoming. The other was a memoir left by my mother's aunt Garnet, Eb's niece and the daughter of my great-grandfather Squier Jones, one of the rare men in the Old West who began with a 160-acre homestead and became a wealthy rancher. Together, the memoirs covered an astonishing period of American history, from the California Gold Rush in 1849 through the Great Depression of the 1930s, encompassing the Civil War, the Indian wars, the settling of the High Plains, and World War I.

In one way or another, members of our immediate family had taken part in many of the great events of that pivotal era. Eb's father, John Milton Jones, had walked to California during the Gold Rush and run a store boat on the Mississippi River in the decade before the siege of Vicksburg; Eb had witnessed the results of the massacre at Wounded Knee, and he and Squier had survived the terrible winter of 1887 in Wyoming, when some ranchers lost 90 percent of their livestock. Garnet Jones Johnson had been a hard-riding cowgirl working for her father, Squier, and as a girl had taken part in long and difficult cattle drives from Ainsworth in the Nebraska sandhills to the Pine Ridge Reservation in South Dakota.

My mother (who spent a lifetime putting up with my semiliterate father while reading Chekhov, Balzac, and Tolstoy in her rare quiet moments) thought the memoirs might serve as the basis for a novel. I disagreed. My literary heroes were Ezra Pound, James Joyce, and Thomas Pynchon; I was in search of great and complex themes. I had no interest in a homespun narrative of life on the frontier, no matter how colorful. In pursuit of my own *Gravity's Rainbow*, I shed fragmentary novels the way trees shed their leaves, scattering thousands of pages of unfinished works to the four winds. Along the way, I also managed to lose the memoirs my mother had sent.

Another twenty years went by before my interest was piqued by a conversation with one of my sisters, Linda Dittmar; with Linda's help I tracked down copies of the memoirs to replace those I had lost along with letters, notes, and newspaper clippings provided by other family members. There it was: a sweeping historical epic with a personal and heartbreaking narrative at its core. There was also, in certain events that took place along the Powder River in Wyoming, an opportunity to pay tribute to the westerns I had devoured in junior high school. At the heart of this story was a real-life cowgirl, my grandmother Velma, and a real-life cowboy turned rancher, her father, Squier Jones. The clash between the implacable Squier and the star-crossed Velma drew me more than anything else: With her sisters, Velma had taken part year after year in the arduous cattle drives that helped to make Squier a wealthy man—but when she crossed him, she found herself exiled from his ranch and left to raise her children alone.

Eb and Squier had been raised by their mother (who was either part or entirely Lakota) to speak Lakota and to feel a sympathy for the First Peoples which was rare in that time. Eb became a scout for the U.S. Cavalry in the period leading up to the Wounded Knee massacre, perhaps the most notorious of all the murderous encounters between the U.S. Cavalry and the High Plains Indians. His account of that massacre, ungrammatical and confusing though it is, burned with rage.

All the major events in this novel are based on truth, or at least that truth handed down in family lore either through the diaries and memoirs or through the stories my mother told. The truth here is in the lives of four generations of Americans over nearly a century of headlong expansion from the Mississippi River to the High Plains.

I am indebted to many, not least the great Nebraska writer Mari Sandoz, whose father, Jules (title character of her wonderful portrait, *Old Jules*), was an acquaintance of my great-uncle Eb Jones. The title itself comes from a collection of Sandoz's work: "Sun-Going-Down" is a song written by a Cheyenne chief being held in chains in a Florida prison and translated by Sandoz. It seemed an appropriate title for a novel set in a time when the arrival of Europeans on the High Plains meant that the sun went down on an entire way of life.

In this case, "based on a true story" is entirely accurate. The truth of that story sometimes defies belief, but it is true nonetheless. The High Plains were not settled without bloodshed, conflict, tragedy, and sorrow; triumph for the white man meant disaster for the First Peoples; and the ascendance of powerful men with the skill, imagination, and implacable will to thrive in such a hostile setting often meant a commensurate degree of pain and suffering for those they loved most.

MAY 2007

Acknowledgments

I am indebted first to a family of storytellers, to those who kept diaries, wrote letters and memoirs, and talked to newspaper reporters who were curious about the Old West: Eb Jones, Squier Jones, Tavie Jones Kipp, Garnet Jones Johnson, Alta Johnson Snodderly, Dorothy Randall, and Frieda Todd. I am grateful to my sister, Linda Dittmar, who helped me to pull together the materials I needed to tell it. I must thank all those who first read this book and offered encouragement and advice: Mick Lowe, Celine Boisvenue, Elaine Pfefferblit, Indra Prashad, Eugene Marc, Jeanne Dennison, Lauren Welsh, the wrangler Mike Darnell; and as always, my friend and mentor Dr. John X. Cooper of the University of British Columbia. For help with the research I am indebted to Laurie Mitchell, to John Irwin, formerly of the Denver Public Library, to the Nebraska State Historical Society and the South Dakota State Historical Society, and to Dr. Maya Marc. I am especially grateful to my agent, Hilary McMahon, my Canadian editor Nicole Winstanley, my American editor (and distant cousin) Trish Todd; to Wayne Spotted War Bonnet and George White Magpie, friends of my youth; and to my wife, Irene Marc, for her unshakable optimism and unwavering support.

Among the dozens of books on this period of American history which helped me to understand a time before my own, the most useful were Mark Twain's incomparable *Life on the Mississippi*; Louis C. Hunter's *Steamboats on the Western Rivers*; Shelby Foote's *The*

Beleaguered City: The Vicksburg Campaign; Peter Matthiessen's *In the Spirit of Crazy Horse*; Evan S. Connell's *Son of the Morning Star: Custer and the Little Bighorn*; Gregory F. Michno's *Lakota Noon: The Indian Narrative of Custer's Defeat*; Dee Brown's *Bury My Heart at Wounded Knee*; John G. Neihardt's *Black Elk Speaks*; John D. McDermott's *Gold Rush: The Black Hills Story*; Wayne Fanebust's *Where the Sioux River Bends*; Helena Huntington Smith's *The War on Powder River*; Ed Lemmon's *Boss Cowman*; Elinore Pruitt Stewart's *Letters of a Woman Homesteader*; Edith Eudora Kohl's *Land of the Burnt Thigh*; Lois Phillips Hudson's *Reapers of the Dust*; Ian Frazier's *Great Plains*; and Mari Sandoz's *Old Jules*. This book was made possible in part by a grant from the Canada Council for the Arts.

Sun Going Down

FOR DISCUSSION

1. *Sun Going Down* is populated with a lively, colorful cast of characters, but nature also plays an essential role in the novel. In many ways, it helps determine the plot, providing an element of suspense or affording the characters certain opportunities. Discuss three examples that exist throughout *Sun Going Down* in which nature determines a character's fate.

2. Discuss courtship and marriage as it is portrayed in *Sun Going Down*. When Eb Paint marries Cora, she has already been married twice and they have not spent much more than a few months together. How would you react if you were forced to decide to marry someone you'd known only for a few months? Although Eli and Livvy also only knew each other for a short time before they were married, they have a successful marriage. What makes their marriage work?

3. When Eli marries Livvy, he tells her that the bruises and scars around his neck are not from his attempted hanging for stealing horses but from a joke that went too far. Why did he lie to her? Given the harsh times in which they lived, would she understand the need to steal horses in order to survive or to make up for what was already owed Eli and Ezra?

4. Why does Eli banish Velma from the Fanciful when she becomes pregnant, especially given the fact that everything that he has was built on what he called his "black money"—

the money he earned from stealing horses? Is this a double standard? Would his actions be more acceptable in today's world?

5. Why does Velma refuse to reconcile with Eli, even when she realizes that she needs help caring for her children? When Eli runs Frank off after he breaks Velma's arm, she has the chance to reconcile but refuses to do so. Why?

6. After Livvy's death, Eli eventually marries Ida Mae and has another family. Why does it seem that partners and families are so easily replaceable? Why do you think the author does not focus on this new family except to mention Ida Mae and two of the children's eventual descent into madness or depression?

7. How do you imagine that Emaline's and Eli's relationship progressed after Velma's death? Did Emaline forgive Eli for being absent for so long? Was a relationship possible?

8. For the most part, the characters in this novel have a gritty tenacity, necessitated by their hardscrabble existence. Nevertheless, the female characters are particularly distinct. Discuss the similarities and differences between the women that father and son Eb and Eli choose to marry—Cora, Livvy, and Ida Mae. How are the lives of father (Eb), and sons (Eli and Ezra) similar?

9. Discuss the various ways in which religion is perceived in *Sun Going Down*, whether from the perspective of God-fearing, churchgoing characters, or that of those who revere nature and fate, or those who follw the Native American tradition. How do the characters' faiths serve them throughout the novel?

Any sweeping novel about the American West is bound to be compared to *Lonesome Dove*. How do you feel about *Sun Going Down* being compared to McMurtry's epic novel?

Obviously, I'm gratified and a little embarrassed to find *Sun Going Down* compared with an American classic such as *Lonesome Dove*. At the same time, I should point out that they are very different books. Both are sweeping tales set partially or entirely in the Old West, but apart from that, I think, the similarities really aren't there. I had read *Lonesome Dove* when it first came out years ago but didn't remember much about it. I have since re-read it and read *Comanche Moon*, and I might have done some things differently if I had read these books while I was writing *Sun Going Down*, which was much more influenced by Mark Twain, Cormac McCarthy, and the Nebraska writer Mari Sandoz.

You've managed to tell the story of four generations of one family in just over four hundred pages, yet the novel doesn't feel rushed or hurried. How did you edit yourself and decide to move on to the next plot or storyline? Given the scope of the novel, did you outline the story first? Did your research or writing process evolve at all while working on *Sun Going Down*?

The greatest difficulty in writing this book was to get so much story between two covers. The first draft was nine hundred pages long in manuscript; it was then cut by a third and then cut to half that length before some one hundred twenty pages were restored for the final version. I didn't really do an outline; I was following the story of the family as handed down in diaries and memoirs, so the outline was there from the beginning. In the original plan, however, the Mississippi and Big Sioux sections took up no more than a couple of chapters; it was when those sections expanded to their current form that I began to develop a very different and more ambitious version of the book. I knew that two things would be very difficult: the shift from generation to generation, when one set of characters die or move offstage and are replaced by another; and the gradual shift from a largely male to a female perspective as Eb, Eli, and Ezra are replaced as the central characters by Velma and Emaline. For the most part, I tried to trust the story as it was and let it unfold as I felt it needed to and hope that readers would come with me on the journey.

Sun Going Down is based on memoirs left by your family, and the character of Velma is based upon one of your grandmothers, with the "Paint girls" being your great aunts. Beside your family's first hand accounts, what other research did you do?

The early sections required much more research than later sections closer to our own time, but my method remained pretty much the same: I relied on family diaries and memoirs for the basic structure but read dozens of other histories and memoirs written by settlers and cowboys as well as some of the great literature from the period, then I tried to let it all seep into the work. I also spent significant time at the Nebraska Historical Society and the Denver public library, reading newspapers from Ainsworth, Sioux Falls, Denver, Sheridan, Scottsbluff, and other cities mentioned in the book, going through public documents (I found the marriage certificate for Frank and Velma, for instance) and reading letters written by other settlers. I often do what I call "backfilling," working in more detail from my research during the rewrite phase. I write very quickly, sometimes 4,000 or 5,000 words in a day, but most of the chapters in this book have been reworked at least a half-dozen times and some as many as forty or fifty times.

In conducting your research, did you come upon discrepancies or differences between the family memoirs and notes you received and what you may have found in historical reference books and materials?

I didn't find discrepancies between the memoirs and histories from outside the family so much as I found lively arguments within the family over certain issues, especially the race of the Cora character, based on the real-life Sophia Swift. When I was a boy, I was told that Sophia, my great-great grandmother, was Jewish. But when I had a Jewish roommate in university and he began telling me about "our" heritage, my mother decided to tell the truth. She said that her grandfather Squier Jones, the real-life model for Eli Paint, told people that his mother was Jewish to explain the dark color of his skin, because he would not have been accepted in business if people knew he was part Sioux. Squier's youngest son Lyle Jones, born in 1920, published a memoir before his death in 2007 in which he said that Sophia Swift was a descendant of the "Jewish" Swift Packing Co. family from Chicago. That Swift family, however, is old New England Anglo-Saxon, not Jewish and if Sophia was their heir, it's hard to explain why she was living in one-room cabins in South Dakota and harder still to explain why she knew Lakota and was willing to take her sons on a summer-long trip with a band of Sioux at a time when white women would never go traveling with the Sioux. Of her sons, Eb Jones (whose account of the trip to Devil's Lake is the source of much of this material was especially fluent in Lakota and his reaction to the Wounded Knee massacre was hardly typical of white opinion at the time. I've decided to accept my mother's version, which is that Sophia/Cora was part Sioux. One of my researchers suggested that I have a DNA test to settle it but I declined for two reasons: first, my father was part Cherokee, which might muddle the result. Second, I'd rather have the mystery and a good argument.

In researching the book and your family tree, did you come upon some people or incidents that were surprising to you or slightly unsavory? If so, did you work any of those elements into the book?

The librarian in Ainsworth said that Squier Jones was a bit like Tony Soprano. She came up with the story of the mysterious hanging which some people blamed on Squier; it has been worked into the Valley of the Shadow section.

Each of the six sections of the book is set on or near a different river. Why did you choose to utilize rivers as a plot device?

The rivers were a natural, organic device to link the disparate sections of the book. The early settlers were entirely dependent on the rivers for everything from irrigation to transport; John Milton Jones, the model for Eb Paint, did ruen a store boat on the Mississippi River and everything else flowed from there. The rivers flow through the story like the veins and arteries through our bodies and to me, nineteenth century North America was very much like a living organism—the land and the rivers are also like characters in this book.

You wrote in your author's note that you at first had set out in search of your own *Gravity's Rainbow*. How did you come to instead write a great narrative of the birth and growth of the American West? Do you think that *Sun Going Down* shares any similarities with Thomas Pynchon's novel?

I suppose that *Sun Going Down* and *Gravity's Rainbow* share at least the quality that they are both long and ambitious but I wouldn't claim anything else in common with Thomas Pynchon's novel. I do know that I did not become a writer until I realized that I could *not* be Thomas Pynchon or Ezra Pound or James Joyce, nor did I want to be. The writers you most admire are not necessarily the best models for young writers, because their very greatness can be discouraging.

Nature plays a central role in the novel, either being a harsh and bitter enemy or a boon companion to your characters, and it is portrayed in vivid detail. Do you have any firsthand experience with some of the difficult weather conditions described in the book?

As a three-year-old, I was lost for a time behind a snowdrift in the blizzard of '49 in Nebraska. From that time until I left home to go to the University of Nebraska, I spent mornings, evenings, and most of my free days from school working beside my father through blizzards, bitter cold, dust storms, and searing summer heat. I also witnessed with the rest of my family the famous Scottsbluff tornado during the 1950s, a photo of which appeared in national magazines such as *Life* and the *Saturday Evening Post* as part of an insurance advertisement for years after. My father took us to the top of Scotts Bluff when he saw the tornado coming and we watched it slash through the valley, an unforgettable and terrifying experience of the power of nature. I've helped to deliver a calf in -20 degree weather on Christmas Eve, towed cattle out of snowbanks and ridden through thunderstorms, all experiences that were difficult at the time but probably helpful when I began to write this book.

Though Eli and Ezra Paint provide much of the central thread to the novel, some of the strongest characters in the story are women, especially those who lead rough, hard lives, and work as hard as the men. As a man, how difficult or how easy was it to write such convincing female characters?

I think it was very hard to write convincing female characters, if indeed I have succeeded. I knew from the beginning that it would be difficult. But I had the personal example of my mother Maxine (Emaline in the fictional version) along with numerous stories of the courage of women in the Old West. Pioneer life was difficult for everyone but it was most difficult for the women; the more I read about them, the more I wanted to write a novel that would show at least part of what their lives were like.

Can you share with the reader a bit more about what became of your grandmother Velma, her sisters and their descendants?

Velma's story is pretty much in the book in its entirety, although she died in 1936, not 1933. In fact, I could never quite get comfortable with any other name so she remains Velma, although in life she was Velma Morgan. I spent many happy months in my youth staying on the farm run by her wonderful third husband, the gentle Swedish farmer Jim Lindquist, and

I have kept his real name in tribute for his kindness to me. I knew Velma's sister Garnet (Ruby in *Sun Going Down*) well and was once banned from her ranch on Sheep Creek for insulting her cooking. Her memoir and another left by her daughter Alta were also central to the writing of this book. My middle name, Edwin, was taken from Garnet's son, killed on a destroyer in the Pacific in World War II. Velma's sisters Marguerite and Kate (their real names) were also regular visitors to our house, genteel women who led long, full lives. The last time I saw Kate I was eighteen years old and my mother had been bragging about how her son was going to be a journalist or a writer as they rode in from the airport. I was out mowing the lawn when they arrived and I hollered at my mother: "Mom, I ain't got no guess for this lawnmower!" Her embarrassment knew no bounds. Kate's daughter Dorothy also provided much help with the writing of this book. Blind Daniel, their brother Dale Jones, really did teach generations of kids to swim at the swimming pool in Torrington, Wyoming, despite his limited vision. If you visit Torrington today, you'll see his name on the Dale Jones Municipal Pool. More of the fate of some of these characters and their descendants will be told in the novel I'm now writing, a sequel to *Sun Going Down*. It also seems strange to me that Eli/Squier's youngest son Lyle lived until 2007, and that I met Squier several times myself when I was very young. He used to come by the house once or twice a year in his big white Cadillac, but all I remember of his was his car and his big Stetson hat.

So you are working on a sequel? What is it about and where is it set? If *Sun Going Down* were to be turned into a movie or mini-series, would you be interested in writing the screenplay and helping with the casting?

Yes, I am working on the sequel, tentatively titled *Fire on the Water,* and it's proving to have at least as many challenges in the writing as *Sun Going Down*. *Fire on the Water* is set primarily between Velma's death in 1933 and Pearl Harbor in 1941, where her son (Bobby in *Sun Going Down*) was a machine-gunner on the battleship *Tennessee*. I don't think I would be interested in writing a screenplay; it is hard enough to write fiction.

As *Sun Going Down* is based on your own ancestors, do you feel that the entrepreneurial spirit is something that runs through your family? How has it been passed down to you? In what ways has it exhibited itself with your other living family members?

Unfortunately, none of the entrepreneurial spirit of John Milton Jones and his son Squier was passed down to my immediate family. We have no talent for business whatsoever, although one or two of us are pretty good with horses—but that comes from my father, who ironically was pretty much just like Frank Hughes.